The Black

A Novel of International Intrigue and Revolution

Armando Interiano

Published by

A Fiction Imprint from Adducent

www.AdducentCreative.com

Titles Distributed In

North America

United Kingdom

Western Europe

South America

Australia

China

India

The Black Crusade

A Novel of International Intrigue and Revolution

Armando Interiano

Published by

Escrire

A Fiction Imprint from Adducent

The Black Crusade

A Novel of International Intrigue and Revolution

Armando Interiano

ISBN: 9781937592882 (paperback, English)

Published by Adducent, Inc. under its *Escrire* fiction imprint
Jacksonville, Florida
www.AdducentCreative.com
Published in the United States of America

ISBN: 9781937592899 (paperback, Spanish)
A Spanish language version is also available translated by Interiano-Hubbard, Inc.
www.ihtranslations.com

This book is a work of fiction. This story is--in part--inspired by historical events, people and locations relating to those events. It is a work of fiction intended to discuss and explain relevant events that did happen, which runs counter to the propaganda of the time and in the region the events occurred. This construct--the story--is a product of the author's imagination where names, characters, and locations have been used fictitiously.

Acknowledgments

The Black Crusade couldn't have been written without the unflagging encouragement and support of my beloved wife Leslie and my beloved daughters Marcela, Lucía and Nicole.

I'm also grateful to Dennis Lowery, whose expertise helped me turn my rough draft into a bona-fide novel; to Professor Agapito de la Garza, whose literary expertise allowed me to fine-tune my story into the best literary work I'm capable of producing; to Joaquín Ventura, for his invaluable research, to Camilo Hernández for sharing his memories and to Susana Font-Fontenot for all her editing help, suggestions and contributions.

Table of Contents

Chapter 1

The Order

Colonel López received a call that afternoon.

The voice asked, "You know who I am, right?"

Colonel López replied, "Yes, sir."

"Here's an order from the very top. Go kill the Jesuits at the Catholic University. Make it look like there was a battle."

"Are you serious?" The Commander of the Signal Battalion, Colonel Ciro López, couldn't believe anybody in the High Command would give the order to kill Jesuits of the Catholic University, more commonly known by its acronym 'UCA.'

"Yes I am. They're the head of the movement. Send one of your units. Yours are the only ones available right now because everybody else is combating in the city."

The night before, the guerrillas had entered residences throughout the city of San Salvador, the capital of El Salvador, and used them as bases to attack Security Forces and military units in the city. Their clandestine radio station, Radio *Venceremos* [We Will Win], had proclaimed the invasion of the capital city, calling it *La Ofensiva Hasta El Tope* [The Offensive to the Hilt].

By the next morning, the Ministry of Defense had gotten word that there were rapes and abuses being perpetrated against the civilians in their residences. And there were rumors of child combatants. Naturally, the Salvadoran Army had immediately moved to dislodge the guerrillas from the residences and from the capital.

"Sir, can you please tell me more? I'm going to be remembered as the one who had them killed. Can't I just capture them? I mean, do we even know they're there? If they're the head of the movement, they may be in *Colonia Escalón* [Escalón Residential Neighborhood] in a mansion, directing operations."

"Colonel, if they're in *Escalón,* the 1st Infantry Brigade will get them. If they're not, you will. You have your orders."

"Yes, sir."

Col. López hung up, upset. As Commander of the Signal Battalion, he had units strung out all over the country in support of brigades and battalions, to provide them with reliable military communications. All he had available at his garrison, known as *El Zapote*, was the company that was on duty to secure the garrison and his reserve platoon, consisting of thirty soldiers.

Colonel López weighed the odds of his Signal troops, which were more used to manning repeater stations on mountaintops than engaging in house-to-house combat, being able to overcome a guerrilla unit that might be in a defensive position at the UCA to protect the Jesuits.

And he only had one experienced officer available to take the reserve platoon on this extracurricular mission: Captain Ezequiel Sánchez, the West Pointer, who was out on the soccer field waiting for a helicopter from the Ilopango Air Base to take him to *El Picacho,* the communication station at the very top of the San Salvador Volcano.

His mission was to ensure that that communication station, which provided the necessary command and control to defeat the guerrilla's latest desperate offensive in the capital, did not fail. The fact that he was also an electrical engineer made Captain Sánchez the best man for that job.

But the mission at the UCA took priority over that. The West Pointer would have to go after the Jesuits.

There was one problem, though: Sánchez was, after all, a West Pointer. He was probably going to refuse. But then the Colonel smiled. He might yet turn out to be the best man for this job anyway. He'd find somebody else to send to *Picacho*.

Down on the garrison's soccer field, Captain Sánchez was notified by a soldier that the Commander wanted to see him. The Captain looked at his watch and realized that the helicopter wasn't going to be coming anyway. The Air Force probably didn't have a helicopter available, with all the firefighting going on all over San Salvador.

The Captain ran up the stairs of the soccer field all the way to the Commander's office. "Captain Sánchez reporting, sir!"

"Captain, I've received an order to go kill the Jesuits at the UCA. I need you to do it. Make it look like a battle."

"The UCA Jesuits? Why?"

"Do not question why! Do it! Take the reserve platoon."

"Sir, can I have that order in writing?"

"Listen to me, Sánchez, this is not the U.S. Army. Do you realize that your family may be in danger right now, just like all our families are, with these guerrillas in the capital? We've received reports of raping and what not. The High Command has determined that the Jesuits are directing this operation, and that they must die. And no, you're not getting this in writing."

Sánchez knew that this was an illegal order, and that it was downright stupid. For all he knew, the Jesuits were indeed the masterminds. They had to be, they were the only ones with the brains and international connections to be able to keep this war going, given the guerrillas' woeful inability to win the hearts and minds of the Salvadoran people. The all-out attack on San Salvador was their final act of desperation because of their ongoing losses. It was their 'Battle of the Bulge'—Hitler's final desperate offensive against the Allies in the winter of 1944.

But killing Jesuits wasn't what he'd been trained for at West Point. But he wasn't going to win this argument with his Commanding Officer. It was evident that Col. López wasn't too happy with the order, either. But it had been given, and now it had been given to Sánchez.

"Fine, sir. Do we have any intelligence on them? Are there guerrillas there?"

"All we know is that they probably have a command center there. Do a reconnaissance. Use cover and concealment. You went to West Point, remember?"

A few hours later, under cover of night, Captain Sánchez and his platoon were advancing on the Jesuit Residence inside the gates of the Catholic University.

No building on campus looked like it was a command and control center. The campus looked vacant, like a ghost town. The Jesuit Residence had a light on, and as they approached, they could hear what sounded like a small electric generator going. After ascertaining that the Jesuits were indeed alone there, the Captain told his faithful Sergeant and friend, Efraín Zelayandía, to commandeer the very first ambulance that drove by the boulevard and to drive it back here.

An hour later, Sergeant Zelayandía drove up in an ambulance. In that hour, the Jesuit Residence had shown no movement at all. Nobody coming out, and nobody coming in. It was like there was nothing going on. That order was indeed a big blunder. But who on earth had given it? He didn't know one single Salvadoran officer who'd be willing to give such an order.

The Captain and his men silently approached the residence. When he knocked on the door, a servant opened it and Sánchez walked right in. Two Jesuit priests, Ignacio Ellacuría and Segundo Montes, were sitting in the living room, listening to radio reports. When they saw the military man approaching them, they stood up.

Sánchez walked up to the two Jesuits and asked, "Are you two gentlemen the only ones here?"

"Yes, but what on earth are you doing here?" Ellacuría asked, visibly upset.

"Gentlemen, you will accompany me to that ambulance over there."

Ellacuría refused. "We'll do no such thing."

Sánchez nodded to his troops behind him, and they sprang into action to seize the priests.

"Gentlemen, believe me, I'm doing you a favor."

They were escorted into the ambulance. The Captain turned to the housekeeper. "Who else is here?"

"Just me and my daughter."

"Grab a few necessities, put them in the bag, and come with me. You'll be safer with me than if you stay here. Do you understand?" The shaken servant just nodded, gave instructions to her daughter, and soon after joined the two priests in the back of the ambulance.

The Captain thought for a moment and then ordered Zelayandía to bring Ellacuría back to the Jesuit Residence. Once there, Sánchez instructed him to leave a message on the answering machine, telling the other Jesuits to stay away.

When Ellacuría didn't budge, the Captain said, very calmly but firmly, "Priest, there's an order to kill the UCA Jesuits. I'm here to prevent that. I'm taking you and Montes and the ladies to a place where you'll be safe and protected by us. But I can't protect the others should they decide to come here. Leave a message that says, 'Montes and I are safe. Stay away.' Do it now."

Ellacuría hesitated. But he had to trust this military goon. If he really wanted the Jesuits dead, he could've killed them already and just waited for the others to return to the Residence. So he left that message on the answering machine.

Having done that, they got inside the ambulance and sped off, with the rest of the troops following in the truck.

"Where to, sir?" shouted Zelayandía, who was up front in the driver's seat.

The Captain raised his voice to be heard from the back of the ambulance as well. "Let's go to La Libertad. A friend of mine's got a beach home there. Let's go have oysters and shrimp."

"But sir, the Colonel said that...."

"Sergeant, you really just want to obey my orders. You'll thank me later."

"Yes, sir."

Sánchez turned to the priests. "There's an order to kill you. I'm not about to do that. We're going to protect you. I expect your unflinching cooperation so that we can all get out of this alive."

The ambulance and truck sped down the winding road toward the coast. It was 11 pm, November 12, 1989. The day before, the guerrillas had launched a desperate assault on the capital city because they no longer had the numbers to do anything else.

They had gone into residences. Perhaps they wanted to have fun with rich Salvadoran women and girls before they died. Because there could be no military gain from such an action.

Nevertheless, it did have the effect of portraying strength, a strength that would get magnified by journalists writing from the comfort of their hotel rooms, who merely repeated everything that the guerrilla propaganda station, Radio *Venceremos*, was broadcasting.

The Captain thought about his family. He hadn't heard from his parents. He had no wife and children. For once, he was grateful the love of his life had refused to marry him, because who knows if he'd be conducting himself this way if he'd had a wife and any children in harm's way.

But he didn't. So he said a little prayer for his parents' safety, and then turned his entire attention to the mission at hand: to keep these Jesuits alive. In his mind, preventing this monumental blunder of an order took precedence over everything else.

The ride to the port city of La Libertad was quick and silent. There was no traffic to fight. Everybody was staying put inside their homes because of the flying bullets. And the Captain was counting on that to be able to hide these people from the Army until the High Command regained their senses.

Ellacuría was the first to ask, "Who gave that order, Captain?"

Ellacuría was a tall, distinguished-looking fellow. Very aristocratic. He was dressed in civilian attire, but then again, he had rarely, if ever, seen this Jesuit dressed in Jesuit black. Not even when he was dean of the UCA, where Sánchez had been a student for a semester before leaving for West Point.

"Priest, I wish I knew who the numbskull was who gave such an order. I personally don't know anybody who would give it."

Segundo Montes snorted. "Come now, Captain, anybody in the High Command could've given that order," he said.

The Captain looked at him. If there was ever a guy who looked like Don Quixote de la Mancha, it was Montes. All he was missing was a fat sidekick like Sancho Panza. Don Quixote painted by El Greco. That was Montes.

"Priest, I know the members of the High Command. You know what they all are? Fervent Catholics. Rosary-praying, Sunday Mass-going Catholics. They've heard leftist sermons for decades now and unlike me, they keep going to mass. So don't tell me they gave the order. I'm quite certain that order came from another realm."

Ellacuría asked, "You mean President Cristiani?" Alfredo Cristiani had assumed the Office of the President on June 1, 1989. He'd been the candidate of the right-wing party ARENA, the party founded by Major Roberto D'Aubuisson.

"Father Ellacuría, he's Commander in Chief. He has to know, at the very least. But whoever came up with this stupid idea, that I don't know."

The priests fell silent again. They were uneasy about this Offensive. They hadn't been consulted about it. This was something spawned by the guerrillas themselves, certainly not by the Jesuits. Ellacuría had been in Spain when it had started. He'd caught the first plane back, arriving just a few hours ago.

Upon arriving at the Coastal Highway, the Sergeant asked, "Captain, do we turn left or right?"

"Turn right, keep going till you see the sign that says 'Xanadú.'

'Xanadú' was a private beachfront development where friends of the Captain had a home. It provided a desirable defensive position because once inside, the road bifurcated: to the right it led up a fairly large hill, with houses on either side; to the left the road led down to the beach. The last house on the hill was just on the other side of its crest and therefore couldn't be seen from the Coastal Highway. It would be the temporary residence of the Jesuits.

Sánchez had been to Xanadú several times, and he even knew the custodian of the development, who was an elderly Salvadoran army veteran named Juan. He was very well-liked by everybody. The Captain hoped to find him there.

Segundo Montes broke the priests' silence. "So why are you taking us there, Captain? Why don't you just obey your orders and be done with it?"

The Captain shook his head. "Priest, your forces are going to get destroyed in this offensive and I wouldn't want our military victory to be tainted with an unnecessary murder that would have devastating consequences for us.

"Besides, I have a special place in my heart for Father Ellacuría—I went to the UCA one semester before heading for West Point."

Before the priests could express their surprise, the ambulance came to a stop. The Captain got out and to speak with the custodian.

"Sergeant Juan, is that you?"

"Yes, who's this?"

"It's me, Captain Ezequiel Sánchez, I'm often a guest of the Gameros here."

"Yes of course! What are you doing here, Captain? Shouldn't you be fighting?"

"Sergeant Juan, we're here to stay for a few days while the hostilities continue. We're here to protect some civilians and I couldn't think of a better place. This is very important and I know I can count on a former artillery Sergeant to help us."

The old man snapped to and saluted. "At your service, Captain!"

Captain Sánchez came to attention and squarely saluted the custodian back, saying, “An honor, Sergeant!”

Then he took the old sergeant aside to talk to him. “Sergeant, is there anybody here?”

“No, Captain, nobody here. Since it’s late Sunday night, they’re all gone now. But many left as soon as they heard there was an offensive in San Salvador.”

The Captain thanked his lucky stars for that. The odds of this adventure have a happy ending had just spiked.

“Great! Sergeant Juan, we’re going to try to go as unnoticed as possible here, so we won’t want to let anybody in. My men will be ready to assist you if need be, but all we need for you to say is that entrance is forbidden until you’re notified that it’s OK. Do you understand?”

“Yes, Captain.”

“Do you have lodging in this compound, Sergeant?”

“Yes, sir, down by the pool near the beach.”

“So you don’t need to leave for any reason?”

“No, just to get provisions, but I went yesterday, so I don’t need anything for another week.”

“Can you let us into some of the homes? We just want to see if there are any canned goods that we can eat for a few days.”

“Yes I can, and yes there are.”

“Good.” The Captain turned to call his trusted brother in arms, Sergeant Zelayandía, who got out of the ambulance and rushed over.

“Master Sergeant Zelayandía, this is Sergeant Juan, who used to be in artillery.” The two sergeants shook hands

“He’s going to be our first line of defense by not letting anybody in, but I want you to deploy the men in the houses going up the hill to support him. I don’t think anybody’s going to risk leaving their homes in San Salvador to come here any time soon, though. Coordinate with Sergeant Juan here to get inside the homes to get some chow. I’ll drive the ambulance up the hill while you do that.”

The Captain took two soldiers with him and drove the ambulance up to the Jesuits’ temporary residence.

It was a house that overlooked the ocean, atop a 200-foot cliff. Captain Sánchez posted the two soldiers escorting the priests in the front of the house because they'd never be able to escape going out the back. Not unless they survived the 200-foot fall.

"Step inside, ladies and gentlemen, this'll be your home until I decide that it's safe to take you back." He helped everybody out of the ambulance.

The house was very open, with a large living, dining and kitchen area combined. It was more like a large hut, but with a shingled roof–not thatched. It had bedrooms, but it was really designed for people to sleep in hammocks out in the ample living area. And there were plenty of hammocks, hanging from the accessible wooden beams because there was no ceiling.

The Captain then drove the ambulance down the hill to coordinate the defenses with Zelayandía. If anybody broke through the gate, they'd face an uphill fight. He ordered the military truck to block the gate, but only at night. He didn't want to call attention to the military being in Xanadú during the day. He knew that they'd eventually be discovered. What he was hoping for was enough time for the military brass to reconsider their stupid order.

He had Zelayandía park the ambulance inside a big hut down by the pool, so it was undetectable from the road and from the air. They then walked the compound, and when Sánchez was satisfied that all avenues of approach were covered, he went back to the priests.

He said to them, "Ladies and gentlemen, please make yourselves as comfortable as possible. Please don't try to escape. My soldiers are in defensive mode right now, and you don't want to give them an excuse to shoot. I'll be moving from house to house, so if you need anything, just tell a sentinel, and he'll find me."

With that, he started to walk down the hill. The wait had begun.

CHAPTER 2

IGNACIO ELLACURÍA

Ignacio Ellacuría, the son of a well-known ophthalmologist, was born November 9, 1930, in Portugalete, in the Spanish province of Vizcaya, also known as the Basque Country. He was raised in a fervently catholic family, which was doing far better now under the government of the victorious Francisco Franco than it had been under the former Republican Government, which was anti-religious and socialist. It was no coincidence that the Catholic Church had allied itself with Franco in the Spanish Civil War.

Like his brothers, Ignacio studied in the boarding school of San Javier de Tudela, after which, upon graduation, he joined the Jesuits. He had recently been informed that he would be sent to do his novitiate in El Salvador, of all places.

When he gave his parents the news that spring night in 1949, his mother tried to put the best face possible on the situation. "Ignacio, you have chosen the godly path. It's never easy and your superiors, in their God-inspired wisdom, have decided to send you to Salvador, Brazil."

"No, mom, it's El Salvador, Central America."

"Really? What's in El Salvador?"

"That's my question. Why El Salvador, of all places? After the war, wouldn't a place like the Philippines need more help than El Salvador?"

Dr. Ellacuría finished his last spoonful of gazpacho. Clearing his throat, he offered this plausible explanation.

"Ignacio, Spain is in ruins. We have no treasure. Franco is looking to see where he can get treasure from, and the Americas, our former colonies, are a logical place for him to look. After all, the Americas were largely unscathed by the war.

"He's aware of the large number of Spaniards who fled the Civil War in Spain to the Americas. Educated Spaniards will most certainly take advantage of the cheap labor there, consisting of sub-literate *indios* [natives] that make up the large mass of the Latin American population, to prosper and send money back.

"The other characteristic of the *indios* is that they are very Catholic. Protestantism has gone nowhere in Latin America, and the Jesuits most certainly want to keep it that way. After all, that was the reason why Ignatius of Loyola was allowed to form the Society of Jesus by the Pope: to combat Protestantism.

"And all of a sudden, what do we have? A Second Conquest, only instead of military men as *Conquistadors*, we have businessmen. But just like in the First Conquest, we'll have an active Catholic Church down there, this time as an ally of Franco.

"So you're part of a grandiose plan to return Spain to glory!"

Ignacio shook his head. "But how can the Church be interested in such mundane things, dad? We have to be interested in the souls of people."

Dr. Ellacuría admonished his son. "Ignacio, don't be naïve. Think! The Church has proven to be very mundane. It went to war—to war!—alongside Franco because it lost its worldly possessions to the Republican Government."

Ignacio bowed his head. He had never been required to think, just regurgitate. His schooling was such that others had already done the thinking for him, and it was his task to memorize and parrot such information. The grades he got were passing, which is why the priesthood seemed a way up for him, given that he wasn't much good at math or science.

Dr. Ellacuría put his hand on his arm's son and squeezed it. "Ignacio, look at this as a great opportunity! From what I hear, priests are considered deities there. Even by the well-educated landed gentry. You can be a priest and say that the sun is green, and the people will say 'why yes, it's green, it must be green, and if I don't see it green, there must be something wrong with my eyes.'"

Dr. Ellacuría, the ophthalmologist, laughed at his own little joke, before continuing. "Whether it's Franco's idea, or the Jesuits' idea, it's a damn good idea. If you don't want to go, don't become a priest. But just remember, you don't have the brains to get into medical school, so at best it's either the army or journalism school for you. And you know what I think of journalists."

Dr. Ellacuría got up from the table. He nodded to his wife and congratulated her: "Great gazpacho, Mother." Then he looked at his crestfallen son. "Listen to me, Ignacio: here in Spain, you'd be a nobody. Over there, you'll be a somebody. Do your very best to become a Jesuit priest because they're reputed to be very intelligent. And take advantage of the fact that they're having a hard time recruiting thanks to our Civil War. God has sent you this opportunity; therefore, run with it!" He kissed his son good night.

When Ignacio finally went to bed that night, he read from his newest book, *Das Kapital*. The only course he excelled in was philosophy. While most of his classmates recoiled at what they called 'mumbo-jumbo,' he dove headfirst into its bombastic and flamboyant vocabulary, no matter what language it was in, such as Nietzsche's *Übermensch*, Hobbes' *Bellum omnium contra omnes*, and other wondrous and inscrutable terminology. His dominance of such vocabulary, whether he understood it or not, made him sound far more intellectual than his peers.

Perhaps his love of philosophy was why the Jesuits were so avidly recruiting him. The priest who was his counselor had told him: "Ignacio, philosophers are what we need more of. You're perfect for us." And then he'd reached into a drawer and taken out a book.

"Here's a book Franco won't let us teach from: *Das Kapital,* by Karl Marx. It represents the future of the Jesuits. Start reading it now and you'll go far."

Of course, he hadn't revealed this to his pro-Franco parents. They hated the communists. But his dad was right: he didn't have much talent for anything else, and he loved to read. He felt certain this was the right path for him. He felt certain that the Jesuits would turn him into an intellectual, somehow.

A few weeks later, he'd landed at El Salvador's Ilopango airport, where Father Elizondo was waiting for him. An hour later, they were at the Church of El Carmen in Santa Tecla.

Founded in 1854, Santa Tecla is a small town west of San Salvador, also at the foot of the San Salvador Volcano. It was founded as *Nueva San Salvador* [New San Salvador] on August 8, 1854, by then-president José María San Martín after the capital had been destroyed by an earthquake. It served as the capital of the republic from 1855 to 1859 and became departmental capital in 1865. The town's growth was directly related to the success of the local coffee industry.

Soon after the government returned to San Salvador, it was renamed *Santa Tecla*, after Thecla, the follower of the apostle Paul. The Spanish conquest of Latin America, being more religious than political, instilled the custom of naming towns and places after saints. So it came naturally for Salvadorans to name something Saint this and Saint that or Holy this or Holy that. Apparently, all other saint names had already been used to name something in El Salvador and so the only name available was *Tecla*.

But the coffee riches of Santa Tecla didn't lead to its development beyond a cluster of small businesses for the landed gentry to go shopping without having to go all the way to San Salvador. The main reason was that most of the profits from the coffee industry were expatriated, or spent on paintings, Arabian horses and other imported goods. They would be spent on anything and everything, except in the education of the peasants.

* * *

In 1949, almost a century after its foundation, a prominent landmark of Santa Tecla was the Church of El Carmen, built in 1855 by Colonel León Castillo, a soldier who had served under the great General Francisco Morazán. Wounded in Guatemala in 1840, Colonel Castillo had managed to crawl to a nearby church, the Church of El Carmen del Cerrito, built in honor Our Lady of El Carmen, where he promised her that if she saved his life, he would build a church for her.

On its 94th anniversary, the pastor of the Church of El Carmen was a Jesuit priest named Miguel Elizondo, an old-school Jesuit who took his vows of chastity, poverty, and obedience very seriously; especially his obedience to the Pope. His education had been gospel-centric. He was a Thomist, a faithful follower of the teachings of St. Thomas Aquinas.

Father Elizondo was aware of the Modernist push within the Society of Jesus at the time, encouraging a Church that was more in tune with modern-day philosophy, rather than anchored by the traditional and what they considered antiquated teachings of St. Thomas Aquinas and Jesus himself.

But to him, Modernism was nothing but a distant wave out at sea, which would crash and dissipate when it arrived at the shore; it never crossed his mind that it could be a powerful tsunami that could cause so much death and destruction.

In February of that year, Father Elizondo had received a letter from the Society of Jesus in Orduña, Spain, asking him if he needed any assistance with his parochial duties; if so, would he accept Ignacio Ellacuría, a Jesuit novice, for a span of one year, in exchange for a nice stipend?

Father Elizondo had accepted the offer without any hesitation. A couple of months later, he had his novice with him. And a much-needed stipend to go with him.

On his way from Ilopango to Santa Tecla, Ignacio Ellacuría saw poverty of a kind he could have never imagined. He couldn't believe the number of naked and dirty native children that were begging for money. He saw the decrepit makeshift huts called *champas* populating the sides of the road and the hillside. He concluded that the reputed hell of the afterlife couldn't be worse than this. It was appalling.

But then he saw the mansions that lined the street named after Franklin Delano Roosevelt, which included a castle, and suddenly, the meaning of Karl Marx's term, 'exploitation,' became crystal-clear to him.

He wondered if Santa Tecla would be worse. When he arrived, he found the streets to be cleaner and had with fewer beggars.

The extreme poverty he'd seen on the way over here was the first issue he'd broached with Father Elizondo. In response, Father Elizondo recited Luke 6:20-21, "Then he looked up at his disciples and said: 'Blessed are you who are poor, for yours is the kingdom of God.'"

Father Elizondo reminded him that thanks to the Spanish *Conquistadors*, El Salvador had become nothing but an underdeveloped coffee-producing nation, a nation of peasants. And that as a priest, he needed to help them achieve as much as they could in this life, but with the certainty that they would be rich in Heaven.

Ignacio was dismayed to hear Father Elizondo's words but said nothing. His authoritarian dad had taught him to submit to his superiors and he understood immediately that Father Miguel Elizondo was to be his superior for the next twelve months.

But because he'd resorted to quoting scripture, rather than any of the philosophers he was so fond of studying, Ignacio decided that Father

Elizondo was not 'intellectual' enough; therefore, the intellectual guidance that he sought would have to come from books.

Therefore, during his entire time with Father Elizondo, he performed his pastoral duties mechanically. He didn't connect with the people at any level. And this prompted Father Elizondo to have a little chat with him. "Ignacio, my son, tell me what you like so much about philosophy."

Ignacio's eyes lit up. "Ah, Father Elizondo, philosophy is what the greatest minds study."

Father Elizondo was amused. "I don't think Einstein studied philosophy because he was too busy studying physics and sciences. Isn't his mind great?"

"He would've been a greater mind had he studied philosophy."

Father Elizondo chuckled at his naiveté. "Ignacio, philosophy produces no tangible benefits to mankind. It's based on opinion, not proof. How can you claim that something is true, if you can't prove it?"

Ignacio's mind erupted with the thought, "We believe in a God that we can't see!" But that was something a Jesuit novice simply couldn't utter. So he said nothing.

Father Elizondo continued. "What is it that you intend to do with your studies in philosophy?"

The young Ellacuría didn't hesitate. "First and foremost, Father Elizondo, to develop my mind." Ignacio was of the firm belief that studying philosophy would make him the intellectual that his parents' genes had kept him from becoming.

"To do what? To serve the people?"

Ignacio couldn't hide his incredulity at hearing the word 'serve.' "Father Elizondo, great minds are leaders. I intend to lead the people."

"So leadership is your goal? That's not a bad goal to have. Where are you going to lead them to, Ignacio?"

"Enlightenment and understanding!"

Although Father Elizondo was amused by the intellectual idealism of the lad, he opted to bring him down to earth.

"Ignacio, you're here to learn to be a priest. A Jesuit priest."

"Father Elizondo, I've been taught by Jesuit priests all my life. They're intellectuals, first and foremost."

Father Elizondo shook his head. "Ignacio, please realize that they're intellectuals second, priests first. So whatever their intellectual prowess, they had to connect with non-intellectuals (students like you) to get them to understand the lesson, didn't they? And since you did pass the general high school exam required by the Spanish government, they must've connected with you, at your level, to teach you useful things, like math, science and the other subjects that were necessary for you to obtain the Spanish high school diploma."

Ignacio seemed unconvinced.

Father Elizondo continued. "Intellectualism, leadership and pastorship aren't mutually exclusive. But before you lead, you need to learn how to follow. It would seem to me that your chosen profession, the priesthood, is uniquely suited to enable you to experience followership so that you can understand what you need to do to lead effectively when the time comes."

Father Elizondo paused. He could tell that he wasn't getting through to the novice. He tried a different tack.

"Ignacio, I'm a Jesuit priest. I've studied what the great philosophers propose. And although philosophy does 'grow the brain,' so to speak, my duties as pastor require me not to lose sight of the reality of the past, present and near future of the people who are my flock. Those whom I am called to lead. And so are you, because you're a novice on the way to becoming a priest."

The novice started to shake his head but thought better of it.

Father Elizondo asked, "Ignacio, what do you think would happen if you started speaking metaphysics and ontology to our flock?"

Ignacio realized that the question was a trap. There could be no answer to this question that would support his arguments. So he just reverted the question to the priest. "What do you think they'd do, Father?"

Father Elizondo replied, with just a hint of exasperation, "You know what they wouldn't do? They wouldn't hang around to hear you talk gibberish to them and to feel like you're talking down to them. And then you will have failed as a leader, as a pastor and as a Jesuit, because Ignatius of Loyola founded the Society of Jesus to keep people from becoming Protestants, but that's precisely what they'll become if you can't even be a pastor to them."

The novice didn't wish to acknowledge such compelling reasoning. So he remained silent, waiting for the opportunity to extricate himself from this most uncomfortable situation.

Father Elizondo put on the kindest face he could and reached out to touch the young man's arm, before asking, "Ignacio, why do you think the Society sent you to Santa Tecla, El Salvador, of all places? It had to be for you to learn service, followership and humility, right? Look around you What else can El Salvador possibly offer you?"

Young Ignacio was capable of teaching stubbornness to a mule. "Father my goal isn't to be a pastor like you. I want to write treatises on philosophy To be a leading mind like Marx and Engels."

Now it was Father Elizondo's turn to exert some self-control. "Ignacio what about Jesus? As a priest, wouldn't you want to study the teachings of Jesus, first and foremost? After all, isn't the path to God through the resurrected Jesus? And aren't Marx and Engels still dead?"

The novice shrugged. "Of course I'll study that. But just how much Gospel do you have to study to become an expert? I already know the part of Jesus turning water into wine, and the Parable of the Prodigal Son, and the part about Doubting Thomas, and all that. And that's just from listening to mass for 17 years. So studying Jesus is fine, if all you want to be is the pastor of fairly uneducated people. It's not like I'm going to learn how to turn water into wine, or how to resurrect the dead, am I?"

Father Elizondo decided then and there that he and this snobbish kid just weren't going to get along.

"Ignacio, it's a privilege to be able to lead these people through life and towards God Almighty. It's an honor."

But the young man was unreceptive. "Father Elizondo, if that's all I wanted to do, I wouldn't have joined the Jesuits. I would've become a simple diocesan priest."

The very next day Father Elizondo fired off a letter to Spain, stating that this young man was more suitable to be a university philosophy professor than a priest. That he saw no vocation in him whatsoever.

A month later, he received a letter from Guipúzcoa, Spain, informing Father Elizondo that they were sure Father Elizondo would guide him so that his desire to serve would match his desire become an intellectual.

So Father Elizondo was stuck with Ignacio for the remainder of his year He convinced himself that the stipend he was getting did fairly compensate him for putting up with this arrogant Spaniard. Money didn't grow on trees

Especially in El Salvador.

Time went by quickly, with the young Ellacuría doing what was expected of him and nothing more. He made no effort to mingle with the flock, not even at feasts and *fiestas*. As soon as he was done with his duties, he'd run back to his room to read his beloved Marx, Engels and his new hero, Teilhard de Chardin.

After one year of this, he could quote Marx better than the Bible.

Father Elizondo was none too sad to see the aloof young man get on the plane to go to Quito, Ecuador, where he would spend the next five years of his life.

CHAPTER 3

PHILOSOPHY AND NOTHING BUT PHILOSOPHY

The *Pontificia Universidad Católica del Ecuador* [Pontifical Catholic University of Ecuador] (PUCE) was founded in 1946, with the first rector being Aurelio Espinosa Pólit, a Jesuit priest. In 1946, the academic year started with 54 students and just one school, the School of Jurisprudence. In 1949, the School of Economics was created.

The school of philosophy of PUCE, the Saint Gregory Ecclesiastical School of Philosophy, was founded in 1950, under the direction of the Society of Jesus.

Ignacio Ellacuría was one of its first students. The young novice spent five years studying Humanities and Philosophy, taking courses like Humanistic Education, Christian Humanism, Metaphysical and Philosophical Anthropology, History of Ancient Philosophy, History of Medieval Philosophy, Social Sciences, Philosophical Theology, Social Philosophy, Gnoseology, History of Modern Philosophy, History of Contemporary Philosophy, Latin American Philosophy, and six Philosophy Seminars, with one course in Theology for good measure.

A student would've normally obtained his *Licenciatura* [Licentiate or bachelor's degree] in Philosophy in four years. The fact that it took Ellacuría five years to get a four-year degree was noted by his superiors. He was definitely not Rome material. But he was fine for El Salvador.

Upon returning to El Salvador with his shiny bachelor's degree in Philosophy, he was immediately assigned to the Jesuit-run San José de la Montaña Seminary in San Salvador, to teach (what else?) philosophy. Only in the Seminary, it was called theology.

Ignacio was definitely needed there because the incoming classes were getting larger. Most of the seminarians were of humble origins, yet they had somehow managed to complete their secondary school education to qualify to enter the seminary.

The theology he taught was Marx and Engels. His bachelor's degree had essentially been in 'class struggle,' the basis for Marxism. So, in fact, he could teach nothing else. But nothing else was required of him. The fact that this was being taught in a Seminary, rather than the Word of God, didn't seem to bother anybody.

'Class struggle' had found fertile ground in El Salvador and in all of Latin America. After all, the widespread exploitation of the *indio* was an enduring legacy of the Spaniards, his countrymen. Of course, the Spaniard Ignacio Ellacuría tried very hard to avoid any mention of that particular aspect of it.

So his courses were quite simple, really. The rich landowners in El Salvador were the oppressors, and everybody else was the oppressed, and therefore, there needed to be a class struggle between the rich and the poor, with, as they had taught him in Quito, a 'preferential option for the poor.' After one entire course of Ignacio Ellacuría's classes, the seminarians couldn't help but come away believing that to embrace Marxism was their duty as priests, to be able to help the poor in their struggle against the rich. There was no other way.

And that's how the San José de la Montaña Seminary began to mass-produce Marxist priests.

But this wasn't Licenciate Ellacuría's plan. He was merely following the orders that came from the Church of the Gesù, the headquarters of the Society of Jesus, which is located in Rome and which is headed by the Father Superior General of the Jesuits. The Father Superior General of the Jesuits is also known as the 'Black Pope' because he lives in Rome and dresses in black; as opposed to the 'White Pope' who dresses in white and lives but a few blocks away, just across the Tiber River, in the Vatican.

Chapter 4

Segundo Montes

In 1938, when Segundo Montes was 6 years old, his pregnant mother and father were walking him down the *Acera de los Recoletos* toward the train station of Valladolid. They were on their way to visit his ailing grandmother, Genoveva, in Oviedo.

Since the start of the Spanish Civil War, Valladolid had been safely in the hands of the *Franquistas,* although battles were raging just to the south, toward Madrid. But to the north, it was 'safe.'

So the Montes family felt secure taking the train north to Oviedo. As they approached the train station, little Segundo looked up to see where that engine noise was coming from. He saw the shiny planes for a few seconds, and then he heard the explosions. And then he heard no more.

When he awoke, he was in a hospital. A nurse saw him and asked him how he felt.

“Where are *mamá* and *papá*?” he asked. Tears welled up in the nurse’s eyes. “They’re in heaven, my dear, they didn’t survive the bombing, but you’re safe here.”

That January 25th, 1938, 15 Tupolev SB-2, under the orders of Hidalgo de Cisneros (the commander of the government Air Force), and those of Yakov Vladislavovich Smushkievich, 'Douglas' (the general in charge of Soviet Aviation in Spain), targeted the train station and the munitions depots around it, with devastating effect and huge collateral damage that included the parents and unborn sibling of Segundo Montes.

Without fully understanding the magnitude of what had happened, little Segundo cried himself to sleep.

A few weeks later, he was entering the *Hospicio Provincial de Oviedo* [Provincial Orphanage of Oviedo]. Getting him into the premier orphanage of Asturias before she too passed away was one of the last acts of his ailing grandmother.

The orphanage included children of all ages, to include teenagers, who were cared for and taught by nuns and some priests, because although the law of the land was that no religious orders could run centers of learning in Spain, Asturias was safely *Franquista*, and there the Catholic Church ruled.

And rule they did. Strict discipline was enforced at all times, with yardsticks. Spanked bottoms, male and female, were unceremoniously exposed. Reverence toward Franco, Jesus, Mary and God (sometimes in that order) was instilled.

Segundo endured all until one day in 1946 when it was announced that the Company of Jesus was looking to fund the high school studies of anybody who would then go on to be a priest. Segundo jumped at the opportunity and left for Valladolid again, to live and study in the Colegio San José, where he graduated from high school and immediately joined the Society of Jesus in Orduña. One year later, in 1951, he was in Santa Tecla, El Salvador, as an assistant to Father Miguel Elizondo, at the Church of El Carmen.

"Welcome, Segundo, funny your name is Segundo because you're the *segundo* [second] Jesuit novice that I host here; the first was Ignacio Ellacuría."

"Yes, Father, it was based on his glowing report that I was sent here."

"Really? I didn't think he had a good time here. He was singularly uninterested in dealing with people. All he would ever do was read."

"The Bible? Sure."

"No, he liked to read Karl Marx."

Unlike Ignacio, Segundo was more interested in playing soccer with the local peasant boys than doing anything else, so he was constantly reprimanded. Yet the faithful loved the young novice and people flocked to the masses at El Carmen. Especially the young ladies, just to catch a glimpse of the good-looking Spaniard with the funny lisp (stemming from the way Spaniards pronounce the letters 'c' and 'z').

After soccer games, or during festivities, Segundo would seek out the peasant men and women and befriend them. Despite the educational gap that separated them, he would find a way to bridge it, and had the patience to wait for the uneducated to complete their thoughts, to thus grasp, to the fullest extent possible, the trials and tribulations of these people.

Which would lead to many dinner discussions and arguments between the passionate young novice and his older mentor.

"These people have no education, no skills. It would seem to me that the military government has been derelict in its duty to educate them."

Father Elizondo absolutely loved this young novice's interest in the welfare of his people.

"Segundo, our government is made up of human beings with different interests, most of which aren't altruistic but rather self-serving. But this also describes the government of Spain and the government of every other nation on the planet, doesn't it? It's up to us to convince them to allocate more funds to schools, for example, than to their own bank accounts and to the military. I take great pride in the fact that more and more peasant children are graduating from high school as opposed to a generation ago, when most of them would've been elementary school dropouts."

"Are you satisfied with the status quo, Father Elizondo?"

"I'm never satisfied, Segundo, but we do what we can with the system we inherited from the Spanish *Conquistadors*, unfortunately."

"You can't blame the Spaniards for bringing civilization to what used to be nothing but heathens!"

"Heathens? These people worshiped a deity, although they didn't call him Jehovah."

"No, Father, they had multiple gods."

"How different were they from us, who believe in a Father, Son and Holy Ghost, and, I might add, a Mother?"

"They made human sacrifices!"

"And what did the Spanish Inquisition do, burning Jews at the stake?"

Segundo had to admire this man's defense of his people but above all his common sense. His was a devotion to God that didn't verge on the fanatical. He measured progress in inches, and was grateful for each inch, and so were his people. His sermons reflected this; nevertheless, like most traditional sermons, they emphasized rewards in Heaven.

But to Segundo, waiting for Heaven seemed like a huge waste of time. It was almost as if Father Elizondo had bought into the mantra of the rich: 'this is your station in life, accept it,' to keep them from doing anything to dramatically improve the lot of the coffee-picking peasants who lived in thatched huts with no running water, in conditions that were anything but sanitary.

It was difficult for Segundo to understand how in the first century A.D., the Romans could have running water in every home in every one of their cities, even in Africa, where water was scarce, but nineteen centuries later, the Salvadoran masses could not. And in El Salvador, water was abundant. How could anybody not be appalled by that?

But things weren't half as bad in Santa Tecla as they were in San Salvador. In the capital, people lived in ravines called *barrancos,* and any time it rained heavily, the thatched huts and all their contents would be washed down to the bottom of the ravines. Literally, they built huts out of discarded sheet metal, mud, thatch, tires to hold down the sheet metal and cardboard roofs, and they would go to the bathroom at the bottom of the *barranco*, which was the easiest place for them to get water as well. The number of city children with huge bellies, due to *kwashiorkor* [severe malnutrition], was shocking.

This necessarily led to other extended discussions with Father Elizondo.

"You absolutely can't blame the Spanish *Conquistadors* for the appalling conditions in the *barrancos*, the lack of water, the *kwashiorkor*, etc."

"Of course not, but tell me, Segundo, who's to blame?"

"The military government." Segundo was referring to the government of El Salvador, whose president was Colonel Oscar Osorio at the time.

"But don't you have a military government in Spain? You have a dictator, Generalissimo Francisco Franco. Do you have the poverty over there that we have over here?"

"No, but..."

"Then it really isn't the military government, is it?"

"No, but..."

"So let's not consider the military government to be responsible for this poverty, for the time being. Who else do you think might be to blame?"

The young Segundo Montes knew he was being treated like a young schoolboy by his elder, but he was here as a novice to learn and he was in the presence of a master teacher. So he ventured, "The rich landowners."

The parish priest was expecting more out of the young novice.

"Any Salvadoran high school student could've said that. I'm asking you to think. If you want to be a leader of men, a spiritual leader of men, you have to be smarter than the flock. So think a little first, then answer my question."

Segundo thought for a bit before admitting, "Father, I guess I've been conditioned to blame the rich and the military for everything. If there's another reason for this widespread poverty, please tell me what it is."

Father Elizondo, pleased with the young man's intellectual honesty, continued. "Segundo, if the rich landowners disappeared, would the people be more or less poor?"

Segundo replied, as thoughtfully as he could, "Well, if this country's only real source of jobs disappeared, there would be huge unemployment and poverty would increase."

Father Elizondo nodded. "Correct. And if the military disappeared?"

"Well, the military pays their peasant soldiers and teaches them to read and write, discipline and sometimes even a trade. So the disappearance of the military would create more poverty, initially. But that would free up money to go to things that are far more necessary, such as schools."

Father Elizondo seized upon this cogent reply. "Let's go down that path. Let's assume that we can turn every military garrison into a school. Let's replace every military officer with a teacher. Let's assume we can transfer the military budget to an education budget, and that we can make enough teachers and schools available for the children. Let's even assume that we can feed and clothe such children for twelve years, and pay their books and utensils, and (why not?) even house them, so that they're able to have electricity to read and do homework at night, to enable them to actually learn and pass the courses. Are you satisfied with these premises for going forward with this discussion?"

Segundo nodded.

"Fine. We transform guns into classrooms, and we have all the classrooms and teachers and books that you want, and that still wouldn't be enough. Why?"

The young man looked puzzled. "Not enough? But it would be light years better than what we have now."

"Would it? What if I told you they'd be overwhelmed by the population growth faster than you can say *Don Quixote de la Mancha*? Because our women are producing more children that need to be educated and your solution can't possibly keep up with that birth rate. You know that. You've seen all the women with bellies around here. So then what do you do? Eliminate the police? What other necessary government agencies are you going to get rid of to create the classrooms and teachers that you would need?"

The young man's puzzlement increased. "But Father, you can't possibly be absolving the rich landowners and the military government from blame, can you?"

"I'm saying they're not the main cause for the poverty."

"Then who is?"

"We are."

And puzzlement exploded into full-fledged incredulity. "We priests?"

"The Catholic Church."

Segundo's eyelids flew open wide. "How can the teachings of the Holy Church be culpable of anything?"

The parish priest knew that, for the novice, what he was about to say would border on blasphemy.

"We teach that masturbation is a sin, we teach that preventing the conception of a child by any means is a sin, and we tell every woman that she must bear 'every child God sends her' when God really has nothing to do with it."

Segundo's mouth opened but said nothing. Father Elizondo continued.

"We tell the men that they can't use condoms and we tell the women that they can't use diaphragms, even though the last thing they want or need is a sixth or seventh child. Which may, by the way, endanger the mother's life. And we tell them they can't abort the fetus."

Segundo couldn't believe his ears. "Don't tell me that you're in favor of abortion?"

"Of course not. I'm all for prevention, not abortion, but the Church doesn't allow me to preach that, does it? All we can advise is abstention, or the so-called rhythm method, which will never work here.

"Why not?" The novice had to ask.

"These people lack the bare necessities in life, and they suffer to make ends meet, and they work hard if they can find the work, and we expect them to deny themselves the only pleasure this life has given them, which is sex? Impossible. It goes against human nature."

The novice was young enough to attempt to dispute this. "Father Elizondo, you and I abstain."

"Do we? You don't have to confess anything, but if you go to Antigua,

Guatemala, you'll see colonial-era convents and seminaries. And you'll learn of the maze of underground tunnels that were dug so that the young male novices could meet with the young female novices. And in the convents, you'll see the cells where the pregnant novices were punished. Quite unfairly, don't you think? After all, all they did was act in the way God intended them to."

A bewildered Segundo could do nothing but ask, "Father, what do you propose then?"

"The only way to create enough resources to meet a growing population's demand is to create the monetary resources to pay for them."

Segundo couldn't believe that he'd heard this from a Jesuit. "Capitalism? How can you say that the only solution is a capitalist one?"

"Easy, my young friend, look north. Look at the United States. El Salvador was conquered by the Spanish military in the sixteenth century. The Pilgrims, who were civilians, arrived in the New World in 1620. The evolution of the United States versus El Salvador and Latin America couldn't be more divergent. The founders of the thirteen colonies were fleeing the religious persecution they were suffering in Europe, in the form of the 'Holy' Inquisition.

"Latin America, on the other hand, was conquered by military conquerors, the *Conquistadors*. They organized everything militarily, to the point that the city of Guatemala was the 'General Captaincy' of the territory, not the capital, as civilians would've called it. Their goal was to pacify the *indios*, and the role of the Catholic Church was to convert them to Catholicism to keep them pacified. You can bet the farm that 'Thou shalt not kill' was taught almost as much as 'Thou shalt have no other gods before me.'

"Now then, did the Spanish Crown work toward the development of these people? Absolutely not. All they did was pacify them so that Spain could plunder Latin America's riches, which impoverished us."

Father Elizondo could tell that these facts weren't among those taught in Spanish classrooms, judging by the young Spaniard's expression.

Father Elizondo continued. "Those constraints didn't exist in the thirteen colonies and that country prospered through unbridled capitalism. And when the English Crown started to try to do to them what the Spanish Crown had done to us, they had a war of independence and that was the end of any English Crown meddling.

"So oblivious to any decrees from afar, including religious ones, the USA started to control birth rates through advances in science since the middle of the 19th century. Nowadays, in the middle of the twentieth century, men wear condoms, made cheaper through technological advances, and women can use diaphragms without fearing going to hell for having any type of sex that prevents conception. And those who want to have large families are expected to be able to afford them. And their poverty rates are far, far, far lower than ours."

Segundo listened raptly to the same history that he had been taught; only this time, told from the perspective of a conquered person, not a conqueror.

But Segundo felt compelled to mount a defense against this onslaught. "I just can't believe that what you're saying is that the Mother Church is responsible for the poverty."

Father Elizondo understood the young novice. His idealism was excusable. But it needed to be tempered. "If we as a Church stopped meddling in the lives of Salvadorans, if they were actually able to prevent having children (unless they were absolutely desired), there would be two immediate results: first, the number of poor would decrease, and second, there would be fewer young ladies derailed from completing their education.

"Then, all these educated minds would create businesses and wealth, and employ people, and the poverty rate would plummet."

The novice still didn't see a way forward, though. "That may be true, Father Elizondo, but things being as they are in El Salvador, how do you create wealth beyond what agriculture produces?"

"Well, to begin with, Spain could give back all that it took from us, with interest."

Segundo's opened wide, and then he blushed a little before grinning sheepishly and laughing nervously, asking himself, "Is this man serious?"

Father Elizondo winked at him. "Don't worry, young man, that has to be a joke because it'll never happen, so that can't be a solution."

Segundo felt relieved. So he pressed on. "Father, my question therefore stands. How can El Salvador create the wealth it needs, if not through agriculture?"

"How does Spain do it, Segundo, now that it has nobody to plunder?"

The novice was quick to respond. "Well, fortunately, the education system in Spain is adequate for the population."

"So you're all Einsteins over there? I hear *Gallegos* aren't very bright."

Segundo couldn't help but smile: *Gallegos* (residents of the province of Galicia, Spain) were often made fun of because of their alleged dim wit.

Father Elizondo kept going. "The fact is that Spain is a tourist center. With the gold and silver and riches you plundered from Latin America, you built palaces like El Escorial, and you managed to preserve many of the antiquities, including the Roman aqueducts. Your kings massively funded the arts, built monumental cathedrals, and God blessed you with the Spanish Riviera, where rich people from all over the world vacation, almost twelve months a year."

Segundo latched on to that, enthusiastically. "You've got beautiful beaches here, too, with really warm waters, all year long!"

Father Elizondo smiled. "Now you're thinking!"

A few weeks before, Father Elizondo had taken him on the parish truck all along the Coastal Highway, from Ahuachapán to La Union. There were beautiful, pristine beaches with waters that were a lot warmer than those of Spanish beaches. Segundo recalled how chilly the water of the Cantabrian sea was, when the Orphanage would take the children to the beach near Oviedo in summer. El Salvador's 200 kilometers of warm-water beautiful beaches, year-round, could be a huge source of income for Salvadorans.

The rest of the country, with its majestic volcanoes, would also be a very beautiful vacation destination.

The young novice enthusiastically endorsed 'his' idea. "The tourism industry would employ massive numbers of Salvadorans if it were developed on a scale such as in Marbella and Torremolinos, even those without education. That certainly would bring an influx of dollars and pesetas and marks!"

But then he asked the obvious question: "So, Father Elizondo, why hasn't this been done already?"

Father Elizondo shrugged. "Good question. The obvious answer is that the rich want the beautiful Salvadoran beaches to themselves. But a political case can be made to have the government take over privately-owned beachfront property and bid it out to international hotel chains. The dispossessed owners would then be reimbursed from what the winning bidders pay. Sort of like a 'Beach Reform.' Just like they did in Marbella and Torremolinos, in the French Riviera, the Venetian Lido, Miami and other tourist spots. That might be something you can apply your education to if what you really want to do is to improve the lives of our people."

Father Elizondo ended the conversation with, "You have a fine head on your shoulders, young man!"

The novice and the priest had many such conversations that year. When it was over, Segundo Montes was sent to Quito, Ecuador, to study philosophy. He earned his bachelor's degree in just four years.

After that, he returned to teach at the Jesuit school known as the *Externado de San José*, in San Salvador.

Chapter 5

Hide and Seek

As instructed, the sentinel woke the Captain up at 5 a.m., after barely two hours of sleep. Sánchez washed his face in the bathroom of the house that was his temporary headquarters, put on his gear and then went to check on his men. He made sure that the Army truck was removed from its gate-blocking position, so it couldn't be seen from the road during the day. He ordered it parked where the ambulance was parked. Then he made sure that all his troops had canned food or sacks of rice and beans available to them, and that they had running water for them to shower. Nobody was allowed to go down to the beach, because doing so could blow their cover.

The Captain knew that the military presence at Xanadú would eventually leak out, but that would've been the case anywhere else as well. The fact that the Salvadoran Army and the guerrillas were engaged in battle in the capital bought him time. He felt bad about not being with his comrades in arms in this potentially final battle, but his mission of protecting these priests was equally important. There had been nothing at the Jesuit Residence at the UCA to indicate that it was a command post. He was right about the order being illegal.

The platoon was effectively cut off from regular military line-of-sight communications. The coastal mountain range between the antennas at *El Picacho* and the beach made sure of that. That's why he'd brought a portable HF radio, which would allow him to communicate with his Commanding Officer in spite of that, but only during the day, when the ionosphere was closest to the surface of the earth. The closeness of the ionosphere during the day allowed for the signal to bounce off of it over shorter distances and remain strong enough for good reception. At night, when the ionosphere was most distant from the earth's surface, the signal would bounce back too weak to be detected.

But Sánchez had also brought a secure UHF radio, which was indeed line-of-sight, and that's what he wanted to use to make his first call to Colonel López. Because if Sánchez only used the HF radio, López and the

High Command would figure out that he was in a low-lying area, where he couldn't use line-of-sight, and it wouldn't take a rocket scientist to deduce that such low-lying area could be a beach.

He also wanted to make the call over the UHF radio before daylight, to minimize the chances of being seen, because he was going to have to leave the Xanadú compound to make it.

He called Sergeant Recinos over. He'd been with then-Corporal Recinos in a military operation in Usulután under the command of Col. Domingo Monterrosa back in 1983 where he and Recinos had climbed the only existing tower in the town of Berlín, to install an antenna to enable Col. Monterrosa to communicate with the Chief of Staff. An enemy fighter had started shooting at them while they were on the tower, but Monterrosa's troops had dealt with the shooter swiftly.

Sergeant Recinos arrived and stood at attention. "Yes, sir?"

"Recinos, you and I are going to do something crazy again. We're going to get down to our underwear and nothing else. You're going to leave your M-16 with your buddy, take my MP-5 [the Heckler & Koch automatic weapon issued to officers, which was smaller than an M-16], and wrap it in a towel. I'm going to take this UHF radio and my Browning 9 mm pistol, also wrapped in a towel, and we're both going to run up that hill that's on the other side of the road. Beyond the crest of the hill, with any luck, we'll find a tall tree that we can climb and hopefully be able to hit any of the repeaters at El Picacho, Apaneca or Las Pavas, so that I can communicate with Colonel López."

"But sir, isn't that what the HF radio's for?"

"You're absolutely right, Recinos, but we have to make this first radio transmission using the UHF, to buy us time. And we have to do it before daylight so we're not seen."

The Captain called Sergeant Zelayandía over, using his phonetic alphabet call sign. "Sierra Zulu!"

The 'sierra' was the letter 's' (for Sergeant) and the 'zulu' was for the letter 'z' (for Zelayandía).

Zelayandía came over. Sánchez told him of his plan, and told him that no matter what happened, he was to remain inside Xanadú, because his mission was to protect the priests. The Sergeant laughed. Life had always been an adventure when he was with Captain Sánchez. Why would it be any different this time?

"Hey, Sierra Zulu, why are you laughing? This was all the rage when I was at the Academy. They called it 'streaking.'"

"But sir, do you really have to go in your underwear? It's dark still."

The Captain looked at his watch, and said, "Yes, but it might not be dark anymore by the time we get back. So we want to look like beach-goers, don't we?"

Zelayandía mouthed an 'oh,' and then said, "That's true."

"OK, Sierra Zulu, go tell Sergeant Juan to open the gate."

As soon as the gate was opened, Sánchez and Recinos ran out the gate and started running up the hill. It was hell on their feet but they eventually got to the crest of the hill. Just beyond it they found a *ceiba* tree that the Captain began climbing while Recinos remained at its foot, as a lookout.

As he was climbing, Sánchez kept saying into the radio, "Charlie Lima, this is *Padrino*, over."

Charlie Lima was Colonel López's call sign. *Padrino* [Godfather] was his.

The Captain had almost reached the uppermost branch when he heard, "*Padrino*, this is Charlie Lima. Where the hell are you?"

"I'm here in Apaneca, sir." Apaneca was a town and an elevation in Ahuachapán, the westernmost department of El Salvador, where the Signal Battalion had a UHF repeater. And although at West Point 'a cadet will not lie, cheat, steal or tolerate those who do,' he wasn't about to reveal his actual position. They couldn't 'un-graduate' him, could they?

Sánchez expected to get cussed out, but instead, a very calm Colonel López said, "I didn't know they had a campus all the way out there in Ahuachapán, *Padrino*."

"Well sir, that's why I brought two of them with me here, to start one."

"What about the others?"

"I couldn't find them, sir. But we did bring their two servants with us, to help."

"Did you disobey my order, *Padrino*?"

Captain Sánchez, sitting on a *ceiba* tree branch, in his underwear, had to laugh, but not before removing his thumb from the push-to-talk button.

This transmission was being heard by all garrisons and the Chief of Staff. So Colonel López had to enter CYA ('Cover Your Ass') mode.

"Yes, sir. I disobeyed your order. It's an illegal order, and if the High Command really wants their hides, they're going to have to have mine, too."

Back in *El Zapote*, Col. López was glad. He knew Sánchez wouldn't do it. And that was fine by him. As a graduate of Liceo Salvadoreño, a school run by Marist brothers, he considered priests to be off-limits—even the Jesuits who ran the Externado, their hated rivals in high school basketball.

The Colonel said, perfunctorily, "*Padrino*, I expect you to obey my order."

"I will not, sir. But please tell the High Command this: I've got two of them out of circulation, setting up a campus here in Apaneca, and not doing anything else, and that can only serve our side well."

Then the Colonel surprised Sánchez with the following question: "Padrino, those two servants there, what are their ages please?"

Sánchez wanted to respond, "How the hell would I know?" but realized that he couldn't. They were supposed to be with him, and if they were, he could easily ask them. But they weren't so he had to give made-up ages.

Then a light bulb came on in the Captain's head. "Hold on, sir, let me ask them." He did a mental calculation and said, "The mother is 37 and the daughter is 20 and a half, sir."

"Thanks, *Padrino*."

Sánchez ended the transmission with, "I'm on batteries right now, sir, so I have to go. *Padrino* out." He also wanted to keep the transmission short to keep them from being located through direction-finding techniques.

Since his time as acting head of the C-VI (communications) department at the Joint Chiefs of Staff under General Blandón, everybody knew who *Padrino* was: a hated guy because General Blandón had had the guts to appoint him, a Lieutenant at the time, to a position that should have been filled by a full Colonel. That was a cardinal sin because the Salvadoran military was ruled by *tandas* (military school graduating classes). You occupied a position of leadership (head of a garrison, of a brigade, for example) not necessarily because of merits, but because it was your *tanda's* turn to occupy such positions. As a graduate of West Point, Sánchez didn't belong to any *tanda*.

Sánchez loathed the idea of *tandas* because in 1984, he'd seen the 4th Infantry Brigade at El Paraíso infiltrated and hit by ten guerrillas, all of whom lost their lives, but not before killing several dozen sleeping (off-duty) soldiers, just because an inept member of an older *tanda* was leading that Brigade. It was a minor victory for the guerrillas, militarily-speaking. They lost all their men in that action, but the media had turned it into a huge victory, depicting great strength at a time when it was actually waning, and public support that was non-existent. The Salvadoran Armed Forces must've been the only armed forces in the world that didn't promote by merit.

Now, here were these members of the ruling *Tandona* (the largest-ever military school graduating class), either coming up with or not opposing this stupid decision to kill these priests. If the 4th Brigade attack wasn't proof enough, this latest decision certainly was the ultimate proof that promotion by *tandas*, rather than by merits, could yet be the downfall of the Salvadoran Army because it could very well snatch defeat from the jaws of victory.

So not belonging to any *tanda* was no big deal for Sánchez. Since he'd been sent back to the Signal Battalion, replaced by a full *Tandona* Colonel assisted by an American advisor, he'd remained at the Signal Battalion, eventually becoming Company Commander. And that was fine by him. He had no intention of making a career out of the military. He was ready to move on to a post-war, normal civilian life.

The transition would hopefully come via a final victory, but a negotiated settlement would also do just fine. A negotiated settlement was something the government of El Salvador had attempted many times, to get the depleted guerrillas to incorporate themselves into El Salvador's new democracy, as a political party, but to no avail.

When Sánchez and Recinos got back to Xanadú, Sánchez thanked Recinos and told him to go have some chow. Sánchez then told Zelayandía to set the HF radio frequency to 57.5 MHz and leave it there.

"Why that frequency, sir?"

"Because that's the frequency Col. López and I will communicate on from now on." Sánchez didn't feel the need to tell him that it was the sum of the servants' ages that he had transmitted.

Sánchez went into the house to shower, put on his gear, and when he came out, he asked Zelayandía whether all the men had eaten.

"Yes, sir. You're the only one who hasn't had any chow. Do you want me to get you something?"

The Captain said, "Thanks, Sierra Zulu, but I think I'd better go break bread with the priests."

Chapter 6

Perhaps He's Right?

Colonel René Emilio Ponce was born in Sensuntepeque, El Salvador, in 1947, and from a very early age knew that he wanted to be a military man. There would be no other career for him. It came as no surprise to anybody when he announced that he was applying to the *Escuela Militar Gerardo Barrios* [Gerardo Barrios Military School], and it came as no surprise to anybody when he graduated 1st in his class in 1966, the top man of the *Tandona.* He proved to be a brave warrior as a Second Lieutenant during the 'Soccer War' with Honduras in 1969. His was a stellar career that perfectly combined prudence and bravery. As Commander of the Immediate Reaction Battalion 'Ramón Belloso,' he was one of the first to consistently inflict heavy casualties on the guerrillas. But his destiny was not to be a battalion commander: it was to be Chief of Staff, his current position, and then Minister of Defense. That was what was in the cards for the top man of each *tanda.*

But when he hung up the phone with Colonel López, the Signal Battalion Commander, he lost his normal cool. "Damn Sánchez. It had to be a West Pointer!" Colonel Ponce wasn't partial to West Pointers. He understood that they had to send a cadet every so often, and every so often, one would actually graduate. But they weren't cut out for the Salvadoran Armed Forces. Most of them asked for their discharge immediately. Not Sánchez, despite the fact that he was blind as a bat without his contacts, and that those thick glasses of his made him look out of place in the Salvadoran Armed Forces. So for him to fit in, he had to wear his contacts, and that made him a bad candidate for infantry. It was the Signal Battalion for him.

At least he'd stayed in, which couldn't be said for most other West Pointers. Some just took advantage of the scholarship and refused to serve in the Salvadoran Army. Two or three had stayed in. But as far as Ponce was concerned, the only good West Pointers were discharged West Pointers.

He dialed the office of his boss, the Minister of Defense.

"Larios here."

"General, Captain Sánchez has disobeyed the order to kill the Jesuits. His commander reports that he has two of the Jesuits with him, in Apaneca. He said it was an illegal order."

"I don't fucking believe it. This order comes from the very top, and that son of a bitch disobeys it?"

"I don't know why Ciro chose him. He must've been the only one available. He was on his way to El Picacho to reinforce the communication station there, but the helicopter was delayed."

"So send someone else to get Sánchez's Jesuits and the others."

"We're sending in the Commandos, sir. We hope they'll be ready today."

"Why weren't they ready yesterday?"

Ponce felt kind of sheepish. They should've been ready. But he had a good reason: "Sir, nobody wants to go kill the Jesuits."

General Larios was furious. "How is it that we now have thousands of officers, yet we can't find anybody to go kill the Jesuits?"

"Sir, with all due respect, he's got two of them out of circulation, disconnected from the Offensive. Maybe we should just leave it at that."

Larios was having none of it. "Ponce, those Jesuits could've made the guerrillas join the political system, when invited to do so by President Duarte, and most recently by President Cristiani, with all sorts of guarantees, especially from the U.S. government. But they didn't, and so now we have these guerrilla units invading homes and attacking with armed children! That's Satanic, Ponce. Not to mention the reports of what they're doing to families whose homes they've taken over. Those Jesuits have lost any sort of immunity they had. They have to pay for that."

"Yes, sir, you're right."

The Minister of Defense paused, and then said, "Ponce, leave the organization of the Commandos to me, you understand?"

This took Ponce by surprise. But ever a good soldier, he complied. "Yes, sir!"

"Good. Now, did anybody see anything last night?"

"One of the sentries at the military residential neighborhood across from the Catholic University reported seeing an ambulance go into the University and come out followed by an Army truck."

That was good information. "So we must assume that they were put in an ambulance and driven away, then. Has anybody seen an ambulance and an army truck in Apaneca?"

"Sir, Col. Méndez, the commander at Ahuachapán, says that no ambulance with troop trucks have been seen anywhere. So he's probably not there."

"What do you think, Ponce?"

"Well, since he used the UHF repeater system, he could be anywhere that's within line of sight of any of the repeaters."

General Larios thought about this, and then he asked, "Ponce, where would you go if you were a Signal Captain?"

"Sir, the road to the Comalapa airport and the coast is under their jurisdiction. That's where I'd go."

"But he wouldn't be able to communicate from the beach over the UHF. I've tried it and it doesn't work."

"Sir, this is Sánchez we're talking about. Communications are his specialty."

Larios had heard enough. "Ponce, you're the Chief of Staff. Find out where that SOB is!"

"Yes, sir."

Larios hung up.

Ponce decided to get some more information.

"Get me Colonel Zepeda."

Five minutes later, Colonel Juan Orlando Zepeda, Vice Minister of Defense and a fellow *Tandona* member, was on the line.

Zepeda had graduated way below him, so Ponce should've been Zepeda's boss. But Zepeda's performance during the 1981 guerrilla offensive had made President Cristiani appoint him his Vice Minister of Defense, leapfrogging Ponce. Which was unheard of.

Ponce gave his other boss a rundown of the situation.

Zepeda asked, "Why on earth did we give the order to Signal? I thought the Commando Unit was ready to go." The Commando Unit had been formed the day before, as a sort of a military SWAT team, under the orders of Colonel Benavides, another *Tandona* member, who was the Director of the Gerardo Barrios Military School. It was a temporary arrangement, to be able to have a local reserve unit ready.

Ponce replied, "The Minister said to leave the Commando Unit up to him."

Zepeda couldn't believe that. "To him? Why?"

Ponce informed him of the inability to get any officers to go kill the Jesuits.

Zepeda didn't like that at all. "René Emilio, there's raping and pillaging going on out there; that's why they invaded residences. Plus, many of the guerrillas are little kids. We have civilian eyewitnesses of that. That's an infamy! Plus, you know that the Nun had told us that the Jesuits were the real heads of the movement anyway. We want to cut that head off right away."

"I know, Juan Orlando. The Nun was the best. And she's why you're Vice Minister of Defense today."

Chapter 7

Praying on Her Knees

In Krakow, in the middle of the winter of early 1945, the Red Army sought the warmth of Polish women. If there were any husbands or fathers, they were made to watch the violation of their womenfolk and then shot. It wasn't that Colonel Vladislav Fedoseyev was unmerciful or cruel by nature. These were orders from Stalin himself, and nobody disobeys Stalin if they want to stay alive.

Unfortunately for the women, there was nobody to protect them, so they fled with their families on foot, and because of the snow, they had to flee along the roads, which made them easy pickings for a Red Army traveling on trucks. And when the Soviet units caught up to them, the women would be rounded up, made to strip, and raped right then and there, in front of the men, until every Soviet soldier had had his turn at the women, regardless of their ages. Then everybody would get shot. And the unit would move on toward Berlin.

Fedoseyev preferred to do his raping indoors. The bearded regimental commander chose a young blonde girl out of all the stripped women that were ready to receive Soviet sperm. She was the most beautiful young lady he'd ever seen. As she looked pleadingly up at his bearded face, with her emerald eyes, he put was put a coat over her nakedness and made her ride up front with him in the truck, back to his makeshift headquarters.

The young girl wept silently all the way. She knew what would happen to her. She'd seen what they'd done to her mother and sisters. She pleaded to Jesus and Mary to spare her. She prayed for a miracle.

The Colonel took her up to a sparsely-furnished apartment on the second floor, recently abandoned by fleeing residents, posting two men outside. He made the frightened girl drink some vodka to warm her up, and then removed her coat. Her beautiful girlish figure was his to enjoy. She made no attempt to cover up because she was too busy praying, with her eyes shut, "Dear Jesus, I'll dedicate my life to you if you save me."

She started praying harder and felt him push her down to her knees.

She opened her eyes and saw him drop his trousers and expose his erect organ, along with four red letters spread out in the form of an arc, along the contour of his pubic hair. From her vantage point, the tattoo looked like a crown for his penis. It spelled 'CCCP,' the Russian initials for the Union of Soviet Socialist Republics.

The young girl knew what to expect. She'd seen her mother and sisters forced to do this with their mouths, and if they refused, the soldiers would hit her dad with the butts of their rifles. So the women complied. But she had no reason not to bite down hard on this Soviet prick, if she could only muster the courage to do so.

But just then, all hell broke loose. Explosions shook the building. Machine gun fire was heard everywhere. The guards outside the door screamed, "Polkovnik Fedoseyev, *Partizany* [Colonel Fedoseyev, partisans]!"

Fedoseyev ran out the door to organize his men to fight off the attack.

The remnants of the Polish Home Army called the *Partizany*, after inflicting several casualties on the Soviets, catching them with their pants down, were eventually killed. But by the time Colonel Fedoseyev got back, the beautiful young girl had vanished.

Fedoseyev lamented her loss. He had looked forward to enjoying her thoroughly.

He would have many other girls and women as his Regiment rolled on toward Berlin. But he'd always remember that beauty from Krakow as 'the one that got away.'

* * *

In the mayhem that ensued just as she was about to soil her mouth with that Russian's manhood, the young lady put on the coat and jumped out a window, running away from the sounds of the battle. She was barefoot, but her adrenaline kept her moving fast in the snow. After a while, she found the body of a naked dead woman, with her clothes and shoes near it. She put them on and continued her westward flight, but this time far off the road.

When nightfall came, she was hungry. But all she could do was continue to pray to God for the energy to keep moving, because in this cold, if she stopped to rest, she might never get up again. Fortunately, it started snowing, and that made it less cold, even in the Western Carpathian Mountains that she was going over, because she would never make the mistake of traveling along the roads again.

She was fortunate that these mountains were more like rolling hills—not steep at all.

At dawn she found a vacant hunter's cabin. She crawled inside through a window to see if there was anything to eat. Her dad would take jerky with him on hunting trips in the mountains.

She was in luck. She found a jar with frozen venison jerky. She put a frozen piece in her mouth and took the jar with her. She needed to keep moving.

The jerky fueled her that day and night, and just before dawn the next morning she reached the Oder river. She knew that if she crossed the river, she'd be in German-controlled Czechoslovakia. It was the Sudetenland, Hitler's first territorial conquest. She didn't want to run into Germans so she hid in the woods but in full sight of the riverbank. After a while, she saw a fisherman on a boat. She ran out to the riverbank and signaled to him. He pointed further north along the bank. She figured he was telling her where to go, where it would be safe.

About a kilometer north of where she'd seen the fisherman, she came across a cabin with smoke coming out of its chimney. A woman in her fifties opened the door and immediately let her in. When offered food, she declined. She lay down on the floor near the fireplace and fell asleep.

She was famished when she woke up that evening. The fisherman was there, and they fed her fish and bread and water. She identified herself as Alicja Kowalewicz. After she'd eaten ravenously, they asked her if it was true of the advancing Soviets and their atrocities. Alicja told them how a group of Soviet soldiers had entered her home and raped her mom and two sisters while she'd remained hiding in the attic. She was fortunate the soldiers hadn't found her.

From her hiding place, she could see everything. She'd heard her dad acting like he was pleading with the soldiers, but actually pleading with her, "*Córka, nie wydaje dźwięk, proszę* [daughter don't make a sound, please]." Which the Soviets didn't understand. When they were done, they shot everybody, hoarded the cupboards and left.

Half an hour later she'd come out of hiding, covered the remains of her family, clothed herself heavily and started heading west, in the snow, until she met up with a group of fleeing persons who welcomed her. But soon a Russian unit caught up with them and raped and shot everybody but her because she'd been saved by a *partizany* attack.

They all looked at each other without the need to utter the question on their mind: Why were the Polish people being savaged like that? They could understand why Germans might get that treatment, but why Poles?

The fisherman, named Makary Nowak, told his wife Wioletta that they had to leave. If the Russians were such savages, they would do the same to them. They would cross the Oder River before dawn and head southwest, with enough food supplies to allow them to remain in the mountains. They wanted to avoid Ostrava, because it was full of Germans, and it would probably get attacked by the Russians. Makary took his bow and arrows with him, to be able to hunt for food. He wanted to avoid the use of guns with soldiers all around them.

Two days later, Makary, Wioletta and Alicja arrived at the town of Olomouc, in eastern Czechoslovakia, where some Ursuline nuns were serving watered down soup to those fleeing the Soviet onslaught. Alicja immediately told Makary and Wioletta this is where she would be staying, hugged them both good-bye, and approached the first nun she saw, informing her in Polish that she wanted to be a nun.

The nun responded, "*Nie rozumiem Polskiej* [I don't understand Polish]," and so Alicja told her in makeshift sign language that she wanted to wear the habit. The nun responded in kind that there was a higher-up who decided that, who wasn't there just then. So Alicja went to sit at the entrance to the convent, to wait for the higher-up, hoping that she could speak Polish. She sat there all day, watching the endless parade of hungry, filthy refugees (like herself) passing through Olomouc, and she grew angry. She promised the Lord a life of service to him. But she also wanted revenge. She'd seen her mother and sisters raped then shot and watched her dad watch and lose his mind most assuredly because he was unable, as the man of the house, to prevent the ultimate dishonor and harm to his women.

She'd get her revenge, and she asked God to help her get it, right then and there.

Mother Margareta appeared later that afternoon. After being told about the young girl, she approached Alicja, and in passable Polish asked her what she wanted.

"I want to become a nun. I promised God that I'd be at His service for the rest of my life if He allowed me to escape from Krakow with my life. So here I am."

Mother Margareta was thinking that it was going to be hard to reject this child's petition but reject it she must, because there was no budget, no resources.

As if reading her mind, Alicja pleaded her case with all the cunning she could muster: "Mother, when that Soviet officer was going to violate me, I prayed to God, and He saved me. Do you really think God Almighty saved me then, just to sacrifice me to them a few days later? Keep me here. The Soviets won't come this way. You'll be safe."

The young girl had touched a raw nerve. The convent was ablaze with debate about staying or going. She wanted to stay but many sisters wanted to leave. The certainty, nay, the faith of this child, was reassuring to her.

"You may stay as a novice, but you're on probation."

"Thank you, Mother, you won't regret it."

"What's your name?"

"Alicja..." She paused. She didn't really want to use her Polish last name.

"Here in Czechoslovakia, it's 'Alice,' pronounced 'ah-LI-suh.' What's your last name, Alice?" Alice decided to use Makary's last name: "Nowak."

"Here, we say Novak."

"Fine, Mother. I'm Alice Novak."

The Soviets never entered the town of Olomouc in their push toward Berlin.

But by the end of 1945, it was clear to Alice that the hated Soviets wouldn't be going back to the USSR. They remained occupying Eastern Europe. This she couldn't bear.

But if she asked Mother Margareta for a transfer anywhere, it would be refused, because she was still a novice.

The worst part of Mother Margareta was that, amazingly, she'd started buying into the socialist equality that was the excuse for the Soviets to subjugate everybody. Socialism was the benign face of the communist boot. Alice was committed to serving out her promise, but in freedom, not under the control of the hated Soviets.

Fortunately for her, she picked up the Czech language quite quickly. After a year, she was able to present herself to the authorities to ask for a Czech passport, claiming that all her paperwork had been lost when the Germans had invaded her hometown of Ostrava, in the Sudetenland, Czechoslovakia, one year before the blitzkrieg against Poland.

The official asked her in Czech: “Are you a nun?”

And she replied in perfect Czech: “No, I’m a novice.”

“And why would you need a passport?”

“They intend to send me on missions to different convents, some in Poland, some in Germany, and some in Italy, of course.”

“But you have no papers?”

“The Germans took them when they came to Ostrava, sir.”

The Czech looked at her from head to toe.

“I’ll have to take a photograph of you. Step through that door and undress completely.”

Alice paled. “Sir, I don’t see why you want to have me undress for a passport picture. I have a right to...”

“Ms. Alice Novak, if that’s your real name, you have no papers, and you have a Polish accent. I could easily think you’re just like every other person who’s wanting to flee to the West, who shows up without papers and gives me pretty much the same story you gave me. I could send you away empty-handed, or you could leave here with a passport. So you decide whether you do as I say or you leave empty-handed.”

Alice was shaken. How can this man be doing this to a human being in need? But did she have a choice?

“Sir, I’m a novice.”

“They all are, dear.”

Alice closed her eyes and fought back the tears. But something told her that the God that had saved her from the Soviets would protect her here. She walked into the room that the official had indicated. There was a photographic apparatus with hood and lamp at one end of the small and narrow room. At the other end, there was a bench. It was dimly lit. He walked in after her and shut the door.

He turned on the single light bulb above and stood behind the apparatus. Then he told her to undress.

Alice didn't make a move. She couldn't.

"I'm going to count to three. I don't have any time to waste."

She started to undress. As she was down to her brassiere and knickers, she stopped.

"One."

Off came her underwear. She was naked and ashamed. She covered her breasts and pubis.

The official approached her, admiring her nubile body. "Drop your hands to your side."

As she obeyed, she knew what was next. "Kneel."

She knelt and saw him take out his manhood. She was thinking, "I could bite it off."

Apparently, so was he. He grabbed his erection and started stroking it, six inches away from her face, making no attempt to get any closer. Alice looked up at his face and saw that he was focused on his thing, not on her. She felt better. That lasted for a couple of minutes. Then he grunted: "Keep your hands down" and ejaculated all over her face.

Afraid to open her eyes because they were already stinging from his liquid, she reached out blindly for a towel.

He commanded, "Hands to the side!" and when she complied, she saw flashes of light through her eyelids. He was taking pictures of her that way.

Next thing she knew, he'd flung a towel at her. "Clean yourself up. Get dressed. I'll take your passport picture now."

He didn't even watch her dress. When she was done, he told her to sit on the bench. He took one more photograph, and said, "Fill out the information on this sheet. When you're done, leave, and come back tomorrow morning for your passport. Don't worry about the fee."

She did as she was told. But she felt so unclean and smelly because of that man's liquid, that she hurried back to the convent to bathe, not letting anybody get too close to her.

The next day she returned, and he handed her her passport. She offered to pay but he shook his head, saying "Your payment was your first picture. Would you like to see it?"

Before she could say no, he showed her a picture of a girl, her features blurred by a white liquid on much of her face, from her eyes down to her breasts. She felt relieved: it didn't necessarily resemble her. That could've been any girl.

"People pay good money for pictures like these. So I'm grateful to you. Now, run along, have a nice life and make sure you think kindly of me."

So in the summer of 1947, on a trip to gather supplies from Bratislava, Alice crossed the border into Austria. From there she hopped on the first train she could, to Vienna.

Dressed in Ursuline attire, she took the train from Vienna to Paris, which was as far as her savings could take her. She'd studied French in school in Krakow, and so at the Paris *gare* [train station], she was able to tell a taxi to take her to *Les Petites Sœurs de l'Assomption* [The Little Sisters of the Assumption], where she would take her vows. Their motto: *Thy Kingdom Come.*

Ten years later, in 1957, Sister Alice Novak was teaching in *Colegio La Asunción* [School of the Assumption], in San Salvador, El Salvador, fulfilling her promise to Jesus for saving her from that Soviet prick.

There, she was known as Sister *Licha* [the Spanish endearing nickname for Alicia, the Spanish equivalent of Alice], teacher of math, science and physical education. Her busy schedule kept her from thinking about her past and most of all, about the bearded Red Army officer who came so close to raping her.

Chapter 8

The Traveling Tovarich

At 9:45 a.m., on a beautiful, sunny yet chilly morning on the fourth Monday of October 1949, Vladislav Fedoseyev was sitting outside the office of Victor Semyonovich Abakumov, Minister of the *Ministerstvo gosudarstvennoy bezopasnosti* [Ministry of State Security (MGB)] under Stalin, ready to present his plan in person.

Abakumov was a very feared man, almost as feared as Lavrentiy Beria because it was Abakumov who had personally carried out the purges of 'cowardly' officers who had lost the initial battles of the invasion of the Soviet Union by Germany. He would apprehend the officers and then torture and rape their female relatives, personally, making them watch, before executing them.

Vladislav Fedoseyev had first arrived at the MGB in late 1948, with a letter of recommendation from General Vassiliy Chuikov, the hero of the Soviet Union who won the Battle of Stalingrad. No longer the bearded warrior, Fedoseyev cleaned up nicely and looked like a perfect bureaucrat in a coat and tie. After his honorable discharge from the Red Army, Abakumov hired him immediately, but the only opening he had was the Latin American section, charging Fedoseyev with organizing it. For such purpose, Fedoseyev was assigned a generous budget.

The first two things Fedoseyev had requested was the hiring of a Spanish-speaking secretary and permission to travel throughout Latin America, for knowledge-gathering purposes. His secretary would travel with him initially to help him with the language, but when he considered himself to be sufficiently fluent at it, he would travel alone. Until he had a secretary, he would receive Spanish lessons from a professor from the University of Moscow. He was anxious to start. If only because many people who worked for his boss often ended up dead.

Abakumov was only too glad to allow Fedoseyev to travel throughout Latin America because that would mean one less potential enemy to be looking behind his back for. Needless to say, Abakumov had no interest in Latin America, which is why he gave Fedoseyev free rein.

Two months after submitting the request, Olga Petrenko appeared at his office. She was prettier than the average Soviet woman, and she spoke Castilian Spanish. At the interview, she told him that her Soviet parents had been stationed in Spain ever since the onset of the Second Spanish Republic in 1931. Of course, Olga learned the language fluently, having gone to school there.

She'd married Timur Petrenko in Moscow and had a child with him before he was conscripted to serve in Stalingrad, where he'd been killed in action. Upon his death she and her son had moved in with her parents. But her parents had moved to Tula City, because they couldn't get a job anywhere else but at the munitions factory there. So Olga now lived alone with her eight-year-old son Viktor in her parents' old apartment in Moscow.

Fedoseyev immediately took a liking to this lady, mainly because she was the widow of a hero of the Soviet Union and also because there could be no better secretary for the head of the Latin American section of the MGB.

"Mrs. Petrenko, I need to ask you if you're willing to travel, at least initially, because if we both want to keep our jobs, I need to learn Spanish quickly and gain as much useful knowledge as I can about Latin America."

"Please, Comrade Fedoseyev, call me Olga, and I had already been informed that to keep this job, I would have to be willing to do anything. So yes."

"Really, Olga? Who told you that?"

"Minister Abakumov."

"When?"

"When he interviewed me last Friday."

"Why did he interview you?"

"He said he interviews everybody who works at the Ministry."

That seemed strange to Fedoseyev. Unless...

"Did he interview you over the weekend?"

She looked down and barely nodded, her thorough embarrassment telling the story. His boss had taken advantage of this woman, and only when satisfied did he allow her to interview with him.

"My dear Olga, there's no need for embarrassment with me. I understand how things work, and having seen what I've seen, let me tell you, there are worse things in life." Olga raised her eyes and smiled gratefully.

"So you're hired, but since you're going to be traveling with me at least for the next six months, it's probably best if your son goes to stay at Tula City for this school year. I'll make sure you receive every assistance to get this done quickly. Then you'll come back and prepare our first itinerary. Welcome aboard."

Vladislav stood up to shake her hand. She thanked him profusely. He accompanied Olga to the hiring office of the Ministry and gave instructions about her employment and the transfer of her son to Tula City and to his new school. The clerk jumped to it.

Two weeks later, Olga and Vladislav were in Madrid, and a week after that, they were in Mexico. From Mexico, they had driven through Central America to the Panama Canal. From there they took a plane to Colombia, and then to Peru.

Since the standing order was for Olga to speak in Spanish only, that month traveling abroad served as an immersion course in Spanish for Vladislav.

Upon their return, he gave Olga leave to go stay with her son in Tula City, while he prepared a report for Minister Abakumov. Abakumov never said anything about it. Much less call him in to discuss it.

Upon Olga's return from Tula City, they embarked upon another trip together again, to visit other Latin American countries.

After which he prepared another report, but this time he felt like he was missing something. One thing that stood out for him in his travels was the extensive poverty throughout the region and the huge disparity between the wealthy and the poor. The pro-U.S. military governments of the region were doing a poor job of providing even basic housing for their peoples, many of whom lived in utter squalor.

There had to be a way to take advantage of this to achieve the Soviet Union's goal: to annihilate the United States of America.

The other thing that stood out was the overwhelming Catholicism in those countries, which made priests powerful. Especially because of the Catholic custom of confession. The priests knew everything. However, it seemed that there weren't enough priests and nuns to serve the flocks. Apparently, interest in joining a life of 'poverty and celibacy' was severely waning among the world population. The do-nothing attitude of the Holy See in light of the known Nazi atrocities probably didn't help them replenish their rank and file either.

Seeking to build a plan around his two major findings in Latin America, Fedoseyev focused on the Jesuits, only because they seemed to be the Catholic order that was most actively involved in education in Latin America. They had educational centers in most Latin American countries, from grade schools to universities. He learned all about their history, from their founding by Ignatius of Loyola, to their current operation under the leadership of Jean Baptiste Janssens, their 'Superior General.'

It only stood to reason that many of the next generation of leaders throughout Latin America would be educated by Jesuits. But by and large, Jesuits were conservative. After all, they'd sided wholeheartedly with Franco, after being dispossessed by the Republican Government, which was anti-religious, socialist, and pro-Soviet Union.

So this promising approach appeared to have a dead end. There was, of course, another approach toward the same goal: the funding of local revolutionary movements, given the fertile ground for revolutions in that part of the world. But such a recommendation wouldn't distinguish Fedoseyev at all because any low-level *apparatchik* could offer the same recommendation. And it wasn't a good one: local communist parties had huge bullseyes painted on their backs everywhere. There was nothing subtle about that approach. He preferred finesse over brute force. He preferred a check-mate that the opponent never saw coming. After all, weren't the Soviets the best chess players in the world?

Fedoseyev was convinced the checkmate could come from Latin America, from where the Americans would never expect it. After all, they were focusing all their efforts on surrounding the Soviet Union. They had forces in Europe, in Japan and Korea, and they were developing allies in Turkey and Iran, right on the border with the Soviet Union. While doing that, they were leaving their Latin American flank exposed.

So the question had to be asked: "Why leave that flank exposed?" And the only possible answer was that the arrogance that had drafted the Monroe Doctrine, against European colonialism in the Americas, was still in effect. Although the Monroe Doctrine had served to kick the French out of Mexico and the Spanish out of the Caribbean, such doctrine wasn't designed to keep local populations from rebelling against their oppressors if their oppressors were local governments, not foreign ones.

And since the only way to activate the Monroe Doctrine was to go plant a Soviet flag on Latin American territory, that was precisely what couldn't be done. Therefore, the subtlety that Fedoseyev sought had gone from being a personal preference... to a national requirement!

There can be no greater subtlety than to spawn revolutions in Latin America without leaving any Soviet fingerprints. And for that, an agent was needed. And the Jesuits, because of their presence in Latin America, would've made ideal agents, except for their alliance with Franco.

But since duty required that he seek other alternatives, Fedoseyev began to investigate other Catholic orders with schools in Latin America, like the Salesians.

He was in the middle of doing that when the heaven he didn't believe in sent him a gift. Olga put the following on his desk:

'INSTRUCTION on the SOCIAL APOSTOLATE'

It was a thirteen-page document signed by 'Ioannes Baptista Janssens, S.I.,' in Rome, dated October 10, 1949.

Straight from the desk of the Superior General of the Jesuits, a.k.a. The Black Pope.

And in this document, the term 'poor' or variations thereof was mentioned at least two dozen times; the same for the word "worker" or variations thereof. It amounted to marching orders for the Society of Jesus, for all Jesuits, to side with the poor over the rich. It literally stated: "To prevent our Society from justly being classified with the rich and the capitalists, we must direct with utmost zeal many of our ministries towards the poorer classes."

And then, "Teach them... to hunger and thirst after justice; the justice which sees to it that all men receive the due reward of their labors and that there be a more just distribution of temporal goods."

The dead end had become a boulevard. The Jesuits had become the vehicle for the 'check-mating social justice' that would defeat the Americans.

All his research had enabled Fedoseyev to write the plan that he'd submitted to Minister Abakumov a week earlier, for which he'd been summoned today, Monday, October 24, 1949. Unlike his previous report, this plan did have something useful for him.

The secretary informed him that he could go inside.

"Come in, Comrade Fedoseyev. Please sit down. I want to commend you for taking your job so seriously and for this excellent plan. I've spoken with Comrade Stalin about it, and he too commends you for the uniqueness of this approach."

He paused. Fedoseyev knew that a 'but' was coming.

"But this requires diplomatic finesse and thought, and my expertise lies elsewhere."

Fedoseyev was about to offer assurances that he could handle it, but Abakumov raised his hand to prevent any potential blunder.

"We feel that the best person to discuss this plan with is our current Ambassador to the United States of America, Alexander Panyushkin."

Abakumov enjoyed Fedoseyev's puzzled look. He proceeded to explain. "You see, Panyushkin is about to end his Ambassadorship and move back to Moscow, where he will serve in a government position that will take advantage of his expertise. He therefore offers the continuity a plan such as yours needs." He paused, and then said, somewhat sheepishly, "Plus, he can speak multiple languages, whereas I do not."

"I understand, Comrade Minister. Thank you."

"No, it is I who thanks you, Comrade Fedoseyev. Every other desk of this Ministry poses only problems, and I'm overjoyed that you're a man who comes up with solutions. Solutions that impress Comrade Stalin even."

"It is my distinct privilege and honor to serve the Motherland under your guidance, Comrade Minister."

The Minister looked at the clock on his wall. Fedoseyev took this as a sign to leave. But the Minister waved him back into his seat.

Abakumov's countenance turned serious. "Fedoseyev, your expense report indicates that your secretary Mrs. Petrenko travels with you but stays in separate hotel rooms. She also informs me that you've never approached her for some well-deserved stress relief. And then your file says that you're not married." He needed to say no more. The implication was blatant and nefarious.

It took every ounce of Fedoseyev's willpower not to react as he would've wanted to. "Sir, Comrade Olga is the widow of a hero of Stalingrad, where I also fought. Although I find her very desirable, it's merely out of respect for her that I keep a professional distance from her."

Abakumov shook his head. "Fedoseyev, it's my business to make sure that no secret of the Soviet Union falls into the hands of our enemies. Now, here you are, the creator of a plan endorsed by Comrade Stalin himself, and if you have sexual urges and you don't satisfy them with Comrade Olga, you might satisfy them with an outside person, and you might talk in your sleep, for example."

This man was good at his profession. The best, maybe. So Fedoseyev felt he had to put this to rest immediately.

"You are absolutely right, Comrade Abakumov. I thank you for showing me the error of my ways. In this trip to Washington, I'll be staying in the same room with Comrade Olga."

Abakumov smiled again, only now his smile had a chilling effect. "Good. Otherwise, please let me know and we'll get you a male secretary. Have a good trip."

As he walked back to his office, sweating, all Fedoseyev could think of was that in all probability, the policy of raping women by the Red Army could only have been hatched by a monster like Abakumov.

He also felt betrayed by Olga, for reporting on him, but then he realized that as long as he worked for Abakumov, things would be that way: constant intrigue and espionage. It was certainly not Olga's fault. So by the time he got to his office, he was calm again and asked Olga to prepare their trip to Washington D.C., after coordinating with Ambassador Panyushkin's office as to when he could receive them.

"Oh, and Olga?"

"Yes, Comrade Fedoseyev?"

"Only one room for the both of us from now on. Do you understand?"

She blushed instantly. "Yes, sir."

"Good. Get on that."

Chapter 9

The Rasputins

One week later, they were landing in Washington International Airport, in Washington D.C. They took a taxicab to the Soviet Embassy, just to report that they had arrived. The Ambassador had informed them that he was uncertain when his schedule would allow him to meet them. The Americans were suspecting the Soviets of having stolen sensitive information about their atomic program, the Manhattan Project, and so he'd be busy with U.S. officials for the foreseeable future.

Fedoseyev and Olga went to stay at the Willard Hotel, where they would wait to be summoned by the Ambassador.

It was a small hotel room, with one large bed and one bathroom. Fedoseyev wasn't about to let awkwardness permeate his stay.

"Olga, undress completely. You will remain undressed in my presence for the rest of our stay. Is that understood?"

"Yes, Comrade." Her clothes were off in no time flat.

Fedoseyev undressed as well. When he was naked, he said, "I'm going to take a shower. You stay out here in case the phone rings."

"I will, Comrade."

But the phone didn't ring for two whole days. In the meantime, Fedoseyev and Olga fucked like honeymooning rabbits. Fedoseyev wanted to make sure Olga reported to Abakumov that her boss was a heterosexual stallion. He even had to go out and buy American condoms because he'd run out of his.

The phone finally rang. Fedoseyev made sure he was at Panyushkin's office half an hour early.

After a while, the secretary told him that the Ambassador was ready to receive him. As he went inside, he came face-to-face with a fairly slim man, maybe ten or fifteen years older than Fedoseyev, with brown hair combed straight toward the back, with enough Vaseline to keep it in place for the rest of his life. He had all the Slavic facial features of a Russian from the center of the country, not softened like those of Russians whose bloodline included European ancestors. Fedoseyev had seen newspaper pictures of the Ambassador with and without glasses. At the time, he wasn't wearing any.

"Mr. Ambassador, good morning."

"Good morning, Comrade Fedoseyev. You're here to discuss a plan involving Latin America, *da*?"

"*Da*, Mr. Ambassador."

"So how is Latin America, Fedoseyev?"

"Ripe for the plucking, Mr. Ambassador."

"How so, Vladislav? They're all vassals of the United States, with their military regimes fiercely loyal to the Anti-Communist USA."

"But they are more loyal to God, Comrade Ambassador."

"Have we recruited God, Vladislav? That would be quite a coup."

"We're about to, Comrade Ambassador."

Skeptically, the Ambassador asked, "Tell me, Vladislav, how are we going to instill a revolutionary fervor into Christians who unlike us, believe in a God, and whose main hero, Jesus Christ, was the ultimate man of peace? Who essentially told his followers, 'Blessed are the poor, because they will find riches in Heaven,' or some such nonsense?"

"Mr. Ambassador, if anything, the Bolshevik Revolution proved that a very religious people, such as ours, do throw religion out the window whenever there is hunger. And the military governments in Latin America do a woeful job of feeding their people."

"Why do you think, Vladislav? They are open, capitalist societies. Why would companies not just sprout all over the place?"

"Mr. Ambassador, one would think that. But the predominant 'private enterprise' in Latin America is agriculture. It's a very curious thing. The rich landowners send their children overseas to get an education in Europe and in the United States, and they get degrees in engineering, finance, and such. But when they graduate and return home, they go into the family business, which is agriculture. So there's no widespread establishment of factories and businesses and such, to hire people away from agriculture. The children of the rich party all week and then they go pay their peons on the weekend, and that's it. By and large, they're stuck in nineteenth-century agriculture. They haven't gone beyond what their Spanish conquerors bequeathed them."

The Ambassador absorbed all this information. "So the peasants are born peasants, and since they don't have what the Americans call 'upward mobility,' they die peasants."

"That's right, Mr. Ambassador."

"This sounds like fertile ground for revolution, Vladislav."

"My thoughts precisely, Mr. Ambassador."

"But the Bolshevik Revolution was assisted by our navy's humiliation at the hands of the Japanese in 1905, a failed effort in World War I, and bold leaders like Lenin and Trotsky. Who would the Latin American poor have as their leaders?"

Fedoseyev was of course prepared for this question. "Mr. Ambassador, as I've stated in the plan before you, my research has revealed that there is a group that is present in every Latin American country, which is capable of exerting much influence locally. It's a religious sect of mavericks within the Catholic Church, which is the religion followed by the vast majority of Latin Americans. They're the Jesuits."

Panyushkin nodded. "The famous Society of Jesus, founded by the wounded soldier Ignatius of Loyola."

"Precisely, Mr. Ambassador. I call them the Rasputins."

"Oh?" Ambassador Panyushkin chuckled at this reference to the legend of Grigori Rasputin, who had entered the inner circle of Czar Nicholas II, because of his son's hemophilia. The convenient, juicy rumors were that he bedded the Czarina, Alexandra.

"Yes, Mr. Ambassador, like Rasputin, the modus operandi of the Jesuits has always been to encrust themselves in or near the throne, that is, at the very source of power of every nation they have been in, to educate the children of the wealthy and exert their influence that way."

"For what reason, Vladislav?"

"The sheer pursuit of power, Mr. Ambassador."

"Power?"

"Why yes, Mr. Ambassador. The mission of the Jesuits was to spread Catholicism and combat Protestantism worldwide. That placed them in the courts of even the most far-flung places, like China and Japan. They not only became advisors to the rulers, but they also educated their children, through whom they could influence future governments."

The Ambassador listened attentively.

"However, once far from the supervision of Rome, they engaged in more than just teaching Catholicism; they engaged in the pursuit of power."

"How so, Vladislav?"

"Mr. Ambassador, the best example I can provide of the Jesuit pursuit of power is their history in Paraguay and Bolivia, in the era of the Spanish Conquest of South America. You see, the most popular 'drink' in South America at the time was a sort of tea, called *yerba mate*, which couldn't be produced on an industrial scale because the plant grew in the wild.

"But the Jesuits discovered a way to produce *yerba mate* in industrial quantities on plantations that they called *Reducciones*. All that was needed was mass labor. Who better than the Guaraní indigenous peoples? Under the guise of teaching catechism, the Guaraní peoples were herded into the *Reducciones* and used as slave labor to produce and export *yerba mate*, which became known as 'Jesuit Tea,' the most popular beverage in all of South America, which also gained popularity among the Portuguese.

"Although the official explanation and excuse for the formation of the *Reducciones* was to better organize and convert the Guaraní indigenous peoples to Catholicism, the truth is that the *Reducciones* were the precursors to the plantations of the southern states of the United States of America in the 19th century, only instead of cotton, they grew *yerba mate*."

The Ambassador's interest was evidently growing. This fascinating history was certainly never taught in Russian schools, or anywhere else, given the Jesuits' reputation.

Fedoseyev continued. "With profit came military power. The Jesuits formed Guaraní militias and sent them into battle against the *Bandeirantes* (Portuguese slave traders from Brazil), and also against the Spanish Crown. You see, Mr. Ambassador, at the behest of the Spanish governors and the Viceroy of Peru, King Charles III of Spain had ordered the seizure of Jesuit property and their expulsion from South America in February of 1767. So the Jesuits sent their Guaraní militias against the Crown's forces as well.

"They lost that two-front war and they were finally expelled. The power grab of the Jesuits was so blatant, and their activities so contrary to the teachings of the Catholic Church, that in 1773 Pope Clement XIV dissolved the Society of Jesus. The Order managed to subsist in Russia, of all places, until Pope Pius VI reinstated them in 1814."

"They were in Russia?"

"Yes, sir."

"Go on."

"The ability of the Jesuits to get away with mundane and unspiritual activities is because they respond only to their Jesuit bosses and to the Pope. They fall outside the hierarchy of the Catholic Church; outside of the jurisdiction of bishops, archbishops and cardinals. In Spain, they fought alongside the butcher Franco against the Socialist government. Yet they're extremely clever. They get their hands bloody but wipe them clean and make everybody forget their deeds.

"These are worthy allies to have, Mr. Ambassador. They can spearhead our relatively inexpensive thrust into the underbelly of the United States: Latin America."

"It sure seems like it, Vladislav, but why would the Jesuits be interested in helping us in our endeavors, which can hardly be described as religious or spiritual?"

"There's a new breed of Jesuits influencing Jesuit thought, sir. They're the so-called 'Modernists,' who are open to the blending of Marxism and Catholicism. The Modernists are fast taking over the Society of Jesus, flushing out the traditionalists who are loyal to the Vatican."

"How so?"

"Allow me to be brief Mr. Ambassador, but a more extensive answer to your question lies in the dossier I've prepared for you."

The Ambassador picked up the dossier, leafed through it, and put it back down. "Summarize it for me."

"The Jesuits' modernist theology is based on the apostle Paul's call for Christians to see themselves not as separate individuals but as one body—the body of Christ. Said otherwise, Christ is in everybody. The Modernists, led by Teilhard de Chardin, now say that no longer is Christ in Heaven, waiting to come in Glory, as the Gospels claim. They claim that Christ is born every day, among the poor. So it behooves the Catholic Church to protect and fight for every Christ that is born in poverty and uplift the child to a position of equality among peers, and not condemn that little Christ to poverty and suffering. It's obvious that Chardin wasn't satisfied with what Christ actually taught. He tried to find an ulterior meaning to Christ's time on earth."

"But why go to all that length?"

"Chardin is a paleontologist by training. He was in China assisting in the discovery of the 'Peking Man,' an ancestor of the human race. Given the difference in the physiognomy of the Peking Man when compared to Homo Sapiens, he became a firm believer in Evolution. That immediately placed him at odds with traditional Catholic thought, which is, of course, that God formed man out of clay, and woman out of his rib, in God's likeness. In light of the evidence before him, traditional theology didn't work for him, so he proceeded to develop his own. And in this new and improved theology, a predominant notion is that Christ is born every day, among the poor."

"Nonsense."

His abruptness caught Fedoseyev by surprise. "That's the cornerstone of their new theology, Mr. Ambassador," he was quick to respond.

"That may be so, but it's still nonsense, Vladislav. I wasn't born rich. I can assure you that I'm not Jesus Christ. None of my children is Jesus Christ. When the Red Army had their way with the millions of Eastern European and German women, were we creating Jesus Christs? When many of those poor women decided they couldn't live with themselves, after being raped repeatedly by Soviet Cossacks, did they also kill Jesus Christ when they committed suicide?"

Vladislav blushed at this. He wondered how many little Fedoseyevs had resulted from his many encounters with such women. And how many suicides? It was best not to dwell on that.

But Ambassador Panyushkin was determined to continue to have fun with this concept.

"I'm fascinated by this, Vladislav, and almost wish that it were true. Because if all these babies grow up to be armed revolutionaries, sure, they could be shot, but then they would come back to life three days later, to keep fighting!"

Both men laughed, but Vladislav's laughter was nervous. He felt that he was on the brink of being ridiculed and kicked out of the Embassy. That wouldn't be a good career move. He proceeded to look somber.

"Of course, you're correct, Mr. Ambassador. Which is why we, you and I, aren't religious. Leaders Lenin and Stalin were right in rejecting religious tenets. But the only reason we're talking about this is that Catholic priests and Jesuits exert influence over the masses in Latin America. Although we don't speak that language, the Jesuits do. To the extent they're capable of moving those masses in a direction that favors our interests, the Jesuits are highly valuable to us."

Fedoseyev's words had the intended effect, which was to temper the levity of the moment. So Fedoseyev continued. "What the Jesuits believe can only serve our purpose because it is now their moral imperative to fight for these poor Christs, so that they gain equality.

"And because Teilhard de Chardin's other predominant notion is that mankind will be unworthy of God if the current inequalities persist, Chardin and the Modernists have essentially declared war on what they perceive to be the world's greatest creator of inequality: capitalism and the U.S.A."

The Ambassador nodded vigorously. "You're right, Vladislav, absolutely. That does serve our purposes. I didn't mean to imply otherwise. Please continue."

Relieved, Fedoseyev continued. "Chardin's influence being what it is, his concepts have been fully embraced by the Superior General of the Jesuits, who has issued written orders to all Jesuits to act in favor of the poor, not of the rich, as they used to. This, without seeking permission from the Vatican. A copy of such orders is in the dossier, along with a translation into Russian."

The Ambassador took out the document, read the part that had been highlighted by Fedoseyev, and said, "Vladislav, first of all, don't bother translating anymore, I'm fully fluent in all European languages, including Spanish."

Fedoseyev was glad to hear that.

The Ambassador continued reading, and then asked, "Fedoseyev, don't you think that it's a tad presumptuous and arrogant for the leader of an Order to call himself a 'Superior General?'"

Fortunately for Fedoseyev, he'd asked himself the same question, and had a ready answer. "Not really, Mr. Ambassador, if you consider that their spiritual leader, Jesus Christ, was called the King of the Jews."

This got a laugh out of the Ambassador. Fedoseyev felt relieved: he had regained control of the discussion.

Panyushkin asked another question. "So does this Superior General have power of his own, apart from the Vatican Pope?"

"He does in the sense of commanding a vast army of fanatics that have historically been at the service of the Papacy, with self-sustaining resources. The Superior General is often referred to as the Black Pope because he is elected by the Jesuits themselves, in so-called 'Congregations,' and because he dresses in traditional Jesuit black; in contrast to the traditional Pope elected by Cardinals, who wears white."

This seemed to pique the Ambassador's interest. "So what you're saying, Vladislav, is that there are no Jesuit Bishops, Archbishops or Cardinals, right?"

"Correct, Mr. Ambassador."

The Ambassador seemed to store this away for future use. He then said, "You bring up another good point: the Jesuits are very resourceful. They own real property, like schools, which are hard assets that can sustain them."

"The Ambassador is correct, but recent history, as in the case of the Spanish Civil War, proves that they can be dispossessed of such assets. They had to side with the butcher Franco to defeat the socialist government of Spain that had dispossessed them, to recover their possessions."

"Is there any evidence that they fear dispossession now, Vladislav?"

"As of now, Jesuits are in good standing with the governments of the respective countries where they operate. But even if their status quo doesn't change, they won't be able to finance their turn toward the poor."

"Can't they just raise their tuition and use the difference to fund education for the poor?"

"As you know, Mr. Ambassador, private education in capitalist nations is subject to market forces. If parents consider that the Jesuit school is too expensive, they'll send their children to a competing private school. That's why they're going to need money."

"What would their usual source for this extra income be?"

"The Vatican Bank, more formally known as the *Istituto per le Opere di Religione.*"

"The Catholic Church has a bank? You mean to tell me, these people with vows of poverty are rich?"

"Yes, sir. The Vatican founded the bank in 1942."

"In the middle of World War II?"

"Yes, sir."

"How did they get money during World War II, when all hell was breaking loose, and there was no actual business being done?"

"How did the Swiss banks make their fortune, sir?"

"With Nazi money?"

"With Jewish money, gold, jewelry, and assets that the Nazis took from their victims. It's particularly noteworthy that the Vatican never condemned or actively opposed the Nazis. The way the Nazis financed their operations was by dispossessing the Jews, who were wealthy. If there was one institution that should've railed against what was happening to the Jews, it was the Vatican. It never did. And then, all of a sudden, it had enough money to start a bank in World War II, when it didn't produce anything to sell, when the populations of the world were economically suffering due to the war, at a time when jobs and income were practically non-existent outside of the military."

"The filthy Vatican!"

"The filthy Vatican is right, sir. But officially, the way the Vatican got paid was through a 1933 Concordat between Nazi Germany and the Vatican, which stipulated that a 9% tax on the income of all Catholics in Germany would be paid to the Vatican. This worked out to approximately US$100 million a year.

"Of course, Hitler wasn't going to use the hard-earned income of Germans to pay such huge amounts of money to a 'foreign power,' when he needed to build up the Wehrmacht and develop its new weapons, and feed and fund a two-front war. The most convenient way to pay the Vatican to keep its mouth shut was through the dispossession of the Jews.

"The Vatican kept its side of the bargain, becoming vastly wealthy from that blood money. The same goes for the Swiss: the only way they could've made such fabulous amounts of money was to be involved in the war effort, like manufacturing and selling weapons, which they did not. The Swiss were left alone because they agreed to hold Nazi gold and money and valuables. The surviving Jews have sued to get their money back from Swiss banks but they lost. Apparently, it's hard to prove that the money in the Swiss vaults is misappropriated Jew money. And that's how those yodeling nobodies became an economic powerhouse."

Panyushkin chuckled. Then he asked, "So if the Vatican has all that money, why wouldn't they want to finance something as noble as helping out the poor?"

Fedoseyev was of course prepared for this. "Sir, this goes to the very heart of Catholicism. The Vatican is on the side of the teachings of St. Thomas of Aquinas, which are essentially the teachings of Christ, who essentially said, 'Blessed are the poor, who will be rich in Heaven.' The Jesuits now reject that, having embraced Modernism, and believe that the poor need not wait for any reward in Heaven, they need to get their rewards now, here on earth, in this life."

Panyushkin nodded and finished making Fedoseyev's argument. "Therefore, under no circumstance will the Thomists in the Vatican finance the Modernists in the Jesuits who seek to overthrow them for control of the Church."

"Exactly, Mr. Ambassador."

Panyushkin seemed satisfied with Fedoseyev's presentation. But Fedoseyev could tell that he wasn't done trying to figure out all the angles.

Panyushkin then said, "The traditional way for us to do this would be to sponsor the local communist parties in each country. Is there a reason you haven't opted for that approach?"

Fedoseyev nodded. "Yes, Mr. Ambassador, you see, Communist Parties in Latin America are the very reason why Military Governments exist: to fight Communism. All we're doing is throwing money down the drain, because all those Communist Parties have a big bullseye on their backs."

He paused for effect and smiled, before continuing. "Jesuits, on the other hand, not only don't have a bullseye painted on their backs, they are almost invisible and invulnerable."

Panyushkin had to admire Fedoseyev's analysis. He'd obviously left no stone unturned. To summarize the presentation so far, he said, "So rather than spend money on revolutionary organizations that would be targeted by the military governments, you propose to spend it on the Jesuits because you believe that they're going to require financial assistance to enable them to help the poor, who can't possibly pay them back?"

"That's the plan, sir."

Panyushkin looked at him skeptically. "Comrade Stalin doesn't have the reputation of being a charitable man, Vladislav. So if we're going to ask him to cut a huge check out of the Soviet Union's Treasury, we have to portray it in a way that makes him come to the realization that it would be folly for him not to cut that check."

Fedoseyev smiled broadly and nodded. The effect on the Ambassador was to make his skepticism vanish.

"You've got that reason, don't you?" he asked.

"Indeed, Mr. Ambassador. You see, with our decision to remain in Eastern Europe, our standing army is going to remain at current levels of 5 million men. At a cost of at least 50 billion rubles a year."

Panyushkin did a quick calculation in his head. "That's about 10 billion U.S. dollars."

Fedoseyev nodded and continued. "That's 10 billion U.S. dollars to maintain 5 million men."

He paused for effect, and then let the hammer fall.

"If we finance the Jesuits, we can raise an army of a hundred million pro-Soviet Latinos, at a mere fraction of that cost."

The look that came over Panyushkin's face was priceless. "You're right, Fedoseyev, if we can back that up, he'd be foolish not to cut that check!"

Fedoseyev nodded. "I don't have the hard numbers yet, Mr. Ambassador. My purpose here is to discuss the concept, and if you agree with it, getting the hard numbers will be my next task."

Which prompted Panyushkin to ask, "So what is the concept, Vladislav? You've laid out the reasons why the Jesuits are a potential partner, but not how we'll use them to raise a pro-Soviet army of a hundred million Latinos."

"Mr. Ambassador, the Jesuits' main assets are their schools, which consist of grade schools, universities and seminaries. Right now, they're producing normal high school graduates, who go on to universities to become lawyers, engineers and doctors, among others.

"Now then, the concept that I have come up with is to have these Jesuits use their schools to produce revolutionaries, at all levels. Even revolutionary priests, who, in turn, would instill revolutionary fervor in their flocks. With our financing, they can build more schools, to create more revolutionaries, a lot faster."

He paused for effect, and then finished his presentation. "And soon, we'd have a hundred million-man army of pro-Soviet revolutionaries to overthrow the pro-U.S. military governments in Latin America, at the doorstep of the U.S.A."

The Ambassador leaned back in his chair to do a little analysis. What

Abakumov's lieutenant was saying made sense to him, but Abakumov and Stalin had sent Fedoseyev to him because they couldn't understand it themselves. He needed something else to sell this plan to Stalin and Abakumov, whose areas of expertise were brute force and violence, not finesse.

The Ambassador posed the following question to Fedoseyev: "Vladislav, let's assume that we fund the Jesuits for the objectives that you've stated. The final act, which is way into the future, would be the defeat of the USA. But that may take a long time to achieve. What would be some shorter-term advantages for the Soviet Union if pro-Soviet governments started to pop up in Latin America as a result of this plan?"

Fedoseyev wasn't prepared for this question. But he had to act as if he was, if this was going to work out for him. "Short of the defeat of the U.S.A., Mr. Ambassador?"

"Yes, Fedoseyev, short of that."

Fedoseyev wished he believed in God, so he could pray for Him to put the right words in his mouth. In the absence of that, he said, "Mr. Ambassador, I'm nothing but an infantryman, so allow me to resort to my military experience to answer this. The best military tactic ever is the ambush, where you lay in waiting, overlooking the probable path an enemy will take, to surprise them with ample firepower. If you look at our bases on the Black Sea, if they come out through the strait of Bosphorus, they can easily be ambushed there from land, with artillery. If we can get out into the Mediterranean, that's just another ambush zone by enemy vessels, from both Europe and Africa, like between Tunis and Sicily. And then to get out of there, we must go either through the Strait of Gibraltar or through the Suez Canal. In infantry terms, those are ambush areas, which can preclude our Navy from ever reaching their intended destination."

The Ambassador nodded and added, "And the same applies if our vessels depart from ports on the Bering Sea, from countries under our control but who don't necessarily want us there."

"Exactly, sir. Our vessels would have to go through the Danish Straits and again, can be ambushed via artillery from land. So for us to reach the Atlantic, we need to depart from Murmansk, on the Arctic Circle. And to get to the Pacific, we have to pass through the Panama Canal (under American control) or go all the way down to Cape Horn. There aren't any

Soviet naval bases anywhere.

"And if our Naval vessels depart from Vladivostok, to patrol the Pacific, the largest ocean in the world, just how far could we go if we have no base to go to, to resupply?

"In both cases, it would be different if we had Naval Bases in friendly countries, such as Mexico, the Caribbean, any of the Central American countries, or in Ecuador, Peru or Chile, wouldn't it?"

The Ambassador nodded. Just from a military viewpoint, the fruits of this plan would be very desirable.

"From a non-military standpoint, Your Excellency, the capitalist United States of America is a source of jobs, and Latin America is a source of cheap labor. That means that the American capitalist will prefer to employ the cheaper Latin worker, to the more expensive American worker. That means that Latin Americans will flock to the United States, via Mexico, across a largely unprotected border, procreate and eventually become a huge voting bloc. If the voting bloc has been 'educated' by Jesuits, we may never have to fire a shot to bring the U.S. down."

The Ambassador agreed. "We have many Jesuit institutions here in the USA as well, Vladislav."

The Ambassador had gotten the bait with which to hook Stalin and Abakumov. This plan was worthy of his time and effort.

The Ambassador stood up. "Comrade Fedoseyev, it would seem to me that your goal today was to propose a way for achieving the interests of the Motherland in a way that is entirely cost-effective and practically undetectable."

He paused, and then smiled widely.

"And you have succeeded! Let me study your dossier, and do my own research on the Jesuits, since they do operate out of Rome, which falls under my general area of expertise. Also, let's explore ways to let them know that there are funds available to them from us; perhaps there's a way to get them to avoid having to go to the Vatican begging for money."

"Yes, sir!" It was hard for Vladislav to contain his enthusiasm.

"After my study of the situation, I'll contact you to set up our next meeting. Thank you and good work."

The Ambassador offered his hand, and Fedoseyev shook it.

Fedoseyev left the office with the goal of celebrating this success very much. Perhaps he'd take Olga to Georgetown, the oldest district of Washington D.C., famous for its night life and for the Jesuit University of the same name.

Chapter 10

"Thou Shalt Not Bear False Witness"

Captain Sánchez finished the rice and beans that the Jesuits' servants had scrounged up and cooked. The pantries of these kitchens were well stocked. Nobody wanted to fight the crowds at supermarkets on weekends before coming to the beach. It took too long, and that was time better spent lying on a hammock, enjoying the sea breeze.

The eldest of the servants, the mother, Mrs. Elba Ramos, returned to the table to take his plate. "Many thanks, ma'am, it was delicious," he said to her. She smiled at him and replied, "You're welcome, Captain."

Sánchez then turned to the priests. "I trust you're all OK, given the circumstances?"

Ellacuría asked, "Captain, we were wondering why they picked you for the assignment? Was there nobody else available, some typical '*chafarote*,' who would've obeyed the order blindly?" That was quite an insult, to call a military man a '*chafarote*' or '*chafa*.' It actually meant a sword or *machete*. But it was addressed to the wielder of such a weapon, implying an 'ignorant thug' or a 'goon.'

Considering that they could've all been dead by now, the Captain considered that to be a tad rude. He looked squarely at Ellacuría.

"Listen to me, priest, you may feel contempt toward your enemies, as evidenced by that pejorative you just used, but all it confirms is how badly you overestimate yourselves and underestimate the Salvadoran military. The Salvadoran military is composed of people of humble origins, to begin with. Then, they lack any sort of higher education, so intellectually, in the book-learning sense, they're no match for you. And yet, you can't defeat them, not even intellectually. I've seen you on TV, debating an ex-military man: Major Roberto D'Aubuisson. I kept asking myself, wait, who was the guy with the decades of higher education? Because I didn't see you roll over him, like everyone expected, considering he's got the minimum education El Salvador can provide, and you have a Ph.D. from a European university."

The priest laughed sardonically. "Come on, I was only being considerate to him."

The Captain thoroughly enjoyed it when his opponent left his flank wide open.

"Really? Was D'Aubuisson worthy of your consideration? Wasn't he the guy you publicly accused of murdering Monsignor Romero in 1980?"

Ellacuría said nothing. He knew he'd stepped in it.

The Captain pressed on. "To accuse D'Aubuisson of such a crime, you had to have proof, right?"

Still no response. Fire at will.

"Because leveling false accusations is considered a crime in Spain, isn't it? They call it a crime against honor. It's called slander and in Spain you'd be in jail right now. By the way, it's a crime here in El Salvador as well. D'Aubuisson was, and continues to be, entitled to take you to court for defamation or slander, given that you accused him of such a crime without proof.

"Because had you had any proof, he'd be in jail, and not free to debate you on TV. And had you known for a fact that he had murdered Monsignor Romero, you wouldn't have dignified him not only with your presence at the debate, but with your obvious camaraderie, which everybody witnessed."

Ellacuría couldn't say a thing. Hoisted by his own petard.

The Captain wasn't out of ammo. "Perhaps he was the one who was being considerate to you. But the one who wasn't considerate with you at all was the ex-Jesuit Tacarello, am I right?"

Ellacuría's face turned dark. Fire for effect. "The former Jesuit Mario Tacarello, somebody with your same academic credentials, who took apart each of your Marxist/Liberationist points with facts, which led you to lose your temper spectacularly. I say spectacularly because it was quite a spectacle. ¿And all you could do was to blame the CIA for everything? Let's just say that that wasn't your finest hour, priest."

Ellacuría stood up, livid. "Tacarello was a goddamn traitor!"

The Captain could feel the eruption coming. "Traitor? Just whom did he betray, priest? All he did was to point out that the Agrarian Reform of 1980 had essentially defeated the guerrilla movement, and that its accomplishment, along with the embarrassing failure that was the January 1981 guerrilla offensive, was the first great opportunity for you to take to the airwaves and call for a permanent ceasefire and to encourage the guerrillas to form a political party, which you refused to do."

Ellacuría was tired of the relentless attack and needed to fire back. So he replied, with all the disdain he could muster, "What Agrarian Reform, Captain? The fourteen families remained the fourteen owners of this country."

The 'fourteen families' were the fourteen richest families in El Salvador who, prior to the Agrarian Reform, owned most of the agricultural land in the country. They were commonly referred to as the *Fourteen*.

The Captain did not hesitate. "The Agrarian Reform Tacarello was talking about, which is the same Agrarian Reform in which my men and I participated, priest. And if the Fourteen retain control, it's over crumbs of what they used to own. We massively dispossessed them. Yours truly got called a communist by several of them, for having participated in that marvelous act of justice. It's what I'm most proud of."

Sánchez recalled that on March 6, 1980, the Junta had promulgated Decree 153, expropriating all farms of 500 hectares (1250 acres) or more and the creation of peasant-run cooperatives on the expropriated land. And then, on April 28, 1980, it had passed Decree 207, the 'Land to the Tiller' program, to train small tenant farmers to become owners of the plots they had only rented until then.

Segundo Montes chimed in. "Come on, Captain, nobody took away their mansions here or their homes in Miami."

The Captain replied, "I see. Did you have your eye on a couple of *Fourteen* mansions that you wanted to move into? Like the Nicaraguan Jesuit brothers, Fernando and Ernesto Cardenal did in Managua, after having their owners executed?"

"We want the poor to move into those mansions!" claimed Ellacuría.

Sánchez laughed sardonically. "That's exactly what every single socialist that's ever existed in the history of mankind has said, and yet they always live in the lap of luxury, while the people they're supposed to care for live in squalor. Neither Lenin, Stalin, Khrushchev or Brezhnev lived in the pigsties they forced millions to live in. Without going too far, Fidel Castro has several mansions and a private island, while his people live in crumbling buildings. And true to form, the Cardenal Jesuits and the Maryknoll Brockmann live in huge mansions, without sharing them with the couple of dozen families that could easily reside there, am I right?"

This was the time to deny it. But no denial was forthcoming. Sánchez continued. "So what you just said is just another falsehood—propaganda. And when propaganda meets reality... well... it loses. And that's why you lost that debate to Tacarello."

Ellacuría could not refute the lives of luxury of revolutionary leaders, but he could refute Tacarello. "Captain, has it ever occurred to you that Tacarello was maliciously lying?"

Sánchez acted shocked. "Ohhh... you mean like...slandering you? Just whom might he have learned to do that from, priest?"

Again Ellacuría couldn't reply. Again the Captain charged. "Was he slandering you when he said that your claims to intellectualism were undercut by the fact that you hadn't written any books, in contrast to Tacarello, who, at a far younger age, had already written two?"

Ellacuría opened his mouth to talk about his thesis, but he opted not to. Instead, he said, "I've written countless articles."

"Yes, that's what you told him, and that's when he mentioned that all you did was plagiarize Zubiri, who, according to Tacarello, was nothing but a pseudo-intellectual."

Ellacuría was about to blow his top. Ellacuría was considered an intellectual god in El Salvador. He wasn't accustomed to having his intellect questioned. But since Captain Sánchez didn't share that opinion, he had no problem lighting this fuse. So Sánchez asked him, "Or was that slander as well?"

A torrent of Basque words erupted from the priest's mouth, much to the Captain's delight.

Unfortunately, Montes was doing his very best to ruin the show by trying to calm his boss down, which he eventually did.

After a brief moment of silence, Montes said, "Let's let Tacarello rest in peace. He was a good Jesuit."

But Sánchez wasn't done. "Such a shame guerrilla *chafas* gunned him down when he was on his way to a radio station, to keep him from continuing to tell the truth, the day right after his thorough humiliation of you, priest."

Sánchez debated whether to stop or go on. He went on. "Or were they Jesuit *chafas*?"

Sánchez was done, for now. He'd leave the slight matter of Ellacuría's thesis for another occasion.

CHAPTER 11

PROTECTING THE FAMILY JEWELS

In 1939, the policies of Benito Mussolini had thrown Italy into a severe economic depression. Business was suffering, including the Neapolitan hardware store *Ferramentas Napoli,* handed down to Albino Tacarello by his father Pietro, may he rest in peace. The Tacarello family lived on the second floor of the hardware store building.

The Tacarellos were four: Albino, his wife Maria, his 22-year-old daughter Lina and his older son Giuseppe, 24, a *caporale* [corporal] in the Italian army. Giuseppe was the family hero, having been wounded in his upper left thigh in the campaign in Ethiopia. He had been sent back home to recover.

The topic at the dinner table was always business, and how the imminent war would affect it.

"The Jews are some of our best customers, and they're getting nervous with what's going on in Germany, and the fact that *Il Duce* is becoming good friends with that monster, Herr Hitler. Many of them are leaving for America," Albino said.

His wife didn't like the idea of fleeing. Naples was her home. "America? What on earth for! They're in a depression!"

"Those with relatives in the USA are going there, but the rest seem to be heading to Latin America, where the cost of living is cheap, and where there aren't any brown shirts persecuting you."

With trepidation, Maria asked, "So what are you planning to do?"

"I want to send Giuseppe to Mexico."

"What?"

"*Moglie* [wife], the way I see it, it's either send him to Mexico or get him killed in a stupid war. It is right to serve the Motherland, and Giuseppe's done his duty. But I don't want him to be serving the German Motherland. Hitler is poised to take over Europe, and *Il Duce* is going to help him, as evidenced by the Pact of Steel they just signed. So once Giuseppe is declared rehabilitated, they will certainly send him to the front, wherever that may be."

Albino looked at his son with much love. Giuseppe was his pride and joy. Then he looked back at his wife. "He was wounded in the upper thigh, very near the family jewels. I'd say he's served his nation enough. Plus, money and customers are moving to Latin America, so having hardware stores in Latin America may keep us afloat if business suffers here due to war. Giuseppe's a smart boy. He knows the hardware business inside and out. Also, Spanish is very similar to Italian, so he'll pick it up very quickly."

Maria's consternation had not diminished. So Albino tried another tack.

"*Moglie*, consider that we're probably saving Giuseppe's life by doing so."

Maria's intuition told her she'd probably never see her son again. But keeping her boy safe from the precipice Europe was about to fall into was paramount. She'd suffered enough while he was in Ethiopia.

So one fine Sunday in August 1939, Giuseppe tearfully bid farewell to his family and boarded the boat that would take him into his future.

Several days later, as they were approaching the Gulf of Mexico, a severe tropical storm developed, so the ship changed course to dock in Puerto Cortés, Honduras for a few days, to wait out the storm. Those few days gave Giuseppe some time to make inquiries. He loved the laid-back setting of Puerto Cortés. But it was too laid back. Somebody at a local bar told him the place that was hopping was El Salvador because everything was so nearby because of the size of the tiny country. You could work in San Salvador and be at the beach in 30 minutes.

That also meant that Giuseppe would be 30 minutes away from the port where his imported wares would arrive. That was a huge benefit for his business.

Having thought about it, he went to the local telegram office and sent this message to his father: "Going to El Salvador. Not continuing to Mexico. Explain later."

He was, after all, financially independent. His underwear contained small diamonds in small pockets that his mother had stitched, which he could easily convert to local currency anywhere. His father had also converted enough liras to U.S. dollars, so that he need not stay at cheap places, to avoid getting robbed.

The next day he got on a bus and headed south to San Salvador, a long but worthwhile trip, because, after all, he was discovering a new world. The landscape became more attractive when the bus started climbing the mountains of the Sierra Madre, in the Honduran Department of Ocotepeque, which bordered on El Salvador. The border crossing led to still higher elevations in the Salvadoran department of Chalatenango, which reminded Giuseppe of the Apennines in Italy. The bus crested in El Pital, the highest elevation in El Salvador, before starting down toward La Palma, Chalatenango, where they stayed overnight in a small motel.

What Giuseppe had seen so far evoked memories of his native Italy, but when he saw the outline of the San Salvador Volcano at noon the next day, he couldn't help thinking about the Vesuvius near his beloved Naples.

When he arrived in San Salvador at 5 pm that day, he knew he'd found his home. It was a bustling little town, in a valley, surrounded by magnificent elevations, where the San Salvador Volcano stood out majestically, but also the Guazapa Volcano to the northeast, the Las Pavas mountain to the east, and with a mountain range to the south. The city lay in a perfect valley called the 'Valley of the Hammocks,' because of the constant tremors that shook the city. But he was used to tremors in southern Italy, many of them due to the rumblings from Mount Vesuvius.

In no time flat he'd rented a locale, along with an apartment on the second floor, in downtown San Salvador. Soon after, he'd opened his hardware business, which he named *Ferretería Vesubio* [Vesuvius Hardware Store]. After a few telegrams to his father, he started importing his wares through the Port of La Libertad just half an hour from the city. With his heavily-accented Spanish and his charming personality, his business started booming, and he was able to start sending money to his family in Naples.

To his customers, he became known as *Pepe*, a lot simpler to pronounce than Giuseppe.

But young Pepe didn't have much of a social life, because his only refuge from the ever-worsening news from Europe was his work.

Chapter 12

Life is not a Beach

In his spare time, Pepe would read up on the history of this tiny nation. The Spaniards came to Latin America to beat the natives into submission and in the process, copulated with the native women, creating a breed of *mestizos*. The *mestizos* were born into good families, and if they weren't bastards, they'd rule over the bastards and the natives. Eventually, it came to be that the Spanish and mestizos were the masters, and the natives were their subjects. The whites and mestizos became the owners of large tracts of farmland, and the *indios* farmed the land for them, receiving a pittance as payment. While the rest of the world progressed, nothing changed in El Salvador: its economy was based on agriculture, where the landowners would make huge profits at the expense of paying their workers next to nothing. This was true in the late eighteenth century, and it continued to be true in the mid-twentieth century.

All Latin American nations gained their independence from Spain in the early 19th century, as a result of the invasion of Spain by Napoleon. But in Central America, the only thing it did was drop the Spanish crown from the economic equation: now the landowners could keep all the profits, and they set up a government that not only allowed their selfish use of the huge wealth they amassed, but also protected it.

Guatemala, El Salvador, Honduras, and Nicaragua became nothing more than large, locally-owned *haciendas* posing as nations.

The military now followed the orders of the local President, not the Crown. The President was a person placed by the landowners for the purpose of improving the lot of the rich few, and not that of the large masses. And the role of the military would be to protect this money-making machine for the few, from anybody with half a heart.

Naturally, in time, there were far more *indios* than mestizos and whites. But the sources of employment didn't multiply commensurately because the Salvadoran economy continued to be based on agriculture, and there wasn't any more land being created. Although a middle class started developing by providing services for the landed gentry, the masses were intentionally left without education and without being taught trades and therefore, without the ability to move up and out of poverty. This was so because from the viewpoint of the ruling class, the country didn't need more attorneys, engineers, doctors, teachers, etc.: all it needed was more peasants.

Eventually, poverty exploded, and masses started moving to the city from the countryside. Without being able to afford a home, they built their own shanties and hovels out of available materials on the outskirts of the city.

With the onset of World War II and the Spanish Civil War, many Europeans moved to Latin America, including El Salvador, bringing other ideas and other business opportunities, with limited industrialization, but alas, it was never enough: an under-educated population translates to ill-qualified labor and tends to attract too few industries.

So poverty kept increasing.

One of the ways for a young peasant woman to move up in El Salvador was to become a *sirvienta* [servant].

If the family was lower middle class, they'd usually have only one who did everything. But most homes in San Salvador had at least two.

The *sirvienta* got paid a pittance, ostensibly because she got free food and lodging. But that didn't come close to compensating her for the fact that she was on duty 24 hours a day, 6 days a week, with usually one day off. If the *sirvienta* needed to travel longer distances to go home, she would get from Friday to Sunday off every two months, instead of a day off every week.

No law had been passed to give any labor rights or recognition to the servants. There was no social security paid for them, no medical insurance, no retirement, nothing. It was up to the munificence of the employer, but only if she'd been with the family for quite a while. The world had evolved in its treatment of employees, but in El Salvador, the treatment could be described as nothing short of exploitation.

The presence of a poor female in the house, who needed the job to help her family in some distant part of the country, invited sexual abuse. Such relationship could never be classified as consensual if she had to submit to keep her job, given her lack of education and skills to do anything else.

Chapter 13

Rumbles in the Vesuvius

Marta Elena Carrillo, known by her nickname Nena, was born in Intipucá, department of La Union, the easternmost department in El Salvador, in 1923. She was the third in a family of seven children, all living in a dirt hut. Her dad was a jack of all trades, and her mom was necessarily a housewife, doing whatever it took to make ends meet. The hut had one single room, with an earthen oven and wash basin outside. Mr. Carrillo had built an outhouse for everybody to use, but more often than not, people went to the bathroom wherever they were at, behind a bush. The local stream would be where people bathed and washed clothes. There was a public spigot for gathering potable water in small tanks, in the middle of the town square. If it was more convenient for people to gather water from the stream, than from the spigot, that's where they'd get their water as well.

Nena grew up selling bread at the local outdoor market in Intipucá. Because of her chores, she had no time for education, which was provided by a local school in a small warehouse, under suffocating conditions, and only up to the sixth grade. She went there for the first few grades, and then essentially taught herself to read while sitting at the bread sale stand, studying old magazines or newspapers.

When she turned 13, she was told by her mom to go find a job to help sustain the family. Her first job was at an old folks' home, an *asilo*, in San Miguel, the largest city in eastern El Salvador, an hour away from Intipucá by bus. There she would clean, sweep, mop, but immediately realized that her way up was to learn to cook, so she managed to ingratiate herself with the cook and soon she was officially made a cooking assistant.

But the pay was still miserable. She heard that in San Salvador the pay was much higher. So when she turned 17, she headed to San Salvador with whatever savings she had left after sending money to her family in Intipucá.

When she got off the bus terminal, she started walking the streets of downtown San Salvador. She passed a hardware store with a sign that said 'Vesubio,' which also had a 'Help wanted' sign. When she walked in, a tall young man greeted her, speaking broken Spanish. She informed him that she wanted to inquire about the job.

He asked her what skills she had. When she said she could cook, he immediately realized that she could help him in the store and also in his apartment above the store, which he never had time to clean up. He asked her if she could be a live-in, and that he would pay her for being a live-in servant, and also for being a store assistant. What he offered her was double what she was making at the *asilo*. She'd struck gold!

But it was nothing for the amount of work she was required to do. During the day she had to learn every aspect of the business; during the night she had to cook and clean up. Fortunately, it wasn't a big apartment, and she had her own room behind the kitchen. It was a huge step up from the flea-infested, dirty world in which she'd grown up in Intipucá.

And Don Pepe was a very nice young man, always courteous, grateful for her help. When business was good, her pay would increase a little. Like her, all he did was work, work, work so he could send money to his family in Italy. But that December he learned that his father had died in a bombing in the war in Europe when he was at the port of Naples receiving a shipment for the store.

Pepe became despondent and began drinking heavily.

She would tend to the shop alone because he wouldn't come down. She understood he was grieving, but the days went by, and a shipment was coming to the port of La Libertad, and he had to take steps to clear customs and bring the goods to the store.

She never went into his room if he was there, but there was no other way to inform him that business was about to suffer if he didn't spring into action.

She knocked on his door, softly. "Don Pepe, they need you at La Libertad." No answer.

After repeating this a few times, with the same result, she opened the door. Pepe had obviously been drinking, and he was passed out, completely naked on top of his bed. She felt chagrined at having seen this and left the room immediately. But hours went by, and people came and asked for Don Pepe. If she didn't move him, he'd lose his customers, and she'd lose her job.

Nudity was not foreign to her since she'd grown up with no privacy whatsoever in her hut and everybody saw everything. But seeing her employer's nudity was not right. And she'd always been warned about the precarious position live-ins often find themselves in: at the mercy of their employers. She'd heard what had happened to other servants. She didn't want that to happen to her.

But she was going to have to walk into that room and wake her naked boss up.

So at lunch, she put the 'out to lunch' sign on the door, walked up the stairs, prepared a light lunch for Don Pepe, and walked in with the tray. She put the tray on the nightstand and nudged him until he stirred, and when he sat up, she saw in his eyes that he realized how exposed he was but made no move to cover himself. Instead, he said, "Nena, I need to shower, and you're going to have to help me because I'm hungover."

Nena knew she had to refuse this but couldn't. She helped the naked young man to the shower and was unable to refuse when he told her to bathe him all over.

She washed his hair with shampoo and soaped his chest and back but wouldn't go further down. She gave him the soap and said, "Don Pepe, please soap yourself there."

Pepe looked at her and said, "No, you do it."

Nena felt the heat rush to her face. It was something every fiber in her body told her to refuse. But she wasn't about to risk this great job. She took the soap back and applied it to his manhood. She knew she was entering forbidden territory but couldn't step back.

His manhood grew in her hands. Soon it was as tall and sturdy as an oak. As she tried to move on to his legs, he held her hand there.

Nena pleaded with him. "Please, Don Pepe, I'm pure, this isn't right."

Pepe's alcohol-ravaged brain didn't care. He provided for her, didn't he? Food, shelter, a far better salary than she'd be able to make anywhere else with her education? Maybe she ought to feel grateful for the opportunity to help him deal with his grief.

Nena wasn't his type of woman: she was too dark, too short, too *india*-looking. Not someone he'd like to be seen in public with. But inside these walls, she'd do just nicely.

"Stroke it." And he moved her hand to show her what to do.

Ten minutes later she ran out of the bathroom, leaving him quite satisfied.

He came down to the shop in his usual, professional demeanor, for which Nena was grateful. He told her to tend shop while he was off to La Libertad.

When he got back that evening, he brought her some flowers, and a note that said, "Thank you for all you do."

Things went well at Vesuvius. Money and people were flowing into the country from Europe. Houses needed to be built. Hardware flew off the shelves. He was grateful for Nena's presence. She was a quick learner. She got a raise and was promoted to manager. With that, she was able to send more money back to Intipucá. She was very happy in the shop.

Upstairs, not so much.

Chapter 14

Begetting while Getting

Late one spring afternoon in 1941, a charming young lady walked into the store, to buy some sandpaper, paint, wood, and nails. She had lovely flowing chestnut hair, dark haunting pools for eyes, and lovely olive skin.

"*Signorina*, what's this for?"

"I have to repair a window frame, it has water damage," she answered in a voice that reminded him of his mamma's.

"*Signorina*, I close up in fifteen minutes. I can go do this work for you if you let me."

"That would be most kind of you, Mr. Tacarello."

"Please, call me Pepe."

"Fine, Pepe, my name is Belinda, Belinda Torres."

Belinda and Pepe walked the fifteen minutes to Belinda's home. Rosa, her mom, opened the door, surprised to see her youngest daughter accompanied by an unknown but handsome young man. Upon the customary introductions, Belinda took Pepe to the window that needed repair, at which time Pepe immediately got to work.

In a couple of hours, the window and sill had been fully repaired and painted, and Belinda asked him to stay for dinner. He begged off, because he was sweaty, but asked to be able to call on her that Saturday, which she accepted.

He returned to his apartment elated. What a charming *signorina* she was!

Nena was waiting for him, dinner served. Unlike the rest of the Salvadoran households, at Pepe's, not only did Nena have a normal room of her own, and not one for servants, but she also sat at the table with her boss to eat, not by herself in the kitchen.

They discussed the business of the day, and then Nena asked him about the *signorina*.

"What is it to you, Nena?"

"I'd just like to know, Don Pepe." What she really wanted to know was if she'd finally be left alone if Pepe took her as his girlfriend.

"I like her, Nena, but that doesn't affect you and me in any way."

Nena mustered all the courage she could to say, "Don Pepe, I'm grateful to you for what you've taught me to do professionally. But you don't love me and I don't love you and yet you force me to do things that not even a whore would do. You take advantage of my need to make a living."

"I see where this is going, Nena. I owe you an explanation, but please, let's finish our meal and then we can talk in the living room."

The meal finished, Pepe got up and went to the living room, while Nena took the dishes, washed them, dried them, and then went to the living room where she found Pepe stark naked, stroking his erection. "Get undressed, Nena."

"No, Don Pepe, please we were going to talk...."

"Do it now."

The voice of the *patrón* [boss] activated her natural submission, seared into her genes by generations of servitude to Spaniards. Her conscience was screaming at her "Don't," but her need to secure the good income she received overcame it, not without tears welling in her eyes. He'd seen her naked countless times, but that didn't mitigate her shame. And what if somebody back home found out?

She tried to cover her privates, but her hands flew to behind her head when he commanded: "*Manos arriba* [hands up]." Pepe loved the way she obeyed.

"Now Nena, how can you say that you're mistreated by me, considering that number one, I pay you as if you were a professional bookkeeper and manager, which you're not; number two, I give you food and shelter for free; number three, you share in the profits and number four, you go back home whenever you feel like it? Compared to the universe of Salvadoran girls with your upbringing and background, are you better off, or not?"

"Yes, Don Pepe, but you shame me!"

"Nobody else knows how you repay my generosity, Nena, and nobody ever will. So why are you ashamed?"

"Only whores suck a man's penis and swallow his god-awful milk."

"Are you a whore, Nena?"

"No!"

"Then your statement can't possibly be true."

"You violate my rear."

"So you won't get pregnant, dear. I'm doing you a favor."

"A favor? Then why do I feel so bad?"

Pepe jumped off the sofa and slapped her across her breasts.

"Because you're an ungrateful bitch!"

She knew better than to protect herself. He continued slapping her breasts, so as not to mark up her face. She was petite, but she had sizeable breasts, and they swayed heavily as he slapped them.

"Get on all fours!"

Once she was on all fours, he spanked her bottom with his hand. He loved to see the red imprints of his hand appear, as she cried out begging him to stop.

When he did, he reached over for the jar of Vaseline he had ready nearby, applied some to his erect member, and plowed into her rectum. He didn't last long because of her tightness and because her cries excited him so.

Spent, he lay beside her. "Whom do you belong to, Nena?"

"To you, Don Pepe."

"Don't ever forget that. Now clean me up."

That Saturday, Belinda received Pepe at her home. He regaled her with flowers, a bottle of Chianti, stories about Italy and about the craziness of Benito Mussolini. Belinda enjoyed it all, enraptured by his worldliness.

The following day, they went to church together, and it wasn't long before they became engaged. Six months after Belinda walked into the hardware store, they were married and honeymooning in Acapulco, Mexico.

When they got back, Pepe moved out of the apartment he shared with Nena, leaving its title to her. He promoted her to General Manager of *Ferretería Vesubio* in San Salvador. He was already making plans to expand in Santa Ana, the second largest city in El Salvador.

Nine months later, Carmen María Tacarello Torres was born. She had beautiful white skin, green eyes, just like his mother, Maria.

From San Salvador, Pepe sent a photograph of their granddaughter and niece to his mother and sister, asking them to move to San Salvador, because Naples was turning out to be one of the most bombed cities in the war. But they wouldn't budge.

While at work, Pepe would leave most of the day-to-day to Nena. At noon, Pepe would usually go home for lunch. But sometimes he would go upstairs and make Nena submit to him, just to remind her of her place in the world. But that was occurring less frequently now. For the first time in her life, Nena was happy.

In time, Belinda became pregnant again, with the baby due in August 1943. When August arrived, Pepe was anxiously awaiting the birth of a son, whom he would name Mario, because it was the masculine version of María. He was fairly certain it would be a boy, because all the womenfolk looked at the shape of Belinda's belly, and said: "It's a boy." The baby was scheduled to be born on August 3rd but came one night early. But it wasn't a boy. They named her Rosa Lina, after his sister and Belinda's mother. That was a sleepless night for Pepe, as he stayed at the hospital during Belinda's labor.

After the birth, the doctor wanted to keep Belinda at the hospital. Belinda told Pepe to go home to sleep, she'd be OK. Pepe decided that he would bring the eldest of his servants, Roxana, the cook, to stay with Belinda. His first-born, Carmen María who was almost two now, wanted to go see her mom. Roxana assured Pepe that the little girl would be all right with her. So after dropping both off at the hospital, Pepe returned home for the evening.

The younger servant, Gladys, who did the housekeeping, served him dinner, and Pepe saw that she was an attractive *india*. He asked her how old she was and where she was from. She said, "I'm almost 15, from Sonsonate." Pepe, realizing she was innocent and underage, decided for a lucid moment to forego his instincts. He finished his dinner and told Gladys he would retire. At which point the young servant said, "Don Pepe, I haven't turned down your bed yet, please let me go do that." He followed her up to the bedroom, and there he saw her budding womanhood in the soft light of the lamps, and what finally sentenced her was the brilliant yet innocent smile she gave him when she was done.

Quickly, Pepe's little head did the following calculations: the Tacarello household was a prize for any servant to work in and so she would dare not rock the boat in any way; if she did, she had no legal recourse, and Belinda would kick her out and make sure she didn't work in this desirable neighborhood again. Would she risk all that? Probably not. But if she did, there'd be no authority that would go against the great Pepe Tacarello. So he told the young servant to prepare a bath for him, and while she was filling up the tub, in walked Pepe with two wine glasses in one hand, a bottle of Chianti in the other, wearing nothing but a smile. The young servant turned crimson at this blatant exhibition but continued preparing the bath.

"You drink wine, Gladys?"

"No, *señor*," she stuttered wishing she could get out of there but his naked frame blocked the door.

"This is Italian wine I imported to celebrate the birth of my son, but I now have two daughters, so I'll use it to celebrate that. I want you to celebrate with me, Gladys, will you do that?"

What could she say? She was in no position to say no. Her mental calculations were similar to Pepe's a few seconds before.

She smiled bravely and said, "Of course, *señor*!"

Pepe slid into the lukewarm water and told Gladys to get in as well. At that point, poor, undereducated Gladys was smart enough to know that if she ran out that door, she may as well keep on running, because she would no longer have a future in this home.

She looked imploringly at him, and said: "Please, Don Pepe, I'm pure, don't dishonor me."

"My child, I give you my word you won't be dishonored, if you give me your word that you won't breathe a word to anybody, much less Mrs. Tacarello."

With that, she did as she was told.

As her slender dark body slid into the bathtub, Pepe told her she was in luck, because she was about to learn some Italian.

Later that night, as Pepe lay in bed alone, he smiled at how useful Gladys had found that Chianti to be, to wash his taste from her mouth. She'd left that bathtub pure, as promised, but far less innocent, although more cognizant of the Italian language. Smiling, he fell asleep.

Only to wake up screaming. He'd had a terrible nightmare. His *mamma* and Lina had appeared to him, dressed in white, and had told him how much they loved him... then they turned somber and said *adio* [good-bye] and started retreating as if floating in the air. In the dream, Pepe had run after them, but couldn't catch up, they kept looking up and shouting in Italian "Stay away!" when suddenly they had disappeared in a fireball.

The screams brought Gladys running to his room. "Don Pepe, *qué pasa, qué pasa*?"

Pepe told her his dream. Gladys instinctively embraced him and tried to soothe him, telling him it was nothing but a dream. Pepe calmed down and, grateful for her ministrations, told her to go get the Chianti.

The following morning, over the radio, news came that Naples had been bombed.

Pepe ran to the local telegraph agency to send a telegram to his *mamma*. When a week passed without a response, he feared the worse. He became despondent. He told Belinda he was leaving for Italy.

"What? Have you gone absolutely *loco*? You have no certainty that they've been harmed. For all we know, the telegraph office was bombed, not them. But regardless, you have a family here. your obligation is to us. If you go to Italy, you won't come back. You'll get shot or bombed or captured or God knows what."

Pepe had to give credit to his wife's logic. But on August 23, he received a telegram from the municipal government of Naples: Maria and Lina were among the dead who died in the Church of Santa Chiara, which had been bombed while they were at a service there.

The only way to keep his mind off the tragedy was to work incessantly. Since the San Salvador shop was well tended to by Nena, he decided to open a hardware store in Santa Ana, the second largest city in the country. Every day he'd leave at 6 am for Santa Ana, and every night he'd be back home by 8 pm. Although the distances were relatively short, Belinda worried that her husband could get into an accident by driving back and forth so much. Especially now that he'd started drinking as a result of his loss.

"Pepe, get yourself a manager for Santa Ana, especially if you've decided to start drowning your sorrows in alcohol, like a typical Salvadoran male."

"*Moglie,* why do you berate me? It wasn't you who lost your *mamma* and sister in a war. Now you're angry because I grieve?"

"Not angry. I just don't want to lose my husband and I don't want my children to lose their father in a car accident because he was drunk. What are they going to say, 'your husband, your father was nothing but a drunk?'"

Somehow this got through to Pepe. The very next day he took Gladys with him to Santa Ana and made her distribute flyers advertising for a job as a manager at Vesuvius of Santa Ana.

The response was not long in coming, and it was overwhelming. Pepe asked Gladys to mind the store while he interviewed candidates in the back office.

The process was somewhat tedious. Most Salvadorans weren't sufficiently educated to take over managerial operations successfully, and hardly any of them had the requisite experience, although none lacked enthusiasm. After three days of interviewing, he'd just about lost hope when a well-dressed lady walked in.

"*Buona sera, Don Giuseppe, io sono María Josefina Pérez vedova de Rossi, e sono interessata a questo lavoro* [Good afternoon, Don Giuseppe, my name is María Josefina Pérez widow of Rossi, and I'm interested in this job]."

Pepe was stunned. Here was this olive-skinned beauty, speaking perfect Italian. And named Maria, like his *mamma*!

"María Josefina, I'm sorry for your widowhood, but where did you learn such perfect Italian?"

"Please, Don Giuseppe, call me Fina."

"Fine, Fina. People call me Pepe."

But Fina knew better than not to call this man 'Don.' She said, "Don Pepe, I studied economics at the *Università degli Studi di Napoli Federico II*, in Naples, where I graduated and met and then married my late husband, Orlando Rossi."

"My sincerest condolences, again, but how did your husband die?"

"He was conscripted by Mussolini and was killed in action in Africa. I remained in Italy as long as I could, but the situation became untenable for me, and I returned to my native Santa Ana recently."

"I got wounded in that war. What a coincidence."

Her eyes filled with tears. "What a stupid war that was. What a useless waste of a life."

"Were you in Naples during the bombings?"

"No, Don Pepe, when my husband was conscripted in 1940, he told me to move to Milan with his parents, where I remained until the news of his demise. At that point, there was nothing left for me to do in Italy, so I came home."

Here, Pepe shared his story with her, right up to the demise of his mother and sister in an Allied bombing. By the time he'd ended his story, it was dark. Gladys popped in to ask if she could close the store. He told her to go get them some coffee and something to eat for the trip home, that he would close the shop. As he got up to do so, he asked the following questions of her:

"Have you ever been in the hardware business?"

"No."

"Have you kept books for any business at any time in your life?"

"No."

"Have you ever managed subordinates, or dealt with customers?"

"No."

Pepe sighed. He'd really hoped for a yes to any of those basic questions. He went to unfurl the aluminum curtains that covered the displays and as he unfurled the last one, he heard Fina say, "But I'm a quick learner, and I'm willing to do whatever it takes to land this job."

Of that, he had no doubt. A graduate of the Federico II University should turn out to be an asset. As Pepe turned around to respond, he was awestruck by the sight of her, completely naked. It was a thing of beauty, large, round breasts, crowned with dark chocolate-colored nipples, no tummy, and a tantalizing black bush ensconced between perfect thighs. Pepe felt dizzy.

She walked toward him, resolute. "What do I need to do to get this job, Don Pepe?"

Pepe's shocked mind and emotions prevented him from responding.

"Do I have to beg, Don Pepe?"

Before any word could leave his throat, she was kneeling before him. "I'm begging, Don Pepe."

When next she unzipped his pants, he knew he'd found his manager for Ferretería Vesubio of Santa Ana. Or that she'd found him.

After this, the fact that Pepe and Belinda ever had a third child was nothing short of a miracle.

It wasn't until 1953 that Belinda gave birth to Mario, the son Pepe always wanted. That would be his final offspring with Belinda.

Holding him in his arms, he promised his son he would always have the best of everything! A most solemn Italian oath.

Chapter 15

Humiliatism

After completing his studies in Quito, Segundo Montes returned to San Salvador to teach 4th-grade at the school named the *Externado de San José* [St. Joseph's Out-Student School]. The Externado de San José was founded in 1921 by the Society of Jesus in San Salvador, as the *Seminario de San José* [St. Joseph's Seminary], which was located in downtown San Salvador, next to the *Iglesia de San José* [St. Joseph's Church]. The purpose of such Jesuit institution was the formation of youths who aspired to be priests.

But a group of parents approached the Jesuits to propose the admittance of students who didn't aspire to the priesthood. That was when the school also became an *externado* [out-student school] for regular students who lived in their own homes and not at the school, as opposed to exclusively being a boarding school (or an in-student school) for aspiring priests, who lived at the school.

Years later, the boarders were sent to live at the newly-built *Seminario de San José de la Montaña* [St. Joseph of the Mountain Seminary], leaving only regular out-students at the original campus. The original campus was thus officially named *Externado* de San José.

In the 1950s, because of the need to expand the facilities and provide better educational services, certain properties were acquired in what was then outer San Salvador to build a new school.

By 1955, the new Externado de San José had been completed. The Jesuits then built the Loyola Academy, for underprivileged, working-class students.

Segundo enjoyed teaching at the Externado. He found the interaction of the Salvadoran boys particularly interesting: they all wanted to become men so soon. They got into fist fights often, accusing each other of being a fag. In the fourth grade?

Sixth graders talked about having sex with whores. What kind of homes were they coming from? And these were the future of this country?

There seemed to be quite an emphasis on manhood and not brains among Salvadorans. Which explained why the country couldn't go beyond producing coffee and sugar and whatever the land produced.

Riches were being created for a few, off the sweat of the many, who got paid a pittance. If you were fortunate enough to be born in a family that got rich that way, the only way to stay rich was to keep your labor costs as low as possible, for which you had to convince your laborers to be content with the crumbs they received.

The rich had even come up with a mantra for it: 'This is your station in life. Accept it.'

Fortunately for them, they'd found an unwitting ally in the Catholic Church, when priests quoted Luke 6:20: "Looking at his disciples, he said: 'Blessed are you who are poor, for yours is the kingdom of God.'"

Said another way, 'you'll get your upward mobility when you die, but not before, Juan.'

And this attitude was certainly reflected in the children. They needed to eliminate any perceived threat to their social standing. And they did so by creating a 'caste system,' enforced by fisticuffs.

Said another way, if you knock somebody down, keep kicking him to keep him down, because, obviously, that's where he belongs. No upward mobility for you, Juan. Not in this life.

But in light of such system that favored the powerful, but humiliated everybody else, no mantra can be effective. Farabundo Martí proved it.

Farabundo Martí was born in Teotepeque, a peasant community in the Department of La Libertad. After graduating from the Saint Cecilia School in Santa Tecla, run by the Salesian Fathers, he entered the University of El Salvador in San Salvador.

Martí had realized that El Salvador's political system, far from caring for the welfare of all, cared for the good of the very few, and humiliated everybody else.

After helping to organize the Central American Communist Party, he cut his studies short to dedicate himself exclusively to politics. He became very popular among the peasants, and it was rumored that he would postulate himself as a presidential candidate. He was assisted immensely by the worldwide economic depression the product of the U.S. depression since 1929.

The government of the time exiled him to Guatemala, but when a new left-leaning government was elected in 1931, he returned to El Salvador to help the poor politically. But that didn't last long because the military, under the orders of the rich landowners, staged a coup, leaving General Maximiliano Hernández Martínez in power.

Martí returned to Guatemala, but this time to organize an army of peasants. The reason was simple: the only way to get up off the canvas in El Salvador was to fight your way up. There was no other choice.

Martí returned to El Salvador at the head of a peasant army in 1932. Although he had military successes initially, the Salvadoran army defeated them, in what is known today as *La Matanza* [The Slaughter], because over 30,000 peasants were killed.

Farabundo Martí was captured, tried and executed. Only then was he free to be upwardly mobile or be rich even, according to the ruling class.

Segundo Montes knew that the next step in his education would be a master's in theology. But after seeing these social interactions, he knew that he definitely wanted to do his doctoral dissertation on social anthropology.

* * *

After a few years, Segundo became headmaster of the school. As he was doing his rounds one day, he saw one of the 4th grade students praying in the school chapel, during recess, while his classmates were playing outside. His name was Mario Tacarello. And this boy would come pray in the chapel several times a day, not only during recess. Upon inquiring about him, Father Montes learned that his teachers were aware of his devotion to Jesus and Mary, but that because of it, he got picked on by some of his 4th-grade classmates, who'd call him a *culero* or *marica* [fag].

One day at the chapel, Segundo sat down next to the child in the pew. Segundo asked him about Jesus and Mary, and after chatting about them for a while, Segundo asked Mario why he didn't fight back when they called him a fag. The child just looked up at him and said, "Jesus Christ wasn't a fighter. I want to be like Jesus."

If there was ever anybody with a calling, it was little Mario Tacarello; Segundo was certain of that. He invited his parents to come talk to him about the child, but only his mother showed up.

"Mrs. Tacarello, your son seems to have a strong calling for the priesthood, are you aware of that?"

"Father Montes, yes, and I celebrate it, but my husband disapproves."

Father Montes nodded, but insisted on conveying how extraordinary the child's calling was. "Well, I've rarely seen somebody so devoted, even in the face of derision by his classmates. His soul belongs to God, and I felt strongly you should realize this and perhaps encourage it. It's not going to go away."

Belinda didn't hear anything beyond 'derision by his classmates.'

"Derision by his classmates?"

Segundo could see this woman's countenance overcome with indignant fury. "Were you unaware of this?"

"How is he derided, Father Montes?"

Segundo blushed. "Well, they call him names. You know, the usual stuff of boys his age. Questioning his manhood."

Belinda couldn't say anything because of the fury she felt. And it was a good thing, all that she'd be able to utter would be a string of profanities against everybody, for doing it and for allowing it.

Segundo continued. "I've encouraged him to fight back, but he says Jesus wasn't a fighter. Believe me, he handles it well, he completely ignores them."

Belinda willed herself to calm down. "Well, thanks for telling me, Father. I don't think it's healthy for a boy to withstand derision. I'll have to do something about that."

Belinda left that meeting seething. When she got home, she dialed the shop and told Pepe to come home immediately.

"But *Cara Mia* [my dear], I have business..."

"Pepe, you let your fucking whore take care of the business! You come home this very minute! *Capisci*?"

Fifteen minutes later, Pepe walked in the door.

"*Moglie*, what could be more important than business?"

"Pepe, listen to me carefully. They're calling your son a *marica* in school. The kids of all those nobodies are insulting him, and I'll be damned if I'm going to let anybody insult a son of mine! Do you understand me?

"Well, what do you want me to do?"

"I want you to teach our son to kick ass! If anybody dares insult him, I want that son of a fucking bitch close to dead, maimed or mutilated! Do you understand me?"

"Ok *Cara*, consider it done. I'll make sure Mario understands the importance of being respected. Please don't be upset anymore."

"OK."

"Just one more question, Belinda."

"What."

"You sure you're not Sicilian?"

He barely escaped the shoe thrown at him as he fled out the door.

Pepe got in the car and drove up the Alameda Roosevelt, to a small Karate gym he'd seen. The sign above its door read 'Karate Choi.'

There he asked to speak to the owner, Master Chong-yul Choi. He had to wait for about 10 minutes until the Master had concluded his class.

In Spanish with a very oriental accent, Master Choi offered him tea and asked what he could do for Mr. Tacarello.

"My son is being picked on at his school, and I'd like to pay you to teach him to defend himself as soon as possible."

"Mr. Tacarello, the teachings of Tae Kwon Do are mostly spiritual in nature. We first teach fortitude of spirit and then..."

Pepe cut him off immediately. "Master Choi, you have a very humble place of business here, and I'm sure the physical limitations of the place directly impact your ability expand it. A nice infusion of cash, in the form of private lessons for my son, might allow you to get a bigger, newer place; to hire or train new instructors. Take on more students.

"I'm asking you to kindly take on my son and dispense with the spiritual part. I need for him to make people respect him, and as soon as possible. I'll pay the cost of a session with many students for each session alone with my son. Do we have a deal?"

The oriental looked at him impassively. All he asked was, "So what is it exactly that you want?"

"If he gets attacked or abused, that should be the last time that happens, because the perpetrators will rue the day they ever messed with a Tacarello; and I'm just paraphrasing my wife here."

Master Choi seemed hesitant. 'That is not our custom."

Pepe stood up. "Thank you for your time."

But Master Choi had wanted to be able to take on more students. And he did have competition. There were other *dojos* starting to appear in town.

Mostly judo. There was even a Brazilian jujitsu gym that had opened on the road to Santa Tecla.

So he said, "Wait, Mr. Tacarello."

Pepe turned. "What, Master Choi?"

"Will you sign a paper in which you relieve me of any liability if your son hurts anybody?"

"Gladly."

"Then I accept. Please let me type the agreement."

When it was ready, Pepe read it and signed it. He took out his checkbook and wrote a generous check to Master Choi. They shook hands, and Master Choi told him he expected young Mario at 5 a.m. the next morning.

Chapter 16

A Kick-Ass Scholarship

"Mrs. Tacarello, this is Father Segundo Montes, Headmaster at Externado."

"Yes, Father what can I do for you?"

"I need you to come to pick up your son. He's being expelled from school."

Belinda raised her fist in triumph, mentally shouting, "Yes!"

But she controlled herself and merely asked why, knowing full well what the answer would be.

"He broke the jaw of one of his classmates and knocked another one out cold with a karate kick."

"So? I'm sure they had it coming to them, right?"

"Please come over, Mrs. Tacarello, this is too serious to be discussed over the phone."

Half an hour later, Mrs. Tacarello was walking into Father Montes' office. The irate mothers of the injured students had just left. Lucky for them: Belinda would've torn them apart had they crossed her path.

"Please sit down, Mrs. Tacarello. Mario will be here soon."

"So what happened?"

"They were in the playground during recess and apparently two boys accosted Mario, fully expecting him to walk away. He asked them to stop. They didn't. He asked them again, they accosted him further. Two crosses and a kick later, the boys were on the ground, seriously injured. We can't tolerate such behavior in this school, Mrs. Tacarello."

"Oh really, Father Montes? It seems that Externado has been part and parcel to this incident and is equally guilty because it allowed that accosting behavior to occur, without punishing the perpetrators. Thereby requiring a sweet child like my son to learn how to defend himself, because Externado certainly wasn't going to."

"Mrs. Tacarello, it's the policy of this school that whoever injures other students, willfully and intentionally, must be expelled. I'm sorry."

Belinda didn't mind throwing caution to the wind. She was ecstatic that her son had kicked some serious ass. So she said, "Listen to me, Montes. We'll have absolutely no problem putting our son in any of the other schools that are popping up like mushrooms all over San Salvador. Given his natural inclination toward the cloth, I'm sure the Marist Brothers at Liceo Salvadoreño would be glad to receive him with open arms. It will most definitely be Externado's loss."

Segundo Montes pondered this. Mrs. Tacarello was absolutely right, the boys had it coming. Nevertheless, the school policy was clear. If the boy isn't expelled, the other parents will create problems for the school.

But a Jesuit light bulb came on in his head. "Mrs. Tacarello, there are two months left in the Academic year. We'll expel Mario for the remainder of the academic year. That will give us time to convince the parents that their children were at fault. In the meantime, I'll personally go over to your house every day, and quickly keep Mario up to date with his assignments, so that he passes the year well. Does that seem doable to you?"

"Father Montes, I'm not an unreasonable woman. If all that you will do is remove my son physically for two months but take care of him academically at home, that's acceptable. See you tomorrow, what time?"

"3 p.m."

At 3 p.m. the next day, Father Segundo Montes began the two-month-long home schooling of young Mario. They'd begin each session with a Rosary, at the request of the boy. Hard to believe this boy had injured those two boys so ruthlessly.

It was during these lessons that Segundo had no doubt that this boy was headed for the priesthood.

Mario was an avid learner, and the 3 hours a day Montes spent with him were more than enough for him to absorb the material. After the last lesson of the day, he'd want to talk about Jesus and Mary. He loved to talk about the apparitions of Mary in Fatima. He would pray for Mary to appear to him.

Segundo had no doubt that it would be Externado's privilege to have this boy join the ranks of the Jesuits one day.

When the academic year was over, Father Montes asked to speak with Mario's parents.

"I'd like to prepare you for the real possibility that your son is going to pursue a religious life."

Pepe didn't like the idea of his son denying himself the pleasures that he so thoroughly enjoyed. Being in a country like El Salvador and not having sex was like owning a bakery and denying yourself pies and cakes. Life was tough, and sex was a God-given gift, at least for men. He didn't think that it was healthy to deny yourself those urges.

Belinda came from a system where having a child in the priesthood was an honor for the family. So she was more open to the idea of her son following a religious life. However, Mario had her husband's genes, and Pepe was a womanizer. She was hoping he could become a Protestant pastor, allowed to marry. The problem was her son's devotion to Mary, which was at odds with Protestantism.

Pepe stated his concerns to Father Montes. "Look, I don't mind if my son pursues a religious career, Father. He'll always have the family business to fall back on. I just don't think celibacy is a healthy thing."

Father Montes smiled. "Mr. Tacarello, please be aware that celibacy was never mandated by Our Lord Jesus Christ. It was ordered by a Pope in the Middle Ages, and not necessarily followed religiously, not even by the Popes themselves, many of whom were married and had children."

Belinda asked, with much hope, "Are you saying he'll be able to make me a grandmother?"

Father Montes raised his hand in caution. "Mrs. Tacarello, the Church is evolving. Right now, the Second Vatican Council is underway, and significant changes are being made to bring the Church into the modern era. So to address your point, Mrs. Tacarello: celibacy may no longer be a requirement for priests, but I don't believe that the Church will allow its priests to marry. If he gives you grandchildren, he won't be able to remain a priest. But then again, I can't see that far into the future, so who knows?"

Father Montes paused. He was unsure about broaching another subject with them. But then he decided to proceed because he didn't want to ruin Mario's chances of becoming a Jesuit on account of a failure to disclose.

"However, what I can foresee is that a future priest will be required to make sacrifices and devote himself to the Church's mission. Having a family or children may be the furthest thing from his mind, and he may not even have the time for that."

"How so, Father?" Belinda was anxious to know all the angles.

"As things seem to be evolving, priests may be required to become more militant in their efforts to redress social inequalities. And redressing social inequalities usually requires some sort of violence, as the French and Soviet revolutions have taught us."

This alarmed Belinda. "You mean, fight with weapons, like a soldier? Like the military?"

Montes knew this reaction would come. He addressed it as best he could.

"No, ma'am, we're not about to start forming military academies for priests, rest assured. But priests are leaders of their flocks, and given the Church's turn toward achieving social justice, they may become the spiritual leaders of social justice warriors. Without doing the actual fighting themselves."

There. He'd said it. But now he would emphasize the good part.

"The great benefit of becoming a Jesuit is an education in the best universities of Europe, as a pre-condition to becoming ordained. All expenses paid. That education will serve him no matter what he does in his life. Should he decide to give you grandchildren and start a family, if the Church doesn't allow it, then he will have gotten the best education money can buy, and it won't have cost you a penny. How can you say no to that?"

Indeed, that was an offer that was hard to refuse, but it wasn't received as enthusiastically as he wanted.

So he added the clincher: "Starting right now."

Although the Tacarellos weren't poor, they weren't one of the Fourteen and tuition at Externado wasn't cheap.

"You would do that for Mario?"

"Consider it done. But we need you to sign a commitment soon."

"Why soon, Father?"

"Because I'm leaving to obtain my master's degree in theology at the University of Innsbruck next year, and I want my replacement to have something in writing, so everybody is on the same page."

Chapter 17

Letters from Innsbruck

Innsbruck, Austria, May 26, 1963

Father Miguel Elizondo, S.J.
Pastor
Church of El Carmen
Santa Tecla, El Salvador

"Dear Father Elizondo,

I trust this letter finds you well. You've always been my true mentor, my compass that always points north. For that, I'll always be grateful.

I've been meaning to write to you for a while, ever since the Cuban Missile Crisis. Once again, you were right about Castro, and I was wrong. Thankfully, cooler heads prevailed!

But what I really want to write to you about is how miserable I am, here at the University of Innsbruck. I'm having a hell of a time with the language. Some of us weren't meant to be linguists, I guess.

There's also the issue of the language within the language: one can dominate the German language and still not understand the writings and teachings of Karl Rahner.

Yes, I'm being taught by the great Karl Rahner, the 'Architect of Vatican II,' but this is my fourth semester here, and I've yet to learn anything that's more useful than anything I learned from you in El Salvador. There is wisdom, and there is bullshit, and apparently, they don't give diplomas for wisdom here.

Here's a summary of the beliefs of the 'great' Karl Rahner:

'The task of the theologian is to explain everything through God and to explain God as unexplainable' – Karl Rahner.

I ask you, Father Elizondo: why am I being sent here for three years, to study theology with this man, who bases his whole 'theology' on a God that can't be explained?

But then he proceeds to try to explain God, which he's already defined to be unexplainable, with this:

'The Word is, by definition, immanent in the divinity and active in the world, and as such the Father's revelation. A revelation of the Father without the Logos and his incarnation would be like speaking without words.'

So which is it? Is the Word of God a revelation of the Father? If so, the Father has revealed himself in Scripture and is therefore not 'unexplainable.'

But do you think we study scripture? Nope. We study everything but. We study Marx, Engels, Nietzsche, Hegel, Heidegger, Teilhard de Chardin, Henri de Lubac, and, of course, everything that Rahner writes, and believe me, he's a writing machine. It's all very incomprehensible to me, and you know me: I'm not dumb.

Also, I'd like to see some proof of all these notions, but in this realm of studies, there is no proof, and so all we study is the opinion of somebody who can write.

In that case, I would prefer to study (are you sitting down?) Americans like Mark Twain, who imparted wisdom with humor, rather than this bunch of opinionated philosophers (because that's really all it is: it isn't theology, even though that's what my master's will be in).

And in the end, I have to ask myself: what is it that I can possibly do with what I'm being taught here? The answer is this: to spawn a revolution. Because there's absolutely no other use for this. It's like the Soviet Union designed our syllabus.

On another note, guess who else is here? Your favorite, Ignacio Ellacuría. He's here for his doctoral thesis. But guess what? He's not going to make it. He's having a worse time with German than I am and he, who thinks he already knows everything, is facing someone who does know everything (after all, Rahner is his professor) and Ellacuría isn't going to win that confrontation.

In such circumstances, instead of studying harder and exercising a bit of humility, he's going to transfer to another university. The last time I saw him, he said he's planning to transfer to the Complutense University of Madrid, to do his thesis under someone named Xavier Zubiri (whom I've never heard of) because, according to Ellacuría, 'he's a real philosopher—

unlike Rahner.' Well, I interpreted this to mean, 'I'm having a hell of a time with German, and even if I could understand it, I still wouldn't be able to understand Rahner and so he's probably going to flunk me.' As the saying goes, 'a leopard can't change his spots.'

That's all for now, my dearest Father Elizondo. I can't wait to see you again, but it won't be until after I graduate because I have to stay here between semesters to perfect my German language skills.

With my sincerest affection,

Segundo.

P.S. You should see my living quarters! We live like royalty here. I never knew the Society had so much money!"

* * *

Innsbruck, Austria, March 3, 1963

Dr. Xavier Zubiri
School of Philosophy
Complutense University of Madrid
Madrid, Spain

"Dear Dr. Zubiri,

I trust this letter finds you well. My name is Ignacio Ellacuría, and I'm a Jesuit priest. I'm here at the University of Innsbruck, studying under Karl Rahner.

Although the plan was for me to do my doctoral thesis here, I find that Karl Rahner's work is too esoteric and not anchored to 20th-century reality, especially 20th-century Latin American reality.

You see, as soon as I get my Ph.D., I'm slated to become the Dean of the Catholic University of El Salvador. And as you may have already surmised, especially since the Cuban revolution, Latin America is entering a phase of fundamental change.

Therefore, my goal is to do my doctoral thesis on something that is more useful to a nation like El Salvador, to be able to play a leadership role in the transformation of its society, and by extension, that of Latin America.

It seems to me that the philosophy of the author of '*Le reel et les mathematiques—Un probleme de philosophie*' [Reality and mathematics – a philosophical problem], '*Naturaleza, Historia, Dios*' [Nature, History, God] offers a vision that is far more suitable to our reality than the philosophy of a man who never did quite get past Martin Heidegger, who was your teacher as well, and whom you have obviously surpassed.

Yes, I know, Rahner is the 'Architect of Vatican II.' But you and I both know that it wasn't his ideas that permeated *Lumen Gentium* [Latin for 'Light of the Nations']; it was somebody else's, and he was just a tool.

So despite your work being far more useful than his, it's his work that's known and not yours.

If you mentor my doctoral thesis, I'll change that. My name will inextricably be tied to yours, and anything I write as Dean of the Catholic University of El Salvador, will be influenced by you, and in the fullness of time, you'll be far more recognized than Karl Rahner. I guarantee it.

Besides, judging from the Cuban Revolution, the eyes of the world will be on Latin America, and the name at the center of the philosophical basis for the imminent change will be yours, and not Rahner's.

Here's what I propose for my doctoral thesis:

'*La Principialidad de la Esencia en Xavier Zubiri*' [The Primariness of the Essence in Xavier Zubiri].

If you accept, I'll transfer my credits to the Universidad Complutense and begin my work with you immediately.

Your admirer from El Salvador,

Ignacio Ellacuría, S.J."

Chapter 18

Letter from Santa Tecla

Santa Tecla, El Salvador, August 2, 1963

Father Segundo Montes
Canisiaum Collegium
University of Innsbruck
Innsbruck, Austria

"Dear Segundo,

I was overjoyed to hear from you. Your letter made my day, month and year!

Yes, I remember our conversations about Castro, in whom you seemed to place a lot of hope, and I always attributed that to your youthful exuberance. But gray hair gives you a healthy dose of realism, and it's my gray hair that's dictating this letter to you.

I urge you to heed it because youthfulness is only excusable in the young, and you're not getting any younger.

When Castro didn't call for free elections immediately, I knew right then and there that he was going to install a Marxist dictatorship.

Segundo, this man didn't take power by force just to abdicate power and cede it to whomever the people want. In his mind, he's earned the right to stay in power for life, because he risked his life to get it. Franco's done the same thing, hasn't he? He didn't defeat the Spanish Socialists just to allow a vote and risk the return to power of the very people he risked his life to defeat, did he?

Lenin left power in a coffin. So did Stalin. So will Franco. Why would Castro be any different?

But to stay in power, you have to eliminate your opposition. And it needs to be done thoroughly. That is something Lenin and Stalin knew too well, and so they eliminated huge swaths of the population, whether they were proven opponents or not. They left nobody willing to revolt against their dictatorships. This lesson was not lost on Fidel Castro. His forces started executing perceived enemies of the Revolution immediately. Who's got the time for a fair and adversarial trial, where you can face and cross-examine your accusers? Not Castro.

But I have to admit that I was completely unprepared for the extent of the ruthlessness of that Argentine physician, Dr. Ernesto Guevara, the one they call *Ché*, a man trained to save lives. And I would've never thought that Castro would've let this Argentine murder his fellow Cubans at whim.

I guess no Cuban would've been able to kill Cubans with the needed ruthlessness, so he relied on the foreigner Guevara to do so. Evidence of such thorough ruthlessness is twofold:

They say the Bay of Pigs invasion failed because President Kennedy withdrew support. I don't believe that for a second. The Bay of Pigs failed because anybody in Cuba who would've otherwise been willing and able to support that operation was long dead and buried. There were no Castro opponents left on the island to help the invading force.

The second and most telling piece of evidence is the fact that Castro didn't think twice about risking a nuclear confrontation with the USA, by inviting the USSR to place nuclear missiles in Cuba, because there was nobody left in Cuba to tell him what a foolish thing that was.

So if you agree with me that he eliminated his opposition ruthlessly, you have to agree with me that those who were left alive were admirers or sympathizers of his. People he was supposed to have helped. Otherwise, why have a revolution?

So why was he doing everything to kill them, massively? That is a betrayal on a scale never seen before, Segundo!

But you already know this, right? So why am I even bringing it up? The reason is because in your letter you wrote that the only thing that you could do with what you were learning over there was to 'spawn a revolution.' Segundo, in my mind, I can't see a revolution happening in El Salvador without the guidance and participation of that crazy man Castro and his butcher lieutenant Guevara. And once the Castro-led revolution triumphs in El Salvador, if he didn't give a damn about killing Cubans massively, what makes you think he'll give a damn about killing Salvadorans massively?

I can almost hear you say to me, 'Oh no, it won't be like that.'

Are you sure?

First of all, what makes you think anybody in any government is endowed with a divine sense of fairness? Here and everywhere, people who are part of government want power. Once they have the power, you'd be hard-pressed to point out anybody who won't use that power to benefit himself or themselves first, especially in a country such as this one. The only antidote to that is the power residing with the people, not with the government or any 'vanguard.'

That's why the most prosperous nation in the world is the United States. In World War II, the capitalists under Roosevelt mass-produced weaponry almost at the drop of a hat and supplied all its allies with weaponry, including the USSR. It wasn't the U.S. government who developed the assembly line for mass production, it was a private citizen named Henry Ford. But more importantly, Henry Ford and other capitalists like Leroy Grumman, William Boeing, Donald Douglas, and Howard Hughes found workers who were sufficiently educated and skilled to do the work that was required, quickly and efficiently, to produce the weaponry needed to win the war.

Now then, Segundo, although the USA has people who make fortunes and people who make minimum wage, all these capitalists, like the Rockefellers, Rothschilds, J.P. Morgans and various other ultra-millionaires—the villains in your courses, no doubt—, create employment and pay taxes so that more people can get educated and improve their lives. The taxes they pay also fund the government. If the government eliminates the rich, where is it going to get funds?

This is a very important question that needs to be answered, Segundo, because the only way to address poverty is to lift people out of poverty and from what I can gather, there's only one system that's been successful at that, and it's not the one you're studying.

Yes, I know you're studying theology but if it's a theology that's going to bring misery and death, then, by all means, stop studying that! Maybe that's why Karl Rahner sounds so confused: he's trying to teach that which is not. He's teaching fantasy, not reality. Because here's what reality looks like, as created by God the Father:

God's 10th Commandment to Moses was, 'Thou shalt not covet thy neighbor's house, thou shalt not covet thy neighbor's wife, nor his manservant, nor his maidservant, nor his ox, nor his ass, nor anything that belongs to your neighbor.'

God the Father was, in fact, acknowledging that some people, because of their talents or circumstances, would have more donkeys and servants than others. God knew that there would be servants. Barely a few generations removed from Eden, God was already recognizing that as humans, we were going to have differences. That some humans would serve others.

If what you strive for is a reduction in the number of servants, a reduction in the differences among humans (a noble endeavor, by the way), then wouldn't you want to start by giving all persons the tools to avoid becoming servants, like a useful education?

Have you noticed that Daimler Benz makes cars in Germany, Ford makes them in the USA, Ferrari in Italy, but nobody makes cars in El Salvador? Why is that? A car is an engine, four wheels, and a chassis. It's very old technology. I would've hoped that your European education would enable you to come back and teach science to Salvadoran kids; instead, you plan on teaching them to kill. Because that's what the Soviets advocate, right? Because that's what Fidel Castro is doing and will continue to do?

Segundo, do you really want that kind of bloodshed in El Salvador? Is that really why you became a priest?

I have a better idea, Segundo, why don't you go do that in Spain instead? Don't you have a dictator there—Francisco Franco?

Because if you do come back here to advocate bloodshed, won't it be the blood of *indios* that will be spilled at the hands of Spaniards, again?

If you really want to be a revolutionary, Segundo, at least be one with brains. If you put your mind to it, you could revolutionize the education system in El Salvador; make it similar to Costa Rica's, or even better!

Fill our people's minds with knowledge! Don't fill our people's heart with hate! And above all, don't spill their blood again!

I pray to God Almighty that you change course, my beloved Segundo, and that when you see the light, you convince Ignacio Ellacuría to see it as well, although I won't hold my breath for that.

Your brother in Christ,

Miguel Elizondo, S.J."

Chapter 19

Green Light

At eleven in the morning of November 7, 1949, Olga walked into his new office with an envelope that had arrived via diplomatic pouch from Washington D.C.

"Would you care for some more tea, Comrade Director?"

He even had a new title. His hard work was being rewarded. Abakumov had called him in soon after he'd returned from the trip and informed him that he was making him Director of the 2nd Department – Latin America, based on a glowing recommendation from the Ambassador.

"No, thank you, Olga." She left.

He opened the envelope. It was a memorandum from Panyushkin labeled 'Top Secret.'

'To: Vladislav Fedoseyev, Director, Second Department (Latin America), MGB

From: Aleksander Panyushkin, Ambassador, USSR Embassy in Washington D.C.

Subject: The J Plan

Please prepare for a meeting at my office on Monday, November 14, 1949, at 9:00 a.m. Please be prepared to provide the following information:

Cost of funding the J Plan at all relevant levels.

Regards,

Panyushkin'

This was Panyushkin's way of telling him that he'd gotten the green light from Stalin, and that this meeting for which Vladislav was being summoned wasn't going to be just another exchange of ideas. He wanted cold hard numbers. And although he had most of that information, he wasn't going to be able to leave any question unanswered. His future depended on his work over the next few days.

He called the Ministry's administrative department and said he wanted a 10% pay increase for Mrs. Petrenko immediately.

Then he called the manager of the Tula City plant and made arrangements for the transfer of Olga's parents to a food-canning factory on the outskirts of Moscow. He then called the Tula City school administrator to coordinate young Viktor Petrenko's transfer to his old school in Moscow.

Upon receiving confirmation of compliance with all his instructions, he called Olga in.

"Olga, I've arranged for your parents to be transferred to work at the 'Red Front' plant here in Moscow, as of next Monday, with a salary increase and more relaxed shifts, effective immediately. Of course, your son will come with them and start school at his old school. I need you to contact them to immediately get over here, because for the next few days, you and I are going to be working non-stop, preparing a very important presentation that we're going to make in Washington next Monday. Do you understand?"

Olga could barely keep calm. "Yes, Comrade Director!"

"Also, you're getting a 10% pay increase starting immediately."

Olga couldn't believe this string of good news. "Thank you, Comrade Director!"

"As you know, I'm not married, so I'm going to need someone to be doing the cooking at my apartment, besides helping me prepare this important presentation. Are you up to the task?"

"Of course, Comrade Director!"

"Here are some rubles and the keys to my apartment. Go prepare my apartment and stock it up with food and vodka enough for the next few days. Take all office supplies that you may need. We'll work here during the day and work there during the night. You need not come back to the office today. When your parents and son get here from Tula City, return to my apartment. Do you understand?"

"Yes, sir!" She took the keys and left for his apartment, walking on air. But when she got there, the realization that her performance over the next few days would seal her future made her come back down to earth. It swim-or-sink time.

At the Ministry, Fedoseyev worked all day. He didn't arrive at his apartment until 8 pm that night. He opened the door to find a place that differed vastly from the one he'd left that morning. It was clean, orderly and there was a fragrance in the air. It had definitely received a woman's touch.

There was a plate set for him at the table. Leaning against the bottle of vodka was a note that read: "Comrade Director, your dinner is in the oven, I intend to be back as soon as I can to warm it up and serve you. But if you get hungry, just heat it up for five minutes."

Fedoseyev smiled. Mrs. Petrenko sure knew how to take good care of a man. He poured himself a glass of vodka. He needed it to relax a bit.

Just then Olga let herself in.

"Good evening, Comrade Director. I want to thank you because my parents are home with my son. They understand they will take care of him for the next few days, because of my assignment. I am at your disposal."

"Good, Olga. Now please undress."

Olga didn't hesitate.

"As long as you're in this apartment, you'll be like Eve, just like in Washington, OK?"

"Yes, Comrade."

"Now, let's have my dinner, and afterward, you can show me how grateful you are to me for transferring your son, your parents and for that salary increase."

Chapter 20

30 Silver Pieces

On November 14, 1949, Fedoseyev was at the Ambassador's office at the indicated time.

"Come in, Vladislav. Sit down."

"Thank you, Mr. Ambassador."

"Let's have the numbers."

Vladislav handed over the thick dossier to Panyushkin and then proceeded to use a portable stand to place larger versions of each chart for the Ambassador to see. The Ambassador ordered his secretary to bring in a stand. When it was available, Fedoseyev placed the first chart on it, which portrayed a pyramid divided into three sections: upper, middle and base.

"As the Ambassador can see, the upper part of the pyramid consists of the Headquarters and the 80 provinces worldwide. The best estimate I have for the financing of the headquarters (F.H.) is approximately 2 million rubles a year, considering current costs. The financing of the Provinces (F.P.) would amount to one million rubles a year per Province."

"I didn't think we'd be funding the entire Order, Vladislav?"

"Mr. Ambassador, I decided to account for all levels, knowing that some figures may be disregarded, reduced or increased. I included a general financing for all Provinces, just in case it was convenient to do so to avoid political problems, such as a Province feeling left out, for instance."

"Fine, continue."

"The next level, the middle one, is what I've called the university level. He changed chart. "This level has three components: European, American and Latin American.

"The North America has the following Jesuit Provinces: the California Province of the Society of Jesus, the Chicago-Detroit Province, the French-Speaking Canada Jesuits, the English-Speaking Canada Jesuits, the Maryland Province, New England Province, the New Orleans Province, the New York Province, the Oregon Province and the Wisconsin Province. These provinces have under them major Jesuit education centers, such as

Georgetown University, Gonzaga University, Xavier University and Fordham University."

The Ambassador interrupted him. "Vladislav, I'm willing to accept that your dossier contains the financing for every member of the Society of Jesus, down to the maids. And I agree with your premise that it is good to have it in hand. But a financing for the Province of French-Speaking Canada will contribute nothing to your army of a hundred million pro-Soviet Latin Americans massed on the southern bank of the Rio Grande."

When he saw Fedoseyev's reaction, he adopted a more light-hearted attitude. "Vladislav, I already know you're good. You don't have to show off!"

Fedoseyev laughed with the Ambassador, but he'd gotten the message: get to the meat of it. He looked for the chart that would satisfy this requirement: the Latin American university component chart.

When he found it, he placed it on the stand and said, "The Latin American University component includes major Jesuit Universities such as the Pontifical Xavieran University of Colombia, the Pontifical Catholic University of Ecuador, the Pontifical Catholic University of Rio de Janeiro and the Catholic University of Uruguay. and others that are run by Jesuits, and where the Spanish and Latin American Jesuit novices go to get their 'formation,' culminating in their bachelor's degrees. They then go back to their assigned countries to perform their 'regencies,' wherein the regent lives and works in a typical Jesuit community, usually teaching in a secondary school, or else in a seminary, where they train diocesan priests. Diocesan priests are priests who don't belong to any order."

Fedoseyev replace that chart with another, which illustrated the following point: "The Ambassador can see the advantage of imposing our preferred syllabus into these Latin American Jesuit universities because their graduates go on to impart their knowledge either to young high school students, who may become revolutionary leaders, or to seminarians, who may become revolutionary diocesan priests."

The Ambassador nodded. This was what he wanted to see.

"Very good, Vladislav. Please go on."

"After their regency stage, they go on to their theological stage, which is the final stage before ordination. European universities are at the core of the theological stage. Here is where the new Jesuit thought is formed. Here is where the giant Jesuit minds, such as Pierre Teilhard de Chardin and Henri de Lubac, come up with their modernist theology that is rejected by the Vatican."

The Ambassador raised his hand to stop him. "This is a very important component, Vladislav, but let's leave it for later. Right now tell me about the base of the pyramid."

Fedoseyev put the original chart back on the stand, and said, "Mr. Ambassador, here is where General Janssens' order materializes. And here is where we can have the most impact."

"All right, let's hear it."

"General Janssen's order is to turn toward the poor. As I see it, every Jesuit educational institution school in Latin America, which now caters to the well-to-do, must expand to cater to the poor. This means to build a parallel school for the poor to fulfill their commitment."

"That's it? One school per country?"

"No sir, in Latin America, religious orders usually teach on a gender basis. Jesuits have school for boys, and religious orders have schools for girls. As such, the plan is to build a new Jesuit school for poor boys, and a school for poor girls under any or the religious orders having schools in the country, such as the Little Sisters of the Assumption."

"Don't tell me we're going to have to deal with the Little Sisters of the Assumption, Vladislav?"

"No, Mr. Ambassador, only with the Jesuits. And since the Jesuits are the ones who are going to finance the poor girls' school, with our money, they will impose the syllabus for the poor girls' school, pursuant to our terms."

"What do you foresee our terms being, Vladislav?"

"At this level, Mr. Ambassador, our goal is to produce the priest and nun candidates that are needed to feed the system and output potential revolutionary leaders."

"Needed?"

"Mr. Ambassador, a telling event occurred after World War II in the Catholic Church. Pope Pius XII seemingly encouraged Lutheran priests to become Catholic priests. Lutheran priests are allowed to be married, and they were married when they became Catholic priests. They got to keep their wives. There can only be one reason for this."

"A shortage of priests."

"Exactly, Mr. Ambassador."

Panyushkin asked the logical question. "Is there a shortage of nuns?"

"I'm sure there is, Mr. Ambassador. But more importantly, there will be."

"Why do you say so, Vladislav?"

"During World War II, which lasted about six years, women entered the factories to take the place of the men who were fighting, and so they became economically independent. Especially in America and in Europe. Therefore, the number of European and American women who will seek to pursue careers as nuns will necessarily be less, because now they have a slew of other careers they can pursue. That means that when the current European nuns who are teaching at the existing schools in Latin America retire, the existing schools won't be able to replace them with European nuns. Technically, that constitutes a shortage."

Panyushkin completed the thought. "That shortage will be more acute when we start building more girl schools."

"Precisely, Mr. Ambassador. The only nuns that will be available will be our Revolutionary nuns, which the Jesuits will be charged with recruiting, training and producing."

Panyushkin added, "At a far more rapid rate than current nuns are produced, because we will tell them to dispense with math and science and stick to Revolution/Marxism/Stalinism."

"Precisely, Mr. Ambassador."

The Ambassador put on his glasses and turned to look at the pyramid. Then he asked, "Since the base of the pyramid is to finance the construction of schools for the poor, which countries are you targeting?"

"Mr. Ambassador, the dossier contains a list of 15 Latin American countries, from Mexico to Argentina, most of which have military governments and all of which have a huge number of poor. But this is merely for budgeting purposes. If better targets of opportunity should arise, the distribution of funds may favor certain countries over others."

"And how much would these buildings cost, Vladislav?"

"Based on best available building construction estimates obtained in Mexico, Mr. Ambassador, I would say that we should plan one million rubles per construction, plus the cost of land, so I estimate two million rubles per new school. This, of course, will be a one-time initial expenditure. The scholarships for the poor students will be the yearly expenditure."

Panyushkin perused the chart.

"And I see you say 4 million rubles per country per year should cover the scholarships for paying the students to complete high school and enter the seminar or convents, correct?"

"Yes, Mr. Ambassador. Four million rubles per country per year covers meals, books and uniforms for high school age students who agree to join convents and seminars, plus a stipend for their parents, from ninth grade till they graduate from the seminar and the convent."

The Ambassador grabbed a pencil and paper. "So the plan calls for the building of two schools per year in each of those nations, plus scholarships, that's 15 x [4 million rubles (infrastructure) + 4 million rubles (scholarships)] = 15 x 8 million rubles = 120 million rubles per year. At the current dollar/ruble exchange rate, that's equal to 24 million dollars per year, approximately, for the base of your pyramid."

The Ambassador asked Vladislav to put the chart of the Latin American university component up again. When it was up, he asked, "How many Latin American universities are there to influence their syllabi, Vladislav?

"Five, Mr. Ambassador: two in Colombia, one in Ecuador, one in Brazil and one in Uruguay. However, in the plan I propose to double this number because, with our financing, the Jesuits would be able to offer the financing of the creation of new theology/philosophy schools at existing or future universities."

The Ambassador liked this idea. "You're right, Vladislav! To the extent the demand grows due to the effectiveness of the base of the pyramid, we would be able to create more Jesuit Schools of Theology/Philosophy, not universities! How much have you allocated to that?"

"For budgeting purposes, Mr. Ambassador, I believe that the Latin American university component could be influenced and made to grow, with a budget of 2 million rubles per university for ten universities: five already in existence, and another five to be developed, in terms of schools of theology and philosophy, directed by Jesuits. And that would include the salary of the professors.

The Ambassador nodded and did the calculations. He then said, "This is 2 million rubles times 10 Latin American universities per year = 20 million rubles per year = 4 million dollars a year. Add this to the 24 million dollars of the base of the pyramid, we have that the Latin American component in both levels amounts to 28 million dollars a year."

The Ambassador looked at the numbers and nodded silently. He then looked at Fedoseyev and said, "So far, everything makes sense, Vladislav. But now it's time to look at the European university component."

Fedoseyev stood up and placed the corresponding chart on the stand. He then proceeded to organize his documentation to give a presentation, but the Ambassador asked him to sit down and take notes. Fedoseyev got ready to.

The Ambassador walked over to the stand. He turned to Fedoseyev and said, "Vladislav, let's examine the circumstances of the relevant European universities. The Vatican has forbidden Teilhard de Chardin from teaching there, but it can't stop him from writing. Therefore, he continues to be the greatest influence on the thought and theology of the Jesuits, as you have pointed out, because his writings continue to be read by them."

He stopped for a second to look for a name on the chart. When he found it, he said, "Henri de Lubac is a professor at the Catholic University of Lyon, but he's under fire from the Vatican as well, so he'll probably get the Chardin treatment soon. Yet their influence still permeates, despite being reduced to spreading 'underground.'

"Perversely, the more the Vatican forbids something, the more the Universities wish to have that 'forbidden fruit,' so to speak."

Fedoseyev smiled at the Ambassador's mocking of the Christian mythology called 'Genesis,' where a talking serpent convinced Eve to eat a knowledge-inducing 'apple.'

"So much so, Vladislav, that last year, Columbia University invited Teilhard de Chardin to lecture there, but he was denied permission to do so. Why was he invited? Because people hunger for what he has to offer."

Fedoseyev nodded.

"Just what does he have to offer? Unbridled intellectualism that is free from the Vatican's chains. You see, Vladislav, what's the use of being a Jesuit, the most intellectual order of Christendom, if you're only permitted to say or write the same things that the dumbest diocesan priest in Latin America says or writes?"

Fedoseyev nodded. "Precisely, Mr. Ambassador: he's busted the dam that was holding the Jesuits back."

"Exactly! Now they truly are the pioneers of Catholicism. And as such, they expect the rest of the Catholic world to follow them. And if the Vatican is in the way, then they must move it aside."

Fedoseyev could only think that the Ambassador was creating a symphony out of a simple melody. A worthy countryman of Tchaikovsky, no doubt.

"Now then," continued the Ambassador, "your friend the Superior General is seeing all this going on in his Order, and he asks himself: 'How can I make this Jesuit intellectual movement the official Jesuit policy, without crossing the Pope, the man we've sworn allegiance to?' And his brilliant resolution was to issue instructions for every Jesuit to 'direct their efforts toward the poor,' in a brilliant paraphrasing of Teilhard de Chardin's statement that 'The Christian God on high and the Marxist God of Progress are reconciled in Christ,' without having to mention Chardin at all."

Fedoseyev wanted to applaud. The Ambassador had nailed this. Instead, he just nodded vigorously.

"There's another interesting element about this European university component: all these priests who come to European universities, including Chardin and Lubac, they don't get taught 'theology' by Catholic 'theologians,' do they? They all don't go to the Catholic University of Lyon. Hell, they certainly don't go to the Vatican, where the true Catholic 'theologians' should be residing.

"My point being, these priests who come to Europe to study 'theology' a) aren't being taught by true theologians, but rather by philosophers, or as the Church would call them, laymen; and b) they are definitely not studying theology, because otherwise, they'd be studying the Bible, or the Jewish Talmud, or those Dead Sea Scrolls discovered in Judea a couple of years ago, or St. Augustine and St. Thomas, exclusively."

Now it was Fedoseyev's turn to add his two cents: "The Ambassador is right: they come here to study philosophies that even deny the existence of God, such as the German Nietzsche's, who proclaimed that God was dead."

"Exactly, Vladislav! And the reason is simple: the Vatican has a series of documents, including the Bible, which describe God and what God expects from Christians, such as the Ten Commandments. The Jesuits, by denying the validity of the Bible and the Ten Commandments, all because the paleontologist Chardin decided to believe in Evolution, need to resort to philosophy because they've got nothing else."

"To philosophy and to the writings of Teilhard de Chardin," Fedoseyev added.

"Correct, Vladislav, but Teilhard himself bases himself on philosophy, not on divine inspiration or wisdom! For example: Nietzsche postulated the development of an '*ubermensch'* or superman. Teilhard de Chardin copied this concept when he said that Man would achieve divinity when he developed to his maximum point, called the 'Omega Point,' which will be when all men will be equal and when Man will most resemble Christ."

Fedoseyev came to the logical conclusion: "So Nietzsche's Superman and Chardin's Omega Point are the same thing."

"Exactly, Vladislav! Only when Nietzsche says it, it's philosophy, but when the Jesuit Teilhard de Chardin says it, it's theology!"

Fedoseyev nodded enthusiastically. Although he could've never said it as eloquently as the Ambassador—he was the first to have discovered this philosophy-turned-theology that moved the Jesuits.

Panyushkin continued. "Henri de Lubac studied four years of theology at a Jesuit College: the first two years in Ore Place, England, and the last two years in Lyon, where it was moved to. After that, he was ordained a Jesuit. His first teaching job after that was at the Catholic University of Lyon, as professor of Fundamental Theology, for which he required a Doctorate, which he didn't have, because he hadn't studied beyond a master's degree.

"So what happened? Your friend the Black Pope, General Janssens, ordered the Gregorian University of Rome to confer the required Ph.D. in Theology to him, without him ever setting foot in that University, without ever taking a single course, much less writing a thesis. Why didn't Janssens require Lubac to do any of that? Obviously, because whatever Lubac had studied for his master's degree had sufficed."

Fedoseyev was impressed. The Ambassador had been doing some valuable research.

Panyushkin continued driving toward his point. "What exactly had Lubac studied, to be worth of an exalted Ph.D. in Theology? He studied Nietzsche, Marx, Hegel, Heidegger, Lukács' *History and Class*

Consciousness and Karl Korsch's *Marxism and Philosophy*, for example."

Panyushkin feigned scratching his head. "Tell me, Vladislav, does that sound like theology to you?"

Fedoseyev shook his head.

"So tell me, Vladislav, are Jesuit 'theologians' students of the word of God, or of the word of mere mortals?"

Fedoseyev's reply was, "Mortals."

"Exactly, Vladislav. That is why Jesuit 'theologians' like Lubac are merely parroting what Marxist laymen are enunciating. Since Lubac has studied four entire years of Marxism, was there a need to study two or three more years?

"Not at all."

"That's exactly what the Black Pope thought. Which is why he gifted him the Ph.D. in Theology: there really wasn't anything more to learn. And it's precisely for that reason that we won't need to finance beyond the master's in theology: a Ph.D. is worthless."

After pausing to drink some much-needed water, Panyushkin resumed this discourse. "What this means, Vladislav, is that the European University component of your plan is already working. There's no need for us to impose our preferred syllabi on these universities because they already teach it!"

Fedoseyev was glad because anything that reduced costs increased the chances of his plan getting implemented.

Panyushkin continued. "Since European universities are rebuilding on account of the war, we could provide some assistance to them but only for that reason and nothing else. And don't need to do anything with the American university level component. There's a lot of money in the U.S.A.—there's no need to spend Soviet treasury here.

"All we need to do is provide scholarships, for as many priests as we can, to European universities with philosophy/theology schools. We must ensure that the Latin American priests who are about to enter their Theology stage, a) come to Europe, and b) get a degree in 'theology,' not philosophy. It's in our interest for people to think that every time priests open their mouths, that they're speaking for God... especially when they advocate armed revolution!"

Vladislav hid it, but he felt giddy inside. He'd conceived this baby.

Panyushkin was just its placenta.

The Ambassador returned to the rubles and kopeks of the matter. "Did you figure out the tuition costs for universities in Europe, Vladislav?"

"Mr. Ambassador, it's hard to establish an average because many universities in Europe do not charge, and some do. So for budgeting purpose, I took one that does charge in the USA: Georgetown University, which costs approximately 800 dollars a year, including tuition, room and board and books."

"That's good enough, Fedoseyev. U.S. universities will be more expensive because they're in more demand for now, given that Europe is still rebuilding. So we can base our estimates on 800 dollars a year, for the European University component, per student. If it's less, then we can offer scholarships to more theology-stage priests, and if it's free, well that's even better because we'll have a monetary reserve."

Fedoseyev asked, "What do you suggest for the top of the pyramid, Mr. Ambassador?"

"Let's first figure out the cost of the two most important components: the middle and the bottom. For the bottom we have 28 million dollars per year. Let's assume that we have four theological-stage priests per country from Latin America per year. That's 60 theological-stage priests that are ready to study their Ph.D.'s in Theology per year, from Latin America. Let's round your 800 dollars up to 1000 dollars. That's 60,000 dollars per year, which is nothing."

Fedoseyev did the math. "The total I have is 28,060,000 U.S. dollars per year for the plan so far, Mr. Ambassador."

"As reconstruction assistance, let's allocate the same to the European university component that we did to the Latin American: 4 million dollars per year. That puts us at $28,060,000 + $4,000,000 = $32,060,000 U.S. dollars per year, Vladislav."

Fedoseyev made the conversion to rubles. "This amounts to 32 million dollars times 5 rubles per dollar = 160 million rubles per year."

Panyushkin smiled broadly. "Vladislav, I will propose double this amount per year, because 320 million rubles is equal to 320/50,000 =.006, which is six tenths of one percent of what it costs us to maintain an army of 5 million men per year!"

Both men looked very pleased. It was a major selling point for Comrade

Stalin.

But then the Ambassador looked at the pyramid and frowned. "Vladislav, there's an important element of your plan missing." Fedoseyev shook his head. The Ambassador said, "You're missing the salaries for the revolutionary priests and nuns, once they graduate."

Fedoseyev's eyes twinkled. "No sir, I'm not. You see, once they become full-fledged priests and nuns, it's the local bishops and archbishops who have to pay them. And that's Vatican money!"

The Ambassador reached out to shake Fedoseyev's hand. "Brilliant, Fedoseyev! Just brilliant!"

After the strong handshake, the Ambassador poured them both a glass of vodka.

He raised his glass and said, "*Nazdarovye*! [To your health]"

Fedoseyev returned the toast. "*Nazdarovye*!"

They downed the glasses in one swallow.

The Ambassador concluded the meeting with, "You've done well, Vladislav."

"Under your sage guidance, Mr. Ambassador."

"I'll be presenting this plan to the General Secretary. Be figuring out a way to bring the Jesuits in."

"Yes, Mr. Ambassador. I will."

"Oh, one more thing, Vladislav. We need a code name for this project. What do you suggest?"

Vladislav thought back to his research of the Catholic Church. Its most famous endeavors were the Crusades and the Inquisition. He immediately decided against Inquisition because it was too cruel.

"Perhaps a Crusade, Mr. Ambassador?"

"The Jesuit Crusade?"

A light went on in Fedoseyev's head. "How about the 'Black Crusade,' Mr. Ambassador?"

Panyushkin liked it. "Of course! It'll be directed by the 'Black Pope,' the Jesuit Superior General, won't it?"

"Indeed."

"Perfect. The Black Crusade it is."

Vladislav had never been happier. He'd celebrate with Olga that night again, at another one of the famous restaurants of Georgetown.

Chapter 21

God or Mammon?

The Superior General of the Jesuits in 1949 was Father Jean Baptiste Janssens, born in Mechelen, Belgium in 1889. He seemed far younger than his 60 years of age, possibly because of his slimness. At first glance, he looked like a walking daguerreotype: his skin and hair looked too white, in contrast with his soutane, which looked too black. But if somebody were asked to describe him, the answer would probably be that he looked like the grandfather everybody would like to have. Not even the years of war had made his features lose their sweetness, possibly because he'd spent them in Belgium, far from the heaviest bombardments and bloodiest battles.

When his immediate predecessor, Superior General Wlodimir Ledóchowski had died in 1942, the Jesuits were unable to call to a Congregation to elect the new Father Superior General until late 1945. Janssens was elected the Father Superior General of the Society of Jesus in September 1946. No doubt he was elected because he looked like the grandfather that all the Jesuits would've wanted to have.

As Superior General of the Society of Jesus, he had his office in the General Curia of the Jesuits, next to the Church of the Gesù. Which is precisely where Father Giacomo Benzini was coming from, after giving mass there.

You could hear the plump and talkative Italian Jesuit coming from a mile away, because of the loud orders he'd impart to clean this, throw away that, open a window, in his very passionate Neapolitan Italian. Was it any wonder that he was from where Enrico Caruso was? They even looked alike! Only Father Benzini was plumper and shorter.

The Italian Jesuit did not wait to be announced.

"Come on in, Father Benzini. Take a seat. Take mine, if you want."

"*Grazie*, General Jean, but this is urgent so let's set all kidding aside."

"All right, what's so urgent?"

"General, I received a donation of 260,000 Austrian Schillings in the collection basket while giving mass here in Gesù today."

He handed over an opened envelope, with a check for 260,000 Austrian Schillings from a bank in Austria, the Erste Nationalbank, dated November 27, 1949, and a note that read, in Italian:

'We understand you want to educate the poor. What a noble endeavor! We'd like to help.' It was signed '*I. Freunden.*'

"Have you ever heard of this person?"

"No, General Jean, but we figure it stands for 'Ihre Freunden,' which means 'your friends' in German."

"Is the bank real?"

"Yes, it's a small bank in the part of Austria occupied by the Soviets."

"The Austrian Schilling-U.S. Dollar exchange ratio is 26 Austrian Schillings per dollar. So this donation amounts to 10,000 dollars."

General Janssens thought that this could be heaven-sent.

Father Benzini continued. "Since 'I. Freunden' is a fictitious name, if the check is cashed successfully, we must assume that this donation is from the Soviets."

Father Benzini looked at his General, expecting him to put an end to this and tear the check up.

But the General had other plans. "You know our history with the Russians, Father Benz."

The Russians had hosted the Society of Jesus when the Pope had dissolved them two centuries ago. Their sudden offer of help, right when a potentially divisive confrontation was developing with the Vatican, because of the Jesuits' turn toward the poor, was no coincidence.

As if reading his mind, Father Benzini pointed out that "Your Instruction was no secret, General. They're putting two and two together and getting that we're going to need financial assistance if we're going to go our own way."

Janssens nodded. "You're right. Unfortunately, if this becomes known, it would only give credence to the accusations of the Vatican traditionalists, that the Society of Jesus is going Marxist."

Father Benzini cut to the chase. "So... do we tear up the check?"

Father Janssens poured himself some wine. The blowback from the Vatican because of his Instruction had been fierce. It was unfortunate that this turn towards the poor, which could be interpreted benignly, was being interpreted entirely another way.

But there was no dam that could hold back the Jesuit Modernism led by Teilhard de Chardin any longer. It didn't matter whether he, Janssens agreed with what Chardin wrote or not; what mattered was that the vast majority of the Jesuits that he headed clamored for release from the Vatican's traditionalist yoke. But the Vatican knew that, and it wasn't about to acquiesce.

It had tried to silence Teilhard by keeping him from teaching at universities. But that had only made him more popular. Now they were threatening to cut back the financing of the Order. So it was indeed true that they would need financial assistance. It was unfortunate that it was coming from the Soviets, who were in the process of enslaving half of Europe, behind Churchill's famous 'Iron Curtain,' after committing atrocities that hadn't been discovered until recently. Fortunately for them, their atrocities paled in comparison to the horror of the much-publicized genocide of millions of Jews by the Nazis. So those atrocities were being ignored.

Nevertheless, if the Jesuits were going to go down the path of the wave of Modernism led by Teilhard de Chardin, which had gripped the rank and file of the Order, they were going to need funds.

"No, let's not tear up that check just yet, Father Benz."

"General Jean, please reconsider. I hate to put it this way, but when you sleep with dogs, you wake up with fleas."

"There's an ointment for fleabites, Father Benz. They don't kill you." General Janssens got up from his chair and walked over to the window overlooking Gesù. He was weighing the best way to convince his faithful subordinate. Without losing sight of Gesù, he said, over his shoulder, "Let's examine the lay of the land, Father Benz. For different reasons, certainly none of them spiritual, the Soviets have the same goal as we do, to fight inequality. For that, they consider it imperative for the state to control the means of production. In capitalism, the means of production are in private hands, where the owners get wealthy, while the workers do not, thus creating the inequality that we loathe as well."

Father Benz was not sold. "General Jean, let's be frank: in the Soviet system, only the members of the Politburo get rich and nobody else. The so-called 'Vanguard of the Proletariat' live like royalty while the masses form long lines for a loaf of bread. Also, the means of production in the hands of the Soviet state didn't do them much good, because were it not for the production capacity of capitalist America, they would've faced the Nazi war machine with slingshots. Frankly, it's astonishing how they were able to recover from Pearl Harbor so quickly."

General Janssens had to give credit to Father Benzini's assessment. But he was undeterred. "Yet we see the Soviets conquering half of Europe and espousing the ideals that we espouse.

He went back to his chair to see his friend eye-to-eye, before continuing. "And they're offering money… which we'll soon need. But the Soviets aren't financiers. So they're not in this for profit, in the sense of monetary return on their investment. So the question isn't whether we tear the check up, Father Benz. The question is, what terms do they want for their investment?"

"General Jean, this is Stalin we're talking about. He purged his own ranks while the German columns were advancing toward Moscow. Do we really want to get in bed with him?"

General Janssens sighed. These Italians turned every situation into a sexual one. There was no cure for that. But he continued. "Father Benz, Stalin won't live forever. Our project will outlive him, I can assure you of that. As it will outlive us. We must look to the future. So the question is, what kind of return do they want on their investment in us?"

Father Benz decided to have a drink of wine. Why he of all people was being asked this question was beyond him. The 53-year-old Father Benzini headed the human resources department of the Society of Jesus and his expertise lay in dealing with personnel issues, because of the time he'd spent on the job. He wasn't the moneyman. Father Higinio Fuentevivas was the moneyman.

But if General Jean was going to embark on this risky adventure, he was going to do so with someone of his utmost trust, and Fuentevivas didn't fit that bill.

But Father Benz didn't want to do it, so he invoked Scripture to try to get out of it. "General Jean, allow me to quote Matthew 6:24: 'No man can serve two masters: for either he will hate the one, and love the other; or else he will hold to the one, and despise the other. Ye cannot serve God and Mammon.'"

General Jean smiled at Father Benz's use of 'Mammon,' the more fearsome Biblical synonym for 'money.' It referred to the god of riches, or even to Lucifer himself. Nevertheless, the Society of Jesus had wholeheartedly and enthusiastically adopted Teilhard de Chardin's new theology, so it would be unwise to start relying on old theology at this stage of the game; certainly not after the 'Instruction.'

The Superior General of the Jesuits replied, "Father Benz, if anybody can figure out a way to serve both God and Mammon, it's the Society of Jesus."

Last attempt: "General Jean, the moment you sign on the dotted line, it won't matter. We'll be at the mercy of those who must not even have the word mercy in their vocabulary."

"Well, in that case, I guess we'll have to negotiate the best possible terms. If we can't come to terms, we'll simply refund their 260,000 Austrian Schillings."

After a few seconds, Janssens spoke the words Benzini feared the most: "Go to Austria and cash the check. Take this with you." He wrote a note in Italian, on Society of Jesus letterhead, then signed it, stamped his seal on it and put it in an envelope, giving it to his friend.

"Floor it, Father Benz."

Chapter 22

Mammon

Father Benzini took a cab to the address in the check, on Graben Strasse. He got out, paid the taxicab driver and when he turned around, he saw a tall and sinewy man, some thirty-five years old, who was waiting for him at the entrance. His short brown hair and pale blue eyes, his Slavic traits and the whiteness of his skin convinced the priest that he was Russian.

The Jesuit knew a little bit of several languages, but his forte was Italian and Spanish. He assumed there'd be a translator inside. But after nodding to each other as a greeting, once inside, Father Benzini realized that they were completely alone. The Russian used a hand gesture to invite him to sit down on a sofa in the lobby. After both had sat down, he handed a card over to the priest. It read: 'Blas Pérez, Bank Manager,' with the rest of the information in perfect Spanish.

Father Benzini assumed they could speak in Spanish. "Mr. Pérez, I am Giacomo Benzini, Jesuit Priest. It is a pleasure to meet you."

Pérez replied in perfect Spanish. "Father Benzini, I'm the bank manager. I assume you came to cash the check, correct?"

"Yes, somebody deposited it in the collection basket of the Church of the Gesù, with this note." He tried to hand the not over but Blas Pérez indicated with his hand that he didn't need to see it.

Blas Pérez asked, "So, Father Benzini, are you interested in the assistance?"

Benzini studied the man before him. He wasn't that old, but he had eyes that seemed to have seen a lot. More than a banker, he looked like a military man.

Father Benzini then replied, "We are definitely interested, but first, please tell me: Why are the Soviets offering us assistance?"

Blas Pérez didn't lose his commercial serenity, but he was jumping for joy on the inside. The gambit had worked perfectly. They had deduced that it was the Soviets who were offering them money, yet they came anyway.

"Father Benzini, you're at an Austrian bank that has been appropriated as Soviet Property by the Administration for Soviet Property in Austria, or ASPA, which was formed in June 1946 and is, in fact, a state corporation, in charge of over four hundred expropriated Austrian factories, transportation and trading companies. Now, as you may have surmised, I'm no banker, but I am trying to make this work, and from my standpoint, it's easier to manage one large, reliable customer, than many small ones. And the Society of Jesus fits my business plan perfectly."

He then stood up to go over and pour some tea for both. After thanking him for the cup, Father Benzini took two sips and, to his surprise... it was *yerba mate*!—Jesuit Tea, the tea that had been produced massively at the Guaraní Reductions, and which eventually led to the dissolution of the Society of Jesus in the late eighteenth century.

It was a very smooth maneuver to let him know that the Soviets knew full well that when it had been dissolved by a Pope, the Society of Jesus had sought refuge in Russia, which had granted it, until they were reinstated as an Order by another Pope. Father Benzini had to admire the subtle act and raised his cup, saluting him.

The perfect-Spanish-speaking Soviet smiled and said, "As you may have realized, it's not the first time that the Jesuits do business with us. And it's usually when they run into trouble with the Vatican."

"And you used the 10,000 dollars to remind us."

"What are 10,000 dollars among friends?"

"It's a lot of money, Mr. Pérez."

"Please, call me Don Blas." It was a calculated move to make the priest know who the superior in this meeting was, with the prénom 'Don,' a sign of great respect, in Spanish and in Italian.

"Fine, Don Blas, ten thousand dollars is substantial."

"It's nothing for ASPA, Father Benzini. I would think the former owners of this bank, and of other ASPA-controlled Austrian companies, would only be too happy to help atone for their crimes against humanity by doing something in favor of humanity, like educating it, wouldn't you agree?"

Father Benzini received the message loud and clear. There were ample funds available.

"If we were to be interested, what would the next step be?"

"Father Benzini, you have come here to cash the check. The next step is to let me cash it for you."

Don Blas came back with an attaché containing ten thousand US. Dollars in cash, in hundred-dollar bills.

“Please count it, and please accept the attaché as a token of our appreciation for your business.”

“Thank you, Don Blas. No need to count it. But where do we go from here?”

“That’s entirely up to you. You have my card, but I don’t have anything from you?”

Father Benzini took out the letter signed and sealed by Superior General Janssens and handed it to Don Blas along with his card. The letter said, in Italian:

“To whom it may concern. The bearer of this letter is my official emissary, and he speaks with my full authority.”

It had the same signature and seal that had been on the 'Instruction.'

“Would you care for more tea, Father Benzini?”

“No, thank you, I’m fine.”

“Well then, since I understand that you represent the Superior General of the Jesuits, I would propose a meeting, here in Austria, at a place of your choosing outside of Vienna, off the beaten path. Perhaps one of the many monasteries that will offer us security and discretion.”

“That can be arranged, Don Blas.”

“I don’t suppose I have to tell you that the quantity of funding you require will probably need to be detailed.”

“You can count on that.”

“Good. That’s the next step if you decide you want to get funding from us.”

Father Benzini stood up. They shook hands.

Don Blas escorted him to the door.

As he saw him depart in a taxicab, he locked the door to the office and took a taxi himself to the airport. Vladislav couldn’t wait to deliver the news to the Ambassador.

Chapter 23

Wisdom to Know the Difference

Superior General Janssens quickly reread the Jesuits' proposal, written in Spanish because Don Blas Pérez was obviously a Spanish name. It basically presented an itemized budget to keep the Society operating, at bare minimum levels, until such time the armies demobilized, economies got back in gear, and the schools became self-sustainable. The budget was for approximately four million dollars per year for the next ten years.

Only Benzini and himself knew of this arrangement. But now they had to bring in Father Würzburg, the Abbot of the Klosterneuburg Monastery, in Soviet-occupied Austria, where the meeting with the Soviets would take place.

Jesuit priest Franz Würzburg was about the same age as General Janssens. They'd gotten their Licenciate in Philosophy together at St. Aloysius University in Brussels in 1907, and they'd remained good friends ever since. Superior General Janssens had gotten the Pope to make him the Abbott here in 1947.

Abbott Würzburg was very bald, very thin and very Austrian, with his blue eyes and his love of the music of Strauss. A native of Salzburg, he could have easily played the part of jovial Friar Tuck in the 1938 film 'The Adventures of Robin Hood' starring Erroll Flynn, had he packed on a couple of hundred pounds more.

But this evening, on the eve of the meeting with the Soviets, he wasn't very jovial. He'd even lost his appetite. He was stating his concern about the Soviet financing while dining on a terrace of the monastery overlooking the majestic Danube River. They spoke in Italian to keep the Monastery personnel from understanding what was being spoken.

"General Janssens," he warned his superior, "you have no idea whom you're entering into an alliance with. The atrocities that the Soviet soldiers have committed, and continue to commit, are heart-stopping in magnitude. They're doing to our women what they're doing to Austria. They've dismantled every major Austrian industry and shipped it to the Soviet

Union. They're ruthless. They have no soul. It is infamy."

The Superior General was prepared for this. "My dear Abbott, the Society of Jesus must look to the future in all matters. We're the intellectuals of Christendom. Our best minds have deciphered what Catholic Doctrine used to call 'mysteries,' and point the way toward the future, toward God. Under a condition of equality for all men, which is something that only one country is actively seeking: the Soviet Union.

Abbot Würzburg could only shake his head, disbelieving what he was hearing. But then again, Rome wasn't in Soviet hands, so these two couldn't possibly gauge the magnitude of what the Soviets were capable of doing.

But the Superior General wasn't ignorant; he simply didn't assign the same weight to the actions of victorious soldiers that their victims did. And the future of the Jesuits was far more important than all of that. He went on, saying: "Abbot Würz, the latest and most savage conflict involved nations where moneyed elites made war decisions. Imperial Japan (a throwback to the Middle Ages), set out to conquer the peaceful nations of Southeast Asia, in search of raw materials they lacked back home. The Fascist Dictators of Germany and Italy proceeded to conquer Europe. The United States entered the war because their elites didn't pay attention to their people, who wanted to stay out of it. Not coincidentally, their industries profited and thanks to the war, they went from depression to prosperity. Their excuse was Imperial Japan's attack on Pearl Harbor."

General Janssens asked Father Benz to pass him the plate with *Liptauer* and the breadbasket. After helping himself to more, he continued. "In contrast, the Soviet Union got invaded. A nation without elites didn't provoke this war. And this hasn't been lost on the survivors of this disaster, which is why you see communist parties sprouting everywhere."

Father Würzburg wasn't buying it. "But they're hell-bent on quashing freedom, which is the engine of prosperity. It's their way or death."

General Jean was also firm. "Let's tally the dead at the hands of the Soviets, shall we? It's easy: two German armies, roughly 200,000 soldiers. How many men, women and children, civilians, were killed in Hiroshima and Nagasaki, with two bombs?"

"But the raping...."

"Raping isn't killing, and all armies do it. It's been the custom of armies since forever. The Romans did it after a siege. The Vikings did it."

The Abbott pointed out that, "There are no stories of American or British rapes."

"Not yet. And should any come out, we'll profess our righteous indignation. But let's keep in mind that in 1917, Russia decided to start caring for the poor, to eliminate rich elites, to create a fairer society. And, Abbot Würz, please recognize that all we want to do, as Jesuits, is to create a fairer, more moral and godlier world. Capitalist America, Fascist Germany and Italy and Imperial Japan caused more death and destruction than the communist nation. A nation whose main concern is the elimination of poverty, the care, and education of its people, didn't cause all the recent death and destruction."

Abbot Würzburg had a headache from all that head-shaking. He'd said all that he was going to say. He'd known General Janssens for a long time, ever since they'd both been ordained Jesuits. He knew that Janssens, being the good Jesuit that he was, would only arrive at a decision after a thorough analysis. It was obvious that Janssens had arrived at such decision and that his mind was made up. He wasn't going to be able to change it.

After asking for more *Tafelspitz*, the General continued. "History has taught us that elites cause problems that are paid for with the lives of the poor. We are for the elimination of elites. The Vatican disagrees with us. They will employ every means to combat us, including the power of the purse. With this treaty, we'll be ready."

Abbot Würzburg continued to believe in his vow of obedience to the Pope. So to him, the break from the Vatican that General Janssens was planning was monumental and momentous. So the question that needed to be asked was, why is General Janssens doing this?

Had the Superior General of the Jesuits decided to disregard the core beliefs of Christianity, which was, essentially, the Word of God the Father stated in the Ten Commandments and the teachings of God the Son in the Gospel? Had he essentially thrown out 60 years of faith in such beliefs, only to replace them with the unsubstantiated proposals of Teilhard de Chardin, Henri de Lubac, and others, who claimed that to reach God, Man first had to attain earthly equality? If that were true, then why hadn't God the Son said so during his three-year ministry here on earth? Not even once?

Abbott Würzburg didn't for a minute believe that Janssens believed all that. Therefore, if the Superior General didn't believe Chardin's nonsense, but nevertheless embraced it, then he must have an ulterior motive for doing so.

If it were true that the Superior General hated elites, because they caused the death of non-elites; and if he truly believed that capitalism was the greatest generator of inequality in the world, then why not focus his efforts to combat such capitalism in the United States—the Sodom and Gemorrah of capitalism?

The logic of his conclusion was so devastating that he shrugged his shoulders and nodded his head, which seemed curious to his two guests because neither of them had said anything for a while. Embarrassed, he offered both more wine, and poured himself another glass, but then continued his silent analysis.

What made his conclusion even more devastating was that the Society of Jesus had a huge number of Jesuit institutions throughout the United States, at his beck and call. If he really wanted to confront U.S. capitalism, he already had an army in the USA, and he didn't need a single penny from the Soviet Union to do so.

Therefore, that couldn't be what was motivating the Superior General either. And so his motivation could only lie in his past. It had to have been some transformational event in his life.

Abbott Würzburg recalled that what had been said at the Jesuit Congregation that ended up electing him Superior General in 1946, was that Janssens had spent most of World War II saving the lives of many Jews in Belgium. And that he'd been very upset at not being able to save all, or enough of them.

If that was the transformational event, then he must have felt unholy rage at the Vatican for not doing anything to help the Jews or to confront and call out the perpetrators of their extermination. Moreover, it seemed that the Nazis had paid the Vatican so much hush money, that it was able to start a bank in 1942. Otherwise, what other money could they start a bank with, if the Vatican didn't manufacture and sell war materiel?

The Vatican had allowed itself to be bought off by the Nazis, and General Janssens did not forgive it for that.

Again the Abbott gestured with his head and shoulders, and again his guests were amused by it. But Würzburg didn't care. He'd nailed it: The Superior General of the Jesuits, Jean Baptiste Janssens, the Black Pope, needed Soviet money to go to war against the Vatican. Period.

But what about the poor? Didn't Jesus say, 'The poor you will always have with you?' But what about the equality of man? Again, 'The poor you will always have with you.'

If Janssens believed the same as the Abbot, that Jesus wasn't wrong with respect to the impossibility of eradicating poverty and achieving universal equality, then all he wanted to do was to use such excuses to punish the one entity that should've confronted evil and didn't: the Vatican.

The Abbott stood up, seemingly very happy. He bade good night to Father Benzini, who was perplexed at such a change in attitude, which had been anything but jovial before dinner. And then he hugged General Janssens, whispering in his ear, in German, "*Ich verstehe alles* [I understand everything]."

Before going to sleep, the Abbott felt proud of two things: being a Jesuit, to be able to have the reasoning power to arrive at his correct conclusion; and having General Janssens as a leader, because of his noble cause, and because he was sure that the Black Pope was going to get everything he wanted out of the Soviets, and make it seem like it was their idea.

Chapter 24

The Black Pope Gambit

The next morning, at 10 a.m. sharp, a black limousine stopped in front of the entrance of the Klosterneuburg Monastery. Ambassador Panyushkin, Vladislav Fedoseyev and General Ivan Konev, Soviet Commander of Soviet-occupied Austria stepped out of it. Konev and Fedoseyev were old army buddies, having commanded regiments under General Fyodor Tolbukhin. Konev had accompanied them only as a courtesy to the Ambassador. He didn't go inside.

The two Soviet officials were shown to their quarters by two nuns. At noon, the same two nouns took them to meet with Janssens, Benzini, and Würzburg for lunch. After lunch, Würzburg led them in a tour of the monastery, narrating its history to them. It had been built in 1114 by Saint Leopold III of Babenberg, the Patron Saint of Austria, and his second wife, Agnes of Germany. In 1949, the monastery was still recovering from the ravages of the war. But the original construction from 1114 A.D. and the twin gothic steeples that had been built in 1879, had survived intact.

His tour included the famous Verdun Altar, built in 1181 by Nicholas of Verdun, with 45 gilded copper plates modeled on Byzantine paragons, which had been originally manufactured as panels, but which had been assembled as an altar around 1330. They had been configured into three parts: the left part depicting the eras of Adam and Noah, the right part depicting the eras of Abraham, David, and the Babylonian captivity, and finally, the central part, depicting the life of Jesus.

After the tour, Abbot Würzburg departed, leaving the four to begin their meeting. The Ambassador introduced himself with his true name, but Fedoseyev remained Don Blas Pérez.

Ambassador Panyushkin was the first to intervene, in Spanish, as it was the language known to all.

"Gentlemen, the Jesuits have once again come to seek the assistance of Russia, like they did when they were dissolved by Pope Clement XIV in 1773. We were informed by Father Benzini that it was for economic assistance. My first question is, why us?"

General Janssens pointed out that the Soviet Union, with its lack of elites, was the innocent nation in World War II. Its pursuit of social equality since 1917, went hand-in-hand with current Jesuit thought, as enunciated by Teilhard de Chardin. However, such Jesuit thought was not accepted by the Vatican, which had begun to use their power of then purse against them. And how could the Society educate the poor without additional funds?

Panyushkin reminded General Janssens that if the current Pope decided to dissolve the Society, it would have to dissolve. A dissolved Society of Jesus wouldn't be as worthy an investment as a functioning one. How did the Society intend to avoid such a possibility?

General Janssens didn't hesitate in his response. "Ambassador, we plan to hold Congregations in Rome, under the very nose of the Pope, with his full knowledge. Therefore we won't be doing anything he can claim ignorance of, and we'll make it very difficult for him to get rid of one of the few allies he has left, after his unfortunate conduct during the Second World War. He will therefore have to accept our metamorphosis, even if he disagrees with it."

The Ambassador raised an eyebrow. "If that's his perception of you, then why would he cut you off financially?"

"Mr. Ambassador, the power to turn funding on or off doesn't necessarily reside in the Pope. The Pope alone can dissolve us. But the funneling of funds is done by a committee of Cardinals who are no friends of ours. Hopefully, we'll be able to convince these people to be our friends, but that's in the future, not in the present. Right now, a deviation from traditional Catholic doctrine would be met with 'checks in the mail' that never arrive, promises that aren't kept and an annual slashing of our budget because of 'lack of funds.' Progressive Jesuits would continue to be removed from university teaching positions because it's not the Society that's financing them; it's the Vatican."

Ambassador Panyushkin appreciated the subtle, yet valid differentiation between political power and budgetary power. But that's not the answer he wanted to hear.

"Fine, General Janssens, but why us?"

Somewhat surprised, General Janssens replied, "Mr. Ambassador, I thought I'd answered that question when I praised your 1917 revolution?"

"General Janssens, if you're implying that you're now full-blown socialists, that's something that I can't take to my superiors and expect to be taken seriously. That's something that you'll have to prove to all in time before anybody believes you because not long ago, you fought alongside Franco against the legitimate government of Spain, an ally of the Soviet Union."

Father Benzini spoke up. "Mr. Ambassador, we were lured to you through a considerable donation in Austrian coin, as you know. Upon my conversation with Don Blas, at the Austrian Bank, we agreed to explore greater financing of our goal of expanding our education to the poor of the world."

Ambassador Panyushkin looked at Benzini with a touch of exasperation, as if asking, 'How on earth did these Jesuits get their reputation for being so bright?'

Fedoseyev decided to throw them a lifeline. "Gentlemen, what the Ambassador is asking is, very simply, why wouldn't you want to get financing elsewhere?"

It was the perfect lifeline. Janssens spoke up. "Gentlemen, all our goals, which necessarily separate us from the traditional Vatican-led path, require subtlety. They are best achieved discretely. If we were to go to a commercial bank in New York, for example, we would immediately be associated with the Vatican, and our desired discretion would not be achieved, because inquiries and securities would be sought from our 'parent company.' Our association with the Vatican in the market is inescapable. We feel that you offer the best way to escape the Vatican's grip."

"By coming under our grip, gentlemen?" Fedoseyev cringed at this totally unexpected, undiplomatic riposte by the ambassador.

The Jesuit Superior General had a prepared response for this: "Mr. Ambassador, an association with us can only enhance the reputation of the sponsor of the education of the poor."

Again, the Ambassador's countenance cracked a tiny second to denote exasperation.

"Superior General, if all we wanted was to burnish our reputation, we could simply opt for donating a minuscule portion of the money you require, in exchange for a thank you published in the Vatican's *Corriere della Sera* newspaper, and avoid ourselves all this cloak and dagger with followers of a God we don't believe in. You can go begging other nations, groups and organizations for the donations that complement the money that you require."

General Janssens took the budget out of their dossier and slid it to the other side of the table, saying, "Gentlemen, there you have the needs of the Society of Jesus for the next ten years. They amount to a total of 40 million dollars, or four million dollars a year. It's not much, and if you desire absolute secrecy, I will sign my commitment to that."

The Ambassador took the budget, glanced at it and passed it over to Don Blas, who compared it to the pyramid calculations. He then looked back at the Ambassador and shrugged.

The Ambassador then turned to General Janssens and said, "Gentlemen, we are the Soviet Union, and as such, we think strategically. With four million dollars a year, you'll be able to pay for the construction of one or two schools for poor children and then you'll have no money left to pay for their teachers. Forgive us, but we were under the impression that you were serious about helping the poor. We certainly are."

All Janssens said was, "Gentlemen, we've just presented a proposal to you. Shouldn't we be expecting a counterproposal from you?"

This caught the Ambassador by surprise, and this pleased the Superior General, who knew full well that financial negotiations weren't the Soviets' forte, and who knew full well that in every negotiation it was important to gain control. Janssens had just gained it because he hadn't revealed anything that they didn't already know. If this negotiation was going to continue, it would be the Soviets who'd have to show their hand.

Ambassador Panyushkin recognized the Black Pope's gambit too late. Begrudgingly, he admired the man's intelligence for it. The truth was that in order to achieve their goals, it was preferable to have intelligent partners, and Janssens had just confirmed that he was.

He replied, "General Janssens, you are definitely entitled to a counterproposal, but I need to prepare you for it, by emphasizing the term 'to think strategically.' A synonymous term would be 'to think big.' Usually, thinking small leads to disastrous results. Had Hitler headed for the Caucasus to take over the oil fields, we'd probably be speaking German right now. But he thought small and focused on Stalingrad, with the results that we're all aware of.

Janssens nodded, not saying anything, but thinking 'Go on, go on.'

The Ambassador continued. "To us, thinking big is to defeat the United States of America, which is something that can't be a surprise to you. They are our enemies."

General Janssens replied, "Mr. Ambassador, we thought that turning toward the poor, and building schools to educate them, was big enough. That's what's reflected in our proposal. But I understand that that's not big enough for you. As such, I would ask for some guidance, because the only scenario that I can come up with, that would be equivalent to your situation vis-à-vis the United States, is if we suddenly decided that the Franciscan Order was our enemy, and that we needed to eradicate them."

The Soviets laughed at this. And although on the outside Janssens was laughing along with them, on the inside he was praying to the God of the Ten Commandments and to the Jesus of the Gospel for them to see the door that he'd just opened for them.

The Ambassador, anxious to recover the control of the negotiation, magnanimously satisfied the Jesuit's petition. "General Janssens, you're closer to thinking strategically than you realize. I'm quite certain that you would've come to this realization by yourself, had you had more time: your strategic enemy is not the Franciscan Order, but those who are forcing you to seek financing elsewhere, because they are unfairly denying it to you: the Vatican."

Both Father Benzini and General Janssens opened their mouths in astonishment. Except that Janssen's astonishment was an Oscar-worthy performance. His thoughts were, "Gentlemen, make yourselves at home. Would you like a cup of coffee?"

But before the Superior General could say anything, Father Benzini said, "Mr. Ambassador, the Vatican cannot be our enemy. We've taken vows of obedience to the Pope!"

General Janssens nodded in agreement, validating what his colleague had stated.

The Ambassador decided to tackle the vow thing head on. "Vows, Father Benzini? Don't you get something in return for your obedience? It seems to me that all you're getting in return are rejections and censures, and if the Pope were a leader worthy of your allegiance, the idea of turning to help the poor should have been his, am I right?"

Father Benzini turned toward General Janssens, expecting his support.

The Ambassador continued. "It wasn't the White Pope who came up with this most noble of ideas—to help the poor. It was the Black Pope—your own Superior General Janssens." And he nodded to General Janssens.

At that moment Don Blas stood up and started clapping, a slow, steady clap. The Ambassador joined in. Father Benzini figured he might as well join in as well.

The Black Pope didn't know what to do. He hated calling attention to himself. But if the Soviets were paying tribute to him, he had to do the polite thing. He stood up and bowed, and then raised his hands, as if saying, 'Please, enough.'

When the tribute had subsided, Ambassador Panyushkin looked directly at Father Benzini and said, "It seems to me that if you wanted to vow allegiance to a worthy leader, you need not look across the chessboard at the white pieces, Father Benzini." The prelate nodded in agreement.

General Janssens sat pensively for a moment, and then asked, "Gentlemen, if we were to agree with you, which we cannot for the reason Father Benzini gave, what form would the strategic action that corresponds to the strategic thought take? Would you give us Soviet artillery to fire on the Vatican from our headquarters, or what?"

Laughter all around. The Ambassador eventually replied, "Mr. Black Pope, as chess players, we prefer a good checkmate over raining artillery shells on someone. So if you're asking me what a good checkmate would be versus the Vatican, I'd tell you that it would be a Jesuit Pope."

Once again, the Jesuits' mouths opened in astonishment; once again, only one was sincere. General Janssens quickly pointed out, "Gentlemen, that's impossible because we don't have and we can't have a Jesuit cardinal. The reason is that that's what Ignatius of Loyola and Pope Paul III agreed to in 1534: in exchange for obedience to the Pope, we would respond only to the Pope, and not to any cardinal, archbishop, bishop, parish priest or anybody in the ecclesiastical hierarchy. And since we aren't part of the ecclesiastical hierarchy, we have no cardinals and therefore we can't be pope. So that checkmate is impossible."

Don Blas was ready for this, though. "Gentlemen, it would seem to me that far more impossible than having a Jesuit Pope is for the Vicar of Christ on earth to remain silent and look the other way while Hitler is exterminating the Jews under his very nose."

The Ambassador nodded. "General Janssens, I agree with Don Blas: nothing is impossible, especially in the political arena."

But Janssens kept shaking his head.

The Ambassador shrugged and said, "Mr. Black Pope, the only thing that will be impossible will be to give you financing, if you aren't capable of resolving such a matter in a way that makes it possible."

It was Father Benzini who replied, looking sideways at Don Blas, "It can't be done, Mr. Ambassador! The only thing I lament is that Don Blas didn't inform me of this requirement in Vienna, where I would've told him of such impossibility! It would've saved us all this time and effort!"

The Ambassador looked directly at General Janssens, and asked, "Is that true, General Janssens? That it can't be done?"

Janssens made it seem like he was pondering it, and then asked the following question: "Gentlemen, why do you say that it would be impossible to give us financing if we can't have a Jesuit Pope?"

Again it was Don Blas who answered: "General Janssens, did you really think that we were going to ask Comrade Stalin to write a huge check to the Society of Jesus from the Treasury of the Soviet Union, without him asking us how you were going to repay us?"

General Janssens feigned sudden awareness. "Gentlemen... forgive me for not realizing it sooner. You're entirely correct: the way you see it, to have a Jesuit Pope is essential to be able to reimburse you with funds from the Vatican Bank."

"Yes, but there's more," said the Ambassador, ominously.

"What else, Mr. Ambassador?" asked the General, with trepidation.

"We're going to choose your next Superior General."

This caught both priests by surprise, although it seemed to affect Benzini more, because it sounded like he was choking on something.

"How would that work exactly, Mr. Ambassador?" General Janssens couldn't hide his bewilderment.

"Superior General, in a chess game, which could take hours, the purpose is to checkmate the opponent. When I reach for my queen to attack my opponent, it's got to be there. But in real life, you may die, for any reason, although I hope it's of very old age. Or did you expect to live forever?"

This touch of levity dissipated a lot of the tension that had filled the room. Nevertheless, the Ambassador continued with the chess analogy. "In a chess game, the pieces don't resist the will of the player. But in real life, they not only can resist, they can also oppose. We simply can't allow that. Which is why we need to choose your next Superior General."

General Janssens shook his head, repeating that it was impossible.

The Ambassador pressed on. "General Janssens, we are simply trying to control all the variables that we can, to be able to achieve our goals. Anybody who agreed to finance you would do that."

The irrepressible Father Benzini spoke up just then. "Gentlemen, there's another way to frame this, and it's as a service agreement, not a finance agreement. Under a service agreement, we get paid for services rendered, and once rendered, we owe nothing to anybody."

Don Blas was about to reply, but Panyushkin shot him a look that stopped him in his tracks. He turned to Father Benzini and cheerfully said, "Father Benzini, I agree. Let's consider this a service agreement. As such, we won't pay the Society of Jesus a single kopek until the completion of your services to our satisfaction. And that will only occur when either the United States of America has fallen to us, or a Jesuit Pope has been elected."

Panyushkin then turned to Don Blas and said, "Let's go type this service agreement up. Comrade Stalin is going to love this!"

But General Janssens stopped them, saying, "Gentlemen, let's get serious, shall we? We've all used humor to punctuate our arguments, and that's all Father Benzini's done. It's obvious that this has to be a finance agreement, with all possible guarantees, which is something all financiers seek. It's also obvious that this agreement won't end until a Jesuit is elected Pope, because the Jesuit Pope would reimburse the Soviet Union for the financing received, with funds from the Vatican Bank."

General Janssens paused to drink water, and to give himself time to fine-tune what he was about to say. "Since we don't have a Jesuit cardinal, and since the authorization to have one would have to come from the Hierarchical Church to which we don't belong, and which opposes us right now, the appointment of a Jesuit cardinal is going to take a long time. It'll probably take longer than the rest of my life, and that makes it necessary for the financier to appoint the next Superior General, who is going to have to be someone who is fully onboard with the plan."

Everybody nodded. Janssens then asked, “How would that come to be? Would I have to find him for you?”

The Ambassador replied, “No, General Janssens, we’ve already chosen him. His name is Pedro Arrupe.”

The Superior General had heard of him. “He was in Hiroshima in 1945. How do you know of him?”

Don Blas replied, “General Janssens, we’ve just taken over one of Japan’s major islands. Please rest assured that we have eyes and ears over there.”

The Ambassador went on. “Arrupe is the most anti-American Jesuit we know. He was one of the first to reach downtown Hiroshima to see the horrors of the American atomic bomb up close and to help the survivors. Now, then, General Janssens, you may be an intellectual or spiritual opponent of American capitalism, but Arrupe’s hatred of America is visceral. You may want equality and the elimination of elites, but all Arrupe wants is to destroy America. With what he saw and lived through... who can blame him?”

General Janssens nodded. “Pedro Arrupe it is, then. I’ll groom him for the position.”

The Ambassador looked very happy. He reiterated, “Superior General, we both have goals that go hand-in-hand. All we want is to minimize our risks by controlling as many factors as we can. Any finance institution would do that. Only they’d give you a grace period of no more than two years, and then you’d have to start paying back principal and interest. Our grace period ends when you achieve the crown jewel of your existence as an Order: the Papacy and the control of your Church. Do we have a deal?”

“No, Mr. Ambassador, we don’t.”

The Soviets’ faces fell. They could’ve sworn that this was a done deal. Ambassador Panyushkin asked, with trepidation, “Why not, General Janssens?”

“First of all, Mr. Ambassador, nothing that is said will be valid until it is written and signed. Only then will we have a deal.”

The Soviets nodded.

“Secondly, before signing, I’ll have to see how much you’re willing to invest for us to do everything that we have to do, to get a Jesuit to become a cardinal. The obstacles are huge, and although, as Don Blas pointed out, they may not be impossible to overcome, it will cost a lot of money."

The Ambassador felt relieved. "Superior General, we're in complete agreement with you, and we're prepared to do so."

But General Janssens wasn't done. "Gentlemen, there can be no agreement until you've explained to us, in full, what you expect from us for your checkmate of the United States."

For the first time, the Ambassador smiled broadly. He turned and gestured to Don Blas, who took out three copies of a document titled 'The Black Crusade Finance Project.' He put two copies on the table in front of the priests. The document had a pyramid on its cover.

The Ambassador said, "Gentlemen, this document contains all the information that you require. We can start going over it now, or we can take a recess and a stroll down by the Danube and do it when we get back."

Having decided to take a recess, the four then left for the town of Klosterneuburg, feeling satisfied. But none more satisfied than the Superior General of the Society of Jesus, Jean Baptiste Janssens, the Black Pope.

Chapter 25

Another Children's Crusade

The HF crackled. Exactly on the frequency that was the sum of the alleged ages of the Jesuits' servants. Which was not the frequency the garrisons were on. This conversation would be about as private as you could get on HF.

"Charlie Lima, this is *Padrino,* over."

"*Padrino,* Charlie Lima. How are things over there... nice and breezy?"

"Absolutely, sir. Why don't you come over to Apaneca?"

"*Padrino,* there's a Commando Unit looking for you and your prisoners right now."

"Well sir, I'm here at the newly inaugurated Catholic University of Apaneca, waiting for them."

The Colonel laughed. "*Padrino,* always playing with fire."

"Yes, sir, I know. But this time you're going to thank me. If there's a unit looking for us instead of fighting the guerrillas, that means that the situation in the capital must be under control. Having the head honchos out of circulation must be working."

"Perhaps. But the reports are that they can't fight very well because of the quality of their troops."

"What do you mean?"

"*Padrino,* they have nine- and ten-year-old boys and girls fighting; using them as cannon fodder. The First Brigade troops, after a street battle, found many of them—their bodies—clutching AK-47s. Many civilians witnessed that, too. I doubt the guerrilla movement is going to survive this offensive after this becomes known."

This didn't come as a complete surprise to Sánchez, who'd heard rumors of children guerrillas before. But this was no longer a rumor. This was proof. And that only strengthened his resolve. "Charlie Lima, then please tell the high command not to kill the Jesuits, sir. If they're involved, then they're responsible for the deaths of those children and they should be brought to justice."

The Colonel was having a hard time arguing with the Captain, especially since he agreed with him. "I hear you, but I'm just following orders."

Sánchez offered him a way out. "If I may respectfully suggest something, Charlie Lima. If this turns out well, you could be the one to take credit for saving the lives of these priests, to make our victory complete. *Padrino* out."

He thought about the news. It seemed like such an infamy to him, to recruit girls and boys to send them into war, instead of educating them to become productive citizens? There had to be a more suitable word than infamy.

He decided to trek up the hill, greeting the soldiers as they poked their heads out of the houses. When he arrived at the priests' house, he found them lying in hammocks.

Ellacuría got up immediately. "Any news, Captain?"

"Battles in the city continue with gains made by our troops against your underage guerrillas."

"You keep saying that they're 'ours.' They're not under our command."

"I do want very much to believe that 'men of God' had nothing to do with sending nine-, ten- and eleven-year-old boys and girls into combat to die, instead of educating them."

"Of course not!"

"But it seems—from reports—that you've armed children to fight well-trained troops. And according to civilian witnesses... those children aren't doing too well. They're dying because of you. Those civilians will spread the word. What you've done—are doing—violates many conventions, doesn't it? When this final battle is over, the captured guerrillas, to save their hides, could—likely will—point the finger at you."

Segundo Montes got up and joined the conversation.

"I assure you, Captain, we would never approve of that."

The Captain looked squarely at Montes. "Really? Because it wouldn't be the first time, would it?"

Both Montes and Ellacuría blanched. This surprised the Captain, but that curious reaction didn't stop him from saying what he wanted to say: "Didn't Pope Innocent III have a 'Children's Crusade' in 1212?"

Color rushed back to the priests' faces, along with relief.

"Look, Captain..." Ellacuría started to explain.

But the Captain cut him off. "Priest, I'm not debating this... what I stated are facts as reported. I'm certain there are photographs to prove what I told you. If you bear any responsibility, you should be brought to justice. I'm no judge, so save your explanations for somebody who is. My job is to keep you alive so you can be judged for this."

Sánchez turned to walk away then stopped and faced them again. "You know what the sad part is, gentlemen? This could've all been avoided."

Ellacuría was about to reply, but it was Montes who asked, "Why do you say that, Captain?"

"Father Montes, the High Command is shocked at the use of children as soldiers. We all are. And the world will certainly be when they find out. But you must've known about it." The priests protested, but the Captain raised his hand. "Please, it doesn't take a genius to figure out that you two knew about it. But I'm willing to grant that it wasn't your decision. And that you may have even opposed it passionately, for moral reasons, when the guerrilla commanders decided to recruit or kidnap or do whatever they do to round up children and arm them."

The Captain's suspicions were confirmed when they each started to say something but didn't. He continued. "What I'm driving at is... it would be obvious to any casual observer that things can't be going well for the guerrillas militarily if they have to use children. It would also be obvious to the same casual observer that if the government is offering such depleted guerrillas a way to join the democratic process as a political party, with guarantees from the USA, that they'd be crazy not to accept the offer."

Ellacuría had heard enough. "We don't trust the army, Captain. Didn't they order us killed? Isn't that the reason we find ourselves in this predicament?"

The Captain shook his head. "Isn't that too facile, priest? I admit I haven't thought this through, but that's because I don't need to. When confronted with the order to kill you, I instantly made the decision to protect you. That's all the thought I needed to put into it. It wasn't even a thought process. My gut, every fiber in my being, told me to protect you before my brain did. It was literally a no-brainer for me."

He pointed directly at Ellacuría when he said, "You, on the other hand, you do have to try to figure out why you ended up in this predicament, don't you? Because I have the feeling that this offensive took you by surprise; that you weren't consulted."

The two priests kept wanting to say something but didn't. The Captain was right. They weren't consulted, and they still hadn't figured things out. So it was best not to say anything for now.

The Captain could've left it at that. But there was something that he wanted to air out. And rather than tackle it head-on, he decided to go about it tangentially.

He started with, "The great boxer Mohammed Ali rose to fame thanks to his fights with Sonny Liston, which he won fairly easily. This surprised many people because Liston was a punishing boxer. One explanation given later was that Liston considered Mohammed Ali to be 'crazy,' and that Liston was 'afraid of crazy people.'

"And I can understand such fear because such people are unstable, unreliable, undependable, and prone to making and repeating costly mistakes. In that sense, Sonny Liston was right: crazy people should be feared."

The priests looked puzzled, clueless as to where the Captain was going with this.

The Captain continued. "Let me give you an example of crazy: less than a month ago, while peace talks were being held in Costa Rica, in which the Government again invited the depleted and weakened guerrillas to join the democratic process as a political party, guerrillas in Santa Tecla intercepted the car of 23-year-old miss Ana Isabel Casanova and riddled her with bullets. In broad daylight."

The priests knew where he was going now. Sánchez pressed on. "I have many adjectives to describe such an attack, all stemming from the fact that she was innocent, not a military target, and that the target in any case should have been her father, Colonel Oscar Casanova Véjar, not her. After all, her father was instrumental in transferring lands from the Fourteen to the peasants over nine years ago. I know this because I was the Signal officer providing communications to his battalion while he and his troops were carrying out the Agrarian Reform in the Department of La Paz."

The Captain choked up. He'd known the young lady personally. "Was this her sin? To be the daughter of a man who helped empower peasants?"

He paused long enough to regain his composure. Then he continued.

"But the subject of this conversation is 'crazy,' and considering the degraded military situation of the guerrillas, killing her was especially crazy because the results of such action would've been foreseeable by any person of sound mind: the tanking of the guerrillas' already pitiful standing with the population, the withdrawal of the offer to join the democratic process and the elimination of all alternatives other than military action, like the attack on San Salvador."

The Captain shook his head. "But if that's not crazy enough for you, get a load of this: these same people launched an offensive in San Salvador last Saturday, somehow expecting to achieve with children, what they couldn't achieve with men in 1981. Gentlemen, that's awfully crazy."

Ellacuría replied with what must've been the only thing his vaunted intellect could come up with: "What about the daughters who've died at the hands of the Army, Captain?"

The Captain looked at him, shaking his head. But all he said was, "Priest, if the Army were in the business of killing daughters and noncombatants, as your side always claims, we would've fallen faster than Batista and Somoza, and we would've fallen ten years ago. Or else we'd be the ones having to fill our ranks with children, not you."

The Captain ended with this earnest request: "Priests, I urge you not to defend 'crazy.' Whoever killed Ana Isabel Casanova, with premeditation, and whoever attacked San Salvador with children, also with premeditation, are the same crazies who have put you in this predicament. They're the ones you ought to worry about, not the Army." He turned to walk away and this time he didn't stop.

As he walked down the hill, Sánchez allowed himself to get emotional. Ana Isabel Casanova had been nothing short of amazing. He wished that he could've done for her, what he'd been able to do for Major D'Aubuisson.

Chapter 26

Majanismo

Sánchez harkened back to those days, 10 years ago.

The seat of the executive in 1979 was the complex known as *Casa Presidencial*, in the Barrio known as San Jacinto. Next to it stands the Military Garrison known as *El Zapote*. In 1979, it was the headquarters of the Salvadoran Signal Battalion.

On October 15, 1979, the military commanders who headed those garrisons were ousted along with the President, General Carlos Romero, and they were replaced by subordinates who were supportive of the coup. It was called the coup of the 'Military Youth,' led by Colonel Adolfo Majano, who formed a Revolutionary Government *Junta*.

The other members of the Junta were Col. Abdul Gutiérrez and three civilians: Guillermo Ungo, representing the 'Popular Organizations,' i.e., the organizations that represented the underprivileged masses, Mario Antonio Andino, as a representative of the private sector, and Román Mayorga Quirós, an MIT-educated engineer, who was the non-Jesuit Dean of the Jesuit-run Catholic University.

That day, the new commander of the Signal Battalion, Major Francisco 'Sammy' Samayoa assembled the Battalion and gave an impassioned speech about social justice, Agrarian Reform and a move toward civilian rule. A couple of hours later, the Civilian-Military Junta that assumed the government of El Salvador said pretty much the same thing to the nation.

It was obvious that of the two military men in the Junta, Majano was the most left-leaning. Col. Abdul Gutiérrez was a moderate. Most of the new commanders of the Armed Forces and the Air Force identified with him more than with Majano. But the two main San Salvador garrisons, the Signal Battalion and the First Infantry Brigade, were definitely pro-Majano or *Majanistas*.

Nevertheless, the influence of Majano was deeper than it was wide. Most of the Lieutenants and Captains in the Army had had Majano as their instructor at the Gerardo Barrios Military School, and he was much beloved. Every garrison in the Republic had many officers that supported Majano, even though their commanding officers did not. And their commanding officers knew that. Majano had real power.

The coup would've never gone as smoothly as it did had everybody not felt represented by the Junta, and that's why many garrisons required someone other than Majano to represent them. The true force behind the coup, Majano, was forced to share power with Gutiérrez.

Although the proximate catalyst for the October coup had been the fall of Anastasio Somoza in July 1979, and the takeover of Nicaragua by the hard-line Sandinistas, Majano's outlook, *Majanismo,* had already grown and matured and was waiting for the right time to step onto the big stage. To understand it, one just needed to drive around San Salvador, and see the misery in which people lived: in shantytowns without toilets, in homes made out of cardboard and aluminum sheets, in *barrancos* with no running water and all the naked kids running around with kwashiorkor bellies.

In contrast, lying on the slopes of the San Salvador volcano, overlooking that sea of misery without doing anything about it, were the posh San Benito and Escalón neighborhoods, where people lived in luxurious mansions. Such contrast clearly depicted the concept of 'social injustice' that spawned *Majanismo*.

Unfortunately, it also spawned *Comunismo*, and although many equated *Majanismo* with *Comunismo*, it was clear to Sánchez that *Majanismo* was a good thing; a necessary thing. Nay, a vital thing. Majano wanted to place the main wealth-generating engine of El Salvador, the farms, in the hands of the peasants, by law. The current owners would be compensated, and the new owners would be trained to become successful farmers. This was the Agrarian Reform that the Revolutionary Junta, led by Majano, had promised the nation.

His opponents on the left, which were the guerrilla leaders and the Jesuits, wanted to take the farms by force, to have the State own them and have the peasants work them as State employees—not as their owners. And whoever opposed such a takeover would be executed, just like Fidel executed his opponents in Cuba in 1959, and just like the Sandinistas were doing in Nicaragua, since the fall of Somoza in July of 1979. Majano's opponents on the left considered the Agrarian Reform to be something to be opposed at all costs.

His opponents on the right, the Fourteen, also considered the Agrarian Reform to be something to be opposed at all costs, because they were the ones being dispossessed. And since *Majanismo* sought to have things done legally, by passing laws to that effect, and not arbitrarily, the Agrarian Reform would not happen overnight. This gave plenty of time for the Fourteen to exert influence anywhere they could, including among the Armed Forces.

And in stepped Major Roberto D'Aubuisson Arrieta, a member of the Gerardo Barrios class of 1963, to fill that need for them. At the time of the coup, he was a Major stationed at the Joints Chief of Staff of the Armed Forces, in the Military Intelligence Section, under a Colonel. A few days later, he resigned from the Army and entered the political arena, in opposition to the Junta. A charismatic man who was universally liked, he decided that the time had come to dedicate himself to what came naturally to him. As a result, Sánchez never got to meet the man. Of course, so early in his career, 2nd Lt. Sánchez hardly knew anybody outside the Signal Battalion anyway.

In D'Aubuisson, the Fourteen had found their man. D'Aubuisson began to work against the interests of the Junta by speaking constantly and often, in person and through videos, against communism in general and against the *Comunistas* on the Junta.

D'Aubuisson became a major opponent of the Agrarian Reform and the other social justice goals of *Majanismo*. Roberto D'Aubuisson was far too intelligent a man not to understand the goals of *Majanismo*. But if his ambition was to become a politician, the only space available to him was right of center, where he would feel at home, and where a lot of cash awaited him.

To that part of the political spectrum, anybody who wanted Agrarian Reform and Bank Nationalization, and the Nationalization of Exterior Commerce, the proclaimed goals of the Junta, was a *Comunista*. It was far too simplistic, but it also made for a simple message: *Patria Sí, Comunismo No* [Homeland Yes, Communism no]. And so wherever D'Aubuisson spoke, after warming up the crowds with his sense of humor and his *bonhomie*, he would convey his simple, yet effective message.

And his message didn't change when the first Junta dissolved because, although the actual communist, Ungo, was gone, his replacement, a Christian Democrat, also wanted the Agrarian Reform. So D'Aubuisson continued to hammer away: the Junta was a bunch of *Comunistas*. Their Agrarian Reform was nothing but *Comunismo*.

Col. Adolfo Majano knew full well that the survival of the nation as a democracy depended on the Agrarian Reform. If the Junta didn't follow through with it, the *Comunistas* would gain the upper hand. If so, El Salvador would be next domino to fall.

Col. Majano would do anything in his power to prevent that. Absolutely anything.

CHAPTER 27

HOMICIDIUM INTERRUPTUS

May 7, 1980 was *Día del Soldado* [Soldier's Day] in El Salvador. At *El Zapote*, it was a day of festivities, with the relatives of the soldiers allowed inside the garrison from noon till 6 p.m. When the festivities were over, 2nd Lt. Sánchez went to his quarters, changed into civilian clothes, and proceeded to get into his car to leave. He wasn't on duty that night.

Suddenly a soldier ran up to him, saluted him, and informed him that he was to get back into uniform for a mission, by order of Major Rodríguez, the Battalion's operations officer.

Major Roberto Rodríguez was a natural leader. He was direct, to the point, and very professional in uniform. But he sure knew how to party when off duty. He was a fun guy to be around.

It was with Major Rodríguez that he'd been on duty the night of March 23, listening to Monsignor Romero's 'Homily of Fire,' to which Sánchez had reacted furiously, proclaiming, "Sir, that man ought to get shot." To which Rodríguez had only laughed, and said, "Hell, all priests say the same thing, you know that."

When news came the next night that Monsignor Romero had indeed been shot, Major Rodríguez walked up to him and said, "Hey, Sánchez, don't ever let me get on your bad side, ok?"

But tonight, Rodríguez was indeed getting on Sánchez's bad side. Sánchez had a hot date that night, damn it! But that didn't prevent him from getting ready and reporting to Rodríguez.

All Rodríguez said to him was "Stand by. I'll call you when we're ready to leave."

So he went to the Officer's Mess, which was empty. He started not to like this. Shouldn't he be preparing equipment and troops, if they were going on a mission? Outside the Mess, there was movement. Somebody was preparing them, but not him. ¿How could he, if he didn't know what the mission was? If he was going to get sent into San Marcos or other neighboring shanty towns where he'd picked up guerrillas before and where he'd had his first skirmish, then why not say it? Why the secrecy?

About half an hour later Major Rodríguez summoned him and told him to get on the second truck of the convoy of trucks because he'd be on the first one and Master Sergeant Hernández would be on the third troop truck.

"Where are we going, sir?"

"You don't need to know that."

"Yes, sir." And with that, he did as he was told. But he was liking it less and less. They were a signal battalion and so their mission was to provide communications support to combat troops. They had only one radio for about 60 men. This wasn't a signal support mission; this was an infantry mission.

The convoy headed west, not south or east. South would've been toward San Marcos, east would've been toward Cojutepeque, where some guerrilla activity had occurred in the past few days. However, under no circumstance would the garrison at Cojutepeque require any Signal support beyond a two-man team, due to the magnificent *Las Pavas* hill towering over the city, crowned by the microwave station of ANTEL, the State communications company.

But out west? Nothing was happening there. Everybody always joked that the garrisons in western El Salvador were on extended leave. So why were we heading west?

And then it dawned on Sánchez: perhaps the Signal unit wasn't being used as a military unit; perhaps it was being used as *Majanista* unit. If so, the target was political, not military. And if it was political, then it could be argued that what was about to unfold was a murder, and he didn't go to West Point to be a murderer.

The convoy rolled through San Salvador, past the Chief of Staff building, out to Santa Tecla, past Santa Tecla and suddenly stopped, in the middle of nowhere, with a hill to one side of them and dense vegetation on the other side. And then, they just sat there.

Sánchez sprung to action. "Everybody out, get a squad up that hill! Get a squad to the other side of the road! The rest of you set up security in front and in back of the trucks!"

Rodríguez came out and shouted. "Belay that order! Stay in the trucks!"

Sánchez couldn't believe this. He started to approach the Major, but the Major reiterated his order.

Sánchez was glad this was the west, where absolutely nothing was happening. Because pretty soon, the entire population would know that there were three military trucks parked on the road outside Santa Tecla, as sitting ducks.

Then a car stopped next to Rodríguez's truck. It was Major Domingo Monterrosa, who would later become the Hero of the Army, Colonel Domingo Monterrosa. He got into a heated discussion with Rodríguez. He left after about fifteen minutes. And then Rodríguez called Sánchez over.

"Take a platoon down that path." He pointed to a path that was hard to see in the dark. Sánchez had to squint to see it.

"You'll get to a house. Apprehend everybody there, and when you've got everything under control, send word to me with a soldier. Take Master Sergeant Hernández with you."

For some reason, the imposition of Hernández, who'd never been in an operation with Sánchez, and whom he really didn't trust, didn't sit well with him. So Sánchez replied, "Yes, sir, but I'd rather just take subsergeant Zelayandía with me. I've never worked with Hernández before."

Major Rodríguez's eyes flashed in anger. "Listen to me, Second Lieutenant, you will do as ordered, do you understand me?"

"Yes, sir!" Sánchez went back to the truck and ordered Sergeant Zelayandía to tell the men to form two columns. He then told Master Sergeant Hernández to bring up the rear. Sánchez never saw when Sergeant Hernández signaled Sergeant Delgado to come along.

When the men were assembled, he went to the front and said, "Double time" and took off down the path at a brisk pace. They passed an open gate that had a sign that said "*Finca San Luis* [San Luis Farm]." About 200 yards down the path, they saw a house with a light at its entrance, with a man sweeping the pavement in front of it. The man saw the soldiers running toward him and didn't make any sudden movements. He acted like it was the most natural thing in the world, to see thirty armed soldiers running toward him at night. Sánchez reached him first and said: "Please step aside, and don't make any sound." He should've apprehended the man, but something told him that this poor humble peon wasn't the target.

The man did as he was told. Then Sánchez and his men ran through the door, down a short hallway which opened up into a large open living room to their left. The living room had no western wall, which opened up into either a large garden or the farm itself. It was too dark to tell because there was insufficient outside lighting. All one could see was the outline of shrubs and trees.

At the far end of the living room, there were about a dozen men, sitting down with weapons at their side, most in military uniform, drinking and having a good old time. They seemed to be celebrating Soldier's Day. And they didn't act surprised when they saw the soldiers come in.

Not until Sánchez shouted at them, "Stand up, get away from your weapons. Get up against the wall, facing it, hands behind your heads! Don't make any attempt to reach for your weapons or we'll shoot!"

The men obeyed. Meantime, Master Sergeant Hernández had had the soldiers fan out behind Sánchez.

"Sergeant, collect their weapons."

Hernández did so.

The men in uniform started insulting Sánchez. "Why aren't you after guerrillas, you worthless *gringo*?"

"Beat Army," said one who wore a Salvadoran naval uniform in English, repeating the favorite sports saying of the U.S. Naval Academy.

Sánchez felt at a disadvantage. They knew him, but he didn't know any of them. Well, he did know one: a guy with red hair who had hazed him mercilessly when he spent a few weeks at the Gerardo Barrios military school before leaving for West Point. He only remembered his nickname "*Fosforito* [Little Match]."

Sánchez wasn't going to allow this to continue. "You will remain silent and give me your names." But they continued insulting him. After all, they'd been drinking and they all outranked Sánchez.

The thin man who wasn't in uniform said, "People, let's obey the lieutenant, he's only following orders." They immediately shut up.

When told to, they gave their names: Lt. so-and-so, Capt. so-and-so, Ensign so-and-so, Navy Captain so-and-so, Major so-and-so and then the thin man said, "Major Roberto D'Aubuisson."

Sánchez almost dropped the pen. He knew then that his gut had been right: he was in the middle of something bad.

So Sánchez decided to address his captives: "Gentlemen, I believe we're all in a situation that we'd rather not be in. So I ask for your complete cooperation so we can all get out of this predicament." His gut kept telling him something could go terribly wrong.

At that moment, out of the corner of his eye, he saw Master Sergeant Hernández and Sergeant Delgado lift their weapons and aim them at the captives. And then Master Sergeant Hernández said, at the top of his voice, "Aren't we supposed to kill these bastards?"

Sánchez lunged at the Master Sergeant, wrested his weapon away from him, and shouted as loud as he could, "Nobody does any shooting here unless I give the order! Lower your weapons, all of you!"

When they all obeyed, Sánchez ordered Hernández and Delgado back to major Rodríguez, with the list of the detainees' names. He put Subsergeant Zelayandía in charge of the platoon.

All of a sudden, the outlines of the shrubs and trees to the west of the large living room started to move, and silhouettes emerged from behind them. They were camouflaged soldiers. Their commander stepped forward: he was a Captain from the First Infantry Brigade, from the *San Carlos* garrison – another *Majanista* unit! How long had they been there?

Their commander walked up to Sánchez and said, "I'm Captain León. We'll take over now, Lieutenant."

Sánchez said, "Excuse me, sir, but Major Rodríguez is my commanding officer. I won't take any orders unless they come from him."

Just then, Major Rodríguez entered the room.

One of the men up against the wall was a good friend of Major Rodríguez and started to insult him.

"Rodríguez, you pathetic son of a bitch. Have you no shame for turning your weapons against your classmates and comrades in arms?"

Major Rodríguez walked towards them, and said, "Calm down, we're just following orders."

Captain León approached Major Rodríguez but Sánchez couldn't hear what was said because Rodríguez's classmate, *El Toro* [the Bull] Staben, kept shouting at him. Captain León then went with a soldier with a radio on his back. Sánchez walked toward them with the hope of hearing something.

All he could hear was the Captain say, "No, Colonel, can't do that anymore. What do you want me to do? Nope, can't do that anymore."

Just then he felt someone tug at his sleeve. It was *Fosforito*. Apparently, Major Rodríguez had let the detainees walk away from what they now considered their wall of execution. *Fosforito* said, "Sánchez, don't let them kill us, please."

"No sir, I won't."

He left to be with the other detainees, who were all talking to Major Rodríguez. So while Sánchez was standing there, waiting on new orders, he analyzed everything that had happened.

It was clear to him that since only Majanista units had been involved, that it was Col. Majano himself who had ordered this operation. He deduced that the person Captain León had been talking to on the radio must have been Colonel Majano himself.

Furthermore, the operation must have been leaked because Major Monterrosa, who was not serving in either *El Zapote* or *San Carlos*, had confronted Major Rodríguez in the middle of the road. That heated discussion had probably been long enough to mess up the timing of the two units that were involved.

Which meant that Sánchez's unit was late. In all probability, the First Brigade unit was already hiding behind the bushes when Sánchez's unit got there. So it couldn't have been their mission to kill D'Aubuisson, could it? They could have done it easily, from behind the bushes, while D'Aubuisson and his buddies were celebrating Soldier's Day.

Conclusion: It was Sánchez's unit that had the mission to kill D'Aubuisson. But Major Rodríguez couldn't tell Sánchez because he knew Sánchez would refuse. So the order had been given to Master Sergeant Hernández, who had most likely served under Col. Majano and would do anything for him, like many others in the Armed Forces would. And Hernández had chosen Delgado probably for the same reason. Majano was much beloved in the Army. No doubt about it.

So what was the First Brigade unit there for? Probably just in case D'Aubuisson and his buddies proved too much for the Signal troops. They were there to finish the job if the Signal troops couldn't.

So Sánchez was satisfied with his deductions, but there was still one thing he couldn't figure out: Why had he been chosen for this mission?

Just then, Major Rodríguez ordered the Signal soldiers back to the trucks. As they were leaving, the Signal troops saw the First Brigade troops load the prisoners onto one of their trucks and take off with them.

Sánchez and his troops got back to the barracks at midnight. Sánchez went to his quarters and crashed.

The next morning, the whole Army was on alert. Some garrisons were threatening rebellion if the First Brigade didn't release its prisoners.

Sánchez's parents called him, worried because they were getting threats from people saying that Sánchez had been the one who captured D'Aubuisson.

All Sánchez could say was, "No, that's not true, and I can't say anything else." But he definitely didn't like his family getting threats.

Later that day, it was learned that D'Aubuisson and his friends had been released, unharmed. And then the calls started coming in that Sánchez had actually saved his life.

Sánchez still hadn't figured out why he'd been chosen for this assignment, because he wasn't on duty and he wasn't the company commander. With a company-sized outfit, the company commander should have been there, and 2nd Lt. Sánchez should have been under Captain Palomo's command, who in turn would've followed the instructions of Major Sammy, the Battalion Commander, or Major Arriaza, the Battalion Executive Officer.

Also, Santa Tecla was under the jurisdiction of the Cavalry Regiment, in Opico. It certainly wasn't under Signal or First Brigade jurisdiction.

So given that every sound military practice had been violated, Sanchez had come to the following conclusion: it was Major Sammy's intention to get 2nd Lt. Sánchez inextricably involved in the *Majanismo* cause. How? By making Sánchez complicit in the murder of the number one anti-*Majanista,* Major Roberto D'Aubuisson.

But why? Sánchez had done his duty at every turn and had never been involved in any extracurricular activities with any anti-Majano elements of the Armed Forces. There was no reason to doubt his commitment to *Majanismo*. So what had prompted this bizarre move?

After racking his brains, he came to the only plausible conclusion: The Women's March of December 10, 1979.

Chapter 28

The Stronger Sex

The Women's March was being organized by the anti-communist groups, as a demonstration against *Majanismo*. But it was cleverly being promoted as 'Pro-Peace.' And since the left-wing organizations, despite being represented in the Revolutionary Junta, had not stopped protesting and creating violent situations, this was an opportunity for the part of the population that didn't see violence as the means to an end to let their voices be heard. And it attracted women from all walks of life, even the *sirvienta* class. The participation fever had gripped the Tacarello women as well.

"*Moglie*, it's too risky. All those women on the Women's March will be sitting ducks. I don't want to lose you."

"Just so you know, your daughters Carmen María and Rosa Lina are going also."

Just then, Gladys came in with the coffee and biscuits. After serving them, she said, "If you don't mind, Mrs. Tacarello, my mother and I would like to go with you on the Women's March."

Pepe almost spilled his coffee. "What? Why on earth would you want to go? This has nothing to do with you!"

Gladys spoke up. "Don Pepe, I'm for peace, my mother is for peace. Every other *sirvienta* in the neighborhood here is for peace. I pray to God that war never comes to this country, so that my son doesn't have to fight. He's all I've got. No sir, this march for peace deserves our complete support."

Pepe understood. Like every mother, Gladys was very protective of her son.

"I understand you, ladies, but please understand that I can't let you get exposed to danger. Every time there are marches in this country, people die. So forgive me if I don't want my loved ones dead."

He finished his cup of coffee and went to Vesuvius to talk to Nena. It amazed him how this woman had gone from the semi-literate *india* (she had only gotten to the 6th grade), to becoming Director, all on her own merits. As Pepe had given her more independence, Nena had started to dedicate more time to improving herself, taking courses at night. She didn't do it to get any degree; she just wanted to have the necessary knowledge to deal with customers and run the store better. She even took a Dale Carnegie course. Within a few years, she'd become a very polished manager. Her future was to be the President of Vesuvius if Pepe ever retired.

In one of the night courses she took she'd met a young man who was studying to become an accountant. As normal, his sentiments of friendship soon bloomed into something else, but she was too ashamed of what she'd done with Pepe to allow it to go any further.

Pepe had noticed her sullen demeanor and asked her about it, but she didn't want to talk about it. When a few days had passed and her demeanor had not improved, he decided that it was time to get to the bottom of this.

At noon one day, he told Nena to shut the store for lunch. Nena felt her heart sink. This could only mean that Don Pepe was going to dominate her, and she had hoped that that would never happen again. Her newfound self-assuredness, based on her success, pushed her to refuse. But her heritage-induced meekness was more powerful, and at noon she shut the store and went upstairs.

When Pepe got to the apartment, he told her to undress completely. She did so but couldn't hold back the tears. Pepe ignored the tears and told her to undress him, which she promptly did. He sat down on the couch and told her to kneel before him and suck. She did so without hesitation.

Then he told her to stop. This surprised her. She stopped and just knelt there, looking up at him.

Pepe looked at her sternly and told her to tell him what was wrong, or he would beat it out of her.

Nena blurted it all out. Pepe listened to her and when she was done, told her to get dressed and compose herself, because he was going to take her out to lunch.

Half an hour later, they were sitting at *Nanette's Café*, ordering lunch. Nena assumed he wanted a rundown of the business, but he told her to be quiet and to listen.

"Nena, you're a wonderful young lady whom I took advantage of. Why did I do it? Because I could. Because in this backward country, your rights as a woman aren't protected. You come from an impoverished town, with hardly any education, and men like me will take advantage of you. I have acted like a monster toward you. For that, I apologize.

"But I don't see how it could've happened any other way. Your lack of education was made up for, in spades, by your desire to learn, and the fact that you were willing to stay in the apartment gave you a leg up on every other candidate, who would've probably charged me more for less work, who would've left at 6 p.m., whereas you would go upstairs to cook dinner for me. You were the far better option because I was alone. You understand me, don't you?"

Nena nodded. She knew why it had happened, and why, despite the humiliations she had endured at his expense, she was still grateful to him. After all, most of her contemporaries from Intipucá were far worse off than she was: they were poor, but now they had children and no responsible father. She'd been spared that.

As if reading her mind, he finished her thoughts. "But I didn't get you pregnant. I didn't take your virginity. Yes, I did everything else to you, but that's something your future husband need never know. Nobody will ever know it. And that's precisely why I didn't take your virginity, when I could have. I didn't so that one day you could start a life with a man you love, without any regrets."

She began to say something but he didn't let her.

"Everybody has secrets, Nena. Everybody. I have mine, and you have yours, and your young man probably has his. But with all such secrets, men and women have been marrying and procreating and leading happy lives. Some get divorced, but that's just human nature. So what am I saying? Live life to the fullest. On your wedding night, the sheets will be stained red, and your husband will be a proud man. And you should be a proud wife. And whatever happened between us will be a secret we take to our graves."

Nena was overcome with joy at these words. But then she asked what she'd been wanting to ask all along: "Don Pepe, could you please stop using me for sex?"

Pepe shook his head somberly, as if she was asking too much. Then he smiled and said, "Only if you promise you're going to stop moping and walking around with such a long face."

Six months later, Nena became Mrs. Marta Elena de Domínguez, and her husband moved into the apartment above the Vesuvius. Nine months later, the first of the Domínguez children was born.

That was several years ago. Right now he was coming to Vesuvius not to inquire about the business, which couldn't be in more capable hands, but to ask her about something else. And now she wasn't Nena anymore; she was Mrs. Domínguez. That had been Pepe's idea, to bury the past for good.

He knocked on the door to her office, which had a sign with her full name and her title of 'Director.'

"Mrs. Domínguez, do you have a minute?"

Mrs. Domínguez got up to greet Don Pepe. She looked so elegant and professional.

"What can I do for you, Don Pepe?"

"I wanted to ask you if you had any plans to deal with the Women's March that's going to pass by here."

Mrs. Domínguez lost her normal self-assuredness and seemed uncomfortable with the question. She hesitated before saying, "Don Pepe, I believe it's best if we close that day. I'm having some of our handymen over the night before to put wooden plans in front of the glass, as extra reinforcement between the glass and the external aluminum curtain we bring down at close of business every day."

Pepe thought that the steps she was taking were commercially sound and logical, so why wouldn't she look him in the eye?

"Don't tell me you're planning on marching as well?"

Mrs. Domínguez nodded. "Yes, I am, Don Pepe. I don't want war in this country. Nobody does. My husband objected, but since he knows I'm going, he's planning on marching with me as well, to protect me."

"With his bare hands?"

"Oh no, he'll have a gun and I'll have a kitchen knife on me."

Surprised, Pepe had to recognize that this march was an opportunity for the women of the country to demand a peaceful solution to the problems of the country. As such, although it was being organized by D'Aubuisson against *Majanismo*, it was actually an endorsement of *Majanismo,* because his Agrarian Reform was the only way to achieve social justice without bloodshed. Maybe that would keep the *Majanistas* from disrupting the march.

But all Pepe said was, "Well, then I guess I'm going to have to march with my wife as well. For the same reasons as your husband. I'd better go buy me a gun."

And he went back home to give his approval. And to start planning the protection of his women.

He then called his son, Father Mario Tacarello, to tell him that all the women of the Tacarello household were going to participate in the Women's March, with the hope that Mario could call off any attacks from the left.

Father Mario Tacarello had recently returned from the University of Münster, where he'd gotten his bachelor's degree in philosophy, and he was now undergoing the stage that the Jesuits called 'regency,' by teaching at the Externado de San José.

But he was also very much involved in the planning of the Salvadoran revolution which, had it not been for the coup of October 15, 1979, would've already triumphed in El Salvador. He wasn't doing it because he was a revolutionary himself, but because every Jesuit in El Salvador was working hand-in-hand with the guerrillas toward such revolution—it came with the territory.

He had been working so close with the guerrillas, that he'd even been given his own *nom-de-guerre* [war name]—*Eliseo*—because he'd led a couple of Externado's students to join the guerrillas. But it wasn't his doing: he was merely following the instructions of his boss, Father Segundo Montes, who was following the instructions of his boss, Father Ignacio Ellacuría, who in turn was following the orders of his boss, Pedro Arrupe, the Superior General of the Jesuits, also known as the Black Pope. Arrupe had been elected Black Pope upon the death of his predecessor, Jean Baptiste Janssens, in 1964.

The new Black Pope's first order of business had been to order the creation of the new Jesuit Bible: 'Liberation Theology.' This was a necessary step to foster revolution because it justified any and all actions that poor people took to satisfy their needs on earth, and that included killing.

So young Father Tacarello told his dad not to let them participate, because might get attacked by forces on the left, and there was nothing he could do about it.

When Pepe relayed that message to them, his women just laughed at him. Nothing was going to stop them. Which was a testimony to the bravery of those women.

Those women included Second Lieutenant Sánchez's mother, who called her son to inform him of her participation.

"Hi, son, I just wanted to tell you that I might be stopping by your garrison next Monday."

"Oh no... are you going to be on that march?"

"Yes, me, your aunts, some friends. We're all going to go dressed in white. The march is going down Alameda Roosevelt, through downtown and then we're headed south to Barrio San Jacinto, to *Casa Presidencial*."

"Mom, don't stop by to see me."

"You can't expect me not to drop by and see my son, do you?"

"Ok, but it'll have to be quick. We'll be confined to quarters that day, I'm sure."

"Instead of being out in force to protect us?"

"Mom, we're *Majanistas*. That march is against *Majanismo*. The garrisons of the capital aren't going to be out to protect you. As a matter of fact, I would prefer it if you didn't go. Every time there's a march in San Salvador, people get killed."

"Sorry, son, everybody I know is going, and the men are going to follow right behind us, to protect us. Hey, it's the least I can do for my country."

"Mom! You've already done enough, with the Cerebral Palsy Shelter you founded."

When Sánchez's sister Claudia Marcela was born, the doctor screwed up. As a consequence, Claudia Marcela suffered from cerebral palsy. His mom, after seeking the best help in the USA for her daughter to no avail, had founded the *Hogar de Parálisis Cerebral* [Cerebral Palsy Home] for children such as Claudia Marcela. It was a successful non-profit organization that she had raised money for and which had endured for over a decade. In Sánchez's mind, she'd done enough.

"Sorry, son, there's no way I'm not going. We want peace. It's a pro-peace march."

And so that day, tens of thousands of women from all walks of Salvadoran life gathered at the *Salvador del Mundo* [Savior of the World] monument and began their eastward march toward downtown, down the *Alameda Roosevelt*, escorted by many men walking next to and behind them, trying to prevent or ward off any attacks on the women.

Near a park, the women started to get pelted with plastic bags filled with urine, with rocks and with other projectiles. The men folk ran after such biological warriors, and the women were able to go on, proud of having withstood this first attack.

The emboldened women continued their march, singing the national anthem or shouting pre-packaged sayings, such as 'Homeland Yes, Communism No!' made famous by Major D'Aubuisson, but what the women most chanted was what they carried in their hearts: "We want peace!"

When they reached the *Plaza Libertad* [Freedom Plaza] right before making a turn toward the south, to head toward the *Barrio San Jacinto* neighborhood and *Casa Presidencial*, a large mob of left-wing men and women were waiting for them. When the bulk of the march had gotten there, they pounced.

A battle royal ensued. Carmen María, Father Mario Tacarello's oldest sister, started to get kicked by a man and a woman. That didn't last long because the lady next to her, a street merchant, took out a machete from under her skirt and started hitting the two attackers with it.

Don Pepe got into a fight with a guy who grabbed his wife's bottom, and so did Celso Díaz, when two men tried to drag his wife Rosa Lina away. Gladys and her mother, Estela, got into a fight with two women who'd ripped the white t-shirt off an old lady, recovering it.

These scenes repeated themselves up and down the march. Not all the women were able to continue toward *Casa Presidencial*: many were seriously injured, and so were some of their men, who had to be taken to hospitals.

But two thirds of the women emerged victorious from the battle, and managed to get to their destination, to share their views with the Revolutionary Junta, and especially with Col. Majano, over megaphones. Again, most of what they said was that they wanted peace. Majano should've considered this an indirect endorsement of his *Majanismo*.

But perhaps that fact that it was organized by D'Aubuisson precluded him, and his supporters in the *El Zapote* garrison next door, from seeing it that way.

At around 5 pm, a soldier came looking for Lt. Sánchez, informing him that his mother was waiting for him at the entrance gate.

Sánchez went to his commanding officer, Captain Palomo, for

permission to go see his mother at the gate. Palomo looked up and said, "Oh no, go ask Major Rodríguez about this."

Major Rodríguez chuckled and said, "Go ask Major Sammy."

Major Sammy wasn't happy at all. He said, "Officer, those marchers today are opposed to everything that we're trying to accomplish. They're shouting at Col. Majano that they don't want the Agrarian Reform. Don't you want to have the Agrarian Reform, officer?"

"Sir, with all due respect, all I hear is that they want peace! And if they want peace, they have to be endorsing the Agrarian Reform, right? Because if there's no Agrarian Reform, war is exactly what we're going to get!"

Sammy hated it when this uppity West Pointer made sense. But he didn't want to grant him his request, so he asked, "Sánchez, if you're seen with those women, wouldn't that undermine your *Majanista* credentials?"

"Sir, with all due respect, that's a negative way of viewing this. A positive way of viewing this is that the lady who wants to see me at the entrance to this garrison gave birth to a *Majanista*. That being the case, shouldn't you not only give me permission to go see her, but also come with me to thank her for her contribution to democracy?"

For a millionth of a second, the commander of the Signal Battalion smiled. But his seriousness returned quickly because he knew full well that the future of El Salvador might well depend on his preventing this second lieutenant from seeing his mother.

"Just whose side are you on, officer? Majano's or your mother's?"

"Both, sir."

"Why didn't you advise her not to go on this march?

"I did, sir."

"Why didn't you advise her not to come here?"

"I did, but technically she's at *Casa Presidencial*, not here."

Sammy was obviously concerned about how Majano would react to a display of affection between one of his *Majanista* officers and a woman that was part of D'Aubuisson's march.

So the second lieutenant decided to alleviate his concerns. "Sir, those women are dirty, smelly, and who knows what else, after they faced the Salvadoran version of the Sandinista 'divine mobs' at *Plaza Libertad*. I would be very grateful to you if you denied me permission to go embrace my mother, because I may get my uniform dirty."

Major Sammy had been informed of the attacks leveled at those brave women who'd marched today and realized that there might be a downside to not allowing one of those women to see her son who was a member of the army. Besides, those women were more anti-guerrilla than anti-Majano.

"Officer, go see your mom. Make it quick."

"Thank you, sir."

When he got to the gate, he saw his mother outside with friends of hers. They were dressed in white, but they looked dirty and beat-up. Nevertheless, they were beaming with pride at what they'd accomplished.

Sánchez was glad to see his mom and went out to embrace her. And then he embraced her friends.

A Spanish news crew was filming the entire scene.

Majano must've seen that report on TV and called Sammy.

That's why he'd been sent on the D'Aubuisson mission.

As good fortune would have it, he'd been accepted at a U.S. university in Texas to get a master's degree in electrical engineering. Classes started in August. Sánchez asked for an audience with Colonel Abdul Gutiérrez, member of the Junta, for permission to attend that university. He told him that it was because of his unwitting involvement in the D'Aubuisson assassination attempt.

The Colonel smiled and said, "It's an honor for a member of the Salvadoran military to be accepted into a U.S. university. Say no more. Go."

When Sammy found out that Sánchez was leaving in August, he sent deployed him to the Engineer Battalion in Zacatecoluca, to be the Signal Officer for Lt. Col. Casanova Véjar, who was about to start the execution of the Agrarian Reform in the Department of Zacatecoluca.

2nd Lt. Sánchez spent all of June and July of 1980 there, assisting in such transfer of land to the peasants—his greatest pride.

Chapter 29

The Black Indulgence

"Would you like some coffee, Captain?" Ellacuría probably wanted to know if Sánchez had any more news. He was kicking himself for not bringing a transistor radio. And the darn house didn't have any, having looked as thoroughly as he could for one.

"Sure, Father."

"Come on over and sit down. Elba, can you bring the Captain a cup of coffee?"

"Coming!"

Elba Ramos brought over a cup on a saucer.

"Sugar?"

"No, just black, thank you." The Captain was about to take a sip, but then he stopped and asked the lady, "You're not from Izalco, are you?" Izalco was known as the 'witch capital' of El Salvador.

Elba immediately caught the captain's gist and decided to play along. "I used to live near there, Captain."

The Captain immediately gave the cup of coffee back. "Oh no, who knows what kind of potion you put in it," he said, only half-seriously. Elba giggled.

Just to show that he wasn't completely serious, Sánchez took a sip of the coffee, placed the cup down, and smiled at her. Suddenly he raised his hands to his throat, making choking sounds. Elba started laughing out loud. Her daughter Celina came out to see what was so funny.

Elba then said, "No, Captain, we don't want to kill you, we just want to turn you into a frog."

To which Sánchez replied, "My gosh, is that why my uniform is turning green?" Both ladies loved it. They started giggling.

The Captain continued. "But seriously, ladies, everybody knows that those are just old wives' tales." He then took a hand to his throat, opened his eyes wide, and said, "Brrribit! Brrribit!"

Elba and Celina couldn't contain their laughter.

Captain Sánchez then said, faking difficulty in talking, "Ok, but promise me that when I finish turning into a frog, one of you will kiss me and I'll turn into a prince!"

Their laughter traveled was heard throughout the beach complex and it must've been heard by fishermen out at sea. The soldiers wondered how those women could be having so much fun in their situation.

Party-pooping Ellacuría put an end to it by asking the ladies to leave so he could talk business with the Captain. They left, but they could still be heard laughing in the kitchen and imitating the Captain's 'brribit.'

Ellacuría brought his cup of coffee over as he sat down next to the Captain. "So you went to the UCA, Captain?" Ellacuría was curious about what he thought of 'his' university.

"Yes, for one semester. And I got to read that composition of yours extolling Marx, and not mentioning Jesus even once. A most amazing piece of work, coming from a priest, in a 'catholic' university. But when I read that, I really paid no mind to it. I was head and shoulders above my peers in math classes, and soon I felt like I was repeating tenth grade. So I prayed fervently for an opportunity to study abroad."

Father Montes had joined Ellacuría and the Captain by that time. He probably figured there'd be fireworks again. He wasn't wrong.

The first punch came from Ellacuría. "Who'd you pray to, Captain? Mars, the god of war?" He just couldn't help himself.

The Captain cupped his ear, as if to hear better. "Did you say Marx? The guy you praised in your manifesto? Marx is the god of the Jesuits. I prayed to Jesus, and Mary, and God Our Father. And they came through."

Ellacuría snorted. "That's blasphemy: praying to God to become a killing machine."

This guy obviously never took a Dale Carnegie course.

"Priest, if I've ever killed, it's been only when attacked and only to defend myself and my troops and my country. My troops and I had to kill some of our attackers when we were atop Cacahuatique mountain in order to survive. I can assure you that they were attacking us with AK-47s and mortars, not sticks and stones. Also, on occasion, we'd get attacked with mortar fire at the 3rd Infantry Brigade in San Miguel. We responded in kind."

But enough defense. Time to go on offense.

"You described me as a killing machine. Pray tell, what would an actual killing machine look like? What would it do? It would produce countless deaths, wouldn't it? Like the grim reaper with the sickle? Well, priest, that certainly doesn't describe the Salvadoran Army at all. Certainly not the one who took land from the Fourteen and to give it to the poor. And it doesn't describe me because look at you: you're alive and well. And I'm prepared to die so that you may live. This entire platoon of men is."

But it was hammer time. "But can there be a deadlier killing machine than one that promises you Heaven if you kill? An Indulgence? Such as what Pope Urban II gave out, in France, when he launched the First Crusade in 1095? So no matter what you did, like rape, pillage, plunder, torture, you were guaranteed entrance to Heaven? Wasn't that what the 1st Crusaders did, and the 2nd Crusaders, all the way up to the Ninth Crusade, in 1291? There are accounts of how the 1st Crusade killed 70,000 people when they got to Jerusalem. Imagine how many hundreds of thousands, if not millions, died in the Nine Crusades ordered by the Catholic Church? Plus the children's crusade; which children never returned."

Ellacuría took a sip of his coffee and said, "Come now, Captain, that was to recover the Holy Land, a noble endeavor."

"Noble? More fun than noble, especially since no matter how many women you raped, you'd go to Heaven anyway, right? Since the Holy Land wasn't recovered, it seems that the Crusades attracted more criminals and rapists than good soldiers. On top of that, the enemy was anxious to avenge what had been done to their women.

"Not only were they unable to recover the Holy Land, they also infuriated the Muslims, who launched their own crusade against Europe, only they called it a *jihad*. Many Europeans started to blame the Pope, who said, 'Oh yeah? Screw you!' (but in Italian), and in 1184 AD Pope Lucius ordered bishops to start inquisitions in their local dioceses, against those who dared criticize him, also known as 'heretics.'

"But that didn't work out because some bishops refused. So in 1227, Pope Gregory IX appointed the first papal inquisitors, mostly from the ranks of Franciscan and Dominican friars. In 1252 Pope Innocent (oh, the irony!) IV allowed inquisitors to torture whoever was considered to be a heretic.

"This had been going on for almost 300 years already, by the time the

'Catholic King and Queen,' Fernando and Isabel, received permission from Pope Sixtus IV to name inquisitors throughout Spain—inquisitors of the Crown, because Spain already had religious inquisitors.

"Which came to be known as the 'Spanish Inquisition,' which spawned the term '*Auto de fe*,' which means 'act of faith,' which in reality meant execution of heretics at the stake. Those heretics were mostly Jews, but also included political enemies of the Crown."

Sánchez finished his cup of coffee and awaited any comment from the Jesuits. They had the look of, "How is it that this military goon knows so much history?"

He went on. "The idea of being able to eliminate its enemies by simply accusing them of being heretics was appealing to the Portuguese Crown as well, and so the Inquisition was taken to the Americas by both Spanish and Portuguese conquerors. And could there be a more fertile ground for the Inquisition, than the Americas, where no *indio* had ever heard of Jesus Christ and any European deity?"

Segundo Montes reacted to this. "Look, Captain, what was done during the Conquest was to catechize, not torture."

The Captain shook his head, incredulously, and asked, "So how did that happen, according to you, Father Montes? The conquerors got off their boats and told the *indios*: 'Hey, let yourselves be catechized while we take all your treasures back to Spain,' is that it? And their answer was OK? Because your answer apparently ignores the military component of the Conquest, necessary to militarily subjugate the *indios*, before being able to catechize them. And then, if they preferred to continue worshiping their own gods, as they were entitled to, then you'd turn them into wraiths, through acts of faith!"

Montes said nothing. The name Hernan Cortez came to his mind, which only proved the Captain's point. And the Catholic Church had helped another military man in 1936: General Francisco Franco.

The Captain continued. "How many *indios* did the Inquisition kill in the Americas, priests? Just imagine how many, considering a population of heretics from California to Patagonia, and considering that the Spanish Inquisition didn't end until 1834, when the Royal Decree abolishing it was signed."

Sánchez looked directly at Ellacuría when he asked, "How many people from all over the world were executed under the Inquisition, priest? Who knows? We know that the Portuguese executed 'acts of faith' in as faraway places as India. And we know that the Inquisition lasted seven centuries. We also know that the Inquisition went from being only a religious weapon, to being a political one as well. And the number of such countless executions doesn't take into account the deaths caused by the internal wars that erupted in places like England and France between Protestants and Catholics, which spawned a war between England and Spain, culminating with the defeat of the Spanish Armada.

"Gentlemen, if we go back to the Crusades, the Catholic Church isn't just a killing machine, it seems to be a perpetual killing machine!"

Ellacuría was undaunted. "The Holy See has stated that only 32,000 people were executed under the 'Autos de Fe' and the Salvadoran Army has certainly killed more than that in a decade."

Sánchez addressed the first part of his claim. "First of all, priest that 'See' that you talk about is far from Holy, as we've already proven. Secondly, because of the sheer enormity of the atrocities committed over a period spanning seven centuries, of course they're going to try to say they were less. But since they are as unintellectual as the rest of the priests that I know, they fail to see that admitting the torture and burning of even 32,000 already condemns them and makes my argument for me: that men of the cloth tortured and killed in the name of God—a killing machine."

The Jesuits said nothing. Even they didn't believe that seven centuries of Inquisition had produced only 32,000 deaths.

Sánchez then addressed the second part of his claim: "As for your accusation that we've killed 32,000 in a decade, I understand that that's what your propaganda radio in Nicaragua says, which is repeated by left-wing American newspapers and movie producers. But the problem with propaganda is that it's easily debunked by reality. Because this is what reality looks like, in November 1989: the guerrilla forces launched a desperate attack on San Salvador with children combatants, and they left their greatest allies, the Jesuits, unprotected.

"Had we done any of the things you accuse us of doing, me and every other member of the army would've been executed ten years ago, by orders of a Jesuit, just like they did in Nicaragua, because we would've fallen faster than Somoza."

This reality described by the military man affected the Jesuits. They still hadn't figured out why they were in this predicament; why they hadn't been told of this offensive.

Sánchez then went on. "It wasn't only the Inquisition that was killing *indios* in the Americas, because the Catholic Killing Machine had opened up another front, this time under the command of the Jesuits."

The Jesuits exploded as if the captain had questioned their mother's virtue. He couldn't understand what Ellacuría was saying in Basque, but he understood when Montes asked, "Just because Ignatius of Loyola used to be a soldier?"

The Captain replied, "Ignatius of Loyola pledged obedience only to the Pope and got the Pope to allow his organization not to obey parish priests, bishops, archbishops and cardinals. That allowed them to do whatever they wanted. And what they wanted to do in the early 1600s, half a century after the death of Ignacio, was to establish slave plantations called 'Reductions,' for the production of the popular tea-like drink called *yerba mate*, which plant grew in the wild in Bolivia and Paraguay.

"You see, because *yerba mate* grew in the wild, it couldn't be produced in industrial quantities. But the well-educated and clever Jesuits discovered a way to grow it on plantations, to be able to produce it and sell it in industrial quantities. But since there wasn't any mechanized agriculture back then, the only way they could produce the industrial quantities that would make them rich and powerful, was to do what the plantations of the U.S. south would do to grow cotton in the 1800s: use slave labor. Only the Jesuits didn't need to import African slaves, because they already had available labor that cost them nothing in Bolivia and Paraguay: the Guaraní *indios*.

The Captain got up to get a glass of water. His throat was drying up from so much talking, and he still had a lot to say. "Of course, Jesuits couldn't enslave a man, ¿could they? Enslaving men is for Pharaohs and Romans and bad men, certainly not men of the cloth. So to get these *indios* to grow their crops for nothing, the Jesuits herded them into plantations called 'Reductions,' claiming that they were missions to catechize. With that excuse, the made them grow and harvest *yerba mate* throughout Latin America, with so much success, that the *yerba mate* became known as 'Jesuit Tea.'"

Ellacuría didn't attempt to deny it. "So they were capitalists back then. Big deal."

"No, priest, you weren't capitalists; you were slave owners. And I'm not the one who says it; the facts do. Because just what did the Jesuits do with the fabulous sales of Jesuit Tea? I'll tell you what they didn't do: they didn't pay taxes. And since those Jesuits weren't any smarter than the current ones, it never occurred to them that all of South America was going to be drinking their product, including the Viceroy of Peru, who would inform the King, and the King would say, hey, they're not paying taxes on that!

"The other thing they didn't do, which would've reduced their taxes, was to take part of their profits and invest in educating the Guaraní *indios*. Because had they done that, the Guaraní *indios* would've done what all educated people do: prosper. Somebody who's educated doesn't stay to grow and harvest yerba mate all their lives. And just how long were those plantations operational? From 1609 to 1767. Which is 158 years of enslaving the Guaraní *indios*, and profiting massively."

This time it was Montes who tried to defend his Order. "Captain, you're twisting our history because of your animus toward us."

The Captain had to laugh. "Father Montes, I'm an engineer, so I necessarily deal in reality and not feelings. As such, everything I say must be proven. And if I say you enslaved them, it's because unfolding events proved it.

"So let me go on. The Jesuit slave-owners had to face two enemies: the Spanish Crown, who had ordered the confiscation of the Jesuit assets because they owed taxes; and the Portuguese slave traders called *Bandeirantes*, who wanted the Jesuits' Guaraní slaves.

"Since the Jesuits back then weren't any smarter than the Jesuits I know, it never occurred to them that if they paid the taxes they owed, that it would've been the Spanish Crown who would've fought against the Bandeirantes. Instead, they opted to form an army of Guaraní *indios*, and sent them to fight and die to protect the economic interests of the Jesuits, in a two-front war.

"And since those Jesuits had about as much knowledge about war as the Jesuits that I know, they didn't know that a two-front war is a lost cause, and so they lost. How many thousands of poor *indios* died to protect Jesuit profits? Before the Jesuits were finally captured and expelled by the

Spanish Crown?"

They had no answer for that. How could they?

"Second question: What happened to the Reductions when the Jesuits got captured and expelled from the Americas? Answer: they failed. The Jesuits gave no knowledge to the Guaraní *indios*, not even how to continue to grow *yerba mate*. So after 158 years of fidelity to the Jesuits, those who survived the Jesuit wars were left as ignorant and as poor as when they'd begun."

Sánchez looked at Montes and said, "I'm not twisting anything, priest." He went on. "The next question has to be, what did they do with all the profits of more than a century and a half of industrial sales of Jesuit Tea? We know that the money didn't go to the Crown; we know that it wasn't invested in the *indios*. And we know that Pope Clement XIV dissolved them as an order in 1773. Answer: they used the money they made to pay Russia to house them, and to be able to live there, because at the time, nobody else wanted the Jesuits. They lived off of that money from 1773 to 1814, when Pope Pius VII reinstated them."

Even Ellacuría had to admit, "You know your history, Captain."

Montes nodded, "It wasn't our finest moment."

The Captain remarked, "Look, priests, you accused me of being a killing machine, and all I'm doing is making the case that the only killing machine I know of is the one you belong to. Look at what happened in Spain. You got dispossessed of worldly goods, by a socialist government. That's what socialists do. So instead of engaging the courts or other ways to fight the dispossession, you endorsed General Francisco Franco, to overthrow the government that dispossessed you through bloodshed, because you value earthly assets more than human lives, and you can't deny it because you did exactly the same thing in Bolivia and Paraguay. Not only did you endorse Franco, you also preached that all of Franco's actions were blessed by God, or something like that.

"In other words, Francisco Franco was granted an indulgence. So the Catholic Killing Machine reaped 500,000 lives during the Spanish Civil War."

All Ellacuría could say was, "Captain, the end justifies the means."

The Captain shook his head. "Father Ellacuría, it's obvious that long ago, the Jesuits changed their original motto 'for the greater glory of God' to their new motto, 'the end justifies the means.'

"But let me go on. An ally of Franco and therefore an ally of the Catholic Church as well, was Nazi Germany. And while Nazi Germany proceeded to exterminate over 6 million Jews, the Catholic Church looked the other way. We now know that it was because part of what was being expropriated from the Jews was being paid to the Vatican, in the form of a tax allegedly levied on German Catholics. Either way, it was hush money, and the Catholic Killing Machine reaped 6 million more lives."

"Come now, Captain, that's quite a stretch," said Father Montes.

"Is it, Father? You spent 7 centuries killing Jews with the Inquisition. Hitler was exterminating Jews by gassing them. Do you really think it's a coincidence?"

They shrugged. Sánchez continued. "The Catholic Killing Machine didn't stop there. In the 1960s, the Jesuit Karl Rahner, the 'Architect of Vatican II' has as his lover the most influential advocate of abortion of West Germany: Luise Rinser. Through Karl Rahner, Luise Rinser was also part of Vatican II, and during Vatican II she also had relations with another participant at Vatican II: an Abbot. No chance she had any influence on them, right?"

"Come now, Captain, the Catholic Church has never endorsed abortion," said Ellacuría.

"Father Ellacuría, before Vatican II, the Catholic Church condemned it. After Vatican II, because of the liberalization of the Church, it tolerates it, and since Vatican II, abortions have gone up exponentially. So after Vatican II, the Catholic Killing Machine is now a party to the killing of millions of human beings inside the womb, every year."

The priests said nothing. Abortion had indeed become a plague, worse than any other plague in the history of the world.

"But wait, there's more. In 1959, a Jesuit-educated attorney named Fidel Castro ousted Fulgencio Batista in Cuba and took power. We now know that he proceeded to eliminate all his opponents through his butcher friend, Ché Guevara. And when there was nobody left to kill in Cuba, he sent Ché to Bolivia, to continue killing over there. Fidel Castro executed so many Cubans that in a few short years there was no opposition left to tell him that inviting Soviets to install nuclear missiles on the Island, aimed at the United States, was not a good idea."

Ellacuría decided to speak up. "Come on, Captain, that was in response to the Bay of Pigs! An attempted invasion organized by the CIA!"

Sánchez laughed and replied, "Look, priest, the CIA didn't attack Cuba with nuclear missiles, did it?"

Montes indignantly asked, "You can't seriously be saying that we were endorsing Castro at the time, are you?"

The Captain shrugged. "Castro was Jesuit-educated, priest. That can't be a coincidence, can it? His Jesuit education must have included some assurances that he'd get an Indulgence to allow him to do everything he did, because we now know that when the missiles got discovered, and Kennedy imposed a blockade, Castro wrote to Khrushchev assuring him that Cubans were willing to give their lives in the upcoming nuclear war. Now then, gentlemen, the population of Cuba in 1962 was approximately 7.5 million people. Your current partner in the liberation wars of Latin America, Fidel Castro, thought nothing of sacrificing 7.5 million Cuban lives, and countless millions more had the Soviets decided to heed his pleadings, both in American lives, Soviet lives, and how many more, if there was a nuclear war between superpowers?"

The Captain let this unbelievable fact sink in. Then he said, "Castro acted like he had the mother of all Indulgences, didn't he? If he killed millions upon millions, he'd still go to Heaven, no sweat. But that Indulgence wasn't given by the White Pope at the time, John XXIII, an Italian who was so weak, that he was convinced to call to Vatican II because he didn't have the moral backbone to defend the word of God against the nonsense of German philosophers. No sir. Castro's Indulgence must've been granted to him by the Black Pope of the time, your Superior General, Jean Baptiste Janssens. It was a Black Indulgence."

Montes said, "He didn't act rationally, Captain. We Jesuits act rationally."

The Captain was enjoying this. "Do you, priest? Because fully aware of 'irrational' Castro's actions, the Catholic Killing Machine, this time led by the new Black Pope, Pedro Arrupe, decided that Fidel Castro was exactly who was needed to execute his Liberation Theology and free the poor of... Asia? No. Africa? No. India, with its institutionalized poverty through castes? No. The poor of the poorest nation in Latin America, Cuba, where they stick twenty into a small, crumbling apartment and pay them with rum? Of course not, because although the Catholic Killing Machine likes to kill, it always has somebody else do it for them, to keep their hands clean.

"In this case, although Liberation Theology is designed to free the poor from dictators that impoverish them, they make an exception with the poorest country in Latin America, because its dictator is willing to kill on behalf of the Catholic Killing Machine. This time in Colombia, Nicaragua and El Salvador, where there is far less poverty than in Cuba. I'm sure he's got a new and improved Black Indulgence from the Black Pope. That's one hell of a killing machine you've got, Jesuits!"

"I have never...," began Ellacuría with his standard excuse.

"Priest, I have never heard you tell anybody to stop any abduction, assassination, anything. If you have, you must have used sign language and your audience must have been blind."

The ladies could be heard laughing in the kitchen. The Captain had a cheering section!

"But let me go on: Fidel Castro's Black Indulgence must've been made extensive to all of Fidel Castro's minions, such as the Nicaraguan Jesuits, Fernando and Ernesto Cardenal, who not only replicated the brutal executions that Castro carried out in 1959 and beyond; they also exported their revolution to El Salvador, just as Fidel did with Ché Guevara in Bolivia."

"Furthermore, Fidel Castro's minions in El Salvador didn't think twice about kidnapping, torturing and killing Ernesto Regalado, a decent man, a philanthropist, in the most hideous way possible, sticking pins in his eyes and genitals. They also kidnapped and killed Roberto Poma, an industrialist who was trying to increase tourism to El Salvador. And also Mauricio Borgonovo, working as Minister of Foreign Relations, looking to bring jobs to El Salvador and to open markets for Salvadoran products. Those who killed Regalado must've had a Black Indulgence autographed by the Black Pope, don't you think?"

No comment. So he continued. "They kidnapped Mrs. Elena Chiurato, a very distinguished and pretty mother of two, involved in the coffee business, and nobody ever heard from her again. Somebody must've had fun with her, huh? With their Black Indulgence? Because they refused to give her body back, to allow the world to see what torture and violations she'd been subjected to, am I right?"

Silence.

"And then they went international, kidnapping and murdering the South African Ambassador, Archibald Dunn, and the two Japanese heads of INSINCA, a massive textile factory employing hundreds of Salvadorans.

"As the Contras started becoming effective against the Sandinistas, less resources started to flow to the Salvadoran guerrillas, so they continued kidnapping for ransom, like the kidnapping of Teófilo Simán, the President of the Salvadoran Red Cross."

The Captain interrupted his litany to say, "Do you realize that Teófilo Simán is a philanthropist who helps the poor massively? My gosh, how many kids were left without books, without tuition, without clothes, because of all the ransom money he had to pay the Black Indulgence-holders who kidnapped him?"

Only Father Montes seemed to care.

The Captain decided to end his litany. "I could go on, gentlemen, but suffice it to say that the kidnappings continued, to include a poor lady mayor of a small town in San Miguel, and that poor woman, what could she offer besides her body?"

Ellacuría made one final futile attempt to defend himself. "You keep saying 'you,' Captain, as if we had anything to do with it. We never endorsed such kidnappings and killings."

"But I never heard you demand that they stop, unlike Monsignor Romero, who not only demanded that such kidnappings be halted, he also offered to negotiate the freedom of abductees. And he wasn't a Jesuit."

The Captain stood up and looked squarely at Ellacuría. "You dare call me a killing machine, priest? When it's you who's involved in another deadly Crusade, a Black Crusade?"

He then laughed and said, "You're lucky Dante Alighieri wrote his Divine Comedy with its nine circles of hell, in the 1300s, two centuries before Ignatius of Loyola founded the Society of Jesus. Had he written it in the 1700s, he would've had to include a tenth circle of hell, just for Jesuits."

The Captain smiled, winked at them and said, "Don't lose your Black Indulgences. You're going to need them."

Then he went over to the kitchen, found the two ladies, and said "Brribit!"

They laughed merrily again.

Chapter 30

Make Me an Instrument of Your War

Sister Licha couldn't believe her ears. Sister Belén was the new Director? Upon Sister Marguerite's retirement, Sister Licha should have been the next Director at Asunción.

Nobody knew where the new nuns had come from. Well, they knew they were Salvadoran, but they hadn't received the rigorous, European academic training that the old guard of nuns had. They knew more about Karl Marx than about Jesus Christ. Yet the Archdiocese was allowing them in.

Since Licha had arrived in El Salvador, real progress had been made, particularly during the administration of General Fidel Sánchez Hernández, with his Minister of the Economy, Dr. Armando Interiano, hammering out a Central American Common Market Treaty. She had always wondered why Central America was so divided, because together they could be so much stronger: the economic opportunities for everybody would multiply with a far larger market.

But then came the Soccer War between Honduras and El Salvador in 1969 and the Central American Common Market had been shattered. Apparently, the main instigator had been Anastasio Somoza, the Nicaraguan leader who liked his fiefdom, and probably figured he wouldn't be able to keep it in a united Central America.

The Sisters of the Assumption kept on teaching the values of charity and concern for the poor. If with the education you get, you amass a fortune, share it. Be charitable. Do good with it. If you become an entrepreneur, share profits with employees. Set up schools for their children. Offer upward mobility.

That hadn't worked out as well as everybody would've wanted.

It was 1977. For years the nuns had been remarking that their replacements would have to be local nuns because interest in religious life in Europe had waned considerably. But the influx of local young ladies into the religious life, trained in the facilities of the old Asunción school in Santa Ana, was overwhelming. It was as if every other high school graduate young lady was wanting to become a nun. And their training focused on humanities and social issues. And the Jesuits were handling that. Just like they were handling the Seminary.

It wasn't as if there was no place for them, though. In 1963, Asunción had built a sister school for poor girls in the Barrio San Esteban, named "Our Lady of Lourdes." So they had a place where they were needed. It's just that the European nuns were disappearing.

But the new priests and nuns were militant: well-versed in Marx and class-struggle and the preferential treatment of the poor. They weren't particularly knowledgeable about science, math, art and literature, but it didn't matter: their mission was to indoctrinate, not educate. They were going to produce militant high school graduates who were anti-government and anti-military.

Sister Licha started praying for guidance. It was like the Church was preparing to go to war... in favor of communism! Licha felt that she was in El Salvador because God wanted her there. Her path since her near-rape had been set for her by God. So if this was where God wanted her, she couldn't leave. Her heart was known to the Almighty. Surely He wanted her to play a role in the coming events. But what role?

Outnumbered at the school, they would shun her and drive her out unless she gained their trust. She would be of no use if she remained an outsider.

So unlike the other European nuns, she went to extremes to try to gain the trust of Sister Belén. And she'd get two chances to do so.

The first chance came when Sister Belén announced that they would start constructing a warehouse-like structure underground, on school premises. As a math and science teacher, Sister Licha volunteered to oversee that. Sister Belén couldn't say no because no other nun was better suited for that; certainly none of the new nuns.

The second had to do with *Don Nico*: Nicolás Chávez, an old policeman who was on the verge of retiring from the police force. Because he was so well-liked, he was given a cushy final assignment at Asunción, where he received the girls as they came to school and helped them depart as they were picked up in the afternoon.

He did his job well. But the newly-arrived nuns found him annoying. Sister Belén had tried to remove the policeman, favoring a 'private' security firm of her choosing instead, but the moment she had floated the idea, the parents had shot it down. Don Nico was too well-liked.

But Don Nico had to be removed. That 'warehouse' wasn't going to remain a secret if he was around. Having that policeman on the premises was like having a spy by the government. But how to get rid of him?

Since Sister Licha was working on that project, she decided to enlist her help for the Don Nico problem. At noon, as she made her rounds, Sister Belén entered the cafeteria and saw Sister Licha chatting with some students. She called her over.

"Sister Licha, you've been here the longest, and I'd like your advice."

"Of course, Sister Director! Anything I can do to help!"

Sister Licha, unlike the other older nuns, had tried to befriend the newcomers. Although the new nuns had been urging Sister Belén to get rid of her, Sister Belén felt that it was a better idea to retain the math and science teacher, to be able to say that Asunción taught more than just Marx. Plus, the new Director believed there needed to be some sort of link to the school's past, so as not to seem too radical.

The Jesuits at the convent had warned the novices that changes would have to come hard and fast, and that the faster they did away with the past, the faster they could lead this country into its inevitable future, where the poor, not the rich, ruled. But it was easier said than done. So she'd keep Sister Licha.

They walked into the Director's Office together and sat facing each other.

Sister Belén was the exact opposite of Sister Licha: Licha was tall, she was short; Licha was European, Belén *india.* Nevertheless, Belén's leadership abilities enlarged her. Licha recognized that attribute and accepted it.

Sister Belén asked her why she'd stayed, when she could've easily gone to another one of the schools of the Little Sisters of the Assumption in any part of the world.

Sister Licha was somewhat taken aback by this bluntness. But she had already rehearsed her response.

"Sister Director, I've been trying all these years to get our graduates to be good and kind and charitable to the poor and to get them to realize that greatness is defined by how many lives they can improve. Unfortunately,

I've failed. The system has failed. Salvadoran society has failed. The poor are getting poorer while the rich are getting richer. Some of the families of our girls own entire provinces of this country, and they do nothing to educate the peasants so that they might have a better life."

Sister Belén nodded. She'd be poor and getting poorer herself were it not for the Jesuits who had recruited her from the slopes of Guazapa and paid her and her family all her expenses to finish school and join the religious life, with a nice little stipend for her poor family. She wasn't the only one who'd been recruited. Several boys and girls were actively recruited by Father Rutilio Grande in the Guazapa area. They were in need of people to join the ranks of the church. Were it not for them, she'd be plowing the fields of the rich, making little to no money, like her parents and grandparents before her.

How did the Jesuits get the money to pay all the expenses for so many poor children? She didn't know and she didn't care.

Sister Licha continued. "So now you, the new generation of nuns, come along, and you want to change things. You want to shake them up. Why wouldn't I want to be a part of that? It's like a rebirth. Or as they say in golf, a mulligan."

Sister Belén seemed pleased with her answer. "Sister Licha, I'm glad you want change, but do you realize that this change is going to be like Noah's flood, to cleanse El Salvador from evil? In that flood, many good people drowned, but God's purpose was to start with the new, thereby doing away with the old. That's the goal here."

"Sister Director, I find no fault in that reasoning."

"Then I need your help to start cleansing the School. The first element that must go is the policeman they call Don Nico. Come up with a plan. Earn your position among us."

Sister Licha understood full well that this was her test of fire. If she passed, she was 'in.' If she didn't, she might as well leave El Salvador, like the other nuns did.

She slept on it and woke up with a plan.

The next day, during recess, she approached a student named Gracia Flamenco. Here was a middle-class student who had openly espoused her admiration for *El Grupo*, the revolutionary group that had abducted, tortured and killed the rich industrialist Ernesto Regalado. She would often wear a Ché Guevara t-shirt under her uniform. The guerrilla movement beckoned to her.

"Good morning, Ms. Flamenco. I wanted to talk to you about your goals. I understand you want to be a revolutionary?"

The question surprised Ms. Flamenco, especially coming from an old-guard nun.

Sister Licha continued. "What is it that you expect to achieve with your ideas? Do you want a bloodbath for this country?"

"Sister Licha, blood is a requirement in all human events of birth and this country needs a rebirth."

"Ms. Flamenco, aren't you afraid that it may be your blood?"

"I'm not afraid to die for a noble cause, Sister Licha."

"You have two more years until you graduate."

"I'm here only because my parents have me here. My destiny has nothing to do with getting a high school degree."

"But the guerrilla movement is happening outside these walls. I don't understand why you remain here."

"I've tried to contact people but they look at me with distrust. I'm not poor enough."

"I can understand why you feel that way. If I were sixteen, I'd probably feel exactly like you. I'd like for you to come talk to Sister Belén with me after school. I think it would help your cause."

Ms. Flamenco looked at her skeptically. "I've approached Sister Belén before. She ignores me."

"She won't now."

That very afternoon, Sister Licha walked Ms. Flamenco into the Director's Office. "Sister Director, Ms. Flamenco has earnestly wanted to help the revolutionary cause in El Salvador, and I believe she can be of assistance with Don Nico."

"How?"

"Ms. Flamenco has no interest remaining in school. She feels the revolutionary call. She wants to be a guerrilla. But because of her middle-class status and her age, nobody takes her seriously. But she could certainly make her bones with the problem we have."

Sister Belén understood Sister Licha's plan immediately. She turned her full attention to Ms. Flamenco.

"What do you think of the police, Ms. Flamenco?"

"They're repressive agents of the military dictatorship, Sister Belén."

"So the elimination of police agents is a legitimate need for social justice to be achieved, in your view?"

"Absolutely, Sister Belén."

"Even Don Nico?"

"I can't stand seeing him with his uniform, Sister Belén."

"Well, for the role of this school in the upcoming revolution, we need him gone, sooner than later."

There was silence in the room, as this sunk in.

"If I do this, what do I get?" Ms. Flamenco was eager to start upon her manifest destiny.

"I'll see to it that you get military leadership training in Cuba. I'll guarantee your safe passage out of the country, so when you come back, you will no longer be Ms. Flamenco, but Commander something, once you pass the training you receive. Does that sound agreeable to you?"

"That's all I ever wanted, Sister Belén."

After a lengthy discussion, it was agreed: Sister Belén would have a 22-caliber pistol ready for Ms. Flamenco to shoot the policeman in the thigh. Just to get him out of the picture and be able to replace the Asunción policeman with personnel who were sympathetic to the cause.

The next afternoon, Ms. Flamenco approached Don Nico and shot him right in the head with a .45-caliber revolver. And she was never heard from again.

Sister Licha went pale when she heard that Don Nico was dead, his head almost blown off. That wasn't the plan. But she didn't say a word. She was now 'in.' But not completely. Not yet.

Chapter 31

Deja Who?

"How is the underground construction in La Asunción going, Sister Belén?"

"Father Montes, it's complete. Allow me to introduce Sister Licha. Since she started supervising the construction, it went faster and better, and it's done. Thank God she decided to stay with us to help us with her knowledge, instead of leaving like the other European sisters did."

Father Montes raised an eyebrow. She wasn't like the other European nuns he'd known. She was tall and quite beautiful.

"How do you do Sister Licha. Where do you hail from?"

"Olomouc, Czechoslovakia, Father Montes."

"Welcome." He then turned to the group as a whole, and said, in a louder voice, "Please take a seat, sisters and brothers, so we can begin this meeting."

The group of priests and nuns was sizeable. They were representatives of most of the private schools and universities run by the Catholic Church. They took their seats in the first pews of the Externado de San José Chapel.

Father Montes went up the stairs of the altar, removed the microphone from the pulpit, and said, "A little bit of history. We've been unsuccessful at turning this otherwise devout Catholic nation into a people that value social justice. Although we've been teaching Catholic values, we've seen our graduates continue the exploitative habits. That's because we haven't been frank enough in our exposé of the dire poverty that exists in this nation. In part it's because teachers feared upsetting parents if a syllabus with greater emphasis on social justice was implemented. Well... there's no such reticence anymore. The staff of teachers that has displaced the old guard comes from such exploited strata of society. You're not European and you're not afraid to tell the truth!"

A brief applause. But then nun from the *Sagrado Corazón* [Sacred Heart] school stood up. "But Father Montes, we still have one of those nuns here. One of the old guard: Sister Licha. She's been teaching with the reticence you speak of and all of a sudden she's here among us? How do we know she won't betray us?"

Her question drew a murmur endorsing her question. Sister Licha was expecting this. She started to get up, but Sister Belén held her down.

The diminutive Sister Belén rose to respond, instead. "Brothers and sisters, I come from Guazapa. Like you, I pledged my service to the Catholic Church many years ago, in exchange for an education, and the opportunity to serve my people. Which is what this meeting is all about. Now, I've come too long a way, and climbed too high a mountain, to fight for this cause, to be bringing somebody here who could sabotage our efforts. Sister Licha has been tried by fire. She's been baptized in blood. We couldn't have completed our clandestine warehouse/hospital project without her help, for which I and all of us should thank God. You should doubt me before you doubt her."

And with that, she sat down. The Sagrado Corazón nun stood up. "My apologies to Sister Licha. But she must understand that we have but one loyalty here, and that is to the poor. And we're prepared to die for the poor. The old guard had their loyalties elsewhere. But if Sister Belén says she is one of us, then I welcome her."

A murmur of consent followed. Then Father Montes proceeded with the main subject of this meeting.

"Brothers and sisters, by relentlessly pounding into our students the notion that there is social injustice in this country, every single hour of every single school day, we'll accomplish several objectives:

"First. We'll have the students relaying the message to the heart of their homes every single day. They'll start questioning the validity and legitimacy of their parents' position in society. They'll undoubtedly get into arguments, but we'll be giving them the weapons to win those arguments.

"Second. By winning such arguments, we'll make the population at large aware of the inequity, iniquity, and injustice of the Salvadoran system, which is based on exploitative capitalism, a legacy of the *Conquistadors.* Yes, my native Spain is at fault, as a mentor of mine in Santa Tecla pointed out, but we're obviously here to rectify the situation.

"Third. What is being taught in the classroom, discussed at the dinner table, will also be preached from the pulpits at every church in this land. The message will penetrate the subconscious of every Salvadoran. Remember, even the tyrants of this nation go to mass.

"Fourth. By such social awareness, we'll attempt to bring change to this country peacefully. But change will come, even if not peacefully, because, through our efforts, we're creating the leaders of the guerrilla movement that will once and for all topple the military and their masters, the landowners.

"So you're at the forefront of this upcoming revolution, whether peaceful or not. It's for this purpose that you were selected, given scholarships and trained in the religious life, at no economic cost to you. But it's time to pay back what you received, with your devotion to this cause. The People will take over this nation. And you'll be the vanguard of this revolution."

The cheers and applause were deafening, amplified by the acoustics of the chapel. When the cheers subside, Father Montes announced: "And now, may I introduce Don Blas Pérez. He's an Eastern European businessman with considerable mining interest holdings. He's a member of an international group of businessmen actively sponsoring our movement.

"The son of a Spanish father and Romanian mother, don't be surprised by his perfect Spanish."

Onto the altar stepped a tall, tanned and sinewy man with gray hair. From where Licha was sitting, it seemed that he had pale blue eyes. He seemed to be in his early sixties, but he moved with agility for his age. He wore coat and tie, pastel colored; not austere black like the Jesuits wore. A shiver ran up Sister Licha's spine. There was something about this man that seemed... familiar?

Don Blas took the microphone and began speaking in perfect Castilian Spanish, encouraging to give it all for the cause, assuring them that the entire world was supportive of their efforts, and finally thanking Father Montes for the opportunity to address them.

After another short applause, Father Montes adjourned the meeting.

As everybody was leaving the chapel, Father Montes approached Sister Licha with Don Blas. The priest addressed her first. "Sister, we're going to need more underground warehouse/hospitals throughout the nation. Are you so attached to the Asunción, that you couldn't work outside its walls?"

"Father, I'll go where I'm needed, but my Director's going to have to approve of that."

Don Blas then addressed her, saying, "Sister Licha, we're fortunate that we have someone of your education and knowledge on our side."

Lowering his voice, he continued, "The new religious and priests aren't well-versed in math and sciences, but rather in social justice, which is what is needed most. And we could hardly keep our infrastructure projects secret if we hired outside engineering firms. And with the experience you gained in the Asunción underground, you're our 'lead engineer' for other underground projects that we'll undertake nationwide. If the revolution doesn't come peacefully, we'll need places where our fighters can be medically taken care of. That's the purpose."

Sister Licha nodded but couldn't shake the feeling of unease this man produced in her, for no apparent reason. So she asked, "Thank you, sir, but how do you know so much about what I do?"

Don Blas smiled. "I'm afraid I don't have much time to tell you. Sister, but I did tell Father Montes I wanted to meet you to congratulate you on the excellent work you've done."

The man looked at her admiringly. She was definitely not like most of the women he'd met in Latin America, including women of European origin, which abounded after World War II. Although he usually liked his women younger, this Czechoslovakian Sister looked far younger than her nearly fifty years of age, according to their files in Moscow. And for him, she was perfect.

Of course, there was the problem of the vows. Saving herself for the Lord and all that. But revolutionary nuns didn't have such commitments.

He took her hand in both of his, and said, "Sister Licha, I must run along, but hopefully we'll have the opportunity to talk further shortly. Again, you have all my gratitude and admiration." He then walked away.

The encounter with this man unnerved her, although she couldn't understand why. He was just another foreigner, like the Jesuits and herself.

The very next day she was informed by Sister Belén that she'd be reporting directly to Father Montes, who'd be sending a vehicle for her when needed.

That news didn't sit well with her. She associated it with that man, Don Blas. But hey, she wanted to be 'in,' didn't she?

Chapter 32

Consummatum Est

Good Friday of the year 1979 fell on April 13, which also made it Friday the 13th. Sister Licha was summoned to the Externado early that morning. That seemed strange to her, but then again, the Revolution didn't take a holiday, much less a religious holiday, even less with the imminent fall of Somoza in Nicaragua. The Sandinistas would start to send weapons and they needed to be stored somewhere.

Sister Licha had gone beyond clandestine constructions in Asunción. She was the de facto lead engineer for the construction of a clandestine hospital at another catholic school and at two other strategic locations in the city. It was extra work because most of the work was done at night.

On one of those nights, however, she'd been visited by Don Blas Pérez. It was a professional visit, in which he was asking about the budget and the grade of the steel that was being used. He didn't want any of her constructions to succumb to earthquakes. That's what his mouth said; his eyes told her that he didn't want her to end up under a ton of rubble.

The man still unnerved her, though, for some reason.

Father Montes had warned her that a project under a church would be coming soon. But the church hadn't been identified yet. She figured that's why she'd been summoned today. Although she needed some rest and she'd been looking forward to getting some this Easter Weekend. She needed it.

Father Montes greeted her at the Externado, but all he did was to introduce a young Jesuit priest that she'd seen only once or twice before: Father Mario Tacarello. He was very nice, in his mid-twenties, very *mestizo* and very effusive.

"I've heard of the magnificent job you're doing, Sister. And commend you for staying instead of leaving, like the other European nuns did. Let me assure you, Sister Licha, this is the purest form of revolution that the world will ever see. We'll overthrow the military puppets of the Fourteen and give the land to the peasants. It will be as if Christ himself decided to govern a nation."

Sister Licha's exterior nodded, but inside, she was wondering, first of all, what this pipsqueak was doing lecturing her about anything. Secondly, the kidnap, torture, and murder of Ernesto Regalado and Ernesto Poma and Mauricio Borgonovo and people who used their fortunes for the betterment of a nation, indicated the existence of a violent element that wasn't going to stop until it gained absolute power. To believe that after committing such heinous crimes, they would become angels of the Lord, was more than mildly delusional.

She recalled that the Russian revolution was similarly well-intentioned. But the ruthless element had immediately eliminated the royal family and the democratic element, enthroning Lenin as a dictator.

Then Father Montes said, "Father Tacarello represents a new generation of Jesuits in El Salvador. He's my right-hand man and he'll be representing me from now on, whenever I'm not available."

Licha got the message loud and clear. This pipsqueak was her boss. She'd wanted to be 'in,' hadn't she?

But the surprises had not ended. Father Montes told her that she and Father Tacarello would be going to the beach today.

This surprised Sister Licha. "Father, I don't have anything suitable to wear."

Montes told her they could go to Asunción first, so she could dress appropriately.

Sister Licha still tried to beg off. "Father, I have some pressing work to do."

"Nonsense. Today is Good Friday and in El Salvador, good Catholics go to the beach on Good Friday. Besides, this isn't a petition."

Alarm bells rang inside Sister Licha. This was totally out of the blue.

Mario took the wheel of a Volkswagen Beetle and took her first to Asunción, where she changed into clothes that were more suitable for the beach. When she went to look for Sister Belén to inform her of her destination, she was nowhere to be found. Although that seemed odd to her, it was the least of her worries.

Once back in the car, they traveled eastward toward San Miguel, to a beautiful beach known as *El Cuco*. Since it was about three hours away, Sister Licha decided to get some much-needed shuteye. She awoke when the car started going over the rough dirt road off the main highway that would take them to the beach.

"We'll be there in about 15 minutes. The ride is going to be rough for a while."

"Where are we going, Father?"

"Sister, you're going to have to forget that I'm a priest right now. We're all comrades. We're revolutionaries."

Her alarms went off again. "That's fine but why do I get a sense of foreboding?"

"Good instincts. You see, you're going to have to prove yourself."

"What? Why? I masterminded the policeman's death in La Asunción! I..."

"Sister, you didn't kill him. Many are of the belief, despite Sister Belén's protestations to the contrary, that you may be a spy."

"A spy? For whom?"

"For the government. For the military. For the Americans."

"Come on, Father. The Asunción underground is nothing but a weapons depot right now, and the government doesn't have a clue."

"That's a plus for you, but one of the commanders is very distrusting. And he wants to meet you. This has to happen. Men and women are going to be trusting you with their lives, and they want you to be worthy of that trust."

She looked at Father Tacarello. He looked uncomfortable. Sister Licha started praying.

They arrived at a typical Salvadoran beach hut: fairly ample, circular, with thatched roof and wide-open spaces for hammocks, a small kitchen to the side, a bathroom and an outside shower to get rid of the sand before coming inside. Walls made of grey concrete blocks. Nothing pretentious. This obviously belonged to a middle-class person.

The hut was fairly distant from its neighbors and set back from the beach. The reason was that although it was a beautiful beach, it was too far away from San Salvador to be as developed as the beaches that were closer to the capital.

There were several coconut trees and *almendro* trees to provide even more cover and concealment. But this hut also had green translucent mosquito nets that hung from the outer beams of the roof, for even more privacy.

And all that privacy was needed to prevent any outsider from seeing what was going on inside: sitting on a sofa was a guerrilla Commander who wore glasses, a black beret and a red scarf that indicated his rank. Deployed along the circumference of the hut were four other guerrillas, armed with AK-47s. The Commander was dressed, but his trousers were open from the waist down, exposing his genitals.

Kneeling in front of him was Sister Belén, completely nude. Two other naked Asunción nuns were sitting on two armchairs on either side of the sofa, facing each other Another armchair faced the sofa. It was empty, and that's where Father Tacarello took her. As she approached the chair, Sister Belén released the Commander's organ to mouth a silent hello to her, and then resumed her chores.

Once seated, she couldn't help noticing how good Sister Belén looked, with her long black hair all the way down to her buttocks, with a slim, well-proportioned body. But what stood out the most was how comfortable she seemed in such a state, and orally pleasing the Commander. It was as if it was nothing new for her.

The Commander stopped Belén for a second to be able to address Sister Licha. Fortunately for Licha, Belén didn't move aside, she just stopped. The last thing Licha wanted to do was have a conversation with a penis pointed at her.

The Commander greeted her with a smile. "Sister Licha, I've been wanting to meet you. My name is Marcial. You're obviously a holdover from the old guard of the nuns."

"Commander Marcial, it is nice to meet you." She mustered all her willpower to ignore the obscenity in front of her and lie.

"Marcial is my *nom de guerre*, of course. And when this day is over, perhaps we'll be baptizing you with a *nom de guerre* of your own. For example, Sister Belén's *nom de guerre* is Inés."

Stoically, she lied again. "Commander, it would be my privilege to be baptized as such." Honesty was not the weapon of choice here.

"We'll see. First of all, I need to explain some realities to you. We're all here because we're tired of the misery that permeates this land, while the Fourteen live in European monarchy-type opulence, protected by the Security Forces and the Army. Their health is guaranteed by the national health system and their money, which allows them to get the best medical attention from the best doctors in the world. In the meantime, our children could die of a simple flu, due to lack of care, not to mention malnutrition. And that's not fair.

He put her hand on Inés' head for her to continue sucking. He then continued to address Licha. "We've tried other means of achieving social justice, peaceful ones, but they haven't worked out very well. Farabundo Martí tried the peaceful way in the 1930s, and they exiled him to Guatemala. When he had no other recourse left, he armed himself and thousands of peasants, and engaged the Government I battle, only to have them slaughtered by the Army in *La Matanza*, in which thirty thousand peasants died. We're not going to make that mistake again."

Sister Licha had to agree with the Commander. It made sense.

"Although some talk about a political solution, I disagree with that because with their money, the Fourteen are able to buy their security, both private and public. To get to them, we have to fight through that security and defeat it. Which is why the Revolution must be armed and not political."

He looked down at Inés to say, "Honey, don't bite."

Belén disengaged to apologize.

The Commander continued talking to Licha.

"But we don't produce weapons. We have to import them and that means that we need allies. Fortunately, we have Cuba, and their sponsor, the Soviet Union. Soon we'll have another ally, the Sandinistas of Nicaragua."

Sister Licha wanted to say, "Don't forget the Jesuits." But didn't. She just nodded.

Marcial continued. "Although we're not quite ready, we're going to have to strike soon, because right now, we have an unlikely ally in President Jimmy Carter, with his human rights policy, and his very progressive ambassador, Robert White, who absolutely loathes the military. So now is the perfect time for our revolution to triumph, before the U.S. elects a right-wing president, which gives us a realistic window of now until January 1981. Any questions, Sister Licha?"

"Commander, why am I here?"

"In part, to thank you for your collaboration, but more importantly, to guarantee your secrecy."

"What have I done to earn your mistrust? Sister Belén can vouch for me. As far as anybody can tell, the government doesn't have a clue as to our clandestine activities."

Commander Marcial smiled. "That's what Sister Belén is doing so well right now, vouching for you. You see, we have learned lessons from the Colombian conflict. In Colombia, the FARC is tightly knit. Said another way, there are no traitors. There are woman combatants, along with males. They live in the border mountains between Colombia and Venezuela. The women and the men mate, as is natural. That makes the FARC a family. Such an arrangement guarantees secrecy."

"But Commander, of what use is a pregnant woman as a combatant?"

"Sister, it's not like before. We have doctors who take care of unwanted pregnancies."

Sister Licha was shocked. They aborted if they needed to. But the shock was overcome by the urge to confront this man. Screw the sexual obscenity in front of her. They'd entered a realm in which she held the moral high ground.

"Commander, I understand why revolutions exist. And this country is in dire need of one, on that we all agree. But when Pope Paul VI published his encyclical *Humanae Vitae,* which is Latin for Human Life, he enshrined the sanctity of human relations and even forbade the use of any kind of contraceptives, not to mention abortion. So we as a Church cannot be a part of this."

Father Tacarello felt compelled to get involved in this, even though he preferred to stay out of it. He didn't want this conversation to deviate from its main purpose. Besides, he was anxious to see Sister Licha nude. She may be approaching fifty, but she was in great shape. And she was Czech, who, in his experience, were sexual firecrackers.

Father Tacarello therefore regurgitated what he'd learned from his mentor, the Jesuit Karl Rahner, at the University of Münster. "Sister Licha, a product of Vatican II was that the Church would not oppose the gaining and implementation of knowledge to improve the human condition, which is the condition of the people of God, the poor. Paul VI never set foot in El Salvador, the current Pope hasn't either. And Pope John Paul II is far more concerned with the nascent pro-democracy movement in Poland than he is with the plight of the Salvadoran poor, which is our main concern. So thanks to Vatican II, the people of God are allowed to freely act according to their own needs in pursuit of their improvement, locally, and we're allowed to consider the Pope's encyclical to be nothing but his own opinion, with which we disagree."

She was taken aback by this admonishment and dismissal of the Pope. John Paul II was a beloved Pope and her countryman. Although John Paul II hadn't visited El Salvador, since he had only recently been inaugurated on October 22, 1978, she was certain that this prostitution of women of the cloth would be condemned by him; not to mention the abortion of fetuses that were inconvenient to the Revolution.

As if reading her mind, Father Tacarello attempted to assuage her. "Sister Licha, I'll gladly explain to you when we return, why all of this is allowed. If it weren't, why would we be involved?"

Licha wanted to give this pipsqueak a piece of her mind. Jesuits had proven to be ill-suited to be arbiters of what was moral and what was not. Alliance with Cuba? Where poverty was massively greater than in El Salvador? Where the dictator was infinitely more despotic than anything El Salvador had? And then to let their religious comrades be humiliated this way, without lifting a finger? He'd do well to shut up and admit that this was nothing but a power grab. Just like the Jesuits had done so many times throughout their history.

But instead, she turned to Marcial. "Forgive me, Commander. I'm just taken aback by this departure from what I was taught. I'm sure you can understand that, and please don't let my surprise define me or my commitment to this cause."

Marcial smiled and gestured to her that there was no problem. "What Father Tacarello says about the Pope is right, Sister Licha. If a European Pope visited our shantytowns, and huts, and utility-less villages in the hills and *barrancos* and saw our naked children with worms in their bellies and smelled the stench that pervades those dwellings where people defecate and urinate out in the open, he'd be one of us, I'm sure."

That wasn't far from the truth, Licha acknowledged.

Marcial continued. "Sister Belén and the new breed of nuns were recruited from the villages and shantytowns all over the country. They didn't have a 'calling,' they had an empty stomach. Our sponsors provided them with a full high school education, and then a crash course in religious studies in the old School of the Assumption in Santa Ana. When they weren't studying academics, they were studying Marx and the recently-developed Liberation Theology, but above all, the meaning and dimensions of social justice, the goal of our revolution."

For some reason, the word 'sponsors' made Licha think of Don Blas.

Marcial continued. "Therefore, these nuns didn't receive your same academic and spiritual education, Sister Licha. But don't for a second believe that you're better than them. And as you can see, they're naked and willing to serve the Revolution."

He gestured the other two nuns to come over to him. They didn't hesitate and took turns at sucking the guerrilla's penis. He then looked at Licha and said, "If you want to be a part of us, Sister Licha, we expect you to do the same, now."

The nuns stopped sucking and looked at Licha expectantly.

Licha was not about to go meekly into the slaughter. "Commander, you're right. I'm not one of the new breed of nuns. I have devoted far more years of my life to my Lord, Jesus Christ, than these three nuns put together, preaching His message of salvation. I've taken a vow of chastity. Perhaps the sisters here, whom I very much admire, were not required to, but I was. I'm not about to violate that oath to the Lord my God, just to satisfy a *machista* desire to prove who's who here. Frankly, it is disappointing to me that you're acting no differently than any other male in this country, because the women you take advantage of, Commander, are poor women, who deserve your best, and not your penis."

Marcial's eyes flashed in anger but he didn't allow himself to lose control. "Sister Licha, I've got blood on my hands. Many of the things you've read about in the newspaper have been done by me, or on my orders. If there is a God, then I'm on His blacklist because of my sins, and if there's a hell that's worse than being poor in El Salvador (which I doubt), then I guess I'm headed that way, but I'm not losing any sleep over it. So forgive me if I choose not to include God in my decisions. While you and the old guard religious were educated to believe power came from above, Mao Tse Tung had it right when he said power comes out of the barrel of a gun. In this Revolution, first, come fighters, then comes everybody else including you and the Church. I also find your elitism revolting, because your words indicate that you somehow feel superior to these religious women who support the revolution with every fiber in their bodies."

Licha wished she could take her words back. But how is one supposed to react perfectly to such a situation? How does life prepare you for this scenario?

She attempted to apologize. "Please, Commander, I didn't mean in any way to..."

But Marcial cut her off. "However, I'll respect your vows."

He signaled to another one of the nude sisters, who got a satchel and brought it to the Commander. He took out her passport and an airline ticket; the passport had been withdrawn from her belongings by Sister Belén, no doubt.

"Sister Licha, you may walk out of here with our gratitude for your help to this date, but you won't stop until you've reached the airport, gotten on the plane and departed El Salvador forever. Or, you can formally join the Revolution. Your choice."

Sister Licha looked at Father Tacarello. He was looking at her as if he were watching an action movie, wondering how the hero would get out of danger. But completely unwilling to lend a hand.

Her eyes went back to Marcial. "I was told by Father Montes that my education was an asset, it allowed me to effectively supervise and manage the construction projects. Won't you miss that if I leave?"

"Dear Sister, we'll find a replacement for you, rest assured of that. Please let us know your decision, now." Inés had stopped sucking to look at her. Her pleading eyes said everything.

Licha's racing mind flew back to Krakow, to the vow she had made back then. And how her vow had paved the way to this moment in her life. Back then, it was life or death. Here, it's Revolution or a flight to Paris... maybe. Would they actually let her live, after witnessing the unholy alliance between Church and Marxists? And if she'd been saved in Krakow for a greater good, would it go unfulfilled if she refused to do what every other new nun in El Salvador apparently did without a second thought: suck and fuck?

If she refused, would she put the three sisters' lives at risk, especially Sister Belén's, because she'd vouched for her?

Or might this just be a way to atone for Don Nico?

"Commander, I..." But her attempt was cut off immediately.

"Are you staying or are you going?"

At that very instant, she realized that she had nothing to show for her life yet; something that would've made it worthwhile for her to be saved in Krakow. And that perhaps, by leaving, she would end her days without any accomplishments whatsoever.

"I'm staying."

"Then come take Sister Belén's place. Do it now."

* * *

The ride back to San Salvador the next afternoon was thick with silence. She had endured stoically, despite the shame and the pain. They pounded the elitism right out of her, every which way they could, enthusiastically.

She understood now why so many German women who had been raped by the Red Army had committed suicide. Only faith in a greater purpose would allow her to overcome this ordeal.

After she had knelt, she had closed her eyes, rather than look at that member inches away from her. She hoped it was a repeat of Olomouc. But she felt hands push her head, and the penis enter her mouth. The hands made her mouth move forward and she completed the motion when she recoiled every time she felt she was about to gag on it. Then she heard the same grunt as in Olomouc, and tasted the foul, salty, mucus-like substance that filled her mouth. As in Olomouc, she didn't know what to do.

"Don't you dare let a single drop fall, Sister Licha."

She swallowed that foulness. When she opened her watery eyes, Marcial told her to undress.

She had to suck all the guerrilla fighters. She swallowed so much sperm, she hadn't eaten anything since. But the onlookers would cheer her. They were celebrating an induction, not a gang rape. But to herself, was thinking that perhaps it would've been preferable to let the Soviet use and kill her, because at least she'd be with her family.

When she was done servicing all the fighters orally, Marcial put a sheath on his manhood and deflowered her. It was painful. And when he finally grunted, he pulled out, and her blood was all over his manhood and his sheath. Everybody applauded. The four other fighters inducted her as well.

When the last guerrilla had pulled out of her, she wondered if Father

Tacarello would join in. But he didn't.

When the 'ceremony' was over, Commander Marcial walked over to her, hugged her and said, "You're now *Juana*."

She finally broke the silence in the automobile. Her soreness had subsided enough to let her speak.

"Father Tacarello, why did you take me there to have them violate me?"

"I did no such thing. You could've walked out of there. You allowed that yourself. But let me tell you why you did it. You too believe in the Revolution. That blood between your legs was proof to everybody that you valued the Revolution above God. You have unimpeachable credibility now. When the time comes, you'll be seated at the negotiating table, as one of us, and then you will help guide the poor out of their miserable existence with your superior education and intelligence. You will have lost a hymen but gained a nation. All those nuns you've been meeting recently... not one hymen among them. It's just the way of the Revolution. It reigns supreme ... for now."

"Is that why you didn't partake? With all us naked nuns at your disposal?"

"You weren't at my disposal, and I don't condone what happened, and the sole purpose of that entire scenario was your induction into the Revolution. You belong to the Revolution now."

What Father Tacarello left unsaid was, "And it's too bad, because I would've loved to enjoy that splendid body of yours."

Silence resumed. She understood why she'd been put through all that. That was the final test she had to pass to prove that she was a revolutionary. But anybody who knew her in El Salvador already knew she was trustworthy. She really didn't need to sexually service the entire guerrilla high command to prove that.

The car turned toward the Asunción. As they were arriving, Juana asked, "Do you have a *nom de guerre*, Father?"

Father Tacarello replied, "My *nom de guerre* is 'Eliseo.'"

Juana smiled and asked, "Oh? And when were you inducted?"

Eliseo grinned, shifted the car into first gear, and said, "I'll tell you some other day, Juana."

Chapter 33

Another Sacred Band

The Ministry of Defense was located next to the Chief of Staff building, on the road to Santa Tecla, near the El Salvador International Fairgrounds. The six young men had been summoned by Minister Larios. They used to be outstanding cadets in the Military School, who had gotten expelled because they had been seen socializing with gay men while on leave.

The Minister of Defense, General Humberto Larios, had obtained this information from the Director of the Military School, Col. Benavides, who was also the head of the Commando unit that hadn't been completed yet because no active military officer to go after the Jesuits.

The other thing that the ex-cadets had in common was that they had all gone to all-boys Catholic schools.

"Gentlemen, please have a seat. We all know of the circumstances under which you were unable to graduate and frankly, your personal life is none of my business, or the business of anybody else. You're here because the country is in peril, and because you swore to serve the country while you were cadets. Unfortunately, standing policy had you expelled. But the country needs your service now."

The young men were sitting at attention, back straight, hands palm down on their thighs, feet flat on the floor.

The Minister studied the files of the ex-cadets, and told them, "It says here all of you went to all-boys Catholic schools. Did your activities with men begin there?"

One of them, Remberto Fiallos, stood up and said, "Mr. Minister, allow me to speak for all because our experiences are very similar. We were all induced into homosexuality by priests."

"Thank you, Mr. Fiallos." He looked at all. "Every one of you?"

They all nodded.

"Please sit down, Mr. Fiallos. The reason I suspected so and called you in, was because our Military Attaché in Mexico informed me that there was news of a prominent priest in Mexico named Marcial Maciel who was being accused of sexually abusing boys. Doing further research on the subject, the ex-consul of El Salvador in New Orleans, a friend of mine, informed me that in 1985, a priest named Gilbert Gauthe pleaded guilty to molesting 11 boys in Louisiana. And I've heard of other cases occurring all over the world, like in Ireland."

The six former cadets were very interested. They had no idea this was turning out to be a worldwide phenomenon.

"In 1983, a group of Baptist young men and women came to El Salvador from Florida, to help the poor. I was at the Artillery Brigade in Opico and being one of the least conflictive zones out west, the local Baptist church asked me if I would allow the American group to meet with me. Of course, I accepted.

"There was this very tall distinguished gentleman, who was there as the chaperone of the group of youths. He was a Spaniard by the name of Juan Font, who was now living in Florida. His daughter Susana was an active member of the group and, given the false news about El Salvador that the U.S. media was publishing, he decided to travel with his daughter and the group."

The Minister tried to get the ex-cadets to relax a little bit. He could only imagine the turmoil of emotions and shame they might be experiencing. He hoped this story would have the desired effect.

"It turns out he was from Catalonia and served in the military in Spain, and he was very interested in talking about military affairs. He induced me to talk with a bottle of *jerez* [sherry] that he brought as a gift. We cracked it open and started to enjoy it, and pretty soon we spoke as if we had been long lost friends.

"It occurred to me to ask him how he'd become a Baptist, because hadn't he been raised a Catholic in Spain? And he went from happy to somber in no time flat. He downed the glass of sherry in his hand and poured himself another one. Then he looked at me in anger."

"Juan," I said, "please forgive me if I asked something inappropriate. It's none of my business."

Juan Font relaxed his stern face a bit. "No, no, Colonel, you didn't ask anything inappropriate. It's just that it's something so odious, that I can't help but get upset when I recall it."

The Colonel again apologized. Juan gestured with his hand that it was

OK. He then said, "Let me tell you, and you'll see. I was an altar boy at a local Catholic church in Barcelona, and one Sunday, after the last mass of the day, the priest called me into the sacristy, saying he wanted to talk to me. I'd spilled some holy wine earlier that day and I was sure that he was going to reprimand me. I was ten years old in 1935, and everybody was always reprimanding me for something."

The Colonel smiled and told him how at that age his mom would often spank his behind with her shoe.

"I entered the sacristy as he was changing. He asked me to sit down on a couch. He was dressed in t-shirt and trousers when he went into the bathroom. A minute later he walked out completely naked, fully erect. He sat down on the couch next to me, grabbed my hand and pulled it toward his penis, saying that God wanted me to touch it."

The Colonel couldn't hide his astonishment. "Oh my, Juan, what did you do?"

"I right out of there as fast as I could. Right out of that church, and right out of Catholicism. For a while I was churchless, but when I got to America, I joined the local church, which was Baptist, and that's where I've stayed."

The Colonel knew that priests in El Salvador had female lovers, and in *machista* El Salvador, that wasn't frowned upon. But homosexuality with kids? That would've never crossed his mind.

"Juan, did you report him?"

"No. I didn't say a word; I was too afraid."

"Didn't your parents think it strange that you stopped being an altar boy?"

"Perhaps, but then the Spanish Civil War broke out, and the Catholic Church took sides with Franco, and we weren't about to take sides with anybody, so we all stopped going to mass anyway."

The Minister ended his story there and looked at the ex-cadets.

"Gentlemen, apparently, what happened to you has been happening since 1935. Why do they do it? I don't know. I'm no psychologist. But I do believe they count on their victims being too young and too ashamed to say anything. And who could possibly believe a 'holy man' or a 'man of God' would do such a thing?"

Remberto Fiallos spoke up again. "Mr. Minister, I can speak for all when I say that it's been a living hell for all of us after we were outed. El

Salvador is too small for things not to get known. People talk about us and then our friends leave us because they might say that they're fags, too, by association. In a *machista* society such as this one, it's hard to get back up from such a blow."

The Minister suspected as much. That's why they were there. "Tell me, gentlemen, if I give you the opportunity to clear your names and gain a measure of revenge for what has been done to you and to this nation, would you take it?"

The response was a unanimous yes.

"You will all become 2nd Lieutenants *de fila* to do this mission."

This was well-received by the ex-cadets. The *de fila* classification was given to the officers who had not graduated from any military school but had risen in the ranks as non-commissioned officers. Their status would be the same as any other 2nd Lieutenant, except that they wouldn't belong to any *tanda*.

"When you're sworn in, I'll tell you what your mission is."

CHAPTER 34

THE PROMISE

"Mario, business has been booming at Vesuvius because of a large demand for construction material. But I don't see many new homes being built in San Salvador."

Mario didn't respond, knowing full well that all the new construction wasn't in plain sight because it was underground: clandestine hospitals/warehouses were being built, not homes. And it was all under Juana's care. And that's why Vesuvius was doing well.

He thought, "It's too bad you're not in the medical supplies business because that's the next business to boom."

He had scurried away from the Externado for the evening. Things were hopping because Somoza was expected to fall any day now. There had been an increase in marches and therefore an increase in wounded, many of whom would be dead but for Juana's clandestine clinics.

"Mario, you look haggard. Have they been overworking you at Externado, making you lift too much chalk?" That was his dad's sardonic way of trying to get information out of him.

Mario just kept eating. "Dad, as a Jesuit, I do much more than teach lessons."

This was the opportunity his sister Rosa Lina was looking for. "You aren't teaching, Mario, you're indoctrinating. Your nephew Freddy is accusing his dad Celso and me of being rich capitalist pigs who exploit the poor. My lord, his dad is a cattle rancher, he built a school and a clinic at the ranch, for the workers. He couldn't be a better *patrón* [employer]. But Freddy comes in one evening and says that we should just hand the ranch over to the peons!"

Mario just kept on eating his dinner, knowing his sister was right. Segundo Montes had implemented a social justice-focused curriculum at Externado, rather than a math and sciences-focused curriculum, and it was bearing its intended fruits: it was shocking Salvadoran families into becoming aware of the social inequality that existed, and it was also inducing high school students to join the guerrillas. The same type of curriculum was being implemented in other private catholic schools.

Rosa Lina continued. "And there's no reasoning with him. Celso tells him that he pays the peons way more than what the law requires. They share in the profits. He put one of the foreman's daughters through accounting school, and now she's the property's accountant: she keeps track of what goes in and what goes out, she tallies the profits and losses, and she distributes part of the profits to the workers, and what's left over is ours, to put Freddy and his siblings through school."

Everybody at the table agreed with her. But Celso Díaz was a rarity in El Salvador. He was the exception to the rule. The rule was that the peasants were paid a pittance, and in many cases, they were paid less than what corresponded to them. For many Salvadoran peasants, the coffee harvest was when they'd make most of their yearly income. They would go, pick coffee and have their pickings weighed and they would get paid according to the weight of their pickings. But many landowners skewed the scales to measure less than what was actually picked. In other words, landowners were capable of stealing from some miserable peasants! Everybody knew this was going on, and nobody did a damn thing about it!

For many Salvadorans, what they picked during the coffee season was the only real income they'd have for that year. And even though the owners of the coffee farms made obscene profits selling the coffee at far more than 1 *peso* per *arroba*, they still swindled the poor peasants out of their rightful earnings.

And people still wondered why there was a revolution brewing.

Mario spoke up. "I was honestly trying to get away from all of that this evening. It's been stressful, and I want to relax. What better place than home sweet home to relax?" And he gave a meaningful look to his dad, who understood perfectly.

Mario continued. "But to your point, Rosa Lina, we've talked about this before. More people like Celso should fight to pass laws that rectify injustices. Costa Rica did that. They're not suffering any revolutionary breakouts. They passed laws forcing the landowners and business owners to facilitate the education of their peasants. Every other Central American nation has guerrilla problems, to a greater or lesser degree, but not Costa Rica. They're certainly reaping the rewards of forward thinking."

But Rosa Lina wasn't through. "Mario, if Freddy becomes a guerrilla, I'll never forgive you."

Cacophony. Everybody talking at once. Somebody invoking the 'Three Divine Persons.'

Mario took a spoon and hit his glass a few times with it, as a sign that he wanted to speak. When everybody had piped down, he said, "Rosa Lina, I hardly see Freddy at the Externado. If I do, I'll tell him that the people who are the brains behind our revolutionary movement and Nicaragua's, have never pulled a trigger. I'd advise him to stick to the intellectual field and not the military field."

With that, he excused himself from the table and went to his old room. His father joined him shortly.

"Stressful, huh? Your mom and I are going to go to Carmen María's house just to spend a few hours. We'll be back by curfew." Carmen María was Mario's oldest sister, who had become an artist and had never married, to Belinda's despair. But her paintings were works of art!

"What time is the curfew set by the Junta now?"

"Eleven p.m. So you'll have about four hours to relax, ok?" His dad winked at him.

"OK, dad, thanks."

He went out to say goodbye to everybody, and when they had left, he went over to the maids' quarters. Estela was there, ironing.

There had never been anything pretty about Estela. But he loved her hands.

Estela was now a lady in her early 60s, who had arrived at the Tacarello household a few months before Gladys had her son. When Gladys was taking care of her newborn, whose dad had died in an accident, Estela cooked and cleaned, and whenever Mr. and Mrs. Tacarello went out to dinner or to parties, she'd wait up for them watching TV.

One evening, when Mario was around twelve years old and his parents were out, Mario prayed the Rosary and went to bed. But that night he was unable to fall asleep. So he went over to watch TV with Estela, in his pajamas. The movie she was watching was "From Here to Eternity" with Burt Lancaster and Deborah Kerr, dubbed in Spanish. When they came out of the water and kissed on the beach, lying on the sand, Mario's penis popped out of his pajamas to watch TV as well.

He looked down at his erection, surprised, and so did Estela, who said, "Oh, look, Marito you're becoming a man." And she touched it.

Her touch was the purest thrill he had ever felt. It seared his entire body with a perfect combination of heat and sweet. He'd never felt anything like it before.

Estela whispered, "It's nice and stiff, Marito. Have you ever played with it?"

Mario, in ecstasy, just shook his head.

She took his foreskin between her thumb and index fingers and pulled down.

The thrill was almost unbearable. She continued playing with it.

"Have you ever had the milk come out?"

"Milk?" He could barely get the word out.

"A white liquid."

"No."

"Look, Marito. I'll do this for you, but you can't make any noise because you'll wake your sisters or Gladys or her son. OK?"

He nodded.

"When I sense that the milk is going to come out, I'm going to cover your mouth, OK?"

He nodded again.

A minute later she was covering his mouth with her other hand, as he was spurting 'milk' all over the place. He'd never forget that pleasure. When it was over, he couldn't believe he was still whole, or alive.

As he lay there panting, while Estela was getting some cloth to wipe everything clean, he realized that he'd found something that was more vital to him than a Rosary: an addiction.

The years had gone by and he'd always come back for more. All his sexual encounters with European girls had yet to produce a pleasure as exquisite as Estela's hands could.

And that's what he was after when he entered the room to greet Estela, who jumped out of her skin when she heard the unexpected greeting.

"Marito!!! You scared me, I thought everybody had left." She came over to hug him.

After their embrace, Mario told her, "We're alone, and I need you to take care of me, Estela."

"No, Marito, Gladys will be back any second now, she went out for a little while."

"How's Gladys?"

"She's fine. She went to see Neto at the boarding school."

"How's Neto?"

"My Neto is fine."

"What is he, 16 years old now?"

"Yes. Look, this is him, this picture was taken last month."

Mario looked at the picture. When he gave it back, he asked her, "You sure you can't help me quickly?"

"Are you that desperate, Marito?"

"Yes, I need your magical hands."

"OK, but let's go to your room."

Once there, Mario undressed immediately. He loved that sensation of freedom he had with Estela. He lay down on bed, and Estela sat on the edge of the bed. He then wrapped his right leg around her body, giving her maximum access to his genitals. Before she started touching him, he touched one of her breasts and said, "Take them out, Estela."

"No, Marito. What if Gladys comes and sees us? And this has to be quick."

"Ok, Estela, go."

Estela started stroking him. It felt marvelous.

She cupped his testicles with her other hand. He opened his legs wider and closed his eyes and let himself be taken to heaven on earth. As he was getting there, he heard a voice. And it wasn't St. Peter's!

"Hello, Marito."

Mario's eyelids flew wide open, as Estela jumped, startled. His hands reached down to cover himself.

Gladys walked right in to kiss her mom and then to hug completely naked Mario, who could do nothing but ask, "How long have you been here?"

"I just got back."

"I thought you'd gone to see Neto?"

"I did, gave him some money, and came back."

Estela could say nothing but, "That was quick."

The awkward situation had made Mario go limp and look for his clothes to get dressed. He'd never been so exposed to Gladys, and he felt ashamed.

"What are you doing?" Gladys asked with a mischievous smile.

"Well, I'm kind of embarrassed."

Gladys took her top off immediately. Her bountiful, age-defying breasts were exposed completely and immediately, because she didn't even need a bra.

"Are you still embarrassed, Marito?"

The answer was yes, but the situation had become intriguing. He stopped attempting to get dressed and said, "Ok, I guess not, but I don't understand this. Weren't you upset at seeing your mother stroking me?"

"You don't think I knew about my mom 'milking' you?"

He looked at Estela in astonishment. "You told her?"

Estela laughed. "Oh Marito, come on! The house is big, but it's not big enough for people not to find out. Gladys saw me touching you, and I had to tell her. Your mother has seen me doing you more than once, and she's never said a word. Remember, you got hooked on it for a solid year."

The reference to his mother was very believable. She'd always hoped to find a way to make a man out of him, especially since they'd called him a fag in Externado. And although he hadn't realized it back then, his dad was the greatest instigator for him to enjoy sex, because although his mom wanted him to be a Protestant pastor to be able to have grandkids, his dad simply didn't want him to be a chaste priest.

But he stopped reminiscing and started focusing on Gladys' tits, because it was inappropriate to have her exposed and him limp. Focusing on her tits finally made his blood flow to where it was most needed at the time.

But the Jesuit in him had to ask, "Gladys, I hope that you won't take it the wrong way: why on earth would you choose to remain here, exposed, with your mom present?"

Mother and daughter looked at each other and started laughing, which definitely puzzled Mario. When the laughter ceased, Gladys just said, "Why don't you lie down, open your legs, and let *Mamá* and me take care of you, while I explain?"

How could he say no to that? Estela sat on the bed, Mario wrapped a leg around her and she resumed her ministrations.

"Do you remember when I asked your parents to hire my mom, and your dad refused, but a few days later, he relinquished?"

"Yes, I think I remember that."

"Do you know why he refused?"

"Why?"

"Because I was servicing your dad and with my mother here that would've been more difficult."

"Yes, I can see how that would be an inconvenience for him. Why didn't you talk to him before you made the request?"

"I was just a dumb *sirvienta*, Marito. And I was scared."

"Why? Would dad mistreat you?"

Gladys opened her eyes wide, genuinely astonished by the question. "No, heavens, no. Your dad may be sex-crazed, but he's the nicest and most generous man I know."

"So what were you afraid of?"

"My period was late."

Mario understood immediately. "Neto is my dad's son?"

"Neto Suárez is your half-brother." His name was Ernesto Manuel Suárez, Suárez being Gladys' last name.

Limp city. Estela tried to revive it by stroking faster.

"Your mom knows. Your sisters don't. So, I wouldn't say anything to them."

"Not to worry about that. I won't even mention it to my dad."

"Thank you, Marito."

"I'll start visiting him at the boarding school."

"No. Please. Let's let things continue as they are. If there's ever a time to reveal it, your father will do it. That's what we've all agreed to. Thanks to your father, my son is getting a first-rate education and has a bright future ahead of him."

"Ok, but Neto doesn't know either, right?"

"No. I always told him his dad had died. He doesn't know he's your half-brother, or that Don Pepe is his dad."

Estela complained. "Marito, my arm is getting tired, and you're not hard."

Gladys volunteered to take over. "Let me do it, mom."

Mario jumped. "No! You're my half-brother's mother!"

"And your beloved Estela is his grandmother. So what?"

Deep inside, Mario's voice was telling him to get up and get dressed. But there was another voice that said you're horny and you've never done a mother-daughter combo.

Gladys took over and pushed him back onto the bed.

The mother-daughter voice had won.

As she was exerting herself, Mario asked, "So how did you resolve your problem? How did Estela get hired?"

"Let me explain," Estela interjected. "You take care of Marito."

"At the time, your father was trying to hire someone for the San Miguel store, and he was taking Gladys whenever the store needed re-stocking or cleaning. The next time Gladys went with him, she told him she was not feeling that well, but that I could go with them to help out since I was available. So the next day the three of us left for San Miguel."

Mario was enjoying the story, but more so because Gladys was an expert with her hands. She must've done this often to his dad. It felt intoxicating.

"When we got to San Miguel, Gladys told me what to do, because she really wasn't feeling well, and I did everything quickly and efficiently. I did in half a day what it was taking Gladys all day to do. Your father was impressed. At that point, Gladys asked him again to hire me, in front of me. He hemmed and hawed, and said that there was really no need for me at the house, but that he could use me on an as-needed basis, like that day."

She paused but Mario urged her to go on.

"It was then that Gladys told him that she was pregnant with her child and that she was going to need help in the house because if she was indisposed because of her state, she wouldn't be able to, and so who was going to help Mrs. Tacarello, especially when the baby came? And since Don Pepe was in shock, saying nothing, Gladys said, 'unless you're going to kick me out like other employers do with their pregnant servants.'"

Mario stopped Gladys' hand to ask her, "You seriously said that?"

Gladys smiled proudly. "Yes. Not bad for an uneducated *india*, huh?"

Mario nodded. "And what did he say?"

"When he got over the shock, he was ecstatic. He promised to take care of the child and me forever, and of course. But then I asked him about Mrs. Tacarello, and he said that whether she supported him or not, he would help raise the child because it was his."

Estela said, "I've blessed your dad every day since he said that, Mario.

Not many *indias* in Gladys' position are that lucky. Don Pepe has a heart of gold, and so the rest doesn't matter."

Mario was bemused. "Everything else?"

Gladys was about to explain, but Estela insisted, "Let me explain, Gladys. You keep going with Marito."

Upon Gladys' resumption of her magnificent touching, Estela continued.

"Gladys asked him again if I could be employed. He got that mischievous look he gets and said that I could be hired on one condition: if Gladys wasn't able to service him, that I would."

"So you agreed?"

"Marito, I wouldn't be here if I hadn't agreed to it."

"And you serviced him?"

"Right then and there!"

"You're kidding!"

"No, I let him have me whichever way he wanted."

He turned to Gladys, "Did you watch that?"

"Marito, my goal was to make sure my mom got the job. So when Don Pepe told me to stay and watch, I stayed and watched."

Mario looked astonished.

"Marito," Gladys explained, "you have no idea how having a child inside you helps set your priorities. I was going to need help, and I needed mom to be hired. Having achieved that, I really couldn't have cared less what he did with mom."

Mario was curious and excited. "What did he ask you to do, Estela?"

Gladys stopped her mom from answering. "Let me show him."

Gladys started performing fellatio on Mario. After a while, she stopped just to say, "Give me all of Neto's nieces and nephews, Marito," and clamped down on his manhood, on time to receive spurt after spurt of Neto's nieces and nephews, which she swallowed entirely.

After Mario stopped experiencing what the French call the 'small death,' he lay there, panting. It was the most intense orgasm he'd ever had.

Gladys smiled and said, "Does that answer your question?"

Mario just nodded. He hadn't recovered from his earth-shattering orgasm.

Estela said, "We love your father, Marito. We have a home in

Sonsonate. He's funded our pension plan. He pays us very well."

"But you're his..."

"Whores? Sure. Small price to pay. I have no formal education. Neither does mom. But many women with a formal education would give anything to have what we have, thanks to your dad."

Although the energy depletion wasn't letting him think clearly yet, Mario knew that the story hadn't ended yet. So he asked, "Why do you think my mom accepted the three of you?"

Gladys thought for a few moments, then said, "Well, your mother is a good woman, to begin with, and very reasonable. Don Pepe told me that he had made a deal with his wife, which was: no other women. He knew he was a womanizer, and she didn't want to catch some sort of sickness from him, and so if he accepted that condition, plus a couple of others, we could stay. Another condition was that we would have to be the servants of the house and act accordingly. Otherwise, if there was any whiff of insubordination, she would terminate our employment, and if need be, her marriage. We kept our end of the bargain."

"Any other condition?"

"No, I had to agree to something else."

Gladys grew very somber. "She demanded that I get my tubes tied when I gave birth so that I couldn't have any more babies."

"My lord, my mother demanded that?"

"Yes and I agreed. I was in no position to say no. And anyway, with so many orphans in El Salvador, I could just adopt."

"I'm sorry, Gladys. It was unfair of my mom to demand that of you."

Mario thought of something else to ask. "Did she also demand that Neto not know?"

"Yes, Neto doesn't know that he's related to you, that he has a half-brother and two half-sisters. I told him his dad died in an accident. Your mother also demanded that he go to a boarding school as soon as he was old enough."

"To keep him out of her family and have as much normalcy as she possibly could, under the circumstances."

"Yes. All those conditions were met by us."

Mario remembered the young child Neto but couldn't remember the last time he'd seen him. He wouldn't have recognized him after all these years without seeing the picture that Estela showed him.

Again, Mario apologized.

Estela tried to inject some levity into the situation. "Marito, with the way women are treated in this country, the ability not to get pregnant is a blessing in disguise." And she smiled.

"If you say so, grandma."

Mario looked at his watch. 9:00 p.m.

"My parents won't be home for another couple of hours. Can you both lie with me for a while? I've never been with a mother and daughter together."

The women laughed. "We've never been with a father and son either!" They undressed and hopped into bed with him.

He embraced them both.

Gladys turned to him and asked: "Is this a sin, Marito?"

He turned his head to kiss Gladys's forehead, saying, "*Ego te absolvo*, Gladys." Then he turned to kiss Estela's forehead, and said, "*Ego te absolvo*, Estela."

He was anxious to reassure them. "You, my dear ladies, are completely devoid of sin. Sin truly lies with those who failed to give you a sound education, to protect your rights as women, and who've taken advantage of you. You both are lucky you're appreciated and taken care of. But how many countless poor Salvadoran women have been forced to submit, and then disposed of like used trash, especially if they're pregnant? Or forced to commit a greater sin, like abortion?"

He embraced both fiercely. "No, my beloved Gladys and Estela. You are definitely not the sinners."

He had just finished saying that when he realized which issue was left to be discussed. He sat up between the women and turned to Gladys. "Gladys, why did you tell me about Neto? You were allegedly instructed not to. Yet that was your intention tonight. And you ambushed me with your splendid body, to make sure that I heard your message loud and clear. sexually here not because you find me attractive, but because you find me useful. So tell me why."

Gladys' lowered her eyes, somewhat embarrassed. But embarrassment was quickly replaced by anxiety. "Marito, your father would do anything for Neto, within the rules imposed by your mother. But the country is heading toward violence and I'm afraid for my Neto."

"We both are, Marito," asserted an equally anxious Estela.

Gladys continued. "I had a very frightening nightmare recently. In it, Neto was a wounded guerrilla. Before he died, he reached out to hold the crucifix on my necklace, the blessed one you gave me as a present for Christmas a few years ago, and he began to pray. Then he closed his eyes forever."

"God forbid, God forbid!" cried Estela.

Mario tried to sound reassuring. "Come now, ladies, that's a common nightmare nowadays."

Gladys was having none of it. "Look, Marito, Neto is all we have. He's the most precious thing in our lives. Do you understand me?"

Her eyes were answering his question, in ways her mouth never could. Gladys had decided to give herself to Mario to obtain some sort of guarantee that he would do everything he could to keep Neto safe. She had obtained everything she'd needed out of life with her body and that was all she'd done tonight.

She felt she'd needed to do it because if Neto was captured by the army, or the police or somebody on that side, Pepe would move heaven and earth for him. But if Neto were captured by guerrillas, Don Pepe was impotent. But Mario was not. After all, Mario was on the side of the guerrillas.

Mario stood up, so both women could see him make this solemn promise: "Gladys and Estela, I promise I'll do everything in my power to keep Neto safe. I solemnly promise."

Half an hour later, it was Estela who was receiving Neto's nieces and nephews. It was an earth-shattering orgasm as well... not because Estela was that good, but because he was imagining that it was the naked Juana that he'd seen on the beach who as doing him.

As soon as Mario fell asleep, both women got up, dressed and went back to their room.

Mission accomplished!

Chapter 35

Odium

Inés entered her office. Sister Licha stood up to show the proper respect to her superior. But rather than assert her superiority, she tightly embraced Sister Licha. "I haven't had the opportunity to thank you for pulling through for the cause at the beach."

Sister Licha felt her face turn red. "Sister, I believe in the cause. I didn't know there were so many skeptics about my commitment."

"Nobody's doubting you, Juana. Those commanders just wanted new meat, and they hadn't eaten you yet. And look at you, you're tall, blond, European; certainly not an *india.*"

Juana shrugged. For whatever reason, it happened.

"You know who wanted you, too? That Jesuit."

For some reason, she was very grateful that Father Tacarello hadn't partaken. Juana remarked, "Father Tacarello behaved decently."

Inés countenance was overcome with fury. "No, Juana, the Jesuits are nothing but a bunch of assholes!"

Juana was surprised by such a heartfelt and disparaging remark towards those who had taken her out of poverty and helped her family financially. "Why do you say that, Inés?", she had to ask.

Inés took her by the hand and led her to a couch where they both sat down. She explained, "Juana, the only good Jesuit I've known as Rutilio Grande, may he rest in peace. That man was a saint, and he was certainly respectful of all of us peasants. Do you know why? Because he was one of us. Pure *indio.* But when they killed him, we were left in the hands of Spanish Jesuits, and they look down on all of us.

"The Spanish Jesuits that taught us in Santa Ana, at the so-called convent, had no patience with us when we found to understand the concepts that they wanted us to learn—things like ontology, metaphysics, gnoseology and other 'ologies' that I still don't understand."

"We'd done so bad in one of those courses, that when he gave us the final grades, this priest named Father Pueyrredón told us that he couldn't understand how Spain had lost its colonies to such mentally-handicapped people, and that normally, we would've all flunked out. But that since the Revolution needed us, that we were going to get the chance to redeem ourselves that weekend."

Juana shook her head, incredulous. She knew how this story was going to end. "They took you to service guerrillas, didn't they?"

Inés eyes filled with tears. She bravely continued. "It was on a farm in Chalatenango, near the border with Honduras. They kept us there from Friday to Sunday. They did everything to us, like what happened to you, only unlike Tacarello at *El Cuco*, Father Pueyrredón did participate. He didn't care—he was going back to Spain soon.

The guerrilla commander was Marcial—yes, the same one at *Cuco* who gave us the same spiel he gave you—and when we finally agreed to service them for the sake of the blessed Revolution, Father Pueyrredón told Marcial that he wanted me, because I was the smartest, which actually meant that I was the less stupid of the bunch."

"Inés, please, don't go on. You don't have to."

"Juana, let me continue because I want you to understand why I'm going to say what I'm going to say. That goddamn son of a bitch took me aside and violated my rear. He told me that he wasn't interested in female parts, only asses. He did boys as well!"

Juana wanted to throw up. But she stoically controlled herself, because she wasn't the one who was suffering right now.

"A couple of months after it was over, the Jesuits brought in a doctor, to take care of a few unwanted pregnancies that were the result of that weekend. I was lucky. The others who used me only used my mouth." Seeing Juana's astonishment, she has to reiterate, "It's true. They took an abortion doctor."

Inés ended her story, saying, "The commanders believe that they're in charge. Not at all. They're *indios*, and therefore, they're puppets of the Jesuits, like we are. When the shooting starts, only *indios* are going to die. And when the shooting is over, they'll be the ones sitting on the throne of power, without having sacrificed a goddamn thing."

She paused for a second, looking at Juana with eyes that no longer brimmed with tears, but with anger. "I'm willing to die for the Revolution, for my people. But they're not, because we're not their people. They see us as inferior. And let me tell you something, Juana: if I had but one bullet left, and I had to choose between shooting a rich man or a Jesuit... I'd shoot the goddamn Jesuit!"

The last thing Inés did before returning to her office was to embrace Juana tightly again, as she whispered in her ear: "We owe you our lives. Marcial is a butcher. Had you left us there, he would've killed all three of us!"

It took Juana a while to get over the shock. She understood why people like Marcial were savages; after all, life hadn't been good to them. But what excuse could the Jesuits have, living the life of the rich, the life of the well-kept?

Although she couldn't blame Inés for feeling the way she did, she knew that there was somebody above the Jesuits, personified by Don Blas. So they too followed orders.

And that was what she intended to find out. If God had allowed her to be humiliated so mercilessly at the beach, it must have been for a greater purpose. Achieving that greater purpose was the only thing that spurred her on.

Chapter 36

All Shook Up

When she returned from lunch, Licha found a message on the answering machine: "Hello Juana, this is Eliseo. We've been invited to dinner. I'll pick you up at 8 pm tonight. If you don't have a dress for the occasion, which is formal, please go to *Simán* and ask for Miss Evelyn Santamaría, and she'll take care of you. See you then." *Simán* was the largest department store in El Salvador.

Juana felt relieved. It didn't sound like it was going to be another gangbang. She put on a blouse, slacks, tennis shoes and sunglasses and walked over to director's office to inform her that she'd be going out. Inés looked up at her and waved her away. Her deflowering at *Cuco* had brought them closer.

She took a taxi to Simán downtown, where she asked for Miss Santamaría. Shortly, a very elegant lady came to greet her. She led Juana to the ladies' clothing section, where they picked out and Licha tried on a very elegant blue dress and matching high heels. A Simán seamstress made the necessary adjustments to the dress, and while she was doing that, Miss Santamaría took her to the jewelry department, where they picked out a pearl necklace.

An hour later, everything was ready and Miss Santamaría packed everything carefully. She handed the bags to Licha, informing her that everything had already been paid for. She then said good-bye and left, without giving Licha a chance to ask who'd paid for all that.

But Licha supposed that whoever had paid for all that would be at the dinner that night.

At 8 pm on the dot, Mario picked her up in his Volkswagen and they took off to the west, getting onto the Escalón Boulevard which was the main artery going into that posh district. When they reached the restaurant *El Bodegón* [The Tavern], which was famous for its Spanish fare and its wine cellar, they turned right to park in the parking lot.

When they went inside, Eliseo and Juana looked like movie stars—

that's how elegant they were dressed. Nobody in a million years would've guessed that they were a priest and a nun—which was the purpose, of course! The owner, Mr. Angel García, greeted them and walked them over to the private dining room in the back of the restaurant. But until then, all the eyes of the patrons were on them, asking themselves who that spectacular couple was, that nobody'd ever seen before.

Don Angel opened the door to the private dining room. Facing the entrance was a man who, at first blush, reminded Licha of the Mexican singer Pedro Infante. A tall gray-haired man had his back to the entrance, and when he turned around, it turned out to be ... Don Blas!

Eliseo made the introductions. "Juana, this is Don Polo, and he is Don Blas." Everybody shook hands. Don Blas held on to hers and kissed it. That struck Juana as strange. Didn't he know she was a nun?

The purpose of the dinner was to expand Juana's 'construction' expertise outside of San Salvador, to more 'strategic' places. They would all be under schools, and would Juana be capable of directing the construction of schools first, if need be?

They continued to talk shop over a sumptuous dinner of *Paella*, which was quite possibly the best *Paella* in the world.

During the conversation, Don Polo said, "Juana, the places where the new schools/clandestine hospitals/warehouses will be built, will be on land owned by me. We're merely reproducing what I've done at my large *hacienda* in Sonsonate, to the other strategic places that we decide upon."

Juana had to say, "Don Polo, if there's ever an Agrarian Reform in El Salvador, you may lose those lands."

Don Polo smiled, and said, "Which is why we have to start right away, Juana."

Juana didn't mind, but had to ask, "Fine, I'm only too glad to help. But gentlemen, why are you relying on me? Why not hire a civil engineer from the University of El Salvador?"

Don Blas answered that in his exquisite Castilian Spanish. "They're well-versed in Marxism, but not in engineering, Juana. And anybody else, from a private, established and reputable firm, is simply unreliable. Case in point: one of those engineering firms built one of the buildings that got flattened like a pancake in one of the latest earthquakes in San Salvador. They exist to make a profit, and to do so, they often cut corners. You're a better engineer than the others because you're doing it for a cause beyond profit. And also, what could be more inconspicuous than a nun working to educate poor children?"

Eliseo was amused by all this. It was obvious to anybody who wasn't blind that Don Blas was smitten by Juana. If he ever had any desire for Juana, it was put on indefinite hold from that moment on. One of the main sponsors of the revolutionary movement had laid a very public claim to her. She was officially 'off limits.' And it was too bad. That body of hers was spectacular.

Juana had one more question. "Gentlemen, I work at Asunción. Will that continue to be my base?"

Don Polo replied, "Juana, this is a small country, distances are short. You'll have a driver and a jeep at your disposal. He'll take you wherever you need to go. If you're ever stopped, you'll identify yourself as an Asunción nun and teacher, working on building a new school in such-and-such a place. And the chauffeur will identify himself as working for me. You'll get a generous allowance every week so that you always have cash on hand if you need it."

She had one last question. But it was one Don Blas was expecting. So when he saw the pained expression on her face, due to the difficulty of having to ask such a question, he cut her off at the pass. "Juana, nobody is going to bother you, for any reason."

The way he said it, it was as if God had given an eleventh commandment: "Thou shalt not mess with Juana."

Dinner eaten, business discussed, they parted ways, but not before another lingering kiss on the hand by Don Blas, and not before he gave her a note in an envelope.

After Mario dropped her off, she opened the envelope. "Dear Juana, if you ever get a letter from a Marcos Arévalo, please read it. Thank you for all you continue to do." It was signed 'Marcos Arévalo.'

The next day, a courier arrived at La Asunción, with a note from Marcos Arévalo. It said to be ready Saturday at 6 a.m., because her driver would pick her up to take her to 'El Jobo,' the *hacienda* of Enrique Alvarez Córdova. Now she knew who Don Polo was! Although he had seemed familiar, she was unsure, and since everybody was using only their aliases, she'd been afraid to ask. The mustache and the years had thrown her off—

she remembered him younger and thinner, when he was Minister of Agriculture back in 1970.

The purpose of the visit was to review what had been built in 'El Jobo,' to obtain a copy of the 'As-Built' drawings, and to use them as a blueprint for the other sites where construction would begin.

Enrique Alvarez Córdova was known for instituting profit-sharing and other progressive capitalist measures for his workers, such as schools and clinics for the workers and their families. In that sense, he was a true capitalist and not the communist that people accused him of. What landed him in hot water was that none of the other rich landowners did that. The others got rich exploiting their workers.

Alvarez Córdova was among the very few who'd studied in the United States and had returned to put the knowledge gained into practice. His *nom-de-guerre* 'Don Polo' was given to him probably because he liked to play that aristocratic game—polo. And although *noms-de-guerre* weren't supposed to say anything about the individual, polo was a fairly unknown sport to the masses (how could it be otherwise?) and in El Salvador, Polo was the nickname given to men named 'Leopoldo,' which was the only connection Juana's mind had tried to make. So it was an effective *nom-de-guerre.*

The two-hour ride to El Jobo was uneventful. When she arrived, Don Polo and Don Blas were there to greet her.

Most of the day went by with a tour of the *hacienda.* Don Polo was very proud of the facilities he had built for his workers. And they absolutely loved him. Both Juana and Don Blas were very impressed.

But it was all business when Don Polo produced the 'As-Built' drawings. Juana dove into their analysis. After a while it became clear to Juana that Don Polo had spared no expense in order to build the best possible infrastructure for his workers. But it was also clear to Juana that there were cheaper alternatives for building the structures that the Revolution would need. But every time Juana would suggest it, Don Blas would ask, "But which alternative stands a better chance of surviving an earthquake, Juana—Don Polo's or yours?"

This question got asked so often, that Juana had to ask, "Don Blas, have you ever lived through an earthquake?"

Don Blas turned to her somberly. "Juana, on May 31, 1970, I was in

Peru, north of Lima, in the Ancash region, when a massive earthquake struck. I had no idea what to do. The building I was in withstood it but many others collapsed."

"Wasn't there a massive landslide?" Don Polo asked.

"Yes, and about seventy thousand people died."

Juana recalled reading about that. "But that was a 7.9 earthquake on the Richter scale. It's hard to survive that."

"Yes but not all buildings crumbled, Juana. Just the poorly-built ones."

Juana wanted to say that nothing could withstand thousands of tons of dirt slamming into it, but there was no refuting his point that a better-built building stood a better chance of surviving than one where corners had been cut.

But Don Blas wasn't done with his telluric experiences yet. "A couple of years later, I'm in Managua, Nicaragua, ready to spend Christmas with a *señorita* who had caught my eye, when the Managua earthquake hit on December 23. It was only a magnitude 6.3, but it leveled a lot of buildings, killing about 10,000 people, leaving 300,000 homeless. And it left me without my *señorita*. So yes, Juana, I'm very earthquake-averse, and I, I mean the Revolution, wouldn't want to lose you to one. Or lose anybody who may be inside any of our structures. I can rest easier knowing that you're under a structure you built, and not built by corner-cutting, Marx-spouting civil engineers."

Juana raised her arms, as if saying, 'I give up!' and said, "Don Blas, there's nothing more important for me, than for you to rest easy. As such, I have no recourse but to inform you that I'm no longer going to use steel. Instead, I'm going to use tungsten, which is harder than steel. It's also more expensive but, who cares? Certainly not you!"

Don Polo started to laugh. Don Blas seemed surprised. It was obvious that he wasn't used to someone talking to him that way.

Juana went on. "On the other hand, Don Blas, if you see that tungsten is too expensive and you tell me, 'Juana, please go back to using steel,' I need to inform you that I will refuse to do so, unless you solemnly swear that you will never set foot on Salvadoran soil again, because it is obvious, even to the most casual of observers, that wherever you go, disastrous earthquakes follow, and there's no steel structure that can withstand them!"

Don Polo was laughing his head off, and Don Blas couldn't keep a straight face any longer.

Juana ended her fun-poking with, "Now I know why the Sandinistas are going to win: you lost your *señorita* in an earthquake, and you blamed Somoza. But don't worry: I won't tell a soul that the one who was truly responsible for the Managua earthquake was you!"

Everybody laughed hard. But while he was laughing, all Don Blas could think of was, "I love this woman!"

At the end of the day, Don Blas concluded the proceedings. "Ok, we've discussed everything we need to discuss. Juana has everything she needs to start in Sensuntepeque. Don Polo, thank you for this day, for your magnificent work and for your assistance to the cause. But now I'd like to take Juana to dinner before she departs for San Salvador. If she'll accept my invitation, of course."

What was Juana going to do, say no?

Later that evening, they rendezvoused at a tiny *pupusa* restaurant in downtown Sonsonate, called *Tía Tala*. Don Blas ordered for the both of them, two orders of cheese and pork *pupusas*.

"I figured you wanted something totally different from *paella*, Juana."

"Absolutely, Don Blas, variety is the spice of life."

"So tell me about yourself, Juana?"

"No, Don Blas, because first of all, you already know most of what there is to know about me, and secondly, that would require that you tell me more about yourself, to be fair, and I'm pretty certain you can't, so why don't you tell me about the revolution in Nicaragua, instead? I keep hearing about Sandinista victories, but they haven't been able to seal the deal yet. After all, it all started with the Managua earthquake, didn't it? Where you lost someone near and dear to you?"

He loved this woman's character and brains. And she was a beauty. But Don Blas wasn't ready to tell her anything that wasn't in the public domain. For her to know more confidential things, she had to be in love with him. Till death did them part.

"Well, Juana, first I'll tell you what I suspect: Somoza's fall is imminent, which is to say, within a month, in June, or else in July, at the latest. You can take that to the bank."

Juana nodded, because she had no reason to doubt that. Not from everything she'd heard.

Don Blas continued. "The dictatorship of Nicaragua started with Somoza's father. It had been going on way before Anastasio Somoza came to power. Nevertheless, people weren't ready to rise up against him, despite the growing opposition spearheaded by the newspaper 'La Prensa,' run by the Chamorro family. But then the earthquake hit, devastating Managua, and the world rushed aid to that nation."

"And Somoza, instead of distributing it to the needy, hoarded it and sold it, for a profit." Juana knew that part.

"And then only companies in which he held a controlling interest rebuilt the city, so he made a fortune off that earthquake," added Don Blas.

Juana had to agree that Somoza was worthy of being taken down. He was heartless.

Juana then said, "And yet the Sandinista revolution didn't gain any traction until years later, when Somoza killed Chamorro." Juana was just repeating what was considered common knowledge.

Don Blas jumped at this opportunity to give her the real story, to gain credibility in her eyes.

"Actually, it wasn't Somoza who killed Chamorro."

"What? But that was what was broadcast the world over!"

Don Blas smiled. "Propaganda works, doesn't it?"

"If it's true that Somoza didn't kill Chamorro, then I guess it does, Don Blas."

Don Blas replied: "It would've been folly for Somoza to do it. After the earthquake, Pedro Joaquin Chamorro stepped up his attacks against Somoza in his newspaper, proclaiming that Somoza was robbing the nation at the expense of the poor. Still, no uprising. So why kill him? And Somoza relied on the existence of Chamorro and 'La Prensa,' to be able to say, 'Look, I'm no dictator, I have an active opposition.' Nevertheless, the relentless drumbeat did spawn a broad coalition against Somoza, led by two Jesuit priests, Fernando and Ernesto Cardenal, who are brothers, a Maryknoll priest, Miguel D'Escoto Brockmann, and, frankly speaking, most of the new clergy."

Juana stopped him for a second, to ask, "New clergy... like Sister Belén and the other revolutionary priests and nuns here in El Salvador"?

"Exactly. Fernando Cardenal, because of his brainpower, became the de facto leader of the opposition to Somoza, but he works behind the scenes. He travels abroad to obtain support from the U.S. left, the Soviet Union, Cuba, Spain, and other nations; he has many contacts in the press. He's like the Ellacuría of Nicaragua, only far smarter."

"Wait, what did you just say? 'Far smarter than Ellacuría?' I thought Ellacuría was the smartest man alive, according to everybody in El Salvador."

"Oh please. He's not even the smartest priest in El Salvador. The Jesuits have him in El Salvador because he's too unqualified to be anywhere else. It took him a year longer than normal to get his bachelor's degree in Ecuador. They sent him to study under Karl Rahner, at the University of Innsbruck, and he couldn't make it. He had to transfer to some Madrid University to write a thesis about his professor at the university, to get his Ph.D. in philosophy."

Licha was astonished. "What do you mean, a thesis about his professor? Would a University allow that?"

Don Blas' winked at her when he said, "Not normally." And then he smiled broadly.

Juana didn't understand why he was smiling as if he'd had something to do with it, but instead she asked, "So what was his thesis about?" She really wanted to know.

"I can't remember the exact title, but you can paraphrase it like 'The greatness of my teacher Zubiri.'"

"My gosh, that's such an undignified way to get a PhD!"

Don Blas nodded. "Isn't it? Ignacio Ellacuría is not very intellectual, is he?"

"But they say that he writes articles in the Catholic University magazine."

"Sure, but he's mostly regurgitating whatever his thesis professor, Zubiri, is thinking at the time. After all, he visits him fairly often."

"How do you know that he visits Zubiri?"

Don Blas smiled. "My organization foots his travel expenses."

"Oh my!" Juana was genuinely surprised because everybody who ever graduated from UCA sang the praises of Ellacuría's intellectual prowess.

Don Blas was only too happy to share some insight with her to gain her trust.

Juana wanted to get back to Chamorro. “So go on with Chamorro’s murder.”

“OK. A few weeks before his death, Chamorro discovered that this Cuban exile living in Nicaragua, Dr. Pedro Ramos, was taking blood from peasants, paying them a pittance, and selling plasma abroad, making a fortune off it. So Chamorro started publishing editorials against him, accusing him of being a vampire. So much so, that his business went downhill fast. So Ramos hired a thug named Silvio Peña, and Peña and his gang shot Chamorro dead in his car.”

“¡You don’t say!”

“Oh yes. But the Jesuit priest, Fernando Cardenal, being as smart and well-connected as he is, started the ‘Somoza killed Chamorro’ theme in every national and international news outlet, and since Somoza was a heartless bastard to begin with, it was easily believable, and it was believed. By the time they found Peña and his gang and jailed them, it was too late for Somoza. The tide had turned.”

The *pupusas* arrived. Don Blas ate them expertly, adding the right amount of *curtido* [pickled cabbage slaw], and with his hands. Like a native. Which meant that he’d been to El Salvador quite a few times. His 'organization' must be loaded, to keep so many people, like Fernando Cardenal, Ellacuría and himself, traveling all over the world so much. But that wasn’t a question that she was ready to ask yet.

Juana changed subjects. “The Americans often talk about a ‘Domino Theory’ to explain the expansion of communism. After Cuba, Bolivia seemed to be the next domino to fall, until they killed Ché Guevara. Then, the next domino was going to be Chile, with Allende, but Pinochet quashed that. So then it was going to be Colombia, but they haven’t made any gains whatsoever. Which makes Nicaragua the crown jewel of dominos, doesn’t it? And we’re next?”

At the mention of Pinochet, Don Blas almost winced. Juana made a note of that. She’d bring the subject up in the future.

Don Blas pondered his answer a little, before saying, “Juana, what I’m supporting is social justice, not communism. I could care less about communism. It just so happens that the only ones massively in favor of social justice, are communists. But witness what’s happening in Nicaragua. The most famous military leader of the Sandinistas is Edén Pastora, known as *Comandante Cero*. He led daring attacks on the Somoza institutions like the National Assembly. And he's no communist. He just seeks to overthrow the dictator."

"But the communists always end up in power."

Don Blas shook his head. "No, the true leaders of the Sandinista movement are Jesuits. If the Sandinistas win, and it sure does look like they will, they'll be in power."

"And that's the plan for El Salvador?"

"Yes."

"With all due respect, Don Blas, I got told recently by a guerrilla commander that power comes out of the barrel of a gun, and that the church was to be subordinate to the gun holders."

Don Blas reached out to hold her hand. "So I heard."

Juana gently removed her hand from his grasp. "I'm a nun, Don Blas, I resent being put in that position, with all the humiliation it entailed."

Don Blas raced to put out this fire, before it became a conflagration that would end this budding relationship.

"Juana, being a nun isn't who you are. It's what you do."

Tears welled in Juana's eyes. "Well, now I suck and fuck. So I guess I'm a whore now."

"Juana, you didn't do that voluntarily, you were coerced. You were put in a spot where the only noble thing to do was to submit. Why noble? Because your fellow nuns were at risk. Do you honestly believe that had you left, Marcial wouldn't have taken it out on all of them—especially with Inés, who vouched for you? And you would've probably never made it to the airport. You probably saved her life and yours."

He moved next to her and said, "I'm so grateful that you did what you did, because... what would I do without you?" And he kissed her.

Juana didn't know how long it lasted, but she enjoyed every second of it. She didn't love this man or want to be kissed, but it was what she needed—to be wanted and valued by someone who didn't care at all about what had happened to her.

Soon after they parted ways, not before another kiss, and a reminder that Marcos Arévalo would continue writing to her.

CHAPTER 37

BOOLEAN THEOLOGY

"*Padrino* here."

"*Padrino*, you still in hiding?"

"Not at all, sir. I'm here in Apaneca, but nobody's come to visit us."

"You're going to have a Commando unit visiting you soon. Why don't you just come on in?"

"No way, sir. I won't obey an illegal order. You might ask whoever gave that order whether they realize that the cold-blooded murder of priests could lose us the war."

"*Padrino*, the guerrillas are committing all sorts of abuses, against women and against alleged informants. The Treasury Police just found the body of civilian who'd been skinned alive by the guerrillas because they thought he was an informant. Since they couldn't get any information out of him, before they shot him, they made him watch as they raped and killed his daughter. Those people are worth more than your two Spanish Jesuits, don't you think?"

"Oh yes, I agree, but they're untouchable, can't you see?"

Of course Col. López could see. And he wanted to help Sánchez but he needed Sánchez to trust him enough to give him information about his location.

"*Padrino*, you're in way over your head in this. From what I gather, a platoon won't be able to withstand the Commando force they're going to throw at you."

Sánchez thought about it. Perhaps he'd miscalculated. Perhaps the more guerrilla atrocities were discovered, the more the hostility against them would rise, not subside.

"Sir, with all due respect, those resources are better spent getting the murdering and torturing guerrillas, than coming after the priests and me. And excuse me I need to conserve batteries, sir. *Padrino* out."

"Wait, *Padrino*."

"Yes, sir?"

"Send me a message if you want me to help you. You know how."

Sánchez knew he was offering to escort them in. But he'd have to reveal his position, and that would place everybody at the mercy of whoever was hell-bent on killing the priests. Besides, so far, there was no need to. Regardless, his best chance of survival was in a defensive position behind the concrete walls of these homes, holding the high ground. They wouldn't last five minutes if they were ambushed on the highway.

"Thank you, sir, I'll keep that in mind. Oh, by the way, I was wrong about the age of the daughter. She's exactly twenty-one years old. *Padrino* out."

He turned to Sergeant Zelayandía. "Sierra Zulu, let's do what you wanted to do earlier, put a couple of sentinels on that hill across the road, so they can signal us in case somebody's coming."

"Yes, sir!"

"Have them take my MP-5 and Browning 9 mm pistol, wrapped in towels, instead of their M-16s. Make sure they look like beach-goers. Plan the shifts, and if you get bored over here, you can go, too."

"Yes, sir."

"But first, change the HF radio frequency to 58.00 MHz exactly." The Sergeant complied.

Sánchez went up the hill again. It wasn't doing anything for his blood pressure, but it was good exercise.

As usual, Ellacuría was anxious for any news.

Sánchez told the priests of the alleged informant who'd been skinned alive by the guerrillas, and what they did to his daughter.

Ellacuría looked shocked. "That is most unfortunate," he said.

The Captain went to the point: "Don't act so shocked, priest. They're just doing what you're advocating, aren't they? The use of violence in the pursuit of the satisfaction of social needs is allowed by God, according to Liberation Theology. After all, you're both Liberation Theologians, aren't you?"

"Yes, we're Liberation Theologians," Segundo Montes replied. "We're not the authors of Liberation Theology, but we're certainly endorsers. Our colleague Jon Sobrino was one of its drafters. He's traveling abroad right now."

The Captain said, "Here's what I know about Liberation Theology: its main proponents, like the Jesuit Teilhard de Chardin, developed their theology from philosophers such as Hegel, Nietzsche, Marx, Engels, and others. Now then, I'm not going to say that I remember much about what those philosophers said, despite studying them at West Point. However, what I do remember quite clearly is that nobody ever called their work anything but philosophy. They certainly didn't call it theology!"

Ignacio Ellacuría didn't want to miss the opportunity to educate this *chafa*. "Actually, Liberation Theology stems from the writings of St. Thomas Aquinas, but modified from the perspective of philosophical thought."

"The thought of Zubiri, I take it?"

"Yes, among others."

The Captain summarized it as follows: "So Arrupe, Rahner, Jon Sobrino and that Peruvian whose name I can't remember, took the 'theology' of St. Thomas Aquinas, modified it with the 'philosophies' of Marx, Hegels, Nietzsche, Chardin and others, and produced Liberation 'Theology,' is that correct?"

"Yes, in broad strokes, that's it, and the Peruvian's name is Gustavo Gutiérrez," replied Ellacuría.

"Oh? Forgive me, it's just that we didn't study him at West point. I wonder why?" Sánchez then proceeded to look for a grassless patch of dirt to draw on with his bayonet.

When he'd found one, he called the priests over and said, "Forgive me for not being as quick on the uptake as any philosopher might be. I'm just a lowly engineer, so I'd rather go mathematical on this if you don't mind?"

Ellacuría magnanimously said, "Please do." You can act magnanimously when dripping sarcasm escapes you.

"First, let's separate the wheat from the chaff, shall we? In his 'Summa Theologica,' St. Thomas basically promotes the teachings of God and Christ as found in the Old and New Testament does he not? So let's proceed to call St. Thomas' work the Word of God or 'WG,' is that OK?"

Condescendingly, Ellacuría accepted, saying, "It's a rather simplistic way of interpreting it, but it'll do."

So the Captain drew a WG on the ground with his bayonet, and then he said, "Now, let's represent the philosophical thought of Marx, Hegel, Nietzsche and Engels, Gutiérrez, Zubiri, Arrupe, Rahner and Jon Sobrino, with the variable '-WG,' or 'Not the Word of God.'" The Captain looked up at the priests, who didn't know what to say.

So the Captain explained: "You see, we can't have what a philosopher like Nietzsche said, which was that 'God is dead,' be a Word of God because that would mean that God also said, 'I am dead,' because if He were dead, He wouldn't be able to say anything, am I right?"

The logic was devastating enough to silence the Jesuits. So the Captain drew '-PD' on the ground.

Sánchez continued. "You, as educators, must be familiar with Boolean Algebra, right? It's the mathematics of logic, used for the design of digital machines, like personal computers." No response. They had no clue, mainly because they couldn't find the notion of digital machines in Marx's *Das Kapital*, written in 1867. But they finally ended up nodding because, what else were they going to do? And the stench of magnanimity disappeared.

"In Boolean Algebra, you have two states: 1, or true, and Ø, or false." The Captain, squatting to draw on the ground, saw the priests' shadows nod, but without much conviction.

"Finally, let's represent Liberation Theology with the variable 'LT.'" And he drew 'LT' on the ground.

"Now, let's put them all in an equation that reflects your claim, which is that Liberation Theology is the work of St. Thomas of Aquinas 'modified by philosophical thought.' Father Montes, please correct me if I'm wrong: the mathematical representation of 'modifying' is multiplication, am I right?"

Father Montes reluctantly nodded.

"Now then, let's stipulated that WG = 1 [one] or true (after all, we are believers, aren't we?) and let's stipulate that the teachings of a philosopher like Nietzsche, who said, 'God is dead,' let's call that a Ø or false." The Captain drew the 1 and the Ø on the ground and put the multiplication sign between them.

He continued. "In Boolean Algebra 1 x Ø = Ø, or 'false.' So if you modify a truth with falsehood, you get a falsehood. Here, LT = 1 x Ø = Ø, which means that Liberation Theology is false."

The priests were about to protest, but the Captain raised his hand and said, "Hold on gentlemen, there's still hope that it may not be false. Let's see what happens if we multiply WG and –WG." The Captain wrote: LT=

WG x –WG.

He then looked up at the priests and shook his head. "Sorry, liberation theologians, in Boolean Algebra, multiplying a truth (1) by its opposite (Ø), results in Ø or false. Therefore, LT= WG x –WG= Ø or false or a lie. Once again, the result of modifying the Word of God by Not the Word of God produces a falsehood or lie."

He stood up and put his bayonet back in its sheath. "Do I need to go on, gentlemen? In the world of the mathematics of logic, Liberation Theology is a falsehood. A damnable lie."

Ellacuría dismissed it all with a wave of his hand, saying, "You've oversimplified the complex thoughts of great minds."

Sánchez pondered the priest's comment and took out his bayonet again. "I beg your pardon, priest, but we can fix that immediately." He squatted again in front of the equations, and said, "According to Father Ellacuría, I've failed to provide an amplifying factor that accounts for the greatness of the minds of the components of -WG. And since I don't want to make that mistake again, I'm going to multiply -WG by the factor ALAFEWI, which means, 'as large as Father Ellacuría wants it.' Are you OK with that?"

Sánchez didn't wait for an answer, to draw the following equation on the ground:

LT = WG x (-WG x ALAFEWI) = (WG x -WG) x ALAFEWI = (Ø) x ALAFEWI = (Ø)

The Captain stood and put his bayonet back in its scabbard. "Gentlemen, I've proven that, after rectifying the oversimplification, Liberation Theology continues to be false, or a damnable lie."

The Jesuits just stared at the equations. Before they could say anything, Sánchez pointed out the following: "Gentlemen, as you can see, we never could that rid of that negative sign in the equations. Why? Because Liberation Theology is, in and of itself, a negation. And that negative sign is going to affect everything that Liberationists do. For example, if what you want to do is eliminate hunger, that negative sign is going to negate that effort."

Segundo Montes questioned that. "Captain, you know full well that if you multiply two negatives, you get a positive result."

"Father Montes, don't confuse the mathematics of logic with the mathematics of numbers. In logic, you have a true or a false. If you multiply two logical negatives, you're multiplying two falsehoods, i.e, two zeros. Therefore (Ø x Ø) = Ø or false. The falsehood persists. And that falsehood is a negation of the truth which, once again, is intrinsic to Liberation Theology."

Ellacuría had had enough of so much logic and mathematics. He tried to put an end to this attempt by a lesser mind to lecture a greater mind. He said, "Captain, of what use is so much logic to the hungry poor of this nation? You can talk all the Boolean Algebra that you want, till you're blue in the face, but that won't feed the hungry. It is therefore useless and irrelevant."

Sánchez shrugged and said, "Father Ellacuría, Boolean Algebra, because it's the mathematics of logic, is entirely a design and analysis tool. I've used it only to analyze Liberation Theology, and I've identified why it won't work. It's got a negative sign in it. Anything you do with that negative sign, will negate your desired outcome."

Sánchez decided that it was time to cheer the priests up. "But there's some good news, Father Ellacuría: your true specialty—education—has no negative sign. It's all positive. Which only goes to show that your decision to give up education in favor of violent liberation was... illogical."

Segundo Montes seemed receptive to his words, but they bounced right off of Ellacuría. The Basque Jesuit was sick and tired of so much logic from a goddamn *chafa indio*! So he spat at Sánchez:

"Look, Captain, there's far more at play than what can be represented in a couple of two-variable equations. We Jesuits analyze multiple variables, all with positive signs, which lead to superior results. You're just going to have to take my word for it, because you are completely incapable of understanding them."

The Captain let the insult bounce off of him. "Fine, but let me tell you what I do understand, priest: Liberation Theology is the instrument to justify the imposition of a dictatorship via armed struggle. Once such dictatorship is imposed, the dictators will do what they do best: perpetuate themselves in power, by eliminating all real and perceived opposition. By doing so, they cause widespread misery and hunger, because they invariably eliminate those who do know how to make the means of production produce and replace them with those who don't. That is exactly what's happened in Cuba under Castro, but for some reason, you've turned a blind eye to that.

"But you can't turn a blind eye to what happened last week. On November 9, 1989, when the widespread misery and poverty was too much to bear, people behind the Iron Curtain, tired of making long lines to obtain a loaf of bread or a gallon of milk of bad quality, attacked the Berlin Wall, the symbol of the dictatorship. These people did so because they had nothing to lose—except for their miserable lives. The surprising part was that the guards joined them, instead of shooting them. And the Berlin Wall fell.

"You have to realize that it was a communist dictatorship in a country with 8.65 million square miles of gold, silver, minerals, oil and other resources, and that wasn't enough to prevent the widespread misery and huger of socialism from gripping the Soviet Union and the Iron Curtain countries.

"Therefore, priests, knowing full well that the path that you have set for this country is going to end exactly the same way, for exactly the same reasons, the question I have is this: Why do you want to inflict upon the people that you claim to want to help, a misery that is far greater than the one they already have?"

Ellacuría, having had enough of these lectures from this intellectual inferior, only repeated: "You're just not capable of understanding these things, Captain."

Sánchez saw exposed flanks. His eyes lit up. He began his attack with: "Is it because you think I'm dumb?"

In response, Ellacuría looked at him as condescendingly as he could, and shrugged, as if saying, 'If the shoe fits, wear it.'"

Sánchez smiled. "Let me tell you how wrong you are, priest. You see, I had to write a thesis. One of my professors, Dr. John Navratil, suggested that I do research on Voice Recognition, which was of interest because it would enable people who are paraplegic to be able to use a computer by using their voice, instead of the keyboard that such people are incapable of using. It wasn't anything that Professor Navratil had ever done any work on. You see, in 1981, the field was very new."

Ellacuría smug countenance didn't change. He didn't give a damn what this *indio*, or any *indio*, studied or wrote. The Captain continued. "I ended up writing my thesis on 'Fast Fourier Transforms for Voice-Recognition

Systems,' with John Navratil as my thesis sponsor, which was judged by a panel of professors to be well-researched, original and valid, and qualified me to get my master's degree."

Ellacuría couldn't have cared less. The Captain pressed on. "Does that make me smart? Not necessarily. But it definitely doesn't make me dumb. Because dumb would've been to lack the brains to do my own research and propose an original solution, right?"

Ellacuría's look of contempt began to morph into a mask of anger. He realized where this was heading. The Captain continued. "Had I been dumb, I wouldn't have had the brains to do anything besides take my professor's work and praise it, am I right?"

Ellacuría's lower lip started to tremble. The Captain had him in his sights and started to squeeze the trigger. "That's something that I couldn't have done at the University I went to. I would've never been able to write a thesis like: 'The Accuracy of the Circuits of John Navratil,' because that would've constituted fraud. Not only would they have labeled me a fraud and intellectually-lacking, they would've labeled my professor and the entire university the same way, wouldn't you agree?"

Ellacuría's countenance went from angry to volcanic. How dare this *indio* make fun of his marvelous thesis, 'The Primariness of the Essence in Xavier Zubiri,' with the great Xavier Zubiri being his thesis sponsor? He couldn't hold back: he let go with a slew of Basque curse words!

The Captain had one more round in his chamber: "Look, priest, I don't understand Basque, but you'd better not be calling me dumb, because it wasn't me who had kiss his professor's ass to get a degree!"

Montes intervened. "Captain, you haven't read his thesis, you can't judge."

"I don't really have to read it, do I, Montes? The 'great revolutionary,' the 'intellectual genius' that everybody says he is, had to write a tribute to this thesis sponsor to get his doctorate? I'd be ashamed of that... wouldn't you?"

And with that, the Captain left them. He didn't want to be the cause of the priest having a stroke. That would be self-defeating.

He was here to protect Ellacuría, not kill him.

CHAPTER 38

ROMERISMO

After the heated discussion with Ellacuría, Sánchez did his rounds and then decided to rest in a hammock in a house where two of his soldiers were posted. One of them, Corporal Alvarado, happened to be writing a letter.

"Is that letter to your girlfriend, Alvarado?"

Corporal Alvarado started to stand at attention to respond, but the Captain told him to sit down and remain at ease.

"No sir, it's to my parents in Ciudad Barrios, San Miguel."

"You're from all the way over there?"

"Yes, sir, from the city where Monsignor Romero was born."

"Really? They must've loved him over there."

"Oh yes, sir! He was a hero. He was beloved. And he wasn't a communist, I assure you!"

The Captain nodded in agreement. "You're right about that, Alvarado. He certainly wasn't!" But Sánchez still couldn't explain that last sermon he gave. That was so uncharacteristic of him.

Sánchez recalled what he'd learned about Monsignor Romero and his beliefs, which Sánchez liked to call *Romerismo.*

Oscar Arnulfo Romero was born on August 15, 1917, in Ciudad Barrios, San Miguel. He entered the priesthood as a way to achieve upward mobility, which was as scarce back then as it is today in El Salvador.

He didn't finish his studies in the national seminary in San Salvador because he was sent to complete his studies at the Gregorian University in Rome, receiving his Licentiate in Theology *cum laude* in 1941, but wasn't ordained until a year later when he achieved the age for ordination. Nevertheless, he immediately began studying toward a doctoral degree in Ascetical Theology, which is the organized study or presentation of spiritual teachings found in Christian Scripture, to help the faithful more perfectly follow Christ to Christian Perfection. Said another way, Ascetical Theology encouraged Christians to act according to the New Testament, according to the Sermon on the Mount, the pillars of which included Beatitudes such as: 'Blessed are the poor in spirit, for theirs is the Kingdom of Heaven.'

Romero's theology was precisely what the Modernist movement, headed by Teilhard de Chardin, Lubac and the entire Society of Jesus, was trying to do away with.

Shortly before finishing his doctorate, Romero was called back to El Salvador by his Archbishop, where he became parish priest for the town of Anamorós, in the easternmost Salvadoran department of La Unión. He was then transferred to the city of San Miguel, where he remained for over 20 years.

Oscar Romero wasn't even in San Salvador when the takeover of the Church in Europe by the Modernists was taking place. He was out in eastern El Salvador organizing support for 'Our Lady of Peace,' and establishing Alcoholics Anonymous groups. Romero was never exposed to Teilhard de Chardin, Henri de Lubac, or even Karl Rahner when they were at their peak of influence. He remained a Thomist all his life.

In 1966, he became the director of the newspaper of the San Salvador Archdiocese *Orientación* [Guidance], which defended the traditional 'Magisterium' of the Catholic Church while he was its editor. In 1970, Romero was appointed auxiliary bishop for the Archdiocese of San Salvador, a bureaucratic, non-influential position. In 1974, he was appointed Bishop of the Diocese of Santiago de María, a poor rural town in the eastern province of Usulután.

While Romero was in Usulután, the influx of 'modernist' priests and nuns into El Salvador, trained by Jesuits, continued. Only now, after the publication of the book "A Theology of Liberation," by the Peruvian priest Gustavo Gutiérrez, they called themselves Liberation Theologians. The result of this was that most of the parishes in El Salvador began to be headed by the new Liberation Theology priests.

So it came as a shock for the Jesuits and most of the religious corps of El Salvador when somebody who was not one of them, a conservative like Romero, was appointed Archbishop of San Salvador in 1977.

And that's when Romero first came face to face with his ecclesiastical nemeses, the Liberation Theology Jesuits.

Understanding that he was the leader of the Catholic Church of El Salvador as it was constituted at that time, and that the Jesuits had in fact molded the next generation of priests and nuns that he was appointed to lead, he developed his *Romerismo*, which consisted of staying true to his Thomist theology, while bending where he could to accommodate his liberationist flock in their call for social justice. His *Romerismo* was to Liberation Theology the foil that *Majanismo* was to *Comunismo.*

Certain events tested him early, like the murder of his friend the Jesuit Rutilio Grande barely one month after his appointment. His liberationist flock, headed by the Jesuits, immediately demanded that he blame the Government. But the Government of his friend, Col. Arturo Armando Molina, immediately denied that it was a government action, both publicly and privately, and then proclaimed that the Government would do whatever it could to bring the perpetrators of the crime to justice. Nobody was every captured, though.

These assurances allowed Romero to continue with his middle of the road path. Yes, he wanted social justice, but he didn't want to supplant the rule of law with the rule of the gun, which was what Castro had done in Cuba. He wanted to improve the laws to promote social justice. Like Majanismo, Romero wanted to achieve the Church's goals legally.

The Archbishop held the moral high ground over his nemeses by being the sole ecclesiastical voice in El Salvador who condemned the heinous murders and kidnappings committed by the nascent guerrillas, something the liberationists refused to do. The only member of the Church to ever try to mediate for the victims of kidnappings was Archbishop Romero and nobody else; certainly not the Jesuits.

But with the revolutionary fervor reaching a crescendo after his friend President Molina left office, *Romerismo* was going to need some help, especially in light of the ineptitude of Molina's successor, General Carlos Romero, and in light of the Sandinista victory in Nicaragua in July 1979.

That help came on October 15, 1979, in the form of the proclamation of the Revolutionary Junta, which brought forth *Majanismo*, which was exactly what Romero needed to follow his non-revolutionary path.

Years after he'd left the Junta, Majano would tell people that Archbishop Romero had been one of the greatest supporters of the coup of October 15, 1979.

Chapter 39

Forsaken

“Damn! How the hell did Ungo and Román accept to become part of the Junta?” Ellacuría was livid. Things were going so well for the movement in El Salvador after the fall of Somoza in Nicaragua, but now this coup d’état by the Salvadoran 'Military Youth' had blown the rails off the tracks of the revolutionary train that had been gathering steam.

Segundo Montes, as usual, tried to exert a calming influence. “Father, Román will be representing us as the current dean of the UCA.” Román Mayorga was a gifted Salvadoran, a graduate of the prestigious Massachusetts Institute of Technology, M.I.T.

“But why didn’t Román tell us anything?”

“Father Ellacuría, this had to be done in secrecy, and I’m sure the coup was sprung before Román could tell us anything, and since the Archbishop was involved, why wouldn’t he believe that it had our blessing as well?”

Ellacuría exploded. “Because we don’t need any damn junta! The Nicaraguan Jesuits never needed a junta to gain power! Had Ungo and Román refused, it would’ve just been a change from one military dictator to another, who would’ve been just as easy to overthrow as Somoza was. But they accepted? My Lord, my Lord, why hast thou forsaken me?”

Segundo wanted to laugh. It was comical to invoke the words of Jesus Christ as He was dying on the cross when Ellacuría lived comfortably in a splendid Jesuit Residence in San Salvador, served like a king, and having his every word obeyed, all while being invulnerable to the forces he had helped to unleash.

But the powers that be had installed Ellacuría as the leader of this revolution, and therefore his superior, and he would treat him with the respect that he would otherwise not command.

“Father, let’s look at the bright side, shall we?”

“What bright side, Montes? Why, the Archbishop of San Salvador himself, Monsignor Romero, has blessed this coup and its Junta! I always knew Romero would be trouble. Had Rivera y Damas been appointed

Archbishop, instead of Romero, we'd have been the first to install a Revolutionary Government in Central America. But Rivera y Damas only got appointed Auxiliary Archbishop, and now we're further away than ever!"

Ellacuría had lost his cool in his normally grandiose way. But Montes had enough cool for the both of them. "Father, they have to produce. They've set lofty goals for themselves that aren't easily attainable. If they fail, it'll be like rolling out the red carpet for the Revolution."

That mollified Ellacuría somewhat. Montes did have a point. Implementing an Agrarian Reform against the Fourteen was easier said than done. They would put up a fight that they could win. Especially if the revolutionary forces opposed the Agrarian Reform as well. In that case, the new Junta would fail and fail miserably, thereby proving to the world that the only way to transfer land to the peasants, was through a bona fide armed revolution, like Nicaragua's.

Suddenly, Ellacuría felt better. "The first thing we need to do, Montes, is to make sure that Ungo and Román are aware that the announced Agrarian Reform must never be allowed to go forward."

Montes disagreed. "Father, wouldn't it be wiser to make sure Román Mayorga understands your goals first? As Dean of the UCA, whenever he speaks to the other Junta members, his words will carry our weight."

"Fine, you talk to Mayorga, and I'll talk to Romero."

"Father, given the situation, don't you think it would be best if we both talked to them? That way, there can be no doubt as to our stance, our message."

Ellacuría had calmed down enough to see the validity of Montes' point. This warranted some serious thinking. And wasn't he a great thinker?

But the next day, Ellacuría went to see Monsignor Romero alone.

His secretary announced him. "Monsignor, Father Ellacuría is here."

"Let him in."

Tall and lanky Ignacio Ellacuría walked in, looking a little bit off-kilter.

"Monsignor, there's been a coup!"

"So I hear. That's a good thing, no?"

Ellacuría towered over the diminutive archbishop. "No, it's not. It's nothing but a trick to deceive the people into believing that there's another way forward when there is none."

The Archbishop of San Salvador disliked being talked down to, literally. "Father, please sit down."

"I don't have time to sit down, Monsignor. And neither do you, you must..."

"I must do nothing, Father. Now, you will either sit down and calm down, or you will come back when you're less agitated."

Father Ellacuría sat down, fuming inside because he had to obey this *indio*. But he willed himself to calm down. There was an overriding goal to which his personal sentiments needed to subordinate themselves.

"Monsignor, I'm sorry, but this sets us back."

"Sets who back?"

"The revolutionary movement."

"You mean the violent takeover of power and the mass executions like the Sandinistas have been doing for the past 4 months?"

"I don't know what you've been hearing, but things are going very well in Nicaragua."

"Not for the poor souls who are being executed, by order of the Jesuits."

"They were members of the oppressive Somoza regime, Monsignor."

"They were poor people who had to earn a living somehow, and military service offered them a way out of misery, which, by the way, occurs the world over. I would've thought that a Jesuit-led revolution would've minimized bloodshed. I guess not."

"Monsignor, I can assure you that we'll learn from the Sandinista experience, and make things better here."

"Father Ellacuría, fortunately for us, Salvadorans have learned from the Sandinista experience already. That's why this coup was led by a military man, Colonel Adolfo Majano, a man of very humble origins, who also believes that there's a better way than the Cuban way of doing things."

"But they're lying when they promise a better way!"

"Father Ellacuría, they promise Agrarian Reform. That's huge! That means that the military, by law, will dispossess the Fourteen of their huge tracts of land and distribute them to the peasants. How can you expect me to oppose achieving the goal we all seek, without bloodshed?"

Ellacuría could barely contain his anger. But he somehow did. "Monsignor, you can't believe that this Junta is going to achieve that, do you? Colonel Majano may have the benefit of the poor in mind, but the other Colonel, Abdul Gutiérrez, is said to be right-wing."

Romero had to laugh. "Does the name *Abdul* sound like a *Fourteen* name? I don't think so. He's also a man of humble origins. But let's assume that he is indeed right-wing: he can't be that right-wing, can he? I mean, didn't he just overthrow a right-wing despot and invite Ungo and Mayorga to co-govern with him and Majano?"

To this Ellacuría had no response.

Monsignor continued. "But what should really put your mind at ease is that the five-member junta has a left-wing majority. So the revolutionary left has achieved more power than it ever had, thanks to the military, and without shedding any blood."

He let this sink in.

"I want to remind you of something, Father Ellacuría. His Holiness, Pope John Paul II, your boss and mine, instructed me to act with prudence when I visited him last May. Let's exercise prudence, you and I, because if with the intent of helping the poor, we fan the flames of violence, only the poor will die. Or do you think the rich will hang around to fight?"

In the absence of a response, Monsignor asked, "So tell me again why we shouldn't give the Junta a chance?"

A few minutes later Ellacuría was leaving the Archbishop's office. It was obvious that this coup was a setback, especially because it had given the Archbishop a reason to return to his conservative, pacifist roots. That was a problem for which they would have to find a solution.

Chapter 40

Ayatollahed

Guillermo Manuel Ungo, the most left-wing member of the Junta, had convened an emergency meeting of the yet-to-be-unified revolutionary groups for the night of November 10, 1979 at the Externado de San José. In attendance were Commander Marcial and other guerrilla commanders, Leoncio Pichinte and other leaders of the Popular Organizations, Ignacio Ellacuría and Segundo Montes. Ungo had phoned in, at the eleventh hour, asking them to start without him, because he'd be late.

Things weren't going as planned for the Revolution. The Junta was saying all the right things, and the impetus that had been building before October 15, 1979, had turned into a general wait-and-see attitude by the population.

Segundo Montes was the first to speak, to greet the audience and to inform them that Ungo would be late because of pressing official matters.

Marcial asked to speak. He informed the gathering that recruitment had gone down, because of the willingness of the population to give the Junta a chance, and that this was a problem. With the Sandinistas sending them weapons, the guerrillas had what to go to war with, but not whom.

Then Ellacuría stood up and said, "Since we're all gathered here, and while we wait for the arrival of Mr. Ungo, I'd like to take advantage of the opportunity to present a plan that is being developed in conjunction with the Sandinistas. Please take note of the action items that apply to each of you.

"Number 1. Cuban communications experts in Nicaragua are setting up an AM radio station in Managua, with enough power to be heard all over El Salvador.

"Number 2. Its programming will be designed to a) instill a revolutionary fervor in the listeners, and b) ridicule and expose the Salvadoran government and military. We'll call this station: Radio *Venceremos* [We Will Win].

"Number 3. Cuban advisors will train Marcial's personnel to configure local repeaters to retransmit the AM signal to FM, from elevations that we control." Marcial took note of this action item that he'd have to act on.

"Number 4. The Popular Organizations need to nominate people who will be traveling to Nicaragua to get trained by Cuban advisors to develop the daily programming for Radio *Venceremos*. Please note that the Radio Venceremos team will end up operating out of Managua." The Popular Organization representatives there took note of this action item.

Just then Guillermo Ungo arrived, signaling that Father Ellacuría should continue.

"Number 5. Father Fernando Cardenal, the Jesuit Sandinista leader, has pledged to place his vast foreign press network at our disposal, so the press covers us like it covered them: we can do no wrong, and our enemies can do no right."

Everybody nodded their approval. They were glad that the Jesuits were taking care of things internationally.

"Number 6. Messrs. Ungo and Mayorga must resign from the Junta to prevent the implementation of the Agrarian Reform."

When Segundo Montes heard this, he shook his head and thought, "Ignacio... why are you jumping the gun like this?" Had Montes known that he was going to include this sixth point, he would've attempted to dissuade him. Because it would come across as arrogant and meddlesome.

But it was hard to dissuade someone who thinks he knows everything.

Guillermo Manuel Ungo immediately stood up and took the microphone from Father Ellacuría, thanking him for his intervention. Ungo had been Napoleón Duarte's running mate for the 1972 election that they had won, but which had been stolen from them. After the failed coup to rectify the fraud, Duarte left for Venezuela but Ungo hung around.

The veteran Ungo said, "No, comrades, we must not resign. The problem with us resigning is that we've heard that Napoleón Duarte, the winner of the 1972 presidential election, is coming back to the country from his exile in Venezuela. He was always a proponent of the Agrarian Reform, and the moment we leave the Junta, Colonels Majano and Gutiérrez will no doubt call him and some other center-left member to take our place. And the Agrarian Reform will start immediately. That's precisely what we don't want."

He paused to see if anybody would comment. In the absence of comments, he went on. "The other advantage to our staying in the Junta is this: a large part of the Armed Forces is very pro-democracy, but there are still a substantial number of right-wingers who do not want to cede power to civilians and who want to preserve the status quo. I'm talking about the Security Forces. And this is only natural because most of the people who've died so far in this undeclared war have been National Guards, with their measly two-to-three men outposts in the towns out east and up north along the border with Honduras, which have been easy pickings for our forces. They're out for blood.

"And so our stay in the Junta can keep this Security Forces - Armed Forces schism alive because Mayorga and I are going to be able to accuse the Security Forces of killing several of our members in our marches, even though we know that they aren't the ones who start the shooting. Duarte, on the other hand, would not."

There was a murmur agreeing with Ungo. It was a tactic of the Popular Organizations to cause shootouts with the Security Forces who were standing buy, to then be able to accuse them of having fired first.

Ungo continued. "So I want to commend Father Ellacuría for his coordination with the Jesuit leaders of the Sandinista Revolution, but I'll be the one who determines what the best political course of action for our movement is."

Everybody nodded, but Ellacuría was incensed. Here was another *indio* who thought he was smarter than him! But he controlled himself.

Ungo went on. "So the Popular Organizations' marches are of utmost importance, to enable us to say that nothing's changed from the last regimen. I'm sorry to have to say this because we're causing the death of our own people, but we have no other way to vilify the Junta."

The representatives of the Popular Organizations nodded.

"We will resign when the time is right, and that will be when we can say to the world that, despite our best efforts, the colonels are too recalcitrant and right-wing to deal with. It wouldn't help our cause if we didn't give ourselves time to give our best efforts, would it?"

Everybody agreed.

Ungo then looked directly at Ellacuría, and then he said: "By then, hopefully, the Archbishop will have been convinced to stand squarely with us—that's the most important mission the Jesuits have."

Ellacuría felt humiliated. The nerve of these *indios*! But it wasn't a moment to argue, but rather, to collaborate. So he stood up and said, "Believe me, engineer Ungo, we're working on that. We are confident that sooner, rather than later, the Archbishop will be on our side, decisively. Our efforts include enlisting the help of our Jesuit brothers in Nicaragua to join our efforts in petitioning our international contacts and members of our order to exert pressure on the Archbishop, through letters and phone calls that urge him to decidedly stand on the side of the poor in all matters. And they've agreed to do so."

Ungo applauded this, and the audience joined in. But for some reason, Ellacuría felt more chagrined.

When the applause stopped, Ungo continued. Nobody had ever accused him of being brief. "If all these factors line up, we'll be doing our part to stop the Agrarian Reform, which is a top political priority. The others who will do their part to stop it will be the Fourteen, because they're going to be dispossessed. We're lucky that they've put a face on their movement: Major Roberto D'Aubuisson, someone who is an easy target, because he's a right-wing military man, even if he's now retired.

"So gentlemen, rest assured that, politically, we're doing everything we can to achieve the victory we all desire."

There was applause, but an applause by people who thought the speeches had concluded. But Ungo continued. "But the reason I called you here today is the following: everything we've talked about today becomes more urgent because last Sunday, November 4, 1979, the new government of Iran, led by a Muslim cleric, Ayatollah Khomeini, took 40 members of the US embassy in Iran as hostages. And throngs came out to shout 'Death to America.'"

A muted celebratory murmur arose from the audience. After all, the enemy of the enemy is a friend. But that was precisely what Ungo wanted to address: "Gentlemen, this isn't good for us. Our de facto ally, President Carter, is going to feel the heat from his political opponents, especially because he's up for re-election. They'll accuse him of losing Iran, losing Nicaragua, getting the hostages taken, and possibly the loss of El Salvador.

"Now then, the freedom of those hostages is not in his hands but preventing the loss of El Salvador is. And he's going to start sending the aid to the Junta that he refused to do so far."

He let his words sink in. Judging by the somber attitude of the audience, they did. He concluded with, "The longer this hostage situation continues, the more difficult it will be for the press to cover us, because the most interesting story will be on the other side of the world. So it is more urgent than ever for us to double our efforts, especially the marches, and to get Monsignor Romero to get full square behind our cause. Thank you."

There was applause, but not enthusiastic, just realistic. A chastened Father Ellacuría took the microphone only to adjourn the meeting. Ungo may be an *indio*, but he was right: they'd just been Ayatollahed, and only he'd been smart enough to figure it out.

Perhaps it wasn't too late to take Father Elizondo's advice on humility from years ago.

Chapter 41

The Immovable Object

"... the Junta's armed forces have massacred peasants in Guazapa and Ayutuxtepeque, mowing down peaceful demonstrators who only asked for higher salary, better education, better healthcare, and an immediate and fair agrarian reform, which was nothing but what the murderous Junta had promised when it usurped power from the butcher General Romero..."

"I don't want to listen to that anymore, Father Ellacuría. Turn it off."

Father Ellacuría turned off YSAX, the Archdiocese radio station, which was retransmitting what was being fed to them by the Radio *Venceremos* team, the antenna for which was not yet operational, even though the programming team was. Letting their programming team use YSAX was one of the Archbishop's concession to his Marxist flock.

Ellacuría earnestly said, "Your Eminence, those things are indeed happening. The enemy only put on a nicer, softer mask, but they're the same bunch of butchers that the previous military government was."

The Archbishop was not buying it. "Well, the other side of that story is that the marchers were armed, and my question is, why?"

"Armed? Only with signs!" said the Jesuit, grateful that Pinocchio was just a fairy tale.

"Father Ellacuría, I'm sick and tired of getting propaganda from you, too! From you, I expect the truth!"

"He's telling you the truth, your Eminence," said the Auxiliary Archbishop, Arturo Rivera y Damas, who was far more in tune with the Jesuits than the Archbishop was. Everybody knew that the Revolution would be much further along if Rivera y Damas were the Archbishop, and not Romero.

Rivera y Damas continued. "All they were doing was exercising their right to demand the Agrarian Reform that was promised. And the Security Forces started shooting at them. They're nothing but butchers!"

The Archbishop looked at his subordinate in exasperation. It was obvious that the Jesuits were getting to him.

Father Ellacuría pressed on. "Your Eminence, what we've been telling you has also been appearing in the international press. The radio isn't inventing this."

Monsignor Romero sighed and looked at them with a sad smile. "Gentlemen... I implore you. Stop trying to feed me falsehoods. I don't see San Salvador crawling with foreign reporters. They're covering the Iran hostage crisis and the Sandinista Revolution. Even little old me can figure out that the foreign press is only repeating what's being fed to them by the guerrilla's propaganda team."

He paused, trying to find the right words to strike the right balance, which had been his trademark all his life.

"I understand that the priests and nuns of this nation, who work directly with the poor, are all for the poor. I understand that they're the body and soul of the Catholic Church in El Salvador, which I've been charged to lead. But I am the head. I have to use reason, not just my heart. I will act forcefully if I see that the Junta isn't working toward the Agrarian Reform. If all of a sudden, the Popular Organizations aren't represented, I'll be the first to represent them. That hasn't happened yet."

The two prelates were about to say something when Monsignor Romero raised his hand to stop them. "Gentlemen, don't we want peace in this land? Don't we want to avoid more deaths? As men of the cloth, shouldn't this be our overriding goal? But we won't be able to achieve peace here if all we do is to demand that only one side stop shooting, right?"

Then the diminutive Archbishop stood up and spoke with an authority that made him seem ten feet tall and silenced any further debate. "This may not be in the news, but nevertheless, it is a fact: all the popular organizations have their own small armies, who accompany them on the marches—the Communist Party has the *Fuerzas Populares de Liberación* [Popular Liberation Forces] - FPL; the National Resistance has the *Fuerzas Armadas de la Resistancia Nacional* [National Resistance Armed Forces] – FARN, etc.

"Now then, gentlemen, I may be an *indio,* short and malnourished, not tall and European-looking like you two fine fellows, but you can't feed me the complete nonsense that these groups go out on the streets with their armed people and that they have nothing to do with the violence that always seems to be the result of those marches!

"And what should move us to disarm the Popular Organizations is that whoever is directing these marches, is intentionally sacrificing their own sympathizers!" The Archbishop's face was a combination of astonishment and incredulity.

He continued. "How is it that I'm the only one who sees this great betrayal of some poor peasants who are convinced to participate, promising them benefits if they do so... only to be turned into cannon fodder in a shootout that the same organizers of the march provoked! And then, all of a sudden, a family whose meager income depended on the work of the dead peasant, is left father-less and income-less!"

Neither of the two priests he was addressing seemed too heartbroken by it.

The Archbishop concluded with, "Therefore, my office, the Office of the Archbishop of San Salvador, demands that as long as there is a Revolutionary Junta that is taking the necessary steps to peacefully take land from the rich and give it to the people, that these groups put away their weapons. Am I clear?"

Ellacuría nodded, thinking to himself, "As clear as an obstacle can be."

Chapter 42

Honor Where Honor Is Due

On December 28, 1979, the First Revolutionary Junta was dissolved, with the resignation of Guillermo Manuel Ungo, Román Mayorga Quirós and the representative of the private sector, Mario Andino. They were replaced by José Antonio Morales Ehrlich, of the Christian Democratic Party (PDC—the party headed by Napoleón Duarte), by Héctor Dada Hirezi, who had been Minister of Foreign Relations during the First Junta, and by Ramón Avalos Navarrete, a physician without political affiliations. The three new members, plus the two original colonels, formed the Second Revolutionary Junta.

As far as the Archbishop was concerned, the Popular Organizations were no longer represented in the Junta, and therefore, true to his word, the Archbishop assumed their representation, which began to be exerted in his homilies, in which he pressed the new Junta to keep its word to the people.

Although that constituted a deviation from his middle of the road path, it wasn't enough for the Jesuits and the liberationists. Rivera y Damas would remind him, every chance he could, that the priests and nuns under him were getting restless.

Monsignor Romero had learned to take whatever his Auxiliary Archbishop said with a grain of salt. Moreover, he no longer got upset at him whenever he opened his mouth, because he was only repeating what the Jesuits had told him, and it was better to hear it from him than from the insufferable Ellacuría.

Moreover, Monsignor had enough friends among the priests and nuns to know he enjoyed enough support among his subordinates, who, like him, also believed that the Agrarian Reform was going to occur.

Besides, Majano continued to lead the Junta, and he'd invited members of the PDC, the party founded by Napoleón Duarte, a true center-left leader who was a graduate of the University of Notre Dame, to join the Junta.

Finally, Col. Majano had managed to rein in the right-wing factions of the Armed Forces and therefore, he deserved all his support.

But other voices were more strident. And the Archbishop was receiving a huge influx of letters from foreign ecclesiastical authorities urging him to be more forceful with the Junta.

He stuck to his instincts. As interim representative of the Popular Organizations, he would bend to the left, but not that far: not more than one standard deviation from the norm, statistically-speaking. After all, the Second Junta was focused on the Agrarian Reform and on the nationalization of the banks and the coffee trade. It was gunning for the source of power of the rich. Majano had personally told him that everybody was aware of its importance. He'd also promised him that the Security Forces would do whatever they could to avoid having to fire upon demonstrators, even if they fired. All Romero had told him as that the Reform needed to be done sooner than later.

In mid-January, Monsignor Romero got an invitation to travel to Belgium, to receive an Honorary Doctorate Degree for his work for the poor from the Catholic University of Leuven. He was surprised by this, but the Jesuits weren't: they'd been lobbying their network to pressure Romero to join them in the revolution. And this helped their cause.

The Archbishop wasn't comfortable with this because he didn't think he'd done a whole lot for the poor, certainly not more than any other priest. He did some research to see who else had gotten this honorary degree from that university.

He found that another Honorary Doctorate Degree recipient was Nadine Gordimer, an anti-apartheid writer, but who identified herself as an atheist. An atheist?

Other honorary degree recipients granted by that university were two kings of Belgium. The Archbishop wasn't impressed. Number one: What has any King of Belgium done for mankind, ever? And number two: they could've very well been buttering the kings up for some infusion of cash. Pure and simple ass-kissing.

The other honorary degree recipient was Eugène Ionesco, a playwright who was half French and half Romanian and who wrote plays that harp on the insignificance of human existence.

It seemed incongruent to the Archbishop that he was being honored for his work for the poor, by a University that had honored Ionesco, someone who had values that were in opposition to his. If human existence was significant, why fight to improve it?

Perhaps he was being too picky? "Come on, Oscar, they're honoring you!" he said to himself.

"But this University will honor any Tom, Dick and Harry," he replied to himself.

"But you got called back to El Salvador before you completed your doctorate! Don't you want the doctorate you deserve?" he insisted.

"I do," he replied to himself

There was nobody more insistent to get him to accept the honorary degree than Father Ellacuría. "Your Eminence, this is quite an honor! They are recognizing you to be a Church Leader who is fighting for the poor in El Salvador!"

Monsignor Romero replied, with his typical calm, "There are others who are far worthier than me, who ought to get honored instead."

When Ellacuría heard this, his first thought was, "He's going to mention me! And for the first time in his life, he'd be right!" He swelled up with pride.

Monsignor Romero then said, "Colonel Arturo Armando Molina had a policy of building one school per week when he was President. That man did more to help the poor, through education, than any other President in our history."

Ellacuría started coughing.

"Is something wrong, Father?" The Archbishop called his secretary over. "Please bring Father Ellacuría some water."

"No, I'm fine. I'm fine." But he took the glass of water anyway, downing it all in a few gulps.

Monsignor Romero continued. "Another person who is worthier than me is Mr. Teófilo Simán, the founder of the Simán Corporation, who takes a huge chunk of his annual profits and spends it on educating the poor."

Father Ellacuría couldn't believe his ears. "Monsignor, you've nominated a military goon and an oligarch. Why on earth?"

Monsignor Romero shook his head. "Father Ellacuría, both these persons have done more for the poor than you and I have. Isn't the only way to help the poor, to educate them and give them the necessary skills to get them out of poverty?"

Monsignor observed how upset Ellacuría was getting. He didn't care. "I'm not rich, Father Ellacuría. I wish I were so I could do what Mr. Simán is doing. Let me tell you why. Because when the Simán family came from Palestine, they had nothing but the clothes on their back and the desire to work. And they worked hard and created wealth. And now they share part of that wealth with the poor. They give back to the community. Please tell me what part of this story is objectionable, from your standpoint?"

Ellacuría icily said, "Monsignor Romero, since Vatican II, the teachings of the Church have been to emphasize action rather than faith. It is clearly stated in *Lumen Gentium*, the Summary of Vatican II, which was signed by all the Bishops and the Pope. So that is the official policy of the Catholic Church to which you belong. You mention Mr. Simán, and I don't dispute that he's a charitable man, but we need more than charity. He helps maybe a thousand poor, but we have millions of poor. What about those other millions of poor? We need to take action!"

Monsignor Romero corrected him immediately but with a beatific smile. "Father, that's not the official policy of the Church. What you just quoted to me is not *Lumen Gentium*, it is Liberation Theology." He summoned his secretary again. "Mercedes, please bring Father Ellacuría my copy of *Lumen Gentium*, he's going to take it with him today, to study."

Father Ellacuría sat stone faced, but inside he was seething. How dare this *indio* purport to lecture him? Vatican II paved the way for Liberation Theology. He ought to know better. But he said nothing. He just thanked the secretary when she gave him the document.

Monsignor Romero continued. "As far as taking action through any means necessary, Father Ellacuría, that's not what our Lord Jesus Christ advocated in the Beatitudes is it? Since it's not in Scripture, then it's not Christian, and I am under no obligation to follow or advocate that.

"But since you bring it up, let's examine why Jesus never advocated the satisfaction of needs here on earth. What actions could a blind person in Jesus' time take to recover his or her sight? None. How about in our time? None as well. Where will that person achieve eyesight? According to Jesus, he'll find it in Heaven.

"What your Liberation Theology is telling handicapped people is, don't pay attention to what that Jesus fellow said. Ignore the Beatitudes. Take any action, even violent action, to get what you need now. Oh, you're blind? Tough luck, kiddo.

"That's quite callous, isn't it? But more importantly, that's not Christian or Christ-like."

But Ellacuría was faithful to action, not faith. "Monsignor, we need to take action against a system that is unjust!"

"Certainly, Father Ellacuría, but you keep advocating means that aren't what Christ advocated. In Jesus' time, Israel was subjugated by Rome. Did Jesus become 'Ché' Jesus and start killing Romans? Not at all. He even let himself get captured, tortured and murdered to prove to us that there was a better life after this one. So he didn't advocate what you advocate either by action or by word."

Ellacuría started to say something but Monsignor cut him off. "Father Ellacuría. I may still end up going to that University to receive that Honorary Degree, but only because it may help put pressure on the Junta to expedite the Agrarian Reform. But if I go, I want you to promise me one thing. If the Junta passes the Agrarian Reform, you and all the Jesuits will endorse it, and you will publicly call for the Popular Organizations and their little armies to incorporate themselves into the political process as a political party."

"Why would I do that, Monsignor?"

"Because the Junta will have achieved without bloodshed, what you wanted to achieve with bloodshed."

Ellacuría stood up and bid the Archbishop good-bye. He didn't even take *Lumen Gentium* with him.

Monsignor Romero did travel to Belgium. He received his honorary degree on February 2, 1980, and in his acceptance speech, he said, "The world of the poor teaches us that the sublimeness of Christian love must go through the imperious need for justice for the majorities and must not avoid honest struggle."

Chapter 43

The Irresistible Force

Ellacuría threw the paper down and looked at Rivera y Damas in exasperation. "'Honest struggle,' Arturo? What does 'honest' mean to him, go to court? Litigate? What on earth prevented him from taking a more militant stance? After all we've told him? After all we've shown him?"

Arturo Rivera y Damas replied, "Ignacio, the man is almost 62. All his life he's been conservative. He's too old to change. It'll take a far greater effort and far more time to convince him thoroughly."

Ignacio didn't hesitate to render a verdict. "We don't have that time, Arturo. Monsignor Romero's no revolutionary. But you are."

Rivera y Damas acted surprised. But he knew where this was leading: to a promotion! So he played along, saying, "I'm a liberationist, Ignacio. The Salvadoran rich won't cede anything, it'll have to be taken from them. If the Agrarian Reform was meant to be, it would've already happened. What's to stop the military from invading a property and forcibly handing over the land to the peasants? Only the rich. We're the ones who are going to have to take it from them by force."

Ellacuría was happy to have him as an ally. So he didn't hesitate to ask him, "How do you propose that we handle Romero, then?"

Rivera y Damas had already thought about this. "Write a letter for him. Addressed to the President of the United States. I'll convince him to sign it. The goal is to ask the President to stop sending military aid to the Junta."

Ignacio liked the idea. "Ok, I'll do that, but I'll also write a homily for him. A firebrand homily. And I need you to convince him to read it in mass."

"Why do you want to do that? Let's nudge him one step at a time."

Ellacuría stood up. "Because can't wait anymore, Arturo. Monsignor Romero has never been right for the movement. We need a man like you as Archbishop. You know why? Because El Salvador is too small to effectively hide a revolutionary army. We're going to need every church in the nation to shelter revolutionaries and only the Archbishop can give that order. Do you honestly think Monsignor Romero would do that?"

Rivera y Damas was sure that he wouldn't. But there was one slight problem: "But for me to become Archbishop, he'd have to resign, or die."

"My friend, all we have to do is have him read the *Homily of Fire* that I'll write, and the death squads will do the rest."

Rivera was not convinced. "What if they don't? He won't be the first priest to give a sermon against the military—they all do. And they've been doing so for several years now. The funny thing is that the military keep going to mass! It's like they don't realize we're preaching against them!"

Ellacuría grew impatient. "Is Romero an obstacle, yes or no?"

"Yes."

"Then the obstacle must be removed because this Revolution can't wait any further."

And with that, he walked out of Rivera y Damas' office.

After receiving his honorary doctorate degree in Belgium, Archbishop Romero traveled to Rome to visit Pope John Paul II. Again the Pope cautioned prudence because of what was going on in Nicaragua and urged Romero to give the Junta a chance.

As soon as Romero arrived in El Salvador, his Auxiliary Archbishop and the Jesuits received him with terrible news. All hell was breaking loose. The Security Forces and 'death squads' were murdering left and right, according to them.

Monsignor Romero shook his head, and said, incredulously, "I kept following the news in Europe, and I thought things were peaceful. The Pope even congratulated me on how things were better."

Rivera y Damas said, "Monsignor, Jimmy Carter is sending weapons to the military again. We have a letter addressed to him, for you to sign and send off immediately. Such aid needs to stop."

Romero read the letter. "Wait, Arturo, what's this about the Junta 'in general has only resorted to repressive violence producing dead and wounded in far greater amounts than past military regimes?' I can't sign this because it's not true!

"And then the letter says: 'If it's true that last November a group of six Americans was in El Salvador delivering 200,000 dollars' worth of gas masks and bullet-proof vests...' — I'm not going to put my signature on rumors!"

Rivera y Damas was insistent. "Monsignor, I urge you not to lose sight of the forest for the trees—the receipt of more weapons by the government will do nothing but increase the spilling of the blood of the poor that we seek to protect!" Rivera y Damas knew that his future depended on Monsignor signing this letter.

Monsignor Romero finally signed it and Rivera y Damas mailed it. Although he had doubts about the quality of the veracity of that letter, stopping the military aid to the government forces was the overriding concern. In the end, it was a concession to his liberationist flock. He had to stay on his tightrope, not fall off of it.

Then, on February 23, 1980, six days after he'd mailed the letter, the Christian Democrat who was the Attorney General under the Second Junta, Mario Zamora, was assassinated in his home by a 'death squad.'

Of course, the assassination was very high profile, and all the propaganda outlets for the left blamed the Security Forces, claiming that they didn't obey the Junta, and that the Junta really had no power and would not be allowed to carry out the Agrarian Reform. Which was what the letter to Jimmy Carter said, among other things.

Romero was under pressure to deliver a scathing homily in light of such a murder, for which purpose Rivera y Damas had given him the *Homily of Fire* written by Ellacuría. But Romero had doubts. Deep down, he doubted that such 'death squads' were Security Forces because Security Forces were clumsy. That's why they were easy pickings for the guerrillas up north and out east. Security forces were good only when they were the only ones who were armed.

The murderers of the Attorney General had gotten past his armed security without firing a shot, so as not to alert anybody inside. They'd entered his home, taken him from the living room to another room, shot him and left without a trace. Nobody in the Security Forces had that type of skill. So he seriously doubted that the men who entered the home of Zamora were Salvadoran Security Forces. Or even Salvadorans—this had every indication that it was an elite force with years of training, and the only elite forces in this part of the world were Cuban.

So the *Homily of Fire* remained stuck in a drawer.

Ellacuría wasn't happy. Rivera y Damas advised him to keep putting pressure on him from abroad, with letters and phone calls, etc.

In the meantime, the Popular Organizations were creating martyrs by sacrificing their own people in marches and takeover of private property, provoking firefights. The propaganda referred to the reaction of the Security Forces, when fired upon by the marchers, as 'repression.'

But Romero had as his ally his soul brother, colonel Majano. And Majano calmed the situation by inviting the maximum opposition leader in El Salvador, José Napoleón Duarte, to join the Junta and preside over it.

To date, this charismatic leader had only been working behind the scenes. But the man who'd first proposed the Agrarian Reform in the electoral campaign of 1972, had decided that if he didn't lead it, that it wasn't going to happen. And Majano, ever a good soldier of the motherland, recognized that his abilities had reached their limit, and for the good of the country, he handed real power over to Duarte.

Duarte was much loved, even within the Popular Organizations. The revolutionary fervor seemed to drop a notch, when he joined the Junta.

Every fiber in Romero's being said, "Give him a chance."

The Jesuits felt snakebitten. Things just weren't going their way.

And then, on top of that, on March 8, 1980, the Revolutionary Junta, with Napoleón Duarte as its member, approved the Agrarian Reform law and the Bank Nationalization law. That meant that not only were the peasants going to own their land, they were also going to get financing to work them. Monsignor Romero congratulated Duarte and the Junta.

Segundo Montes tried to calm the despondent Ellacuría. "Father Ellacuría, this can be interpreted another way: if there's anyone responsible for the Junta to act in favor of the people, it's you. Were it not for your tireless effort and pressure, throughout all these years, we wouldn't be on the verge of endowing the peasants with the land they till, and which is rightfully theirs, would we?"

But Ellacuría wasn't in the mood for praise because in his heart of hearts, he couldn't care less about the peasants. All he wanted was to gain power, like the Nicaraguan Jesuits had. But that wasn't something he could admit to anybody, much less Montes, who was too much of a goody two-shoes.

But just when Montes had begun to believe that Ellacuría wasn't going to be easy to get along with for the foreseeable future, the gods the Jesuits pray to came through for them. Jimmy Carter had responded to Romero's letter, but not in a formal letter signed by him, but through a telegram signed by Secretary of State, Cyrus Vance, dated March 10, 1980, which, among other things, stated: “We believe the Reform Program of the Revolutionary Junta of Government offers the best prospect for peaceful change toward a more just society. We, therefore, have responded to the Junta’s request for our assistance to help carry out its goals... We appreciate your warnings about the dangers of providing military assistance given the traditional role of the security forces in El Salvador. As we consider any request for such assistance, I can assure you that whatever military assistance may be provided will be directed at helping the Government to break with this tradition and to defend and carry forward its announced program of reform and development... Therefore, any equipment and training which we might provide would be designed to overcome the most serious deficiencies of the armed forces: enhancing their professionalism so that they can fulfill their essential role of maintaining order with a minimum of lethal force... I believe there is no real contradiction between proper law enforcement and respect for human rights... We hope you will agree that a less confrontational environment is necessary to implement the kind of meaningful reform program you have long advocated.... Sincerely, Cyrus Vance.”

Upon reading this measly telegram, signed by a Jimmy Carter subordinate, Archbishop Romero, the Honorary Doctor, felt slighted, disdained, and roundly rejected by Carter, who hadn’t even had the decency to reply to him personally, but rather through a Secretary. More importantly, Carter seemed to have abandoned his human rights policy and adopted the normal 'imperialist' US stance that all of Latin America resented. Including the Archbishop of San Salvador.

True to form, though, he didn’t rush into any decision. He pondered it for a few days. Finally, he called in Rivera y Damas and said, “Invite the Jesuits to have dinner with us this coming Saturday, March 22. Have *El Bodegón* prepare a banquet and bring it over. Also, have some Spanish wines and some *jerez* for them.”

He saw the surprise on Rivera y Damas’ face. Romero shrugged and said, “It’s time to join the Revolution, Arturo.”

Chapter 44

The Last Supper

"Gentlemen, as you know, I've bent over backwards to give the Junta a chance to come through with their promises. And I was counting on the active collaboration of the government of Jimmy Carter to pressure them to do so. But then I got this telegram from Cyrus Vance, in response to the letter requesting that the U.S. government stop providing military aid to the Junta."

Monsignor Romero handed then handed the telegram to Ellacuría, who merely glanced at it and passed it on to Montes. This surprised Romero, but that night was not to accentuate the negative; it was a night to seize what joined them and jettison what did not.

After all had read it, Ellacuría took another sip of his *Rioja* wine, before asking, "So Oscar"—not Your Eminence, or Monsignor, or Mr. Archbishop, but just 'Oscar'—I didn't think your ego was that fragile. What did you expect? An invitation to go to Washington D.C. with a red-carpet ceremony and a dinner at the White House?"

This gross lack of respect didn't go unperceived by Segundo Montes, who promptly tried to make the Archbishop forget Ellacuría's slight. "Your Eminence, what was it about the telegram that has prompted you to change your mind?"

Romero took a sip of the *Rioja*. He wanted to say to Ellacuría, "Yes, frankly, I did want to have a sit-down with the President of the United States, because so far, all he's done is listen to those who aren't representing the poor! I now have a Doctorate in helping the poor and they send me a telegram that essentially says, 'don't bother us, you're a nobody?'"

But instead of verbalizing all that, he said to Montes, "Father, there is nobody more qualified to speak for the poor, than the Salvadoran church. We tend to their needs every single day. They are the reason for our existence. It seems to me that Secretary Vance's telegram was saying, 'We believe Napoleon Duarte speaks for the poor better than you do; plus, he's got a shiny degree from the University of Notre Dame!'"

Rivera y Damas asked, "You're going to show Carter and Vance how wrong they are, am I right, Monsignor?"

He looked squarely at Rivera y Damas, somebody he also had to create stronger bonds with, and said, "Arturo, you saw me jump in to represent the Popular Organizations when Ungo left the Junta, because they no longer had a seat at the table. Well, from that telegram it seems to me that the poor of El Salvador no longer have a seat at the table with the United States, either, and we'll never get such a seat by playing nice, are we?"

"Hey, Oscar! You want to play nasty? Just read that homily I wrote for you. You'll get their attention then!" said Ellacuría, right before he downed his glass of *Rioja*.

Romero continued to take Ellacuría's lack of respect in stride. But Montes and Rivera y Damas were alarmed. The head of the Salvadoran Church was on the verge of coming over to their side, and Ellacuría was going to blow it?

Rivera y Damas got up, took the bottle of *Rioja*, and went around the table to pour some more wine in Ellacuría's glass. But he tripped and poured it all over Ellacuría instead. Ellacuría jumped up and went apoplectic, saying something in Basque that didn't sound too nice. Rivera y Damas asked him to forgive his clumsiness. Montes got up and escorted him to the bathroom.

There, he turned to Ellacuría and said, "Father, you're a great man. You're the leader of the Revolution in Central America, but you aren't thinking straight right now. You may despise Romero because he's thwarted our efforts so far, but if he's planning to come over to our side now, I beg you, don't give him any excuse to change his mind!"

Ellacuría kept trying to remove the excess wine with toilet paper.

Montes continued his pleading. "Father, please, don't worry about that. Fortunately, we wear black, and you can't even see it. Listen to me, please."

Ellacuría finished wiping himself. "You're right. You can't notice it." Then he turned to Montes and said, "OK, Montes, I hear you. I'll call him Monsignor for the rest of this night. Fortunately, I won't have to call him that ever again."

Montes was alarmed. "What do you mean?"

"It's too late, Montes. This guy may now be on our side, but he's never going to do for us what Rivera y Damas is prepared to do. We need to make Rivera y Damas the Archbishop."

"Yes, I agree that Rivera would be a better Archbishop for the cause. But you're not realizing the value of having Monsignor Romero, someone who was so obviously Pro-Junta, turn against them."

"I am, and that's why by the time we leave tonight, this guy will have agreed to read my *Homily of Fire*. That'll be my mission. After that, he's toast."

When the two Jesuits returned to the table, the famous *Bodegón Paella* was waiting for them.

Ellacuría turned on the charm. "Your Eminence, forgive me if I failed to show the proper respect before, but that's some powerful *Rioja* you ambushed us with. It even made Rivera trip."

Laughter all around. All was forgiven.

Ellacuría continued. "Your Eminence, you have always told both sides to lay down their arms, which is only fair, which is what the head of the Salvadoran church should do. But now, one side is not only not laying down their arms, they are arming themselves further, despite your timely request not to. In the Homily I wrote for you, I've given you the key to thwart this increase in weaponry. Not only will it do that, but it'll also place you at the forefront of the movement for the poor, which to date is a mantle that has undeservedly been assumed by others, while you gave the Junta a chance."

Rivera y Damas put in his two cents' worth. "Your Eminence, the entire world is witness to the utmost fairness you have displayed. They know you to be a fair man. So if you give a Homily such as the one Father Ellacuría wrote for you, it'll have an amplifying effect that only you can provide. And the *gringos* will hear it loud and clear."

Romero smiled. "It's a hell of a homily, for sure." He raised his glass to toast Ellacuría.

Everybody raised their glasses, saying, "Bravo!"

Ellacuría pressed on. "Your Eminence, if I may humbly suggest..."

Romero had to laugh out loud. "You, humble, Father? I think we just witnessed a miracle!"

Montes laughed the hardest of them all.

Ellacuría seethed. How dare this *indio* make fun of him? But for once, he remained under perfect control. But he couldn't resist a fine riposte: "Yes, Your Eminence, it's almost as big a miracle as your conversion to our cause!"

Now Rivera y Damas laughed the hardest.

As soon as he could, Ellacuría returned to his persuasive efforts. "Your Eminence, what I was about to suggest was that you continue to proclaim the same message at every venue where you give mass. Like if you give a mass on Monday the 24th, that you essentially repeat the message of the *Homily of Fire* again, so everybody knows that this is serious and not a passing fad."

"What's my schedule look like for Monday, Arturo?"

"Sir, you have a fundraising event for an orphanage, but you hadn't decided whether that was it for Monday, or whether you were also going to give mass at the *Divina Providencia* Hospital chapel that evening."

"Yes, I haven't made up my mind on that, it just depends on how long the charity event goes on. Such events can be long and tiresome."

Ellacuría wasn't going to let up. "Your Eminence, forgive me, but the impact of the Homily will decrease in time, so I respectfully beseech you not to let a day go by without reiterating it."

Since the main course was over, Monsignor Romero was already sipping *jerez*. He took another sip and said, "Father Ellacuría, I've failed to listen to you for too long. I pledge to you that I'll read your *Homily of Fire* tomorrow, word for word, and that I'll repeat the message at *Divina Providencia* on Monday evening."

Everybody at the table stood up to clap. Ellacuría went one step further. He walked over toward the Archbishop, kneeled, and kissed his ring, saying, "I pledge my loyalty to you for as long as you live, Your Eminence."

Everybody else followed suit.

As soon as Ellacuría arrived at the Jesuit Residence at the UCA that night, he placed a call. "*Divina Provid*encia Hospital Chapel, Monday evening mass." And then he hung up.

On Sunday, March 23, 1980, Monsignor Romero read the *Homily of Fire*.

It was like every other homily that every priest had given in El Salvador, thousands of times before, in the last few years, except for this part:

"I would like to especially address the men of the army. Specifically, the members of the National Guard, of the Police, and the soldiers in the garrisons... Brothers, you are one of us, we're one and the same people. You are killing your peasant brothers. When you receive an order to kill from a man, keep in mind that the Law of God must prevail, which says: 'Do not kill.' No soldier is obligated to obey an order that goes against the Law of God. Nobody is obligated to carry out an immoral law. It's time for you to recover your conscience, and for you to obey your conscience rather than the order to sin. The Church, the defender of God's rights, of God's Law, of human dignity, of the person, can't remain silent in light of such abomination. We want the government to seriously realize that blood-soaked reforms are no good to anybody. In the name of God, then, and in the name of these suffering people, whose laments go up to heaven every day more and more tumultuously, I plead with you, I beseech you, I order you in the name of God: stop the repression!"

The fire in this homily was that it was telling soldiers to disobey orders. To refuse to shoot. To refuse to fight. It upset many members of the military who heard it. Secondly, the ones doing most of the killing were the left themselves, seeking to create martyrs to discredit the government. But more importantly: Why was it against the Law of God when policemen shot back, but not when armed revolutionaries shot, killed, tortured and maimed?

The evening of the very next day, Monday, March 24, 1980, Monsignor Romero was assassinated while giving mass at a little hospital chapel. A single shot was fired from outside. It was claimed that it was done by a 'death squad,' probably headed by Major D'Aubuisson. But nobody saw anything, because D'Aubuisson was never detained for that. He went on to become a presidential candidate and then a congressman.

One month after the murder of Monsignor Romero, Arturo Rivera y Damas was named Acting Archbishop of San Salvador by Pope John Paul II.

Chapter 45

Man on Base

"Son, we're worried about the turn of events. Can you shed any light?" His mother was worried and so was everybody else. The assassination of Monsignor Romero had shaken the entire nation.

"Mom, crystal ball is as good as mine."

His dad said, "Son, we know some military people. They're all appalled at anybody having the guts to shoot that man. They honestly doubt it was a military man. To begin with, because they've heard thousands of left-wing sermons in the last ten years, because they all go to mass."

Deep down, Mario was certain it hadn't been the military as well. Not that anybody had told him. But recently, Montes hadn't told him anything about the top-level meetings between the Jesuits and the Archdiocese that had been happening, and that wasn't like him. Something was up, and they didn't want him to know. Mario just kept on eating without saying a word.

His dad went on. "One of my customers, a retired colonel, told me that he's convinced it wasn't anybody in the military or Security Forces, because none of them knew in advance that he was going to give such an incendiary homily, and no military man would've been able to plan and execute such a perfect operation for less than 24 hours after the homily. He then said that there would've been no way to know where he was going to be the next day. And whoever killed him had to have known way in advance where he was going to be, to be able to scope out the place, and determine how they were going to carry out the operation, to murder him and escape without being seen."

Mario nodded and Pepe went on. "The colonel told me that the chapel of the *Divina Providencia* hospital is a difficult place to execute an assassination, because it can only be executed from one direction. There are certainly other places that are more open and where a murder would be easier, with less of a risk of detection. Romero's assassination was carried out with a precision and professionalism that is beyond the capability of any military unit, and therefore, the military units would've waited for a better place to do it, than that little chapel."

That comment encouraged Mario to put in his own two cents: "Which also tells me that there was an urgency to kill him. For some reason, it had to be that day and right there."

Pepe was surprised. Not even his military customer had made such an obvious point. Mario continued: "Dad, what's got me convinced that it wasn't military or Security Forces or Major D'Aubuisson or death squads, was the murder of forty poor mourners at Monsignor's funeral, in broad daylight, without anybody seeing anything. There's a force that's active here in El Salvador that's not the government, and I doubt they're guerrillas."

What Mario didn't say was that the people who had the most motivation to eliminate Romero were his Jesuit bosses. Romero may have given that homily, but he had friends in all sectors of the country, even among the military. He was beloved. The only ones that hated him were the Jesuits. For the Jesuits it was much better to have Rivera y Damas, a self-proclaimed liberationist, as Archbishop. Plus, the dead Romero was now a martyr for people to rise against the Junta, because of its inability to control the alleged death squads.

Pepe latched on to Mario's last statement: "You don't think the guerrillas could've done that?"

Mario shook his head. "Dad, I honestly don't know of any Salvadoran, left or right, who would be so heartless as to shoot at mourning countrymen."

"Ah-hah! I knew it! There's a rumor that the 'death squads' are Cubans. You believe that too, don't you?"

"Well, I'd say that there's evidence support that."

Pepe nodded and said, "Well, I believe it. You have to have very-well trained individuals to get into Zamora's house past his security, kill him and escape undetected like they did; to plan and execute such a precise operation against Romero, and then to be so heartless as to murder, in cold blood, over 40 mourners at the Romero funeral! That right there tells me they're foreigners!"

Mario agreed. Whoever murdered those forty civilian mourners had to consider Salvadorans inferior, sub-human and expendable. No, worse than that. Whoever murdered the forty mourners killed them like one would kill cockroaches. Without a second thought, and without mercy. Which reminded him of Argentine Ché Guevara, killing thousands of Cubans, proudly admitting it at the United Nations.

Pepe Tacarello wanted to say something but opted not to. Mario looked at him and knew he was adding two plus two and did not like the four he'd gotten.

But his mother wasn't shy about speaking her mind. Belinda said, "Marito, the only ones in the country who have the sagacity to set in motion all the events of these last few days are the Jesuits. They got rid of an enemy, they gained a tremendous ally in Rivera y Damas, and they turned Romero into a huge martyr. I'd call that Machiavellian, but it's worse than that: it's Jesuit. And their goal is an insurrection before the Agrarian Reform is carried out."

Mario nodded vigorously. He'd inherited his voracious sexual appetite from his dad, but his intelligence was his mother's. She'd come to that conclusion all by herself.

Belinda paused to think about whether to say something, and then said it. "Marito, perhaps you should leave the Jesuits."

Mario had not been happy with the latest turn of events, precisely because of his mother's deductions. Because, in the end, what the Junta wanted to do was to bring about some social justice without bloodshed. But the moment he'd mentioned that to Father Montes, it seemed that he'd been cut out of the loop. Perhaps they thought he needed a refresher course in revolutions, so they were sending him to Europe.

Mario answered his mom. "Mom, if there's an uprising, which is what my bosses are expecting, it'll be good for our family for me to be on the 'winning side.' If there isn't an uprising, then I may just take you up on that. Especially if the Agrarian Reform is carried out."

Silence followed. Estela came and started clearing the table. Finally, Belinda asked him, "What other news do you have, Mario?"

"Well, apparently, they're sending me to Rome."

"What? And when were you going to tell us?"

"Well, I wasn't sure of it till today. Father Montes pulled me aside and told me there were lots of things going on at all levels, and it was best to keep it on a need-to-know basis. But what he could indeed tell me was that I was going to head up the Base Communities effort in El Salvador and that there was going to be a Base Community conference in Rome hosted by the Black Pope himself, and that Karl Rahner's going to be there as well. He told me I was best suited to go.

"I'm kind of looking forward to seeing my teacher, Karl Rahner, again."

Since they seemed to worthy of an international conference, Pepe decided to ask, "What exactly do you mean by Base Communities, son?"

Mario recalled the textbook definition: "It's an autonomous group of around thirty people who worship according to their local needs, not according to what bishops, archbishops, cardinals or popes tell them to. The emphasis is on the term 'autonomous.'"

Pepe had heard something like that. So he asked, "Is this like the building block of what they call the Popular Church?"

"Exactly, Dad. The Popular Church is composed of a set of like-minded Base Communities, that is, they all share the same needs, and emphasize the satisfaction of those needs here on earth, rather than waiting to be compensated in Heaven, which is what the bishops, archbishops, cardinals and popes keep telling them."

His mom asked, "But now that all priests are liberationists, including diocesans, why is it that a Jesuit is charged with Base Communities?"

Mario decided not to sugar-coat it. "Mom, diocesan priests may end up doing it, but for now, the ones who are most interested in the creation of Base Communities are the Jesuits. It's in the Base Communities where we can tell the members that to satisfy their needs here on earth, they're going to have to join the guerrillas or go risk their lives in marches."

And Pepe understood. "It's a Liberation Theology tool and Jesuits are at the forefront of Liberation Theology."

"Exactly, Dad."

Everybody silently digested what Mario had just told them.

Belinda asked, "Are you going alone, or with other priests?"

"I'm going with a nun, Sister Licha of La Asunción."

"Why a nun? Are they doing Base Communities too?"

"She's the one who's been helping to build the clandestine clinics where the wounded of the marches are tended to. I'm sure it's a much-needed vacation for her, and that's why they're sending her."

Pepe asked, "When are you leaving?"

"Saturday afternoon."

"Well, you enjoy, son. You never know what's going to happen here."

His mom asked, "Are going to meet Pope John Paul II?"

Mario shook his head. "Oh no, he's pretty much our enemy."

The silence that followed that statement was very loud. Even Estela stopped what she was doing. John Paul II was beloved in El Salvador. Much beloved.

Mario tried to undo the damage. "Not my enemy, mind you, but he and the Jesuits don't see eye-to-eye."

His mom repeated her earlier advice. "Maybe you should leave the Jesuits, Mario."

"Yes, Marito, leave them!" They were all stunned when Estela said that. Estela hardly ever said anything. She never talked politics and she never reacted that way. It was significant for someone like her to come out so earnestly against the Jesuits.

"Well, if I do, it won't be before this trip to Rome. Just know that I don't take your words lightly."

Chapter 46

Vows that aren't Vows

"Are you leaving, Sister Licha?"

Sister Belén had walked into her quarters in La Asunción, with a knowing smile on her face.

"Yes, Sister Belén, we're flying out this afternoon, to go to Miami and from there take the overnight flight to Rome. Father Montes' driver is picking me up soon."

Sister Belén embraced her, wished her a safe trip, and turned to leave the room.

"Sister Belén?"

"Yes, Sister Licha?"

"Why am I going? Why not somebody else—like you?"

Sister Belén shrugged. "Somebody upstairs likes you, I guess."

But Sister Licha wasn't satisfied. "You can't be more specific?"

Sister Belén paused. "You were selected in Europe, not in El Salvador."

"But why?"

"They didn't tell me, Sister Licha, but considering the great work you've done with the clandestine constructions, they must want to reward you with a vacation. And Rome's not bad."

To Licha, that seemed plausible. But she couldn't shake the premonition that it was Don Blas, who was planning to take up most of her time. He felt sure he was going to ask her to marry him, because he'd been telegraphing that since the first kiss in Sonsonate.

But frankly, she didn't love him and if she was going to leave the religious life, it was going to be for a man she truly loved. And despite all the love letters she got from 'Marcos Arévalo,' she didn't love him like he wanted and like a would-be husband deserved. But at least he didn't give her the willies anymore.

The last time they'd seen each other, he wanted more than kissing, but she'd pushed him away. But the man doesn't seem to take no for an answer.

Furthermore, she was going to meet the higher-ups of the Jesuit movement, Superior General Arrupe and Karl Rahner, and she wanted to learn everything she could about what was about to be inflicted on El Salvador. So she couldn't dedicate too much time to 'Marcos Arévalo.'

Sister Belén hugged her again and said, "Have a nice trip, Sister Licha. Enjoy. Life's going to get a lot tougher when you get back."

On the plane to Miami, she didn't get to ask Father Tacarello the questions she wanted to because First Class was full. They both felt reticent about talking religious matters in first class, because for people of the cloth to fly First Class was at odds with the vow of poverty. So they read for the two and a half hours it took them to get to Miami.

But on the Miami-Rome leg of the flight, First Class was practically empty. So she felt free to engage him in conversation, but not before agreeing to call each other by their *noms de guerre*.

"Tell me, Eliseo, why did you become a Jesuit? You're good-looking, from a wealthy family—you could've been anything you wanted. Why a Jesuit?"

"Juana, I've had a calling ever since I was a child. Father Montes encouraged that calling and convinced my parents to nourish it by giving me a scholarship to Externado. So when I graduated from Externado, I was first sent to Oña, Spain, where I began my bachelor's degree studies, and then to the University of Münster, in Germany, to study under Father Karl Rahner, where I completed them and graduated with my Licentiate in Philosophy."

Juana recalled the conversation with Don Blas. "I thought Rahner was at the University of Innsbruck?"

"Earlier he was, but in the 1970s they moved him to the University of Münster."

That made sense to Juana. Next question: "Eliseo, you took vows, like chastity and obedience to the Pope. Yet the day of my 'induction' into the Revolution, you disparaged him."

Eliseo smiled sadly. "Things have changed in the Jesuit world, Juana. My mentor, Karl Rahner, following the footsteps of Teilhard de Chardin, started a revolution in the Church. We're now free to disobey the Pope and disregard the traditional Catholic teachings that are based on Saint Thomas of Aquinas. And we have the complete freedom not to comply with any of our vows, especially, and obviously, chastity."

"But if you had a calling, how could you opt for such a mundane approach?"

"Opt? I had no choice if I wanted to be a priest. The graduates of the San José de la Montaña Seminary in El Salvador are all like Sister Belén: parrots. They repeat. They don't think for themselves. So for a person of my intellect, the Jesuit route was the only way to go, because it exposes me to ideas that run rampant in the intellectual circles of Europe. It was either the Seminary or Europe. It was a no-brainer."

Juana thought about his response. Then she pointed out the following: "Eliseo, I never had a calling. I had a need. Even so, I managed to remain very chaste until Marcial deflowered me. So I have to wonder, how is it that someone who did have a bona fide calling, became so promiscuous?"

Eliseo understood the question. "Well, four years in Europe will do that to you. My professor Karl Rahner, a Jesuit with a doctorate in philosophy, had a pro-abortion lover, Luise Rinser, whom I met. I would often attend soirées at her apartment. In such a circle, the traditional teachings of the Catholic Church under which you and I grew up and were formed were tossed out the window, replaced instead by a church that was more of this world. The reasoning behind this is simple: if a priest doesn't know the things that the faithful have to go through, how can he be a spiritual leader of the faithful? Stop to think about that."

Juana's perplexed look prompted him to try to explain it better. "You know that couples have to attend priest-imparted courses on marriage, from priests who have never been married. They don't have a clue as to what holds a couple together. My father would often kid my mother saying that the priest who married them had sternly warned my mother that she was to submit completely to the will of her husband or that otherwise, she'd be a sinner.

"But the problem was clear: how can anybody with no experience, advise somebody about something he knows nothing about? So Karl Rahner propounded that you had to wallow in the world, to gain knowledge of it and become a better leader. He'd tell us that the most influential teacher he ever had was Martin Heidegger, who often stated that 'a faith that doesn't constantly expose itself to the possibility of unfaith is no faith at all but a mere convenience.' So to perfect our faith, we have to expose ourselves constantly to the mundane. After all, didn't God himself adopt human form, through Jesus, to show us the way to Him?"

Licha kept her cool. She was going to be spending time with this Jesuit, and she didn't want to forfeit the opportunity to learn more about them. The objections that rose in her throat against such nonsense would have to be left for a more propitious occasion. Instead, she took a less confrontational tack.

"So Jesuits now focus on the human side of Jesus, rather than the divine side."

"That's right. The Creator of the Universe subjected Himself to all the problems of humanity: illnesses, plagues, fleas, mosquitoes, and He became one with the people, to be able to lead them. We can do no less."

She continued to remain calm in the face of such nonsense. Jesus as a human didn't say, 'It's Ok to be promiscuous.' He didn't become human to say, 'spilling your seed on the ground is now OK, but not when Onan did it.' Jesus did say, 'Go and sin no more.'

As she got taught in the Convent in Paris, Jesus came to earth to prove that it was possible to be human and face all the difficulties humans faced, and still be holy. And that His followers—men and women of the cloth, and laymen—were expected to be holy, despite being human.

This was nothing but another attempt by the Jesuits to twist Jesus' life to suit their goals: "If we're going to say that Jesus was a guerrilla, then let's also say that he was a promiscuous guerrilla."

Eliseo continued. "The great theologians of our time: Rahner, Lubac, Chardin, argue that had He been of this time, He would be partaking of the world in the manner we do. He was a leader for the people of that time. We're leaders of the people of this day and age."

Juana shook her head but tried to keep it to a minimum. Theologians? How can they call themselves theologians if all they were doing is following what a German philosopher said? At most, they were 'Heideggerlogians,' following the teachings of a man who died and did not resurrect.

Her outward silence made Eliseo reconsider whether he wanted to get into such a profound discussion with her. He came back to the more mundane. "Juana, my dad was a promiscuous businessman from Italy who came here to escape the Hitler-Mussolini axis. Ever since I reached puberty, he's rewarded servants for satisfying me sexually, because he never wanted me to become a priest. Had my dad been somebody else, and not Pepe Tacarello, I may have been different."

Juana had to ask, "Are there priests among your mom's ancestors?"

Eliseo shook his head.

Juana then noted, "Then you must have priests in your father's side of the family, because they're Italian, and it seems fascinating to me that the same genes that made you so promiscuous gave you your vocation!"

Eliseo had to admire Juana's observation. Her intellect obviously extended beyond knowledge of math and science.

Juana kept looking at him, as if expecting a reaction from Eliseo. Since none came, she told him: "Eliseo, do you know what that means? It means that your calling is so strong, that not even your sex addiction will derail it. In my humble opinion, your love for God will overcome everything else. You'll end up doing something that'll bring glory to God."

Eliseo didn't know what to say. Mostly because the moment Juana said that, he felt something stir inside him. Something that had been asleep, or turned off, since he went to the University of Münster.

Juana went on. "So they sent you to Europe... did your father pay for any of that?"

"No, the Society of Jesus did."

"Four years in Europe, all expenses paid—that's expensive, Eliseo! Where does the Society of Jesus get the funds?"

"I honestly don't know, Juana. Perhaps we'll find out in this conference."

"You know, it can't be sponsors like Don Blas, or many Don Blases. Your education was expensive, and since you weren't the only one and this has been going on for decades... we're talking about a huge fortune!"

Eliseo nodded. "It's expensive, no doubt. I know for a fact that we haven't gotten money from the Vatican for years, much less under this Pope. And although the Jesuits own many educational institutions the world over, the funds they obtain from tuition are used to maintain and operate the schools, and not to fund the lifestyles and education of so many Jesuits."

He asked the stewardess for a glass of water. Then he continued. "While in Europe, I met this Argentine Jesuit named Bergollo. The man had spent many years in European universities. He'd already gotten his master's in theology and was working on a doctorate in philosophy. And judging from the stagnant economy of Argentina, it wasn't Argentina who was paying for his lifestyle and education.

"There were also Jesuits from Peru, Brazil, Colombia, Venezuela... it seemed the plan was to send Latin American Jesuits to study their master's in theology in Europe."

The stewardess brought him the water. He took a pill. He then said, "It would be interesting to find out on this trip where the Society of Jesus gets the funds for all of that."

"And to travel first class to Europe," thought Juana. She recalled her conversation with Don Blas: his 'organization' was paying for Ellacuría's constant trips to Spain to visit Zubiri. She was sure he went first class as well. She was definitely going to get it out of Don Blas.

Mario looked at his watch and said, "It's almost midnight San Salvador time. I took a sleeping pill so I can sleep through turbulence."

With that he went to sleep. Juana did the same.

They were awakened by the Captain announcing that they were about to land at Rome's Fiumicino Airport. After rapidly clearing customs, they took a taxi to the Hassler Hotel, which, in 1945, had been the U.S. Army headquarters in Rome. The exterior gave no inkling of the sumptuousness of its interiors. All Juana could think of was that the Jesuits are rolling in dough. The daily rate of a suite here was something that could feed a Salvadoran family of five for a long, long time.

At the front desk, Eliseo told the clerk of their reservations. The lady looked it up and said, "Sir, there's been a change of plans. You are no longer in the Suite; you have two separate rooms instead."

"Who ordered this, *Signorina*?" Eliseo asked, more out of curiosity than anything else.

"The party paying for your stay, sir: Mr. Blas Pérez."

Eliseo said no more.

When she got to her magnificent room, she found flowers and a welcome note, signed Marcos Arévalo.

Upon opening her closet, she saw beautiful clothes hanging there, and as she started to try them on. She was surprised at how they fit her to a 'tee.'

She figured that Evelyn Santamaría, of Simán, had given her measurements to Don Blas.

Eliseo called her by phone to suggest that they go shopping to look elegant for the dinner that night.

"No, Eliseo, I'm going to rest up and give myself time to get dressed."

"Yes, for which we need to go buy clothes."

"You go ahead. I found a closetful here. They fit me perfectly. See you tonight."

Chapter 47

Arrupe-sama

When the door opened, Eliseo was taken aback. A stunning woman in a long black gown with an uncovered shoulder and pearl necklace opened the door of the room that should have been Juana's. The woman smiled. "It's me, don't worry," and she stepped out with a Gucci purse in her hand.

"I thought you weren't going to go shopping," was all Eliseo could say.

"Believe it or not, this was already in the room. Now then, whom are we dining with tonight?"

"There'll be a reception for the delegates at the banquet hall in the Mezzanine, hosted by the top Jesuit himself, the Superior General, Pedro Arrupe, also known as the Black Pope."

"What's his story?"

Eliseo proceeded to tell her what he had heard about Pedro Arrupe, from wagging tongues:

In 1945, Pedro Arrupe y Gondra was squatting over the Japanese toilet, which is actually a hole in the ground, relieving himself after breakfast, when the blinding light frightened him backward, and then the huge explosion and heat wave finished pushing him further against the lavatory wall made of rice paper, which gave way and he ended up in the garden of the Novitiate he led in Hiroshima, Japan.

He cleaned himself as best he could, lowered his cassock and ran out the door. He called out to his seven subordinate Jesuit novices, five Japanese and two Korean. They were astonished to see the rising mushroom cloud over downtown Hiroshima. Arrupe promptly gave orders to prepare the Novitiate to get ready to receive the wounded and took off with five of his novices toward the cloud on foot, because he figured the streets might not be passable by car. And he was right.

The six Jesuits, led by Pedro Arrupe, who had gone to medical school before joining the Jesuits, worked non-stop, tending to the injured, organizing their transportation back to the Novitiate and also administering last rites. They would rally able-bodied survivors to help them carry or drag the injured back to the Novitiate, in all manners of modes of transportation. Soon the Novitiate was filled with injured and dying.

The horrors he saw would be seared in his mind, heart, and soul for the rest of his life. When he found out that one single American bomb had killed so many, the seed of hatred toward the Americans was planted on that fateful day of August 6, 1945, only to grow sprout and grow roots three days later when the second bomb was dropped on Nagasaki.

He had identified evil, and that was the U.S.A. It didn't matter to him that with the surrender of Japan as a result of the two American atomic bombs, millions of lives had been saved, which would've been lost in the event of a military invasion of Japan by the U.S. armed forces; compared to the two hundred thousand lives that were lost in Hiroshima and Nagasaki.

For his efforts and assistance, Father Arrupe was honored by the Japanese Government. In 1958, he was named the First Jesuit Provincial for Japan, a position he held until being elected Superior General of the Society of Jesus in 1965.

As Provincial for Japan, Father Arrupe frequently traveled to Rome, to the Church of the Gesù. He always flew first class but dressed in civilian clothes because it was unseemly for a priest with vows of poverty to travel like the rich do. Which would also allow him to travel with his faithful companion, Michiko.

Michiko Nakajima was 15 years old when the bomb dropped on Hiroshima. She was at her school halfway between the Ota River and the Novitiate when the bomb exploded. Her entire family was vaporized, as they lived near the Aioi Bridge. She never remembered what happened. She just remembered the blinding light and then she awoke in the chapel of the Novitiate, feeling ill and with all her hair been burned off, including her eyebrows and eyelashes. Father Arrupe ministered to her for months, and she was 16 when she was fully recovered.

She asked Father Arrupe to let her stay, since she had nowhere else to go. She stayed as an assistant to Arrupe-sama (short for Arrupe-*shinpusama*—Father Arrupe in Japanese—, but which also meant Honorable Arrupe, more befitting his earned status), and she studied nursing, with her education paid for by the Novitiate. But her foremost duty from age 16 on, was to tend to Arrupe-sama's every need. And she did it gratefully.

As Arrupe-sama's stature grew, so did hers, because everybody knew he was her favorite. She was given a room next to Arrupe-sama's. Since the novices were Japanese and Korean, they were very oriental in their views of male-female relationships and felt that Arrupe needed a female, vows of chastity be damned. The health of a man was preserved by his relations with a woman, and Arrupe was more than a man: he was a god!

Not that Arrupe-sama took advantage of that. He was indeed a man dedicated to his vows. Having a female in his life was the last thing on his mind. As a matter of fact, it never even crossed it. Not even now that the news from Europe was that Jesuits were having sex. Of course, that was never discussed with Arrupe-sama; the novices only discussed that among themselves.

Until one fateful day when Arrupe-sama's back gave out on him. He couldn't move. Michiko tended to him with dedication. She bathed him, dried him, helped him squat, cleaned him. She did so with all the love in the world, with gratitude for keeping her alive and with a roof over her head.

That night, after Arrupe-sama was asleep, Father Kuzu, one of Arrupe-sama's subordinates at the Novitiate, asked her to come to his room. There he met Father Kuzu's girlfriend, Akari. She was a woman ten years older than her. Father Kuzu commanded her to sit in a chair, to watch and to learn. For the next 2 hours, Michiko watched Akari pleasure Father Kuzu with her mouth, hands and body openings.

When they were done, Father Kuzu asked, "Any questions, Michiko?"

"No, Father Kuzu."

"We need you to keep Arrupe-sama healthy. Part of his health is his manhood. You must tend to it like Akari tended to mine."

"But he hasn't asked for it, Father Kuzu."

"He's too kind and gentle, and perhaps he's mindful of your young age. But those are European, *gaijin* [foreigner] considerations, and he's Japanese now, so we want him healthy and that's your responsibility. And you're failing in your duties because that back seizure is not healthy."

He then sent Akari and Michiko for a walk outside in the gardens, for Michiko to learn the finer details of ministering to Arrupe-sama.

The next day she was alone with Arrupe-sama. Remembering the lesson of the night before, she lay him on a table, to bathe him with a sponge, only this time, she took all his clothes off. This surprised Pedro, but when he tried to react, he hurt his back even more, howling in pain. Now he couldn't move at all.

Akari had warned her this would happen. And that he would be at her mercy. She was to act with devotion, ignoring his admonishments, because what would be done could never be undone. Since it was for his health, nothing could stop it. Not even Arrupe-sama.

She bathed every inch of Pedro's body. Noticing how thin it was, she made a note to herself to feed him better. She touched every part of it, every orifice, making sure it was clean. According to Akari, she had to do that to make sure he knew that she knew him completely. That no part of him was hidden from her. Her eyes and hands on his body had to become natural for him, so that he couldn't live without them.

When she grasped his penis, he weakly muttered "*Iye, iye,*" telling her not to, in her native tongue. She looked at him, smiled as sweetly as she could, and lowered her mouth to it, as she'd seen Akari do to Father Kuzu. One minute later, she was receiving his essence, as Akari had called it. Under no circumstance must she waste a drop of his essence, she'd said. It was sacred.

"Holy Heaven, Holy Heaven, forgive me!" he said in Spanish, which Michiko couldn't understand. Michiko raised her head, looked at him with her eyes shiny with tears, and swallowed.

"Daughter, daughter, what have you done?" The foreign words were now fully understandable to her, thanks to his expression.

She replied, "I owe everything to you. I'll do whatever is necessary to keep you healthy, Arrupe-san."

Then she proceeded to once again wash his privates, dry him and put a pillow under his head. But she didn't dress him. He lay naked for her to see, to get him used to it. She was only following Akari's instructions.

That night she reported to Father Kuzu and Akari. Father Kuzu was very pleased. He advised her to pleasure him only with hand and mouth, initially. But that she was to bathe him in the nude next time. That needed to become the norm between them. For his health's sake.

Michiko was weary, though. "Father Kuzu, how will this affect me? My reputation, my standing. Everybody will know."

Father Kuzu became angry. "Little girl, you'd be worm food were it not for Father Arrupe. Your reputation is secondary. But I give you my word: I'll see to it that you're honored for keeping our father healthy. So you have nothing to worry about. But never let your personal interest come ahead of his. Do you understand?"

"*Hai, Kuzu-shinpusama* [Yes, Father Kuzu]."

"Go tend to your master, *Redi* Michiko-sama."

The *Redi* was her honor. It was the Japanese version of 'Lady.'

From that moment on, in the Novitiate, she would be known as Lady Michiko. Never again would she be a servant.

On October 5, 1964, the Black Pope, Superior General Janssens passed away.

At the thirty-first General Congregation of the Society of Jesus in May 1965, Pedro Arrupe, the hero of Japan, was elected twenty-eighth Father Superior General of the Jesuits, taking office on May 22. He was only the second Basque to be Superior General. The first had been Ignatius of Loyola, the founder of the Society of Jesus.

The world had a new Black Pope.

CHAPTER 48

THE ANTICHRIST

In Rome, the Hassler Hotel was where *Redi* Michiko and Arrupe-sama usually stayed when they traveled from Japan to Rome for frequent meetings with General Janssens. While there, she dressed in a luxury that made her blend in with her surroundings quite well. As did Arrupe-sama when he dressed as a civilian, because it was not well-seen for a priest to have a beautiful bejeweled lady hanging onto this arm. And since money didn't seem to be an issue, why not?

And now the Black Pope and *Redi* Michiko were greeting the guests at the entrance to the banquet hall. He knew the names of every one of the guests. In front of Eliseo and Juana, at the greeting line, was the Argentine Jesuit that Eliseo knew—Jorge Bergollo. They greeted each other and introduced their companions. His was a German lady named Helga, whom Eliseo greeted in German. Then Eliseo introduced Juana, Bergollo's eyes lit up. "Juana! Of course! We've heard so much about you and your works in El Salvador! It is an honor!" And he kissed her hand. Juana and Eliseo were both stunned.

When it was their turn, the Black Pope also greeted Eliseo and Juana by their *noms de guerre*! All Michiko did was smile.

Eliseo and Juana then made their way to their table. All Juana could think of was, "If they know my *nom de guerre* and work, I wonder if they all know of my deflowering at the beach?" And she blushed. The first thing she did when they sat down at the table was to pour herself a glass of wine and down it in one gulp, to calm her nerves.

When everybody was seated, the master of ceremonies went up to the podium. He identified himself as Giovanni. In perfect Spanish, he invited all to start dining as soon as they were served. But to please listen up.

At the head table were Arrupe and Michiko, Giovanni and his female guest, somebody with glasses who looked like a Nazi and his date, and then... Don Blas!

Juana asked Eliseo who the couple next to Don Blas were.

"That's my mentor Karl Rahner and his lover, Luise Rinser."

Karl Rahner was an imposing figure who belonged more in a Nazi uniform than in the exquisitely-tailored suit he was wearing. His thick eyeglasses made him look like one of those concentration camp doctors than a regular Nazi. His lover could have passed for pretty, but she had the hardened features of somebody who advocates the murdering of babies in the womb.

Giovanni started by thanking those in attendance and then proceeded to introduce that night's speaker, Father Lupe. "Don't mind his accent, he's one of us. He started building the cornerstone of our Liberation Theology, the Base Communities, in Honduras, before being expelled by the Honduran Military Government. Please welcome Father Lupe."

A tall redheaded man with a beard, of Irish aspect, stood and walked up to the podium. With a nice tan, he stood out because he looked out of place in a suit. He was too tall and burly. He looked straight out of the wild west.

He spoke in nearly flawless Spanish, but with a decidedly American southern drawl. "Thank you, Father Giovanni. It's an honor to be here, but I'd rather be in Honduras, where I will return soon. But Rome is a nice little vacation, isn't it? Please, how about a round of applause for our hosts, the Black Pope and *Redi* Michiko, Karl Rahner and Luise Rinser, and particularly for our sponsor, Don Blas."

A round of applause erupted, everybody at the head table rose and bowed.

When the acknowledgment had ended, Father Lupe continued. "I was born in the USA to German-Irish parents, with my dad a salesman and my mom a housewife. After high school, I went to college on a football scholarship. I lost my scholarship due to a football injury, and so I was drafted into the army for World War II, where I saw action in Europe. After the war, with the G.I. Bill, I studied theology and then went into a Seminary. Upon graduating, I spent three years as a missionary in Honduras. After returning to graduate with my divinity degree, I was ordained a Jesuit, I was sent to work with impoverished Hondurans by the Missouri Province of the Society of Jesus. I eventually naturalized as a Honduran citizen and renounced U.S. citizenship. Nevertheless, I was expelled by the Honduran government this year, went to Nicaragua, and there I'm preparing my return to Honduras. This hiatus has given me the opportunity to be here today."

A standing ovation followed.

Upon subsiding, the priest continued, "But I'm here to talk about another priest, a true hero whom I can only hope to emulate: Father Camilo Torres Restrepo.

"He was the son of a physician, from a wealthy family, who became a seminarian in Bogotá, becoming a diocesan priest in 1954. He got sent to Belgium, to study at the Catholic University of Leuven, where he earned a bachelor's degree in social sciences. He applied for a doctorate but his thesis was rejected.

"He returned to Colombia in 1959, and when he started working in the shantytowns of Bogotá, he started to organize the faithful into Base Communities, all of which were bound under the University Communal Promotion Movement, the MUNIPROC.

"Ladies and gentlemen, without ever having studied under Teilhard, Lubac or Karl Rahner, father Camilo developed the first Base Communities in the shantytowns of Bogotá, under the first Popular Church, named MUNIPROC! Which is a testimony to the validity of everything sustained by Teilhard, Black Pope Janssens, Black Pope Arrupe, and all the liberationists fighting for the poor in Latin America today!"

"In 1962, he became a member of INCORA, the Colombian Agrarian Reform Institute, based on the Agrarian Reform Law of 1936. With his participation, the government proceeded to expropriate lands from large landowners, to distribute them to peasant farmers. But it didn't go fast enough or far enough for his taste. He wanted social justice right then and there! And having seen what he saw, who could blame him?

"He proceeded to write weekly bulletins encouraging Christians to help the poor, and for the poor to help themselves. He exhorted colleagues and university students to take direct action. Unfortunately, most of those who claimed to be for the poor, didn't feel it as urgently as he did, so he joined the guerrillas in November 1965.

"In February 1966, Father Camilo Torres Restrepo was killed in a military skirmish with a military patrol."

Father Lupe paused to wipe his tears. And then he said in a breaking voice, "I hope my death is as glorious, for a cause that is equally as noble. Thank you."

Thunderous applause erupted, along with shouts of "Liberation or death!"

He bowed and made his way back to his chair. Giovanni got up and invited everybody to mingle, and on their way out, to pick up the schedule for the rest of the week.

Eliseo invited Juana to go talk to everybody he knew, but Juana preferred to stay seated. She didn't feel comfortable in fine garb. Habits were comfortable and that's what she was used to. These clothes could make her trip or show too much and so she decided that the less she moved around, the better. So she stayed put, enjoying sips of her wine.

She also wasn't in the mood to chat. Father Camilo's decision had upset her. He was obviously a political leader, so why on earth would he become a guerrilla? Was the romanticism of living in the mountains, fighting not only better-trained people but also the elements, so overpowering that it overcame common sense?

Being from a wealthy family, engaging in politics and obtaining political victories would've helped more people than shooting bullets. Besides, the two Colombian guerrilla factions, the ELN and the FARC, had never been able to get along and unite. Perhaps Father Torres could have used his political skills to unite the factions. Honestly, what a useless and idiotic death!

"I know what you must be thinking." The deep voice in flawless Spanish startled her, but just for an instant.

She looked up and saw Don Blas standing over her, very well dressed, although not nearly as well-dressed as some of the Jesuits here.

She smiled at him and said, "Nice to see you, Don Blas!"

"Likewise, I was very much looking forward to seeing you again."

"Really? And is it you whom I have to thank for my Versace gown, my matching Gucci purse, and high heels, and this priceless Marco Bicego pearl necklace?"

"No, my secretary Olga chose those for you, once we knew you were coming. She got the measurements from Ms. Evelyn Santamaría, of *Simán*. Remember her?"

Juana nodded and said, "Don Blas, this is all so lavish. You must own a dozen diamond mines somewhere."

Don Blas laughed and sat down next to her.

"How did you like Father Lupe's speech, Juana?"

"I find that Father Camilo transferred his thinking functions to his heart, rather than keeping them in his brains."

Don Blas agreed. "Because he should've stayed in the political realm, correct? He was particularly well-suited for that. He was obviously ill-suited to be a guerrilla."

"But what struck me, Don Blas, is that he held a high position in the Agrarian Reform Program of Colombia, and by all measurable standards, it had started redistributing properties. If it was going too slow for him, then logic dictated that he move heaven and earth to speed it up... not to become a guerrilla!"

Don Blas nodded his agreement, but for some reason, set his sight on her bosom for too long. Juana noticed it and blushed. He tried to correct his faux pas by resuming the conversation, this time looking at her eyes.

"Nevertheless, you're right. The lesson we take from Father Restrepo is that the intelligentsia should stay away from the battlefield. They should remain the 'uber-generals.'"

Juana, in response, asked, "So why did you have as your keynote speaker a man who is obviously another Father Restrepo in the making?"

Don Blas admired the way her mind worked, and replied, "First of all, because he's going to Honduras and there's nothing going on there. He's going to have to do everything himself: do politics and fight!"

Juana smiled mischievously and said, in a low voice: "There must not be any Spanish Jesuits in Honduras, then, Don Blas."

Don Blas first opened his mouth in surprise, and then burst into laughter.

While he was enjoying himself, Eliseo approached the table with Karl Rahner and his lover Luise Rinser. They stopped in front of them, and Juana almost expected Karl Rahner to click his heels, like a good Nazi, before speaking. But he didn't. He just said, "Forgive me, Don Blas, I just wanted to meet Eliseo's lovely date, whom he speaks so highly of." In a heavily German-accented Spanish.

When Don Blas nodded, he addressed Juana, saying, "*Wie geht es Ihnen, liebe Johanna*? [How are you, dear Juana?]"

"Es geht mir sehr gut, danke, Herr Doktor Rahner. Es freut mich sehr, Sie kennenzulernen, und Fraulein Rinser auch [Fine thank you, Dr.

Rahner. I'm very pleased to meet you and Ms. Rinser as well]." She had learned this basic German from the daughter of a West German ambassador to El Salvador who had studied at La Asunción. This was before the German School had opened in San Salvador.

"Impressive indeed, Eliseo. I look forward to speaking further with *Johanna* in the upcoming week."

But Don Blas quashed any such notion. "You'll forgive me, Father Rahner, but I have every intention of continuing our political conversation with Juana while I escort her around Rome. You don't mind, do you, young Eliseo?"

Eliseo was surprised at this question, but had the presence of mind to say, "Of course not, Don Blas. That way Juana will have the best of both worlds!"

Even the great Karl Rahner immediately acquiesced to Don Blas. Juana supposed that it had to be difficult for a man of such ego to accept a rejection of anything that came out of his mouth. But he said nothing. He just nodded and bade everybody good night, before withdrawing and taking Eliseo with them. This didn't go unperceived by Juana. As Salvadorans like to say, "Where captains order, sailors obey."

As the Rahner party withdrew, Don Blas turned to her and said, "I'm glad he left. Rahner's insufferable."

Juana downed the rest of her wine, and asked, "Why did you bring me here, Don Blas? I have work to do at those places you know of, and this nice vacation is going to set us back a whole week that we can ill afford."

"Well, Juana, I'll be just as blunt as you've been. I want to convince you to marry me."

Although Juana sort of expected this, she was shocked at his bluntness. "I am a nun, sir," she said with as much aplomb as she could muster.

"A technicality. You're now married to the revolution, but now, I want you all to myself."

He reached out to touch her hand.

Juana rescued her hand to take another sip of wine. Reminding her that 'she was married to the Revolution' didn't sit well with her. And all of a sudden she had that fear that these people knew of her deflowering at the beach. She was about to reiterate that she was a nun, when the Black Pope himself arrived at the table, with this companion. The Black Pope greeted them both; Michiko only smiled.

Don Blas didn't stand up. He merely turned around, greeted Arrupe back, and asked, "You already know Juana, don't you?"

Juana extended her hand to Arrupe to be shaken, but instead he took it and kissed it. Michiko and her only exchanged smiles.

Don Blas said, "Please join us, Superior General and Lady Michiko," and the Black Pope said, "Thank you, Don Blas," and both sat down.

So now she knew the pecking order: first Don Blas, then Arrupe, then Rahner, because Rahner hadn't even been invited to sit down.

Pedro Arrupe was a thin man, short, very bald, with very white remaining hair. Juana wanted to believe that the repulsive facial features of this man had been attractive once, like when he studied medicine and saved lives in Hiroshima. Because all he saw now was the face of an Antichrist. Why Antichrist?

John 18:10: "Then Simon Peter, who had a sword, drew it and struck the high priest's servant, cutting off his right ear."

What did Christ say? John 18:11: "Jesus commanded Peter, 'Put your sword away!'"

What would the Antichrist have said? "Peter, cut off his other ear!"

And that summarized Liberation Theology perfectly: it was the manual of the Antichrist.

The Antichrist took her hand, while he told Don Blas: "With your permission, Don Blas, I'd like to thank Juana for the magnificent work she's done for us in El Salvador."

Juana could feel her face flush. Don Blas diverted attention from her expertly, saying in a louder voice than normal, "You know, Superior General, after working with Juana, I believe the best engineering school in the world is the convent of *Les Petites Sœurs de l'Assomption* in Paris. Not the Sorbonne, not M.I.T. As you well know, San Salvador is subject to many earthquakes, and her structures don't even feel them."

The Antichrist laughed lightheartedly. Even Lady Michiko laughed, only she didn't know why.

Juana began to feel bad for Lady Michiko. Nobody including you in the conversation because you didn't know the language must be very uncomfortable. So she strived to recall some of the Japanese that she'd learned from the daughter of the Japanese Ambassador to El Salvador who had been a student at La Asunción.

"*Redi Michiko-san, o genki desu ka*? [Honorable Lady Michiko, how are you?]"

Her delicate features lit up. "*Genki desu, Juana-san, domo arigatoo gozaimasu. Anata wa*? [Fine, Honorable Juana, thank you. And you?]"

"*Genki desu, domo arigatoo gozaimasu.* [I'm fine, thank you very much.]"

Pedro Arrupe was stunned. "*Jozu desu ne, Juana-san*! [You are an expert, Honorable Juana!]"

"*Jozu ja nai, Arrupe-sama.* [Not at all, Most Honorable Arrupe]."

Juana was quick to add: "That's about the sum total of what I remember, I had a Japanese student in my classes at La Asunción."

Don Blas was beaming with pride. He may as well have had an 'I'm going to marry you' neon sign glowing on his forehead.

Pedro Arrupe leaned into her closer. He reached for her hand and kissed it, almost whispering, "Juana, your devotion to our cause is well known." At which point the heat returned to her face. He hadn't said it in a low-enough voice, because Don Blas turned to look at him in astonishment.

Juana began to stutter a response, but Don Blas would have none of it. He spit out to the Jesuit, "Hey Pedro, your devotion to little boys is also well known, but nobody says anything about it because we're all too polite to say it in public."

Fortunately for Arrupe, nobody else heard this dressing down, except for Juana and Michiko.

He turned to Lady Michiko, who was no longer smiling: "My lady, keep him away from boys unless you want to be replaced by one. And if you want him to stay alive, keep him away from Russian boys."

The Superior General and his concubine were dumbstruck; he, because he understood everything, and she, because she sensed something bad had happened.

But Don Blas wasn't done. "Now, you two, get up, bow to Juana deeply, and leave politely."

And they did!

After they had left, Don Blas apologized for the embarrassment and escorted her to the lobby.

Juana said, “I don’t think he meant anything bad by it.”

What she was really thinking was, “Russian boys? Why Russian?”

Don Blas said good night, kissed her on her cheek and said, “See you tomorrow at 8:30 a.m. in the lobby.” And he left.

Chapter 49

Revelations I

She got to her room, took off her minimum makeup, undressed, put on her nightgown, called the front desk asking her to be awakened at 7:00 a.m., and fell asleep immediately, certain that this was going to be quite an adventure.

The next morning she opened the closet and found slacks and tops and tennis shoes and sandals, all suitable for tourism. All fit perfectly. She showered, put on some of her new clothes, and went downstairs to the lobby.

It was 8:15, she figured she had time for coffee, but a tap on her shoulder made her turn, and there was Don Blas, dressed like a tourist, smiling. "Good morning! Ready to go see Rome?"

They got into the sleek black Mercedes Benz convertible Don Blas was driving, and went to the Piazza Navona, where they parked and walked over to the *Caffè della Pace*, a hip, classy cafe frequented by artists and tourists since 1891. Because the interior of the cafe is a bit dark, they ordered their cappuccinos and apricot *crostatas* outside.

As she sat there, basking in the sunlight, she asked, "Don Blas, you're a man of the world, why are you spending time with a nun? You could be spending time with the likes of Sofia Loren, or Gina Lollobrigida, why me?"

"I've never met such an enchanting and intelligent nun before, who was so wedded to the cause."

"Do you customarily date nuns?"

"I don't, but then again, you're not a traditional nun, are you? And these aren't traditional times."

"No, they're not. I was forced to wed a revolution and cheat on Christ in doing so."

"That was necessary. Nothing can be accomplished without trust, and trust is of utmost necessity to achieve revolution."

The brought them the cappuccinos. Juan took a sip of the delicious coffee and said, "Don Blas, I'm curious about the fact that everybody seemed to treat you like the boss. Karl Rahner is a heavyweight, and Arrupe is the Black Pope, so how is it that you are their boss, being a simple layman?"

"Please, Juana, let's not talk business quite yet. Let's talk about you."

"Don Blas, don't you know everything about me already?"

"Actually, I know everything about you starting in Paris, when you arrived at the Assumption convent. You stood out in every sense of the word and now I know you're an expert in languages. Extraordinary for a young peasant girl from Olomouc, Czechoslovakia. My question is, why did you leave the Ursulines at Olomouc?"

"I didn't want to remain under the Soviet boot. Theirs is a godless society, and I was not a godless young lady."

Don Blas didn't let that comment affect his demeanor. Fortunately, their *crostatas* arrived, and they ate the Italian pastries with gusto.

After paying the check, Don Blas asked her, "Have you ever been to the Coliseum?"

"Never, Don Blas."

"Let's go visit such an everlasting tribute to Roman cruelty."

The next couple of days were a whirlwind of monuments, museums, bridges, all the way to Florence. The weather was marvelous, and she loved riding in the Mercedes convertible. The Community Bases seminar went forward without them. She didn't need to be among those priests and nuns. She was getting the facts from the horse's mouth, because fortunately for her, Don Blas was quite smitten.

Juana wasn't attracted to him at all, physically, but there was no way for her to dismiss him. What was going on in Latin America was obviously a grandiose, international scheme, and not home-grown. And she was being driven all over Italy by the person who could very well be the '*capo di tutti capi*' as they say in Sicily.

Don Blas was indeed smitten by her because there was something about her... and he couldn't quite put his finger on it. She became an obsession for him. He couldn't wait to be alone with her, and now he finally was!

He always knew that he'd never marry a Russian. Too Slavic for his taste. They were nice, but not nice enough to wed. Which was Olga's problem. She was a wonderful secretary, a wonderful lover, a but not enough to become Mrs. Fedoseyev.

Plus, ever since Panyushkin had been reassigned from the KGB to the embassy in China and Khrushchev had made Fedoseyev head of the Black Crusade, he had traveled constantly, particularly to Peru, where the Soviets were a welcome presence and the women had bosoms one could only dream of. He also traveled frequently to Cuba, of course, where the black women were exquisite. Latinas had ended up displacing the Russian women from his heart, forever.

But their lack of intellect bothered him. For years he had yearned for an intellect to share his pillow with, before and after sex. And he couldn't find a Latina that fit that bill.

Which was no fault of the Latinas. Because Latinos weren't any more intellectual than the Latinas. The deficient public school system throughout Latin America didn't educate anybody well. Too many communities didn't even have a school. And that, despite the education expenses that the Black Crusade had incurred, actually building more schools. But it soon became obvious that there was no realistic way of satisfying the demand for education due to the population growth.

This had forced them to become more selective about where to spend the Black Crusade funds. The Central American and Caribbean region had become ideal because Fidel Castro had no problem exerting his influence outside of his island. Bolivia had proven to be too far away for him, but Colombia, Nicaragua and El Salvador were fine.

And with the redirection of funds to where they were most useful, moneys for the clandestine constructions in El Salvador had become available, and that's how he'd met the beautiful Juana, with her blond hair, green eyes and spectacular intelligence.

Now then, he'd lost the Peruvian girl he liked in an earthquake, and he'd lost the Nicaraguan girl he liked in an earthquake, so he was going to be damned if he let Juana be lost to him in an earthquake as well. That's why he always bugged her not to cut costs. She was someone with whom to share the most important aspects of his life. Someone to respect after sex. Someone who'd fill the biggest void in his life.

He was tired of waking up alone. Six and a half decades of that was too much. Both his parents had gone past a hundred years of age. He had thirty-five years left. He didn't want to spend them alone.

The fact that Juana was a nun was no longer a problem because she had already experienced sex. Don Blas had made damn sure of it. That made his chances of convincing her to leave the religious life to marry him much greater. And things were going well. A gondola ride in Venice should seal the deal.

His KGB voice popped into his brain. "You'll be depriving the revolutionary movement of a valuable asset." To which his heart replied: "Au contraire, we'll put her talents to use at a regional or worldwide level."

This time, his heart won the argument.

In Florence, where he had booked two rooms in the Four Seasons Hotel, they met in the lobby and toured Florence by carriage, visiting the Ponte Vecchio and the Palazzo Vecchio, eating at different mom and pop eateries. There couldn't be a better place in the world to conquer the heart of a woman. On the second day, after visiting Michelangelo's David and the Boboli Gardens, they went to a nearby restaurant where Don Blas asked her if she wanted to go to Venice and the *Lido*.

"What's the *Lido*?"

"The Venice beach my dear. On the Adriatic Sea."

"Oh, I'd like that very much."

"We have a few more days before you fly back home."

"You mean, fly to Rome."

"No dear, why go back to Rome, when I want to spend every second with you? Besides, your time is better spent with me than listening to yet another priest talk about their righteous revolutions and their rightful elimination of all perceived enemies, just like Castro did in Cuba. And how Liberation Theology, which is now the official policy of the Jesuits, allows that."

Juana acted surprised. "Are you serious?"

"Oh please. You already knew that, right? Liberation Theology is God's blessing for the proletariat to take up arms and kill their enemies."

As she had already deduced. But what she didn't know was why Don Blas was involved in all of this. But she wasn't about to ask; he had to want to tell her.

He excused himself to go to a phone. Ten minutes later, he was back.

"I've asked Olga to book us two rooms in downtown Venice for tomorrow, and then the next day at a hotel on the Lido."

"That's fine, Don Blas."

"Please, darling call me Vlad. That's my real name. Vladislav."

"You know who I am, don't you? Alice Novak, but call me Licha."

"Fine, Licha, but I want to you stop being so formal with me, OK?"

Licha nodded and asked, "So, Vlad, what's your real profession?"

Vladislav knew it would come to this. To open up or not to open up—that's the question. But nothing in this woman signaled betrayal. Besides, just how long could he put off answering this brilliant woman's questions?

So he opened up. He headed the Jesuit Bureau of the KGB. He answered only to the Politburo.

She clenched her hands tightly and did everything in her power not to show any emotion. This was the answer to her 'Russian boys' question: Don Blas was Russian.

Licha calmly asked, "Why on earth would the Jesuits have anything to do with you?"

And Vladislav told her that the Jesuits under Janssens knew the Vatican would oppose their modernism because it was a direction contradiction to what the Vatican promulgated, and that they were going to need funds to finance their turn toward the poor. That they only proposed educating the poor, but that Ambassador Panyushkin had convinced them to educate them but with an emphasis on social justice. And that's as far as Janssens was willing to go.

Vladislav didn't tell her about the quest for a Jesuit pope—no need to.

He went on to say that when Panyushkin left the KGB because Khrushchev named him Ambassador to China, it was Vladislav who was left in charge of everything Jesuit, and it was he who negotiated with Arrupe taking the project to where it was now: not the education but the indoctrination of students, with the purpose of fostering revolutions.

Vladislav explained: "To facilitate this, we wrote Liberation Theology, in conjunction with Arrupe and other Jesuits such as Rahner and others. But it couldn't be authored by Arrupe or Rahner— they were too white and too European. We assigned the authorship to the Peruvian priest, Gustavo Gutiérrez, to make it seem that it had its origins in Latin American poverty."

"Seriously? Father Gutiérrez wasn't its author?"

"Not at all. We asked him to contribute something, so he would agree to sign it. Besides, he's not a Jesuit. It was a form of hiding that this was a Jesuit and KGB project."

Licha had to ask, "Why did you choose Latin American poverty? Because there are worse poverties, such as African or Indian, right?"

Vladislav shook his head. "My dear, the oppressor of the masses is the USA. Its back yard is Latin America, with enough poverty to make it a fertile ground for our revolutionary priests and nuns."

Now Licha shook her head. "Vlad, I applaud the elimination of oppression, while applauding even more the elimination of lack of education. So I am with you. But don't expect me not to be amazed that the religious weapon that you're about to use against oppressors was designed exclusively for Latin America, when the poverty of Asia and Africa is far greater, and far more hopeless, as in the case of the lower castes of India."

Vladislav loved this woman's intelligence. But even her intelligence wasn't enough to realize this very important fact: "Dear Licha, do you honestly think that Comrade Stalin would've accepted to spend millions from the Soviet treasury, had the goal been to overturn African tribal chiefs or Indian leaders, and not the defeat of the United States? He would've had Ambassador Panyushkin and me executed, for being fools."

Licha understood. This was all pure Cold War.

But then it occurred to her to ask, without really knowing why,

"Does the operation have a name?"

And Vladislav answered, without really knowing why, "The Black Crusade."

"Because of the Black Pope, Arrupe."

"Actually, it was Arrupe's predecessor, Janssens, who negotiated it. He was the original Black Pope. But it was Arrupe who really turned it into a crusade."

Something was guiding Licha. Because Licha wouldn't have reacted this way: she took his hand, looked at him with much admiration, and said, "But its true name should be the Red Crusade and that would make you the Red Pope, right Vlad?"

All he could think of was, "Where have you been all my life?"

But what he said was, "You're now privy to a top secret of the Soviet Union. You can't disclose this to anybody, ever."

"Oh, Vlad, don't you think I know it? And haven't I proven to you that I know how to keep secrets?"

Vladislav knew it. But he wanted to make sure, so he got up, took a knee next to her at the restaurant, and took out a velvet case. He opened it and gave it to her. Inside was a diamond ring.

"Licha Novak, I love you. I've loved you since I first laid eyes on you. Would you marry me? Would you become Mrs. Vladislav Fedoseyev?"

The diners who witnessed the proposal started clapping. It had been perfect.

But Licha's head reeled, as if from a blow. Fedoseyev? During that ride back to the Russian's apartment in Krakow, she kept hearing 'Polka Fedoseyev,' or something like that. When the partisans had attacked, she'd heard the same: 'Polka Fedoseyev, partizany!' and she remembered it perfectly because it had been the moment of her salvation. Polka, of course, was the national dance of Poland, and partizany is what the Polish resistance called itself, and the Soviet soldiers referred to them by their Polish name. So for her, it was hard to forget.

She shut her eyes hard, to try to stop the spinning. It was life or death all over again. What this man had revealed to her, the Black Crusade, could spell her end if she didn't' play this right.

She opened her eyes and found that Vlad was kissing her. Apparently, what was guiding her had told her mouth to say yes.

She regained control and said, "Yes Vlad, I'm honored. Only a man so in love would've defended my honor like you did last Sunday."

After whispering eternal love in her ear, Vladislav kissed her again and said, "Please let me go see if Olga has the Venice itinerary ready."

He came back 10 minutes later, all smiles. "Ok, Licha, tomorrow first thing in the morning we pack our bags, drive to the airport and take a plane to Venice. Olga booked us two rooms at the Metropole Hotel in downtown Venice. But the Lido hotels are full. She was able to get us one room at the Hotel Des Bains on the Lido. It's a single bed, but I can sleep on the couch. Tomorrow we'll visit the Piazza San Marco, take the perquisite ride on gondola and spend a beautiful evening in the Jewel of the Adriatic. The next day we'll rent a motorboat to go to the Lido. We'll moor our boat on the bay side, and we'll take a cab to the Hotel, a short ride."

"Can I drive the boat?"

"Have you ever done that?"
She shook her head. "I'd love to learn!"

Chapter 50

Revelations II

The next morning they drove the Mercedes to the Florence airport. On the way over, she finally decided to ask about his comment about Arrupe's 'devotion to boys.'

Vladislav gave her a wry look as if it was too distasteful to talk about.

But Licha insisted.

Vladislav relented. "Ok, but I have to warn you: it's not something I want to discuss with the woman I love while we're pre-honeymooning in Italy."

What was guiding her made her say the following: "Look, future husband of mine, you'd better start getting used to not keeping secrets from your future wife."

"OK, my love. Here goes: he makes use of a Roman prostitution ring that caters to the clergy. And we've learned that he would satisfy himself with prostitutes who were boys."

Licha shook her head. Rome hadn't changed a bit since the time of Martin Luther, who opposed the fact that the pope of the time also had fun with boys. But Arrupe?

She had to ask, "Vlad, it's obvious that Arrupe likes women. So why boys?"

Vladislav shook his head, as if not wanting to say anything. Licha poked his shoulder to remind him about the secrets. So Vladislav said, "Part of the deal with Janssens was to groom Arrupe to be his successor. Because of Hiroshima, we knew that Arrupe was ideal for the Black Crusade."

Licha was astonished at that. "Don't tell me you guys killed Janssens?"

This seemed funny to Vladislav and he burst out laughing. When Licha insisted, he composed himself to say: "You've seen too many American movies, darling. We're good to our friends and Janssens was a great friend. He moved heaven and earth to get Rahner into Vatican II, for him to draft and make everybody sign *Lumen Gentium*. *Lumen Gentium* or Light of the Nations is the Vatican II document that paved the way for us to be able to write Liberation Theology under Arrupe. Janssens was vital for the success of Vatican II. We owe him a lot."

Licha understood and urged him to go on with Arrupe. Vladislav accepted. "When Janssens saw that Arrupe traveled to Rome with Michiko, he was horrified, not because he was having sex, but because he might get Michiko pregnant, and that would jeopardize the entire plan. Had Michiko become pregnant, Arrupe would've been expelled from the Order. Do you understand?"

Licha recalled what Belén had told her. So she speculated: "So Arrupe began having sex with Michiko in a way that wouldn't get her pregnant."

Vladislav nodded, always with the wrinkled nose.

So Licha asked the following logical question: "But if he has Michiko, why does he need to have sex with boys?"

Vladislav replied: "She didn't come to Rome with Arrupe when he became Black Pope in 1965. She stayed in Japan."

Licha nodded. "Now I understand."

Then she said, "This may be something good that comes out of the modernists: to allow priest to marry, like protestants do."

What she didn't say was, "That Antichrist is one hell of an Antichrist."

They reached the airport, parked, and soon they were on the plane flying to the Venice airport.

Two hours later they met at the lobby of the hotel, after unpacking in their rooms and freshening up a bit. They walked toward St. Mark's Plaza, where they entered the splendid Basilica. After doing the tourist thing, Vladislav suggested lunch at the Osteria Boccadoro, but Licha suggested pizza instead. "We've been eating all these fancy foods, how about some good old pizza. They must have good pizza in Venice, don't you think?"

"Let's go to Campo Santa Margherita, for pizza."

They walked a few blocks and bridges to the east, across the Grand Canal, to Campo Santa Margherita, where they sat outside, enjoying the art stands and neighborhood, which reminded her of Montmartre, in Paris. It was close to the *Universitá Ca Foscari*, so the mom and pops catered to the students as well. The quaintness of the city, its history, and the number of tourists all fascinated her. So different from San Salvador. An entirely different world that made her feel at home.

They got to the restaurant *Ae Oche*, where they ordered a margherita pizza and a carafe of chilled rosé. While waiting, Licha asked Vladislav, "Why didn't we stay in Rome? Weren't there sufficient places to visit there?"

"Several reasons, my dear. The main one you already know: it's that diamond ring you're wearing. The second one is that the further away I am from Karl Rahner, the better."

"You don't like Karl Rahner? Despite being so essential for Vatican II?"

"He's too German and too arrogant and he thinks he's the smartest man in any room he walks into."

"Vlad, that can be said about most any Jesuit."

"Yeah? Well, all this was my idea, not Rahner's. But he acts as though he's the mastermind."

"And you can't say anything because you have to stay in the background."

"Exactly."

"I can see how he's insufferable. But according to Eliseo, he's quite an intellect."

"Really? How intellectual is it to say that your theology consists of 'go ahead and sin, because to be a good religion, we've got to know sin?' Any Soviet soldier could've come up with the same 'theology.' Where's the intellect in that?"

Licha decided to take advantage of the opening. "Vlad, you mentioned Soviet soldier. Were you in the Red Army in World War II?"

"Yes, I fought in Stalingrad, where we were attacked and underwent a siege by the German Army."

"That must've been brutal."

"You have no idea, but please, let's not talk about sad things."

"OK, dear, but you have to admit that you probably dislike Rahner more for being German than for any other reason. And the poor guy looks very Nazi. So I get it." She reached out to hold Vladislav's hand."

Vladislav thought about that for a minute. Then he said, "You know, darling? Wars only end for the dead. Those of us who survive them, keep fighting them."

Licha was amazed by such a lucid thought coming from this KGB agent. Not only did it describe him, but also her. And probably all of humanity.

Because Adolf Hitler rose to power from the ashes of Germany's humiliation under the Treaty of Versailles that ended World War I.

Just then the pizza and wine arrived. After a few bites, Licha remarked, "Without detracting from the wisdom of your last statement, dear, I wish to point out that the USA was your ally in World War II. And that, although your bravery helped to defeat the evil Nazi regime, you were helped by the invasion of Normandy on June 6, 1944, an act of incredible bravery in which thousands of Americans died attacking the ultra-fortified positions of the Germans head-on. And they didn't really have to do it, did they? It's not like the Germans were attacking New York, Washington or Miami, right?"

This woman's intelligence didn't cease to amaze him. And it warranted an honest answer. "Look, Licha, the war against the USA began when Lenin assumed power. A system that doesn't recognize private property cannot coexist with a system that values private property. That's about the most fundamental war that can exist. If you're a homeowner, and somebody wants to take it away from you, you either fight it or you'll become homeless. There's no middle ground."

Licha nodded. The World War II alliance had been one of convenience, and in the end, communism and capitalism couldn't coexist. But it was too simplistic. She replied, "Although you're right, if you frame it all that way, you're bound to lose."

"Why do you say that, my dear?"

"Because the system that allowed somebody to buy a house is a system that creates riches and resources, whereas the other does not. Case in point: While the Soviet Union is unable to produce enough wheat to feed its people on 8.65 million square miles of land, U.S. private farmers produce more than enough for both populations on a fraction of that land.

"So then the U.S. farmers become rich by selling their surplus wheat, the U.S. government gets richer from the income taxes that those farmers pay, and the result is a net enrichment on their side and a net impoverishment on your side. And if the guy who wants to take your house away from you arrives armed with just a slingshot, and you've got a machine gun to defend it with, nobody's going to take anybody's home away that day."

Vladislav didn't like that analogy. For a second there, he thought of asking for the ring back. But he thought better of it, and he just asked, "So, my love, what would you do, then?"

Licha didn't hesitate. "Number one, Vlad, I'd be a realist. The production of funds and resources is not the Soviet Union's specialty. I'd focus my efforts and resources on targets with a high probability of success and forget the others. Especially since the Soviet Union invaded Afghanistan four months ago, on December 24, 1979."

He continued to be surprised by Licha. He couldn't but agree. No doubt it would curtail his funds, and he'd already spoken with Arrupe about that. This conference in Rome probably shouldn't have happened, but he needed an excuse to bring Licha over!

Licha went on. "When I say forget the others, I mean forget countries like Chile."

Vladislav's countenance changed. His eyes flashed. She'd touched on the sore spot again, but this time intentionally. "Chile was not Black Crusade! Allende was the old way of doing things. A Brezhnev-appointed ambassador sold him on this charismatic leader, Salvador Allende. What the ambassador didn't tell Brezhnev was that Allende was an idiot. Because it was Allende who promoted Pinochet to a position where it was easy for him to overthrow Allende. Let me tell you, Jesuits aren't that dumb."

But he regained his composure, admitting, "No doubt, that was a serious blow. But we were lucky to find Somoza. That's how everybody's supposed to fall!"

Licha kept going. "But you've got to accept that Somoza fell because Jimmy Carter abandoned him. But now, we're just a few months away from a presidential election in the United States, and Carter's prospects aren't looking that good, with the Iran hostage crisis. And his opponent has promised not to let El Salvador fall."

Vladislav nodded vigorously. "Which is why El Salvador must fall before January 1981, or we risk a reverse domino effect: they're going to save El Salvador and take back Nicaragua from us."

Licha took a long swig of the chilled wine to be brave enough to pop the question. "Is that why you had Archbishop Romero killed?"

Vladislav felt like the air had been kicked out of him. Instead of answering, he finished is glass of wine and ordered some more.

Licha insisted. "You authorized that, didn't you?"

Vladislav knew that he had to say something. "I would've authorized it had the request come to me. But it didn't."

"Are you telling me that the Black Pope gave the order to murder Romero, a fellow man of the cloth?"

Vladislav ceased to hesitate. "You must've been too busy with the constructions, my dear, to notice that the Spaniards have nothing but contempt for the *indios*, since 1492. And there was nobody more *indio* than Romero."

Without saying anything further, Licha looked squarely at Vladislav, who did everything he could to avoid her gaze. He even started looking for the waiter with his wine. Finally, Vladislav couldn't avoid it any longer, and practically shouted, "What?"

What was guiding her made her reach out to him, hold his hand and squeeze it. Then it made her make the sweetest, most loving face that she could, and then say, "Vladislav Fedoseyev, if you really want to be my husband, you'd better not lie to me again, comrade."

Vladislav reacted indignantly. "Lie to you? When did I lie to you?"

Licha didn't hesitate. "I don't for a minute believe that the man that you humiliated in Rome that night had the balls to order the murder of Monsignor Romero."

Vladislav looked down at his plate. Then he looked at her, with contrition, and said, "I will never lie to you again."

They finished their meal, and went back to the hotel, with her hanging on to his arm. Halfway there she asked, "Do you know what Pinochet did to spur his economic miracle?"

"What do you say that he did, my love?"

"He emphasized education, and it is my opinion that that's what you should be doing, rather than financing everybody's first class trips all over the globe."

Vladislav looked at her lovingly, kissed her forehead and said, "My dear, I'm not in the business of educating people. I'm in the business of defeating the USA. And since you asked me to be a realist, let me ask you the same thing: if you want to keep your future husband alive and well, don't ask him to go ask Brezhnev for funds to educate the poor of Latin America."

Back at the hotel, each went to their separate rooms. Not that Fedoseyev wanted to, because he knew with 100% certainty that he'd found the right woman for him. He would rather die than continue his life without her at his side.

Chapter 51

Apocalypse

That evening they went on the perquisite gondola ride, with the perquisite singing gondolier, singing 'Sorrento' and 'O Sole Mio' and other famous romantic Italian songs. Vladislav felt like he was in heaven; not her, because she hadn't figured out yet how she wasn't going to marry Vladislav, after telling him that she would. So she prayed for enlightenment and enjoyed the gondola ride. After a great dinner at Osteria Boccadoro, they withdrew to their respective hotel rooms. "For the last time," thought Vladislav.

The next morning, they took a water cab to the motorboat rental, and after paying, Vladislav untied the boat and gunned it away from the pier, then promptly put Licha behind the wheel. An hour and a half of lessons later, Licha was successfully mooring the boat to one of the many piers on the Venetian Lido. A short cab ride later, they were in the Hotel and entering their room, with one queen-sized bed, and a spectacular view of the Adriatic Sea. It was one of those views that stay engraved in one's mind forever. She set aside her misgivings about the Russian and decided that, no matter what happened, she was going to enjoy that day because who knew what tomorrow might bring.

While she was admiring the view, Vladislav had unpacked and gone into the bathroom. He came out wearing normal swim trunks, up to just below the belly button. Licha blushed at the surprising view. For a man north of 60 years of age, he looked good. But she had no time for anything as Vladislav planted a thorough kiss on her lips, allowing it because this was not an unexpected outcome of their sharing a room; plus, it was out of her hands. When he stopped, he looked at her with loving eyes and said, "Where have you been all my life?" And kissed her again.

He finally tore himself away from her, and said, "We have 6 hours of sunlight left, so let's go to the beach, shall we?"

"But I don't have a bathing suit, Vlad!"

"Sure you do. I put one in that drawer," he pointed.

Licha went to the drawer of the armoire he was pointing at, and took out an azure-colored bikini, as flimsy as two strings.

She looked shocked. "I can't wear this!"

Vlad smiled. "It's either that or nudity, dear. Those are your two choices."

With any luck, no Salvadoran would be on the beach that day; after all, it wasn't summer yet. "Remember, enjoy this," she thought to herself. She excused herself and went into the bathroom. Five minutes later, she came out in a bathrobe.

"Let me see."

Off came the bathrobe, and Vlad couldn't believe how beautiful this woman was. So voluptuous.

Licha was relieved that all that exercise all the years of coaching sports at La Asunción had kept her in good shape. She was a strong Polish woman.

"Such beauty is to be exposed, not hidden, my dear. Let's go to the beach."

The rest of that day was just glorious. The sun, the breeze, the waves, everything. She enjoyed the feeling of men's eyes on her scantily-clad body. Vlad's rubbing of sunblock all over could do nothing but ready her loins for what was coming. And she wanted it to come.

As the sun got less fierce, people started to shed their swimwear. Suddenly more women were topless. Even some men exposed themselves. An entire family walked in front of them in the nude.

Vlad untied her bikini top. Before she could stop him, it was gone.

"Let's go for a walk, dear. Hold my hand."

And Licha took a walk on the Venice Lido, exposing her voluptuous breasts to the world. Feelings of guilt, embarrassment shame and sensuality, all bundled into each of her bosoms, gave way to a sense of exhilaration. She started to enjoy it. She just couldn't wait for night to come.

Suddenly, Vlad said, "Let's go swimming," and shed his trunks.

In the blink of an eye, something knocked the air out of her. Her mind saw the CCCP tattoo before her eyes saw it. She looked away, which Vlad interpreted to mean she was shy, but then she took off running toward the water so she could scream underwater where he couldn't hear her. And scream she did, really hard. Only stopping long enough to come up for air. She kept screaming and kicking toward the deep, and she didn't even feel how chilly the water was. Suddenly to strong hands tried to stop her. At that moment she stopped screaming, and she said to herself, "Think!" By the time she got her head out of the water, she'd calmed down because this thought her calmed her: "If this wasn't ordained by God, nothing is. You've got a decision to make."

The decision had been made. She turned to Vlad and kissed him. His hands roamed all over her underwater. She let him because she wanted him to feel like he was in complete control.

They got out of the water and took their nude bodies to the dunes. They had to look around because there were couples already there. They found a spot and copulated in earnest. She did it enthusiastically because she wanted Vladislav to feel like he was in heaven with her. He suddenly roared and collapsed on her. Mission accomplished.

When they got back to the room, they showered together. She knelt to suck him, but it was actually to get a closer look at the red tattoo. When it got erect, it matched the penis back in Krakow in 1945: a penis crowned by the CCCP.

They got dressed and went to dinner. After ordering, Vladislav asked, "So when do we get married, my love?"

"Vlad, I'm still a nun!"

"We can fix that tomorrow."

"When did you want to get married?"

"Tomorrow, the next day, as soon as possible."

That wasn't what Licha had in mind. "Vlad, are you planning on going back to El Salvador with me?"

"No, of course not. You're coming with me to Moscow."

"Vlad, do you really think that that's a good idea?"

"Why, Licha?"

"A lot of people depend on my work. Don Polo is having me build the underground barracks for the future offensive."

When he heard this, Vladislav came back down to earth. It was true. As he himself had said, there was nothing more inconspicuous than a nun at a school for children.

"So what do you propose, my love?"

"Vlad, I already consider myself your wife. As such, I'll do whatever makes you happiest."

Vladislav's eyes filled with tears of happiness. He couldn't ask for anything more out of life.

What was guiding her made her take his hands and say, lovingly, "If you want me to stay, I'll stay. Nevertheless, if you agree with me that it would be best for me to finish my work before the next offensive, which has to be no later than January 1981, then let me go back. When I've finished my work, you can go pick me up in El Salvador at any time, take me to Paris to resign as a nun, and have me at your side for the rest of my life."

Vladislav nodded. "Go back to El Salvador. I'll be going frequently anyway."

Licha agreed. "I'll be waiting for you anxiously, husband of mine."

"So do you want to fly back to Rome by yourself, to return to El Salvador with Eliseo?"

"Just to keep up appearances, my love."

"OK. I'll make arrangements for your ticket to Rome to be waiting for you at the Marco Polo Airport."

"Thank you, my dear Vlad."

"Waiter, your best champagne!"

After ordering their seafood entrées, and after downing her second glass of champagne, Licha asked, "Vlad, can you tell me about the tattoo?"

Vlad looked embarrassed for a second, but then he said, with pride, "My dear, we all have a history, and when I was sent to fight the Nazi invasion, we were so motivated to be fighting Hitler's goons, and so proud after our victory at Stalingrad, that I got a tattoo down there. It was supposed to commemorate Stalingrad."

Or, Licha thought, once you got Stalin's orders, you wanted to make sure that the last thing your victims saw was a prick made in the USSR.

But Licha just nodded and said, "That's understandable. What rank did you achieve in the Red Army?"

"For my valor and ability to lead, and because my valorous commanding officers were killed in action, I was promoted to the rank of Colonel."

"I have to admit, Vlad, with your suave and debonair demeanor, I would've never guessed that you were a warrior. You even had me believing that you were a businessman. What did your men call you, 'Comrade,' or sir, or what?"

"No, they called me 'Polkovnik'—Colonel."

Of course, to the terrified young girl riding on the truck, who didn't speak a lick of Russian, 'Polkovnik' sounded a hell of a lot like 'Polka.' And that's why she remembered him as 'Polka Fedoseyev.'

Licha wanted to know more. "Tell me more of your war experiences. Did you actually go to Berlin?"

"Sure! My regiment was among the first to get there!"

"What route did you take?"

"We had to go through Poland, although it was a very cold January 1945. So we had to stay inside Polish homes when we could."

"Were you treated well?"

"Oh yes, the families were most kind. They saw us as liberators."

"Did you go through Warsaw?"

"No, my regiment went through Krakow, to the south of Warsaw."

Somebody even two months younger couldn't have kept such a semblance of serenity upon hearing that revelation.

"We thought you were going to come through Olomouc in Czechoslovakia."

"No, the Germans were retreating toward Berlin and we had to stay on their heels."

"We had Polish people come through Olomouc talking about Russian atrocities."

"Propaganda, dear, pure propaganda."

"Yes, knowing you as I do now, it had to be."

Vladislav nodded. "We were admirably restrained, considering that we were the ones that had been invaded."

"Yes, that's true. I suppose the Germans committed atrocities on your women and children?"

"Things I can't even bring myself to mention."

A voice was screaming inside her head. "What did the Polish people ever do to you, you son of a bitch?"

At that point, the food arrived. She ate heartily, deciding that she'd gotten enough information for today. And she needed energy. She wanted to make him feel loved and desired. That he had made the right decision. At least for 24 more hours.

They went back to the room and they made love like rabbits.

The next morning, he made the arrangements for only Licha to fly to Rome the next day. He'd fly to Moscow. He also made the arrangements for somebody to pick up the Mercedes at the Florence airport.

He woke her up with the news, and she immediately feigned a headache and stomachache, blaming it on the champagne. She told him she'd go down to get some medicine. He offered to go instead. She gave him an embarrassed smile, telling him she would also need feminine products, so she'd rather go alone.

"Please hurry, my love."

The hotel had no pharmacy, but the front desk told her where she could find one if she took a cab. Upon arrival, she asked for and found Valium. She also purchased rolls of duct tape, a pack of Gillette razors, some vials, and, of course, the Kotex. And then she took a cab and hurried back to the hotel.

In the room, he wanted to make love, but she begged off asking him to wait for later because she didn't feel well yet. She suggested that he go have breakfast and then pick her up because she'd be better by then. Since he was hungry, he went.

Five minutes later, Licha got up and walked the hallways, hoping to find a room service cart. When she found one, she raided it of several large trash bags and towels and hurried back to the room. There, she grabbed the Valium pills and used one of her shoes to ground them into powder. She poured the powder into the vials. She put everything in one of the drawers under her clothes.

Half an hour later, Vlad came back. Since she declared herself to be better, they went to the beach. There, they frolicked a couple of times among the dunes. Vlad was a happy man.

When they got back to the room, Vlad wanted to go out to dinner, but she begged him to have a romantic dinner on the room's terrace. It was their last night together, for the time being, and she wanted to spend it naked with him. How could he say no?

"What would you like to order, dear?"

"I'd like a nice thick juicy steak, the type you need real sharp knives to cut."

"That sounds fine, I'll order two. Would you like a fine Chianti with that?"

"Sure."

When the food came, it was placed on the table in the terrace, and as Vlad poured two glasses of wine, she said, "You know, we're going to need more napkins," so he volunteered to call room service for such purpose. When he got up, she emptied a vial of crushed Valium into his glass of wine.

He came back and toasted the future couple. He drank and gave no indication that his drink tasted funny, which was a relief for Licha. He poured another glass of Chianti, and when room service rang, he got up, and she emptied another vial into his glass.

He came back with the napkins and drank and ate. She kept asking him questions about Moscow and Russia. He was very lively but then started tapering off. He then said he was going to lie down. He fell asleep.

When he woke up, he was lying in the tub, face up, knees bent back and under his torso. It was as if he'd been kneeling and someone had pushed him backward, and he'd been unable to get his legs out from under him. As he struggled some more, he noticed that his wrists were secured to his ankles under him as well. He tried to call out to Licha but realized he had a gag in his mouth, and all he could do was moan. He moaned more when he realized he was naked.

When Licha heard the moans, she entered the bathroom completely naked as well. She went directly to the shower and turned it on so that it was loud. She also went to the wash basin and turned both spigots on full blast. The noise of all the running water would drown out everything else. The shower would wake Fedoseyev up completely. And she wanted him wide awake.

She sat on the edge of the tub and said to the perplexed man, "Polka Fedoseyev, in 1945, in Krakow, you took me to your temporary headquarters to rape me. I was fleeing you animals, after Red Army troops had raped my mother and my sisters, in front of my dad, shot them and then shot my dad.

"You arrived in a truck and saw that I wasn't menstruating, unlike others who were anally raped and then shot. So you chose me. When we got to your headquarters, you made me kneel in front of your penis, where I saw your red CCCP tattoo. Just then the partisans attacked and I escaped. All the way to Olomouc. I joined the Ursulines because I swore to God that if He delivered me from you, I would dedicate my life to Him."

Fedoseyev's eyes confirmed everything. He realized why he was attracted to Licha so much—she was the one that had gotten away.

Licha continued. "I'm a woman of my word, Polka Fedoseyev. I kept my word to God, until your honchos took the virginity that I was saving for God. So I think maybe God might not have liked that. For why else would He deliver you to me, at my complete mercy?"

Fedoseyev said something completely unintelligible, but it sounded desperate. However, his eyes were pleading for mercy, clearly and understandably.

"But I continue to be a nun, Polka Fedoseyev, and it behooves me to be merciful and forgive. So I'm going to ask you a question, and I want you to answer me sincerely, OK?"

Fedoseyev nodded vigorously.

"Fine, Polka Fedoseyev. Did you rape under Stalin's orders?"

Fedoseyev nodded.

What was guiding her made her smile happily, as if with relief. Fedoseyev noticed it and continued to moan with pleading eyes.

As a reward for his sincerity, Licha grabbed his penis and started to stroke it.

"Another question, Vladislav?"

Fedoseyev nodded vigorously again.

"Did you give the order to make me a woman of the revolution at the beach?"

Fedoseyev hesitated a second, and then nodded. Eyes pleading.

Once again, whoever guided Licha painted a smile of happiness on her face. "I knew it, Vladislav. It was to improve your chances of making me your wife—I understand!"

Fedoseyev vigorously agreed. Licha looked at him with merciful eyes and said, "I forgive you, Vladislav. So let's make this a forgiveness ceremony, OK?"

Fedoseyev nodded. Licha stood up and got into the tub, kneeling in front of him. "Let's get this baby hard, first." She bent over to suck it.

Somehow, almost miraculously, Fedoseyev's penis started to get hard in her mouth. When it was hard, Licha let go, looked into his eyes and said, "Polka Fedoseyev, I forgive you. But this is for Monsignor Romero."

She took him in her mouth again and bit down as hard as she could.

Fedoseyev's entire body convulsed in limitless pain as he screamed like crazy into his gag. He tried to bust his binds with the strength of someone who's drowning, but the binds held. While Licha continued biting down on the organ, her left hand sought one of the towels that she'd left next to the tub, and when she found one, put it on top of her head and his abdomen. It was to prevent the blood from spurting outside the tub. She wanted it all to go down the drain.

When she felt the shrunken piece of meat entirely in her mouth, she lifted her head from under the towel, looked into Fedoseyev's crazed eyes, and spit his penis and his blood into his agonizing face. She then reached for the razor blade she'd also left outside the tub and proceeded to amputate the rest of his genitals with it.

She'd thrown his genitals into the toilet bowl, after showing them to him, and then she'd flushed. She then told him: "Good-bye, Polka Fedoseyev. And I'm not done: I'm going to destroy your goddamn Black Crusade." He died quickly after she opened is femoral arteries with a knife.

Removing his head and extremities had been tough, but that's what the steak knives were for. He put everything inside the trash bags and then inside the luggage. After cleaning the bathroom, she showered and dressed.

She made a bellhop take the luggage down to the lobby. At the front desk, she asked for the zero balance receipt. Only Fedoseyev's name was on it.

A taxi took her to the dock where the boat was moored. The taxi driver put the luggage in the boat, and after receiving a nice tip from Fedoseyev's wallet, he untied the boat.

When he did, she gunned it out into the open bay, toward mainland Venice.

Halfway there, she stopped the boat, opened the luggage, took out one of the steak knives she'd used on the body and punched as many holes as she could in the two pieces of luggage to ensure that water seeped in. Then she put the knife and Fedoseyev's wallet inside the luggage, zipped both pieces up and was getting ready to throw them overboard when she noticed the diamond ring on her finger. Did she throw it away or keep it? She took it off and put it in her purse. She'd pawn it in El Salvador and use the proceeds for the schooling of poor children. She'd call it the 'Polka Fund.'

She then threw the two pieces of luggage overboard. She waited until they sank completely.

She gunned the boat again. On the way to Venice, she hoped that the Buddhists were right: that there was no hell—only reincarnation. That way, Polka Fedoseyev could come back as a German woman who got raped many times in 1945. That way, he wouldn't need any penis and balls.

Chapter 52

You Can't Uncall a Calling

On the flight back from Rome, Juana fell asleep almost immediately, as if she'd been up all night. Which was a good thing because you didn't want to get her going with her questions. And that left Mario Tacarello time to reminisce.

When young Tacarello graduated from Externado de San José, Pepe still bore hope that he could persuade his son to engage in more mundane pursuits than the faith. Although he had managed to get his son interested in sex, the priests at Externado had convinced him that in the new Jesuit order, engaging in such activities was not only permitted, it was encouraged.

The opportunity arose when Fina was going to do inventory at Vesuvius Santa Ana but her assistant Sara was on maternity leave, so someone was going to have to mind the store while she was doing the inventory in the back of the store.

Fina had turned out to be a marvelous store manager, as Pepe had expected, because if Nena, with her scant education, had become one, then a graduate of an Italian university certainly could as well. Fina's only problem was that all her husbands seemed to die.

Two years after she'd started working, she had re-married and had a son, but the husband died at childbirth. He'd had a heart attack while she was pushing.

Three years later, she'd married a Guatemalan merchant who traded goods between Guatemala and El Salvador. While expecting his child, he went to Guatemala and never returned. Later, somebody showed her a Guatemalan newspaper: he'd been shot by his Guatemalan wife after discovering him in bed with his Mexican wife.

Her fourth and last husband had been an electrician.

She got tagged with the nickname of *Viuda Negra* [Black Widow], naturally. She'd become so famous, that a Judge in Santa Ana sentenced a murderer to either death by firing squad, or marriage to the Black Widow, if she accepted, of course.

Pepe figured that maybe the Black Widow could end Mario's desire to lead a religious life altogether, so he sent Mario for the to mind the store while Fina did inventory. Mario wasn't supposed to stay beyond a few days in Santa Ana, but he stayed far longer.

Pepe would call the hardware store and Mario would answer, saying that everything was fine, and that Josefina was very nice to him, not to worry.

One Monday while Mario was still in Santa Ana, an engraved invitation arrived at the Tacarello residence. Belinda opened it and read it. The invitation said, "Mr. and Mrs. Demetrio Pérez are pleased to announce the wedding of their daughter, María Josefina Pérez *widow of* Rossi, *widow of* Santos, *widow of* Pacas, *widow of* Zacapa, to the gentleman Mario Tacarello, which ceremony will take place on November 31, of this year, in the Cathedral of Santa Ana. You are cordially invited."

Belinda, upon reading it, screamed and fainted. Gladys read it and started screaming, "*Mamá, mamá,* Marito is marrying the Black Widow!"

"God of Mercy! The Three Divine Persons! Jesus, Jesus, how strong thou cometh!" wailed Estela, invoking the help of all heavenly entities and their assistants.

Belinda, coming to, told Gladys to call Pepe to go to Santa Ana immediately, to rescue her son from the Black Widow!

But then Gladys asked, "But what if she's pregnant?"

Belinda fainted again.

So Gladys called Pepe. "Don Pepe, your wife, before she fainted, told me to tell you to go to Santa Ana to rescue Marito."

Naturally, Pepe wanted to know why.

Gladys read him the invitation. Pepe started cussing in Italian and hung up. He dialed Santa Ana.

"*Ferretería Vesubio,* this is Sara. What can we do for you?"

Pepe didn't think Sara would be back from maternity leave so soon. "Sara, you're back?"

"Yes, Don Pepe, I came back today."

"Where's my son Mario?"

"He is at the Cathedral."

"Tell my son I'm coming for him!" And hung up.

An hour later, Pepe was entering the store through the rear. He found Mario with Sara in the rear office.

Pepe roared, "What the hell is going on Mario? What was that wedding invitation we got?"

Fina ran in. "Shhhhhh! Don Pepe, what's all this scandal? We have customers up front!"

Pepe looked at her angrily. "Fina, what's this about you marrying my son?"

Her look said it all. Mario started laughing.

Pepe looked at Sara. "You told me he was at the Cathedral!"

"Don Pepe, he was. He said he was going to pray."

Don Pepe understood all and sighed, saying, "Ok, perhaps I deserved this." And started laughing as well.

On the way home, Pepe asked, "Did you at least get some?"

"Dad, a gentleman never kisses and tells."

"You know, your mother fainted. You're going to get a whipping when you get home"

"Attention to detail, dad. November only has 30 days, not 31."

"Yeah, but that could've been a typo."

"Of course, there's also the fact that both of her parents are deceased."

"Yeah, I should've known that."

He reached over to muss his son's hair. "I guess this means you're going to be a Jesuit, huh?"

"Yes."

His dad sighed. Although Pepe's hardware businesses had made him a ton of money, it was still attractive for him for the Jesuits to pay for everything dealing with Mario's European education.

He had a problem with the unending study of philosophy for several years, which seemed completely worthless to him, but then again, philosophy-studying Jesuits seemed to be ruling the world. So it must be good for something.

In any case, his son could always fall back on the family business.

Mario recalled conversations between his parents about his calling that he'd overheard. He once heard Belinda tell Pepe, "We can't ignore the fact that our son has always had the calling. It's in his blood. You must be a descendant of one of the many out-of-wedlock children the Borgia pope had."

Mario knew that the fact that Belinda was a devout Salvadoran wife despite her husband's infidelities didn't mean she was stupid. But it didn't mean that she was innocent or a victim, either. It was seared in her genes that a man had to be manly, and that meant having women. The more women he had, the manlier and the better. But the only thing she did with what was to propagate *machismo*, which, among other things, got many Salvadoran young women pregnant, who were forced to leave their studies to take care of their child or children, alone. And whereas the impregnator got praised for being *macho* or a 'rooster,' the poor young lady was labeled a *puta* or whore.

That reality had led his older sister, Carmen María, to refuse to participate in the *machista* system. In that sense, she was the most European of the Tacarello children.

The only thing in which all the Tacarello women coincided was for Mario to have sons to continue the surname Tacarello. And since the Jesuits had said that chastity was a thing of the past, Belinda hoped that Mario wouldn't remain a Jesuit forever

Which was why Belinda would often say to Mario: "Better leave the Jesuits, Marito." Any pretext was good enough for her.

But to leave the Jesuits, he first had to become one, and in 1972, Mario Tacarello embarked on his trip to Spain, to Oña, to the Colegio Máximo, to join the Jesuits as a novice. There he studied two years of philosophy, the humanities, and theology. In 1974, he got sent to the University of Münster, to complete his college under the Jesuit priest Karl Rahner, which was quite an honor, because, in 1962, Pope John XXIII had appointed Karl Rahner as Expert Advisor to the Second Vatican Council. He was known as the 'Architect of Vatican II.'

And Vatican II, under the leadership of Karl Rahner, had officially changed the Catholic Church forever by allowing other interpretations of Christ and God that weren't based on the Old and New Testament, such as the philosophies of Teilhard de Chardin, Henri de Lubac, Yves Congar, and Rahner's philosophy-based theology. As of 1973, those alternative teachings also included Liberation Theology.

The change proposed by Rahner was based on the teachings of the German philosopher Heidegger, and the result was that, instead of encouraging the faithful not to sin, from a non-sinning platform, they were encouraged not to sin from a sinning platform. It didn't take the intelligence of a Mario Tacarello to recognize that all that would result in more sinning, not less.

The intelligence of Mario Tacarello also told him that Rahner's declaration of the 'absolute mystery of God,' was the height of German arrogance, because he set aside everything written about God by Moses, the biblical prophets and Jesus Christ himself, setting himself up as the only one capable of deciphering the indecipherable God.

So how was it that young Tacarello continued to study two years under a man whose teachings he rejected? Easy: he was given an indulgence to be promiscuous.

And he loved to be promiscuous. He was promiscuous with any woman he met: married, single, widow, barely legal, barely alive, pregnant, not pregnant... it didn't matter.

And it sufficed for him to cite some philosopher to uncover what was covered and to open what was shut. For example, Hegel's "Too fair to worship, too divine to love" was a winner; thereafter he'd either pardon their sin at their request, or otherwise convince them that there was no sin, that it all served the purpose of achieving mankind's highest point in the future, Teilhard de Chardin's 'Omega Point.' Which made nobody a sinner and everybody a pioneer.

And whether they believed it or understood it or not, it didn't matter. What the Italian Tacarello spoke was far more interesting than what the typical German spoke. Plus, there was something positively medieval to sin with someone who pardoned your sin immediately.

Two entire years of that.

And then he got back to El Salvador, to teach at the Externado de San Jose, where Father Montes had said to him: "We need you to teach math and science to the students, Father Mario."

"With pleasure, Father Montes, but it'll be the math and science I learned while I was here as a student because my years abroad equipped me for little else but philosophy and sex education." And he laughed.

Father Montes didn't join in the laughter. "Father Mario, let me be clear about something. I expect you to teach our students well. But your being here, as part of your 'Regency' training, is more than teaching, it's a learning experience. And I expect you to learn about the social injustice that is afflicting this miserable country, and pass that on to the students."

"Father Montes, you can count on me."

"Fine. You'll also stay to live with us here, and you'll be involved in community actions, particularly in the establishment of Base Communities."

Mario wasn't prepared to go from playboy to monk in no time flat. "Is that really necessary? My teacher, Karl Rahner, a Jesuit priest, lives with his lover. I don't see my lack of chastity having anything to do with my ability to serve the greater good. Obviously, neither does he."

Montes shook his head. "When you get a doctorate in philosophy, you can do whatever you want. For now your duty comes before any other interest. With what's about to happen in this country, I guarantee that your duty won't leave you time for anything else. Are we clear?"

"Yes, Father Montes, very clear. I'll live here."

"Good. I promise you the next few years will be the most interesting years of your life."

And so far, so true. He looked at the sleeping beauty next to him on the plane. When she'd gotten to the airport, she looked as if she hadn't slept at all last night. Once seated on the plane, she'd looked at him and said, "We'll talk later. I need to sleep." And lights out immediately.

Not just most interesting—most extremely interesting.

Chapter 53

The Second Washing of the Hands

Juana suddenly opened her eyes and winked at Eliseo.

After ordering coffee, she asked Eliseo what she'd missed.

"You missed Karl Rahner's presentation on the movement."

"Did he go into Liberation Theology?"

"No, but he went into his activities in the Second Vatican Council, which paved the way for Liberation Theology. But first tell me, how did it go with Don Blas?"

Juana winked at him and said, "He made a valiant attempt to divest me of my habits, but I wanted to remain a nun."

"Is he upset?"

"Not at all, Eliseo. He's quite at peace. Now tell me about Rahner's presentation."

"Well... he began with the January 25, 1959 announcement by Pope John XXIII that he would call to a Second Vatican Council to try to come up with ways to make the Catholic Church more attractive to modern man."

"Why would he do that?"

"The CELAM (Latin American Episcopal Conference) that was held in Rio de Janeiro in 1955 discussed the glaring shortfall of priests and nuns throughout Latin America. At the time, the Church was dominated by Thomists (adherents to the teachings of St. Thomas of Aquinas), who were rejecting and condemning everything that didn't fit into their narrow moral code."

Juana asked, "The moral code being what, the Gospels and Scripture?"

"Well, yes, but also their narrow interpretation of them. And this was turning people away from the Catholic Church, and naturally reducing the number of people willing to dedicate themselves to the Lord. The Thomists wanted to continue down that path, but the Modernists, headed by the Jesuits, wanted to modernize the Church, to make it more attractive to modern man, doing away with concepts that the Thomists consider to be pillars of the Catholic faith.

"So an ecumenical council was required to figure out how to deal with the growing belief in Darwinism and the theory of evolution; in Marxism, which claimed to be the cure for poverty, while portraying capitalism as its cause; in Freudianism, which explained human behavior as the result of sexual impulses; and atheism, as proclaimed by Nietzsche, when he asserted that God was dead."

Juana interrupted him to ask the obvious: "So the Modernists wanted a Church that kowtowed to man?"

"Well, yes."

Juana shook her head. "History repeats itself."

The bewilderment that overtook Eliseo's face was almost comical. "What? What do you mean by that?"

Juana explained. "Matthew 27:24: 'When Pilate saw that he could prevail nothing, but that rather a tumult was made, he took water, and washed his hands before the multitude, saying, I am innocent of the blood of this just person: see ye to it.'

"Pilate didn't want to crucify Christ. But he didn't have the balls to stand up to the Jews who wanted Christ dead. So he washed his hands. And history repeats itself: Pope John XXIII didn't want Modernism. But he didn't have the balls to resist the Modernists. So he washed his hands and said 'see ye to it.'

"So the Second Vatican Council was nothing more than a Second Washing of the Hands by a Roman. Only this time it was the Pope and not Pilate."

Eliseo was astonished at the intellect and force behind the words of this woman. It would've never crossed his mind to make such an analogy.

Juana gestured for him to go on.

Eliseo went on. "So that was the backdrop for the Second Washing... I mean, Second Vatican Council. And Karl Rahner was invited to be an expert theologian advisor of the bishops at the Council, and through sheer force of personality, he became the dominant force of Vatican II.

Juana nodded and asked, "How is it that Karl Rahner got to such a position?"

"His history, I guess. Karl Rahner, two years after becoming a Jesuit priest, registered for a doctorate in philosophy at the University of Freiburg and attended virtually every lecture course and seminar that Heidegger gave. Karl Rahner used to say that the best of all the professors he'd had, and the only one he called his teacher, was Martin Heidegger.'"

"Remind me who Martin Heidegger was again?"

"He was a German philosopher who was heavily influenced by Friedrich Nietzsche. He said things like: 'Every man is born as many men and dies as a single one.' Also: 'The most thought-provoking thing in our thought-provoking time is that we are still not thinking.'"

Juana couldn't resist laughing. "Are you serious? That sounds to me like Chinese fortune cookie sayings."

Eliseo gasped. How dare she disrespect the great Karl Rahner's mentor?

But Juana wasn't done. "So let me get this straight: this German's *philosophy* inspired Rahner's *theology*? And consequently, all of the *theology* of the Second Washing of the Hands is based on the *Chinese fortune-cookie sayings* of a German *philosopher*? Heidegger is dead, he isn't God. How can anybody who wears a frock or habit (like you and me) accept all that as *theology*?"

Eliseo gasped again. In the two years he spent with Rahner, it never occurred to him to pose that logical question to him. He accepted everything Rahner said as if it was... the Word of God.

Juana asked him to continue to explain how Rahner had been named expert in the Second Washing of the Hands.

Eliseo told her, "In 1962, Karl Rahner was placed under pre-censorship, meaning that he couldn't publish or lecture without prior permission from Rome. But then Pope John XXIII suddenly changed his mind and appointed Rahner to the position of expert advisor to the Second Vatican Council. And then he was chosen as one of seven theologians who would develop *Lumen Gentium*, which is Latin for 'Light of the Nations,' the document that explained the findings of the Second Vatican Council."

His faux pas made Juana smiled, who said, "So let me get this straight, Eliseo: the Vatican had censored Karl Rahner, but all of a sudden, it uncensored him and elevated to the most influential position of the time—*theological expert adviser* for the Second Washing of the Hands—when his doctorate was in *philosophy* and not *theology*? Doesn't that seem strange to you?"

"They wanted the most brilliant mind to be involved?" the Jesuit speculated.

Juana knew that the Black Pope of the time, Janssens, had pressured pusillanimous Pope John XXIIII to do so.

Juana just said, "Ok, go on."

"The Bishops were in charge of drafting *Lumen Gentium*, but the actual drafting was left to the 7 expert advisors, who would then submit their drafts to the vote of the Bishops of the Council. Rahner's goal was to convince the Bishops that the Church needed to evolve with the times, and the guidelines for such evolution would be Teilhard de Chardin's evolutionary view.

"And the way they did it was to write *Lumen Gentium* in Latin, in a way that allowed multiple interpretations."

Juana laughed sardonically. "Eliseo, that's exactly how philosophers write, isn't it? They combine terminology that is either made up, or obscure, to form sentences that are far from clear, precisely to allow multiple interpretations, and then be able to claim that they're the only ones capable of determining which of those interpretations is correct, isn't it so? That can't be news to you, having studied philosophy under Karl Marx."

"Karl Rahner."

"Sorry, Freudian slip."

Eliseo smirked. He knew it was no slip.

Juana continued. "You know why they have to write that way, Eliseo? Because they can't prove a damn thing. For example, Nietzsche said 'God is dead.' Did he ever prove that?"

Eliseo had to shake his head.

Juana nodded. "Exactly. He uttered something he could never prove. Now tell me, Eliseo, in the real world, if somebody says to you, 'Buy this medicine of mine because it will cure you of cancer,' but it doesn't... what is that person? Is he a great philosopher... or is he a fraud?"

Eliseo didn't feel the need to provide the obvious answer.

"Contrast that to Christ, who said he'd be betrayed, crucified till dead, and that he'd rise after three days. Boom! Nailed it. Tell me, Eliseo, if you had to put your trust in the hands of someone, would it be Christ, or would it be Nietzsche?"

Again, Eliseo decided to consider her question rhetorical.

Juana asked him to go on. “Explain to me how Rahner managed to hoodwink the Bishops of the Second Washing of the Hands.”

That’s what Eliseo wanted to do, if only to get a respite from her intellectual onslaught. “Well, in the end, Rahner was successful because *Lumen Gentium* was written in a way that *in Latin*, it said the things that the traditional Bishops and the Pope wanted it to say, but that, when translated to other languages—the languages that the entire world read, write and speak—it said the things that the Modernists wanted it to say. For example:

“*Lumen Gentium* used the Latin word *subsistit* to claim that there’s only one church of Christ and that it’s exclusively the Roman Catholic Church. In other words, in Latin, *Lumen Gentium* says the Church of Christ starts and ends with the Roman Catholic Church. That’s the meaning of the Latin verb *subsisto*.

“Nevertheless, Rahner knew that the translation from Latin to the rest of the languages would be done with its homonym ‘subsists,’ which isn’t the correct translation, and which doesn’t exclude any other entity outside the Roman Catholic Church. This allowed the interpretation that while substantially, the Church is to be found within the Roman Catholic tradition, other parts of Christ’s Church that are outside Roman Catholic tradition.

“The moment it was interpreted that way, other entities outside the Catholic Church that claim to be churches of Christ, such as the Base Communities, were granted equal validity and holiness .”

Juana couldn’t believe her ears. “So the great thinker and theologian, your mentor, Karl Rahner, relied on a mistranslation, and not on original thought, or divine revelation, to fool the Bishops and then the world? Your mentor is nothing but a shyster, Eliseo!”

Eliseo was offended. “Well, if that’s the way you’re going to be, then I’ll stop.”

Juana wasn’t going to leave it at that. She put her fists up to rub her eyes, as if crying, saying, “Oh boo-hoo, you hurt my feelings! You bad, bad nun, how dare you question all the falsehoods I’ve been fed at no cost, in exchange for getting laid more than Hugh Hefner! Boo-hoo-hoo!”

Eliseo honestly didn’t know what to do. He really wanted to stop talking to this woman who had come back from spending time with Don Blas just to make fun of him, his mentor, and the entire basis of the revolutionary movement to which he and she—allegedly—belonged.

But on the other hand, she'd been with Don Blas. That meant that she could very well tell him something about his future that she's learned from Don Blas, which he might never find out. So he walked it back.

"Ok Juana, you got me. I'll continue," he said weakly.

Juana took his arm and pressed it, as if to reassure him. "Good Eliseo, this is going to do us both a lot of good, I assure you. Please continue."

Eliseo did. "*Lumen Gentium* also used the term 'the people of God' to refer to the Church. In Latin, it defined 'People of God' as those who are fully incorporated in the society of the Roman Catholic Church, who accept it as the vehicle for Christ's will, as expressed through the Pope and the bishops.

"However, this term got mistranslated to mean Karl Marx's proletariat. And once you say that the Catholic Church accepts the proletariat, then it opens the door to accepting everything related to the term proletariat."

Juana pointed out, more in wonderment than in scorn, "Do you realize, Eliseo, that if *Lumen Gentium* had been written in any language other than Latin, our entire movement would be nowhere? That nobody could've written Liberation Theology?"

Eliseo continued. "Finally, although *Lumen Gentium* clearly stated in Latin that the Bishops had power but only in conjunction with the Pope, the 'Spirit of Vatican II,' as advertised to those who don't actually read Latin, claimed that the Bishops had achieved power away from the Pope.

The mistranslation took hold, and it was crucial for the Liberation Theologians, who could now act with the acquiescence of local bishops, and not necessarily the acquiescence of the Pope."

Eliseo ended with, "And that was Rahner's presentation."

Juana looked at Eliseo sardonically. "And I'm sure it was received with thunderous applause, was it not?"

"Juana, Rahner is a rock star."

Juana shook her head. "I hate to say this, Eliseo but your Karl Rahner took less from Heidegger than from another German, Joseph Goebbels, who famously said, 'A lie told once remains a lie but a lie told a thousand times becomes the truth.'

"But he might have also taken from Stalin, who famously asked, 'How many divisions does the Pope of Rome have?' Because any Liberationist can ignore the Pope because the Pope has no army divisions to enforce his will. And that's ideal for priests in El Salvador and Nicaragua to be able to ignore Pope John Paul II, because both the Archbishop of Managua and the Archbishop of San Salvador have essentially decided that local churches must respond to 'local forces and circumstances,' and not to Rome. That's quite a set-up, Eliseo."

Eliseo had to concur. "Yes, it is, it's the ultimate justification for not only Jesuits to disobey the Pope, despite swearing an oath to obey him, but also for every priest and nun to disobey him as well."

Eliseo pondered what he'd just said. Disobeying bad popes wasn't a bad thing. A Catholic priest named Martin Luther had disobeyed a bad pope who liked little boys and who sold indulgences or permissions to sin, no matter how awful or grave or mortal the sin.

Disobeying the bad pope who took hush money from the Nazis and looked the other way while the Holocaust was taking place wouldn't have been bad, either.

But disobeying John Paul II? That wasn't just wrong, it was also dangerous. Because if there was ever a man who was under God's protection, it was John Paul II. Here was a man who survived being hit by a tram, and later by a lorry at a quarry, back in 1940. Then he survived being hit by a German truck in 1944. Not only that, he saved Jewish boys and girls from Nazis.

It seemed to Eliseo that logic would dictate that if God was with Pope John Paul II, and the Jesuits were against him, that the Jesuits were against God as well; conversely, if John Paul II was against the Jesuits, then God was against the Jesuits as well.

That could only mean that the Jesuits were bound to lose.

All of a sudden, Eliseo heard his mother's voice, saying, "Marito, perhaps you should leave the Jesuits."

Chapter 54

The Antichrist Manual

Juana wanted to keep going. "Who else spoke, Eliseo?"

"Father Jorge Bergollo of Argentina spoke about Liberation Theology."

"Why him?"

"He was one of the ones who helped draft Liberation Theology."

"But didn't Father Gutiérrez come up with it all by himself?"

"No, Juana, many people contributed to it, like our own fellow Jesuit Jon Sobrino, who graduated from Frankfurt, Germany; Karl Rahner and General Arrupe himself, among others."

Juana thought, "And Polka Fedoseyev, too." But what she said was, "Doesn't it seem strange to you, Eliseo, that a Peruvian Dominican priest is said to have been its author when it was actually the Jesuits?"

"Well, that's probably just to portray it as a Church-wide movement."

Juana asked, "So what did Bergollo say?"

Eliseo took a deep breath as he gathered his thoughts and said, "He explained the key principles of Liberation Theology, the first being the preferential option for the poor, which means that the Church must side with poor people and demand justice for them. Bergollo said that Catholic missionaries helped the European conquerors and that Church leaders sided with the elites for 400 years. So the point is for the Church to shift its loyalties."

This immediately pushed one of Juana's buttons. "Eliseo, stop and think about this, will you? Siding with the poor, to a normal, intelligent being, means to get them out of poverty, because poverty is an undesirable condition. If that's a principle of that 'theology,' then their entire focus should be to effectively educate them, to make a decent living, isn't that so?

"Because otherwise, it would be like saying that you're on the side of the sick, but you don't do anything to cure them, except take away the doctor's instruments, health or life, am I right?"

Eliseo couldn't believe his ears. It made all the sense in the world. Why hadn't he thought about it?

But he just nodded and went on. "Second: Institutional violence. Liberationists see violence in social arrangements that create hunger and poverty. They refuse to endorse the status quo because that would mean continuing to endorse a system that did and does violence to millions of people."

Juana looked at Eliseo intently, as if expecting a light bulb to turn on in his head. Since none did, she reached out to hold his hand, as if to guide him, and said, "Eliseo, if Liberationists 'refuse to endorse a system that did and does violence to millions of people,' wouldn't logic dictate that Liberationists therefore have to endorse non-violence?"

Juana's logic was devastating: you can't promote violence if you reject violence. Wait, who was the one who'd studied years of philosophy, the Jesuit or the nun?

"Go on, Eliseo."

"Third: Structural sin. Since the Church encouraged the current feudal structure between landowners and peasants, it's guilty of structural sin, and therefore that's one of the sins that Christ died on the cross for. The only way for society to the Church to atone for that sin is to get society to eliminate the unjust relationship between the rich landowners and the peasants."

Eliseo looked at her, expecting another intellectual blow. But Juana only embraced him and congratulated him effusively. But Eliseo suspected that this was a setup. And he was right, because Juana asked, "How did they react?"

Eliseo's bewilderment wasn't going to let him respond. So Juana expanded on her question. "How did Bergollo, Arrupe and Rahner react when you told them that the Junta's Agrarian Reform was designed precisely to eliminate the unfair relationship between landowners and peasants? Because you did stand up to tell them, right?"

At that point in time, Eliseo wished that he had.

Juana shook her head and spoke in a tone of disappointment. "So you didn't tell them that the Society of Jesus should publish a full-page ad congratulating the government of El Salvador for its Agrarian Reform, because it satisfied three of the main principles of Liberation Theology, which are the preferential option for the poor, the elimination of the institutional violence and the elimination of the unfair relationship between landowners and peasants—without bloodshed?"

All Eliseo could say was, "I'm sure you would have." And he was sincere.

"Go on, Eliseo."

Eliseo really didn't want to go on. He felt shamed and humiliated for being outthought by this nun. But he did anyway, because she was merely stating what he should have and never did have the guts to do. "Another point was *Orthopraxy*. Liberation Theologians argue that the Church should emphasize correct action, which in our case is an effort to achieve human liberation, rather than emphasizing faith and grace. The reason is clear: the emphasis on faith tends to make people not want to take action."

Eliseo looked at Juana expectantly.

Juana shrugged. "What else are they going to say, Eliseo? They have to hide the fact that God the Father Almighty, Creator of the Universe, did order and write, with His Own Hand: 'Thou shalt not kill,' to justify killing, don't they?"

But Juana didn't wait for a reply. She said, "Look, Eliseo, I'm not going to stand in the way of human liberation. But I have to question why the Liberationists aren't putting the same effort into liberating Cubans from their murderous dictator Castro? The same murderous dictator who turned one hundred percent of his people into the poorest on the planet? Who's got them living in crumbling apartment buildings, twenty people to an apartment? Paying them a pittance, if there's money, or with rum if there isn't? And jailing, torturing and/or killing them if they dare to complain that there's no milk, bread or toilet paper? While he lives in a mansion?

"Don't Cubans need more liberation than Salvadorans?"

Eliseo blushed. The reason that Juana could see things so clearly was because she wasn't wearing the Jesuit blinders he'd been wearing for eight years now.

Juana asked, "Is that all that Bergollo said?"

He only had one more point to go. "Bergollo ended by stressing the need for Base Communities, which are small groups of Christians, usually 10-30 people, who come together to study the Gospel and to engage in reflection leading to action."

Eliseo waited for her comment.

Juana only sighed, and asked the young Jesuit, "Eliseo, when you heard Bergollo say that, please tell me that you stood up and asked him which verse in the Gospel tells someone to go kill?"

All he could do was shake his head.

Juana wasn't done. "Tell me, Eliseo, your calling—which is something that I've never had but which you did since you were a child—called you to serve whom?"

"Jesus Christ."

Juana nodded. "You wanted to follow Christ because when those men wanted to stone that poor woman, Jesus proceeded to stone the men, didn't he?"

She said it so seriously that Eliseo didn't know whether to laugh or not. He finally laughed, nervously, and said, "No, of course not, Christ didn't do that."

Juana lifted an eyebrow, skeptically. "Tell me the truth, Eliseo: you wanted to follow Christ because to finance his anti-Roman guerrilla actions, He'd kidnap the temple moneychangers and ask for ransom, rather than kick them out of the temple, would He not?"

Eliseo kept shaking his head.

"Don't lie to me, Eliseo. You wanted to follow Christ because when the disciples asked him, 'Then who is the most important person in the kingdom of heaven?' Jesus replied, 'You need to become like guerrillas. If you don't, you'll never enter the kingdom of heaven'—am I right?"

Eliseo had to object. "Juana, Christ's reply was, 'You need to become like *children*—he never said *guerrillas*!"

Juana pounced. "Christ may have not said that, but the Antichrist did! said *children*, but the Antichrist said *guerrillas*; Christ saved the woman from being stoned, but the Antichrist stoned the men; Christ kicked the moneychangers out of the temple, but the Antichrist kidnapped them for ransom, to finance his guerrilla operations against the Romans—just like the guerrillas do in El Salvador."

Eliseo just looked at her, not knowing how to respond.

"It's clear to me that your vocation is not for the Antichrist. If so, you can't follow Liberation Theology because it describes the actions of an Antichrist. Because that's all Liberation Theology is: an Antichrist Manual that advocates a violence that Christ never engaged in or advocated."

Juana took his hand and squeezed it, before saying, “But it’s up to you Eliseo. Just know this: if you follow one, you can’t follow the other. Remember Matthew 6: 24: ‘No man can serve two masters: for either he will hate the on and love the other; or else he will hold to the one and despise the other. Ye cannot serve God and Mammon.’”

That’s where the nun ended her spiel.

But Eliseo was full of questions. Now it was his turn.

“Tell me, Juana: you just spent a few days with one of the leaders of the movement, and now you’re rejecting it? How can that be?”

“I’m not rejecting the goal, Eliseo, just the method. I’m surprised that you yourself don’t question whether an armed struggle is the best way to lift these people from their dire conditions.”

He had to ask, “So is it you who wants to replace armed struggle with education? Or is that Don Blas speaking?”

“Do you know who Don Blas is, Eliseo?”

Eliseo replied, “He’s a member of an organization of Eastern European progressive businessmen who want to give back by helping the poor.”

“Really, Eliseo? In Eastern Europe, the only ones capable of financing the Jesuits’ high life are the Soviets, the mighty USSR. Make no mistake, he’s Russian.”

“Did Don Blas admit this to you?”

“Absolutely not. He gave me the same song and dance he gives everybody. Only I’m not buying it.”

That was hard for Eliseo to believe, that Don Blas Pérez was Soviet. Not with his perfect Castilian Spanish. Eliseo always thought he was Romanian, because the Romanian language was so similar to Spanish. But Juana never spoke with a forked tongue. If she says Don Blas is Russian…

He had to ask, “If Don Blas is Russian, that means that the Society of Jesus is partnering with the Russians. Why would the Jesuits do that?”

Juana shrugged. “Money. Resources. The existential struggle between the Modernists and the Thomists, which the Thomists would’ve won had the Jesuits depended on the Vatican financially. For the Jesuits to have confronted the Vatican as they have, and for them to have achieved the victories they’ve achieved, they needed a source of financing that wasn’t the Vatican. And that was the Soviet Union, for which they had to agree to their terms.”

"And Don Blas didn't tell you all this?"

"He didn't need to, Eliseo. I've got enough brains to deduce it on my own, based on all the available evidence. And you would've deduced it too, had they not baited you with free education, all expenses paid in Europe, and more sex than King Henry the Eighth... all of which has softened your intellect... and your vocation."

And there it was! Completely stripped and exposed by Juana. He had been judged correctly.

After a very brief moment of feeling sorry for himself, he asked, "What do you think the Russians' terms were?"

Juana replied, only because she needed this Jesuit to start using his head. The big one, not the small one. "Beyond the obvious? I don't know. But even what's obvious is telling: We're in the middle of a Cold War, and people have taken sides. Apparently we, that is, you, me, Ellacuría, Montes, Rahner, Arrupe, Marcial, the Sandinistas and Castro are on the side of the Soviet Union. So it doesn't take much effort to conclude that the huge amounts of money the Soviets have lavished on you is for you to serve the interests of the Soviet Union, above all.

"Judging from the Cuban Missile Crisis, the Soviet Union's number one target is the USA. So the Jesuits' main mission must be to help the Soviet Union achieve their goal. And that explains why, despite the existence of places with far more poverty than El Salvador, Nicaragua and Colombia—like India, a huge part of Asia and all of Africa, and even Cuba—the Jesuits do nothing against the poverty in those countries. Only against the poverty of countries that are allies of the United States.

"That also explains why they chose a Latin American *indio* like Father Gutiérrez to be the author of the Antichrist Manual, instead of naming its true author... the Black Pope, the Basque Pedro Arrupe, or any other of its European authors." Juana was tempted to say Vladislav Fedoseyev but thought better of it.

As the Jesuit absorbed this information, Juana asked, "Is this what you signed up for, Eliseo? To be a Soviet minion?"

And with that, she closed her eyes to rest.

The silence forced Eliseo to go over everything Juana had told him. He suspected that she knew more, but instead of disclosing it, she'd opted to home in on him and his calling. Why? The only logical conclusion was that she wanted him to reject what was going on—like she already had.

Then he focused on her warning: you can't serve Christ and the Antichrist at the same time. That left him no choice. He had to reject the Antichrist Manual known as Liberation Theology. His calling demanded it.

Just then, the sound system announced: "The Captain asks that you please fasten your seatbelts. We're starting our descent into Miami International Airport."

Chapter 55

The Jesuit Death Squad

The two didn't do much talking at the Miami terminal while they were waiting to board their flight home. Eliseo excused himself and disappeared. Juana went directly to the departure gate for the flight to San Salvador. She spent the time reading a magazine.

When they started to board the flight to San Salvador, she stood to see if she could see Eliseo. She saw him approaching the gate walking quickly. He smiled when he reached her, motioning with his head to get in line.

Juana was happy to see the smile on the Jesuit's face. She knew that she'd torn the young Jesuit down on the flight over. But if she was going to keep her promise to the dying Polka Fedoseyev to 'destroy his goddamn Black Crusade,' she needed to build him back up quickly because she needed an ally.

When they boarded, Juana hung on to his arm. There were only four other people in first class. Juana led the Jesuit to sit in the seats, that were furthest from the other passengers, so they could speak more freely.

When they were seated, she turned to Eliseo and said, "I need your help."

Eliseo looked at her quizzically, because if anybody had proven not to need anybody's help, it was Juana. She explained, "Don Blas told me something that I can't tell you, but I don't know if it's true and so I need you to help me figure out if it's true. Are you up to it?"

Eliseo laughed. "A riddle? Why can't you just tell me outright?"

Juana replied, "Why tell you if it's not true? But if you can help me figure out whether it's true or not, then we'll both know the truth without me having to tell you. If it's not, then the old coot was lying, and you don't need to know what he said because it was a lie. Do you understand?"

Eliseo laughed again. "No but go ahead."

Juana began. "Wasn't Base Communities what Father Rutilio Grande was doing in Aguilares?"

"No, Father Rutilio was a recruiter. The one doing Base Communities in Aguilares was somebody else."

"But they said that they killed him because he was doing Base Communities to organize peasants against the landowners!"

Eliseo shook his head. "Since the 1950s, Jesuits have been recruiting for religious life from among the poorest classes, offering them scholarships. No Spaniard could do that better than Rutilio. So that's what they had him doing.

"In 1977, the priest that was indeed doing Base Communities in the zone of Aguilares, while Father Rutilio was recruiting, was Father Mario Bernal Londoño, a Colombian who was a huge Liberationist, and who advocated armed struggle. But nobody ever did anything to him. The Government simply declared him a *persona non grata* and deported him to Colombia.

"So I very much doubt that a government that didn't kill a proven revolutionary Marxist priest would kill someone who only recruited teenagers to become priests and nuns."

Juana nodded. "So it wasn't Security Forces who killed him." Eliseo concurred and said, "It wasn't anybody on the right either—he had no enemies on the right. Which leaves us two options."

Juana raised an eyebrow. "Two? The only option we have is Marcial's people, right?"

Eliseo adopted a professorial attitude and said, "Let's analyze that. For Marcial's men to have killed Rutilio Grande in 1977, Rutilio Grande would've had to have been one of the Fourteen, like Regalado, Poma or Borgonovo, right?"

Juana was impressed. "Wow, Eliseo. You implemented Occam's Razor: 'simpler solutions are more likely to be correct than complex ones.' You nailed it!"

Eliseo felt proud of himself for the first time in a long time. All was not lost. But then Juana said, "But the fact remains that somebody massacred Rutilio Grande and a little boy and an old man who were with him. Who?"

Eliseo paused before answering. Then he said, "You know, Juana, I've always been afraid to delve too deeply into this, because it might lead to a place I'd rather not go."

Juana knew that already. But she said, "You know what? Me too. But maybe together we can handle it better. Are you game?"

Eliseo liked the idea. "I am!" He got more comfortable in his seat, and then began. "The Jesuits tried hard for Romero not to be named Archbishop, through our contacts in Europe. But the latest popes have been no friends of ours, so they were unsuccessful.

"After his appointment as Archbishop on February 23, 1977, Romero told the Jesuits in no uncertain terms that he was no Marxist, socialist, or anything of the kind. He told the Jesuits that he was an Ascetical Theologian, which is about the most anti-Liberation Theology a priest can be; that he was the purest of the Thomists, which is about the most anti-Modernist a priest can be. In other words, the Archbishop of San Salvador was the most anti-Jesuit Archbishop that an Archbishop could be."

Juana concurred. "I remember all the new nuns complaining that Romero had been made Archbishop. And if they complained, I'm sure Ellacuría did, too."

Eliseo nodded. "According to Montes, he was apoplectic. But then one day Ellacuría went to the Archbishop's Office and found a fellow Jesuit, Rutilio Grande, happily fraternizing with the Jesuits' enemy—Monsignor Romero. It turns out that Romero and Rutilio were best of friends.

"One week later, on March 12, 1977 Rutilio Grande was traveling near Aguilares on a jeep driven by 72-year old Mr. Manuel Solórzano, with 16-year-old Nelson Rutilio Lemus riding in back. All three were riddled with bullets. Massacred."

Juana asked, "Do we know who did it?"

Eliseo crossed his legs, clasped his hands across his lap, and adopted his most pensive pose. Juana would've given anything to give him a pipe to complete the picture of intellectualism. Eliseo said, "You have to ask yourself, what was the motivation? Rutilio Grande was the nicest guy around. And he was a very successful recruiter. So the only motivation I can think of was to affect the Archbishop's anti-Jesuit and anti-revolutionary stance."

Juana nodded. Eliseo continued. "Curiously, without being anywhere near the scene of the crime, and without being able to provide any supporting evidence, Father Ellacuría immediately blamed the Government and the right-wing death squads. But we've already ruled them out, because Rutilio had no enemies on the right.

"Not only that: the President of the Republic at the time, colonel Arturo

Armando Molina, was a good Catholic and a friend of the Archbishop. His government was the one that had expelled the liberationist priest Bernal Londoño. President Molina gave Romero his word that it hadn't been the Government and promised to find the assassins. But they were never found."

Juana said, "President Molina had a 'one school per week' policy. He did a lot of good for the people. He was no despot."

Eliseo agreed. "Therefore, we can see that Ellacuría not only had the motivation to do so, but that he also leveled an accusation to put the focus of the media on those he wanted to blame, which also had the effect of providing cover for the actual guilty parties. All this for the sole purpose of putting the Archbishop at odds with the Government and politically bring him closer to the Jesuits."

Juana asked the obvious question. "OK. Fine. But then who committed the massacre?"

Eliseo said, "Whoever did it didn't think twice about viciously massacring a group of harmless and defenseless Salvadorans consisting of a fifty-year-old priest, a teenager and an old man. I don't know of any Salvadoran who would do that. It had to have been done by someone who views Salvadorans as inferior, sub-human and expendable."

Juana looked shocked. "You think it was foreigners?"

Eliseo nodded. "Yes, and I'll tell you why. Ellacuría could've never approached anybody here in El Salvador to ask them to commit this murder. The reason is simple: he could've been subject to blackmail. Just the mere insinuation that Ellacuría could've ordered something like this would spell the end of any revolutionary goals he and the Society of Jesus had for El Salvador—not to mention the fact that he'd feel very uncomfortable in a Salvadoran jail. So they had to be outsiders.

"But they couldn't be just any outsiders, for the same reason. The only outsiders that Ellacuría could resort to were one that shared is very same interests. And that could only be Fidel Castro's military forces. Therefore, the only ones who could've committed that crime were Cubans, under Ellacuría's local control."

Juana remarked, enthusiastically, "Brilliant deduction, Eliseo! Not even Sherlock Holmes himself could've done any better!"

Eliseo smiled broadly. "Elementary, my dear Juana!" he said, to play along. Feeling better, he continued. "So we know that Ellacuría had the motivation, and we know that he accused the Government falsely in furtherance of his motivation, which was to move Monsignor Romero to the left, toward the Jesuits, and away from the Government.

"The question before us is why risk leveling such an accusation with absolutely no proof, which exposes him to be considered a biased liar, or even an accomplice, if one of the true culprits were ever captured? Let's recall that Ellacuría takes care of his reputation of being for peace, as a cover for the fact that he's for war, and such a revelation would destroy such a carefully cultivated image."

"Tell me why, Professor," Juana asked, very pleased with the development of the conversation.

"Because Ellacuría was certain of three things: First, that the burden of proof fell on the accused, who would be forced to prove that it did not commit the crime; second, that the only way to prove that it did not do the crime was to capture the culprits; and third, that the culprits would never be captured because they had already left the country."

Eliseo concluded his analysis by saying, "Every day that went by without the Government capturing the culprits was a day in which the Archbishop moved further to the left and closer to the Jesuits. It was, in fact, quite brilliant."

Juana said, "No, Eliseo, you're brilliant." And she hugged him.

The stewardess came by to ask their dinner preferences. They told her and she left. Soon afterward, they were eating dinner.

As they ate, Juana said, "Your theory would be validated if there were a pattern of such behavior."

Eliseo said, "Well, let's look at another event. When Monsignor Romero came back from Europe, a few weeks before his death, Ellacuría and Rivera y Damas had a letter addressed to Jimmy Carter for him to sign. The letter stated, among other things, that the Security Forces were committing murders, that the Junta couldn't control them, and that for such reason, Carter shouldn't send weapons to the Junta.

"A few days later, the Attorney General of the Republic, a Christian Democrat, got murdered in his own home, and Ellacuría accused the Security Forces."

Juana recalled that and said, "The murderers got in undetected by the

Attorney General's security, shot the Attorney General, but not in front of his guests, and left, undetected."

Eliseo nodded. "So according to our theory, Ellacuría must first have a motivation. In this case, it was to prove to the Americans that the Security Forces were so out of control, that they even killed members of the party in power, thus giving them a reason not to send weapons to a government that couldn't control its own forces. Motivation? Check.

"Next, there has to be a lie in furtherance of the motivation. In this case, he accused the Security Forces, which, according to the letter, were out of control and were murderous. But in this case, it couldn't have been the Security Forces because they don't have such abilities. The murderers entered the house like ninjas and left like ninjas. So was there a lie in furtherance of the purpose? Check."

Juana pointed out that, "To validate your theory, there must be evidence that they're Cuban. In this case, their skills, which far exceed any local capability. So then... Cubans? Check."

Eliseo concluded, "So it also seems that the murder of the Attorney General was also perpetrated by Cubans, under Ellacuría's local control."

Juana nodded. Then she got to the whole point of this exercise: to make Eliseo realize what had happened to Romero, without disclosing her conversation with Don Blas. She asked, "What about Monsignor Romero's murder?"

Eliseo looked at her less sure of himself and told Juana, nervously, "You know, this was where I didn't want to go."

Juana took his hand and squeezed it. "Go on, Eliseo."

Eliseo went on. "Monsignor Romero got killed with one shot, from outside that chapel, and nobody saw anything (again). Motivation? To create a martyr to spawn a general uprising, because Carter's reelection prospects aren't good, and because the Agrarian Reform is imminent."

Juana nodded—proud that her Jesuit was using his big head again. And she added, "There was another reason: to make Rivera y Damas the new Archbishop, because he's a liberationist like they are. Motivation? Check!"

Eliseo nodded and said, "The lie in furtherance of the motivation was to accuse D'Aubuisson and the death squads. He lied to promote an uprising against a Junta that was either complicit or unable to control D'Aubuisson and the death squads."

Juana added, “We know that it’s a lie because D’Aubuisson, an enemy of the Junta, is free, because nobody saw him at the scene of the crime. Again... a lie in furtherance of the motivation? Check.”

Eliseo continued. “The murderers had to have been informed beforehand of the place the Archbishop would be, to be able to scope out the place and determine the best way to murder him, the routes to get there and the routes to escape. That information could’ve only come from the Archbishop, or people he’d told.

“I know Father Montes and Father Ellacuría had dinner with Monsignor Romero the Saturday before his death. So we know that Ellacuría was in a position to find out, on Saturday, March 22, that a) Romero was going to give the Homily of Fire the next day, and b) where Romero was going to be on Monday, March 24. And that gave the murderers enough time to prepare the operation.”

Juana added, “That was crucial: to know that Romero was going to read the Homily of Fire that Sunday, to be able to say that the Security Forces or death squads killed him because of that Homily.”

Juana then concluded, “Again, that information could’ve only been given to trustworthy foreign assassins... Cuban? Check!

Eliseo looked at Juana and said, “Do you see why I didn’t want to get into this? Everything indicates that my Jesuit superior had Romero murdered!”

Juana just shrugged, saying, “John 8:32: ‘the truth will set you free,’ Jesus said to the Jews.”

Eliseo nodded and said, “Final case study: The murder of 40 mourners at Monsignor Romero’s funeral. I’ll make this easy for you: Motivation? Same as for Monsignor Romero’s murder. Lie in furtherance of the motivation? Nobody saw anything not even Ellacuría, who accused Security Forces and death squads, without evidence, to cause the desired uprising. So lie in furtherance of motivation? Check.”

Eliseo took Juana’s hand, as if to transmit his earnestness not only by voice, but also by touch, and said, “Here’s the clincher: Whoever killed 40 Salvadoran mourners at a funeral must consider Salvadorans inferior, sub-human and expendable. They were killed like one kills cockroaches. I don’t know any Salvadoran capable of doing that. So Cuban? Check."

The stewardess came and removed their trays. When she left, Eliseo said, "Conclusion: The only death squad in El Salvador is the Jesuit Death Squad: Cubans acting under the control of Ellacuría."

Juana nodded, but Eliseo hadn't arrived at the conclusion she wanted him to. Vladislav Fedoseyev had told her that he'd ordered Romero's death. Now, she wasn't about to tell Eliseo that because such a confession can only occur if there is a serious relationship, and she didn't want to admit to that, for self-preservation reasons. She had to make Eliseo reach that conclusion by himself.

So Juana said, "You know, Eliseo, we're forgetting something very important: One of the principles of your theory is that whoever is ordering the massacring of Salvadorans must view them as inferior, sub-human and expendable."

Eliseo shrugged and said, "Ellacuría is a Spaniard, from the Basque Country... he carries his disdain toward *indios* in his genes."

Juana shook her head. She wanted Eliseo to at least consider that Ellacuría didn't have the final say. She said, "Eliseo, are we being too hard on Ellacuría? First of all, he's not in command of that unit—Fidel Castro is. So at most, he makes suggestions, recommendations or just asks permission."

Eliseo nodded. "You're saying that someone above him makes the decision, not him."

Juana nodded and said, "Exactly. His superiors. Ellacuría is a hothead. He flies off the handle too quickly. Such decisions have got to be made by cooler heads than his."

Eliseo held Juana's hand, and said, "Juana, I agree, but our theory still holds, because whomever Ellacuría is recommending to or asking permission from is a foreigner, too..."

Suddenly his eyes opened wide in astonishment and he asked, "Don Blas?"

Juana nodded and said, "That's what I think." But inside, she was shouting, "Bingo!"

Eliseo whistled his amazement. But then Juana took both his hands and looked him squarely in the eyes, and asked, "So what are you going to do about it?"

Eliseo looked down at the clasped hands and closed his eyes. After a few seconds he opened them, looked at her and said, "Do you know where I was at the Miami Airport? I went to the chapel there. I knelt and prayed with all my energies. I asked God for forgiveness for failing him to date. And I swore that I'd serve Him the rest of my life. I took a long time because after I'd asked for forgiveness, I felt like I'd felt when I was little again, and I didn't want it to stop."

He then smiled, squeezed Juana's hands and said, "I'm going to start serving God and not Mammon."

Juana hugged him. Just then the cabin lights dimmed.

Juana asked him: "If you're going to become holy, can you wait until we land, first?"

"What?" was all Eliseo could ask, perplexed.

Juana sat upright, looked around for the stewardess, saw that she was sitting near the cockpit, and said, "Be a good boy and pass me a blanket." He did so

She spread it over both their laps. Then she rested her head on his shoulder, put her hand under the blanket, and unzipped him.

Eliseo jumped a little but let her continue. Juana took his penis out and stroked. While she did so, she asked the enthralled prelate, "Don't you want to know what Don Blas told me, that I need to know if it's true or not?"

"What did he tell you?" he asked, breathlessly.

She replied, "Don Blas told me that I bite. Can you tell me if it's true?"

And then she dove under the blanket.

Chapter 56

Sacrificial Lambs

"Captain, Charlie Lima is calling on the HF!" The soldier had come running to the house where Sánchez had installed his temporary command post. Sánchez went running back to the radio with the soldier.

He took the mike and said, "This is *Padrino*, over."

"*Padrino*, I'm calling you to tell you that now that things aren't going well for the guerrillas, they're accusing us of having murdered Ellacuría and Montes. But you have them alive, right?"

Sánchez was perplexed. "Forgive me, Charlie Lima, but you really ought to know me by now." The question was dumb. If they were dead, why wouldn't he be back at the garrison?

Colonel López wanted to make sure. "Captain, all I want is for you to help me prove that they're alive, to silence their damned propaganda station, which is saying that they're dead."

Sánchez turned to Zelayandía and ordered: "Go get me Segundo Montes. Take a couple of men with you. Only Montes! Nobody else!"

Into the microphone, he said, "Charlie Lima, please understand that I'm not going back until I am fully certain that that stupid order's been rescinded."

"*Padrino,* I'll be the first to let you know when that happens. For now, help us out with this."

"OK, Charlie Lima, get a recorder. Call me back when you have one ready. *Padrino* out."

A couple of minutes later, Segundo Montes was walking down the hill escorted by the soldiers.

"Yes, Captain?"

"Father Montes, the guerrillas are accusing the Army of having abducted and murdered you and Ellacuría. Now then, that leaves me with two choices: either you say into this radio that you and Ellacuría and Elba and Celina are alive and well, or I'll have to take you back to prove that you're alive, in which case I will no longer be able to protect you."

"What would you like me to say, Captain?"

"Identify those who are here and say that you're safe and protected. Say the date and time as well."

"Can I go consult with Father Ellacuría?"

"Do you really want to involve that hothead?"

Montes obviously wanted to discuss this with somebody, so he asked Sánchez, "Have you thought this through, Captain? Because the moment I admit that we're with you, then it's obvious that we've been abducted by you."

Sánchez was willing to concede the point that he hadn't thought things through, but then again, he wasn't expecting this from the guerrillas. "Do you have a better idea, Montes?"

The HF radio crackled alive. "*Padrino*, this is Charlie Lima. I have what you asked for. Ready when you are."

"Charlie Lima, *Padrino* here. I have the second here with me. I just brought him up to date."

"Where's the other guy, *Padrino*?"

"I prefer to deal with the second. He's far more reasonable than the other one."

"OK, *Padrino*, ready when you are."

Sánchez handed the microphone to Father Montes, who refused it. "I don't know how to operate such things, Captain. Perhaps it's better if you operate it, when I'm ready," said the priest.

Sánchez thought this a tad strange—what was there to think about? But he opted not to force him. Montes was cool-headed and he'd reach the best possible conclusion for him. If not, it was a return to the capital if he didn't collaborate. That was the best guarantee Sánchez had. "Fine. Let me know when you're ready," he told the priest.

"Hold on, Charlie, please," Sánchez said into the mike.

The reply was, "No problem... I'm not going anywhere."

Segundo Montes as thinking furiously. He was weighing whether to talk into the mike or not. Although Sánchez was trying to protect him, he'd gotten the order to kill them from the guy on the radio. He thought about it for a second and reached his first decision: he'd talk because the alternative was for the Captain to take them to San Salvador, and there there'd be no protection by anybody.

The second decision he had to make was: What would best serve the cause? But the moment he'd asked himself that, the real question he'd been afraid to ask popped into his mind: What cause? The cause that launched an offensive without notifying them? The cause that left them unprotected?

This last question had the two Jesuits baffled. Not only were they left unprotected because there was no guerrilla detail to protect them. That was the lack of protection that the Captain had referred to in their discussion.

No, the lack of protection was far worse. On Saturday, November 11, at the start of the offensive, Elba and Celina Ramos were at the little house assigned to the groundskeeper of the UCA, who was Obdulio Ramos, their husband and father, respectively. The three were sitting in the living room of their house near the main gate of the UCA—normally left closed and locked at this time of the year because classes were out. Suddenly, all three observed how an FMLN patrol placed a bomb at the gate. The explosion opened and unhinged both gate doors, leaving one of them on the ground. Effectively allowing unfettered access to the University, to whomever wanted to come inside.

The bomb was so strong that it shattered the windows of the Ramos' house. The guerrillas seemed to be ready to come into University premises grounds in their vehicles when they were fired upon by the military police that provides security to the military residential neighborhood and Armed Forces discount store across from the boulevard that the gate faced, and so a firefight developed, which forced the three Ramos to hit the floor and stay there all night.

The next morning, when the only firefights that were heard were far away, the Ramos went outside and found traces of blood but nothing else. To them it was clear that the military security on the other side of the boulevard had thwarted the guerrillas' plans.

They went up to the Jesuit Residence, and the only one there was Father Montes. Montes knew that Ellacuría was on the way back from Spain, and he knew that Jon Sobrino wasn't coming back any time soon. But he didn't know where the other Jesuits were. And when the Ramos told him about the guerrilla bomb, the normally cool Montes had almost lost it. He couldn't reach the Archbishop or anybody to tell him what was going on. In the end all he did was to let the Ramos stay.

But Obdulio said that the house was unprotected because of the shattered windows, and that he needed to go board the windows up, because everything they owned was in there, and now it was open to the street. His women asked him to stay, but he said not to worry, he knew where to get boards. He left and by the time the Captain and his men had arrived, Obdulio hadn't gotten back. But Ellacuría had.

The guerrilla bomb and the fact that nobody warned them of anything, taken together, could only lead to a conclusion that Montes feared arriving at. And before going there, the cerebral Montes wanted to analyze all the facts.

For example, what did he know about this offensive? He knew that it had been launched the week after the fall of the Berlin Wall, which meant the fall of the Soviet Empire, and of the entire support system of the guerrillas. The *Contras* had successfully interrupted the flow from Nicaragua to El Salvador, and now they were talking about free elections in Nicaragua.

So the timing of the offensive was due to that. But what could the objective be? The guerrillas had launched themselves with their few remaining forces into the capital, without any hope of military success because the Government would throw everything they had at them to dislodge them and finish them off in the process. So the objective couldn't be military, in the sense that the capital was not real estate that they could hold on to.

What then... a propagandistic objective? If what the Captain said was true: dead little girls and little boys on the streets, abuses of civilians in the residences... all that would offset by far any positive propagandistic impact.

Since military victory was out of the question, a negotiated peace settlement was all they could hope for. But... what incentive would the government have to sit down to negotiate a peace settlement when they had every reason to annihilate because of everything the guerrillas had done? None.

And if that was all they were looking for, why hadn't they simply accepted the offer to join the political process, which had been offered to them countless times? Well, the Jesuits were at fault there—Ellacuría advised against that, because they'd have to lay down their weapons and without weapons, what would stop the government from finishing them off?

So if the government wasn't going to sit down with them, what was it that the guerrillas sought? A direct negotiation with the United States? But in their weakened condition and with the violations of international norms such as the use of armed children and then the abuse of civilians, why would the triumphant superpower that had just defeated the USSR, sit down with a quasi-defunct guerrilla force to revive them? A guerrilla force that had murdered four off-duty marines who guarded the Embassy while they were chatting at an outside café in the posh Rose Zone of San Salvador in 1985?

His body responded to his question before his mind did. Suddenly, he couldn't breathe and a cold sensation spread from his abdomen to the rest of his body. His whole body started shaking. For the first time in his life, he was experiencing raw fear. He struggled to control himself, to take deep breaths. And to continue thinking. The Captain asked him if he was OK. He signaled that he was.

He was finally able to think clearly: the reason for this offensive was to do as many atrocities and violations as they could, to make the Army have an extreme reaction... like killing the Jesuits!

Because only the murder of the Jesuits by the Army would be capable of overshadowing the atrocities and violations committed by the guerrillas in this offensive. And only the world-wide indignation over the murder of the Jesuits by an ally of the U.S. could force it to sit down with the guerrillas to negotiate a peace settlement—as equals, not as winners and losers!

Every other scenario would end in disaster for the guerrillas. Only the murder of the Jesuits by the Army saved them. This was crystal clear to Montes.

This explained everything: why they hadn't been consulted, why they hadn't been warned, and why they'd been purposefully left unprotected by opening the main gate to the UCA with a bomb—they'd been designated sacrificial lambs.

But... was it possible for the guerrilla high command to come up with such a sophisticated plan? Marcial and Ana María couldn't have. But Joaquín Villalobos and Schafik Handal could.

Villalobos and Handal had taken over when Ana María and Marcial had fought to a mutual demise in Managua, Nicaragua, over their massive defeats at the hands of Colonel Monterrosa.

And it was Joaquín Villalobos who had lured the great Monterrosa into a deadly trap.

The answer had to be that they could. And that they had.

Over the HF radio: "*Padrino*, you there?"

Sánchez turned to Montes: "Priest?"

Montes begged for just a bit more time with his hand. He'd recovered from the shock of this realization. And now that he was one hundred percent sure that the purpose of the guerrilla offensive in San Salvador was the murder of the Jesuits, because no other scenario could save them, he was capable of clearly determining the necessary steps to prevent such an outcome.

There was one thing that didn't quite fit: it was the *guerrillas* who'd bombed open the gate that left them unprotected, on the 11th. The firefight with military security from the military neighborhood across the street had thwarted their plan... which was what? To come inside? To do what?

The Captain had appeared the next night, with an order to kill them. Was the Army going to do it because the guerrillas had been prevented from doing it? And since Sánchez had refused, and was keeping them alive, would it be the guerrillas who'd come looking for them, since it was the guerrillas who needed them dead?

The other question was: since Sánchez repeatedly claims that he doesn't know any military man who'd want to kill the Jesuits, but he'd nevertheless received the order to do so, ¿could a member of the Army High Command have been bribed to do so?

He was going to have to discuss all this with Ellacuría. Montes would have to resort to all the finesse he was capable of, to get him to think clearly and without hatred. Because it was now clear to Montes that Ellacuría's hatred was directed at the wrong people.

Sure, he'd speak on the radio. No sacrificial lamb goes willingly to the slaughter without offering resistance. He wasn't about to be the first. But under one condition.

He turned to the Captain and said, "I agree to speak. I'll just say that we're in a safe place, that we aren't abducted and that we're protected. And that we all want a negotiated settlement of the conflict. In exchange for one thing: don't tell Father Ellacuría. I'm going to have to tell him myself, in my own way. Ok?"

This was even better than the Captain had hoped for, so he accepted the condition. But the Captain warned him: “Just remember, you’ll be speaking into a recording device and they can edit you if they don’t like what you say.”

Father Montes put a hand on his shoulder and said, “Captain, trust me. Let’s do it.”

An hour later the army radio station, Radio Cuscatlán, was transmitting Segundo Montes’ message. And the Captain didn’t tell Ellacuría, as promised.

Chapter 57

The Jesuit Commander

After Estela had lifted his plate, Belinda asked Mario if he wanted dessert.

"No thanks, Mom. But I'll take some coffee if you've got some."

Belinda got up to get the coffee brewer going.

"So how was the trip, son?" Pepe was very curious. He sensed something.

"The trip was fine, very illuminating."

Pepe was surprised at the answer. "Illuminating? When you spent all the time getting your baccalaureate degree in Europe, you visited every monument they had over there. I doubt Europe had anything new to offer."

"No, dad, same old monuments, with the same old sayings."

"So what was so illuminating about it?"

He hadn't rehearsed what he was about to say, because otherwise, he might never say it. But he waited for his mom to bring him his coffee, so she could hear it too. When his mom was sitting down, he told them: "Mom and Dad, I'm guilty of a few things. For one, I'm guilty of not thinking for myself. I've discovered that I've been far too gullible regarding all things that I've been taught. Instead of being closer to God, I find myself further from Him because I let the teachings of the likes of Karl Rahner replace the teachings of God the Father in the Old Testament and the teachings of Jesus Christ in the New Testament."

"By swallowing everything they've fed me, I've become a tool. A tool for death."

Belinda couldn't contain herself any longer. "For death? Marito, whom have you killed?"

Mario rushed to assuage his mom's fears. "Nobody, mom, at least not yet."

"Then explain yourself, Mario." Pepe was also worried by his son's words.

"Mom and Dad, there's going to be a violent revolution in this country, because that's what my teachers, my bosses and their bosses want. All of the new nuns and priests that constitute the vast majority of the Church here in El Salvador also want a war here."

His mother felt relieved. "But Marito, we've known that all along. Why is it a surprise for you?"

"Because I believed my superiors when they told me that all they were doing was for the benefit of the poor. But now I know that their real intention is to send the poor to their deaths, because that's what their bosses, the check-writers want them to do."

Pepe wanted to know what had happened on that trip to prompt this change in him.

"Dad, how much money did you spend on my education in Europe?"

"Zero."

"I can't tell you how many Jesuits and priests from Latin America were studying in Europe, in great comfort, while I was there. When regular students, in contrast, barely get by. And this continues unabated to this date. Now, where do you think that money's coming from, for meals and lodging, tuitions, books, travel, health care, and the rest of their expenses?"

Belinda said, "Well, you were on a scholarship at the Externado since the fifth grade—that's a lot of money that Externado failed to perceive from us, and which we could've easily paid. And that was money could've been used to subsidize the tuition of the students that go to their Loyola Academy, which they founded in 1956, for the children of laborers."

Mario nodded and went on. "In addition, they set up mandatory conferences in Bonn, Munich, Stockholm, Dublin, Rome, Paris, London, Madrid, Barcelona, etc.? Ellacuría travels back and forth to Spain several times a year. That can't be coming from paltry tuition paid by students, can it?"

Pepe asked, "It's not coming from the Vatican?"

Mario shook his head. "Indeed not. The Vatican and the Jesuits are adversaries, in the sense that John Paul II opposes the Modernists that have taken over the Jesuits and want to take over the entire Church."

Belinda asked, "So where's that money coming from? Did you find out?"

Mario replied, "I'm not certain about who's funding the Jesuits, but one would think that whoever's writing the checks for our aristocratic lifestyles, would want something in return, wouldn't you agree?"

"Absolutely," mom and dad said in unison.

"Well, the one writing all these checks for the Jesuits wants war in El Salvador."

His mom reiterated: "Marito, but most people already knew that. What you're saying isn't news to us. Certainly, Major D'Aubuisson has been repeating that this movement is funded by the USSR-Cuba-Nicaragua axis."

Mario sure did feel like a fool. He was the most educated person in the house, in the block, in the entire neighborhood... but people much less educated than him were far wiser and cerebral. The good news was that he'd hit rock bottom, and there was nowhere to go but up.

He went on. "Mom, I became a Jesuit because I felt a calling to serve Christ. I felt sure that I'd be able to serve Christ better if I went to Europe to learn the thoughts of quote-unquote geniuses like Plato, Socrates, Hegel, Nietzsche, and a whole slew of others that I studied.

"But I never did learn to think—only to repeat. The irony of it is that that's precisely why it never crossed my mind to become a diocesan priest, because that's precisely what I accused them of doing—repeating like parrots."

He took a sip of his coffee, perhaps to try to gain strength from the caffeine. Then he said, "Now, I find myself following not the Christ I wanted to serve since I was a child, but rather the Antichrist of Liberation Theology, in whose name my bosses and their bosses want to send thousands of poor to die in a war."

He shook his head vigorously, and said, "I refuse to be a part of that. I didn't become a Jesuit for that."

His mother seemed happy. She asked, full of hope, "Are you going to leave the Jesuits, Marito? You can do anything with that brain of yours. You don't need to be with them."

His dad added his two cents. "Mario, I can send you to Italy to get a master's in Finance, or something useful like that. You're an Italian citizen through me."

But Mario shook his head. "No, Mom and Dad, I'm not going to leave them. I'm going to fight them. They owe me."

There—he'd said it! That was a sufficiently brave thing for him to do. Of course, braver yet would've been for him to tell them that he'd been convinced by a nun who, on paper, was his intellectual inferior, but who in real life was his 'mother superior.'

But that didn't matter. What mattered is that he was on this path now, and he wasn't going back.

Mario went on. "My calling is to serve the Lord, and although in His day and age, He called on us to dress the naked and feed the hungry, in this day and age, to serve the Lord is to educate the uneducated—so they can stop being poor. The irony of all this is that Jesuits have a history of being educators. That's been the reason for our existence. Then, for some reason, the Society of Christ became the Society of the Antichrist.

"And the worst of it is that we've decided to engage in something for which we're woefully unsuited. Because in the military, you go up in rank based on your leadership experience. First, you command small groups, then larger groups, then large units, then whole armies.

"I'm sure our top Jesuit deems himself a 'Commander,' despite having no command experience. Moreover, if he were ever to handle a rifle, he'd probably end up shooting himself, rather than anybody else. But here he is, knowing nothing about war, yet wanting to start one!"

"You know, son, Montes warned us about that when he offered us your scholarship at Externado," his mom recalled.

Pepe nodded. "But he explicitly said that it wasn't going to involve priests fighting like the military."

Mario shrugged. "Well, Montes didn't lie to you back then. But what was unleashed with the Second Vatican Council and then Liberation Theology practically demands it. And why not launch a war? From 'Commander' Ellacuría's standpoint, he's untouchable because he's a priest, whereas the rest of us are all inferior, subhuman and expendable."

"Even you?" Pepe sounded incredulous.

"Especially me, dad. Next time they need a martyr, an *indio* like me is a perfect fit. The Europeans don't mind sending the natives to their deaths."

His mother was surprised. "Are you saying they're racists?"

Mario nodded. "They certainly have a racist history. Their own Liberation Theology admits that the Spanish priests helped to subjugate and do violence against *indios*. Jesuits took it a step further: they were slave-owners in Bolivia and Paraguay during the *Conquista*. So yes: they see us as inferior, subhuman and expendable."

Although they were taken aback by their son's damning words, they knew that only Salvadoran prelates had died in El Salvador—no Europeans.

Mario went on. "And in the Externado, my alma mater, my role went from educating students to indoctrinating them to support the guerrillas one way or another, either as fighters or as revolutionary priests. There is no doubt: my role is to serve the cause of the war. Therefore, they weren't sincere with me. They fooled me. They've turned me into an instrument to send people to kill and die, instead of educating them to be able to earn a decent living in peace."

Silence again ensued, until Belinda asked, "Marito, what are you planning to do?"

Mario looked at both his parents, took a deep breath, and blurted it out: "Mom, I need to get a message to Major Roberto D'Aubuisson. It has to be hand-delivered to him. Can you help me?"

His mom smiled. "Of course, son, I'll find a way to get him that message."

Pepe got up and served them all some wine. They all had a role to play in the upcoming events. His may be the most important one: if something went wrong, he had to get Mario out of the country.

As he was thinking about his, Pepe thought out loud: "You know, Mario, you're absolutely right. They owe you. Because what's the use of being a European-educated Jesuit if you sound exactly like a graduated of the local seminary?"

Mario sipped some of his wine and said, "It's worse than that, dad. What's the use of being an ultra-educated Jesuit with a Ph.D. in philosophy, if you sound exactly like Ché Guevara?"

Both his parents laughed at that—perhaps imagining Ellacuría with a beret and a beard.

But Mario didn't laugh. Instead, he said, almost wistfully, "When Ellacuría could instead sound like Christ... and seek peace!"

Chapter 58

Immaculate Confession

The Church of El Carmen had always occupied a special place in the heart of Segundo Montes. So on weekends when he wanted to brush up on his pastoral duties, he'd go help out the aging Father Elizondo and take confessions and give mass. As he got busier with the revolution, he'd often send Father Tacarello for such pastoral assistance. So it was no surprise to Segundo Montes when Tacarello told him that he wanted to go spend the weekend of May 3 and 4, 1980 at El Carmen.

Father Elizondo was very arthritic and welcomed the help. While Mario went to the Church to prepare it for mass, Sister Licha helped Father Elizondo at his quarters with any chores he usually did on Saturdays, so he could rest.

By 4:15 p.m., Licha had completed her duties and went to the Church to monitor its main entrance. Mario entered the confessional at 4:25 p.m., fully thirty-five minutes before the normal start of confessions. At 4:30 p.m. someone entered the confessional on his right. Sister Licha's voice said, "He's here and don't worry— he's well-disguised."

A few seconds later a person entered the confessional to his left and kneeled. Father Tacarello said: "Hail Mary, Full of Grace."

The unmistakable voice of Major D'Aubuisson replied: "The Lord is with thee since 15 B.C." The 'since 15 B.C.' part was the agreed code phrase.

"Major, welcome. I'm Father Mario and kneeling on the other side of the confessional is Sister Licha. We're glad you came."

D'Aubuisson replied, "Nice to meet you." And then he went directly to the point. He wanted to get this 'confession' over with quickly. He realized this meeting was important, so he'd agreed to disguise himself. Plus, it had been requested of him by a dear friend whom he owed a lot to—a friend of the priest's mother. "Your note said you had information you wanted to share with me. How is it that you're in a position to provide that information?"

Mario replied. "We just returned from Europe, where all the plans were laid bare. The Jesuits and the Soviet Union are hell-bent on El Salvador being the next domino to fall. That means war, no matter what the government does to prevent one. We're here because we don't want this nation to fall into a terrible war in which the vast majority of the dead will be poor."

"We're on the same page, believe me," said D'Aubuisson earnestly.

Mario continued. "I'm close to the Jesuit high command. I work directly for Segundo Montes and I am privy to information discussed with the head of the movement, Ellacuría. Sister Licha, because of her assistance to the movement so far, is also privy. So we needed someone to pass on any information we deem important to, and a secure method to do so. Please understand that if we contact you, it's because we consider it urgent. We're not going to nickel-and-dime you."

There was silence in the confessional booth. Then the Major spoke out: "Why me? I'm no longer in the military. And I'm being accused of doing all these bad things. Your association with me can harm you if it ever becomes known."

Sister Licha intervened. "Major, please tell me what isn't risky in El Salvador nowadays? We die if we do, die if we don't. And in this case, your actions could even be justified, because you're a military man. But violence by the clergy isn't justifiable, and so far, most of the violent acts committed in El Salvador have been masterminded by people who claim to represent God. But more directly to your point, our relationship with you is so unlikely, so improbable, that it could very well be the safest relationship we can have."

The Major was impressed with the Sister.

Mario completed her answer. "We decided to approach you because you're more accessible. Plus, we don't know anybody in the Army."

D'Aubuisson had to get this out of the way: "I take it you don't believe all the things I'm being accused of."

Licha replied before Mario could. "Major, you have powerful enemies in the Junta, due to your opposition to the Agrarian Reform. If they had the tiniest bit of evidence that you did anything wrong, you'd be in jail by now. For me, that's the greatest proof of your innocence."

Mario added, "We're quite certain you didn't pull off the Monsignor Romero murder. The murderers needed to have known, sufficiently in advance, where the Archbishop was going to be that evening, and that information could've only been gotten by people from our side. Who, by the way, were the only ones that knew that he was going to give that Homily of Fire that Sunday, which he had to give in order to try to pin the murder on the Government or death squads or you."

D'Aubuisson nodded in the dark. "You're absolutely right, but in addition to that, nobody in El Salvador has the skill to pull off such a precise operation and disappear, without being able to be identified. That was done by professional foreigners."

"We agree, Major."

The Major said, "In the note you sent me, you say that you'd like me to come up with a reliable communication system."

"Yes, Major, in a way that we can contact you and you can contact us. Is that possible?"

The Major replied, "Yes, it is. I'll come up with a key to decipher the message that will be hidden in biblical passages."

Mario replied, "Perfect! But we're going to have to ask you to bring it to us tomorrow, so you can teach it to us. We'll be here tomorrow but after that, we don't know when we'd be able to get back here at El Carmen, which offers us the security no other place can. We're sorry to be imposing on you, but things are moving so fast due to the Agrarian Reform and the upcoming American elections, that it would be best to have a system in place sooner than later."

"I'll be here tomorrow at the same time." But D'Aubuisson didn't get up. Moments later, he said, "Although people tend to believe me when I speak to them, I'm pretty certain that before any Commander commits his troops to take any action based on information you give me, they're going to want more definite proof than my word. And I don't want to have to tell them about you. Besides, knowing how Catholic they all are, they wouldn't believe me that religious folk do bad things. Can you help me in that sense? What do I say?"

Licha was ready for this one. "Major, you don't need to provide any information about us. Just point to the Nicaraguan revolution, which was planned and executed by Jesuits, and that the Spanish Jesuits in El Salvador want the same thing for this country."

The Major liked that: a simple and independently verifiable

explanation. “That makes sense. That’s what I’ll rely on.”

He got up and said, “I’ll see you tomorrow at the same time.”

With that, he was gone.

CHAPTER 59

U OR UCA?

Major Zepeda, the First Brigade S-2 (Intelligence Officer), was on duty as Officer of the Guard on May 7, 1980. At 6 p.m., the relatives and friends of the soldiers, who'd come to visit and partake of the 'Soldier's Day' celebrations, started to leave.

After supper, he went to his office to look over the latest dispatches from the different garrisons. In May 1980, he was in constant contact with the Security Forces who were keeping an eye on the National University, a haven for communists since its creation.

The kidnap, torture, and murder of Ernesto Regalado, a wealthy philanthropist, had been concocted inside the National University of El Salvador. Most of the Popular Organizations' marches started at the National University. It would've been so easy to shut down the it down, but that would' have angered the non-activist students who just wanted to get a degree. So the decision had been made to keep the University open for now, but to keep it under constant surveillance.

Time passed, and around midnight, he heard activity outside of his office. Two trucks rolled into the central area. Several men, mostly in military uniform, were helped off the trucks. The Brigade Commander, Colonel Blandón, turned to Zepeda and instructed him to interrogate them. Zepeda asked his Commander what their status was. The Colonel said, "Right now, they're enemies of the state, according to the Junta."

Zepeda asked the Colonel if he wanted them thrown in cells.

"No, put them under armed guard in the Officer's mess, while I talk to Majano. Interrogate D'Aubuisson first."

The fact that D'Aubuisson was among them alarmed Zepeda. The darling of the right in El Salvador. Why on earth had he been captured? And why hadn't the S-2 been informed, since it involved units from his Brigade?

As if he could read his mind, Colonel Blandón said, "This was all handled by Majano. I was just ordered to put Captain Leon's unit under his operational control."

Zepeda had to admire Majano's guts for attempting this. D'Aubuisson was an easy target, because of his reputation. And he was retired, which meant that no garrison had a valid excuse to rebel. Removing D'Aubuisson would've silenced the left-wing propaganda that accused the Junta of not being able to control the alleged death squads. Finally, it would've made Majano somebody to fear. He was very much liked, but he wasn't feared. It was good to have your enemies fear you.

But Majano should've killed him. Not doing so meant that D'Aubuisson was going to become some sort of folk hero, a legend. And it meant that Majano was going to lose respect and power, and that he'd end up leaving the Junta sooner than later. With which Zepeda had no problem—it was past time for the government to be in the hands of whomever the people elected, and not in the hands of the military. The military should stick to soldiering, not governing. He firmly believed that.

Zepeda went to the officer's mess of the First Brigade and ordered the prisoners untied. He told them to make themselves comfortable, but that there would be armed guards outside with orders to shoot.

"Zepeda, you piece of shit, we're *Tandona* classmates, where the hell do you get off threatening to have me shot?" asked *El Toro* Staben, a massive man if there was one, who was very popular in the Army.

Zepeda, who was born with a perpetual smirk on his face, accentuated it and said, "Toro, you stupid son of a bitch how did you allow yourself to be captured like this? I'm just following orders so have a drink and shut up."

He turned to Major D'Aubuisson, who, although no longer serving, was senior to him, and addressed him respectfully, "Sir, please accompany me to my office."

"Yes, of course, Zepeda." And D'Aubuisson immediately turned his charm on.

It wasn't an interrogation at all. Soon D'Aubuisson had Major Zepeda laughing with anecdotes and stories. The guy was a natural born politician, he should've never been in the military.

After a while, Zepeda figured that he had a duty to fulfill, and so he said, "Sir, I'm supposed to interrogate you. I don't like the situation that we're in, but I'm just following orders. What were you doing at that farm...

planning a coup?"

D'Aubuisson didn't bat an eye when he said, "Zepeda, it was Soldier's Day, we were celebrating, we weren't planning a damn thing."

Zepeda tried to look serious, but his smirking face didn't let him. He didn't frighten anybody. On the contrary—it used to get him in trouble in the military school, when upperclassmen would haze him, and he tried to look serious, but all the upperclassmen saw was a smirk. They'd scream at him "Mister, you making fun of me?" Was it any wonder he'd set the record for most pushups by a cadet, which hadn't been broken yet?

Nevertheless, he said, with all the seriousness he could muster, "Sir, I hear you want to overthrow the Junta."

Upon hearing that, D'Aubuisson turned dead serious. "Zepeda, we have bigger problems than the damn Junta. I wouldn't waste my time going after simple politicians. Sure, Colonel Majano is a damn socialist, but he's just a puppet. If I'm going to go after somebody, it'll have to be the puppet masters. So you tell your Colonel Majano that he's got nothing to fear from me."

Zepeda laughed. "So... at that farm tonight, you were planning on going after the real puppet masters, Fidel Castro and Brezhnev? And that's why you had some members of the Salvadoran navy with you, to use their boats?"

D'Aubuisson laughed. "Only if they ever show their faces in El Salvador, Zepeda. But they have representatives here, and Majano and Ungo and the rest of the politicians dance to their tune."

Zepeda was curious. "And who might they be, according to you?"

D'Aubuisson shook his head. "That, Zepeda, is information that I'll provide to you once you get us out of here alive. All my friends and me."

Zepeda had to laugh at that. "Come on, sir! You're speaking to the S-2 of the First Brigade, the most all-knowing Intelligence Officer in the Army. So I doubt very much that you know something that I don't already know."

But D'Aubuisson's cocky look said otherwise. This made the S-2 uncomfortable, because if there was something that he didn't know, well... he just had to know it, right?

He continued, to see what he could get out of his prisoner. "Look, you're a brother in arms and I wish you no harm. If it were up to me, I'd say, 'Go and sin no more.'"

D'Aubuisson pounced. "You're getting warmer."

This surprised Zepeda. "What?"

D'Aubuisson had Zepeda where he wanted him. "Tell me, Zepeda, have you ever heard the Sandinista Daniel Ortega talk?" They both knew that Daniel Ortega was the top Sandinista military man.

Zepeda shrugged. "Sure. He's nothing special."

D'Aubuisson nodded. "Of course, nothing special. He's a moron. And a puppet, just like your Majano."

"Of Castro?"

"Of the Church."

"What?"

"Yes Zepeda, the mastermind behind the Sandinista movement isn't Daniel Ortega, it's a Jesuit named Fernando Cardenal."

"How do you know this?"

"Please, let's use our heads here. Somoza had the means and the organization to keep him informed of any possible threat to his corrupt power. Do you think nobodies like the Ortegas could've outfoxed him? The only ones with brains there were the Jesuits because they're all educated in Europe."

"Are you telling me that Jesuits planned the downfall of Somoza?"

D'Aubuisson nodded, smiling. "Yes, and they were the only ones who could. It never occurred to Somoza to keep spies in seminars and convents."

This seemed too far-fetched for the S-2. "But come on, priests are trained to give mass, communion and hear confession, and in the case of the Jesuits, to educate. Not to make revolution or war."

D'Aubuisson looked at Zepeda almost with pity. He shook his head when he said, "Zepeda, set us free and you have my word as a former fellow officer that I'll open your eyes to the reality of the war that is coming our way. And I don't mind because my destiny is to become a politician and become president. So I'll pass on everything I know to you, and I'll get you in touch with my informants."

Zepeda didn't know what to make of this. So all he could ask was, "Does anybody else know about this?"

For the first time, D'Aubuisson lost his cool. "Zepeda, who the hell can I trust? Colonel Majano? Anybody in the Junta? Especially after what happened today? I'd be dead if it weren't for that Lieutenant Sánchez from the Signal Battalion!

"And no, I haven't told anybody. Do you want to know why? Because they're all Catholics who don't believe that a priest or nun can do anything wrong! Just like you!"

Zepeda just shook his head, not ready to believe.

So D'Aubuisson said, "OK Zepeda... tell you what. Prove me wrong. I claim that you have constant surveillance on the National University, but not on the UCA. Go ahead. Tell me I'm wrong."

Zepeda had to nod. He was absolutely right. It had never occurred to him to place the UCA or any catholic institution under surveillance... for the very reasons D'Aubuisson had given!

The prisoner knew he'd won the S-2 over. He continued. "Let me assure you that the sources I have are priceless. Those sources are telling me how things are unfolding with the revolutionary priests and nuns. But right now, I can't trust those sources to anybody."

Zepeda was leaning toward believing him now. This wasn't an invention. This was making sense. D'Aubuisson was indeed aware of something that he was unaware of. He continued his query. "So, is it just the Jesuits, or is it from Archbishop Rivera on down as well?

"Zepeda, you're catholic, aren't you? A mass-going catholic?"

Zepeda nodded and laughed. "My wife drags me to mass every Sunday I'm not on duty. Can't avoid it."

D'Aubuisson pressed on. "When was the last time you went to mass, where the priest didn't talk shit about the military?"

Zepeda laughed. "Since I can remember, they always talk shit about us."

D'Aubuisson nodded. "And those priests aren't Jesuits, are they?"

Zepeda shook his head.

Major D'Aubuisson gave the S-2 his 'I told you so' look. "Does that answer your question?"

Zepeda pondered all this. Just to make sure, he asked, "So the revolution isn't being planned by students of the National University?"

D'Aubuisson shook his head. "Students, Zepeda? Students plan marches. Kidnaps, assassinations, even. But revolutions? You need much smarter people than that, and they don't come much smarter than the Jesuits."

This guy was making more and more sense to Zepeda.

His prisoner continued. "The places where the revolution is being planned are the Catholic University, the Externado de San José and of course, the Seminary of San José de la Montaña."

He paused, and then stated what was now obvious: "And by not placing them under surveillance, we're making the very same mistake that Somoza did."

Zepeda wanted to give excuses for not doing so. "Look, sir, I know lots of priests. They're harmless. They bark but they don't bite."

D'Aubuisson shook his head and explained. "Zepeda, they have this new theology that allows them to go to war. It's called Liberation Theology. And liberationist priests are planning to take over El Salvador like the Jesuits took over Nicaragua."

Zepeda weighed all this. If D'Aubuisson was right, it meant that all this time, the much respected First Brigade S-2, its vaunted Intelligence Officer, had had the wrong intelligence all this time. What's more, he was completely ignorant of everything. Ignorant is not a good thing to be, if you're an S-2. So he asked, "What else can you tell me?"

"Zepeda, that's all you'll hear from me until you set me free. When you do, I'll pass my informants on to you."

Major Zepeda took Major D'Aubuisson back to the Officer's Mess and took another one of the prisoners back to his office. He left his classmate, *El Toro* Staben, for last, and only after he'd made sure that he was too drunk to attempt to strangle him with his bare arms.

At around ten o'clock on the morning of May 8, 1980, the Captain of the Guard entered and saluted smartly. "Major Zepeda, Colonel Blandón's order is to set the prisoners free."

When he went to inform the prisoners that they were free to go, D'Aubuisson approached him to thank him and to tell him that he'd follow through with his promise to pass on his informants to him, after he coordinated with them.

CHAPTER 60

S-2 PLUS 2

The confessional shook when the penitent knelt. He was obviously bigger and heavier than D'Aubuisson, who was as thin as Gandhi. But instead of saying the act of contrition, or saying something purely Catholic, he said, "Is there anybody here?"

Father Tacarello said, "Hail Mary, full of grace."

The penitent said, "Oh, right... I'm supposed to say since 15 B.C. or something like that?"

Father Tacarello said, "How are you Major Zepeda?"

"I'm fine. You must be Father Mario."

"Yes, and Sister Licha is here as well."

"Hello, Major." Sister Licha was kneeling on the other side of the confessional, again.

"Hello, Sister, I'm glad to meet you both."

Mario spoke up first. "We're glad Major D'Aubuisson put you in contact with us, given that we almost lost him a couple of weeks ago. We wouldn't have known whom to turn to, if he was no longer around. Did he tell you about us?"

"Nothing but your names, and only after you'd given the go-ahead for this meeting. He realizes the value of this relationship, but only if it remains secret. As do I."

Everybody nodded.

Zepeda continued. "So now that we're in contact, and that I'm aware of the communication method that D'Aubuisson and you came up with... do you have any information for me?"

Licha took the lead. "Major Zepeda, Major D'Aubuisson told us that you, as the Intelligence Officer of the First Brigade, needed to know that a major offensive is being planned for next January, if not sooner."

Zepeda shrugged. "Maybe so, but the truth is that the Agrarian Reform has begun, and that's going to peel away support from them. In guerrilla warfare, the side that wins the hearts and minds of the people wins. And we're doing that. A people that is grateful for the dispossession of the rich to empower the peasants, won't rise up against the army that made it happen. And without a popular uprising, the guerrillas have no numbers to do anything serious. So forgive me, but I doubt it."

Licha didn't like the disdain with which the major treated that information. But at the same time, she had to consider that he might just be testing them.

She tried another tack. "Major, the Sandinista Revolution has been sending weapons since July 1979. Have you managed to seize all of the weapons that have gone into the 'U?'" The 'U" was what people usually called the National University.

Zepeda was surprised by the question. D'Aubuisson must've told them what he'd been doing. He decided to answer sincerely. "Truth is, we haven't seized any weapons at the U."

Mario injected himself in the conversation with, "Do you know why, Major Zepeda? Because the weapons are being stored in many places, but not the U."

Zepeda was even more surprised by this reply. According to his 'intelligence,' the Sandinistas had yet to send anything; that they were mostly engaged in training guerrilla commanders. He asked the logical question. "So where are they being stored, then?"

Mario replied, "There are several places throughout San Salvador that had to be built, because of your constant surveillance of the U, Major. Sister Licha helped to build them. If we tell you where they are, you'll never see Sister Licha alive again—they'll know who betrayed them."

Zepeda understood that. It did seem odd to him that the Sandinistas hadn't sent anything. Which meant that his intelligence was wrong. And therefore, weapons were indeed coming in and that meant that...

Licha inserted herself in his thought process with her voice. "The weapons are being sent with only one purpose, Major. And that's the offensive that must take place before they inaugurate the next U.S. president. That offensive will take place. And it's so important that a Russian has been coming to the country, to supervise the building of the weapons depots."

This shocked Zepeda. "A Russian? In El Salvador?" He couldn't hide his distress. How was it possible that he, the S-2 of the First Brigade, its

Intelligence Officer, didn't know about a Russian in El Salvador? He had informants everywhere! Well... except, of course, among the priests and nuns, just like D'Aubuisson had said.

Mario said, "Major Zepeda, since July 1979, Nicaragua is in the Russian sphere. More than one Russian must be able to speak Spanish well, to be able to pass himself off as a Spanish Jesuit, wouldn't you agree?" Although Don Blas had never sought to pass himself off as a Jesuit, the white lie had a purpose: to make sure this military man took them seriously.

Zepeda felt humiliated. It was obvious that the enemy was preparing something big, about which he had no clue. But no more.

He said to them, "What you're telling me makes sense. If there are weapons, and there are Russians, that means that the offensive will come. Forgive me for doubting you."

Licha was magnanimous. "Major, it does sound incredible: for men and women of God to be planning a revolution, hand-in-hand with the godless Russians. But that's exactly what's coming our way."

Zepeda shook his head. It had seemed incredible to Zepeda. But not anymore.

Licha continued, "I ask you for two things: the first is that you never doubt us. If we weren't so sure of all this, we wouldn't have sought out Major D'Aubuisson. The second is that you not ask me where the weapons are, for my personal security. Rest assured that when the time is right, I'll let you know."

Mario added, "I also ask you not to stop your surveillance of the U, Major. That will make them sure that nobody knows any better."

Zepeda nodded. "That's a good idea, father, but now what? Do I start putting surveillance on the UCA, too?"

Licha asked, "Major, why expend resources there, when you've got us?"

But Zepeda was a skeptic by nature. "Forgive me, Father and Sister, but D'Aubuisson said that you work at schools, not at the UCA. So that means that whatever is planned at the UCA may go unperceived by you."

Mario replied, "Major Zepeda, we're so close to those people that we're going to find things out a lot sooner than any informant that you may decide to place there—who hasn't earned the trust that Sister Licha and I have earned."

Zepeda relented. "OK, I agree." Zepeda's mind went back to the offensive. Something wasn't adding up. There may be more than enough weapons, but they certainly don't have enough fingers to pull the triggers.

So he said, "If they do have the weapons, what there's missing is manpower. And that manpower is only going to come from a popular uprising. And what could bring about such uprising? If the murder of Monsignor didn't, nothing will."

Mario agreed. "Believe us, Major, that has everybody scratching their heads. The only explanation is the personal popularity of Duarte and that the people really looked forward to getting land. And you're right—now that it's actually starting, that uprising seems more and more remote."

Zepeda felt validated. "You see? Even you agree that, given the circumstances, that offensive won't take place because it can't succeed."

Licha shook her head. "Major, as an expert on military history, can you think of any battle that was engaged by a numerically inferior force against a numerically superior force, even though they knew they were inferior?"

Zepeda could recall several battles: the Battle of the Bulge in 1945, when the depleted German army mounted an attack on the numerically-superior allied forces; Leonidas and his 300 Spartans; the Tet offensive in Vietnam... and he replied, "Yes, many, Sister Licha."

Licha nodded. "Well then, this offensive will take place, whether the popular uprising occurs or not, because the foreign powers that are invested in it are going to ensure that it does. The only thing we can do, Major, is whatever we can to defeat this offensive with minimum bloodshed. And that's why we're here with you now."

Zepeda shook his head, and remarked, "If they do, they're going to wish they hadn't. A lot of them are going to die. They're sending them to a certain slaughter."

To which Mario replied, "Major, that's another aspect that Sister Licha and I have come to realize: those who want this war see Salvadorans as inferior, subhuman and expendable. They don't give a damn how many are left dead, blind, paralyzed, mutilated... nothing. And we're offended by that. That's why we've wanted to establish a relationship with you: to defeat this with as little bloodshed as possible."

Zepeda was impressed by the sincerity of his words. For the first time, he felt at ease with these two religious people. These could very well be the sources that every S-2 dreams of having.

So Zepeda sincerely said, “You are so right, Father. Very well said. I want you to know that I believe you and that, from this moment on, we’ll be in touch. Don’t hesitate to contact me if you need me for anything, as well.”

He was about to get up to leave, but Sister Licha asked him to wait. “Major, there’s something else you need to know. In Europe, they emphasized the history of father Camilo Torres Restrepo, a Colombian priest who died fighting as a guerrilla. Before he joined the Colombian guerrillas, he’d been part of the Colombian Agrarian Reform Institute, which actually did redistribute farms to the peasants, like the Junta is doing now. Only in the case of Colombia, it didn’t go fast enough for father Restrepo. Please take this into account.”

Major Zepeda left the Church of El Carmen, walked a couple of blocks to where his car was parked, got inside and sped off, thinking about the alleged offensive. The enemy would attack with an ill-trained and ill-equipped force, not ready for any frontal assault. Furthermore, since the offensive would involve attacking military garrisons, they would need to have a three to one manpower ratio in their favor to have any probability of success at each garrison. That would require the attackers to number 60,000 well-armed and trained guerrillas to be able to defeat the Armed Forces in a defensive position.

All the intelligence available to him pointed to a guerrilla force one-sixth of that size, not all of whom were well-trained.

So he was right that only a popular uprising could make such an offensive work. Major Zepeda was suddenly very grateful for the reappearance of Duarte, someone whom he, as a lieutenant, had hated for allegedly being a communist. How wrong he’d been—it was actually Duarte, together with Majano, who were saving the country from communism.

The guerrillas had tried to stop the first handovers of expropriated properties to the peasants and faced a determined Army. Never had the Army felt so close to its people, and vice versa.

The significance of that was that in all probability, the population wasn’t going to give any guerrilla offensive any support, much less in the form of an uprising.

But the probability wasn’t zero. And if there was something that he’d learned in the past few days is that if he felt too certain about something, that he was probably in the wrong. So now he had to force himself to consider what could go wrong as well.

He focused on the size of the Armed Forces which, all together, including seamen, airmen, army and Security Forces, didn't amount to more than 20,000 men. That was enough to defeat a frontal attack, but...

He then realized the significance of what Sister Licha had said: with that number of men, the Army was planning on completing the transfer of properties in July of 1981; but if the offensive was going to come in January of 1981, then the Salvadoran Agrarian Reform, like Colombia's, was going too slow!

To make certain that the population didn't rise up in support of the guerrillas, what he had to recommend to his commander, Col. Blandón, was to recommend to the Junta to accelerate the transfer of properties, to complete it by December 1980—not by July 1981.

Since the problem was that there was no way to increase the number of soldiers because there was no budget for it, the only way to accelerate the Agrarian Reform would be to deploy far more soldiers to support it—even at the expense of combating the guerrillas.

But Col. Blandón would want a complete solution, and therefore Zepeda was going to have to tell him how—not just why.

Zepeda knew that the guerrilla was the strongest in the eastern part of the country, because it was the closest to Nicaragua. Therefore, what was logical was to do the Agrarian Reform there, first. Then they could proceed to the north, the central zone and then the western zone of the country. That would allow the Agrarian Reform to be complete by December 1980.

The race for the hearts and minds had suddenly become a sprint.

Chapter 61

The Nightmare Come True

"How are things here in school, son?"

"Things are going well, mom. My grade average is a 90, and I'm doing well on the soccer team.

"Son, focus on studying. That's what's going to get you ahead in this life. Who knows? Maybe Don Pepe will give you a job at the Vesuvius."

Neto shook his head. "No, mom, I want to be a doctor, so that you and grandma don't have to be servants anymore, and I can have you living like queens with me."

Gladys embraced her son. She felt somewhat remorseful for not telling him the truth about his father: that he was alive and that he was the owner of Vesuvius—instead of the lie that his dad had died before he was born.

But in exchange for such lie, his son was receiving a great education at the Rodrigo Borgia Boarding School, which had been founded by several men who found themselves in Don Pepe's situation: fathers of illegitimate children. So whatever money Don Pepe was saving with Mario's scholarship, he was using to pay for the schooling of his other son, Neto.

The school was in the Flor Blanca residential neighborhood, a short bus ride away from the Tacarello residence. It had been named that way in honor of a Pope who had several illegitimate children, and who, when he became Pope, assumed the name of Alexander VI.

After releasing him from her embrace, she asked him, "So what did you need this money for?"

"We're taking a field trip to the Cerrón Grande dam, going through Suchitoto."

"Won't it be dangerous?"

Her son shook his head. "No, mom, the school does it every year."

The two were sitting in the schoolyard, outside of the cafeteria, having lunch under a huge, majestic *maquilishuat* tree. They were eating the turkey sandwiches that Gladys had brought him.

"How's your job, mom?"

"Oh, you know, busy, but it was a lot harder before, when there were children to take care of. By the way, your grandmother Estela sends her love and says that she'll come see you this weekend."

Neto was fully aware of who he was and where he came from. He wasn't' much different than the majority of his classmates—most father- or mother-less, or illegitimate. He also had classmates whose parents had divorced. In the end, everybody there had a good reason to live in a boarding school and not in a normal home.

That made them bond. But what divided them was what they planned to make of themselves. Half of them, like Neto, wanted to be successful in life, to overcome the setbacks life had dealt them early on. The other half resented the fortune of others, and they thought life and society owed them something. These were generally guerrilla-sympathizers. But not enough to go into the hills with them and abandon the comfort and security of their boarding-school lives, where they lacked for nothing, save the warmth of a home.

After lunch, Gladys made the sign of the cross on his forehead with her thumb and bid him farewell. She left certain that he'd be OK. After all, they' be going on yellow school buses and they were like Red Cross ambulances—untouchable.

Two yellow school buses left the school the very next day at 6 a.m., heading to Suchitoto. They left early to avoid the traffic in San Salvador, and the everyday protest marches. By 7 a.m. they had cleared Apopa and were on their way to north to Aguilares, where they would turn east toward Suchitoto and the Cerrón Grande Dam.

The section of highway between Apopa and Suchitoto crossed flat farmland, which eventually turned into to the slopes of Guazapa to the east and the San Salvador volcano to the west. The predominant crop was sugar cane.

About one kilometer before the town of Aguilares, the buses slowed down. They were stopping for what seemed to be a military checkpoint. The boys looked out the window and saw men wearing military uniforms. But something didn't seem right to Neto. They weren't clean shaven with cropped hair like the military was. These had facial hair.

The teacher that was on that bus must've noticed the same, so she shouted to the driver, "Don't stop! Don't stop! They're guerrillas!"

So the driver accelerated past the checkpoint, but to no avail. The bus tires were shot out, and the driver lost control. The bus came to a rest in a ditch. The bus behind them stopped.

Suddenly more armed men emerged from the sugar cane fields, not in uniform, but in peasant garb. They surrounded the buses and made the schoolboys and the teachers get out and go into the tall sugar cane fields.

Just so they understood the consequence of disobeying, the guerrilla leader, wearing military uniform, shot the driver who'd tried to run the checkpoint in the head. The other driver, who was an elderly man, was left behind.

When he found himself alone, the elderly driver got on the bus and drove to Aguilares, to report what had happened to the police.

When he returned with police to the scene of the crime, a policeman told the driver that everybody was probably halfway up Guazapa mountain, to guerrilla camps. Although it did seem strange to them that they'd take to female teachers with them. What on earth for?

The policeman said, "We'll inform the First Infantry Brigade. You'd better go back to the school and tell them what happened."

* * *

"Hello, this is Father Tacarello. May I help you?"

The hysterical voice was incomprehensible, all he could make out was 'Neto.'

"Gladys, if that's you, please calm down. I can't understand you."

His mom took the phone from her and said, "Marito, guerrillas kidnapped Neto and his schoolmates and took them to Guazapa. Gladys wants to know if you can do anything about it."

In the background, he could hear her scream "Please! My son!"

"Mom, I'll get on it right away."

Mario hung up and went directly to the director's office. "Please tell Father Montes that I need to see him at once," he told his secretary.

"I'm sorry, Father, but Father Montes is at the UCA right now."

"When do you expect him back?"

"In the evening."

"Could you please find a substitute for me for the rest of my classes today? I'm going to have to go to the UCA as well."

With that, Mario went to his car and sped off to the UCA. He was extremely upset, but halfway to the UCA, he calmed down enough to think. What was he going to tell the Jesuits, that his half-brother had been captured? What for? To get him released, just because he was his half-brother? There was a good chance that they'd refuse, claiming a greater priority, and if so, why reveal it? Besides, introducing this variable could very well jeopardize the plan he'd concocted with Licha. On top of that, his gut was telling him not to say anything.

Plus there was really no need to make this personal, when it could be left on a moral plane—to kidnap teenagers was amoral. Period.

With that, he turned his Volkswagen Beetle right around and went back to the Externado, to teach his classes normally. He would broach the subject with Father Montes at night, over dinner.

That evening, as he entered the Jesuit dining room, he was surprised to see Father Montes with Father Ellacuría and another priest whom he did not know.

Ellacuría greeted Mario effusively. "How is my Base Communities man?"

Montes introduced him to the other priest, Father Jon Cortina, who was actively involved in recruiting for guerrillas in the field. Mario thanked God for the chance to make his case precisely before all the right people.

As they were eating, Mario brought up the kidnapping as nonchalantly as possible: someone had called his mom to inform her that her son had been kidnapped, along with other boys and their teachers, by the guerrillas near Guazapa, after killing one of the bus drivers.

Ellacuría seemed unconcerned about it. "I understand that poor mother's pain. But as far as the guerrillas are concerned, she's no different than any other mother of any other Salvadoran teenager who has been made to enlist either by the Army or the guerrillas."

It took every ounce of fortitude for Mario to control himself, to be able to say, calmly, "Father Ellacuría, there are about 50 Salvadoran mothers out there who are feeling that pain right now. What's more, all those kids that were kidnapped today were teenagers, minors. The Salvadoran Army certainly isn't doing that, because if they did, we'd already be broadcasting it to the world."

Father Montes wasn't moved. "Look, Mario, for us to go tell Marcial to stop recruiting teenagers is to interfere with his conduct of the armed struggle that will bring a more just society for the very same teenagers and their families. And if we went there to request the release of those teenagers because of their privilege, he'd scoff in our faces, and tell us about the sufferings of kids all over this nation who aren't so privileged. And that's where the conversation would end, and so would his trust in us. We can't take afford that risk—certainly not at this stage of the game."

Mario tried hard to keep his personal interest from showing. "Father Montes, I understand that the revolution is paramount and that everything is subordinate to it. But in this case, morality isn't on our side, is it? God Almighty can't be on the side of the people who act as Marcial's people did in this case. And you know people are going to ask, 'If the movement is a grass-roots movement, why do they have to abduct poor kids, teachers, and murder a poor bus driver?'"

Father Jon Cortina intervened. "As we were telling our Nicaraguan counterparts on the conference call earlier today, we're having a hard time recruiting adults, thanks to this Agrarian Reform. People prefer to be landowners rather than guerrillas."

The phone line they spoke over with Nicaragua was a 'secure' line that had been established by Cuban technicians. To anybody that tried to listen in, they would only hear white noise, the type you hear when a TV station goes off the air. They were pretty sure it was Soviet technology stolen from Americans, because Cubans couldn't even manufacture toilet paper.

Jon Cortina continued. "That's why I asked Father Ellacuría to set up a conference call with Nicaragua today. I don't like our recruiting to be invading forbidden territory, like minors. So we consulted with the Sandinistas about the possibility of lending a hand for the offensive with manpower because of the detrimental effect of the Agrarian Reform on our ability to recruit, which is done from Base Communities. I also coordinate with the local diocesan priests about what to say to encourage the men to sign up. The guerrilla commanders must not be liking the rate at which people are joining them, and so they've taken the step to abduct teenagers."

Father Montes seemed surprised. "But Father Cortina, I thought that that we'd been meeting our recruitment quotas for the guerrillas. Was I wrong?"

Father Cortina nodded. "We have, we have fulfilled our end of the bargain. But they haven't."

"How so?"

"Many recruits can't take it and escape. So their rate of attrition is pretty big. And even if an escaped recruit is captured, he gets shot, to set an example. This must be why they've started recruiting teenagers."

Segundo Montes thought about this. It was early August 1980. The deadline was for January 1981, and as morally abhorrent as recruiting teenagers seemed, they had the physical stamina and trainability to be ready for the January 1981 uprising because they had no wives and families to care for. Actually, they were ideal. Their young minds were malleable. Militarily, this was not a bad solution. But it was amoral, as Mario had pointed out.

Father Ellacuría took over to establish courses of action. "Gentlemen, we need to develop our position in light of these events. But first, let's review what we've learned today: Nicaragua has its Sandinistas spread all over Nicaragua, to bring it under control. In addition to the fact that their territory is six times greater than ours, they seem to be encountering resistance from the Miskito *indios*. And since they were never that large because Somoza's Guard was fairly small, any additions to the Sandinista army must be used internally. They can't spare anybody. We also learned that Cuba can't reinforce us because they're too different from us and the last thing we need is for the world to see big black Cubans killing Salvadoran troops."

Mario knew that Cubans were already operating in El Salvador, under Ellacuría's command. But operating as death squads, with a high probability of not getting caught, was one thing; engaging in sufficient numbers to be killed or caught was something else. That would justify a massive U.S. intervention, with the risk of losing everything that had been gained under pusillanimous Jimmy Carter.

Ellacuría continued. "However, there is a silver lining: the Salvadoran Army is out handing land over to the peasants and so they're not pursuing the guerrillas actively. That means that we have time to train without worrying about the Army attacking our training camps. That will ensure the best possible training for our fighters by the time the offensive is launched.

"We've also learned that to fill their ranks, the guerrillas are abducting minors or teenagers by force. They have to because of their rate of attrition. So while we understand the need for them to fill their ranks, we're going to suffer a huge public opinion hit if this continues. We have to talk to Commander Marcial to come up with a better solution. Mario's same question will be posed by everybody: if this is a popular movement, why are minors being abducted?

Mario nodded. Ellacuría continued. "Also, today was messy. A driver, a poor man making minimum wage was executed by Marcial's men. Two female teachers were taken by force. You can bet that all those affected families won't be joining the uprising. Nor will their friends."

Ellacuría concluded his summary with, "So, Father Cortina, I would recommend that you immediately find Commander Marcial and inform him that this must stop. Both of you should be able to come up with a better way to recruit people. Preferably, young men of legal age. You should consider that because of the Army's greater dedication to the Agrarian Reform, the guerrillas will have the time and resources to train their recruits much better."

Father Cortina nodded. "You make perfect sense, Father Ellacuría. I'll convince Marcial to keep those who are sympathetic to the cause and let the others go. There are enough poor people in El Salvador who won't become landowners who can serve the cause, without having to resort to violent abduction."

Father Ellacuría looked at Mario. "As for you, young Mario, after your European trip, we have pretty much set you on the path to develop Base Communities. Father Rutilio Grande had his headquarters in Aguilares, which would be a good base for you to assist Father Cortina in the recruitment effort."

Mario nodded. He thought this was a splendid idea because it would allow him to get in touch with Neto and coordinate his escape.

But Segundo Montes wasn't comfortable with this. Father Tacarello was his right-hand man and he was instrumental in getting students to join the guerrillas, which had earned him the *nom de guerre* 'Eliseo.' There was nobody more suited than Mario Tacarello to inspire the students to support the cause either physically (a few) or morally (the majority).

In addition, the reason for his trip to Europe wasn't to send him to Aguilares, it was, first and foremost, to accompany Sister Licha to Europe, at Don Blas' request.

But instead of rejecting his superior's idea outright, he offered an alternative: "Father Ellacuría, in reality, our Man on Base right now is Father Cortina. But the guy producing commanders for the guerrillas is Padre Tacarello. Just recently, another student of his joined the guerrillas. So I propose that we take advantage of his youth and energy to do both things: in the school week, that he remain at Externado, but on weekends that he join Father Cortina in the Aguilares zone, starting this Saturday."

Ellacuría had no problem with that. "I concur. The August vacation is coming up, so let's have him spend that week in Aguilares with Father Cortina as well. And that way, you can start implementing the new recruitment plan that you come up with."

Jon Cortina assented. "I have no problem with focusing on the Aguilares/Guazapa area anyway. For any offensive to be successful, it must succeed in the Guazapa area."

Ellacuría stood up. "Gentlemen, we've made important decisions today. Godspeed to all of us."

Mario felt relieved—everything had turned out in the best possible way to fulfill his promise to Gladys and Estela. And though he had yet to study all the possible ramifications, his gut was telling him that this was a promising path, for all his purposes.

But what had really made his day was to learn that the meeting with Major Zepeda had borne fruit: the Army had dived head-first into the Agrarian Reform and that also meant that Neto was less likely to die in an attack by the Army to his camp in Guazapa.

Chapter 62

Making Men out of Boys

That Saturday, Father Cortina and Mario set out for Aguilares early in the morning, wearing their Jesuit-black uniform with clerical collars. They left in a van that belonged to the Archdiocese, for their protection. They were going to stop off at the church of Aguilares to drop off their bags and head up Guazapa Mountain on a jeep that belonged to the parish.

About an hour up the mountain, on the dirt road, guerrillas armed with AK-47s waved them to a stop. Father Cortina got out with his papers signed by Archbishop Rivera y Damas and told them he was coming to discuss the matter of recruitment with Marcial.

Two men frisked the priests for weapons, and two of them hopped on the back of the vehicle, telling the priests to continue up the path.

About fifteen minutes later, the men told the priests to stop the vehicle and get out. They started walking into a wooded area to the side of the road. They could hear loud voices up ahead, barking orders. Then they came to a clearing, where they saw young men marching with sticks in lieu of weapons. They had their heads shaved and they were barefoot, to make running away more difficult.

A quick count revealed to Mario that at most, there were two dozen teenagers there. Neto wasn't among them.

The two guerrillas took them up a path to a cave. The cave was lit inside with Coleman lanterns. It was spacious. It had some cots and in the back part of the cave there was a desk. Sitting behind it was a hairy, dirty, disheveled man with long fingernails and yellow teeth, wearing a green uniform, who was not Marcial. He stood up to greet them and smiled a less than comforting smile. "Gentlemen, I'm Commander Mayo Sibrián. I'm Commander Marcial's executive officer in Guazapa, to use military jargon. What can I do for you?"

After introducing themselves, Jon Cortina asked, "When will Commander Marcial be back, Commander?"

"He's out east and I don't know when he'll be back. We expect him any day now."

Cortina nodded and continued. "Commander Sibrián, we're concerned about the abduction of the teenagers from two school buses last Tuesday."

Sibrián smiled proudly and said, "That was me!"

Cortina continued, unimpressed. "Commander, we don't believe that this is the best way to proceed to recruit people for the cause. The agreement we made with the commanders was to let the Popular Church, through its Base Communities, drive recruits toward you. So this abduction of 50 teenagers using violence has taken us by surprise, and we believe that it's going to hamper our ability to recruit people to the cause."

Mayo Sibrián stopped smiling, and that sent shivers down both priests' spines. He stood up. He wasn't very tall, but he looked very wild, but most of all, very intimidating, despite his short stature.

He said, "It's very easy for you to criticize my actions, sitting in an air-conditioned office or church. Over here, we have to contend with snakes, bugs, mosquitoes and what not. But that's all right because it toughens us up. But your environment has the opposite effect on you: it makes you soft and bourgeois."

He paused for effect. This man wasn't educated, but he knew his craft. He then continued. "You Spanish priests can go home if this cause fails. Back to Spain, or wherever you come from, because you certainly look more like you're from Berlin, Germany than my hometown of Berlin, Usulután. For me, this country is either going to be my home or my grave, gentlemen."

Mario wanted to tell him that he was Salvadoran, but Cortina pressed his arm to prevent him.

Mayo Sibrián continued. "I don't see all these recruits that you're allegedly send us. When the offensive comes, what do you want me to attack with, mannequins? Or ghosts? Perhaps you're better at conjuring ghosts than recruiting guerrillas?"

Father Cortina dared to answer him, despite the rhetorical nature of the question. "Commander Sibrián, we were unaware of these circumstances you're telling us about. But we did realize that with your action, things weren't going as planned. And so my superiors sent me here, along with Father Mario, to come up with a better plan, if we can, but also to pledge to you that we'll work with you to get you the recruits you need. I'll be stationed in Aguilares from now on, and Father Mario will be assisting me on weekends over there, while still doing recruiting work in the capital." He stopped and signaled to Mario to back him up.

"Indeed, Commander Sibrián, we've sent you potential commanders from the Externado."

Sibrián's eyes opened wide. "Are you Eliseo?" When Mario nodded, Sibrián got up to hug him. When he released the priest, he said "You know, commander Zonte is from the Externado and he just got back from Cuba and is now training people to be sappers. Another one of yours just left for Cuba as well." Mario nodded.

Father Cortina was unaware of this, but he was glad that young Mario had been assigned to him. He was certain they'd be able to reach an agreement. And taking advantage of the happy turn of events, Father Cortina said, "Commander Sibrián, in the action of last Tuesday, two female teachers were abducted as well. In the spirit of cooperation, I'd like to ask you to kindly let them go back to Aguilares with us so that we can return them to their husbands and children, who are very anxious."

Mayo Sibrián shook his head and smiled that chilling smile again. "I'm sorry, that won't be possible. They're fulfilling a mission for us, and I'm pretty sure their husbands won't want them back anymore."

Both priests' hearts sank. They knew what was coming.

Sibrián continued. "You see, those fifty new recruits were nothing but crybabies. They wanted to go home to momma. We simply told them that their teachers were there momma, and more."

He smiled more broadly, despite the faces of the priests, and he continued: "The teachers are useful to keep them here. Since the force under my command is not sufficiently large to prevent escapes, we need an incentive for them to want to stay. And thanks to the teachers, the boys are becoming men. And not one of them has attempted to escape in three days, which is a record for us. You see, we've told them that if anybody tries to escape, that we'll kill one of their teachers. And as I said, they really like their teachers a lot now."

The priests couldn't believe their ears. The teachers were being used as comfort women—what the Japanese had done with Chinese women in World War II. And what was worse, they were being used for minors—fifty minors. There was no adjective to adequately describe such evil.

Now it was Mario's turn to hold Cortina's arm, to restrain him from speaking out. Besides being impossible to reason with this commander, it was time for him to find out about his half-brother. Mario said, "We understand, commander. We understand that the main purpose is to overthrow this oppressive government. But when we entered through the forest, all we saw was a couple of dozen young men training. So the others must be around here, if they haven't escaped, right?"

Mayo Sibrián gleamed when he replied, "Not one. This isn't the only camp. We have several camps placed around the mountain. Near the mountaintop. There are natural caves on Guazapa that offer shelter, in case the Air Force comes to try to bomb us. So we've established the camps near such caves. Like we've done here. The recruits are shifted from camp to camp."

"As are the teachers?"

"Of course."

Commander Sibrián got up, slung his weapon over his shoulder and invited them to go with him to the other campsites. He told two guerrillas to come with them.

It was obvious they were circumnavigating the top of the mountain, about a kilometer short of the summit, which offered no tree cover. After a 5-minute brisk walk, they got to another camp. Mario immediately saw Neto drilling, shaved head, and barefoot. With his stick at his shoulder. The Commander led them to the corresponding cave, where the guards saluted Mayo Sibrián. Inside the cave were the two female teachers, covered by blankets, but obviously wearing nothing. That was to prevent them from running away.

When they saw the priests, their faces lit up. The priests represented hope! But then they sank back under the blankets, as they saw Mayo Sibrián walk in.

Mayo Sibrián flew into a rage, shouting, "Haven't you learned by now, comrades, that you are to stand up when in the presence of a superior?" He turned to one of the guerrillas and ordered: "Bring me a *palo* [stick]."

The women stood up in a hurry, and in so doing, stepped on each other's blankets, so that they were fully nude in front of everybody. They attempted to cover themselves with their hands, and then they started to sob.

Mario's heart broke at the sight. What had they done to deserve this? He remembered Marcial's words to Sister Licha to the effect of hell not being worse than being poor in El Salvador. Yet today he realized there was indeed something worse: being a woman in El Salvador.

The guerrilla came back with a branch, gave it to the Commander, who told the women to turn around. Sobbing, they did, and he proceeded to whip their behinds with the branch. Their sobs turned to pleas, but nothing could stop the Commander from disciplining them. Not that the priests attempted to. They felt ashamed for being such cowards.

When he was done, he ordered the women to turn around. "What is our motto, comrades?" The women replied, in unison, "Revolution or Death, Commander."

"Good, now then ladies, we've been drilling our new recruits hard today, and they're going to need to be taken care of. Will you do that?"

The women bravely said "Yes, Commander," through their pain and tears.

"Why will you do that, comrades?"

Again, in unison: "Because the Revolution demands it of us, Commander, and we belong to the Revolution."

"You used to have a bourgeois life, didn't you? You used to have servants, didn't you? You used to lord over your fellow Salvadorans, as if you were superior, didn't you?"

The women kept responding with nods.

"But now you repent, and you're now serving your fellow Salvadorans, just like many servants serve their employers, aren't you?"

"Yes, Commander."

"Proceed then."

With that, the women left the cave, with just the filthy blankets on, picked up some water jugs and went to fill the jugs, probably to bathe the recruits.

The priests and Sibrián spent the rest of the afternoon discussing alternatives so as not to have to resort to kidnapping high school students and their teachers. But Sibrián only committed to not doing more kidnappings for a while, since he had his hands full with these fifty new ones.

After the meeting, the priests when back down to Aguilares.

* * *

Sunday night, Mario returned from Aguilares to his parents' home, where he informed Gladys that he had seen Neto, that he was fine, but that getting him to escape wouldn't be easy.

Gladys started to cry. "I've heard they beat them up, they even shoot them if they try to flee."

Mario explained how they were keeping them there, using the two teachers as comfort women and threatening to shoot them and their classmates if any of them fled. Gladys was inconsolable.

So he tried to calm her with the news that it was highly improbable that they would be attacked by the Army, since it was heavily engaged in the transfer of land under the Agrarian Reform.

That consoled her somewhat.

Pepe stepped in. "Mario, do you think I can pay them something to get him back?"

Mario shook his head. "Dad, I would've offered that if it stood a chance of working. But it doesn't. They're looking for bodies to use to launch a nationwide attack probably in late December, early January. The problem they're having is that people aren't volunteering because the Agrarian Reform is working against them. They seem desperate. They were expecting to get an overwhelming number of volunteers after Monsignor Romero's death, but that never happened."

Pepe nodded. He assumed it would be of no use, but he had to ask, and ask in front of Gladys, so she wouldn't believe Neto's dad wasn't willing to do whatever it took. Which he was.

Gladys asked, "So what happens now, Marito? Does Neto get killed in a stupid attack on a garrison? That would be the end of me!"

Mario did his best to console her. "We pray, Gladys, and we have faith. Here's why: nothing's going as planned for the guerrillas; so their luck would've to change and let's pray that it doesn't.

"Also, there are 100 other parents out there who are doing what they can to recover their loved ones, plus two very upset husbands who will get even more upset when they find out what their wives are being used for. I guarantee you this: the karma that's coming their way is huge.

"Regardless, you have my word—I will not rest until I get Neto out of there."

Gladys hugged him and left, feeling hopeful. She felt certain that Mario would get her son back.

Pepe got a bottle of Chianti and offered some to Mario, who gladly took the glass.

"Mario, from what you're saying, it seems to me that the guerrillas are headed for slaughter if they pull off this attack."

"Undoubtedly. The recruits aren't given weapons because they might be used against their captors, and so how can they train? They'll be cannon fodder."

"So what can I do to prevent Neto from being cannon fodder? He's my son."

"Dad, I don't have a plan to get him out yet. But I'm thinking one up, believe me. Meantime, I'm going to try to convince my Jesuit superiors that the guerrillas are in no position to attack anybody. That time is too short for them to become an effective military force. That they're destined to fail."

"Are you going to tell them to call it off?"

"Yes, but also to give the Agrarian Reform a chance. I don't know if there's anything more astonishing in my life than seeing the Army going in, dispossessing the large landowners, and distributing that land to the peasants. It's really finishing off the guerrilla movement. That really ought to make my superiors reconsider."

"Son, you make sense, but if they disagree with you, what would be the reason for that?"

Mario thought about regurgitating all the reasons having to do with the Cold War, but his Dad already knew that. So Mario summarized it all up with this simple response: "Dad, without a revolution, there's no reason for the Jesuits to even exist."

The simple truth of his son's words almost knocked him over.

All Pepe could say was, "Wow."

And then his eyes opened wide, when he reached this realization: "You're going to betray them, aren't you?"

Mario nodded. "If they don't call the offensive off, then I won't have a choice."

They both sipped Chianti silently. Then Pepe asked, "Is your D'Aubuisson connection of any use?"

Mario hadn't told his parents that it was no longer D'Aubuisson, and he didn't see the need to. But he replied, "Yes, very useful. Maybe it'll help with Neto, I don't know yet."

After another sip, Pepe said, "You know, son, I'm proud of you, but I always wanted a better life for you. If at any point you want to go to Italy and lead a normal life, you can do so, because you're the son of an Italian. Please know that."

"Thanks, dad, but you may want to leave that option available for Neto and Gladys. If Neto escapes, he'll be hunted down."

Pepe thought to himself, "And so will you," but didn't say it. He felt confident that his son would arrive at the same conclusion. But he did make a note to himself to plan on a trip to Italy, to pave the way for any such exodus.

CHAPTER 63

A FRIENDLY CONVERSATION

That night was extra quiet at Xanadú. After doing the rounds, Captain Sánchez settled into a hammock of the home of his friend Gamero, near the top of the hill, and near the house of the Jesuits.

He had an inkling this would not end well. There were forces at work well beyond the control of his measly platoon. So if they wanted to annihilate him, they would. But besides his work on the Agrarian Reform program, nothing had felt as right as this. So let the future come, no matter how lethal.

He was about to doze off when he heard footsteps: in the darkness, he made out the silhouettes of one of his men and Segundo Montes.

"What can I do for you, Father? Please sit down."

"If you don't mind, Captain, I need a break." And he smiled apologetically, as if saying, "You understand."

"Yeah, I can imagine." Ellacuría's intensity must have that group on edge. Ellacuría was definitely not accustomed to being restrained and even less to being talked down to by an *indio*—a military *indio*.

But Segundo Montes was all right. He was far more mellow, probably from so many years of dealing with students. In fact, all the Externado graduates that Sánchez knew liked him very much. And his conduct over the radio earlier that day had been very helpful. Frankly, had he not been cooperative, this whole caper would've probably come to a premature end and probably not to his liking. So he felt he owed it to Montes give him some of his time.

Montes started out the conversation by asking, "If you don't mind, Captain, just tell me about yourself. How did you end up in the military?"

"I don't know, Father. I always wanted to be a musician. My first school years were in the USA, where my dad was a diplomat. One of the first things my parents did was to set me up with piano lessons, and apparently, I was pretty good. Of course, we never had a piano, so all my piano playing was when I was with the teacher. And they weren't but two or three classes, but my parents were convinced that I had it in me to be a musician.

"When we came back from the USA, we couldn't afford a piano, but we could afford a guitar. So my dad arranged for me to take lessons from Professor Jesús Quiroa, who had been a student of Agustín Barrios, the brilliant Paraguayan guitarist and composer known as *Mangoré*, who decided to settle down in El Salvador."

"You don't say!" Montes knew very well that *Mangoré* was on par with Spanish classical guitar giants like Francisco Tárrega and Joaquín Rodrigo.

"But they put me in the classical music lane, which really has a small audience. What would've really opened the doors to a musical career would've been to learn to play electric guitar. It's a different skill set, and I knew this because whenever we got together to form a band, I couldn't perform that well—going from soft nylon strings to steel strings isn't easy.

"When I graduated from high school, my dad informed me that all he could afford to do was to send me to the local Catholic University to study engineering. I went enthusiastically because relatives of mine who'd graduated from there spoke wonders about Father Ellacuría. And I certainly wanted it to be true—I wanted to be a good engineer. That's where I read Father Ellacuría's manifesto, on how the greatest minds in the world studied philosophy.

"I never could buy into that, you know. To me, the greatest minds in the world studied engineering, and put a man on the moon and brought him back safely. Or built skyscrapers, like in New York, where we lived for a year."

Montes nodded. "I can't disagree with you there, Captain. A priest who was a mentor of mine kept saying that I should study useful things to come teach Salvadoran kids how to make cars here."

"That mentor of yours was so right!"

"So how'd it go at the UCA, Captain?"

"The UCA was no challenge at all. The math classes that were taught were so basic compared to what I had learned at the American High School here in San Salvador. I started to feel that I needed to go study at a more challenging place, like, anywhere but El Salvador. And then fate stepped in."

Montes asked, "How did you manage to go to West Point? I thought that was only for Americans."

"Me too. It just so happened that I saw one of the best soccer players at my high school who was from a politically-connected family. He informed me that he'd be going to West Point, on a scholarship. That he'd have to take the test to enter the local Military School, to then go on to West Point.

"I asked, 'Automatically?' and he said, 'No, I'll have to apply to get into West Point, but with my connections...'"

Montes knew a lot about such 'connections' in El Salvador—he'd done his doctoral thesis on such matters.

The Captain continued. "I went directly to the UCA library to do some research on it. It turned out that there was this 'Allied Cadet' program that allowed foreigners to apply to get into any of the Service Academies: Army, Navy, Air Force, and Coast Guard. But these slots were being offered to cadets from allied armies all over the world, like from the Philippines, Nicaragua, Panama, Costa Rica—and Costa Rica didn't even have an army! It was obvious that only the best qualified among these foreign cadets would get in.

"Now then, I knew my soccer-playing buddy, and I knew that academically, I had him beat. So if he got into West Point, I might get into the Naval Academy or the Coast Guard Academy. I knew that I couldn't get into the Air Force because my eyesight was too poor."

"Do you wear glasses now, Captain?"

"I wear contact lenses, and fortunately my eyes can stand them for long periods of time. But at the time I had to wear glasses to see. And they were thick—like the bottoms of coke-bottles."

"Please go on. Your story is quite fascinating."

Sánchez did. "I found out that the local tests were like in a month. And of course, I wasn't an athlete. So I hit the 'Flor Blanca' stadium every morning. Running and doing pushups and sit-ups. But it was hopeless—there was no way to make up in one month's time what I hadn't done for 18 years of my life."

"So what happened?"

"Well that same month I took the SAT, to be able to have everything ready to apply to whichever U.S. military academy I qualified for—if I passed the local military school's physical admissions test."

The priest nodded, knowing full well some of his graduates took the same SAT test to study in the USA.

Sánchez continued. "But then came the two days of physical testing at the Gerardo Barrios military school. That was hell. I had to go through a military obstacle course, and I had definitely not trained for that. I mean, I gave it my best shot, but everybody else climbed up the ropes like pros, whereas I struggled."

Montes shook his head incredulously. "Captain, did angels come down from heaven to help you? It sounds like there was no other way for you to have made it."

The Captain laughed. "Well, the help wasn't heaven-sent. What did help was that they set different standards: one for those of us who'd be going abroad, and another for those who'd stay in the local military school. They had identified us as the *gringos*. And there were only three of us: my soccer buddy, a tall blond guy who was strong, who actually looked *gringo* but was actually from Chalatenango, where there are plenty of blonds; and me.

"Of the three, the one doing the worst was my soccer buddy. But what decided it all was the two-kilometer run: 5 laps around the track. And there, I beat both of them handily. My buddy didn't even finish the run running—he started walking after the first couple of laps."

"So that month at the stadium paid off, Captain."

"It worked better than 'connections.'" They both laughed.

"But you said there were two days of physical tests. What happened the next day?"

The Captain continued. "The next day, we had the swimming test."

"How good a swimmer are you?"

"I swim like a fish. I left everybody way behind. And I got so anxious to prove myself at something that I veritably crashed into the other wall."

"Did you hurt yourself?"

"A little. But I didn't care. I knew then that I would have the first choice of academy."

"And you aced the written exam."

"I sure did. So I was given the first choice, and I chose West Point."

"But given that you're a natural swimmer, why not the Naval Academy?"

"In retrospect, I should have. But West Point had the aura, the prestige."

"But Captain, were your parents OK with this?"

"It didn't matter. This was my decision."

"So then what happened?"

"Well, I had to wait to see if West Point accepted me. That was a painful three months."

"Why painful, were you uncertain?"

"I had no guarantee that I'd get accepted. And if I didn't get accepted, I would've never been able to live it down."

"So how did you get through it?"

"I prayed and abstained—to the point of almost becoming a mystic. One afternoon, I went into my room and kneeled, and started praying feverishly. There I was, all alone, when I felt this hand placed on my back, reassuringly. Instead of being afraid, I felt very much at peace. I just kept kneeling, eyes closed, wondering what would come next.

"Just then, the phone rang. It was my dad, who told me to go to the American Embassy because they had something they wanted to tell me."

"You'd been accepted."

"Yes. The U.S. military attaché gave me the news."

"So a musician turned military man."

"Yes."

"From what you've described, Captain, it seems to me that if you had trouble going up against Salvadoran cadets physically, I could only imagine how hard it was to compete against American cadets, who grew up playing American football."

Sánchez shook his head, recalling those days. "You have no idea, Father Montes. I barely passed gymnastics, and then Greco-Roman wrestling. I did well in boxing—I even participated in an intramural boxing championship, and even won some fights. But that was only because in intramural boxing, I only went up against people in my same weight category—it was easier than in boxing class, where I would have to go up against everybody—even football players."

"So it seems that you had improved physically, Captain."

"I had to or they would've kicked me out. But what really saved me was swimming. They had this beautiful Olympic-sized swimming pool. And they'd throw us in combat uniform and gear and time us on how long it would take us to swim back and forth a few times. I aced that. I left everybody else in my wake. And that prevented me from flunking out due to physical education."

"But would they have really kicked you out?"

The Captain nodded. "There was a cadet from Nicaragua. A really nice guy. Really rich, too. He did worse than me, but more importantly, he didn't try. I would go to remedial gymnastics every chance I got. He didn't. He flunked out."

Montes thought about this. It was obvious to him that the Captain was a man who'd had to struggle long and hard to get to where he was. So he decided to say so. "Congratulations, Captain. You've overcome great obstacles. That is admirable."

But Sánchez shook his head and then denied with his index finger. "No, Father Montes, what I've had to endure is nothing compared to the hardships every other man in uniform in the Salvadoran army has had to endure."

Montes didn't expect this reaction. Not wanting to make the priest uncomfortable, Sánchez thanked him for his kind words, but continued with his explanation. "There can be no doubt about the capacity and valor of the American soldier. The 'D-Day' invasion proves my point. But the truth is that the American soldier has won his battles with far more human, economic and scientific resources than the Salvadoran military has ever had.

"Nevertheless, the performance of these humble Salvadoran soldiers has been no less brave and admirable. I'm honored to wear their same uniform."

Montes couldn't contribute to this conversation. So he stood up to leave. But Sánchez didn't let him. "Hold on, Father, now it's your turn. You went to the University of Innsbruck, didn't you?"

The priest nodded.

"*Wass haben sie studiert? Philosophie, wie jeder andere?* [What did you study? Philosophy, like everybody else?]"

Montes wasn't surprised that this military man knew German. He guessed correctly that he'd learned German at West Point.

"*Ich habe mein Deutsch vergessen, Hauptmann; können wir auf Spanisch sprechen, bitte?* [I've forgotten my German, Captain, can we speak in Spanish, please?]"

"Sure, it's easy to forget if you don't practice it. What did you study?"

The priest replied, "I got my master's in theology degree there, under Karl Rahner."

"The Architect of Vatican II," said the Captain matter-of-factly.

"Exactly, Captain."

"So I take it you didn't spend three years studying the Bible."

Montes laughed an embarrassed smile. "No, we actually studied everything but the Bible." And then he braced for the onslaught.

But it never came. Instead, the Captain said, "You know, Father Montes, I've been as ferocious as you both have been in our arguments, but I'm not going to pretend to be able to have an intelligent conversation about the philosophy studies you undertook at Innsbruck for three entire years; just as you couldn't possibly reciprocate in a conversation about Fourier transforms, wideband filters, integrated circuits, etc. But I feel quite certain that all that knowledge you've acquired can't possibly be used for violence only."

Sensing that his words could be taken the wrong way, he hurried to clarify them. "What I mean is... look, nuclear missiles? Full of electronics. Deadly tanks? Full of electronics. Warplanes? Full of electronics. My chosen field of study can translate into violence, but it can also translate to life-saving intelligent medical devices, to ultrasound machines that can check the health of babies in the womb, to personal computers that can facilitate learning and understanding, to instant communications that save time and money, etc."

Montes nodded. "I understand, what you're saying, Captain. You're asking me what I would be doing with my philosophy if I wasn't trying to seek social justice."

"Yes."

Segundo Montes replied, "The short answer to your question is no unless we're talking about writing books and articles, for consumption by the very few—like you with your classical guitar. Which is why when I got my Ph.D., I got it in Social Anthropology, from the *Complutense* University in Madrid. Although it sounds very technical, *Complutense* University means the University of *Alcalá de Henares* in Madrid, because the Roman name for the city of *Alcalá de Henares* was *Complutum*."

Sánchez exclaimed, "I had no idea! I'll have to remember that."

"My dissertation was in *compadrazgos* [collusive relationships among *compadres* [close friends]] in El Salvador."

As soon as he said that, he smiled mischievously, and said, "And I can assure you, my thesis professor... was not my *compadre*."

They both laughed heartily at this. But the Captain said nothing about it. He didn't want to talk about Ellacuría. His attention was all on Montes, whom he was beginning to like.

When the laughter ceased, Sánchez said, "A *compadrazgo* is a relationship designed to exclude somebody from being able to compete. So I'd like to read it one day, Father Montes, because I abhor anything that goes against free competition and free markets."

The priest nodded, and said, "I don't like capitalism, Captain, but I do have to admit that what we've had in El Salvador wasn't capitalism, but rather a monopoly by the Fourteen."

But realizing that the Captain might dispute that because of the Agrarian Reform, Montes was quick to point out that, "Of course, that was more the case back when I wrote my thesis, than right now."

The Captain didn't want to argue either, so he asked a more academic question: "Don't the Japanese have a similar way of doing business?"

Montes appreciated the Captain's interest. "Indeed, they're called the *keiretsus*. But there's a difference between the Salvadoran *compadrazgos* and the Japanese *keiretsus*. I'll illustrate it with this true story, Captain:

"The owner of a restaurant in San Salvador decided to start selling beer that they brewed on their premises, known as *microbrews*, in competition with *Pilsener, Suprema* and the other beers produced by the single brewing company in El Salvador: *La Constancia*.

"The owner of that restaurant soon got a visit from two representatives of *La Constancia*, demanding that he stop selling his own beer because it competed with their beers. The owner refused."

"Naturally, I would've done the same thing, too," said the Captain.

"Within a week, the owner of the restaurant got an eviction notice from the landlord, a *compadre* of *La Constancia*. And that restaurant is no longer operating."

The Captain whistled his dismay.

"*Keiretsus* in Japan are far less aggressive than the *compadrazgos* in El Salvador. Although they prefer to do business with each other, they don't kill competition. Our *compadrazgos* kill commercial activity in this nation.

They put that restaurant out of business, and you know what? I really liked that restaurant!"

The Captain couldn't resist this: "So that's why you became a revolutionary!"

Again they both laughed at this. But then Sánchez thought of something that he conveyed to the priest in the nicest way he could: "Father Montes, you should have studied what I studied."

Montes was surprised by that statement. "Why do you say that, Captain?"

"Look at where technology is going. With everything going digital and smaller, cell phones are beginning to predominate wherever they're not bombing communication towers. They represent the networking of not only voice but data as well. It won't be long before people are able to see movies on their hand-held devices and so if you can watch a movie on a phone, you can also take a lesson on a phone. And aren't lessons your specialty?"

Montes hadn't thought about that. Life had led him astray from pure education—his true profession. But not enough to preclude him from realizing what a valuable tool technology could be for educational purposes. "I understand what you're saying, Captain; if those devices become so cheap that everybody can have one, then sure, why spend money and time to go to a regular school, when the lesson can be transmitted to the student, wherever he or she may be?"

The Captain was thrilled at how quickly the priest had grasped the notion. "Exactly, Father Montes! The student can be at his home in a hamlet on a mountain like Guazapa or Cacahuatique—far from a school but never far from a lesson."

Both contemplated this possibility in silence until the Captain decided to ask him one more question. "Father Montes, why wasn't it the Jesuits' mission to achieve the promulgation of an education law that was similar to Costa Rica's? There's violence in every Central American country except Costa Rica—thanks to their level of education.

"I have no doubt that you and Ellacuría would've been lionized, if not canonized, had you done that, because you could have saved us all the bloodshed while filling the minds of young Salvadoran men and women with useful knowledge to rid ourselves of the yoke of misery bequeathed to us by Hernán Cortez, Pedro de Alvarado and the rest of the Spanish Conquistadors."

Montes nodded. "Captain, you're not the first to say that to me. A very wise Salvadoran priest said that to me back in 1963."

The Captain ended the conversation with, "You can still do it, Father Montes. While there's life, there's hope!" Having said that, Sánchez accompanied the priest back to his temporary residence, and returned quickly to get at least a couple of hours of shuteye.

Chapter 64

Where in the World is Don Blas?

When Fedoseyev didn't return, Olga started to get worried. She had last spoken to him to make the reservations for his return, without 'Juana,' the nun from El Salvador whom he had become infatuated with. And she didn't dare call anybody from the Jesuits. She was forbidden from doing so. The only reason she'd kept silent about it was that nobody had inquired about him yet. Also, his absence could very well be a part of a plan that everybody knew about except her. After all, this was the KGB.

She also missed him physically. Sure, she recognized that she wasn't anything but a sexual outlet for him, but she didn't care: she was well taken care of, and how many women in the soviet system could say the same thing?

He'd made her very happy and hopeful when he'd informed her that 'Juana' would be going back to El Salvador without him. Olga had made plans to make his return home a memorable one.

But he never came back, and then came the dreaded call. "Comrade Brezhnev would like to summon Comrade Fedoseyev to his office, this afternoon."

"Pardon me, comrade, but he hasn't returned from the Italy trip."

"Hold on."

After several seconds of silence, the lady came back. "Please tell the second in command to come to the meeting to brief the General Secretary. Two p.m. sharp. Thank you."

That would be Vladimir Putyatin. She got up and walked over to Comrade Putyatin's office, knocking and asking permission to come in.

"Please come in."

The diminutive man stood up to greet her. After all, she was a person of respect, due to her proximity to his boss.

"Comrade Putyatin, the General Secretary is summoning you to his office to brief him on the Black Crusade."

"Where is Comrade Fedoseyev?"

"The last time I spoke with him, he was in Venice."

"Venice? Wasn't he supposed to be in Rome?"

Olga's embarrassed look told Putyatin everything he needed to know: there was only one reason Comrade Fedoseyev wasn't in Moscow right now—he was dead.

He didn't share his thoughts with Olga, and he concealed his glee at his imminent promotion. He merely thanked her for the information and asked her to bring him the files.

At 1:45 p.m., Putyatin was sitting outside the office of Premier Brezhnev, and at 2 p.m. sharp, his secretary informed Putyatin that Comrade Brezhnev was ready to see him.

He walked in with the most updated dossier on the Black Crusade, ready to hand it over to him.

Leonid Brezhnev was as tall and as big as Vladimir Putyatin was short and scrawny. He was glad when he was asked to sit down.

"Comrade Putyatin, why isn't Fedoseyev here?"

"Comrade General Secretary, based on the latest information I have available, he left Rome with one of the participants in the Base Communities conference, and we last heard from him from Venice, and that he was headed to Moscow.

"However, he often flies to Latin America to put out any fires that flare up, because he is very dedicated that way. But we haven't heard from him in weeks, and that's unusual. So my KGB experience tells me that the participant probably killed Comrade Fedoseyev, for why else would he be missing an appointment with the most powerful man in the world?"

Leonid Brezhnev took the news very calmly. In his world, killing was a tool of the trade. That's how he'd gotten to power and that's how he'd been able to remain in power. That was something the KGB would sort out and it wasn't anything the General Secretary of the USSR should worry about. Plus, Fedoseyev's Black Crusade, even though it was an attractive alternative to his preferred method, which was to fund revolutionary movements directly, was becoming too expensive anyway.

"How is the Black Crusade coming along, Comrade Putyatin?"

"Sir, the revolutionary fervor is catching on like wildfire among the priests and nuns in Latin America, which is a good thing. The conference in Rome was to display the glory of the movement and the heroism of all who have died. Enthusiasm has never been higher."

"What element of the Black Crusade isn't flying so high, Putyatin?"

"Comrade General Secretary, the only fly in the ointment right now is the impending American election, and the growing probability of a loss for President Carter."

Comrade Brezhnev stood, his concern making his enormous eyebrows form a single massive tarantula leg. He walked over to the large window overlooking Red Square. Over his shoulder, he said, "Comrade Putyatin, we're spending millions of rubles that we can ill afford to spend on Jesuits crisscrossing the world like capitalists. They dress better than we do. Why, have you ever seen even one of them dressed as a priest? Of course not, why should they, when they can buy the most expensive suits, shirts, ties, socks, underwear and shoes, courtesy of the USSR?"

Putyatin acknowledged the truth in this. Whenever he had accompanied Comrade Fedoseyev to meetings, they were always in sumptuous settings, and the priests were dressed like movie stars, never as priests. Especially that Karl Rahner guy.

Nevertheless, money had not been a problem for the USSR until the invasion of Afghanistan, which had occurred on December 24, 1979. Fedoseyev had often complained to Putyatin that it would inevitably lead to budget cuts for the Black Crusade.

Brezhnev continued. "I've always wanted to put an end to this program, but there's something positively Russian about check-mating the Americans when they least expect it. So I'm sort of glad Fedoseyev isn't here, so that I can ask you if this program is worth it? Because from where I stand, it seems to me that all the money we're spending on the Black Crusade, could best be used to help re-elect President Carter."

Before Putyatin could answer, Brezhnev continued. "Because Jimmy Carter gave us the gift of removing our enemy, the Shah of Iran. That was priceless. And on top of that, a fierce enemy of the USA takes power there—an Ayatollah. And we spent not one kopek on that operation. That's why I'm inclined to try to help reelect Carter instead of doing anything else. What say you, Vladimir?"

Putyatin may have been physically ungifted, but his mind functioned awfully well. "Comrade General Secretary, in my opinion, the least expensive way to help re-elect President Carter is to convince our new friend, the Ayatollah Khomeini, to release the hostages. Because that single event is what's dooming President Carter's re-election."

Brezhnev asked him, "Do you think that's feasible, after Carter's disastrous rescue attempt last April 25?" He was referring to the hostage-rescue military operation that had ended so disastrously in the Iranian desert.

Putyatin nodded and said, "A diplomat of ours could approach the Ayatollah to tell him that he's already humiliated the President of the United States enough."

Brezhnev agreed with that. This Putyatin guy was very smart. Putyatin continued. "So what makes President Carter so valuable to us, his romantic notion of Human Rights, is also what's dooming his fate. For example, although Anastasio Somoza of Nicaragua was a murderous dictator in Nicaragua, and Carter's lack of support doomed him, that fact is being used against Carter, for having 'lost' Nicaragua, in addition to having 'lost' Iran.

"And his opposition is now saying that if El Salvador falls, that he will have lost El Salvador, too. Therefore, Carter is now sending weapons to the Salvadoran Junta, to keep it from falling before the election."

Putyatin didn't really want to have to mention the detrimental effects of the invasion of Afghanistan by the USSR. It wasn't prudent. It had been Brezhnev's decision and Putyatin wanted to stay alive.

"The death of Archbishop Romero, wasn't it blamed on the Junta?"

"Yes, Comrade General Secretary. It was designed to create a martyr of enormous proportions, a trigger for an uprising that would overthrow the Junta."

"So where's the uprising, Putyatin? The infamous 'death squads' murdered the beloved Archbishop and no uprising?"

Putyatin thought fast.

"Sir, when the beloved Pedro Joaquin Chamorro was also assassinated by death squads in January of 1978, the downfall of Somoza didn't occur until July 1979, that is, a year and a half later. This time it will occur sooner, but it obviously takes time."

"Well, Putyatin, this uprising better come quick, because I'm considering pulling the plug on this Black Crusade."

Putyatin asked permission to speak frankly.

When Brezhnev consented, Putyatin began the most important speech of his career.

“Sir, the Black Crusade was not my idea. I don’t have the intellectual capacity that its creators had, but I do know this: the clergy of the world moves the masses. You pointed this out when you mentioned the Iranian revolution. Even our closest ally in Latin America, Fidel Castro, is Jesuit-educated. The masterminds behind Somoza’s downfall were the Jesuits Fernando and Ernesto Cardenal, who are brothers. So an alliance with the clergy can only continue to be beneficial for the Soviet Union. If we advocate revolution, the effect is not nearly as great as when the emissaries of God advocate revolution. And these messages are preached every Sunday and every one of their holy days. For only the voice of God can have more impact than the voice of the General Secretary of the Soviet Union.”

Brezhnev let this sink in. He went back to his seat, like a judge about to render a verdict.

“Comrade Putyatin, you make a valid point, but we do have spokespersons that are almost as good as the clergy: the New York Times. So if I pull the plug on this extravagant funding, we have that to fall back on.”

Putyatin bit his tongue. The western media couldn’t be as effective as the General Secretary desired, now that the Soviet Union had invaded Afghanistan. But he didn’t want to say that. Whether he mentioned it or not depended on the next words to come out of Brezhnev’s mouth.

Brezhnev said, “I’ll allow the Black Crusade to continue, Putyatin, provided we start getting results faster. And I’m only doing it because you gave me the brilliant suggestion of using diplomacy on our Iranian friends, which should cost next to nothing. But I also want you to step on the Jesuits to achieve results faster. And try to reduce their expenditures.”

“Yes sir, Comrade General Secretary.”

“Finally, Putyatin, I’m promoting you to head the Black Crusade Project, but you must find out what happened to Fedoseyev. If he died in the line of duty, we need to know. If he defected, we need to know. And if he does reappear, you’ll continue as head of that division of the KGB, because we’re going to retire him.”

“Thank you, Comrade Secretary.” He rose when Brezhnev stood up.

Brezhnev said, “Wait outside, I’ll have my secretary type up your new orders and I’ll sign them. You will leave with them.”

"Yes, sir."

When he got back to his office, he summoned Olga, gave her his orders, and said, "As you can see, Olga, I'm the new Director. But since I don't know a word of Spanish, I'm going to keep you at your current position."

Olga tried hard and successfully not to express her glee. "Thank you, Comrade Director," she said with an equanimity that is only achievable after many years of working at the KGB.

"So you'll be traveling with me often, wherever I go. Will this be a problem? Do you have a family to take care of?"

"No sir, my son is married and lives in Kiev."

"And your husband?"

"I never remarried, sir."

This was perfect for Putyatin's plans. This woman was older than him, but she kept herself in fine shape. He hoped that she was willing to give him the same type of loyalty that she gave to Fedoseyev.

"Step inside my office, Olga and lock the door."

He sat in his chair behind his desk. Olga just stood there, waiting for instructions by the locked door.

"Please undress completely."

She hesitated. It was so unexpected. But she didn't hesitate too long. Her clothes came off in no time flat. But once she was exposed, she felt a shame that she hadn't felt in a long time. She must have been blushing furiously because Putyatin kept looking at her face, instead of her exposed parts, amused.

He finally said, "Very good, Olga. Do you know what's expected of you?"

"Yes, sir."

"Good, get dressed and sit down. We need to talk."

After she sat down, Putyatin asked, "What do you think happened to Fedoseyev, Olga?"

"Well, sir, he took one of the nuns from the Base Communities conference and went all around Italy with her."

"So she was a revolutionary nun from El Salvador?"

"Yes, she was. But he purchased an engagement ring for her."

"Say no more. We now know what happened to him. He fell in love, spilled the beans, and when she didn't like the beans, she killed him."

"With all due respect, Comrade Director, I disagree. This nun had proven her attachment to the cause. So it couldn't have been anything that she heard from Comrade Fedoseyev that could've caused such a reaction."

"What do we know about this nun?"

"She's originally from Czechoslovakia but at age 16 arrived in Paris to become an *Assumption* nun, and ended up in El Salvador, teaching at an all girl's school. She's been very helpful clandestine weapons depots in El Salvador."

Putyatin thought about this. Czechoslovakia?

"Where in Czechoslovakia?"

"A town called Olomouc."

Putyatin stood up and went to a wall map of Europe, pointing to Olomouc. Right across the border from Poland.

"Olga, I believe the odds are very good that our nun fled into Czechoslovakia from the onslaught of the Red Army in Poland. If Fedoseyev told her he'd been a colonel in the Red Army that raped, pillaged and plundered through Poland on its way to Berlin, that could've set her off, don't you agree?"

Olga looked shocked. "But sir, not Comrade Fedoseyev?"

Putyatin shrugged. "Olga, everybody did it. Stalin's orders."

As Olga sat there trying to digest this, Putyatin was pondering what to do next. If this nun was with Fedoseyev at that Hotel in Venice, and he'd died of a natural cause, such as heart failure, then she would've reported it, or the local authorities would've made it public. But there had been no reports.

Had Fedoseyev died after arriving at the Venice airport, then it would've also been known. So Fedoseyev disappeared between the Lido and the airport. Had an Italian thug assaulted him and knocked him into the water, the body would've resurfaced by now.

No, that body was weighed under water, and the nun must've done it.

So the question before him was: Does the KGB spend time, effort and money to go after the nun? Was there a compelling reason to do so?

Compelling reason 1: She knew too much.

Mitigating Circumstances: A. It wouldn't have been more than she would've learned had she stayed at the conference; B. A personal dispute between her and Fedoseyev doesn't disqualify her from the cause; C. If she decided to sabotage the efforts in El Salvador, she would have to enlist the efforts of others to do so and increase her risk of detection. Besides, what was she going to say, "The Soviets are behind this?" That wasn't earth-shattering news in the Cold War era.

Conclusion 1: Compelling reason 1 isn't compelling enough to mobilize resources.

Compelling reason 2: A hero of the Soviet Union, Vladislav Fedoseyev, was missing.

Mitigating Circumstances: Nobody outside the top Soviet circles knows that. He had no wife or children. There's no pressure to clarify his disappearance.

Conclusion 2: Compelling reason 2 isn't compelling enough to mobilize resources.

Compelling reason 3: She may have been acting on instructions from the Americans, in which case, the Americans may be receiving the information.

Sole Mitigating Circumstance: The Americans in El Salvador, under Ambassador Robert White, are on our side.

Conclusion 3: Compelling reason 3 isn't compelling enough to mobilize resources.

So there was no compelling reason for the KGB to mobilize its own resources at this time.

What about having locals take action? No way. If it were known that a nun disposed of a mighty Soviet official, it would turn what was now his department into a laughingstock. This would be extremely counterproductive because he had to deal with these people from a position of strength. They needed to fear him. He wasn't about to risk it.

He turned to Olga. "Comrade, were you close to Comrade Fedoseyev?"

Her blush said it all.

"Well, then I'm sorry for your personal loss, but I must order you never to mention this to anybody. It's in the best interest of this project, and of the Soviet Union, that for now, Comrade Fedoseyev be considered to be alive, well and retired. Is that clear?"

Olga hesitated but nodded.

"You will immediately write a letter to our counterparts explaining that due to mandatory retirement by age, I'm now their main point of contact. Can you sign Comrade Fedoseyev's signature?"

"Yes, sir. I would sign it as Don Blas Pérez."

"Good. Then do so."

"Sir, may I ask a question?"

"Go ahead."

"Comrade Fedoseyev used Don Blas Pérez as his name for doing business with them, with 'Don' being a name that denotes respect in Spanish. Do you want to use some other name?"

Putyatin thought about this and asked, "Is there a name in Spanish that instills fear, Olga?"

Olga thought about it and said, "Torquemada, Tomás de Torquemada—very much feared during the Spanish Inquisition."

Putyatin liked the name. This Olga was worth it. "OK, Olga, I'll be 'Don Torquemada.'"

"Very well, Comrade Director."

"And Olga?"

"Yes, Comrade Director?"

"Be at my apartment tonight to start my Spanish lessons."

"As you wish, Comrade Director."

Chapter 65

Uncle Sam's Nose

Jon Cortina stood up to report on his recruitment efforts.

"The Agrarian reform has hurt our recruitment efforts among adults, but we've found that teenagers are excited to join. Therefore, the bulk of the recruits we are sending our comrades in arms, are teenagers."

"What, eighteen, nineteen-year-olds?" came the inquiry from Ellacuría.

Cortina shook his head. "No, more like 16-17-year-olds."

A silence fell over the room.

Jon Cortina resumed his presentation. "Although the Agrarian Reform is proceeding faster than we had expected, we're still able to recruit well in zones yet to be reached by it. We're sending them to training camps inside the *Bolsones* because no troops from El Salvador or Honduras can enter there."

Father Montes asked the pressing question on everybody's mind. "Father Jon, how ready are we for an offensive?"

"Well, from what we gather from the Commanders, the more we can delay it, the better off we'll be. We may be approaching acceptable numbers, but we need more time to train."

Ellacuría stood up, thanking Father Cortina and asking him to sit down. The head Jesuit said, "The polls still have Jimmy Carter ahead of the actor, which makes sense, and our friends in the US Embassy are fairly certain that such lead will hold. Which is amazing considering Carter's botched rescue operation in Iran, in late April."

He paused to allow for comments. Since there were none, he continued. "This means that we'll have more time to train our forces for them to engage in guerrilla warfare, knowing full well that the government forces will receive very little aid in a second Jimmy Carter term."

Everybody nodded. Nobody actually thought that an offensive was going to work. Certainly not Mario Tacarello, who was paying close attention.

Father Montes asked what was at the fore of everybody's mind. "But what happens if Reagan wins?"

Ellacuría was ready for this. "Gentlemen, the American Embassy insists that we need to heed the lessons of the Tet Offensive in Vietnam. If Carter loses, we'll all have two and a half months to convince the American people that the Salvadoran government forces are too vile to be supported."

"Vile?" asked Montes out loud.

Ellacuría nodded. "Do you remember those scenes on TV of the naked little girl fleeing the napalm dropped by U.S. forces? And where that prisoner got executed with a shot to the head by the South Vietnamese official? Those atrocities, plus the general offensive during Vietnam's Tet season made the American people rescind their support for the war. You see, even though the Tet offensive was a failure in the purely military sense, they projected power, because they attacked everywhere.

"All of which was magnified by a press whose sympathies lay with the enemies of the United States. And as we all know, in this day and age, the U.S. media is even more against the interest of its own nation, capable of magnifying even more any atrocity committed by the Salvadoran government. And this might tie Reagan's hands if and when he assumes office—according to the Embassy."

Father Montes once again asked the question on everybody's mind. "Father Ellacuría, how are we going to make the government forces commit vile acts? There was nothing viler than the murder of Monsignor Romero and 40 mourners and even that didn't work."

There was a murmur of agreement by all the Jesuits present. Montes continued. "Furthermore, it seems to me that the Embassy wants the government forces to commit vile acts not so much to spark a popular insurrection in El Salvador, which is so necessary for an offensive to be victorious, but rather to impact the people of the United States, to hamper the new president."

Again a murmur of agreement. Montes went on. "The only thing that would spark a popular insurrection here is if the Army does a 180-degree turn and returns the land to the Fourteen. And that's just not going to happen."

Father Montes' reasoning was dead-on right. But Ellacuría didn't seem convinced. What that told Mario was that there was a split in the Jesuit high command. And if there was a split in the Jesuits... couldn't there be a split in the guerrilla high command? They'd been talking about unifying all the guerrilla groups and popular organizations into one umbrella organization: the *Farabundo Martí National Liberation Front (FMLN)*. But that still hadn't happened—could it be for this very reason?

Mario had very good reasons to try to dissuade Ellacuría from pushing for an offensive. He stood up and said, "Father Ellacuría, guerrilla warfare is one in which the guerrillas choose when, where and how to confront the enemy so as to inflict maximum casualties to it, while minimizing its own. Wouldn't it be better to adhere to that, regardless of what happens in the U.S. elections?"

The Jesuits seemed to agree with Mario. Father Ellacuría simply said, "My Jesuit brethren, the ones who will make the decision on how to proceed will be the commanders. All I've done here is to inform you that the option of a general offensive has much support, even from the American Embassy, for the reasons I've laid out—foremost among which is the impact of the press." With this Ellacuría had confirmed what Mario had suspected: there was a split in the guerrilla high command.

Ellacuría continued. "To have the press on our side is of great value, and proof of that is the fact that the U.S. media is not informing its public of the Agrarian Reform. As I stated at a previous meeting, they operate under the premise that the Salvadoran government can do no right. That makes the U.S. public expect the worst from the Army and the Security Forces. And that's something we need to take advantage of."

A generalized murmur of agreement. Ellacuría went on, relieved that he'd seemed to have regained control of the meeting. "Now then, Father Montes is right when he says that the Army won't do anything to create the conditions for an insurrection, and the Embassy knows that. But they're certain that the Security Forces will. Our friends at the Embassy said to leave it up to them."

The room went silent as everybody tried to figure out what the Americans would do. The American Embassy was a huge complex in San Salvador, with antennas of all kinds everywhere. They were likely very well informed, and they were willing to put all that information to the service of the revolution. Why? Because Ambassador White absolutely hated the Salvadoran military. Like only a Marxist could.

And since the Embassy was 'watching the Salvadoran government's back,' so to speak, it was the only one capable of plunging a knife into it without the government ever seeing it coming. It was a plan that was more than Machiavellian—it was positively Jesuit, probably the brainchild of Ellacuría.

Mario came to that conclusion because Ellacuría was a man who had done everything he could to achieve a popular insurrection—even planning the death of Monsignor Romero—to no avail. And now time was running out, and as the Agrarian Reform progressed, he was left with fewer and fewer options.

Out of all his remaining options, this one had seemed the best to him: to resort to the man who hated the military as much or even more than he did—U.S. Ambassador Robert White. And White had bought into his plan.

Although Montes was right to say that inducing the Security Forces to commit atrocities would probably cause more impact in the U.S. than over here, Ellacuría did not lose hope that White's hate might induce them to commit the mother of all atrocities, which could spark the much-needed popular uprising.

Anybody else would've abstained from going down this path out of fear of launching an offensive without popular support, in which thousands of ill-trained *indios* would die. But not Ellacuría, because to him, Salvadorans were inferior, subhuman and expendable.

Although Mario understood the why, he needed to know the how. So he asked, "Father Ellacuría, although the Embassy said to leave it to them, that's not realistic is it? No Embassy personnel is going to commit an atrocity, so that means that they're going to have to induce Security Forces to do so."

Ellacuría nodded and said, "Well deduced, Mario. That's why you and Father Cortina are going to go tell the Commanders to intensify their attacks on the National Guard outposts. Our friends at the American Embassy said that this was crucial for the success of the plan."

The National Guard! The most hated security force, and the one that hated them back the most, because they had taken the brunt of the losses at the hands of the guerrillas It was obvious that the American Embassy knew what it was doing.

Ellacuría concluded the meeting in a decidedly upbeat form: "Gentlemen, a storm is gathering, and it's our storm. We'll win, one way or another. Victory or Death!"

And the gathering of Jesuits replied, in unison, "Victory or Death!"

Mario would do as he'd been told to do and transmit the message, not only to the Commanders—but to Licha and Major Zepeda as well.

Chapter 66

In Search of Bastards

The recruits were given their first boots, taken from National Guards killed in action in Chalatenango. They didn't fit well, but the calluses on their feet were so thick, that as long as they went in, it was a huge improvement.

They tried them on that night around a campfire, swapping boots as they swapped stories. These recruits had grown closer after learning that they were going to be co-fathers to the babies that the teachers were carrying in their bellies.

Marcial and Mayo Sibrián had discovered a gold mine. Most if not all these school kids resented their second-class status: children of servants cast away from their true dads to protect their reputations while besmirching the moms and their bastard children. And all their commanders had to say was, "Hey, when we take over, you'll be on top, and they'll serve you and your mothers."

These second class teenagers were first-rate guerrillas. This was their salvation for the final offensive, and that's what they'd told the Jesuits: "We want bastards—we don't need many, just enough to fill a soccer stadium."

With this approach, they would reach the necessary numbers for the offensive. What was also encouraging was the fact that despite all his problems, Carter kept leading the actor Ronald Reagan in all the polls, which would give them more time to train the bastards. Because attacking outnumbered National Guard posts was one thing—to launch a frontal assault on Army garrisons was something else completely.

Of course, they had to wreck some families to do so: the two pregnant teachers had been separated from their bourgeois lives and families and were now getting ready have their revolutionary families. It was regrettable, but the Revolution was paramount. No sacrifice was too big.

While trying on his new boots, Neto was thinking about his mom and the comforts of the city, to which he would return, but in a better position than ever. He'd take over the Vesuvius shops, and his mom and his mother would live like queens. That ambition kept him warm at night, long after one of his teachers had given him the warmth of her body.

About a month into his training in Guazapa he'd been made squad leader, a position he was truly proud of. And they had given him the *nom de guerre* of 'Guevara,' because it went well with his first name, 'Ernesto.' Nobody could claim the *nom de guerre* 'Ché' because it had already been retired.

That night he slept until he was awakened to supervise the sentinels. He put on his new boots, slung his ammo-less weapon over his shoulder, and started to check on the posts overlooking probable avenues of approach. As he was walking, he got to a point on the mountain where he could see the lights of San Salvador. He felt a pang of homesickness, which didn't last as long as his first bout of homesickness did, when he'd seen San Salvador at night a couple of months ago.

As squad leader, he'd been ordered to participate in tactical meetings led by Commander Mayo Sibrián. They had a mockup of the San Carlos garrison of the First Infantry Brigade, their main target for the offensive. They would start going down Guazapa in small groups and inhabit homes that would be ready to house them in the vicinity of the brigade, until they were ready to launch the attack.

Neto's squad would go over the wall on the western side of the garrison, and once inside, they would attack the watchtowers. Then explosives would be used to punch a hole in the wall; that would allow the bulk of the guerrilla force to enter the compound. The wall-punching was not something they were training for in Guazapa; the sappers that would do that were being trained in Cuba.

Although the guerrillas in Guazapa knew that the First Brigade wouldn't necessarily be their target in an offensive, the same plan would apply to the Fourth Brigade in El Paraíso.

As he continued down the path to the next sentinel outpost, the same voice inside Neto popped up again, asking the same question: "Will the population rise with us?"

Otherwise, the only ones pouring in through the wall would be guerrillas, without the numbers to be able to kill off the entire brigade. Without the population to encourage the soldiers to lay down their weapons and join the uprising, the entire attack would be futile. The popular uprising was the key to their success. But that was something the Salvadoran people weren't keen on doing—not even when Monsignor Romero got killed.

Therefore, if no uprising occurred, they'd be cannon fodder. They would be mowed down. No more revolution.

The more he thought about it, the less he liked the idea. Because in the end, why did they have to launch a frontal offensive, when guerrilla warfare was so much more effective?

But he couldn't ask that question. Another squad leader had, and he got demoted and caned in front of everybody.

CHAPTER 67

THE BERMUDA TRIANGLE

Mario had told Licha to dress in civilian clothes, and he'd pick her up at La Asunción at 8 pm sharp. He was there at 7:59 pm, in his Volkswagen.

Licha was waiting for him in a dress of those that she'd brought back from Europe. Not very formal but definitely expensive. Courtesy of Don Blas. "What's going on, Mario?" was the first thing out of her mouth. She knew this sudden date due to something urgent.

"A lot is. But first and foremost, I'm taking you to a place where you and I can relax!" And he winked at her.

Mario Tacarello's look conveyed exactly what he meant. Which was a relief because she too wanted to 'relax.' The tension had been building up: she was always looking over her shoulder for someone sent by the KGB to avenge the death of Don Blas. Although Mario had told her that Don Blas had retired, and that he'd been replaced by somebody named *Don Torquemada*, she knew better and so did the KGB. So spending time with someone she knew for sure wasn't Don Torquemada's agent was a relief.

Licha got close to kiss him on the cheek. "I thought so, Mario. That's why I'm not wearing any underwear."

Mario was glad. Since the trip back from Rome, it was like they had this telepathic nexus between them. He attributed it to the holiness of their cause, even though they were getting ready to commit a sin.

But he needed it. Since Neto's abduction, he couldn't seek any warmth from Estela or Gladys. Even though he'd promised to get him back to them. But before informing Licha of his plan to get Neto back, he wanted to get laid.

They turned southwest toward the coast, and Licha asked, "Are we going to the beach?"

"No, but please put your head on my lap, so you can't be seen." And he pulled her toward him. "We're going to the Bermuda Triangle."

The Bermuda Triangle was the name given to the series of motels that were hidden off the road toward the port of La Libertad, where cars would disappear. The way to get to the motels was to take a feeder to a semi-paved road, called the 'Road of the Crazy Men,' because every car that drove on that road seemed to have a single man in it, who would invariably be talking to himself.

The cars would look for an open garage door, park inside, close the garage door, and the hidden woman would get out and both would walk into a nice clean room, with a nice clean bed, a TV, a radio, and a phone to order food and drinks. The food and drinks would be delivered to you on a tray that was left outside a small opening with sliding doors that could be opened only from the room. That's also where you paid, because if you didn't pay, you couldn't open the garage door.

When their car came to a stop, Mario got out and pulled the garage door down. Then Licha and him went into the room and satiated their sexual hunger immediately.

Twenty minutes later they were lying in bed, thoroughly satisfied.

Licha turned to him to ask, "Ok, Mario, what's going on?" Mario got up and turned up the TV's volume so that they couldn't be overheard.

He came back to the bed and said, "You're going to have to start meeting with Zepeda alone from now on. I'm really busy on weekends in Aguilares, El Paisnal, and Guazapa. So you're going to have to tell him this: if Carter loses, the American Embassy is going to do something to induce the National Guard to commit some heinous crimes. So he needs to alert the National Guard about this plan."

"Do you have any idea what they might attempt?"

"None. But they're going to make it so that it's the vilest thing imaginable, by National Guards who are out for revenge, for all the casualties they've suffered, and those they are about to suffer because the plan is for the guerrillas to intensify their attacks on National Guard outposts in Chalatenango, starting now."

Licha nodded. "Ok. Consider it done. But is that it?" Licha's telepathic powers were telling her there was more.

Mario had laid back on the bed, and was looking at the ceiling, instead of looking at her. It seemed to Licha that he had the weight of the world on his shoulders. She got closer to kiss him on the cheek and asked, "What's bothering you, Mario?"

Mario replied, but with his eyes fixed on the ceiling. "Licha, the U.S. election is just over a month away. I'm praying like crazy for a victory by Carter, but I have this feeling that the actor's going to win."

Licha looked perplexed. "But I thought we wanted Reagan to win?"

"Yes we do, but that's strategic. In the short term, what that means is that they're going to send Neto to his slaughter."

Licha was lost. "Who's Neto?"

Mario told her the story of his half-brother Neto, from how he was conceived to his kidnapping, along with his classmates and two teachers; how he'd seen him in Guazapa the three or four times he'd gone up there in support of Father Cortina's Base Community-recruiting scheme. He told her that the recruits wouldn't even be given ammunition to practice, because the commanders were afraid they'd use the ammo against them. And that, if Reagan were to win, the plan was to send such poorly train kids to attack well-trained soldiers at their garrisons."

Licha asked, "Did he recognize you?"

Mario shook his head. "No, he has no idea that I'm his half-brother. In Guazapa, they know me as Eliseo, not as Father Tacarello. So Neto hasn't made the connection because otherwise, he would've told somebody and Mayo Sibrián would've already asked me about it."

Licha looked at him skeptically. "You're not doing all of this on account of fraternal love, are you?"

Mario replied, "No, Licha, I'm doing it because I gave my word to Gladys and Estela that if anything happened to Neto, that I'd help him."

Licha shook her head and said "No, Mario, you're doing it to defeat the offensive." Mario smiled. There was that telepathic connection again. So he just let Licha finish explaining his plan.

Licha did precisely that. "If Reagan wins, you're going to join Neto in Guazapa, as a guerrilla. And through him, you're going to get the guerrilla battle plans and you're going to get them to me. Am I right?"

Mario's smile widened, nodding. Licha continue. "The only thing you're missing is how to get the plans to me, am I right?"

Mario stopped smiling and admitted it. "I may get them to you by helping the teachers escape, I don't know yet."

Licha hugged Mario and then put her head on the chest of his brave friend, saying “Make sure your plan allows you to survive. I don’t want to be passing on any information to the First Brigade just to get you killed.”

Mario ran his fingers through Licha’s blond hair. “If I do this and Neto and I survive, we’re going to have to leave the country, along with Gladys and Estela, his mom and grandma.”

“Where would you go?”

“To Italy. My dad will get Italian passports for Neto and myself, and permanent visas for Gladys and Estela.”

“Will you be coming back?”

“Not anytime soon. I’ll have to work over there to sustain everybody; otherwise, it’ll be a tremendous financial burden on my dad. But you’re welcome to visit me anytime.”

Licha felt sad. She felt close to young Mario. She would miss him, because either way, he’d be gone. He’d either get killed in the attack, or he’d leave for Italy. She preferred the latter.

They made love again.

Afterward, she asked, “If Reagan wins, the offensive won’t come until January, so why do you want me to meet with Zepeda alone, if we have a few months left?”

“The main reason is that I don’t want to risk being seen near any military man so that I can retain the utmost trust of the Jesuit and guerrilla high commands for this to work. That trust is essential for this to work.”

That made sense to Licha. But she looked at him like she knew there was more to it than that.

Mario obliged. “Look, the way I see it, I have to find the right time, the right moment, to join the guerrillas. It has to be at a meeting with the commanders, where I can go up to Marcial or Sibrián to volunteer. I don’t want to volunteer and get sent to the *Bolsones*, or somewhere where Neto is not.

Licha asked the obvious, “Mario, what makes you think they’re going to accept you? A full Jesuit who recruits commanders for them—wanting to become a recruit himself?”

Mario shrugged. “Licha, they need people. They won’t reject me. And I suppose my Jesuit bosses will think it’s temporary. With luck, I’ll find the best time to do it.”

Licha said no more. She figured it had to be attempted, anyway. Mario continued. "The thing is, I don't know when that opportunity will arise. It could be any time after Reagan's election and I probably won't get the chance to let you know. So you simply have to be prepared for me not to be around, and I had to tell you today, to forewarn you."

Licha pointed out, "You have to have a plan so everybody can follow it, Mario. And you've got to communicate that plan to Zepeda as well."

Mario agreed. He told her, "I want you to go to my house next Friday, for dinner. I'll have everything figured out for you by then. I think it's going to involve Gladys and Estela and so I want you to meet them. Those two ladies will be the most anxious in the world to help you."

Licha wanted to recap. "So tomorrow I need to send a coded message to Zepeda telling him of the planned intensification of the attacks on National Guard units, by recommendation of the American Embassy."

"Yes."

"But you don't want me to tell him of your plan to join Neto in Guazapa."

"No, but also ask him to be at my house next Friday as well, so I can lay out the plan."

"OK."

After showering and getting dressed, Mario paid the bill and Licha crawled into the front of the car. Once they were on the road to San Salvador, she sat up again. She felt very happy. She'd spent a wonderful evening with Mario.

But her happiness was tempered by the fact that she might not be around come January. She fully expected some KGB agent to dispatch her to the next world soon. That didn't bother her: she'd reunite with her family and that would be wonderful.

What bothered her was the possibility that she might not be alive to help Mario. But that was something she couldn't relay to Mario or anybody else. She had to deal with it all by herself.

But then she counted the months since the demise of Don Blas: five months. With any luck, she could hang on three more months, couldn't she?

Chapter 68

Sacrificing the Pawn

"Come in, Vladimir, how is the Black Crusade going?"

"Comrade General Secretary, we're approaching a critical juncture because of the election of Ronald Reagan."

Brezhnev's eyebrows said it all. "Yes, that was a most disappointing turn of events, Comrade. And I blame myself for being unable to convince the Ayatollah to release those hostages. I want you to know that."

"Sir, the very zealotry that is serving us in the Black Crusade, is providing a disservice to us in Iran."

Brezhnev nodded. "Indeed it is. And that helped to elect an actor who calls us the 'Evil Empire' to the Presidency of the United States."

"Which is why, Your Excellency, it's good to have the Black Crusade in your arsenal. A dagger that he'll never see coming."

Brezhnev stood up. Putyatin had learned that that wasn't a good sign. As he walked to the window with a view to the Red Square, he said, "Tell me why we should keep the Black Crusade, Vladimir."

Putyatin was ready for this. "Comrade General Secretary, with the Soviet invasion of Afghanistan on December 24, 1979, the Ayatollah can't be seen to be too friendly with the oppressor of a fellow Muslim nation. There's no doubt that the invasion of Afghanistan was a masterful stroke, which serves the interest of the Motherland in ways I can't even begin to comprehend. Nevertheless, it had the unfortunate consequence of poisoning our relations with the Muslim world."

Putyatin knew that he had better get to the good news really quick. Unfortunately, he had to establish the setting first, and that setting included the boneheaded move to invade Afghanistan, which put the Soviets at odds with the Muslim world, and with the rest of the world.

Putyatin continued. "So here comes Ronald Reagan, and he promises to help the *mujahideen* that oppose us in Afghanistan. Which means that his anti-Soviet efforts will be diluted. The United States may be rich, but it doesn't have a limitless budget, and that necessarily means that he won't have all the resources he wants to support the *mujahideen* and to combat the FMLN and the Sandinistas."

"FMLN?"

"Yes, Comrade Brezhnev, in a report dated October 11, 1980, sent to you that very same day, I respectfully informed you of the following:

"that the Popular Organizations of El Salvador had formed one single umbrella organization, the Democratic Revolutionary Front, better known by its Spanish acronym FDR;

"that the FDR and the guerrilla groups had formed one single organization, the FMLN, which is the Spanish acronym for Farabundo Martí National Liberation Front, named after the leader of the 1932 peasant revolt in El Salvador; and

"that the FMLN had obtained the international recognition of the governments of France and Mexico."

Putyatin put a copy of that report on Brezhnev's desk.

Brezhnev only said, "Proceed."

Putyatin continued. "As you know, Comrade General Secretary, the Americans have a strange way of handing over power. They elect their next President in early November, but the winner doesn't become President until two and a half months later."

Brezhnev sounded exasperated when he asked, "And how does that help our cause, Comrade Putyatin?"

"It allows time for an unlikely ally, the U.S. Ambassador to El Salvador, Robert White, to help our cause."

Brezhnev continued to stand in front of the window over the Red Square, seeing the autumn dusk. He asked, "And why would he want to do that? Have we recruited him?"

"No, Comrade General Secretary, he's one of those left-wing zealots that abound in the U.S. Democrat Party. There's another such Democrat, Senator Ted Kennedy, who has often expressed his sympathy toward our causes."

"So what does he plan to do, Vladimir?"

"To the best of our knowledge, sir, he's engineering events that will so horrify the American public, that the U.S. Congress, which is still in the Democrat Party's hands, will deny Reagan the aid he seeks. And they might even spark a popular uprising in El Salvador."

Brezhnev turned away from the window to look at Putyatin, and said, "I like that, Putyatin, because that guy's achievements will cost us nothing."

"That's right, Your Excellency." Here it comes, thought Putyatin.

Brezhnev said, "Which is why I brought you here, Vladimir. Our resources are being heavily drained by our glorious operation in Afghanistan, and we're going to have to cut back on all programs, including the Black Crusade."

"I understand, Comrade General Secretary."

"I've been irked by our inability to make that uprising happen. Which means that any offensive that takes place in El Salvador before Reagan's inauguration, is doomed to fail."

"Yes, Comrade General Secretary."

Brezhnev went to a wall map and pointed to El Salvador. "This is what is occupying most of our funding right now? When we already have this?" And he pointed to Nicaragua, which was six times larger than El Salvador.

Brezhnev went on. "Ronald Reagan is going to come after Nicaragua, Putyatin. He won't settle for helping El Salvador. So I'm directing you to sacrifice El Salvador to preserve our gains in Nicaragua."

Putyatin had no problem with that. With a reduced budget, it was easier and cheaper to play defense anyway.

"I understand perfectly, Comrade General Secretary."

"I hope you do, Vladimir. You see, although you and I know that our ultimate goal is to preserve the gains in Nicaragua, it helps our cause if the Americans continue to think that we're as obsessed with El Salvador as they are, and that we're hell-bent on making that domino fall, so they're the ones who pour millions into it—millions that they won't spend on Nicaragua."

"Brilliant, Comrade General Secretary!"

Brezhnev smiled and said, "Now then, Vladimir, I'll send you off with this thought: a reduced revenue stream from the Soviet Treasury doesn't mean that you can't make up that revenue shortfall somewhere else."

This was interesting to Putyatin. "Did you have something in mind, Comrade General Secretary?"

"What was your favorite TV series, Vladimir? Mine was 'The Rifleman,' with Chuck Connors."

He meant Hollywood, of course! But he answered the question anyway. "Mine was always Bonanza, comrade General Secretary."

Brezhnev winked. It was not a pleasant thing to see that eye close and open again. But it was the intention that counted.

Vladimir enthusiastically replied to the wink with, "I understand perfectly, Your Excellency!"

He left Brezhnev's office knowing exactly what he had to do.

Chapter 69

Lisa's Tit

"I thank the leadership of the FMLN for having made every effort to meet so soon after the November 4 election. Without the undetected presence of Commanders Marcial, Facundo Guardado, Ana María and the other commanders here at the UCA, this urgent meeting wouldn't have been possible."

Three days before, Ronald Reagan had won the U.S. presidential election. This simple fact required the FMLN leadership to meet to determine the way forward, after considering all available options. Ellacuría was glad that the commanders had decided to have it in a Jesuit enclave. That would give him the opportunity to have a say.

Although Ellacuría was anxious to present his plan to go forward, courtesy demanded that Commander Marcial speak first. After all, he'd be the one leading the attack, risking his life; not Ellacuría.

"Commander Marcial, please take this microphone and tell us how you'll lead us to victory."

Commander Marcial stood up and stepped up to the podium of the auditorium, to the applause of all those present, including Mario Tacarello. He went over to the projector to place the transparencies that would be seen on a large white screen that unfurled from the top of a chalkboard.

Marcial then took the microphone and said, "Thank you Father Ellacuría, and thank you all for being here. I want to tell you that we're ready. The Agrarian Reform has made the enemy focus on transferring properties to the peasants, rather than pursuing us. That gave us the necessary time to train our forces and plan our attack. However, although we would've liked to have attacked all the enemy's garrisons all over the Republic, we don't have the numbers to do so."

The first transparency he put on showed of map of El Salvador with all the garrisons clearly highlighted. "If we opt to attack all the garrisons of the central and eastern zones of the country, we may be able to achieve victory if there is a popular uprising accompanying our attacks.

"In this case, victory is defined as taking over the garrisons and holding on to them. Were we to achieve that, it would still leave the enemy with a strong reserve, which would be all the western garrisons."

He put up a second transparency, showing the western garrisons, and he continued. "These would go into action immediately, and they include heavy weapons such as their cavalry and artillery units, which could level the garrisons in our hands, even if they had to rebuild them later."

His third transparency showed the avenues of approach to be used by the western garrisons. He then said to the audience, "If a popular uprising does occur, which allows us to take over the garrisons of the central and eastern zones, it's possible that it will convince our enemy to put down their weapons or join us. This is the best scenario."

He then put up a fourth transparency, showing the avenues of approach blocked by figures representing the people. And he pointed out that, "If the enemy wants to counterattack, the best way to stop that counterattack is through barricades placed and backed by the people."

And then he put up his fifth and last transparency. Showing three garrisons across the northern part of the country, from Chalatenango to Sensuntepeque. This transparency had the word 'Lisa' written on top of the northern departments of Chalatenango and Cabañas.

Marcial moved away from the projector to give all his attention to the audience. He proclaimed, "We can't put our trust on the occurrence of a popular uprising to carry out our attack. If we were to do that, and the popular uprising doesn't occur, we'll be cannon fodder and we'll suffer staggering losses that we'll never be able to recover from."

The audience started talking among themselves. Marcial had tackled the maw of the matter head-on. Everybody knew the Agrarian Reform had poured cold water on any revolutionary ardor among the population. The effects had been felt not only in the rate of recruitment, but also in surveys that had been taken, showing a high level of satisfaction of the people with the Junta and especially Duarte. Everything indicated that the people wouldn't rise up with the guerrillas.

Marcial went on. "This doesn't mean that we can't use the resources that are under our control to accomplish a similar goal. To take over a dozen garrisons, we do need a popular uprising. But to take over three, all we need is the people who already support us, which make up the popular organizations that consolidated into one single group earlier this year—the Democratic Revolutionary Front or FDR, presided by Don Polo. With Don Polo's help, we'll have 'popular uprisings' in the form of FDR members, at three towns, to allow us to overtake and hold on to the garrisons at El Paraíso, Chalatenango and Sensuntepeque."

The din rose in volume. The audience was liking what they were hearing. Marcial continued. "These won't be the only military targets of our offensive. The number one target will be the Air Force base at Ilopango. We're going to destroy their air weaponry to ensure that they don't have anything with which to dislodge us. The other military targets will be all the bridges over the Lempa River and the Cerrón Grande reservoir.

"This will allow us to control the entire northern strip of the country bordering on the Lempa River, which we will declare to be the Free Socialist Republic of El Salvador. And since we will have cut off all land avenues of approach, the only way they'll be able to get to us will be on *cayucos* [native canoes]."

Laughter and applause. Marcial went on. "This plan, which I've dubbed Lisa, which is short for *Libre Salvador* [Free Salvador] will also allow our forces to be reinforced through the *Bolsones*. When ready, we'll began to expand the borders of Free Salvador to strategic points, such as the mountains of Guazapa, in the central zone, and Cacahuatique, in the eastern zone of the country.

"By the time Reagan wants to send aid, he's going to have to send it to Guatemala, because we'll have the entire territory under our control by then. Thank you."

There was a standing ovation from all who were present, including Mario Tacarello. It was a sensible plan, making use of available resources and not causing a bloodbath, which increased Neto's probability of survival.

Just then Mario saw a figure running toward the podium. It was Commander Facundo Guardado. He playfully took the mike away from Marcial and said, "Comrades, I support this plan, although I don't like the damn name!"

Laughter all around. The reason for the levity was that Marcial's actual name was Salvador Cayetano Carpio, and so it could be interpreted that the

Salvador in 'Libre Salvador' could be referring to Marcial, and not the country.

When the laughter and jokes abated, Marcial announced that the next speaker would be Don Polo, the president of the FDR, to address the politics of the plan.

The election of Don Polo had surprised Mario. After leaving the Junta and alleging that his print shop had been vandalized by death squads, Ungo had moved his family to Panama, and no longer had a residence in El Salvador.

While he was doing that, the Popular Organizations, whom he'd represented in the Junta, had formed the FDR and had elected Don Polo as its president—not Ungo.

Ungo couldn't have liked that because Don Polo was everything that Ungo was not: suave, debonair, tall, a full head of hair, well-educated, a natural in international circles, good-looking and rich. Ungo was short, balding, wore glasses, seemed to wear the same suit every day, and wore his resentment on his sleeve.

Furthermore, in the eyes of Ungo, Don Polo was a Johnny-come-lately. A member of one of the richest families of El Salvador, he'd been nowhere when the going had gotten tough in 1972, when he should have rightfully become the vice president of El Salvador, but the hated military had prevented it.

Mario was certain that if an *indio* had become head of the FDR, Ungo would've been OK with that. But being replaced by a member of the hated oligarchy? That had to hurt.

Just then Mario realized that the person who never once stood up to clap, who was sitting two rows in front of Mario, to his right, was none other than Ungo, wearing a hat. As if to leave no doubt about who he was, just then Ungo took his hat off.

Mario wasn't surprised to see Ungo at the meeting. He'd earned his right to be there because it was thanks to his efforts that the governments of Mexico and France had recognized the FMLN. But even so, he still didn't look like a happy camper.

Don Polo took the floor. Although he was dressed in everyday, fairly modest attire, his elegance showed through. Even his speech sounded carefully manicured. It was far from the Spanish spoken by the lower classes.

"Comrades, the FDR, as the political wing of the FMLN, stands ready to assist the FMLN to achieve victory, once the first shots are fired. Our people will join in with the guerrilla attacks to create the impression that a popular rising is occurring and to encourage the civilian population to join us."

General applause. Don Polo continued. "Commander Marcial has given much thought to the Lisa Plan. Under his guidance, the FDR has all the staging areas where our people will be lodged ready accompany the combatants in the offensive to create the Free Socialist Republic of El Salvador north of the Lempa River."

General applause. It was obvious that the best brains in the movement had put together this sensible plan. Nobody expected the much-desired popular uprising to occur.

Mario was very happy with Lisa. Cooler heads had looked at the situation in El Salvador as it existed at the time and had come up with a plan that the hotheads never could. But that didn't mean that the hotheads had disappeared. Mario knew that they'd get their say.

Just then, Commander Lucho stood up to ask, "Comrades, wouldn't it be better to create the Free Socialist Republic of El Salvador to the east of the Lempa River?" This was a question that everybody had asked themselves, but it was also a question they already knew the answer to.

Commander Marcial took the mike back from Don Polo and replied, "Comrade, out east there are two infantry brigades, the Third and the Sixth. If we aren't able to take both, the one we don't take will constitute an immediate counterattacking reserve for the enemy, without having to wait for reinforcements from the other garrisons. So the answer to your question is, with the number of fighters we have, we wouldn't be able to hold on to the eastern garrisons. That's why we chose the three northern garrisons that we'll easily be able to hold on to."

A din of approval rose. That was the right answer.

Ellacuría then took the mike to announce, "Comrades, our allies in the American Embassy favor a general offensive, not a limited one."

There was immediate disagreement. Commander Mayo Sibrián stood up to say, "Father, what's the U.S. Embassy going to do? Are they going to pay everybody millions to rise up? Because that's really the only way that we're going to get an uprising. Even the assassination of Archbishop Romero couldn't get people to rise up. And that was before the Agrarian Reform!"

The din from the audience mostly agreed with Sibrián. To counter this, Ellacuría replied, "Comrades, I beg you to consider me only a spokesperson for our friends at the American Embassy, since they can't be present for obvious reasons. I'm not capable of substituting the Commanders' criteria with my own, nor would I ever dare."

"Bullshit," thought Mario.

But Ellacuría's words had a calming effect. They could understand that Ellacuría was speaking on behalf of Ambassador White. And they were all curious about what the American Embassy proposed.

Relieved that his words had had the intended effect, Ellacuría proceeded to highlight the press component of the Embassy's plan, recalling how the world had finally come to know about the extent of the mass executions in Cuba, only when Ché Guevara had proudly announced them at the United Nations in 1964. The New York Times and the western media, although aware of such mass executions, had chosen not to disclose such facts, instead writing about how Cuba had become a socialist paradise.

Ellacuría pointed out that, "Fidel Castro himself always said that his revolution wouldn't have been possible without the New York Times, because the New York Times focused on what Castro said, not what he actually did."

The silence with which his words were received sounded favorable to Ellacuría, who plowed on. "Twenty years later, the press is hiding the necessary executions that the Sandinistas had had to carry out in Nicaragua, and all anyone reads about life in Nicaragua is that it's a socialist paradise.

"And so our friends at the American Embassy consider a favorable press to be a force multiplier. That may be the factor that gets us to achieve total victory."

The murmur that arose reflected doubts. So Ellacuría decided to resort to humor. "Since Commander Marcial has brilliantly named his plan the 'Lisa Plan,' allow me to name the Embassy's plan the 'Tet' Plan."

A ripple of laughter arose. In Spanish, 'Tet' was three-quarters of 'teta' [tit], and so no matter how it was pronounced, it sounded like the vulgar way to refer to a woman's breast: tit.

But Commander Facundo Guardado wasn't laughing. "Father, with all due respect, the Tit Offensive was a military disaster. Their forces got decimated. Sure, they attacked everywhere, but they got defeated everywhere as well. It's only because the North Vietnamese had a million men in reserve that they were able to continue the war after losing so many men in that Tit Offensive. We don't have such vast reserves. We have zero reserves. If we launch a Tit-type attack, that'll be the end of the guerrilla movement in El Salvador."

The murmur rose decidedly in favor of Facundo Guardado, a very respected commander who couldn't have been more representative of the indigenous population of El Salvador. And it irked Ellacuría to be given history lessons by this *indio*.

But to Ellacuría's chagrin, Facundo Guardado was not done. "Father Ellacuría, I question the wisdom of relying on the Americans, who haven't won any war since World War II. Also, I doubt very much that your contact at the Embassy is a military man. Because a military man would be dealing with reality, like we guerrilla commanders are. Yes, it's nice to have the press on our side, but it'd be nicer if they were fighting alongside us, to increase the number of our forces. But they won't."

The audience erupted in Guardado's favor. People like the Embassy folks and the Jesuits lived nice, comfortable lives. Very bourgeois. And no bourgeois was going to dictate the guerrilla battle plan.

At that point, Guillermo Ungo walked up to the podium, uninvited to do so, but with the authority of someone who had gained the FMLN's recognition by foreign governments.

Upon receiving the microphone away from Ellacuría, he said, "Comrades, you know who I am. You know my credentials. You know that I've been in this struggle all of my life. I'm no rookie. While I was facing down the coup of 1972, others were playing polo and living it up here and abroad."

Everybody there knew that this was a slap to the face of Don Polo. But Don Polo sat impassively. Mario was sure it wasn't the first time he'd heard this diatribe.

"So as a veteran revolutionary, let me say this. Guillermo Manuel Ungo urges the FMLN to go for it all, just like Father Ellacuría and the U.S. Embassy are proposing!"

A deathly silence gripped the room. There was a rift in the FMLN. That didn't bode well for an offensive.

Dr. Mélida Anaya Montes stood up. Her *nom de guerre* was 'Ana María.' She was the second in Command of the foremost guerrilla group, the Popular Liberation Forces, the 'FPL,' under Commander Marcial. With her Ph.D. in education, she should've been the leader of the FPL. Mario was sure that she wasn't only because she was a woman.

But now there was no longer an FPL, or a FARN, or any other independent guerrilla group—they were all the FMLN, and the leadership of the FMLN was comprised of the leadership of the different guerrilla groups. It occurred to Mario that perhaps this meeting was being used to determine who the actual head of the FMLN would be. Marcial was the frontrunner with his Lisa Plan, but he'd wear the crown only if the FMLN adopted his plan.

The room fell silent as Ana María stepped up to the podium. She took the microphone from Ellacuría and said, "Comrades, this is no time for half-measures. My highly respected Comrade Facundo Guardado claims that there are no reserves. Allow me to disagree with him. We can attack with three-quarters of our forces and have a quarter in reserve."

Mario shook his head. This made no sense. Ana María was proposing attacking more garrisons with even less people. That wasn't the Vietnamese Tet plan; that was the WWII Japanese Kamikaze plan.

You could've heard a pin drop. Now there was dissension among the commanders. Ana María was siding with Ungo and Ellacuría and the Embassy with the Tit Plan.

Marcial stood up to argue, "Ana María, that's suicide and you know it. If we go with the Tit Plan, you're sending Salvadoran fighters to their slaughter, with virtually no chance of achieving victory, because it is a plan drawn up by non-military people who live their lives in air-conditioned residences and offices reading philosophy and history.

"And while brave Salvadorans are dying for no good reason, they will be safe and sound in those places that offer them immunity—like the UCA or the American Embassy—passport at the ready to go back to Spain or the USA if things go wrong."

Marcial stopped facing Ana María and faced the audience, and said, at the top of his voice: "I urge everybody to reject this Tit Plan, which is worthy of the intellect of a baby!"

Ana María retorted, "Marcial if you don't have the balls to lead this offensive, I have the tits to do so!"

Pandemonium.

At that point, Mario Tacarello decided to make his move. Mario had known that this meeting would occur, but not when or where, because that would be determined by the Guerrilla Commanders, not by the Jesuits. So he couldn't provide actionable intelligence to Licha.

The previous day he'd had the strong premonition that it would be today, so he'd gone to his house to say good-bye, and to ask Gladys to inform Licha, to get the plan in motion.

Mario didn't know exactly how the situation would develop, but seeing this dissension, he figured that there couldn't be a better moment to take the leap. So Mario went up to the podium and asked Ana María for the microphone. She acquiesced.

He then addressed the audience, proclaiming, "Comrades, please... don't for a second believe that just because we're not wearing your uniforms, we won't be with you at your side. And as proof, I tell you right now: Commander Marcial, Commander Mayo Sibrián, I'd like to volunteer to participate in your attack, whether it's the Tit Plan or the Lisa Plan, and from this moment on, please don't consider me a priest anymore, but rather a proud fighter of yours!"

And with that, he dropped the microphone, walked over to Commander Marcial and saluted.

Cheers erupted in the UCA. Young Mario had saved the day. Even Ellacuría went over to embrace him and congratulate him.

After the emotions had subsided, Ellacuría took the microphone again. "Comrades, we're all on the same side. We all want what's best for this land that either saw us be born or has adopted us. I'm certainly in no position to impose upon you what the best military option is. Allow me to pledge that I'll support whatever decision the Commanders make."

Applause and cheers.

"Having said that, let's not set any decision in stone yet. According to the Embassy, events are about to happen that may allow us to better decide which plan to adopt. After they do, we'll call a meeting to make the final decision. Let's do that in deference to the U.S. Embassy, which has been a friend of ours."

Commander Marcial took the floor and said, "I can support postponing the decision and letting those events unfold. Anyone opposed?"

In the absence of opposition, the meeting was adjourned.

And Mario headed toward Guazapa, with Marcial and Sibrián.

Chapter 70

The Italian Gambit

Gladys walked up to the entrance of the San Carlos garrison. The guard phoned Major Zepeda to inform him that a Mrs. Gladys Suárez was looking for him at the main gate. A minute later she was allowed inside. When Gladys disappeared from view, the vehicle in which she'd arrived took off toward the Fourth Infantry Brigade in El Paraíso, Chalatenango.

The plan had been set in motion when Mario hadn't called on Saturday. The failure to call was the signal that Mario had joined the guerrillas.

Gladys had said good-bye to her mother and to Pepe in the car, amid hugs, kisses and tears. Estela had traced the sign of the cross on Gladys' forehead, saying, "May God protect you, and we'll see each other soon."

Pepe hugged her as well. "Everything will be all right, Gladys. When this is over, you'll love Italy."

Gladys hugged him back something fierce. She already owed this man a lot, and if everything went according to plan, Estela, Neto and her would be living a life that she had never dreamed of in Naples. She'd then picked up her bag and walked to the entrance gate of the garrison.

When she disappeared inside the gate, Estela began to cry. But when they got to the Main Northern Highway, which led to the 4th Infantry Brigade, Pepe said, "Look, we're on the highway where Neto was abducted, so I need for you to be on the lookout, to see if you see anything that we may have to avoid. Please compose yourself. If we get stopped, with any luck, it'll be Neto's unit."

Estela finally composed herself, and after a while, she asked, "And all this got set in motion because Reagan won last week?"

"Yes."

Estela sat pensive, reminiscing. She'd been poor all her life, although she hadn't always been a servant. She'd married a carpenter, and Gladys had been the fruit of their love. But her husband had died in an automobile accident when they were expecting their second child, and the grief had caused her to lose the baby. So her entire life had been reduced to caring for Gladys, and then Neto.

Neto's abduction had been as big a blow to her as it had been to Gladys. And thanks to that, any sympathy she may have had for the revolution, on account of her poverty, had dissipated immediately. She hated those guerrillas with a white-hot hatred. She wanted them to fail. But more importantly, she wanted Neto back. Once Neto was back, the world could go to hell.

Another question popped into her mind. "But if the Major works at the First Brigade, how is it that he got the Fourth Brigade Major to accept this?"

"Well, basically it's a good plan, and you'll be performing a useful service, giving them what they call intelligence. All those Majors are first and foremost friends because they belong to this huge graduating class. So the friend of Zepeda arranged it to so that you could have lodging and meals for free while you're there. And once the dust settles and you four are reunited at the Fourth Brigade, they'll take all of you up to the border with Honduras, where I'll be waiting for you."

"I pray to God it works."

"It's got to, Estela, it's the only way to get Mario and Neto safely out of this predicament."

Estela was scared. But she was scared that the plan might not work. But if it did work, then she was scared of living abroad, away from her homeland. Sure, she'd be with Neto, Gladys and Mario, but Italy was like another planet for her.

As if reading her mind, Pepe broke the silence. "Estela, you've got nothing to worry about. Number one, you'll love Italy. You'll love Naples. You'll be by the sea, just like over here. There's a big volcano there, just like the volcanoes here. People are friendly. Think of it as your retirement. You've slogged away like a slave all your life. Now, Mario and Neto and Gladys will take care of you with the business they establish."

Estela didn't seem convinced. Pepe understood her perfectly. It was why his mamma never wanted to leave Italy, even in times of peril. She didn't want to be uprooted, not at her age.

"Over there, you'll be the lady of the house, Estela. Not the servant. It's about time, don't you think?"

"But I like being the servant, Don Pepe. I like taking care of all of you, I like being part of the family."

"Wouldn't you rather have your own family? Your own house? Sleep in the main bedroom, rather than in the servants' quarters?"

Estela supposed she would. But that wasn't what she was used to.

"Besides, Estela, let's be clear here. Your true family is Gladys and Neto. We, the Tacarellos, are, if anything, your 'in-laws.' Remember that."

Something about this didn't sit right with Estela.

"No, Don Pepe. You're far more than that. I've had intimacy with you. You're a part of my life."

"Come on, Estela, that was your *patrón* taking advantage of you being needy. That's nothing you should give any value to."

"Is that so, Don Pepe? You had three women in your house, and you enjoyed all of us constantly, even me. And did you force me? Did I ever say no to you?"

Pepe felt his face go flush with shame. "No, I never did force you."

"Do you know why? Because I liked it. A woman needs a man. And you've been the man I needed."

Pepe was blushing seriously. "Come on, Estela, if you needed a man, you could've gotten one of your own."

Estela laughed. "Don Pepe, at my age? With my looks? The only way I could've gotten a man was exactly like you got me, through a mother/daughter fantasy."

Pepe was crimson by now. "That was many years ago, Estela."

Estela opened her eyes and mouth wide, in incredulity. "Oh yeah? How about the week before you left for Italy, when we were practicing the code, and Mrs. Belinda had to go out?"

Pepe feared he might undergo spontaneous combustion and die in flames before being able to help Mario, so he begged Estela not to go on.

"Oh, no, Don Pepe! I rarely have you all to myself to talk freely with you." And she punctuated her freedom by taking off her panties and throwing them in the back seat.

"My God, Estela! What are you doing?"

"Enjoying you, Don Pepe." She unzipped Pepe and took his penis out. She stroked it while she spoke.

"When Mrs. Belinda left, I told you in front of Gladys that I wanted to suck you, remember? Gladys got up to leave, but you told her to stay. So I sucked you while you sucked Gladys' breasts. Who knows what else would've happened, had we hadn't heard Mrs. Belinda open the garage door?"

The memory of it made Pepe real hard.

"You came in my mouth just in time, Don Pepe. It was a lot. But you know what? I didn't get anything in return—you owe me one. So find the first dirt road you can and stop in the middle of a sugar cane field so you can fuck me."

This was too much. Pepe admonished her. "Come on, Estela... we're on an important mission and there's guerrillas...!" But that's as far as he got because she started sucking him. So driving like that was as risky as facing guerrillas, so he found the first dirt road he could and parked among the sugar cane stalks. Estela sat up, opened the door and got out. She immediately undressed and walked into the cane stalks to lie down and open her legs.

Pepe thought, "For God and country," and went to do her bidding.

Twenty minutes later they were on the road again. Only this time Estela had her head on his shoulder, feeling very satisfied. She said to him, "I love you, Don Pepe."

"But I don't love you back, Estela."

"That's fine. I'll never hear you say that you love me, but I'm sure you do. Do you know why?"

"Because I fucked in you the sugar cane field?" He replied, laughing.

She replied, "No, because of everything you're doing for us."

Indeed, Pepe had invested quite a bit of his savings to send Mario, Neto, Gladys, and Estela to Naples, to his family's old apartment above the old store, which he hadn't sold. The first floor had always remained commercial space and several businesses had come and gone throughout the years. Pepe was lucky that the space was vacant when he went to ask the family to vacate the apartment.

It hadn't been till yesterday that Pepe had gotten back from the trip to Italy, where, besides evicting the tenants, he'd opened bank accounts with enough money to sustain everybody until the Naples branch of the Vesuvius hardware store he planned to open on the first floor started generating income. Then he had to pay for the commercial license, and then the biggest expense, which was the Italian passports for everybody, even those who weren't Italian citizens.

He was grateful to Belinda for allowing him to do this, because it was her money, too; money that was going towards maintaining the three people Pepe had imposed on her. He had sworn to her that he would make it up to her.

Of course, they hadn't planned on having to obtain an Italian passport for Sister Licha, for which they'd have no support documents. That cost them a lot more than they'd thought.

Belinda had just looked up to him and said, "You're just never going to be able to retire, my dear." And she'd smiled.

It was a smile that said, "I'll just be happy to get rid of all that excess baggage and have you all to myself again."

With the exodus that was about to happen, that was pretty much guaranteed.

Chapter 71

Sacrificial Ewes

"So while you were at grad school, you missed some very important events, like the rape and murder of the four missionary sisters, on December 2, 1980, didn't you?" Ellacuría's question was perfectly understandable because it was in Spanish, not Basque, which meant he was over his last tantrum.

"Oh, I didn't miss any of that, priest. It was plastered all over the news. Many of my university professors didn't like me, because of my unconditional support for Reagan. With the death of the nuns, I had serious doubt if I'd be able to finish my master's degree."

"Who can blame them?"

"Oh, I can, priest. First of all, journalists are easily paid to write propaganda. Let's recall that the famous journalist Walter Duranty, of the New York Times, who kept writing beautiful things about the communist paradise that the Soviet Union had become after the Bolshevik revolution, when in fact, there were massive executions and famines, which he neglected to mention for over a dozen years. And he got prizes for all those lies!

"So relying on newspapers is the purview of the less-educated folk. When I had to write papers at West Point, we weren't allowed to quote newspapers as sources. Why do you think that was?"

Ellacuría disagreed. "Come now, Captain, I'm pretty sure that the scenes of poverty they showed over there on TV weren't fiction."

Sánchez didn't' deny it but pointed out that "Poverty needs to be addressed with methods that work. So far, a combination of effective education and capitalism has lifted far more people out of poverty than any socialist revolution, because socialism tends to impoverish massively.

"Case in point: Nobody talks about any 'Cuban Economic Miracle,' for instance, and how long has it been since Castro got into power... 21 years? But everybody talks about the 'Chile Economic Miracle' just 7 years after Pinochet took office. But the U.S. press never mentioned how well off Chile is, and how bad off Cuba is. I'd say that's bias, wouldn't you agree?"

The mention of Pinochet didn't sit well with Ellacuría.

Sánchez continued. "Also, while I was there, there was no mention of the massive Agrarian Reform carried out by the Army. That massive dispossession the Fourteen should've been front and center under an unbiased press, am I right?"

Ellacuría wanted to return to the matter that couldn't be disputed: the rape and murder of the missionary nuns.

"Be that as it may, Captain, the Maryknoll nuns were indeed murdered and raped by National Guards. The U.S. Ambassador said so. The press wasn't lying about that."

The Captain disagreed. "Is that so, priest? I saw the pictures of their bodies. They seemed to be fully dressed. Furthermore, initial forensic examinations of the bodies didn't reveal any rape or torture."

The priest persisted. "Please, Captain, the National Guards were found guilty."

"But not of rape. They weren't even charged with rape. Which means two things: first, that the prosecution couldn't find any evidence of any such rape, which also meant that there was none to be found.

"And second, that the U.S. Ambassador to El Salvador in December of 1980 flat-out lied when he proclaimed that they'd been raped. He invented the whole thing, probably with the goal of Congress denying to Reagan any assistance to the Salvadoran military that White hated so much."

Ellacuría ceded to the Captain's logic when he said, "But even if what you say is true, Captain, murdering the missionary sisters was heinous enough. And it's not hard to reach the conclusion that there was no way that those National Guards were capable of making such a decision on their own and that they had to have acted on orders from the very top, then-Colonel Vides Casanova."

The Captain shook his head. It was obvious that Ellacuría's problem wasn't a lack of intellect, it was his tendency to let his passions cloud his brain. The Captain figured the best way to discuss this was with logic and fact. He said. "Let's consider the following: the very first thing Vides Casanova did when he learned of this murder, was to find the culprits, discharge them from the National Guard, and offer them up to civilian justice to be tried.

"And when these men had been released from any tie or loyalty to that institution or Vide Casanova, the former Guardsmen were then able to testify, under oath, that they committed that murder on orders from Vides Casanova, or anybody else in their chain of command—yet not one of them did! Even though they knew that by doing so, their punishment could be lessened."

It was revealing to the Captain that even though the very public trial of those national guards had concluded in 1985, these priests were still regurgitating propaganda, and not fact. It seemed that truth no longer held any value for them, at this stage of the struggle. Perhaps that explained the predicament they found themselves in at this time.

Sánchez continued. "Perhaps you don't know how the National Guard works. The best analogy is this: they're like a sheriff and his deputies were in a town in the old American west. The sheriff and his deputies could've been tough hombres, but they didn't stand a chance when outnumbered and outgunned.

"When I was in the United States in 1980, I saw a Dan Rather report on the CBS Evening News, in which guerrillas had videotaped an attack on a National Guard outpost in some town in Chalatenango. Dan Rather admitted that the film had been shot by the guerrillas, and that they'd passed it on to the U.S. news network. How easy was it to overwhelm a National Guard outpost of at most half a dozen National Guards, that the attackers even had a film crew with them to record it?

"The regional National Guard post, a few kilometers away, probably didn't even know that an attack was happening, because their only means of communication was the phone line, which was easily cut by the attackers. And since the U.S. government didn't provide help for the Security Forces, not even alternative means of communication, they continued to be picked off by the guerrillas.

"And I get it. Guerrilla warfare is attacking the enemy where he's the weakest. If I were a guerrilla, I'd do the same thing. Except for castrating them."

Ellacuría seized this moment. "Oh please, Captain. Castration? I thought only Ambassador White invented things?"

Sánchez ignored his mockery. "I'm inventing nothing, priest. In 1979, the high command received a report on how a National Guard in Arcatao,

Chalatenango, had been captured and castrated in public. Then in a later official record, a local judge, Dr. Inés Taura de Cuchilla, signed and sealed an official record declaring that civilians who had escaped a massacre by guerrillas who had entered the town of Nueva Trinidad, had castrated National Guards and other men."

"That's hard to believe, Captain."

"Is it, priest? Nobody ever disputes that the first group of guerrillas who abducted, tortured and murdered industrialist and philanthropist Ernesto Regalado Dueñas stuck pins in his eyes and testicles, right? Yet now you claim that the same caliber of people who did that, and massacred Ana Isabel Casanova, and kidnapped, tortured and skinned others alive, with the permission of the Black Indulgence, are incapable of castrating the hated National Guards?"

Their silence allowed the Captain to go on. "And finally, ask yourselves this: if the castration isn't true, why would that lady judge dare to officially declare its truth, thus making herself a huge target of the guerrillas?"

Ellacuría's hate-diminished intellect allowed him to say only this: "Years of repression have caused such actions, Captain, and you know it."

The Captain seemed content with the Jesuit's comment and highlighted it. "Good. Remember what you just said, that revenge is a powerful motive."

Father Montes finally inserted himself in the conversation. "But Captain, those national guards had to have known that two of them were returning from Managua, Nicaragua on that day and at that time. They had to have known that they'd be picked up by the other two sisters. How could they have known, if not told by their superiors?"

The captain looked incredulously at his favorite Jesuit. "Father Montes, if they did know that, and it was Vides Casanova who told them, why not say so in court? With their futures on the line? Logic therefore dictates that it wasn't Vides Casanova, or anybody else in their chain of command, who passed such information on to them."

Since Sánchez didn't want to have to embarrass Montes, he went on to a more personal and irrefutable piece of evidence. "Why would Vides Casanova, a man with an impeccable career, order something that was so against his nature and history? His conduct as Minister of Defense has been unimpeachable. Says who? Say members of both parties of the U.S. Congress and the Pentagon, who honored him. I know because I went with him on that trip.

"And to further underscore this, in the first peace meeting between the government and the guerrillas, everybody saw on TV when guerrilla commander Facundo Guardado walked up to General Vides Casanova and saluted, addressing him as *'Mi General'* [My General], in an obvious sign of respect."

Ellacuría waved that away. "Look, Captain, if for the sake of argument we agree with everything you said about Vides Casanova, the question remains: how did they know that the nuns would be coming their way on that day?"

Sánchez shrugged. "There's more than one way to skin a cat. One of them was this way: in June 1983, the Organization of American States, the OAS, published a conclusion, which, among other things, stated that one of the accused National Guards was at the Airport and saw the two nuns acting suspiciously, and alerted his boss, Sergeant Luis Colindres Alemán, who then ordered his men to get into civilian clothes and stop the nuns' vehicle. Now, whether I believe this version of events is neither here nor there. But this version of events explains how they became aware of their arrival, and it doesn't involve Vides Casanova."

Ellacuría grew exasperated. "OK, Captain, I accept that Vides Casanova had nothing to do with this, but then why murder them?"

The Captain wanted logic to answer that, but he first had to make sure that logic eliminated every other option. "Let me remind you what you said a few minutes ago: 'revenge is a powerful motive.' Guerrillas were doing a number on the National Guard, especially in Chalatenango, to include instances of torture. Now, where was it that the slain nuns were working in El Salvador? In Chalatenango, in guerrilla-controlled territory."

Ellacuría sounded indignant. "Captain, there was no basis in logic or fact to make the connection between castration and the nuns."

Montes stepped in. "All that those sisters were doing here was helping the poor in northern Chalatenango, near the border with Honduras."

Sánchez readily replied, "Yes, in territory that was controlled by guerrillas. Aren't there poor children everywhere? The poor in the *barrancos* of Escalón, for instance? Why did they have to go all the way to Chalatenango if all they wanted to do was to help the poor?

Before they could answer, Sánchez said, "And ask yourselves this: since they knew the guerrillas in that area were killing and torturing and castrating National Guards, why didn't they denounce it? Try to stop it? Or at the very least leave because they refused to be a part of such evil?"

This they couldn't answer. Logic had eliminated another option. Segundo Montes admitted as much when he asked something else: "Don't you think that it's strange that missionaries who were guilty of assisting the guerrillas, were so open in their movements—as if they had nothing to hide?"

The Captain didn't want to laugh in Montes' face because he liked him. So he opted to answer this question impersonally. "Priests, let me tell you a story that I learned from a nurse who works at the *Hogar de Parálisis Cerebral* [Home for Children with Cerebral Palsy], founded by my mother."

Ellacuría was impressed. "Your mother founded the *Hogar de Parálisis Cerebral?* That is a magnificent work."

"Yes, it is. She founded it because my sister was born with cerebral palsy because of medical malpractice. And rather than allow that blow to destroy more than one life, she created something to help others in the same condition."

"Captain, there's more to you than meets the eye." Ellacuría was sincerely appreciative.

"Thank you, Father Ellacuría, but all the merit goes to my mother. But allow me to continue. This particular nurse sought other jobs to supplement her income, like many nurses do. As such, she took a job with a family to care for an elderly relative of theirs. The family owned a warehouse and a used-car lot.

"A parish priest they knew acted as a go-between to get the family to lease out their warehouse to a non-profit organization that took care of *damnificados* [victims who'd lost everything in a disaster].

"The attorney of the non-profit said they needed the warehouse only to store things like clothing, canned foods, mattresses, bottled water, and similar, for *damnificados*. And they offered a very generous security deposit.

"The lease agreement was signed for one year, and it was renewable. The rent constituted a nice and welcome income for the family. The rent check always arrived promptly on the first business day of each month. The lease was going well.

"But a few months later, some warehouse neighbors asked the family if they had rented out to the Government, because people in military uniform would arrive at the warehouse at night.

"This worried the family because if the goods were for victims, the only uniforms that should arrive are Red Cross or the Salvadoran Green Cross."

The Jesuits looked like they knew where this story was going but said nothing. Sánchez went on. "Then the earthquake of October 10, 1986 hit mid-morning, and the family was worried about their warehouse. The lady of the house decided to go take a look, because the husband needed to stay at his business. On the way over she saw many flattened buildings, and she expected the worst. But when she got there the warehouse was standing.

"She decided that she wanted to look inside. But according to the agreement, she was required to give a 48-hour advance notice to the non-profit before any such visit. Since the phones weren't working, she went to look for the custodian, an elderly gentleman who greeted her kindly. She explained the situation to him and the custodian winked at her and said, 'I'll let you in if you promise not to tell anybody, ma'am.'

"When she promised, the custodian let her in. There wasn't anything for victims—only ammunition and medicine. She asked the custodian who these things were for. He winked again and said, 'For the *muchachos*.'

"*Muchachos* was another name for guerrillas. So the people coming at night to retrieve ammunition were guerrillas. When she got back home, they decided that they wouldn't say anything. They would simply not renew the lease.

"A month later, they informed the non-profit's attorney of their decision. The attorney then informed them that they would have to seek their last check from the Office of the Archbishop and return any part of the security deposit to them."

The Captain paused to let that sink in. The Jesuits could say nothing. A fact was a fact.

"Priests, I don't see the Archbishop of San Salvador hiding, despite helping the guerrillas so openly. Does that answer your question? The missionary nuns felt invulnerable to the consequences of their actions—just like every other revolutionary priest and nun in the country."

Given the priests' silence, the Captain went to the bottom line. "Since we have logically been able to deduce what didn't happen, we must allow logic to tell us what did happen. Logically: if I'm a National Guard in Comalapa, and I'm told that Maryknoll nuns are coming my way, suspected of helping the Chalatenango guerrillas, who've tortured and murdered fellow National Guards, I tell my commanding officer. Automatically.

"The only way I don't do it is if I'm offered an incentive not to. That incentive must've been an offer they couldn't refuse. So much so that they were willing to risk jail time, or even death. And their reasoning was straightforward: if they got killed in action that day, back then, their families would remain poor. But if they died executed because of what they did, yet their families were far better off—that could've looked like a very good option for them."

Montes asked, "What kind of incentive or offer, Captain?"

"Besides money? Entry to the USA for their families, with green cards to work, for example—things that poor people already do, but paying a pretty penny to *coyotes*.

Montes nodded. The Captain continued. "Those Guards were approached directly and offered something they couldn't refuse, in exchange for killing them and saying nothing."

Montes remembered quite clearly when Ellacuría had told the Jesuits to leave it up to the American Embassy to make the National Guard do something 'vile.' And since he knew that the engineer in Sánchez was going to arrive at the logical conclusion, he helped him by asking, "That type of incentive could only be given by the American Embassy and Ambassador White. Do you believe that he was capable of this?"

"Yes, for two reasons: the first is his lie that they'd been raped. And the second is that I met him personally and experienced first-hand the hatred he has towards the military. At a get-together with the 'military youth' after the October 15 coup, to which he had invited us, I approached him and greeted him in English, identifying myself as a West Point grad. I asked him about aid to El Salvador and he just stared at me with pure hate for about ten seconds, then turned to all the other officers there and said in Spanish, at the top of his lungs, "We don't give aid to murderers who kill thousands of their own people each day!"

"We were all taken aback. His description of us wasn't true—it was propaganda! Like Stalin? Like Pol Pot? Like Mao's Cultural Revolution? Like Che Guevara and Castro? How much hatred did that guy feel, to invite us pro-democracy military men just to insult us?"

Robert White's twin soul asked, "What about the death squads, Captain?"

Sánchez looked at Ellacuría and said, "I'll address that in a minute, priest, but first, I want to finish up with the nuns."

The Captain turned back to Montes to tell him, "Ambassador White had the means, economic and other, to induce those poor National Guards to commit an atrocity of the magnitude of the assassination of four missionary nuns, and to keep quiet about it, in order to create enough revulsion in the U.S. public to prevent Reagan from sending the promised aid to the Salvadoran Army. And it worked didn't it? Congress curtailed the aid, and only 55 American advisers were allowed to help us.

"As for your claim that the National Guards had to know the itinerary of the dead nuns—can you for a second doubt that the U.S. embassy indeed knew it?"

Sánchez then turned to Ellacuría to say, "Look, priest, do you really believe that I'd wear this uniform if I believed that death squads were real? I've never seen, come across, participated in, or otherwise known what you call a death squad. They're nothing but another lie in your propaganda arsenal!

"I took four years of military courses at West Point and never was a course titled 'Death Squads' taught. The School of the Americas in Panama never taught any courses on 'Death Squads.' The local Military School, where Col. Majano, one of the founders of our new democracy taught for years, doesn't teach any courses titled 'Death Squads.' So there is no military basis for any of the graduates of these schools to engage in such an activity."

Ellacuría seemed unconvinced. Sánchez went on. "Let me be clear, priest. Had I become aware, at any point in time, that the Army was acting incorrectly, unprofessionally, or inhumanely, in any way, including through the use of 'death squads,' as a West Pointer I had and have the means to report it.

"I could've reported it to any West Point grad who is a military adviser here in the country, at any of the informal meetings we have; to any of the military advisors in the country; to the Commander of the Military Group in the U.S. Embassy—in short, I had and have a slew of resources I could've made use of to report any such conduct, who would've protected me from any reprisals. But since I never detected any such conduct, much less any death squads, I never had to report a damn thing."

Sánchez stood up to leave, saying, "Priests, I'm very sorry about what happened to the nuns. They were nothing but sacrificial ewes at the altar of Marxism. Although the National Guards were the knife, it was somebody else who planned the sacrifice, not them."

For some reason, the term 'sacrificial ewes' didn't seem to sit well with Montes.

Chapter 72

The Cost of a Visa

Oscar Peralta was a retired National Guard whose children had all left for the USA, using the traditional method of the *coyote*, the person who gets his clients into the USA for a considerable fee. He'd paid for their *coyote* fees by selling his monthly stipend of free gasoline that he got as part of his miserly compensation as National Guard, at market prices.

Now his children wanted him in the USA, and they had gathered enough money to get him and his wife Eulalia over there. For which they needed a visa.

The Consular Official wasn't very willing. He spoke in very accented Spanish. "How would you maintain yourself while in the United States?"

Oscar replied, "Our four children are over there, and they have jobs."

The Official insisted. "We have no record of your children leaving for the United States with a visa from this Embassy. How did they get there?"

"I really don't know."

The Consular Official had him where he wanted him.

"We know. They're illegally in the USA. They're obviously protected by the network of Latinos that has efficiently sprung up in the major cities like Los Angeles and Houston. They probably even have forged social security cards that enable them to work."

"I really don't know, sir."

The American pressed on. "But make no mistake, we can find them and deport them."

Mrs. Peralta spoke up for the first time. "Sir, you represent a magnificent nation. A superpower. The fact that our children were able to find jobs over there means that the superpower economy is creating jobs that aren't being filled by Americans. So our children are doing nothing but contributing to the economy by paying taxes. They're probably helping to pay your salary."

Oscar Peralta turned to his wife in horror. You just don't speak to an Embassy man that way. He tried to keep her from saying anything else, but his wife went on.

"Do you know how many hours we spent outside this Embassy to get in here? Since 3 a.m. this morning. But that's not the galling part. The galling part is how the Marines treated us when we were out in the line, threatening us with bats and sticks. They treated us like cattle. That's not how a superpower should act, sir."

The Consular Official stood up. "Eulalia, please leave the room. Wait outside."

Mrs. Eulalia Peralta left in a huff. Oscar Peralta rose to follow her out.

"Mr. Peralta, please stay. We're not through."

Oscar sat down again, thoroughly crestfallen. No way would he get a visa now. And he was too old to go the *coyote* route.

The Consular Official smiled. "I know what you're thinking, Mr. Peralta. However, I think we can reach an understanding that will be mutually beneficial. You know where the *Café de Don Pedro* is, right?"

Oscar Peralta nodded.

"Be there at 9 pm tonight, alone. And next time you may not have to wait that long to get in here. Have a good day."

"But whom will I see at the Café?"

"Don't worry, we'll find you."

The *Café de Don Pedro* was a popular drive-in restaurant, where people usually arrived, parked and were waited on at their cars by the Café's staff. It was located on Alameda Roosevelt, one of the most important streets of the capital.

Peralta arrived in his old Toyota and parked. It was 8:55 p.m. He'd told his wife he was going to get together with friends. She didn't think twice about it. If he hadn't been unfaithful to her when young, he certainly wasn't going to start at this age.

At 9 pm. sharp, a man in his thirties knocked on the passenger side window, asked to be let in. He was a Latino. He introduced himself as 'Carlos,' who claimed to work for the 'Mister' who had interviewed him earlier that day. Oscar opened the door for him.

Once seated in the car, Carlos said, "You're having difficulties getting a visa to go stay with your children in the U.S., right? The Mister asked me to tell you that all those difficulties will disappear if you collaborate with us."

"Collaborate how?"

"Two ways. We want you to pass on information to certain members of the Security Forces."

"What kind of information?"

"That doesn't concern you. You'll just take a sealed envelope where we tell you."

"When?"

"We'll know for sure after November 4. You may not have to do that to get your visa. But if you do, we want to make sure we can count on you."

"Sure, I want that visa for my wife and me."

"Which brings us to the second way."

"What would that be?"

"Your wife is going to have to suck my dick."

"What?"

"Mr. Peralta, do you want that visa to the US, or not?"

"Yes, of course."

"Does she?"

"Her children are her life."

"Let me explain this to you in no uncertain terms. You're a National Guard. As far as the government of Jimmy Carter is concerned, you're the most *non grata* of *personae non grata*. Not only that, your children are illegally in the United States. We could have them here the day after tomorrow if we wanted to. And to top it all off, your wife disrespects a Consular Official who has the power to deny you or her the desired visa."

"She won't do it."

"Let me finish, Mr. Peralta. We're asking you to pass on sensitive information, and never reveal it to anybody else, ever. Not today, not tomorrow, not ever. We want to make sure that you and your wife will never breathe a word about this to anybody. And that neither will she. Because if you do, we'll make sure her children get pictures of their mom sucking dick, and you will be in them, and the dick won't be yours. Now do you understand?"

Oscar Peralta would've killed this man with his bare hands a few years back. But now he was in no position to do so. All he could do was say, "She won't even suck mine."

"Then you don't get your visas and your children get deported."

He opened the door to leave. Before getting out, he said, "Look, man, we're just trying to make sure everybody gets what everybody wants, and that nobody ever knows about it. And if you and Mrs. Peralta don't do it, there are plenty of other visa applicants who will."

Peralta thought better of it. "Hold on, please."

The man shut the door and stayed.

"I want guarantees."

"Ok."

"If my wife were to do this, I want more than visas. I want a *green card* [document that enables non-citizens to work in the USA] for each of my kids."

"Sure, we can do that. I'll sweeten the deal: you and the wife will get green cards as well."

"Ok."

Then Carlos said, "You and your wife come to this address tomorrow night at 10 p.m."

Peralta raised his hand. "Wait a second! You want me to take my wife to have her used and photographed by you, as security for our silence, without having received anything in return?"

Carlos laughed. "Mr. Peralta, if we don't keep our end of the bargain, you can become a serious millionaire by suing us and exposing everything. If we don't keep our end of the bargain, we risk our careers and our freedoms. I personally would kill all of them if they didn't keep their end of the bargain.

"This is no game, Mr. Peralta. But just so you don't feel you're leaving empty-handed, we'll have your and your wife's visas at this address tomorrow. Then, if you don't keep your end of the bargain, we'll just deport your kids. Sounds fair?"

The two men shook on it.

CHAPTER 73

THE ALL-POWERFUL GREEN CARD

When Oscar Peralta told his wife about the proposal, her face reflected the gamut of feelings, from incredulity to horror, and then... she burst out laughing.

"They want a 55-year-old woman to suck them? They must really be hard up!"

Which surprised Oscar to no end. He had expected the self-righteous woman who had told the Consular Official off to resurface. But to Oscar's amazement, she did nothing but visibly weigh the proposal.

In bed, she asked her husband, "What did you tell him when he first proposed that?"

I told him, "Hell, she won't even do that to me."

"Well then, I'd better make you my first."

Oscar sat up. "You're going to do it?"

"Oscar, what choice do we have? They've got us. They've left us no choice, except to back out and get ready to receive all of our children here, because they're going to get deported. I don't want that. Do you?"

"No."

"My only concern is, how will you feel? Because they're going to make you watch."

"I'll feel terrible. I'll feel like I'm less than a man because I'll be unable to protect my woman."

"Well, don't feel terrible. It's my choice. You have no say. I'm doing it for the children. Now, let me practice on you."

That had been quite a night for him.

He didn't want to recall the next night, though. There were four men there, including Carlos and the Consular Official, and she had to service all of them, with somebody always taking pictures. Oscar appeared in several of the pictures taken, next to his wife sucking a dick that wasn't his. It was definitely an effective way to guarantee their silence forever.

Before anything happened, the Consular Official gave them their passports with their visas. He then said that he'd give them the promised green cards and first class tickets to Los Angeles sometime after November 4, courtesy of the Embassy. He didn't promise when. It would either be soon after November 4, or after completing a task.

After that night, Oscar and Eulalia didn't hear from the Embassy until November fifth, when Carlos summoned Oscar to the *Café de Don Pedro* and gave him a sealed envelope. He was to make sure that the head of the National Guard of Comalapa got it.

Oscar had pointed out, "But Carlos, if I give it to him, he'll know it was me. Whatever happens after that can be pinpointed to me. I don't think you want that."

Carlos had been very courteous and professional with Peralta. Not a word about his wife. Peralta was grateful for that. "*Don* Oscar, you'll find a way to make sure he gets it, without anybody knowing it was you who gave it to him. You've been a National Guardsman, you know how mail is received."

"Fine. But why not just mail it? It'll get there."

"We don't want to risk this falling into the wrong hands. Or being delayed. This is why we're availing ourselves of your expertise."

Understanding perfectly what was expected of him, the next day Peralta traveled all the way to the Guard Post of Comalapa and asked to see the post chief.

The chief was not in, but he was received enthusiastically by a subordinate, Corporal Valladares, whom he knew. After embracing him, he offered him a cup of coffee which Peralta gratefully accepted.

"To what do I owe the honor of this visit, Sergeant Peralta?"

"Well, Valladares, I dropped a relative off at the airport and I remembered that I was short of 9 mm ammo for a Browning pistol that I bought. So it occurred to me to drop by to see you to see if you didn't have any extra ammo that you may have confiscated."

Peralta knew perfectly well that the answer was yes and that he'd have to go to the local storage room to retrieve it.

"Certainly, Sergeant Peralta. Let me go retrieve a couple of boxes. Do you need anything else?"

"Nothing else, Valladares, thank you."

As soon as Valladares left the office, Peralta went to look for the incoming mailbox, which, fortunately, was full. He inserted the envelope near the top of the stack. He could do no more.

He went back to sit down and wait for Valladares. Upon his return, Peralta offered to pay, which Valladares politely refused.

After exchanging a few pleasantries, Peralta bid him good-bye.

Now, he and his wife would have to wait for the Embassy to act.

Chapter 74

Torque-Nada

Don Polo arrived in an old beat-up Nissan at the Aguilares Church. After knocking in the agreed form and after providing the password, he was allowed inside.

He greeted commanders Marcial and Facundo Guardado and the others who were present. He couldn't help but notice that commander Ana María and Guillermo Ungo were not among them.

Guillermo Ungo had played a vital role in getting foreign governments to recognize the FMLN, which gave him every right to be at the meeting at UCA. To Don Polo, it had been obvious that Ungo siding with Ana María and Ellacuría in favor of the Tit offensive—aptly named, if Ana María was going to lead it (not knowing whether that was intentional or not)—was nothing but an attempt to become the political leader of the FMLN, leapfrogging him. To Don Polo, that was laughable—Enrique Alvarez Córdova was not about power; he was about doing the right thing.

That's why he liked Marcial, despite his murderous nature: he too wanted to do the right thing for the revolution he believed in. He actually cared for this troops. Unlike Ana María, who had proven to be a lot more egocentric than troop-centric. Her only reason to support the Tit Plan was to leapfrog Marcial to the supreme command of the FMLN—never mind that after a failed offensive, she'd be left with far fewer people to command.

Siding with Marcial over Ana María was a no-brainer for Don Polo.

And that's why he was here at this meeting, despite being more military than anything else: he wanted to make sure that it was Lisa that got implemented, not the Tit.

As soon as they were done with the greetings, they got down to business immediately.

Commander Marcial spoke first. "I'm glad we agreed to meet without Ana María, Ungo and Ellacuría. Although their contribution is valuable, especially internationally, they seem hell-bent on applying solutions that worked elsewhere, but which won't work here. The Tit Plan—which is probably Ana María's brainchild, for obvious reasons—would best be called 'Man's Tit' because it's just as useful."

Everybody laughed at this joke. Marcial continued. "The fact is that we don't have the numbers to attack everywhere. It seems strange to me that Ana María would've supported that, but I assume she's got her own, very personal reasons."

Everybody concurred. Marcial went on to say, "I summoned all of you here to give you more details about Lisa, so that, aware of the strategy, you can go back and prepare your tactical plans. So for starters, I'd like to give the floor to Don Polo."

Don Polo stood up and said, "Gentlemen, the only challenge for the Lisa plan is a logistical one, because we have to get the 'popular uprising people' to the staging areas near military targets and keep them there until the day of the attack. We've already got the places ready, and they are already stocked up with food and water, so as to lodge and keep everybody there for up to one week. I really have to commend Commander Marcial for his foresight. I'd also like to thank Don Blas Pérez for having channeled the funds to allow us to do so.

"I'd also like to thank Juana for her valuable contribution, because with a slight modification to the blueprints, she enabled us to store enough weapons for the fighters to move to the staging areas unarmed, to escape detection."

Having said that, he unfurled some maps that highlighted the staging areas. And the structures for lodging the uprisers and the weapons.

One of the commanders asked how such constructions had escaped detection with the Army out in the field dispossessing properties.

Marcial replied that all the staging areas were on properties controlled by Don Polo, and that the constructions were dual: above ground they were schools, and underground they were barracks.

The commanders liked that a lot. It was obvious that the Marcial-Don Polo duo was ideal to command the FMLN. This plan had been well-devised.

For the next hour the commanders discussed the different staging areas that their units would occupy, how to get there, when to visit them to deposit the weapons, etc.

The only one who didn't participate in the discussion was Facundo Guardado because it was Facundo Guardado's unit that would attack the Air Force. He required no uprisers for that. Just secrecy. His unit would penetrate the perimeter of the base set charges under each aircraft and leave. He would detonate them remotely. That was it.

Commander Marcial spoke again. "As you can see, comrades, Lisa has everything planned, except for the transportation of the uprisers to the staging area barracks. This was necessarily the last point to plan, because it must necessarily base itself on the date of the attack that is to be determined at the next FMLN meeting.

"Don Blas Pérez had promised us funds for such transportation, but since he retired, we submitted the petition to his replacement, Don Torquemada, who hasn't replied."

Concern pervaded the room. Did the sponsors want the Tit Plan?

Don Polo's moment had come. He stood to address this issue. "Gentlemen, Reagan's inauguration is two months away. Let's not worry about Don Torquemada's money, because I'm going to finance this part of the operation. The transportation of uprisers without detection should be our only concern."

But Commander Zonte stood up to ask the question that was on everybody's mind: "Commander Marcial, with all due respect, what do you attribute this lack of financing to?"

Marcial stood up, took out a handkerchief to clean his glasses, put them on again and said, "Comrades, about a year ago the Soviet Union invaded Afghanistan. Don Blas had warned us that this was going to reduce our budget, but he made it so that the great majority of our funds were advanced to us. That was enough for everything, except for this transportation issue. But Don Polo, ever magnanimous, has offered to resolve this temporary shortfall. There's nothing else to it."

Expressions of gratitude to Don Polo.

Then Don Polo said, "Gentlemen, if there could be one representative from each of your units, we'd have a complete coordination team and we'd be able to finalize it quicker."

Commander Mayo Sibrián said, "Comrades, we really can't spare anybody for this final battle. We need to be getting ready for battle. Let's just trust that Don Polo will do the right thing, as he's done to date. Just tell us where the coordination headquarters will be so we can contact him if need be.

Juan Chacón, one of Don Polo's FDR assistants said, "The National University would've been ideal, but since June it's been taken over by the Security Forces."

Marcial said, "Just don't let it be the UCA. Ellacuría will be breathing down your necks."

Don Polo proposed the Externado. "I used to coach basketball at the Externado de San José. Father Montes and I are good friends. He won't be sticking his nose in our business. Besides, school's out. We'll be safe there." The Salvadoran school year ran from January to October.

They all agreed that Externado would be the logistics headquarters for the offensive. With that, Marcial adjourned the meeting and everybody disappeared into the night, to get ready for Lisa.

Chapter 75

Silence is Golden

Oscar Peralta had just gotten back to his apartment in Los Angeles, from helping his son build a shed for the tools for his plumbing business. His wife received him with a big hug and a Budweiser, a local beer he liked. He went to his favorite chair and turned on the Spanish language news.

A news reporter was saying, "The bodies of Maryknoll Sisters Maura Clarke and Ita Ford, Ursuline Sister Dorothy Kazel, and lay missionary Jean Donovan were found in shallow graves early this morning near the Port of La Libertad, in El Salvador. Ambassador Robert White said that they had been raped and murdered by National Guards who had hijacked their van and taken them to an isolated spot where they were raped and machine-gunned. Two of the nuns had arrived at the local airport, and had been picked up by the other two, and were going home. Local persons dug a shallow grave for them and notified the authorities. When Ambassador White arrived, he immediately accused the National Guard of rape and murder. The nuns worked in northern El Salvador, in territory controlled by guerrillas.

"There's been no independent verification of any rape."

Oscar turned to his wife, who sat petrified there, listening to the horrible news. He turned the TV off.

She asked, "Don't you want to finish listening to this?"

"No, my love, please come sit with me here."

She did so. Oscar looked lovingly into his wife's eyes and took her hands. "My love, listen to me. What they just said is why the American Embassy made us do what they made us do, to make sure we don't tell anybody anything about it."

Eulalia Peralta blanched. "I don't understand. What does this have to do with us?"

"My love, the Embassy sent me to deliver a package to the National Guards who probably did this. I'm positive that the American Embassy set this up."

"To have them raped?"

"No, my love, I'm pretty sure that part's a lie. I know my fellow National Guards, they wouldn't do that."

"How about killing them?"

"Well, somebody killed them so I'm assuming they could've done that. But the National Guard doesn't have any knowledge as to who comes and goes on our highways. That's something the National Police or the Army does. We patrol the streets of towns, not highways. So in all probability, the Embassy had me give the National Guards information that led to this."

"So the American Embassy wanted them killed?"

"It seems to me that the American Embassy wanted the National Guard to kill them."

"Why?"

"So Reagan can't help El Salvador when he gets into office."

"So what do we do?"

"Nothing! You can't say anything to anybody about this, ever. That's why they had you at that party and took pictures of us. To force us not to say anything. So you make sure you say nothing, do you understand?"

"Oscar, are you sure about this?"

Oscar nodded. "You can never say a word to anybody. Ever."

Mrs. Peralta was white as paper. "Excuse me, Oscar, I think I'm going to throw up." She ran to the bathroom and lifted the toilet lid just in time.

Oscar poured a glass of water for her and took it to the bedroom where she sat recovering.

Eulalia started to cry. "Oscar... I sucked assassins, murderers. Those poor nuns are dead because of me!"

Oscar held his wife close. "You did no such thing. Besides, the guy who set this all up said if we didn't do it, other visa applicants would. And where would we be? Stuck in El Salvador, with our deported children. And doing what? There's no opportunity for them there! They have no future there! Their future is here. You did it for them!"

That did lift her spirits a little bit. But she looked at him remorsefully. "Aren't you ashamed of what I did, Oscar?"

"My love, I couldn't be prouder to be the husband of such a brave woman, a mother capable of sacrificing it all for her family."

They embraced in silence for a while.

Then Oscar said, "We both best forget what happened. We were given what we have because of that, our kids have the green cards they always wanted because of that, but now, poof, it's forgotten. I don't remember a damn thing about anything. And neither should you."

But something didn't sit well with Eulalia. "Oscar, that sub-sergeant was your friend, your brother in arms. Couldn't you help him by revealing what we know?"

Oscar thought about this, but his gut was already telling him no. Then his mind came to the same conclusion, because he had no proof—he never looked inside the envelope. He had no clue what was in it.

Besides, they'd say that he was just trying to help his comrades. And then the *Migra* [U.S. Immigration] could appear here and deport parents and kids. And then they could even accuse him of being an accomplice. Or worse, their kids might start getting pictures of their mom naked with somebody's dick in her mouth, which can't be her husband's because that's his face next to hers.

"No dear, I wouldn't be able to help him. And we'd lose everything we've gained in the process. So the best course of action is to forget it."

"Are you sure, Oscar?" She wanted to be reassured thoroughly, completely.

Oscar realized he was going to have to do exactly that, if he ever wanted tranquility to reign in his home again. "Well, dear, let's analyze this together. Let's assume that it was me who received that envelope and read the information in it. The way to deal with this was to call my superiors immediately. This would've been automatic. Why would I want to deal with nuns directly? First of all, they're nuns and secondly, they're American. That's radioactive.

"So I would've immediately contacted my superiors. Knowing my superiors, they would've kicked it all the way up the chain of command. Upon reaching Col. Vides Casanova, he would've dealt with it automatically as well: he would've informed the Vice-Minister of Security.

"The Vice-Minister of Security would've assigned this to the National Police, because that's their jurisdiction. The National Police would've done investigations, like interviewing the National Guards to gather evidence from them. Then they would've interviewed the nuns, etc.

"Finally, if an arrest is warranted, a judge would've had to sign off on that, and then, if the women didn't voluntarily turn themselves in, the National Police could've stopped them on the highway, because they have jurisdiction to do that. The National Guard does not.

"So had the National Guards acted correctly, this wouldn't have happened."

Eulalia nodded. Everything her husband had said made sense.

Oscar continued. "So that's what those National Guards should've done, because that's what they'd been trained to do. There's no way in hell to get that wrong... unless..."

"What?" Mrs. Peralta asked anxiously.

"Unless there was a considerable monetary benefit involved, right?"

Eulalia could relate to that. Hadn't she just prostituted herself for a benefit?

Oscar kept going. "Now then, how did this all happen? I dropped off the envelope and came back home. A couple of weeks later we were given the green cards, and first-class tickets to Los Angeles, were we not? Why do you think they didn't give them to us as soon as I'd made the drop-off?"

Eulalia replied, "The Embassy had to verify that the drop-off had been made, that you had complied."

Oscar nodded. "Exactly. I didn't call them to tell them. I delivered the envelope and waited. So a National Guard opened the envelope and did what the instructions inside told him to do, rather than report it to his chain of command."

"But what were those instructions?"

Oscar took his wife's hand in his. "Sweetheart, there's no way of knowing—I didn't open the envelope to see what was inside."

But Eulalia insisted. "But how is it that the Embassy knew that you'd fulfilled your mission?"

"The instructions probably gave a number to call. One of the National Guards called that number and that was a number he could've only gotten from the envelope."

Eulalia thought about this and asked, "So are you saying that had they kicked it up the chain of command, we wouldn't have gotten compensated as promised?"

Oscar replied, "The moment anybody called that phone number, where a National Guard or a superior, they would've known that I'd delivered the envelope."

"You're so right! Thank you, my love!" She started hugging and kissing him.

Oscar breathed a sigh of relief. His analysis was spot on. Now, they could proceed to live the rest of their lives in peace.

Chapter 76

Our Father

"Eliseo, wake up, you need to go stand guard." Eliseo woke up, saw that it was 1:30 a.m., put on a sweater and a jacket, grabbed his empty carbine, which, for all practical purposes, was nothing but a well-sculpted piece of wood, and took off with the detail to relieve the sentries.

The commander of the relief had a transistor radio on. There was news about the rape and murder of four nuns by the National Guard. Eliseo listened attentively: "The news on YSKL: four American nuns were found raped and murdered by the National Guard near La Libertad in the early morning of December 2, according to U.S. Ambassador Robert White. Independent corroboration of the rape was unable to be obtained, but that's what the Ambassador claims."

Eliseo was pretty sure that this was an American Embassy-induced crime. Its target was not the local population, but the U.S. population. He was pretty sure the Ambassador wouldn't allow the bodies to undergo an autopsy—first, because there was no need to, and second, because he wasn't going to risk being exposed as a liar.

Plus, there wasn't any need to: they were dead, and if the U.S. Ambassador in El Salvador said that they'd been raped, the U.S. media had no reason to attempt to verify it. The media had long ago ceased to be a seeker of truth, becoming instead a propaganda outlet against American interests. And the rape and murder of the four religious women was very much against the American interests enunciated by President-elect Ronald Reagan.

White had accomplished his mission.

Mario had the premonition that it was the Tit Plan that would get implemented. However, if it wasn't accompanied by a popular uprising, the Tit Plan would have disastrous consequences for the guerrillas. Mario recalled and agreed with the words of father Montes: the American Embassy-induced atrocity was intended for Americans, not Salvadorans. Unless Salvadorans were terribly offended by the rape and murder of the

American missionaries, they wouldn't rise up. That made Lisa the logical way to go.

The news made him pray more fervently for Neto, or rather, Commander Guevara, to be the one who checked on the sentries that night. His mission required him to establish contact with Neto. Otherwise it had very little chance of success.

His prayers were answered.

"Sentry, identify yourself!" It was Commander Guevara's command voice.

"Eliseo, of the Heroes of '32 Unit, Commander Guevara."

"Report!"

"Nothing new, Commander. Except that your mother Gladys and your grandmother Estela want you back."

This stunned the young guerrilla.

"And how do you know about my mother and grandmother?"

"Your grandmother was my nanny. I'm Mario Tacarello, your half-brother. My dad, Pepe Tacarello, is your father."

Surprised, Neto could only say, "But my mom said my dad had died."

"No, your dad has been taking care of you all your life, although indirectly. And I just found out about it a few months ago."

It took the young guerrilla a few seconds to recover from this surprise. When he did, he asked, "So why are you here, Eliseo?"

Mario had rehearsed the answer to this very question. "I'm here because we want to get you out of here. By we I mean your mother, your grandmother, your dad and me."

"You want to take me away from my men? To betray the cause?"

"Neto, I mean, Commander Guevara... you're not men, you're kids, teenagers. You didn't volunteer for this, did you? You were abducted. I'm here to convince you to do what makes sense, in light of the information I have for you."

"What's that?"

"Commander Ana María, Guillermo Ungo, the Jesuits and the American Embassy are insisting on a nationwide offensive before Reagan takes office. That means taking all our forces and attacking all the Government's garrisons all over the nation, sometime in early January. Most commanders are against it because it dilutes their strength and guarantees a defeat everywhere. The alternative plan was to attack only three garrisons up north and the Air Force, declare a Free El Salvador, and start expanding to the rest of the country from there.

"The American Embassy had promised an event that might spawn a popular uprising which we need to have a successful offensive, and tonight I heard about the nuns. I doubt if that'll do it. They were designed to impact the American people, not Salvadorans. But the Jesuits and the Embassy want an all-out offensive because they believe that it'll prevent Reagan from helping El Salvador."

Neto nodded and said, "We sort of knew that already when the FDR leadership got taken from the Externado and executed on November 27."

"What?" Now it was Eliseo's turn to be stunned.

"You hadn't heard of that?"

Mario shook his head. "They don't tell us new recruits much."

Neto told Mario that in a precise military operation, what seemed to be Treasury Police commandos had gone into the Externado de San José, at around 11:30 a.m. on Thursday, November 27, exactly to the rooms where the FDR were meeting. They had cuffed and gagged and dragged the members out, put them in a car, and taken them away, all in a matter of 20 minutes. All had been found murdered, execution-style, the next day. Enrique Alvarez Córdova's body was riddled with bullets. A note was left on one of the bodies, claiming that it had been the 'General Maximiliano Hernández Martínez' Brigade, a reputed death squad.

Neto told him that someone had fingered them. And the first suspect was Leoncio Pichinte, who should've been there and was not. Not coincidentally, Guillermo Ungo had been elected President of the FDR almost immediately after that. And then Guillermo Ungo declared that the FMLN would move its decision-making center to Managua, Nicaragua. And to the surprise of nobody, Ana María was in Managua as well.

Mario felt tremendous sadness for the loss of Don Polo. He was such a gentleman, a true social justice warrior. But he'd feel sad later. His priority right now was getting Neto on his side. "I don't know if that was the Embassy, Neto, but it sure looked like it was somebody who wanted the general offensive. And to send the message, they killed the members of the FDR, which were expendable, unlike the commanders, who are needed for the offensive."

Mario new full well that the Externado operation hadn't been the Embassy; an operation that precise and effective could've only been done by the 'Jesuit Death Squad,' under Ellacuría's control. Because Ellacuría definitely had the motivation: with the adoption of his Tit Plan, Commander Ellacuría was now, for all practical purposes, part of the leadership of the FMLN.

Neto voiced his concern, "Well, attacking everywhere is suicide. We haven't even been able to train with live ammo to make sure our men can hit what they aim for. We'll be cannon fodder."

Mario nodded. "Exactly. Now Neto, I'm here because I want to go where you go. If you want to participate in that, then I'll follow you into battle. But if instead, you want to save lives, not just ours, but those of your comrades, then I can help."

Neto looked confused. "You're saying that you are prepared to die with us, but that you are also prepared to defeat us. I don't get it."

"Neto, your mom, your grandma, your dad, we all have a plan to get you out of here. With them. To Italy. Your Dad has obtained the necessary visas to enable you, Estela and Gladys, to become Italian citizens and lead a better life."

"But I'd be betraying my comrades."

"Or saving them. Especially teenagers like you. Look, the U.S. Embassy, the Spanish Jesuits and whoever controls Ana María and Ungo (probably the Cubans), they're all sending you to your deaths. And to mine, too, because I'll follow you. But everybody knows a general offensive will fail. That means the unnecessary deaths of all of us *indios*. I, for one, don't want that. There are better alternatives to the massive spilling of blood. And we can talk about that later."

Neto asked, "What's the plan?"

Mario told Neto that he would feed the guerrilla's offensive's battle plan to the Gladys and Estela, who were at the First and Fourth Brigades to receive the information.

This surprised the young man. "Really? Why are they there?"

"Because their sole mission in life is to get you back safe and sound, Neto. That's why they've been at the Brigades since November 10."

Neto choked up. All Mario could think of was that Major Zepeda was a genius.

Then Neto asked, “What if we get captured?”

“The plan is for everybody who is captured to be questioned, not executed and the teenagers like you will be returned to their families.”

Neto looked at his watch and said he’d have to move along. But he asked, “How are you going to feed them that information?”

“Neto, I’ll show you when you get me the battle plan.”

“Okay, I have to move along now, let me get back to you soon.”

Mario reminded him of this fact: “Neto, remember, you have your family counting on you. And my life depends on your decision as well. But more importantly, so does yours.”

Chapter 77

The Circuit

As he continued to stand guard that night, Mario recalled the events that had led to this very moment.

Major Zepeda had arrived at the Tacarello household that Friday night. He was greeted effusively by Mr. and Mrs. Tacarello, by Gladys, Estela, Sister Licha and Mario.

Mario had laid out the plan, whereby he would join the guerrillas in Guazapa, learn what their battle plans were, and get them down physically, through the teachers, whom he'd help escape. Mario had reached the logical conclusion that they had the greatest probability of being able to escape because they would have compassion for them. In other words, Mario thought the probability of a sentry letting them go, rather than shooting them, was great.

The Major didn't say anything. He seemed to have doubts.

The alternative plan was for Neto to escape, for which he suggested that Gladys be at the First Brigade, and Estela at the Fourth, so that Neto could be positively identified if he got to either garrison. Knowledge of their presence there would also be a motivation for Neto.

Those were Mario's Plan A and Plan B.

Major Zepeda didn't like either Plan A or Plan B. "Look, Father, I'm fine with trying to help the ladies escape, which I think is a worthy plan. But they're going to escape at night, and they're not going to go down the dirt road, but rather down cliffs and precipices, and if a bullet doesn't get them, they could slip and fall and break their necks or any other bone that doesn't let them go on, and you won't find out about that until it's too late. Same goes for Neto. So your physical plan won't work.

"We need a foolproof plan. We need to get you a transmitter."

Mario protested. "Major, if they find a radio on me, this plan is over. And if anybody tries to take one up to me, they'll be frisked. That's not workable."

Major Zepeda thought long and hard about this. He asked to use the phone. Pepe took him to his study and gave him privacy. A while later the military man came back to the living room and told them that, "The Signal Battalion can't think of anything that's not a radio, but a radio is too big to escape detection. But they told me that they had an officer who's studying electrical engineering in the States right now. They gave me his number. I'll call him from my office tomorrow and let you know."

Mario didn't want to wait another day, "Major, please... call him from here."

Zepeda returned to the study and dialed the number in the United States.

Second Lieutenant Sánchez answered. "Hello."

"Lieutenant Sánchez, this is Major Zepeda, First Brigade S-2. The Signal Battalion gave me your number. How are you?"

Sánchez was surprised by the call. Why would a First Brigade major be calling him in the U.S.? Might it have to do with D'Aubuisson? Nevertheless, he only replied, "Doing well, sir."

"OK, Sánchez, let me get to the point. We're mounting an operation here, in which we're going to have to have someone transmit to us from an elevation. However, that person isn't going to be able to carry a radio with him because if they find it on him, the operation's over. Is there a microcircuit or something really small that he can hide on himself? It would have to be really small to escape detection."

Sánchez thought about this. If the transmission was going to be from an elevation, it would require very little power for the signal to reach its destination. There would be line-of-sight between Guazapa and the First Brigade. If it transmitted at a normal Army HF frequency, like 70 MHz, a small crystal would be required to generate the carrier wave. The greater the frequency, the smaller the components of the circuit, and therefore, the smaller the circuit as a whole. But if he wanted to receive, then you'd have to include a receiving circuit, and that would make the circuit too big—might as well take a radio.

Sánchez replied, "Sir, the only way to make it as small as it can be is for it to be a transmitter only—no reception whatsoever."

The major thought about it and replied, "Fine, let's just make it a transmitter."

Sánchez continued. "If the receiver is within 20 kilometers line of sight from the mountain, a Morse Code transmitter would work perfectly. The largest component would be a battery, but he wouldn't have to connect it to the circuit until he's ready to transmit. If he can get the battery locally, then he wouldn't have to carry one on him, and that would be the smallest possible circuit."

Zepeda said, "I think there's a good chance that there are batteries on that elevation, Sánchez. How small would the circuit be?"

"Sir, it could easily be sewn into garments or undergarments.

"Ok, but wouldn't it need an antenna, too?"

"Sir, just a short wire. The mountain acts as an antenna."

Zepeda asked another question, "How are we going to be able to receive the Morse Code transmission?"

"It can be received on the HF radios that all the garrisons have. The person receiving it will only need a paper and pencil to write it down."

Major Zepeda was liking what he was hearing so far. But he had more questions: "Sánchez, we scan frequencies all the time to try to detect their communications. Why can't they do that to us, and detect the Morse Code transmission that way?"

Sánchez answered quickly. "Sir, we don't transmit in HF at night because we can't use the ionosphere as a repeater. They really have no reason to be scanning those frequencies at night. But if they do, they'd have to know Morse Code to understand it."

Zepeda was satisfied. He said, "Very good, Sánchez, this seems like a good solution. Can you fax me a schematic of this Morse Code circuit?"

"Right now?"

"Yes, it's urgent, Sánchez. Can you do that?"

"There are several places I can fax from. Just give me the number."

The Major obtained the fax number from Mario and gave it to Sánchez, adding, "That number is for a fax that's right here next to me. Please fax this circuit as soon as possible. Also be prepared to receive calls from the Signal Battalion. We're going to need you to help them build this circuit and test it."

"Yes, sir."

"Good job, Lieutenant. We'll be in touch."

Zepeda hung up and went back to the living room with the others and told them about the Morse Code circuit, adding, "As soon as the officer faxes the schematic, I'll take it over to our Signal Battalion to see if we can build it. And they'll make sure to test it before we train Father Mario to use it."

Everybody looked uncomfortable because they didn't have the slightest clue about Morse Code.

Zepeda laughed. "You don't know Morse Code? Don't worry, I'll send someone here tomorrow to start teaching you."

There was relief among his hosts, but not that much. Gladys said, "Major, my mother and I didn't get past the eighth grade. Is that enough for us to learn it?"

Zepeda nodded, and said, "Morse Code is a system to transmit letters and numbers. If you know the alphabet and numbers, you're set."

The Major decided to explain the circuit component of the plan in detail. "We'll know tomorrow if we can build that tiny circuit the officer sends over. We're going to have to test it so we're probably not going to have a circuit for Father Mario to play with for another week.

"Assuming Father Mario can make it work, that'll be our Plan A: to transmit the guerrilla battle plan to Gladys and Estela at the brigades, using Morse Code. Gladys will pass the information to me and Estela will give it to the Fourth Brigade S-2."

Everybody nodded. This sounded a lot better than having two women flee down the mountain at night.

Zepeda went on. "Now then, the only one transmitting Morse Code will be Father Mario, who won't be able to receive. Gladys and Estela will only be able to receive Morse Code, not transmit. That's the only way to ensure that the circuit is tiny."

"Assuming the Signal Battalion can build the tiny circuit, we won't be using it until after the November 4 election in the USA. So we have a month to learn and practice Morse Code. After that, Gladys and Estela can still practice it at the garrisons, no problem, and if they need help, all they have to do is ask me."

"But Father Mario isn't going to be able to practice once he's up in Guazapa, and the only time he'll use it is when he transmits the battle plans. This puts the onus on you, Father Mario, to learn it well. I'll have the instructor here every day to teach Morse Code to Gladys and Estela, so they'll have to be the ones who teach it to you when you're able to come home."

Mario replied, "Don't worry, Major, I'll learn it." Then he asked the obvious question: "What if the Signal Battalion can't build it?"

Major Zepeda replied immediately. "Then I'll come up with an alternative plan really quick and I'll come back here to present it to you all. But I can't think of a better plan than your plan with Morse Code, Father Mario. So your duty is to pray like hell that they can build it."

Everybody laughed, except Belinda, who asked, "I'm sorry, could you please tell me why the plan requires Gladys and Estela to be at the garrisons? Especially since Mario will be transmitting in Morse Code and the Salvadoran Army knows Morse Code?"

Zepeda replied, "Mrs. Tacarello, when we capture the guerrillas, Mario and Neto will probably be unrecognizable. We're going to need someone to identify the good guys and it can't be me, if they're captured by the First Brigade. If they're captured by the Fourth Brigade, we need someone there to identify them and that'll be Estela. You see, the last thing we want is for them to get an inkling that they were betrayed by Mario and Neto—that would endanger all the Tacarellos and we don't want that."

Belinda nodded. Zepeda continued, "Another reason for Gladys and Estela to be at the garrisons is for Mario to be able to say to Neto that his mother and grandmother were waiting for him at the garrisons with the required degree of earnestness because it'll be true. This is important to minimize the risk of Neto refusing to cooperate and outing Mario."

This was the clincher for Belinda. To hell with Neto, all she cared about was Mario.

Zepeda went on. "Furthermore, we want a means of communication that is quicker than biblical messages. We'll run a line from a home that we control, which is adjacent to our garrison, to our communications center, which phone will only be answered by Gladys. That way, Sister Licha can call a civilian number, not a military number, and speak with a civilian, not a military person, to pass information to her in real time. When Gladys hangs up, she'll pass the information on to me.

This way we ensure that the Tacarellos—Mr. and Mrs. Tacarello, their home and business—aren't involved in this operation at all. We also protect

Sister Licha this way, because she'll be calling a phone number that isn't associated with either the military or the Tacarellos."

Everybody nodded in agreement. It made sense. Zepeda said, "As you can see, getting Gladys and Estela out of the Tacarello home and placing them in the garrisons will provide security for the Tacarello family, residence and businesses, even after this operation is over."

Everybody had started to appreciate Zepeda. Although Mario's original plan was bold and daring, it was Zepeda who was making it workable.

Zepeda ended his description of the plan with the following, "With this Morse Code plan, we're going to need Morse Code experts ready all night for Father Mario's transmission, because that's the only time he'll be able to transmit to escape being seen. And who better than Neto's mom and grandma, to receive the information that Neto will pass on to Father Mario? They are a guarantee that the message will be received and that it'll be received well."

Mario asked, "Major, how will you tell me that you've received the information, given that I can only transmit and not receive?"

Zepeda replied, "In broad strokes, Father Mario, a simple way to do it would be to use a system of orange and white flares on our boats patrolling the Cerrón Grande dam. We can use a combination of number of flares and colors of flares to let you know if we've received the transmission or not. Also, we will respond quickly, so you can go back to where you need to be fast, without creating suspicion. I'll fine-tune this plan and come up with a final version soon."

Just then, the fax rang, and Sánchez's circuit started to come in.

Zepeda picked it up, looked at it, and smiled. "This is going to work, folks. This is a good plan." He said good night and he left.

That had been over two months ago. Mario reached inside his jacket and felt the tiny circuit board that he would connect a wire and a battery to, to transmit the plan. He'd brought two circuits, one of which he'd hidden in a secure place. He'd already identified the battery storage cave and had access to it. Anyway, if Neto came on board, Neto could get him batteries as well.

CHAPTER 78

JUST LIKE ABRAHAM

Mario looked at his watch. He had an hour to go before being relieved by the third shift sentinel. So he continued to recall the events that had led to his being in Guazapa.

Mario had stopped by the house that Thursday night, because he was pretty sure that the big Commander conference was going to take place the next day. He didn't know the place and time, and so he wasn't going to be able to provide any intelligence to Licha or Zepeda. But since his 'Morse Plan,' as Zepeda had ended up naming it, required that he join the guerrillas, he'd take advantage of this opportunity, because he knew Marcial and Mayo Sibrián would be there.

So he went and bid good-bye to everybody. Pepe wasn't there, though, because he'd left for Italy to make all the arrangements. He was scheduled to come back on Sunday. He wouldn't see his dad until January, with luck.

It was emotional for everybody, especially for Belinda, who would be left all alone. But they all knew that it was the step that had to be taken. He also wanted to make sure everybody was deciphering Morse Code correctly, because the next time he transmitted, it was going to be for real.

Frankly, it had astonished him how quickly Gladys and Estela learned it. Which confirmed to him that Licha was right: education was the only solution to the poverty problem here and everywhere.

And they in turn had taught him well.

So that night he sat down with Gladys and Estela to tap out messages to each other. The signal Battalion had made them some circuits that didn't transmit but did generate the tones for them to practice on.

"OK, Marito, tap us a message, and we'll reply."

Mario tapped out, "I have missed you."

Gladys tapped out, "We need to talk to you in secret."

Mario tapped out, "When?"

Estela tapped out, "After your mom goes to sleep."

Mario tapped out. "In your room?"

Estela tapped out. "Yes."

When he was certain that his mom was asleep, Mario got out of his bed and went downstairs to the bedroom of Gladys and Estela in his pajamas. They were waiting for him and asked him to sit down on Gladys' bed.

Gladys told him, "Marito, your friend Sister Licha came by a couple of days before Don Pepe left for Italy."

"What for?"

"To talk to your dad."

"You mean, to mom and dad?"

"No, just your dad. Your mom was visiting, and we were supposed to be at the market buying provisions that day, because it was 'market day,' but your mom forgot to give us the money, so we stayed here. And then your dad came home unexpectedly, and about a minute later Sister Licha arrived."

"So my dad didn't know you two were here?"

"No."

"Go on."

"Sister Licha asked your dad to take her to Honduras and to Europe."

"She wants to get out of here, too?"

"Yes, she told him she was going to resign as a nun and start a new life in Europe."

This surprised Mario. Why hadn't she said anything to him before? He would've gladly helped her. Something must've happened. Mario asked, "Ok, but why does she need my dad to do that? She's got the visa she got for the Italy trip in April, which is valid for at least one year. Unless..."

Estela finished his sentence. "She wants to travel under the Tacarello name."

Mario pondered this. Licha is very intelligent. If there was any way to do it without involving the Tacarellos, she would have. So she'd approached Pepe as a last resort.

But why hadn't she called him at Externado? The answer had to be because she didn't want to distract him from his mission in Guazapa. Or because she didn't want to involve him?

Mario asked them the logical question: "Why hadn't my parents told me about this?"

Estela replied, "She asked that you not be told, because if you knew the reason, you could be in danger as well."

So his next question had to be, "So why are you two telling me, then?"

Gladys and Estela looked at each other and then at him, somewhat embarrassed. Estela said, "We wanted to spend some time with you here, Marito."

Mario understood perfectly. And to let them know that he'd understood, he got up and closed the door of their room, locking it. He then took off his pajamas and sat down on Gladys' bed completely naked, telling them, "I appreciate this, but before we do anything else, please finish telling me about Licha."

Mario was really curious because, regardless of the reason why she hadn't sought him out, the fact that she wanted to enter Italy under a false identity meant that she was hiding from someone. Who and why?

Gladys continued the story. "Your dad asked her why it needed to be a Tacarello name. And she answered that it couldn't be her own name because she needed to have a residence in Italy and she had none."

Mario shook his head. "No. She needs it for protection. If she doesn't have a valid Italian address, she gets flagged by the Government, and I'm pretty sure that's what she wants to avoid. What did my dad say?"

Estela proceeded to narrate the conversation between Pepe and Licha...

Pepe said, "Sister Licha, you want to travel incognito with me. You want to be a Tacarello, not a Licha Novak. You must have a very good reason to want to enter undetected."

Sister Licha lowered her eyes. "I do, Don Pepe, but I can't tell you what it is. I don't want to endanger you or anybody in your family, much less Mario, and that's why I'm asking you not to say anything to him, either."

Pepe stood up, walked over to Licha, and sat next to her. "Normally, I would require knowing the reason before I agree. However, you're an important part of the plan to extricate my boys from this country, and so for now, I need not insist. Nevertheless, I could deny you in Honduras, or I could deny you even in Italy, once my children are abroad."

Licha's eyes welled up with tears. Pepe wasn't expecting this and immediately tried to make amends, telling her, "Sister Licha, forgive me. That didn't come out like I intended. I would be incapable of doing that, but it would also be very stupid of me because it would expose the role of my family in the Morse Plan, and that could be fatal What I wanted to say, and said clumsily, is that it behooves me to help you if you travel with me as a wife."

Licha's teary eyes opened wide. "As your wife?"

Pepe asked, "Isn't that the best solution? To pose as my wife?"

Licha didn't expect that, and then there was also the fact that she'd been with his son. She couldn't help reacting with hesitancy.

Seeing this, Pepe assured her that, "If you're hesitant because you were with my son in Europe, let me assure you that I really don't care."

Licha didn't want to expose her relationship with Mario, but she felt that she had to respond sincerely in some way to this man, and not just refuse to share information with him. So she told him about El Cuco, and how Mario had taken her, and witnessed it. By the time she was done, she was sobbing uncontrollably.

Pepe felt sorry for her. The men in this country spared no woman, not even women of the cloth. And he felt ashamed for Mario's role as a pimp in it. And now he felt ashamed for desiring her.

He got up, went to the bar, and got her some whiskey, to calm her nerves.

After she'd downed the drink in a few gulps, Pepe said, "You've been through a lot. I'm ashamed for proposing to share a bed. I won't compound your situation. I'm only too glad to help."

Licha looked up at him, gratefully, and said, "Don Pepe, please tell me how much money I have to give you to help me with my papers, and I'll bring it to you tomorrow."

Pepe said, "Sister Licha, I have no idea how much money it's going to cost me to falsify a passport and the papers to make you a Tacarello, and whether it can be done. But I suppose it would be less expensive and more feasible if I say you're my wife."

"Tell me how much, Don Pepe."

Pepe didn't have the heart to take money from her, but he wasn't going to do it for nothing. So he went for broke and said, "It won't cost you a thing if you travel as my wife, Sister Licha."

Licha thought about this. She needed this man's help, and in exchange, he wanted her to sleep with him. Compared to everything she'd gone through, this was insignificant. But there was a problem and she wanted to address it. “Don Pepe, what about your wife?”

Pepe replied pretty sure of himself. “Leave that to me, Sister Licha. I think that with everything I’m doing for this family, I’ve earned the title of Patriarch, like Abraham. And Abraham had two wives.”

This seemed funny to Licha. But Pepe said, very seriously, “The one thing I need from you is that you bring me passport-type photos so I can take them with me. Please do it tomorrow.”

“All right, Don Pepe.”

“And if we’re going to be man and wife, call me Pepe.”

“Please call me Licha, Pepe.”

“All right, Licha now get undressed.”

Licha opened her eyes wide, with incredulity. “Right now? But... isn’t there anybody home?”

Pepe replied, “My wife is visiting friends and Gladys and Estela are at the market».

“What if they come back, Pepe?”

“We’ll be able to hear the car or we’ll her Gladys and Estela opening the rear gate. You’ll have enough time to get dressed.”

... Estela concluded the story with, “And that’s when Don Pepe’s small head took over.”

“He fucked Licha?”

Gladys shook her head and said, “From what we could hear, Licha was sucking Don Pepe when your mom walked in on them.”

Mario exclaimed, “Poor Abraham!”

Both women laughed, but not too loud. They didn’t want to wake Belinda.

Mario asked, “Was Licha sucking so loud that they didn’t hear mom’s car?”

Gladys replied, as she took off her nightgown, “Your mom’s car broke down, so somebody dropped her off.”

“Eliseo, your relief is here.” The new sentinel had arrived, bringing Mario back to the present, in Guazapa. Gladys and Estela hadn’t told him anything else, because they proceeded to thank him in advance for what he was about to do for Neto. He didn’t want to recall that because there was nowhere in the cave where he could satisfy any urge.

However, he couldn't get this out of his mind: "Who are you trying to hide from, Licha?"

Chapter 79

Santa in Guazapa

On December 24, Mario was at the southernmost guard post of the camp, with a breathtaking view of San Salvador to the right, and Cojutepeque to the left. At 12 midnight, fireworks had started to go off everywhere, as part of the traditional Christmas celebration in El Salvador. Mario was glad because the firework vendors had sold a lot of product and they were going to have a merry Christmas.

He heard footsteps behind him and turned around and ordered the approaching party to halt.

"It's me, Neto. I've got the battle plan."

This made Mario very happy. It meant that Neto had decided to cooperate. This was exactly what the Morse Plan needed.

Mario asked, "The love of your mom and grandmother is pulling at your strings, right?"

Neto's voice trembled when he replied, "No, that wasn't it, Mario."

Concerned, Mario asked, "What happened, Neto?"

"Our teachers hung themselves today."

"They what?"

"They tied together some shirts they were washing, to make a couple of makeshift ropes, and used them to hang themselves."

"They were pregnant, right?"

"Yes, almost 4 months." And Neto started to cry hard. Mario embraced him, thinking, "They're just kids!"

When he'd calmed down a bit, he said, "They left a note saying that they couldn't bear spending Christmas without their families and damning the revolution."

Mario's only thought was that their death wasn't going to be in vain, if that had been what had made Neto cooperate with him.

When he was done grieving, he gave Mario some sheets of paper and a flashlight. Then he took off his jacket and put it over both of them, so that, on their knees, they could use the flashlight without being seen.

With the flashlight on, Mario took a quick look at the papers, to determine how many Morse Code transmissions it was going to take. He calculated three, on three different nights.

Then he went over them with greater detail, realizing that his unit would attack the First Brigade. The Fourth Brigade would be attacked by 'BC's. And there was other nomenclature for other garrisons. Mario asked Neto what their meaning was.

Neto replied: "*Bolsones* Camp No. 1, 2, etc."

Mario realized that he'd have to create a glossary. That would be the first thing he'd have to transmit. So now it was going to take him four nights to transmit the whole thing.

Mario explained to Neto that he'd need enough batteries to be able to transmit the battle plan. He showed him the small circuit he'd use. He also showed the tiny pushbutton that the Signal Battalion had added to the circuit to allow him to transmit easily.

He also told Neto that if the attack was scheduled for January 10, he'd have to have four night shifts in which to do the transmissions. And also that it would be preferable for both to be on duty so Neto could provide Mario with cover while he transmitted.

Neto seemed to be very anxious to help. Mario dared to ask him why. Neto replied, "This is suicide. There are too few men to attack, too few civilians to help establish barricades and incite the people to join us."

"Is this your assessment, or that of the Commanders?"

"The Commanders. Apparently, they had a big dustup in Nicaragua. They didn't come back happy."

Mario asked, "Neto, if the Commanders aren't convinced, why are they doing it? I mean, why don't they just refuse to attack?"

Neto replied, "The Sandinistas in Nicaragua are conditioning their future support to an all-out offensive in El Salvador."

"What?"

"Yes. They need an all-out Offensive to try to prevent any and all Reagan aid to any counterrevolutionaries, in El Salvador and in Nicaragua."

Of course. That made all the sense in the world to Mario. The USSR-Cuba axis wanted to protect their one conquered jewel: Nicaragua. And to protect Nicaragua, they were willing to sacrifice El Salvador. If on top of the murder (and alleged rape) of American nuns, a Tet-like attack against every garrison was mounted by the guerrillas, the Democrat-controlled Congress could deny Reagan's aid. That would guarantee the survival of the Sandinista regime, regardless of how many thousands of Salvadoran lives were lost.

Mario told his half-brother, "Neto, we're doing the right thing. Only people who consider Salvadorans inferior, sub-human and expendable can send them to their slaughter."

Neto agreed. Although it could be said that he was about to betray his commanders, it could also be said that commanders were about to betray them. Plus, what they'd done to his teachers was pure evil. They deserved to pay for that. He stood up and said, "Let's do this, brother."

They embraced each other, and then Mario reminded Neto of what he needed to be able to transmit the guerrilla battle plan.

"Count on it."

A few nights later, a naval unit navigating the Cerrón Grande dam, sent up four white flares, just after midnight on January 3, 1981—the signal that all four transmissions had been received.

CHAPTER 80

JUST LIKE HAGAR

Pepe Tacarello opened the door and greeted Sister Licha with a strong hug. She was dressed in travel attire and looked stunning and very non-religious. Belinda only greeted her verbally.

"Do you have any news for us?" Pepe Tacarello had everything ready for his trip to Honduras. But until Sister Licha had called him to say that she was coming over with news, he hadn't heard a thing.

Sister Licha said, "Yes, I do. The offensive will take place the day after tomorrow, January 10. The Colonel has told me to tell you to be ready to receive Neto and Mario at the Honduran border post of El Poy on January 12th."

"Colonel?"

"Yes, Zepeda is a Lt. Colonel as of January 1."

"Sounds like a good omen to me," said Pepe.

Sister Licha continued. "It seems that the plan that was transmitted by Mario is already yielding results."

Belinda got emotional. "So the plan was transmitted, and they're acting on it?"

"Yes."

Mrs. Tacarello started crying for joy. "Thank God, thank God!"

Pepe asked, "And Zepeda feels certain they'll be able to transport my boys and Gladys and Estela to Honduras?"

"Yes."

Belinda turned to her husband to ask, "When do you plan on leaving?"

Pepe replied, "Well, we should leave tomorrow. Number one, because who knows what'll happen after January the tenth, if anybody's going to be able to get in and out of the country, martial law, etc. So we have to leave tomorrow. Number two, under no circumstance can I be late to that appointment on the 12th! It's better to be over there way ahead of time, than to be late."

"Sure," thought Belinda. "You'll be on your honeymoon with your second wife." But instead of saying that, she turned to Licha to ask her, "Are you all packed up?"

"Yes, ma'am, I have my two pieces of luggage in the taxi."

"Let's go bring them in," said Pepe.

While Licha was paying the taxicab driver, Pepe was taking the luggage to his car in the garage, to put them in the trunk.

When they were all back inside, Sister Licha timidly asked Pepe if he had her Italian passport.

Belinda got angry. "You'll get it tomorrow when you leave, Licha. For now, there's only one Mrs. Tacarello, and it's not you." With that, she said good night and took her husband up to their room.

In the guest room, the soon-to-be former Sister Licha undressed and looked at herself in the mirror. For approaching the age of 51, she didn't look bad. She'd go to the Sisters of the Assumption in Paris to resign and collect her pension. And then she'd go to Poland to join the *Solidarity* movement founded by Lech Walesa.

Trouble was, she knew nobody in Poland. And nobody knew her. Perhaps with a little help from her countryman, John Paul II? Who happened to be in Italy?

Feeling good about her chances, she slipped on a t-shirt and went to bed.

Upstairs, in the master bedroom, Pepe was making love to his wife. He was extra tender and extra slow because he didn't want to finish before she did. He wanted to make it memorable for her because they would be apart for a while.

But the prospect of having Sister Licha with him as a travel companion was making it difficult for Pepe not to ejaculate prematurely. So he was having to constantly visualize Pele's header against Italy in the 1970 World Cup final to keep himself from ejaculating.

His wife hadn't lain with him for all these years without gaining the ability to read his mind. "You're thinking of fucking her, aren't you?"

That made Pepe freeze above her. No chance of premature ejaculation now. No chance of anything, since he immediately began to wilt.

Pepe rolled off of her, face up, and said, "*Moglie*, why do you say such things? At my age, I have no such energy left. After this, I won't have the energy to make love until I get back."

Belinda laughed. "Pepe, why do you lie to your wife? Especially a wife who lets you do whatever you want? The only thing that got you this stiff tonight was you thinking of doing her. As if she were Hagar, Abraham's second wife. Despite the fact she's already done all the guerrillas and your son. By the way, how are you going to explain this to him?"

"*Moglie*, I told you: I'll tell him it's part of the overall plan. He need not know more. If Licha want to, she can tell him. I have no need to."

Belinda sat up and looked at her husband's diminished member.

"I must've been right, or it wouldn't have impacted you so much," she said, mocking him. Then she got up and walked out of the room, completely naked.

"Where are you going?"

"I want some wine."

As he waited for her in the dark room, he fell asleep.

Only to be awakened by a mouth sucking his penis. "*Moglie*, I love it when you do that to me," he said, as he put his hands on the head between his legs.

"You know I can't stand the taste of your semen, Pepe," said his wife, who was sitting on the bed next to him.

Startled, Pepe sat up and turned on the lamp next to him. Between his legs was a naked Licha, hands tied behind her back, buttocks glowing red, who wouldn't let go of him with her mouth, as if there were nothing more important in the world.

Belinda had gone downstairs directly to the guest room. Finding it unlocked she'd walked right in and turned on the light. A startled Licha sat up, saw a completely nude Belinda, and thought she must be dreaming.

Belinda reached down and yanked the sheets off of Licha, ordering her to undress. Licha hesitated so Belinda grabbed her by the hair and pulled her off the bed, snarling, "I told you to undress you fucking *puta* [whore]!"

"I will, ma'am," said Licha, as she took off her t-shirt and panties. Licha opened a drawer and took out some old ties. She took a pair and told Licha to turn around, putting both her hands behind her back. Licha hesitated just a bit, and then turned around.

With the palm of her hand, Belinda spanked her four times, hard enough for Licha to cry out. She felt her buttocks were on fire.

"I said, put your hands behind your back, *puta.*"

Licha's protective instinct, not her mind, led her to comply. She really was in no position to cross the lady of the house. And she figured Belinda had every right to call her a whore.

Belinda tied her wrists together tightly behind her back. Then she told Licha to turn around. Belinda inspected her. She was in very good shape for a woman just slightly younger than her. Her husband would enjoy her. But only because she let him. And Belinda wanted to make sure Pepe knew this.

All of a sudden Belinda slapped Licha's breasts. Licha couldn't hold back her tears. Her breasts were on fire.

Belinda ignored them. "Lie down face up on the floor." Licha obeyed, and Belinda sat over her face. "Lick me, *puta.*"

Licha didn't hesitate. After a while Belinda got up, pulled her up by the hair until she was standing. Since Licha was taller, Belinda grabbed her by a nipple to pull her toward the master bedroom upstairs.

As they approached the bedroom, they heard Pepe snoring. Belinda turned to Licha and said, "In the bedroom, you'll do exactly as I say. Do you understand, *puta*?"

"Yes, Mrs. Tacarello."

"Listen to me, *puta*, the only reason you're still alive is that you're helping my son. After this is over, I better not see you again. Do you understand me?"

Licha nodded. Belinda said, "You're going to enter the room and you're going to suck his penis and keep sucking until I tell you to stop, do you understand me?"

"Yes, Mrs. Tacarello."

"Go."

And that's why Licha hadn't stopped when the commotion started. She wouldn't let go until Mrs. Tacarello commanded her.

She kept sucking the already stiff member, as she heard Pepe and Belinda kissing and caressing.

Then she heard "*Puta,* stop sucking."

Licha let go of Pepe with her mouth, saw Belinda's hand grab his penis and pull it toward her vagina, watching Pepe's penis disappear inside her, leaving only his balls outside.

It didn't take him long to unload. When he rolled off his wife, Belinda ordered, "*Puta,* lap his semen from my vagina."

Licha started lapping. It wasn't the best of tastes, but she ignored it. Suddenly Belinda grabbed her head, tensed up, and let out a slow, long moan that lasted about a minute.

Belinda told her to stop. After she'd recovered her breath, she told Licha to stand up. Then Belinda got up and untied her. She then told Licha, "*Puta,* go to that chair by the window, sit down, open your legs wide, and masturbate yourself until you orgasm."

She did precisely that. And she came so hard that she made the dogs outside bark.

"*Puta*, go to bed now."

She obediently walked down to her room and fell asleep with a smile on her lips. She'd earned her passport.

Chapter 81

Head of a Mouse or Tail of a Lion?

The ex-Somoza mansion was a great headquarters for the FMLN in Nicaragua. Located on the outskirts of Managua, it was sufficiently large for the Cubans to establish all the communications that the FMLN headquarters would need to be in contact with its guerrilla units in El Salvador.

And that ex-Somoza estate was sufficiently large to build the Radio *Venceremos* AM antenna there, which couldn't be anywhere else but in Nicaragua, because something that size wasn't going to go unnoticed in El Salvador, and because of the quantity and quality of reliable energy it required. This was so because for an AM signal can only overcome mountainous terrain through power, and that type of power cannot be found in the rural zones of El Salvador, or in the *Bolsones*. That type of power can only be found in places that have an adequate energy infrastructure, such as San Salvador... or Managua.

For the communications with the guerrilla units in El Salvador, a backbone of VHF repeaters was required between Managua and the peaks leading to the Cosiguina volcano, which had line of sight with all the elevations in El Salvador, especially Guazapa.

The Cubans had finally completed the Radio *Venceremos* and tactical communications center for the FMLN headquarters in Managua in December of 2018. It was not a coincidence that at the end of November, 1980, Guillermo Ungo announced that the FMLN Command was moving to Managua.

So everything was ready for the Final Offensive on January 10, 1981.

At 5 pm on January 10, 1981 the following communiqué was transmitted by Radio *Venceremos*, from the FMLN-Managua headquarters: "At 5 pm today, the general offensive was begun. The enemy is lost, it's surrounded. Popular justice has arrived."

This was followed by incessant calls to the population to rise up against their oppressor and assist the attacking guerrilla units.

Ana María and Ungo waited anxiously to hear back from the units. They were tuned into YSKL, the main Salvadoran radio station, but it merely reported that 6 car bombs had exploded in the vicinity of the 1st Brigade, and that was it. No firefights.

Ungo started to get nervous. "Ana María, they should be reporting firefights all over the place."

Ana María replied, "Maybe the government is censoring the broadcast."

That lifted Ungo's spirits. "That must be it!"

A few minutes later, YSKL announced that the 2nd Infantry Brigade in Santa Ana was on fire.

Ungo leapt for joy. "The population will certainly rise up and overrun the Brigade, Ana María!" The normally unflappable Ana María allowed herself to receive a celebratory hug from Ungo.

A few minutes later, YSKL announced that the population was actually helping the soldiers put out the fire.

This deflated Ungo faster than a punctured balloon. "No uprising? How can there be no uprising?"

Ana María was starting to get a bad feeling. If commercial radio transmissions were being censored, they wouldn't have reported the 2nd Brigade fire. Ungo was right. If there were any combats or uprisings, the radio would be reporting them.

All she said was, "Look, we're attacking everywhere, so let's wait for the commanders to report back."

The next three hours were the longest of their lives. YSKL went on and on about an Army captain killing the 2nd Brigade Commander, before fleeing with a few rebel soldiers, but there was no other news. In the meantime, Radio *Venceremos* kept inciting the population to rise up.

Finally, their Yaesu radio crackled. "Base, Base, Mayo here. The 1st Brigade raided the safe houses and were waiting for our fighters there. They captured most of our forces. It's like they knew our plans, over."

"Is there any pursuit of your units, Mayo?"

"None."

Ungo took the mike from Ana María and asked, "Are there any combats anywhere?"

"Negative. Everything is peaceful."

Ungo continued to ask, "Was there any uprising by the population?"

Mayo lost his patience. "What don't you understand? Are you dense? San Salvador, Cojutepeque, Suchitoto—it seems to be a night like any other. I doubt very much that the population is aware of our offensive. I'm high enough on Guazapa now to see that there's power everywhere. It's obvious our attacks to the hydroelectric dams failed."

Ana María took back the mike and said, "Mayo, call us when you get to your base. Ana María out."

By 12 midnight, the only other commanders who'd reported back were Commander Facundo Guardado, who had attacked San Francisco Gotera, and Marcial, who had attacked Chalatenango. Both were retreating back to the *Bolsones*. No civilian population help and most of their men captured. They also said, "It's like they knew our plans."

They never heard again from the commanders that attacked the Third Brigade, Usulután and Zacatecoluca, among others.

Guillermo Ungo was despondent. He couldn't believe that there'd been no popular uprising. Not even the people of Santa Ana with the garrison on fire.

He looked at Ana María, visibly shaken, and cried, "Ana María, this is a nightmare. How could we have miscalculated so badly?"

Ana María remained serene. "Comrade Ungo, we had to do this to maintain the collaboration of the Moscow-Havana-Managua axis. We had no choice."

Ungo was on the verge of tears. "How are we going to spin this massive defeat into a victory? It's a disaster!"

Ana María took her 9 mm piece out and pointed it at Ungo. If she wanted to stop his babbling, it worked.

"Listen to me, Mr. President of the FDR. We eliminated your hated rival, Don Polo, for you to assume the political mantle of the FMLN. But if you're not going to do anything but cry like a little girl, I'm going to eliminate you as well, and appoint any of your subordinates to take your place. Do you understand me?"

A calmer Ungo nodded.

Ana María put away her gun and said, "Go to the Radio *Venceremos* cabin, tell them to stop repeating that idiocy that the enemy is surrounded because they sound like fools, and have them say what we always say when we lose—that there was a massacre of women, children and old folks. Are we clear?"

Ungo still dared to shake his head and say, "But the people in El Salvador will know that it's not true."

Ana María's eyes blazed when she spewed, "I don't give a damn what the people in El Salvador know or don't know to be true! This is what we'll tell the world! Understand?"

Ungo nodded. He understood what was expected of him. "Fine, comrade, I get it. That's what our Sandinista masters expect from us."

Ana María nodded. "Yes. That was always the plan. And remember, the international press is going to say that we projected power anyway. This will be spun favorably for us."

Ungo said, "I'll go prepare the message for Radio *Venceremos*."

As he left the mansion to walk up the hill toward the Radio *Venceremos* cabin, Ana María had a feeling that this wasn't going to end well for her. After all, she was the one who endorsed the Tit Plan, over the protests of practically all of the commanders, who preferred Marcial's Lisa Plan. However, Fidel Castro had made it real clear that we had no alternative but launch a general offensive. When the commanders had protested, the Sandinistas threatened to cut off supplies. There really was no alternative.

The reason was purely geographic: Nicaragua's territory amounted to 50,339 square miles—already revolutionized; El Salvador's: 8,124 square miles—not revolutionized. Geopolitically, El Salvador was the pawn they'd sacrifice to protect queen Nicaragua.

But you couldn't hate Fidel. And you couldn't hate the Jesuits, who had done everything they could short of shooting. And you couldn't hate the Sandinistas who were providing all sorts of supplies and logistics. And you couldn't hate Ambassador White: he gave it his all and was leaving soon anyway.

The only person that anybody could hate, as a result of this disaster, was her.

Chapter 82

Rendezvous

At around 4 pm on January 12, 1981, two army trucks stopped at a restaurant in the town of San Ignacio, 8 km from El Poy. Two men got off of one, and two women got off of the other, each of them carrying one piece of luggage. They entered the restaurant.

Five minutes later they got onto the bed of a pickup truck, which drove them to the border crossing. There, they walked over to the Honduran side, where they presented their Italian passports. After opening their luggage to reveal nothing but clothes, they walked outside the building and into the arms of Pepe Tacarello and Sister Licha.

They got into the rented van and went to a motel in Nuevo Ocotepeque, called *Casa de Yolanda y Chayito*, where they would spend the night before making the long trip back to Tegucigalpa. Their plane to Miami was scheduled to depart Toncontín Airport on the afternoon of January 13. In Miami, they'd board the Alitalia flight to Italy.

At the motel, Estela and Gladys just smothered Neto and each other with hugs and kisses. The hug between Pepe and Mario was eternal. Zepeda, and then the Lieutenant Colonel of the Fourth Brigade had advised them not to fraternize at all, so that nobody could surmise that there was a relationship among them. It was for the Tacarello family's security. It had been hard, but they'd complied. But now, nothing could stop them.

Mario then said he wanted to take a nap. He still hadn't recovered from the trek down the mountain and to the safe house. Since it was around 6 p.m., Pepe suggested that they all rest while Licha and him went looking for some food at a local restaurant. They would order the food for 8 p.m., which gave everybody enough time to rest.

Licha walked around and found a Restaurant called *Niña Adelita*, where they ordered industrial quantities of *baleadas* (Honduran soft tacos) and jugs of *horchata*, asking that the food be delivered to the *Casa Yolanda y Chayito* at 8 that night. Licha asked, "Why so much, Pepe?"

Pepe replied, "Haven't you seen how skeletal those boys are?"

At 8 p.m. they woke everybody up to go eat in Pepe's room. Neto and Mario didn't say a word because they were famished. Pepe warned them to eat slowly, to prevent indigestion.

After eating, Mario answered the question that was on everybody's mind: "What happened?"

"We went down the mountain in pairs, on January 9, without any weapons, so as not to call attention to ourselves. We'd have the necessary weapons at the safe house. We'd get there sufficiently in advance, to rest a bit and then prepare to attack when the car bombs exploded.

"Of course, we got to the safe house, and we were apprehended immediately. They'd captured a radio and with it they communicated with Mayo Sibrián, making him believe that everything was OK. So the combatants continued to arrive, and they continued to be captured. However, Mayo either got suspicious or he was alerted, because he never arrived. About 10% of the attacking force never arrived at the safe houses."

Pepe pointed out that, "That's why your mom told me over the phone that she hadn't heard a thing in San Salvador, that the power hadn't even flickered."

Estela said, "The plan was very clear. The only thing our forces need to do was a search and seizure in the neighborhood of the First Brigade." Everybody looked at Estela, surprised. Two months in the military garrison and she already spoke like a soldier!

Mario continued. "Col. Zepeda told us that in urban areas, these attacks all failed to materialize because starting January 4, the troops started searching homes. Just like the 1st Brigade did.

"In the hinterland, there were no such safe houses, and so their Plan called for a direct attack by armed guerrillas descending from the different camps. Since their Plan specified which camp would attack which garrison, the Army ambushed them.

"He also told us that at the 2nd Infantry Brigade, in Santa Ana, while most of the troops were out seizing weapons and fighters at the safe houses, Army Captain Mena Sandoval killed the commander of the Second Brigade and opened up the headquarters for guerrillas to enter and attempt to take it over. Since it didn't work out that way, he and some rebel soldiers set the garrison on fire before fleeing."

Licha addressed Estela and Gladys: "Ladies, I gave Zepeda the locations of the weapons depots in the city and also the locations of the barracks and weapons depots to be used for the attacks on Chalatenango, El Paraíso and Sensuntepeque, located on farms that belonged to Don Polo. Was that intelligence useful?"

Both ladies nodded but Estela explained further, "That's where our troops went to wait for the enemy. They confiscated the weaponry and removed it. And then they used the barracks as a brig." This time everybody laughed. Estela had that military jargon down pat!

Pepe asked, "So when did Zepeda tell you all of this?"

Mario replied, "Neto and I got treated like every other prisoner. They had us in a central area of the garrison, under guard. Then we saw Gladys walking over to us with Zepeda. She saw us and for a moment she looked like she was going to run toward us but Zepeda held her back.

"She did identify us to Zepeda because about an hour later, we got taken to be interrogated, but instead of going to the room where the interrogations were being carried out, they took us to Zepeda's office, who greeted us effusively, very happy about the way our plan had worked out.

"He let us clean up in his quarters and then we changed into the clothes that Gladys had brought for us, which didn't fit well, of course, because we'd lost a lot of weight. Soon afterwards, we got put on the truck heading for the 4th Brigade, with Gladys sitting up front, and Neto and me sitting in the back with soldiers. But I didn't leave before calling mom first."

Pepe asked, "Was your mom overjoyed?"

Mario nodded. "Yes, but she couldn't say much. She was overtaken by emotion. I told her I'd call her from over here."

Pepe told him they'd call her in a little while.

Gladys spoke up for the first time. "Zepeda had told us that we shouldn't fraternize until we were in Honduras. He said that soldiers talk and he didn't want anybody to make any connection back to the Tacarello family. He told us to act like we didn't know each other."

"It was hard to constrain my mother when we got to the 4th Brigade. The 4th Brigade Colonel put us in two trucks so we didn't fraternize: mom and me in one, and the two boys in the other. He told us that somebody would be waiting for us at the *Luis Diego* Restaurant in San Ignacio to take us to the El Poy border crossing."

Estela indicated that "We didn't even fraternize in the restaurant—they'd really stressed to act like we didn't know each other until we were in Honduras."

After few moments, Pepe said, "What's amazing is that there were no popular uprisings anywhere. I spoke with Mrs. Domínguez yesterday and they said everybody was surprised because there'd been an offensive and nobody heard anything, except for the Second Brigade traitor. But that everything was very normal in San Salvador."

Licha contributed with, "Thanks to the Agrarian Reform. That was the Government's secret weapon."

Mario looked at Licha, tempted to ask her why she was here. But he thought better of it. He'd ask her when they were alone, not in front of everybody. Instead, he asked his dad, "Dad, have you got Fina working on gaining the business of rebuilding the Second Brigade in Santa Ana?"

Pepe laughed. "I did that before I called your mom."

Everybody laughed with him.

Pepe then asked Gladys and Estela how the Morse Code transmission went.

Estela enthusiastically replied, "It was wonderful! Marito began each transmission with, 'Neto is here with me, he sends his love.'" And then she couldn't say anything else. She choked up.

Gladys started to cry as well. Nobody said a word. It was a solemn moment. Neto hugged her and Gladys hugged him back, sobbing, and saying, "You're my life. You're my life."

Estela got up and hugged Mario. "Thank you, my saint, for saving my boy."

Even Licha and Pepe were choked up. It was a moment of catharsis. Such an ordeal everybody had gone through!

After a while, Neto stood up and walked over to Pepe, and said, "Don Pepe, I want to thank you for what you've done for me."

Pepe felt embarrassed. "Neto, you're my son. Call me *Papá*. You have nothing to thank me for. I should've been a better dad to you, but unfortunately, I wasn't man enough to do so. Perhaps offering you a better life in Italy can make up for that. Now give your old man a hug." He did, and they couldn't hold back the tears.

But nobody was crying more than Licha—not of happiness, but of self-pity. She was surrounded by people who appreciated but they weren't her family. She had no family.

Pepe noticed that Licha was being left out, despite the fact that she'd been so instrumental for this happy ending. So he stood up and said, "Please, let's all thank Sister Licha. None of this could've been possible without her."

They all came to hug her, and Licha let them, but she'd never felt so alone in her entire life.

They left for Tegucigalpa at 6 a.m. the next morning. They boarded their plane to Miami at 4:30 pm, departing from the Toncontín airport.

A new life awaited everybody except for Pepe. He'd have to come back and work extra hard to recover this expense. And the best way to recoup his expenditures was earn the Second Brigade repair business. If necessary, Fina would use the same wiles that she'd used on him to get hired.

Nevertheless, he felt certain that because of the massive failure of the general offensive, the guerrillas would never attain power in El Salvador, and that better times awaited Vesuvius. And he had Mario and Licha to thank for that. Which is why he hadn't let Licha spend a penny of her money.

Thanks to her, this expenditure had become an investment.

Chapter 83

Managua Rose

Montes had invited him to eat with them. Of course, with the existing food stock, dinner was the same as lunch was the same as breakfast: rice and beans. But the invitation was kind albeit unnecessary. Unless they'd finally come to the realization that the only person standing between them and God's judgment was Sánchez, because their Black Indulgences had expired, or unless Elba and Celina wanted an encore, because these priests were everything but fun to be around.

Naturally, Ellacuría came to join them. But when Elba and Celina brought the rice and beans over, Sánchez insisted that they sit with them to eat. The ladies looked at Ellacuría, who said, "Please sit, ladies."

The conversation at the table focused on Elba's life, who was originally from Usulután, and who'd moved to Sonsonate with her husband when he got a job at the Port of Acajutla. Because of an economic downturn, they moved back toward the capital, where her husband, Obdulio, got the job as groundskeeper for the UCA. The job came with a little house for them to live in, just inside the main gate.

The Captain had seen that little house, which looked more like a shed, with its windows broken. It was dark when they arrived at the UCA, but he did wonder why the gates were open, when they should've been shut. As a matter of fact, one of the gates was on the ground, discovered by one of his soldiers when he'd tripped over the black iron bars, in the dark. But then again, with what was going on, he hadn't paid much attention to it.

The Captain asked Elba, "Ma'am, why didn't you tell me you had your husband at UCA? We'd have brought him with us!"

Elba replied, "Forgive me, Captain, but when you entered the UCA, didn't you see anybody?"

"No, ma'am, the only persons we found were you four at the Jesuit Residence."

Elba looked dejected. She mumbled, "He must've been purchasing materials..." She then looked at Ellacuría, who slightly shook his head. Elba said no more.

To Sánchez, it seemed that everybody'd gotten tense. The dinner had been going well, but no longer. Sánchez thought, "They're hiding something," but figured that if it was important, it'd come out without him having to prod for it. After all, their lives were at stake.

Sánchez looked at Celina, who was sitting across from him, and asked her if she was studying. Celina was a very pretty young lady, almost 17 years old, and in El Salvador, the fate of good-looking young ladies who were poor was usually to end up pregnant and drop out, which was no good for them and no good for the country, which needed all the educated people it could produce.

"Yes, Captain, I just finished my first year of my commercial high school degree at the José Damián Villacorta Institute."

"Really? Congratulations, young lady!"

Sánchez turned to Elba and said, "Congratulations to you, too, ma'am!" Elba smiled.

Sánchez had to say, "Please, ma'am, don't let any boyfriend derail her from her studies. Your daughter is beautiful, but education is more important than beauty."

The lighthearted conversation that Sánchez had begun dissipated the tension. When they'd all finished eating, Elba and Celina picked up the plates and didn't return.

Then Ellacuría addressed the following question to Sánchez, "When did you return to the country, Captain?"

"In 1982."

"And how did you find the army?"

Sánchez didn't hesitate. "More professional, more numerous and better equipped than before, priest."

"You were in the San Vicente Operation, weren't you, Captain?" Montes' question surprised Sánchez. But he answered matter-of-factly, "Many of us were. Why?"

"I remember seeing a picture of you next to a blonde Time Magazine reporter."

The captain recalled the pretty reporter. "I remember her. She used to be very pro-Sandinista, but then she soured on them. She was very nice to us in San Vicente. She must've approved of the operation."

Ellacuría asked, "What did you think of the operation, Captain? It was the first one mounted by the Americans and it received lots of publicity, saying that it was to win the hearts and minds of the population."

Sánchez didn't hesitate. "Priest, the hearts and minds of the population were won with the Agrarian Reform of 1980. That's why the January 1981 Final Offensive was such an unmitigated disaster. And that's why you're having the Salvadoran Children's Crusade right now."

Ellacuría winced. But so what? Can't walk on eggshells when talking about these things.

But Ellacuría didn't let that keep him from asking, "What did you think about the American advisors, Captain? We heard they were arrogant."

The Captain shrugged. "Some are, most aren't and many are very good. They're not here because of their diplomatic skills, you know. They are very professional and dedicated to the cause. And oftentimes they don't give a damn about their orders, which are only to train and not to participate in combat situations."

"They engage in combat?"

"They expose themselves to combat. The American communications advisor at that time was an Ecuadorian-born American named Giordi Yanez, who went up to the top of the San Vicente volcano with me, in search of a *Managua Rose* repeater. I tried to dissuade him because it was a combat situation. But he said, 'I'm going with you, brother, because I'm bored to death down here.'"

The Jesuits found the term *Managua Rose* strange, but they assumed it was some military code and didn't ask.

Ellacuría asked, "Did you go up with a unit?"

The Captain shook his head. "No, the Commander had given me the order to go up by myself, to see if there was a *Managua Rose* repeater. A helicopter would take me to the unit that was highest up on the slopes of the volcano, but that I was to go up by myself."

Montes arched an eyebrow. "Didn't it seem strange to you, Captain? To get sent on such a dangerous mission all alone?"

The Captain replied, "It's the type of mission every lieutenant dreams of, priest. But I asked him if the helicopter couldn't just take me up there to observe from the air and he said that the helicopter had no weapons to defend itself with in case it was fired upon. So I just saluted and went to get my gear.

"On the way to the soccer field, where the helicopter was, the advisor saw me and asked me where I was going. Since I couldn't dissuade him, he went to get his gear and got on the helicopter with me.

"It dropped us off in a clearing just above the last infantry unit, at an elevation of about 500 meters. That left us with a kilometer and a half climb on foot."

"Did you encounter any guerrillas?"

"No, none. And no repeater either. But I already knew we wouldn't find anything anyway."

That surprised Montes. "Why is that, Captain?"

"Because had I been charged with establishing the communication system for *Managua Rose*, I'd install a very powerful AM transmitter with a huge antenna in a place where power was abundant and reliable, and the only places in El Salvador that provide such abundant and reliable power sources are government-controlled areas.

"Which means that *Managua Rose* could only be in Nicaragua."

Montes had to ask, "Is *Managua Rose* your code name for Radio *Venceremos*?"

"That's what I call it, priest."

The priests didn't' ask why. But Montes did ask why AM.

Sánchez proceeded to explain the virtues of AM to overcome mountainous terrain—it only required more power.

Montes followed up with, "Why not FM?"

"Because if there's no line of sight, it doesn't matter how powerful the signal is, it won't go from one side of the mountain to the other."

Ellacuría pointed out, "But we'd hear it in FM, too. How'd it go from AM to FM?"

The Captain explained that the audio of a cheap AM radio was connected to a battery-powered FM transmitter (like a slightly-modified U.S. Army PRC-77 radio that the US had left in South Vietnam in the tens of thousands), and if that FM transmitter was on an elevation, that signal would reach any receiver having line of sight with that elevation.

So if they heard *Managua Rose* in FM at the UCA, for instance, it was an FM retransmission from a home in any of the surrounding elevations, like Guazapa. And for that, no commercial station was required. Just batteries and elevation.

The captain concluded with, "But without a *Managua Rose* in AM, there'd be no *Managua Rose* in FM."

Ellacuría had had enough *Managua Rose.* "Captain, the name is Radio *Venceremos*, not *Managua Rose.*"

The Captain rolled his yes. "Priest, in World War II, the Japanese forces had a propaganda station, commonly known as *Tokyo Rose.* It did nothing but lie and lie.

"The similarity between that propaganda station and yours is striking. So, just like they named *Tokyo Rose* after its location, I named your propaganda station *Managua Rose* after the capital of Nicaragua, where it's located."

Montes was skeptical. "We've watched TV footage of Radio *Venceremos* being in Perquín, Morazán, El Salvador, not in Nicaragua."

The Captain laughed. "Yeah, I've seen those. Those 'shortwave' civilian radios wouldn't last two days in the dirty, humid and hot conditions shown on that video. Plus, they'd need reliable power, which Perquín doesn't have. And had it been in Perquín, Salvadoran troops would've found it a long time ago. Especially if every time they transmitted, they had to turn on an electric generator, which can be heard miles away.

"No, gentlemen, *Managua Rose* is in Nicaragua, because such a valuable asset, which is also used to transmit messages from the FMLN high command (which is in Managua, by the way), would never be placed in a zone of conflict, when it's far easier and safer to have it in Nicaragua, beyond the reach of Salvadoran troops."

The Jesuits didn't feel the need to say anything. Sánchez continued. "The reason they had to do that propaganda video was to hide the fact that a foreign nation, in this case, Nicaragua, was directly interfering in the Salvadoran conflict. If that were ever established, that could lead to greater action by Reagan and that wouldn't just jeopardize the Salvadoran guerrillas, but also the Sandinista regime in Nicaragua. That's why they had to put out that propaganda video that *Managua Rose* was in El Salvador and not in Nicaragua."

The Jesuits didn't try to attempt to convince him otherwise. The Captain went on. "*Managua Rose* is as much a liar as Tokyo Rose. *Managua Rose*'s first transmission ever was this one, on January 10, 1981: 'At 5 pm today, the general offensive was begun. The enemy is lost, it's surrounded. Popular justice has arrived.'

"And that further proves that those poor liars were in Nicaragua, because in El Salvador, except for the betrayal at the Second Brigade, nothing was going on. They transmitted that for hours, and in San Salvador all anybody could hear was crickets, according to my colleagues, relatives and friends. It wasn't until the FMLN high command began to receive the disastrous situational reports that they shut *Managua Rose* up, because they were making fools of themselves."

Ellacuría kept digging. "Did you ever find any such retransmitter, Captain?"

"That really wasn't part of my mission, priest. My mission was to ensure communications for military units in combat. And nobody ever asked me to shut that radio station down, anyway."

Ellacuría said, "Good, because that allowed the population to listen to it loud and clear."

The Captain shrugged and said, "You know, priest, the Japanese population heard Tokyo Rose all during World War II. She transmitted in English 75 minutes a day, during her program 'The Zero Hour,' on Tokyo Radio. The rest of the day, Tokyo Radio transmitted in Japanese what Tokyo Rose transmitted in English: a whole bunch of Japanese victories and a whole bunch of American defeats."

"Now then, while Tokyo Rose was proclaiming all these Japanese victories and American defeats, Admiral Nimitz was destroying the Japanese naval fleet at Midway, Coral Sea and Leyte Gulf. While those transmissions continued unimpeded, General McArthur was island-hopping, destroying Japanese forces at Iwo Jima, Okinawa and the Philippines."

Ellacuría was thinking, "Here comes another damn history lesson."

The Captain continued. "Do you for a minute believe that Nimitz and MacArthur fretted about Tokyo Radio and Tokyo Rose? Not at all. You know why? Because while Tokyo Radio and Tokyo Rose were proclaiming great victories over the Americans, the letters that Japanese soldiers and pilots and sailors were writing back home basically said, 'I love you but I'm going to die. This is *sayonara*.'

"And you know what? Pretty soon, when young Asoko, Chikao, Haruto, Mitsuo and all those sons, fathers and brothers didn't return home, then whenever Tokyo Radio came on with its propaganda, the surviving family members would say, 'Turn that fucking radio off. It's nothing but a bunch of lies!'

"But they'd say it in Japanese, of course."

Ellacuría was sick and tired of history, so he went directly to the point. "Well, the butcher Monterrosa listened to *Managua Rose*... I mean... Radio *Venceremos*," he said.

The Captain shook his head. "He never once listened to *Managua Rose*, and he never said that he wanted it shut down. You know why? Because while *Managua Rose* was broadcasting all those guerrilla victories and all these Monterrosa defeats, many *Managua Rose* guerrilla listeners would all of a sudden have to get up and flee because Monterrosa's defeated or decimated troops were approaching, pursuing the fleeing triumphant guerrillas.

"And if they were guerrilla moms and pops who were listening, guerrillas would suddenly appear at their door, to tell them that their sons Juan, Francisco or Demetrio had died in battle against Monterrosa.

"And lately, while *Managua Rose* was proclaiming great victories over the Salvadoran Army, guerrilla recruits would come knocking to tell mom and pop Cruz that they needed their 9, 10 or 11-year-old boys and girls to go fight, because their 12, 13 or 14-year-olds had been killed fighting the Salvadoran Army.

"And guess what? Next time somebody turned on the radio and *Managua Rose* was transmitting, proclaiming great victories, the surviving relatives or friends would say, 'Turn that fucking radio off. It's nothing but a bunch of lies!'—only this time, in Spanish."

Chapter 84

Ass-Kicking at El Mozote

"No, Captain, what *Managua Rose*... I mean, Radio *Venceremos*, broadcast about Monterrosa was that he was a butcher."

The Captain replied, "Here's what *Managua Rose* will never admit: Col. Monterrosa kicked guerrilla ass up and down the mountains like the great Carthaginian General Hannibal kicked Roman ass up and down the Italian peninsula."

Ellacuría exclaimed, "Well, your Hannibal committed the El Mozote Massacre!"

This was what Ellacuría wanted to get to.

Sánchez asked, "Priest, who proclaimed the Mozote Massacre?"

"Radio *Venceremos*."

Sánchez laughed. "By definition, if *Managua Rose* proclaimed it, then it's nothing but a lie."

Ellacuría was relentless. "You weren't there, so you don't know the facts! It was a wanton massacre of civilians!"

"Wait a second, priest, were you there?"

"No."

Sánchez laughed. "Well, that makes two of us who weren't there, doesn't it? Three, if you include *Managua Rose*, which couldn't have been there because it's in Nicaragua."

Before Ellacuría's hate-filled mind could formulate a response, the Captain offered him an olive branch. "Father Ellacuría, it's a nice evening. Let's enjoy it. We're on the same side right now, since neither of us were there. Get comfortable and let's let logic clarify what happened at El Mozote. Let me weave a logical thread, and your prodigious mind can tell me where I'm wrong, OK?"

"Sounds fair, Captain," Montes was quick to answer.

The Captain began, "The mission of the immediate reaction infantry battalions (IRIBs) that were trained by or in the USA was to provide an immediate additional infantry battalion to garrisons the organic units of which were insufficient for the guerrilla presence in their area of operations.

"In the case of the Department of Morazán, the only garrison there was the DM-4 [Military Detachment 4] in San Francisco Gotera. The DM-4 had enough units to control south of the Torola River. The guerrilla camps north of the Torola River, such as *El Mozote* and *La Guacamaya*, which were the closest one to the Torola River, trained unperturbed and would engage in guerrilla action south of the Torola River, harassing the DM-4 troops.

"In late 1981, the Atlacatl IRIB, trained by Americans in El Salvador, was ready for action. One of its first missions was to support the DM-4. And the commander of the DM-4 ordered the Atlacatl to attack the guerrilla camps north of the Torola River.

"Under the command of Lt. Col. Monterrosa, the Atlacatl attacked and fought as trained. And the guerrillas, totally unaccustomed to a head-on attack, were unable to stop the Atlacatl juggernaut.

"When it attacked the La Guacamaya guerrilla training camp, the more experienced guerrillas stayed to fight and died. The more inexperienced ones—the majority, who were young teenagers, thanks to the catastrophic failure that was the January 1981 offensive—fled north to the nearest guerrilla camp, which was El Mozote. The Atlacatl Battalion pursued them, as trained.

"The fleeing guerrillas got to El Mozote and reported that there was this Army battalion attacking them, with all sorts of weapons. They reported that there were about 600 soldiers. The *El Mozote* commanders knew the 3 to 1 rule: for an attacking force to be able to defeat a defending force, they had to have three times the number of men that the defenders had.

"They called for reinforcements from the camps of Perquín, San Fernando and the *Bolsones*, knowing that in a short period of time, they could amass 2000 guerrillas at El Mozote to face the Atlacatl. According to the 3 to 1 rule, the defeat of the Atlacatl was assured, because they had about a sixth of the force that they needed to win.

"Why El Mozote? Because it was a tiny village that was the highest elevation of its surroundings. That's why the guerrillas had forcibly taking over that village of 300 civilians. Once there, the guerrillas had prepared the terrain with foxholes, trenches, tunnels and barricades.

"The one time a battalion of 300 men from the DM-4 had attacked El Mozote, all the work they'd done at that camp allowed 200 guerrillas to repel that attack. The 3 to 1 rule had worked perfectly that time. Now they'd have two thousand guerrillas shooting down at the Atlacatl from higher ground. It was the perfect place to destroy the IRIB.

"The guerrilla commanders had an alternative: temporarily moving to Honduras, where the Atlacatl couldn't pursue them. They could then just track the battalion, learn its movements and how to defeat it or harass it.

"But these commanders, from schools like Externado, the National University and the UCA, were really good at numbers. And the numbers were in their favor. So they decided to stay and fight.

"The problem that the guerrilla commanders couldn't foresee was that Monterrosa was never good at math. He was only good at combat. So he attacked with all the weapons his battalion had been trained to use, especially mortars. No matter how good the guerrilla defenses were, they couldn't defend against Monterrosa's mortars.

"With their heads down, the mortar survivors couldn't shoot the Atlacatl soldiers that were advancing up the hill. And when they least expected it, the Atlacatl soldiers were on top of them.

"The guerrillas got their asses kicked royally at El Mozote. The survivors fled, leaving hundreds of dead guerrillas behind, where they lay.

"The Atlacatl battalion, as trained, pursued them all the way to the Honduran border. They didn't stay to bury hundreds of dead guerrillas.

"After finding the Perquín and San Fernando camps empty, because the remaining guerrillas had fled to the safety of Honduras, the Atlacatl received orders to turn southwest, sweeping down the western side of the Cacahuatique Mountain, which is on the border between the Departments of San Miguel and Morazán.

"Upon reaching 3rd Infantry Brigade in the city of San Miguel, they mounted their trucks and went back to their headquarters in western El Salvador."

The Captain paused, to see if the priests had anything to say. They didn't, so he went on. "When the El Mozote civilians, who'd fled before the battle had begun, returned home, they saw and smelled hundreds of dead guerrillas.

"Who was going to bury them? They were! And how did they bury them? Like mankind has been burying massive numbers of dead bodies since King David killed thousands of Philistines—digging shallow trenches, throwing the bodies in the trenches and covering them with dirt.

"But nobody at El Mozote was calling what had happened anything but a great military victory for the Atlacatl Battalion, and a crushing defeat for the guerrillas. They certainly didn't call it a wanton massacre of civilians, because civilians had fled the battle, like civilians tend to do. And the proof that they fled is: who else could've buried the dead guerrillas?

"Now then, the guerrilla high command in Managua was facing a problem: the Atlacatl Battalion was just the *first* of the IRIBs trained by the USA, both there and in El Salvador. More were coming.

"Commanders Ana María and Marcial must have felt cursed by an Izalco witch. They start the year getting their asses kicked (the January 1981 offensive), and now they're ending the year with another ass-kicking, with more coming their way.

"What could they do? The answer came to them after a conversation with the defeated guerrillas that must have gone like this:

'How many died, Commander?'

'Hundreds, Commander Ana María.'

'Who buried them?'

'We didn't, Commander Ana María.'

'So the local civilians probably buried them in shallow trenches. Thanks, commander, we'll be in touch.'

"Ana María and Marcial and Ungo then decided their only chance to survive this war was to stop the training of future IRIBs, by accusing the first U.S.-trained IRIB of a massacre. And that's when *Managua Rose* started claiming a 'massacre' over the airwaves."

"The Americans immediately sent a forensic team to check out El Mozote, now that the DM-4 had recovered control of the zone. They had to have concluded that it was nothing but a great military victory, because the IRIBs, and the U.S. aid, kept coming.

"Now then, gentlemen, these Americans arrived and asked the population there, 'Was there a massacre?' and the population could've answered, 'Yes.' But the people of El Mozote in 1981 never said that it was a massacre. All they could say was, 'the guerrillas got their asses kicked, and damn them for not burying their dead.'

"Heck, those civilians were probably happy to be rid of those guys, so they could go back to their normal lives."

Ellacuría looked like he wanted to call Monterrosa a butcher again, but he didn't want to sound too repetitive, and he couldn't find a suitable synonym anyway, so he said nothing.

The captain made the following point. "You know, priests, I'd never heard of El Mozote since I'd returned in 1982, until about a week ago. Not once. I may have heard somebody say something about the frozen moons of Jupiter, but never a word about El Mozote.

"So why is it that eight years later, they're talking about El Mozote again? Because Reagan's no longer president, the democrats control both houses of Congress (your only hope, now that the Soviet Union has fallen).

"But also because the guerrillas have had eight years to bury many dead there—dead from the neighboring guerrilla campsites like La Guacamaya, where they trained children; women who died at childbirth, babies who died of sickness, children guerrillas that got killed in combat, and old men who died of old age.

"Why? Just to be able to claim, today, that Monterrosa massacred thousands of women, children and old folks—something that they couldn't say in 1981, when the population of El Mozote never exceeded 300 inhabitants.

"Although it's a lie, Joseph Goebbels said that a lie told often enough becomes the truth. And because of the precarious situation of the guerrillas—attacking San Salvador with armed little boys and little girls—they need this lie to become the truth to escape total obliteration.

"And that's my theory on El Mozote. Any questions?"

The priests shook their heads. He was right, especially about the purpose of the lie. And besides, the one who could disprove that lie—colonel Monterrosa—had died in 1984.

CHAPTER 85

MYSTIQUE

But Ellacuría's hate had to surface again. He reiterated: "All the logic in the world can't deny this reality, Captain: Monterrosa was a butcher."

The captain shook his head. "Priest, you listen to *Managua Rose* too much." But then he decided to go on offense. "Let me tell you about a true butcher. I don't know his name, but maybe you can help me identify him.

"You see, in one of those operations where I supported Col. Monterrosa, I had spent the night atop Cacahuatique Mountain, and the next day I hitched a ride down to the Brigade with a supply helicopter. On the way down, the helicopter got rerouted to Usulután to evacuate a wounded soldier.

"The helicopter touched down, and some soldiers carrying the wounded soldier approached the helicopter. Since there was little space, I ended up cradling this poor soldier, who'd been shot in the head. By the time we landed in the Third Brigade, I was completely soaked in his blood.

"The supply officer gave me clean fatigues so I could change. By the time I'd cleaned up and changed, the helicopter had taken off, so I was stuck at the Brigade.

"I was chatting with the Captain of the Guard, who was a friend of mine, when a soldier suddenly ran up to him and told him he was needed at the entrance because a vehicle from the Salvadoran Green Cross, asking for a document that would grant it safe passage up north.

"While the Captain of the Guard was dealing with the Green Cross driver, I wanted to see who was in the vehicle, which was parked inside the Brigade, under the custody of soldiers.

"I approached the young man sitting up front next to the driver's seat. He looked 15, at most 16. And he had no eyes.

"And then I saw that he had no hands either.

"I said, 'My Lord, son, what happened?' I called him son because he was so young!

"He replied, 'We were ordered to make land mines to use against the soldiers, and one of them blew up in our faces. The others that are in the van are blind, too, but I also lost my hands.'"

The Captain paused and looked directly at Ellacuría, pointing out that, "When those kids were making those mines, the Agrarian Reform had already been completed, Duarte had become the duly-elected president, and El Salvador had become a democracy.

"So tell me, priest, who was the abominable butcher who sent those kids to prepare mines to kill or leave legless as many poor *indios* as they could, or to a life without sight and without hands, instead of fighting light hell to have the country turn all its efforts to educate its people—like Costa Rica did last century?

"You know... so they could lead a good, productive life, and go as far as their talents could take them?"

Was that a tear in Ellacuría's eye? A mental visualization of a kid without eyes and without hands had shaken the Jesuit. Perhaps if he'd seen the kid in person, he would've become a true activist for peace, and not for war.

But the Captain had one more point to make. "Gentlemen, do you know what mystique is?"

Before they could give him a dictionary answer, Sánchez explained. "Mystique is to passionately adhere to a code of conduct. None of the IRIBs was created with a mystique of assassinating civilians. What's more, avoiding the killing of civilians is something that has become doctrine in the United States, ever since they were accused of doing so in Vietnam. It was under this doctrine that the IRIBs were created.

"Another component of the mystique of the IRIBs is to win the hearts and minds of the people—again, that is quite the opposite of killing civilians, isn't it?

«And finally, the third organic component of the mystique of the IRIBs was: when you find the enemy, finish him off.

"When Monterrosa became a full colonel, and they made him Third Brigade Commander, he imparted that mystique on the brigade. I remember one operation in which I was monitoring communications and his executive was leading a Third Brigade unit in an operation, and he radioed Monterrosa that he needed to give the unit rest. Monterrosa's reply was, 'No way. Keep going.'

"And the executive kept going. Only when the goal was achieved were the units able to get back to the garrison. I never heard that executive ask for rest for the units again. He'd bought into Monterrosa's mystique.

"That mystique has endured even after his death. Again, it's only till recently that I've heard El Mozote mentioned. All these years, I hadn't once heard the word massacre used, for El Mozote or any other place.

"The logical question is, why wasn't there another massacre? After all, if the mystique of the Atlacatl and Monterrosa was to kill civilians, then hadn't they gotten away with it at El Mozote? Without a reprimand, even? Didn't they have carte blanche to commit more?"

"The answer has to be that it's not their mystique. And the absence of massacres is amplified by the fact that there were five IRIBs operating in the country.

"Gentlemen, the mystique inculcated in the Salvadoran army is a compass that hasn't failed us all these years. To accuse us of what *Managua Rose* accuses us of is one thing—to prove it is quite another.

"And forgive me for saying this one more time: if any of what *Managua Rose* accuses us of were true, we'd have fallen years ago. But since we've won the hearts and minds of the population since the Agrarian Reform, it's been the guerrillas who've had to fill their ranks with little boys and girls—not us."

Ellacuría said, "If everything you've said about Monterrosa is true, Captain, I'm surprised that he fell into Joaquín Villalobos' trap so easily."

Sánchez replied, matter-of-factly, "Well, priest, the ascendancy of Joaquín Villalobos occurred only after commanders Marcial and Ana María killed each other in Managua in 1983, in a mutual recrimination for the massive losses suffered in the general offensive of 1981 and then at the hands of Col. Monterrosa.

"Villalobos stepped in to fill the leadership void, just as the Roman general *Scipius Africanus* stepped into the leadership void caused by Hannibal's ongoing victories over the Romans. Villalobos, like *Scipius Africanus*, learned from Marcial's mistakes, and studied Monterrosa carefully, just like *Scipius Africanus* studied Hannibal.

"Rather than try to defeat the warrior head on, as Marcial had tried, Villalobos decided to set a trap. He feigned an attack on a Monterrosa unit, and upon withdrawing, left a radio with explosives inside, with an inscription that indicated that it was *Managua Rose.*

"The way I heard it, Monterrosa arrived in helicopter and didn't think twice about taking it with him on the helicopter to the Brigade. The bomb exploded in flight."

The Captain went silent. He'd been very fond of Col. Monterrosa.

He then continued. "Villalobos set a trap counting on the fact that Monterrosa's successes against Marcial had accustomed him to a guerrilla incapable acting so ingeniously. Nobody before Villalobos was capable of such cunning. But Joaquín Villalobos was a different breed, as Monterrosa found out too late. Just as Hannibal found out too late that *Scipius Africanus* was unlike any previous Roman General he'd faced."

The Captain's countenance turned from sorrow to bewilderment. "You know what, gentlemen? It's hard to believe that none of those officers said, 'it might be a bomb, let's not put it on the helicopter.' Or, 'it could be a bomb, let's move back and destroy it from afar.

"The two helicopter pilots should've certainly advised against it. The only explanation has to be that ongoing success made them overconfident."

Father Montes surprised the Captain with his next comment. "For about a year after that, we had a hard time listening to Radio *Venceremos.* Did you have anything to do with that?"

The Captain nodded. "The day after Monterrosa's death I got a visit from American advisors, who asked me if I could jam *Managua Rose.* I said, certainly, since I knew how it worked. And I did."

Montes nodded. "We'd find the station and they'd start the program and then it got noisy and then they weren't there anymore. So we went looking and with any luck, we could find them and then the noise would come and they'd disappear again. After that, we just gave up."

"Sure. All I did was jam their frequency in both AM and FM. Once the frequency got jammed, they'd have to change frequency. Every time they changed frequency they lost a lot of their dwindling audience."

Montes pointed out, "But then in 1986 and till now, RV has returned to normal. What happened?"

The Captain shrugged. "The same Americans who asked me to jam came and told me to stop because they couldn't hear the signal, and they wanted to hear it again to obtain intelligence. But I refused. So they talked to the Chief of Staff who relieved me and sent back to the Signal Battalion."

Ellacuría said, "So, in a way, Radio *Venceremos* did a number on you, too."

"Yes, but my refusal to stop jamming was wrong, for the same reasons I gave you before. Its audience was dwindling, and they were probably going to use it to send instructions from the FMLN command post in Managua. Deciphering those messages was more important than jamming it. That's why I'm just a simple Captain, gentlemen."

This admission of mistakes by the Captain probably led Montes to reciprocate, by saying, "Propaganda is overrated, Captain. Except for 1985, *Managua Rose* has transmitted uninterruptedly for almost 9 years, saying the vilest things anybody can say about the Salvadoran Armed Forces. Screaming massacres like El Mozote and ridiculously claiming the existence of piles of civilian bodies in El Playón, death squads and other falsehoods.

"And then even Hollywood got in on the act with that movie that pretty much reproduced everything *Managua Rose* claimed. And despite all that, here we are, in hiding, with the guerrilla reduced to fighting with boys and girls. Like Hitler in his last days, sending kids to their deaths."

Montes ended his soliloquy with, "Nothing beats facts, Captain. Nothing."

The Captain nodded, and then asked, "*Managua Rose* is catchy, isn't it?"—acknowledging the Jesuit's use of the term.

Father Montes looked embarrassed when he said, "I'm just tired of lies, Captain. And given the situation we find ourselves in, to say Radio 'We Will Win,' is to say the worst possible lie, because we're losing, not winning."

Sánchez didn't say anything, wondering why Montes had made such an admission in front of Ellacuría. It was as if he wanted the other Jesuit to hear it from somebody who wasn't a military man.

It also seemed to Sánchez that the Jesuits seemed depressed. Who wouldn't be, in their situation? So Sánchez decided to liven things up a bit. He stood up and called Elba and Celina over.

When they got there, he asked, "You want to hear a joke?"

The ladies nodded their heads vigorously.

"Ok. Jesus was walking along one day, when He came upon a group of people surrounding a lady of the night. It was obvious that the crowd was preparing to stone her, so Jesus of course said, 'Let the person who has no sin cast the first stone.'

"The crowd was shamed and one by one began to turn away. All of a sudden, a woman in her mid forties made her way through the crowd and when she got to the front, she tossed a pebble towards the woman.

"Jesus looked at the pebble-tossing woman and said, 'I really hate it when you do that, Mom.'"

They all laughed heartily. Even Ellacuría.

When the Captain stood up, Montes stood up as well. The two men shook hands. It was a strong, mutual handshake. Suddenly, Elba Ramos hugged him. And then Celina Ramos did, too. The Captain choked up a little bit. So he just waved good evening to them and left.

Chapter 86

From Salsa to Tarantella

The Tacarello group arrived at the empty building, the first floor of which would be the future home of the Italian branch of the Salvadoran Vesuvius Hardware firm, and the second floor of which would be the home of Gladys, Estela, Neto and Mario. Everything was in good shape because it had been occupied and maintained all these years.

All that it was missing was furniture and the public utilities. Mario was put in charge of buying furniture for the apartment, while Pepe went out to try to find suppliers for the hardware store and to apply to get the utilities turned on, such as electricity, gas and phone.

Although Mario had made it clear to him that he didn't want to work in a hardware shop the rest of his life, Pepe had asked him to work there only until Gladys and Estela could get it going. That way, they can sustain themselves while Neto goes to college. Mario could end up doing what he wanted, but for now, his help would be appreciated. Mario agreed.

Licha needed to make arrangements to head off to Paris, to resign from the religious life, and then leave for Poland.

On the very first day, she accompanied Mario in his endeavors. It was the first time that they were going to be able talk alone.

"OK, Licha, how did you end up being Mrs. Tacarello, and why?"

"Is that any way to talk to your new mother, son?" Licha joked.

"Look, I know there must be a reason for your going undercover like that. Who are you hiding from?" Mario insisted.

Licha shook her head. "Mario, I'm not going to be staying here much longer. At most, a couple of months. And I don't really want to give you any information that could compromise you and your family. And if I told you, you'd be compromised."

That must've been the only time Mario ever heard a complete idiocy come out of Licha's mouth. "Damn it, Licha. You and I helped thwart a revolution in El Salvador after you convinced me to do so, so I'm already compromised up to my eyeballs. Tell me."

Licha weighed that. "OK, Mario, I'll tell you, but the moment you know my reason, you'll realize you can't communicate it to anybody, ever."

"Let's hear it."

Licha started to tell of the rape and murder of her family by the Red Army in Poland, and of her near-rape by a bearded Red Army Colonel with the red CCCP tattooed in his genital area.

Mario caught on immediately. "Don Blas?"

"Yes. Only his real name was Vladislav Fedoseyev. Colonel Vladislav Fedoseyev, of the raping and murdering Red Army."

Mario whistled his dismay. "So that's why we got that message that he'd been 'retired' and replaced by 'Don Torquemada.' You killed him?"

Licha proudly answered in the affirmative.

Mario looked at this woman with an awe that was spiking exponentially with each passing second and then embraced her fiercely. He no longer felt bad about the intellectual beatdown he received from this woman. She was his 'mother superior' in every way.

After he released her, he deduced, "And that's why you had to present yourself as Mrs. Tacarello, to escape detection entering Europe."

"Yes, but I hadn't really planned on doing this, otherwise I would've told you, or asked you to bring me here."

"Why didn't you call me?" was the question that Mario had wanted to ask for a long time.

Licha explained, "Had I called you, you would've gotten the truth out of me and I really didn't want to tell anybody. Otherwise, I would've told you a long time ago."

He asked her, "So what prompted this?"

"The day I called your father to ask to see him, it had been a normal day at Asunción, in which we were closing the books for the past academic year. Then, a call came through. The operator said there was a woman who wanted to speak to a Sister 'a-LI-suh.' That's the pronunciation of my name in Czech, which is pretty similar to how Russians pronounce it, which nobody has ever called me since the Ursulines at Olomouc. Because in France it's 'a-LIS,' and in El Salvador it's 'a-LIS-yah'. The operator asked me if that might be me. I told her to patch her through.

"The woman spoke in perfect Castilian Spanish. She claimed that she was being transferred to the Spanish embassy in El Salvador and was thinking about sending her daughter to Asunción. I asked her how she knew about me, and she said it was because a friend of hers had returned from El Salvador recently and that her daughter had gone to La Asunción.

"We've had many Spanish students, Mario, but they all know me as Sister Licha, not as Sister 'a-LI-suh'. In any case, it should've been 'a-LIS-yah,' as the name is pronounced in Spanish. So that made all my alarms go off, and then I started to detect a very slight accent, like Don Blas' accent. Almost non-existent, but it was there. So when I figured out that she was Soviet, I passed her over to the registrar's office and hung up. That's when I called your dad."

"She was locating you."

"Yes. Don Blas' people knew me either as Juana or as Alice Novak, from my records in Czechoslovakia."

Mario could only say, "How lucky that you never tried to get your Polish papers back."

"When I get to Poland, I will get them back. I want to see if I still have family back there. But Alice Novak will be no more."

Mario embraced her again and promised, "Licha, you'll always have your Tacarello family. Always."

When he said that, Licha lost any semblance of levity. She said, "Mario, you father is very enthused with me. Don't interfere."

This surprised Mario. "Look, I wasn't planning on doing or saying anything—why are you telling me this?"

Licha turned a deep hue of red and said, "Your Dad is eccentric. And I don't mind. I'm just saying... I don't want you to mind either."

"Oh no. What's he done?"

"Last night when everybody was asleep, he went and woke up Gladys, and brought her downstairs to where we were sleeping, so we could service him together."

"Why didn't you say no?"

"I can't say no. That's part of the deal."

"Does he know about you and Don Blas?"

"No, but he knows that I have a powerful reason not to come to Europe as Alice Novak, and that I'm in no position to disobey his whims."

Mario shrugged. "Don't worry about me, Licha. On the other hand, you could leave right now. What's stopping you?"

Licha replied, "Like you, I fulfill my promises, and I made promises to be able to be here today. I'll leave after I've fulfilled all of them."

Now Mario was intrigued. "What promises have you made, Licha?"

Licha led him to a nearby café-bar, where they ordered a couple of expressos and sat down to drink them. Then she looked at him, somewhat ashamed, and said, "Mario, your mother walked into the house when I was naked with your dad, because he and I thought we were alone and that we'd hear her car.

"Your mom grabbed my clothes and called Gladys and Estela, who appeared out of nowhere. She gave them my clothes and told them to throw them away."

"I couldn't help but break down. I told them all that I needed their help to get out of the country, that I feared for my life, and that I was willing to do anything. When your mom wanted more details, I told her that if any of them knew, they'd be in danger as well. That mollified your mom a bit."

"I'm sorry you had to go through that."

"Your dad told your mom to back off, that it was he who had requested the sex in exchange for helping me, because the only way to really help me was for me to travel as Mrs. Tacarello."

Mario shook his head. His mom had obviously relented, but she was a tough negotiator. She'd imposed tremendous conditions on Gladys when she had Neto. He asked Licha what his mom's conditions had been.

"Well, your mom said that I had to earn my place in her family, starting at the bottom rung. That I had to comply with anything that anybody in the family requested of me, including Gladys and Estela. I agreed. What was I going to say, standing naked in front of four people?"

"So what did you have to obey?"

Licha looked at him sheepishly and said, "Well, let's just say that there was only one relevant demand made of me, and that was by Gladys." Licha would never reveal the demands Belinda had made on her.

"What did Gladys want?"

"She wanted me to agree to have sex with Neto. To be his woman."

Mario looked incredulous. "Really? Do you want me to talk to Gladys to get you off the hook?"

"No. Which is why I'm telling you, please... don't interfere. Your dad hasn't let me spend a penny. I'm very grateful, and I'm going to fulfill my promise to Gladys."

Mario looked at her skeptically. "Please, Licha, this is me you're talking to. You must have another reason because frankly, you could've left for Paris to resign the minute you arrived here. You had already entered Europe undetected."

Licha smiled slyly and said, "Well, Mario, if you must know... I'm kind of hoping that a 17-year-old boy might have enough strength and vigor and youth... to make a 51-year old woman pregnant."

That stunned Mario into silence.

Licha smiled, took his arm, and said, "So let's go shopping for that bed. If I'm going to be a mother, I want to get impregnated on a nice bed, don't you think?"

CHAPTER 87

WHERE'S BOBBY FISCHER?

"Please come in, Vladimir."

"Thank you, Comrade General Secretary."

"How is the Black Crusade coming, Vladimir?"

"Comrade General Secretary, the general offensive in El Salvador was not as effective as we'd hoped. But that, together with the murder of the nuns, is making it likely that the Congress will approve less aid to the Salvadoran government and the counterrevolutionaries in Nicaragua."

Brezhnev nodded. "El Salvador is expendable, Vladimir. If it helped to protect Nicaragua, then it served its intended purpose."

Putyatin continued. "In addition, we're operating with the reduced revenue stream you have allotted to us, and, following your sage advice, through intermediaries, we've contacted people in Hollywood to produce a movie about the 4 murdered nuns."

"It won't say the U.S. Ambassador set them up, will it?"

"No, Comrade General Secretary, it will blame it all on the murderous Junta and their murderous Armed Forces and Security Forces."

"That's good, Vladimir, but you'll have to use your ingenuity to work under an even lower budget, now that Reagan has effectively begun to arm the opposition in Afghanistan."

Brezhnev didn't seem to be in a good mood. Who could blame him? Things weren't going his way, lately. After a few moments he asked, "What else, Vladimir?"

Putyatin was dreading having to give this report. If this was a chess match, he was about to tell the King that he was about to lose his two bishops. Putyatin said, "The Pope is pushing the Jesuits out of the Government of Nicaragua. Which means that if he's successful, he will effectively deprive us of Nicaragua's best leaders."

"What about the other two brothers. The military ones?"

"The Ortegas, sir. They're faithful communists, but they're dumb as rocks, compared to the Jesuits."

Leonid Brezhnev got up and started pacing the floor. He was deep in thought, with his famous eyebrows clumped together—never a good sign. He stopped to look out the window overlooking Red Square, with his hands clasped behind his back, and asked, “Vladimir?”

“Yes, Comrade General Secretary?”

“Where’s Bobby Fischer?”

Putyatin was caught off guard by this. Bobby Fischer? The only American to have beaten a Russian, Boris Spassky, in the World Chess Championship, in 1972?

After racking his brains mightily, he recalled what he’d read a few weeks back. “Sir, last I heard, he moved to Los Angeles. He used to live in Massachusetts but he got bored because he beat the MIT Supercomputer ‘Greenblatt’ in chess all the time.”

Brezhnev was swaying back and forth on his feet in front of the window. “No, Vladimir, he’s not in Los Angeles.”

Putyatin felt like he was entering a minefield. Had he believed in God, he’d be praying to Him to put the right words in his mouth right about now.

Brezhnev walked back and stood behind his desk. He didn’t look very happy. Putyatin braced for the worst.

Again, he asked, “Do you know where Bobby Fischer is, Vladimir?”

“I can find out for you, Comrade General Secretary. It shouldn’t take me....”

Brezhnev slammed his fist on his desk. “HE’S IN WASHINGTON D.C., IN THE WHITE HOUSE, ADVISING REAGAN!”

Putyatin jumped out of his skin.

Brezhnev’s secretary came running in, asking if everything was all right. One look at Brezhnev and she let herself out again.

Putyatin couldn’t think of anything else to do but nod, and say, “I am at your disposal, ready to do as you command, Comrade General Secretary.”

Brezhnev unbundled his eyebrows and attempted to grin. It was not a pretty sight. He said, “Do you know what I like to do when one course of action fails, Vladimir?”

“What, Comrade General Secretary?”

“I try something else, Vladimir.”

And then Brezhnev smiled, unabashedly showing his crooked yellow teeth. It was the smile of a Cossack who was about to lead a cavalry attack against an enemy unit on foot—not the smile of a chess player.

Putyatin cautiously asked, "Is the Comrade General Secretary suggesting that the obstacles we're facing are better dealt with by eliminating them?"

The Cossack smile didn't go away. "Didn't shooting work with Kennedy? We got the socialist Lyndon Johnson who decided to almost bankrupt the United States with his 'Great Society' socialist program. That vice-president of Reagan's, George Bush? He's a, how do you say *zanudnyy* in American? They have a word for that."

"I believe the word is 'wimp,' sir."

"Yes! It would be better for us if he were the president and not Reagan."

"Is the Comrade General Secretary ordering me to do so? If so, I would be honored."

The Cossack kept smiling. But this time he raised his right index finger and wagged it at Putyatin. "Stay within your field, Vladimir, stay within your field."

"I understand, sir."

"But damn it! Shoot somebody!"

"Yes, sir."

Vladimir left the office excited. The KGB is the KGB. It's not the diplomatic corps, and although the Black Crusade had been founded by a diplomat, Putyatin was its head now, and he loved shooting, too.

"Olga, in my office now," he told Olga as he walked by her desk.

Olga walked in.

"Sit down, please. How are you, Olga?"

"Fine, Comrade Director."

"How is your training in weaponry going, Olga?"

"I am proficient with a Makarov 9 mm, comrade Director."

"Good, Olga. Tell me. Did you love Fedoseyev?"

Her face said it all.

"Would you like to avenge his death?"

Olga hesitated, but then nodded.

"What do you know of the murderer of Fedoseyev, Olga?"

"I believe she's left El Salvador, Comrade Director. After the general offensive. The school where she works hasn't heard from her since early January."

Putyatin nodded. "If she's Polish, she's going to Poland, don't you agree?"

Olga replied, "But no Alice Novak has entered any European port of entry, yet, sir."

"She's surely entered under a false name. What we do know is that to start a life in Poland, she's going to need money and for that she's going to have to go to the headquarters of her order in Paris."

Putyatin paused, then gave her this order: "Write a letter to the KGB Paris Bureau, requesting that they monitor *Les Petites Sœurs de l'Assomption* in Paris. Subject: Alice Novak. I'll sign it."

"Yes, Comrade Director."

"If she goes there, you'll go shoot her."

"Shoot her, Comrade Director?"

"We're going to start shooting people again, Olga. This is, after all, the KGB."

Chapter 88

For the Children

"Come in, men, sit down."

Second Lieutenant Fiallos and his fellow brand new *de fila* Second Lieutenants sat down before the Director of the Gerardo Barrios Military School, Col. Benavides.

"Congratulations on your promotion, gentlemen. I've been put in charge of a special operations unit, the mission of which is to find the Jesuits and kill them. I understand that you have agreed to do so, no matter what the consequences."

Second Lieutenant Fiallos stood up. "Sir, if I may speak frankly, we have a personal score to settle with men who wear frocks and commit crimes and then shield themselves behind those frocks."

"Please sit down, Fiallos. Thank you for reaffirming your commitment to the mission. I must warn you that so far, we haven't had any volunteers for this mission. So I feel the need to tell you why we're doing this.

"Since the arrival of the Jesuits, they have been a driving force for war and not peace. And this isn't something that the High Command is saying, this was disclosed to us by fellow members of the cloth who disagree with them. According to them, the entire Society of Jesus has planned the war for the violent takeover of El Salvador, according to the document they sponsored, titled 'A Theology of Liberation.' They had to create a document outside of the Bible, to claim that God justifies killing in the name of the poor.

"Now then, so far, they've been unsuccessful, due to the love of country and bravery and forethought exhibited by the Government and Armed Forces, especially since October 1979. Because what did we do?

"1. We overthrew a dictatorial government, with the support of Archbishop Romero.

"2. We gave the representatives of the popular organizations two out of the five seats in the Revolutionary Junta.

"3. We passed the Agrarian Reform Law and the Bank Nationalization Law, mandating the transfer of land to the peasants and the availability of financing for their agricultural activities.

"4. We dispossessed the Fourteen of their lands and gave them to the peasants, with a massive Agrarian Reform.

"5. We promoted free and fair elections, which were won in 1983 by Engineer José Napoleón Duarte, and in 1989 by Alfredo Cristiani, offering them every opportunity to join the political process.

"6. Throughout the 1980s, we've frequently sat down with the guerrillas for peace talks, offering them guarantees to incorporate themselves into the Salvadoran political system, as a political party. And each and every time, they've refused.

"Among other things."

The brand-new second lieutenants nodded vigorously.

"And the true leaders of their movement, the Jesuits, have continued to order them to fight, this time with children, to the point of launching an attack against San Salvador with armed 9- and 10- year-old boys and girls, which is a crime against humanity.

"They did this instead of working to incorporate the guerrillas into our new democracy, and to resolve our disputes at the ballot box."

Second Lieutenant Fiallos said, "They've messed with the children of El Salvador in more ways than that, sir. We're proof."

"Good, gentlemen, report to the Situation Room, where you will be briefed on your mission."

CHAPTER 89

THE PEACE INDULGENCE

"Captain, Sergeant Zelayandía is signaling from the hill across the road!" a soldier shouted. Sánchez pointed his binoculars at the hill. Zelayandía was indicating that a helicopter was coming from the east.

Sánchez immediately shouted: "EVERYBODY INSIDE THE HOUSES! NOW! NOW! NOW!" He trusted that Zelayandía and the other sentinel would act normal. After all, they were in underwear and they looked like beachgoers.

Soon the helicopter rotor could be heard by everybody as it passed overhead in a westerly direction. What Sánchez wanted as for it not to turn back.

It didn't.

But what it did mean was that things were under greater control in the capital. More resources were available to look for them.

He called a meeting of Zelayandía, and Sergeant Juan, the custodian, to discuss options.

"Sergeant Juan, I believe that, as soon as they can, some Xanadú homeowners are going to try to come over. Although I don't believe that's going to happen before the weekend, if anybody does come, I need for you not to let them in. How are you going to do that?"

Juan replied immediately. "Captain, all I have to do is tell them that the water system is contaminated and that it hasn't been fixed yet, and for health reasons, nobody can come in yet."

"Good idea, Sergeant. But what if they insist? Can they get out of the car and try to force the gate open?"

"No, Captain, the only way they can force this gate open, is if they ram it."

Sánchez turned to Zelayandía. "Any vehicle that rams this gate must be considered hostile and fired upon, are we clear?"

"Yes, Captain."

He turned to Juan. "Sergeant Juan, the moment a firefight starts, you dive for cover, do you understand? This isn't your fight."

Juan said, "Give me a weapon, Captain, I'll fight."

"Well, we don't have a weapon to spare, Sergeant Juan. Plus, there's a good chance that those who try to come in by force will be wearing the same uniform as us. So it's best if you don't get involved, OK?"

"Understood, Captain."

Meeting over, he went up the hill to talk to the Jesuits.

They were waiting inside the house.

Ellacuría asked if they could come out.

"Come on out, priest."

"What does that helicopter mean, Captain?"

"It has to mean that the situation in the capital is better and that they may be coming after us."

Ellacuría and Montes looked at each other. The Ellacuría gently took the Captain by the arm and invited him to come inside. How could the Captain refuse such unexpected hospitality?

Celina offered him coffee and he accepted.

Ellacuría opened up with, "Captain, why do you think you received the order to kill us?"

Sánchez shrugged. "I have no idea, priest. My best guess is because there's some intelligence that you were the masterminds behind this offensive. But even so, it's awfully hard to believe that anybody in the High Command would order you killed. I did hear a rumor that they wanted to expel you from the country, but that was it."

Ellacuría persisted. "But you received the order to kill us from your military chain of command, Captain."

The Captain nodded. "I received the order from my commander, who was awfully upset about it, and who is relieved that I disobeyed it. You see, most of those officers studied in Catholic schools, such as Liceo Salvadoreño, run by the Marists, and Don Bosco, and Santa Cecilia, run by Salesians. You're untouchable to them."

Ellacuría went to sit next to Sánchez, and said to him, "Captain, after all our conversations, we've reached the conclusion that you're a sincere man."

Sánchez had the premonition that a big revelation was coming.

Ellacuría continued. "You see, Captain, the only way for the guerrillas to survive is to ensure that the Army murders us."

The Captain was surprised by this. "Are you saying that you're being betrayed? Sacrificed?"

Ellacuría reached out to the Captain and pressed his arm, in a friendly manner.

"Captain, we thank you for protecting us, but we believe you're protecting us from the wrong people. We believe that the people who are going to attack your unit here, to get us, won't be the Salvadoran Army."

The Captain tried not to laugh. "Priest, are you telling me that guerrillas (little boys and girls, maybe) who manage to survive the army's onslaught in the capital are going to trek up and down the sierra to get here, and mount an attack on us? In that case, praise the Lord! We're going to take their weapons away after they fire their last two or three rounds, spank them and send them home to mommy, after admonishing them!"

Ellacuría and Montes didn't share the levity of the moment. Ellacuría said, quite earnestly, "Captain, listen to us. Here's what we know. You received an order to kill us. That's a fact. And although we believe you when you say that most of the officers in the Armed Forces would refuse to obey such an order, the order was nevertheless inserted into your Chain of Command, which, by the way, now includes a civilian: the Commander in Chief, the President."

The Captain nodded. "OK. And so?"

The Jesuit went on. "From a military standpoint, the fact that you took two of the foremost Jesuit priests out of circulation should have had the same effect as decapitating the high command of the guerrillas, assuming we are that high command, correct?"

The Captain nodded. Ellacuría went on. "Since the offensive went on without us, it must be obvious that we're not that high command, and yet the order to kill us hasn't been lifted, am I right?"

The Captain shook his head. The priest went on. "Montes informs me that he had to tell your Commanding Officer that we were all right because *Managua Rose* had announced that you'd abducted and killed us."

Sánchez nodded and smiled at Ellacuría's mention of *Managua Rose.* He once again thought that he was going to be told something momentous—perhaps something that had to do with what Elba failed to say last night—because of the way he was trying to ingratiate himself.

Ellacuría insisted, "And still the order hasn't been lifted, correct?"

Ellacuría passed the baton to Montes, who said, "Captain, the reason I collaborated on that radio call was that I came to the inescapable conclusion that this Offensive was ordered by the current guerrilla high command with the sole objective of getting us murdered by the Army, or to make it appear as though we were murdered by the Army."

The Captain asked him how he'd come to that conclusion. So Montes proceeded to explain all that he'd deduced before he made that radio call, except for the guerrilla bomb. He'd leave that for the second inevitable part of this conversation.

He concluded his explanation thusly: "Only our murder is capable of eclipsing all the atrocities that the guerrillas are committing in the city, and only our murder can force the United States to sit at a table with both parties, as equals, not as victor and vanquished, to negotiate a peace agreement."

The Captain merely shrugged. "Well, I guess I thwarted that plan, didn't I?"

Montes looked at him sadly. "For now, Captain. But we were sentenced to death the moment they got your chain of command to issue that order, and it doesn't matter who ends up murdering us, it'll inevitably be blamed on the Salvadoran Army. I wouldn't put it past the guerrilla high command to have paid somebody in your High Command an obscene amount of money to give that order."

The Captain wasn't convinced. "Father Montes, that sounds far-fetched."

Ellacuría rejoined the conversation at that point. "Captain, Montes tells me that your call sign is *Padrino*, from Mario Puzo's '*El Padrino* [The Godfather],' is it not?"

The Captain nodded.

"What was the Godfather's famous line?"

The Jesuit tried to imitate the Marlon Brando character when he said, "I will make him an offer he can't refuse."

Sánchez nodded, laughing.

Ellacuría concluded with, "Somebody from the FMLN made somebody in your High Command an offer he couldn't refuse."

It was hard for the Captain to believe this. "No way, priest. Nobody in the High Command is in need of such money. We're not talking about poor National Guards here. Plus, all that money would be of no use to any of them in jail."

At which point Montes delivered the logical *coup de grace*: "No jail time, Captain, this deal comes with a Peace Indulgence."

The Captain realized that he was getting some of his own medicine back, but all he said was, "Explain yourselves, please."

Montes did just that. "At the negotiating table, the very first thing that both sides will agree to, almost immediately, will be an Amnesty Law, or, to use your terms, an Indulgence Law, which will exonerate every member of both sides from any act they committed during the conflict, and that includes our murder."

The Jesuit's logic was irrefutable. No wonder he was the headmaster at one of the premier schools of Central America.

The Captain had to agree. "Fine, Father Montes. I can't but accept your reasoning, but that still doesn't change the fact that my men and I are here precisely to prevent your murder."

Now Montes handed the baton back to Ellacuría, who said, "Captain, since you've accepted our logic that the only reason for this offensive against the capital can be none other than our murder, you must accept the logical conclusion that whoever ordered this offensive is going to make sure that we're murdered."

Sánchez asked, "Would that be Joaquín Villalobos, your *Scipius Africanus*?"

Ellacuría shrugged. "It could be him, or Schafik Handal, or Leonel González, but they're in the capital. They won't be the ones coming after us."

"Then who?"

Chapter 90

Shadows, Nothing But

Ellacuría took a deep breath. What he was about to disclose was the most guarded secret of his life. The fact that he was willing to disclose it was product of Segundo Montes' persuasive powers, who had finally made him see that Sánchez and his troops were not his enemies at this time. That his true enemies were the guerrillas who had decided to sacrifice them. And Fidel Castro, who had decided to betray them.

Although this disclosure could bring him trouble, it would only be trouble if he survived and, as Montes had told him, he'd always have the excuse that it was others who were issuing orders. Ellacuría merely made recommendations.

Ellacuría lowered his voice to a whisper, when he had no need to, since nobody was nearby, and they weren't talking loudly anyway. He said, "There's a unit of military professionals that go by the name of the Shadows. That unit is capable of doing astonishing military feats."

"How astonishing?" the Captain asked.

Ellacuría replied, "Things like penetrating the guarded home of the Christian Democrat attorney general and killing him, and then escaping undetected and untouched by his security."

The Captain understood. "Priest, you mean like killing Monsignor Romero with a single shot, undetected. And then shooting 40 people who were at his funeral, in broad daylight, undetected."

"Yes, Captain, precisely."

Sánchez continued. "Things like executing the most precise military operation ever witnessed in this nation, in broad daylight, by posing as Treasury Police and National Police, stopping traffic in front of Externado, entering Externado and capturing all the FDR leaders, and whisking them away, all in no more than twenty minutes? And then leaving the bullet-riddled bodies out in the open, with a note in which a death squad claimed responsibility, thus linking the Security Forces to the death squads forever?"

Ellacuría nodded.

The Captain added, "If they can do the very complex, they can also do the very simple, like brutally murdering Father Rutilio Grande and the boy and old man accompanying him, to make it look like the Government did it, am I correct?"

Ellacuría seemed embarrassed, yet nodded again.

"How about Tacarello's murder?"

Ellacuría nodded. At that time, Montes stepped aside. He may have been close to Tacarello. But why didn't he feel bad about the others as well?

It was with some trepidation that Sánchez asked, "How about Ana Isabel Casanova?" If he nodded, he just might...

Ellacuría didn't hesitate. "No, Captain! That was the guerrilla high command who ordered that. They were after Col. Casanova because of the—to use your term—ass-kicking he gave to the guerrillas in the January 1981 offensive. And because her last name was Casanova."

Sánchez thought, "You're lucky you didn't order that, you son of a bitch." He also thought about everything he could spew in Ellacuría's face for all the times he slandered good people. But that recrimination could wait until after they got out of this predicament. Right now, his priority was to gain as much knowledge as he could about the Shadows.

For a moment, there was complete silence: Ellacuría's embarrassed silence and Montes' stricken silence. But it was a useless silence that Sánchez decided to break. "Are they Cuban?" he asked.

Ellacuría didn't hesitate, "Yes, they are."

Sánchez weighed all this. These Jesuits were very afraid of the Shadows. They certainly hadn't been afraid of the Signal Captain and his soldiers who'd walked into their Residence with loaded weapons, in response to which they had been thoroughly confrontational and unafraid. There was a reason for that and he had to find out.

Sánchez asked: "And you're afraid that these Shadows will come after you?"

Ellacuría nodded.

Sánchez deduced, "But if they're Cuban, then they're under the operational command of Fidel Castro." Ellacuría nodded vigorously.

However, if that was true...

"If that's true, priest, then the one who wants you dead is Fidel Castro, or at the very least, Castro has acquiesced to the petition of the guerrilla leader who wants you dead."

Both priests nodded.

Sánchez asked, "Gentlemen... to believe Fidel Castro is betraying you... don't you think that's taking it too far?"

Montes jumped up and asserted, with verve and aplomb, "Not at all!"

Now that he'd gotten the Captain's attention, Montes explained, "Captain, last Saturday, Elba, Celina and Obdulio Ramos were sitting in their little house near the University gate when they saw what they believed to be guerrillas place a bomb at the gate. When the bomb exploded, tearing the gate wide open, the security of the military residential area on the other side of the boulevard opened fire and wounded one of them.

"Now then, had that wounded guerrilla been Salvadoran, the others would've continued their mission, leaving the wounded guerrilla behind. But since he was Cuban, they couldn't leave him behind and so they aborted the mission and evacuated him."

Sánchez wanted to make sure he understood it correctly. "What you're telling me is that those who blew the gate wide open with a bomb last Saturday were Shadows, and that their mission was to kill you?"

They answered in unison: "Yes and yes!"

Montes pointed out the obvious: "What other reason would they have to blow the gate open with a bomb, Captain? It could only be to kill us!"

Sánchez asked, "But didn't you say that the guerrillas wanted the Army to kill you?"

Montes replied, "They were certainly going to make it seem like the Army did it. It can't be that hard, can it?"

This made sense to the Captain. But he had to point out the obvious: "They're not as astonishing as you said, because they failed to take into account the security detail of the military residential area across the street."

To which Ellacuría had the balls to reply, "God punished them for the evil they were about to do."

The Captain guffawed. With that phrase, Ellacuría had proven everything that Sánchez had ever accused the Jesuits of: they would sow winds, reap whirlwinds, and expect the whirlwinds to wreak havoc on everybody but themselves.

Add to that the sheer, unmitigated hubris! It wasn't evil when the priest ordered it; but when the same thing was done to him, it most certainly was!

When Sánchez regained his composure, he said to the priests, "Priests, why on earth didn't you stick to educating? Why on earth did you have to engage in dangerous stuff like war?"

He took out his Browning 9 mm, took some bullets out of the magazine, and said to them, "See these shiny things? They kill, maim, penetrate cloth, tissue, organs and bones, and if you're lucky, you get to see your Maker; but if you're unlucky, you're left paralyzed, blinded or become vegetables."

He reloaded his weapon and said, "Gentlemen, I'm going to take all this information you've given me and analyze it with my sergeants to come up with the best possible deployment of troops to protect you.

"Personally, I want to thank you for all these disclosures because they do exonerate the Armed Forces from everything you've been accusing them of. I'd love to have you say what you told me on the radio, but then they'd say it was a shotgun confession, and that's no good.

"But I do want to ask you this favor: when we get back, safe and sound, I want you to have the guts to tell the world what you told me just now. Not for my sake, but for the sake of every one of these Salvadoran soldiers who put it all on the line for their country, and who deserve to be as proud to wear this uniform as I am right now."

Ellacuría replied, "With pleasure, Captain."

The Captain smiled and said, "Then now we have even more reasons to protect you. Even if it's ten battalions of Shadows, led by Fidel Castro himself, who come for you!"

He turned to go down the hill but stopped to say one more thing: "You know, gentlemen, my radio call sign has always been *Padrino,* and I've been wanting to change it for a while, mostly for security reasons. But I haven't found a name I like. However, if we survive this upcoming battle, I'm going to change it to *Leonidas.*"

As the bewildered priests saw the Captain disappear down the hill, Ellacuría asked Montes, "Was he referring to Leonidas, the King of Sparta, who battled the entire Persian Army of Xerxes at Thermopylae, with only 300 Spartans at his side?"

Montes nodded. “Yes, he was referring to that Leonidas.”

“But... didn’t Leonidas lose his life in that battle, along with all his troops?”

To which Montes replied, “I’m pretty sure the Captain is aware of that.”

Chapter 91

God Isn't Dead

The Mother Superior of *Les Petites Sœurs de l'Assomption* in Paris had such kind eyes. Truly a saintly woman, she had dedicated herself to the education of young ladies the world over. Her eyes filled with sympathy after she heard what Licha had gone through.

She asked, "But dear, are you sure you want to leave us? You're You still have a lot to offer and teach! Plus, with your unique experience, you can help us confront the indoctrination that children are starting to face the world over. Virginity is overrated, compared to knowledge and experience such as yours!"

Licha replied, "Mother, although I agree with you, it's also true that my knowledge and experience can also be put to greater use in my homeland, Poland, which is struggling to be free from the Soviet yoke. And it's a murderous yoke, Mother. Look at the assassination attempt on the President Reagan two months ago."

"But wasn't that a deranged man who did it?"

"Mother Superior, knowing what I know, I don't for a minute believe that man wasn't following somebody's orders."

The kind eyes became worried. "You know whom I pray for fervently, Licha? The Pope."

Licha vigorously nodded. "I'll be in Rome tomorrow, to attempt to speak to him, Mother Superior, because I do want to join Solidarity in Poland. Maybe through him I can be put in touch with the right people there."

The Mother Superior took a card out of her desk, wrote on it and signed it. Then she gave it to Licha, saying, "We have a school in Warsaw, you can start there."

Licha was very grateful. "Mother, I'll definitely keep this in mind, but I really do have to leave the Order. I'm expecting a child."

Surprised, the Mother Superior exclaimed, "Oh, I didn't realize that? How far along?"

"Two months."

"May God bless your child, Alice!"

"Thank you, Mother Superior, just pray that it's not born with Down Syndrome, given my age."

"I will, Alice." And then the Mother Superior started crying. Licha got up to console her. The Mother Superior clung to her, and sobbed, "I wish I could've done something to prevent this from happening to you, Alice!"

Licha consoled her. "Mother Superior, who could've seen this coming? A Soviet-Jesuit alliance? And even in the midst of it, it's still unbelievable!"

Half an hour later, Licha was no longer a nun. Fortunately for her, her pension was generous. She'd be able to raise the child by herself, if need be.

She went directly to the Paris train station to take the train to Rome. John Paul II would be in St. Peter's Square the next day in the afternoon, and she planned to speak to him quickly in Polish, to ask for an urgent audience. There was a low probability of success, but there as zero probability of success if she didn't try.

It was already evening, and the train she got on would get her to Rome around noon. There, she'd meet up with Neto and Gladys, who'd be arriving on a train from Naples. Then they'd go to the Vatican together.

Olga got on the same train. She would look for Licha while everybody was sleeping on the train. And she'd do as she was instructed. "Two bullets to the head, right before the next stop, cover her head with a blanket afterward and get off."

Olga looked at the train's itinerary. The best station to get off on would be Zurich, 4 hours away. Just past midnight.

By 11 pm, she'd found Licha. She took a seat several rows behind her. Licha read for a while, then turned off the light, grabbed a pillow, put a blanket over herself and fell asleep. Perfect.

When Olga felt that the train was slowing down as it approached Zurich, she twisted the silencer onto her gun, and put her hand with the gun in her bag. She got up, walked swiftly towards Licha, took out the gun, placed it inches away from Licha's head, and pulled the trigger.

Nothing.

She pulled it again.

Nothing.

The loudspeaker said, "Zurich" and Licha stirred.

Olga thought fast. She could either turn around and remain on the train, to try it again later at another stop, or get off.

But why would she stay if she didn't have a working weapon?

She put the Makarov pistol away, walked toward the exit and got off at the Zurich train station. Since she had a little time before the train departed again, she quickly went to the ladies' restroom and got into a stall to check the weapon. Perhaps there was something obvious that she could fix so she could get back on the train again. As she was examining it, it fired a bullet straight into her heart, and nobody heard a thing.

* * *

At 12 noon, Licha got off the train in Rome. She went to the train arrival and departure bulletin board and saw that the Naples train hadn't arrived yet. She decided to wait for them in one of the little cafés in the station. But first she put her luggage in a locker. If Neto didn't want anything to do with her after she told him of her pregnancy, there'd be no reason to return to Naples anymore.

As she sat at the café, she recalled everything that had happened since Pepe Tacarello had gone back to El Salvador. When the phone company finally installed their phones, Pepe had called Belinda who was upset because of the delay in returning. She wanted him back right away. That delay had served its purpose though: it had given Pepe time to ascertain that Mario was on top of the business, and that things were going to go well.

The merchant in Mario's blood had taken over, and he worked tirelessly, day and night, to get the hardware store going. Estela worked alongside him to learn and manage the business, because it would become hers and Gladys' to run when Mario returned to the university.

The night after Pepe's departure, Gladys and Neto had come down to the office where Licha and Pepe used to sleep together, and where Licha was now sleeping alone. Gladys woke her up. When Licha had opened her eyes, Gladys said, "Licha, it's time for you to do what you said you'd do."

Licha sat up in bed. In the darkness, she could see the silhouette of Neto standing in the door. Licha told Gladys. "If you want me to do this, Gladys, I will."

"I do."

Licha turned on the lamp on the nightstand. Gladys was in a bathrobe and Neto was in his underwear, looking embarrassed. Licha was wearing a nightshirt.

Gladys sat on her bed. "Licha, last night Neto woke me up because he was touching himself next to me. I didn't say anything because I didn't want to embarrass him. When I woke up this morning, there was a hug stain on the sheets. I had to get my mother to wash them because I didn't want to touch my son's ejaculation.

"So I want him to sleep with you from now on."

"Neto, is this what you want?" Licha asked, giving the young man every chance to say no.

He nodded nervously.

Gladys told Licha that Neto had told her about the way he'd done his teachers in Guazapa, and that sometimes he couldn't even perform because of the shame. According to Gladys, he hadn't experienced the beauty of normal sex yet.

Licha asked, "Does he have a condom? I don't have birth control pills."

Gladys shook her head. "At your age, there's no way he can leave you pregnant. Don't use that as an excuse."

"OK."

Gladys said, "Thank you. I'll leave you two alone now." She stood up, went to Neto kissed him on the cheek and told him, "Learn to be a man, son." She left and shut the door.

Licha got up and removed her nightdress, revealing her 51-year-old body to the young man. The boy's erection sprung upwards. She approached him and kissed him. She led him to the bed, lay back, opened her legs, and said, "Make me your woman, Commander Guevara."

The boy entered her and orgasmed almost immediately. He couldn't hold back his roar.

Neto had indeed learned to become a man, and a good lover, when he'd finally learned how to control his ejaculation. And despite Gladys' birth control theory with respect to age, she was carrying Neto's baby in her womb. Licha couldn't have been happier. She would finally have the family she'd been missing!

It was the first time Licha was experiencing a normal relationship as well. Neto was very intelligent, and she was glad to help him study to take the Italian high school test. He would take the test soon, pass it and then go to college.

But would he go to college in Poland? And how would that work? Would he marry her? If he did, would he try to keep her here in Italy? Mario had advised against telling him.

"But he's the father, Mario. How can I keep it from him?"

Mario shook his head. "Did you two ever discuss marriage? Forming a family together?"

"No."

"Then why does he need to know? I can assure you that he's not interested in fatherhood. Also, from what I hear, at your age, you could suffer a miscarriage. Would there be a reason for either of you to remain married after that? And what's going to happen when you're 60, and he's barely 26? Think he won't want to trade you in for a young 20-year-old?"

She'd changed the subject.

"So what are you planning to do, Mario?"

"As soon as Estela and Gladys can manage the business, I'm going back to the university for a master's in something that will allow me to combat Liberation Theology."

"Mario, you already did that. Start a new phase of your life. God's granted you that gift."

Mario remarked, jokingly, "Look who's talking, Licha. You want to go to Poland to help liberate your country from the Soviet yoke. So please, don't lecture me."

Then he turned serious. "Remember my calling? A calling is for serving the Lord. I can best serve the Lord by exposing the Jesuit's betrayal of the Word of God. God forbid a Jesuit ever becomes a Pope, because then they'll have all the power in the world."

This seemed strange to Licha. "But Mario, Jesuits can't be bishops or cardinals, and therefore, they can't be popes. They're outside the hierarchy of the Church."

Mario smiled, proud of the fact that he'd figured this out, and that the smartest person in the world hadn't. He said, "Licha, the Jesuits are at war with the Pope. The best way for them to win that war is to have a Jesuit become Pope, wouldn't you agree?"

Licha had to agree with that. To her, it was obvious that Mario was hell-bent on going to war with the Jesuits, intellectually. She asked him, "So when you're done with your master's, what will you do?"

"I'll publish my thesis that will expose them and go back to El Salvador to confront them."

"Come on, Mario. They'll kill you if you do that."

"Not before I've outdebated them in public."

Licha had looked at her dear friend, and possible half-brother-in-law, reaching the conclusion that there was no uncalling a calling and said nothing further.

He had accompanied her to the train on which she'd leave for Paris. They said, "See you soon" to each other, but little did they know that that would be the last time they'd ever see each other again.

* * *

Gladys and Neto finally arrived. Their train had been delayed. Neapolitans weren't known for doing anything right. And that included running trains.

Neto had run over to kiss her in the mouth and touch her breast.

"Boy, control yourself," was all Licha could say. It's what you get for being the lover of a young Salvadoran.

Licha asked them, "Have you eaten?"

Gladys replied, "No, not yet."

Licha suggested, "Let's start walking toward the Vatican and see if we can find a place where we can eat a good pizza."

Licha and Neto walked hand in hand. Gladys held onto her son's other arm.

They found a nice *Pizzeria* near the Vatican. They ordered two *margherita* pizzas and the requisite wine, and then Licha told them that she was pregnant.

Gladys and Neto were stunned into silence.

So Licha said, "It's Neto's child, but I'm not forcing anybody to do anything they don't want. I'm surprised I could still get pregnant. I should've taken precautions, so I take full responsibility. Neto, I'm going to let you decide whether you want to form a family with me. If not, I want you to know that you're going to have a son or daughter in Poland, waiting to meet you."

Poor Neto didn't know what to say.

But Gladys did.

"It could be Pepe's. It could be Mario's. Hell, from what I've heard, it could belong to some guerrilla. How dare you threaten my son, you *puta*!"

This reaction didn't surprise her. She'd even foreseen it. What she hadn't foreseen was how relieved she felt. This was a clean break.

Licha got up, put some bills on the table, and said, "Lunch is on me. Neto, if you ever look for me, you'll get to meet your child. If you don't, have a great life, and don't look back."

She looked at both of them and said, "No hard feelings. Good luck."

And she walked into Vatican City, alone.

She did the tourist thing for a couple of hours, but then the crowd started gathering in St. Peter's Square, waiting to see the Pope.

At around 5:15 the Pope appeared in an open Pope Mobile, to wave at the adoring crowd. As the Pope passed her, Licha shouted, in Polish, "*OJCIEC ŚWIĘTY! POTRZEBUJĘ TWOJEJ POMOCY POWRÓT DO POLSKI!* [Holy Father! I need your help to return to Poland!]"

The Pope turned his head, saw Licha, and leaned toward her, but his eyes opened wide as he focused on something just to the right of her.

Licha's instincts made her react, and she shoved whoever was next to her as hard as she could. The first shot missed the Pope and hit an American woman, the second shot hit the Pope's abdomen, the third shot his hand, and the fourth shot hit a Jamaican woman. By then Licha, with superhuman strength, and with the help of others, had disarmed the middle eastern-looking man.

She then turned toward the Pope, and asked, "*Ojciec Święty? Wszystko w porządku?* [Holy Father, are you all right?]"

John Paul II turned to her, and said, "*Dzięki Tobie!* [Thanks to you.]"

The Pope then turned to one of his guards, and said, in Italian, "*Viene con me, hai capito*? [She comes with me, understand?]"

The guard said, "*Capisco, Santo Padre* [I understand, Holy Father]."

And Licha disappeared into the ambulance with the Holy Father.

Chapter 92

It's Hard to See Shadows in the Dark

It was mid-afternoon that day when the HF radio crackled. "*Padrino*, this is Charlie Lima. The Captain was at the truck talking to a soldier, so he just reached over, picked up the mike and replied.

"Charlie Lima this is *Padrino*, over."

"*Padrino*, the guerrillas are claiming that the Army's captured the Jesuits Ignacio Martín Baró, Juan Ramón Moreno, Joaquín López y López, Amando López and the two that are with you, with the intent to murder them. Can your guys help us out here?"

"Have they lifted the order yet, sir?"

"Padrino, I'll let you know when they do."

"You see, sir, it just doesn't make sense to me that you're calling for their help, when you want them dead."

"¡Damn it, Padrino! You know damn well I'm trying to get that order lifted but I'm not a member of the High Command. Can you just do me the favor and ask them if they care to respond? Because if they don't want to, there's nothing we can do about it anyway."

"Will do, Padrino out."

The Captain walked up the hill to get the priests. They seemed to be worried, as if with a premonition. He told them, "Priests, it's time to put your vaunted brains to work. Here's the situation: the guerrillas are accusing the Army of having captured you two and four other Jesuits named Baró, Moreno, and two priests surnamed López, and my Commanding Officer is asking to see if you can make any statement over the radio."

Ellacuría and Montes took this very seriously. They started speaking very quickly, and in a language that must've been Basque.

After a while, Ellacuría turned to the Captain and said, "Those four priests have probably been captured by the Shadows, Captain."

"Is it just you 6 Jesuits who live at that Residence?"

"No, there's also Jon Sobrino, but he's out of the country at a conference."

The Captain said, "Ok. I'm not going to dispute your conclusion, gentlemen. The question is: would you like to say something over the radio, which will get broadcasted over Radio Cuscatlán?"

The priests went back to talking in Basque. Finally, Ellacuría told the Captain that he'd be the one to speak.

"OK, I just want you to know that whatever you say will be heard by somebody before it's put on the air, and so if it's anything that is objectionable to them, it won't air."

They walked down toward the radio on the truck. When they got there, Sánchez called Col. López. "Charlie Lima, this is *Padrino*. The head guy is going to speak."

"Ready when he is."

The Captain handed over the mike to Ellacuría, saying, "Just keep that button pressed."

Ellacuría said, "Good afternoon, it's 3:30 p.m., November 15, 1989, and this is Father Ignacio Ellacuría, a Jesuit priest, and I'm with Father Segundo Montes, Mrs. Elba Ramos, and Ms. Celina Ramos, in the capable hands of the Armed Forces, whose members have been nothing but gracious to us. I pray to God the other Jesuit priests are fine. I urge both sides to cease hostilities. It's time for peace."

The Captain took the mike from the priest. "This is *Padrino*, Charlie Lima. Apparently, that's the message. Now please let me know when you're going to lift that order."

"I'll let you know, Padrino. Charlie Lima out."

The Captain walked them back to the house. "Gentlemen, I'm hoping to take you back tomorrow, because by now it must be obvious to all that the only purpose of this guerrilla 'Battle of the Bulge' was to sacrifice you and force a negotiated settlement."

"Thank you, Captain." The Jesuits didn't seem very happy. They looked concerned.

The Captain tried to lift their spirits. "If you're concerned about the Jesuits captured by the Shadows, don't be, please. As long as they don't have you two, they won't dare lay a finger on them, because then you'd be able to finger the murderers. Talking on the radio saved their lives."

This reanimated the Jesuits who thanked him.

Before he left, Montes asked, "Do you think they'll lift the order, Captain?"

Sánchez nodded. "I'd bet the farm on it."

As he was walking away, Sánchez looked out to sea and saw a large fishing boat, which seemed to be out of the ordinary. He called the sentinels over. "Have you seen boats that large?"

One of the soldiers shrugged, and said, "Captain, we see boats of all sizes every day." With his binoculars, Sánchez saw that it was a trawler dragging fishing nets.

That made him feel better. But regardless, he was going to reinforce the Jesuits' security that night.

After dinner, the Captain went up the hill with Sergeant Zelayandía and ten soldiers, to set up a defense perimeter around the Jesuits' house. The Captain's order to Zelayandía was, "No matter what happens at the gate, you stay here and defend the Jesuits."

Montes again came out to ask about the order. The captain told him that due to the nature of the radio he had, that he wouldn't be able to communicate with his commander just then, but that it was a certainty that the following morning, his commander would tell him that the order was lifted. Sánchez said good night to the Jesuit and went down the hill to be with the group guarding the main gate.

As he lay in a prone position, weapon pointed at the gate, he thought about that announcement by the guerrillas that the Salvadoran Army had captured the priests, and what the purpose of that could be because it was a lie that was easily disproved by Ellacuría's statement over the radio.

He sat upright. Of course! The Shadows must've had direction-finding equipment deployed everywhere they could, waiting for Ellacuría's reply. It was a trap, and they'd fallen into it!

The Captain willed himself to think things through. If the Shadows now knew where they were, they'd have to assume that the Jesuits would be at the house closest to the cliff. Although they're certainly capable of climbing the cliff to get to them, they'd need a distraction, and the only place the distraction can take place is at the main gate of Xanadú.

But how would they get a distraction at the gate? If Shadows attacked the main gate, several would fall to a hail of bullets from the defending soldiers, and since they're Cubans they can't risk that. Therefore, it wasn't the Shadows who were going to attack the main gate.

Sánchez recalled Ellacuría's words: a guerrilla made somebody in the military High Command an offer he couldn't refuse. Therefore, the Shadows passed the whereabouts of the Jesuits to the suborned officer, who probably proceeded to organize the attack to the main gate using Armored Cav units, because they're the only ones who can bust through the gate and the truck and pour into Xanadu with their armored units. Plus, the Signal soldier's bullets would bounce off the Armored Cav vehicles.

Now that Sánchez knew how they were going to attack, he had to determine his best defense against that. And there was only one: the top of the hill. Sánchez stood up and shouted, "Signal troops, up the hill, double time!"

As they were getting ready to move from their current positions, an Armored Cav vehicle crashed through the gate and pushed the Signal truck aside. More Armored Cav vehicles, or 'tankettes,' poured in.

The battle was over in 30 minutes. The Cavalry troops, under the leadership of Captain Benavides, the nephew of the Commando Unit Leader, Colonel Benavides, were able to overcome Sánchez's defensive positions with sheer firepower. The tankettes had 90 mm cannons installed on them, which 90 mm rounds easily penetrated the house walls that provided the cover for the Signal soldiers. One such round left a gaping hole in Captain Sánchez's chest.

Second Lieutenant Fiallos approached Captain Benavides with Sergeant Juan.

"Who's this, Fiallos?"

"This is the custodian of this place, sir. His name is Juan."

Juan recognized the dead body of Captain Sánchez on the ground. He knelt to say a prayer.

But Captain Benavides was having none of that. "Take us where the Jesuits are, now!"

"Yes sir, they're just over the crest of the hill," said Juan, as he led Captain Benavides and Lt. Fiallos there.

It took them less than a minute to get to what had been the Jesuits' temporary residence. All they found were 11 dead Signal troops, including Sergeant Zelayandía, all of whom had bullet wounds to the head.

The Jesuits and their servants were gone.

Fiallos asked, "Were they here, Juan?"

Juan nodded. "Yes they were. They'd been here 3 days. Two Jesuits and two ladies."

They searched inside the house and one of the cavalry soldiers found a woman's purse, with the ID [*cédula*] of Mrs. Elba Ramos. Such an important document would've never been left behind intentionally.

They then heard a motorboat out at sea. Squinting, they saw faint red lights moving over the water very rapidly in an easterly direction. Captain Benavides attempted to use his handheld radio to inform his uncle of the situation. But it was a line-of-sight radio, so he couldn't.

Juan told him what Captain Sánchez had done to be able to communicate. Captain Benavides had to do the same to inform his uncle of the situation.

It took him an hour to report that the Jesuits and their servants had disappeared. Then they had to wait for another hour for a truck to arrive to take the bodies of the Signal soldiers away.

EPILOGUE

The morning of November 16, 1989, five Spanish Jesuits, including Ignacio Ellacuría and Segundo Montes, were found murdered in the campus of the UCA by Mr. Obdulio Ramos, the groundskeeper of the university. He also found the bodies of a Salvadoran Jesuit and of Elba and Celina Ramos, Obdulio's wife and daughter, respectively.

Military men were found guilty of such murders and were imprisoned. But they were freed under the Amnesty Law that was passed as a condition for the signing of the Peace Accords that put an end to the Salvadoran conflict.

It was a bad ending for a glorious chapter of the Salvadoran Armed Forces who, with the coup of October 15, 1979, paved the way for the transition from the feudal and militaristic system that was the legacy of the Spanish Conquest, to a robust democracy.

How robust? Two of the presidents of El Salvador have been from the FMLN, the political party that the guerrillas formed: Mauricio Funes and the former guerrilla commander Salvador Sánchez Cerén.

Why a legacy of the Spanish Conquest? In 1979, fifteen Latin American countries were under military rule. Sixteen, if you include Cuba.

The guerrillas had ample opportunities to incorporate themselves earlier into the Salvadoran political system because it was constantly offered to them by the governments of Duarte and Cristiani, in frequent peace talks held with guerrilla representatives inside and outside the country. Unfortunately, such offers were always rebuffed.

Never did any Spanish Jesuit in El Salvador publicly encourage the guerrillas to join the Salvadoran democracy as a political party. Not once. Not even after the massive 1980 Agrarian Reform that the Army carried out in compliance with a law passed by civilians, whereby it dispossessed the fourteen richest families of El Salvador from most of their lands and transferring them to the possession of the peasants. This by an Army accused of being the fourteen families' bodyguards.

Not even after the José Napoleón Duarte won the country's first democratic election, in which he defeated the candidate of the fourteen families: Major Roberto D'Aubuisson.

If what the Spanish Jesuits really wanted was to help the poor, they couldn't have found a better ally than José Napoleón Duarte. Proof of this is that the Junta presided by Duarte passed the Agrarian Reform Law in March of 1980, just five months after the coup of October 15, 1979, and one year and four months before the Sandinistas passed their Agrarian Reform Law. In contrast, it took the Sandinistas two years to promote their own Agrarian Reform Law, after they came to power in July 1979. One wonders what the Sandinistas were doing for those two years, because they obviously weren't helping the poor.

Although a few military men were guilty of a gross error in judgment, with which they tainted the conduct of their fellow Army brethren, there is plenty of evidence that points to the fact that they were the knife, but not the hand that wielded that knife.

The evidence also shows that they were the exception to the rule. Because the rule was an Army that was absolutely professional, brave and dedicated to implement a democracy in the country, which otherwise would've never been implemented. See Cuba.

Moreover, had the Army not been as professional as it was, and instead committed the atrocities it incessantly got accused of committing both nationally and internationally by the guerrilla propaganda outlets and their accomplices in the media, the population would've risen against the Army, just like it did in Cuba and Nicaragua. No such uprising ever occurred.

Ironically, five Spanish Jesuits had to die to put an end to the abominable guerrilla policy of using children as combatants, a policy endorsed and certainly never denounced by the Jesuits. Evidence of such policy began to accumulate in the decade of the 1980s, becoming fully evident in the Offensive till the End launched on November 11, 1989. Such abomination and crime could only be eclipsed by something like the murder of the Jesuits. And it was.

To find out what actually happened to the murdered Jesuits, a 'Truth Commission' was formed. That Truth Commission failed to do at least three things:

1. It failed to examine the preaching of armed struggle by the Spanish Jesuits in El Salvador, following the precepts of Liberation Theology, one of the authors of which was a Spanish Jesuit living in El Salvador: Jon Sobrino. By creating a parallel church that was independent from the Vatican and their nemesis, Pope John Paul II, the Jesuits openly preached violence and actively recruited for the guerrillas.

2. It failed to examine the Jesuit-endorsed policy of using minors as guerrilla combatants, which necessarily derived from the encouragement of armed struggle over a negotiated political solution, and from the fatal lack of popular support, the best proof of which is the spectacular failure that was the January 1981 offensive.

In light of the losses suffered at the hands of the US-trained IRIBs and the offer by Duarte's government to join the political process, any person who prided himself in being a thinker, educated and with a profound sense of morality, who was also a follower of the teachings of Christ, all of which are attributes normally associated with Jesuits, would've encouraged the acceptance of such peace offer.

¡But not the Spanish Jesuits in El Salvador! They continued promoting armed struggle, and that necessary led to the forceful separation of ten-, eleven- and twelve-year-old boys and girls from their families. There could be no doubt that they were taken by force because a population that does not support guerrillas is not inclined to cheerfully hand over their minor children to them.

Evidence of the use of minors as guerrilla combatants abounds in the printed and social media. If the Truth Commission really wanted to find out the truth, it could reconvene.

3. Finally, the so-called Truth Commission never examined why the guerrillas blew open the entrance gate to the UCA on November 11, 1989, at the start of the Offensive till the End, which was witnessed by Obdulio, Elba and Celina Ramos, and which was told by Mr. Obdulio Ramos.

What's so sad about that guerrilla bomb was that it not only destroyed the entrance gate to the UCA, but it also damaged the home of the Ramos family, which forced Elba and Celina to temporarily and fatefully stay at the Jesuit residence on campus.

A tallying of the results of the murderous Liberation Theology imposed by Spanish Jesuits in El Salvador is warranted to gain a proper perspective:

hundreds of thousands of dead or injured Salvadorans, versus five dead Spanish Jesuits.

An argument can be made that the Spanish Jesuits saw Salvadorans as inferior, subhuman and disposable, since they didn't hesitate to spill so much Salvadoran blood.

In all fairness, Salvadoran *indios* weren't the first to be considered as such. That distinction belongs to the Guaraní *indios* of Bolivia and Paraguay.

In both cases, Spanish Jesuits exploited the *indios*, instead of educating them. In the case of the Guaraní *indios*, they were enslaved to achieve riches, and they were sent to die to protect such riches.

In the case of Salvadorans, they were sent to die to enable them to achieve the political power they desired, such as the power achieved by the Nicaraguan Jesuits—Fernando and Ernesto Cardenal.

They could've covered themselves in glory if, instead of sending so many *indios* to their deaths, they would've educated them, which is something Jesuits have done in every other European and North American country they've been in.

For some reason, they didn't care if Salvadoran *indios* were left dead, blind or handicapped.

Rest in peace, Elba and Celina Ramos.

Author's Note

A few years ago, I got into a discussion with some people who, almost 20 years after the cessation of hostilities, dredged up the same old accusations against the Salvadoran Army, which I of course denied. Not only because I couldn't personally corroborate any of propaganda talking points they repeat like parrots, but also because such propaganda doesn't at all reflect the army I served in, not while I was in it, not afterward.

What do I mean by afterward? Long after the U.S. advisors were gone, Salvadoran officers who were my contemporaries during the Salvadoran conflict that this book discusses, i.e., Captains and Lieutenants, became the Colonels and Generals and leaders of the Salvadoran Army.

The very same captains and lieutenants who fought the guerrillas in the IRIBs and in the regular Army units, were now in charge of the training and readiness of their units.

In 2004, El Salvador sent Salvadoran battalions to participate in the international coalition that ousted the Saddam Hussein regime to implement a democracy in Iraq.

Which was the same thing that the Army had done in 1979: it overthrew a dictator and paved the way for a democracy in El Salvador.

How did the Salvadoran battalions trained and led by my contemporaries do? They were universally praised, as evidenced by the following: Washington Times, Monday, May 3, 2004 edition: "Salvadoran Soldiers Praised for Iraqi Role," by none other than Secretary of State, General Colin Powell, among others.

They acted the way they'd always acted: like professional soldiers.

About the Author

Armando Interiano is an electrical engineer with patents to his name, a multi-language translator and a published musician who is a graduate of the United States Military Academy at West Point and of Rice University in Houston, Texas.

He fulfilled his military commitment in El Salvador and is proud of his role in the Agrarian Reform of 1980, in which the Salvadoran Army played a crucial role in transferring properties from large estate owners to peasants.

He is also proud of helping turn El Salvador into a legitimate democracy, breaking once and for all with the military-feudal system bequeathed by the Spanish.

He's written several published articles on the need for an educational revolution everywhere, particularly in Central America.

BIBLIOGRAPHY

Ignacio Ellacuría, Filosofía, ¿para qué?, Abra 11 (1976) 42-48, UCA Editores.

"Instructions for the Social Apostolate", Jean Baptiste Janssens.

"Sacrificios Humanos contra Derechos Humanos", by Luis Escalante Arce. Edilit, S.A. de C.V.

"The Jesuits", Malachi Martin. THE LINDEN PRESS, Simon and Schuster, New York, 1987

CPSIA information can be obtained
at www.ICGtesting.com
Printed in the USA
BVHW041507040819
555030BV00002B/1/P